The LABYRIS

-: Tales of the *El Defensor* :-
Book Two.

A Novel.

Copyright © 2019 by Adam Derbyshire
First Published in April 2019

ISBN: 9781095268537

Dedication

This book is dedicated to
Margaret Reid
1948-2018

She always loved tales of high adventure and sorcery.
I think you would have enjoyed this one mum...

And as always

To my three Musketeers,
Nicola, Ryan and Owain.
When we are together
our lives are always one rich adventure.

To peter.

because heros come in all
shapes and sizes.

ADAM

Prologue

In that moment when a storm ends, time almost stands still; the air feels scrubbed, clean and fresh, hinting at new beginnings, endless possibilities and whispered promises of what the future has yet to bring.

In that moment, when nature pauses to catch its breath, many a sailor has looked to the heavens and thanked their gods that they are still alive to face the challenges of another day. Counted their blessings for surviving the terrors that have placed them on the very cusp of death and destruction, elated they could now return to their families and huddle together for warmth and comfort, promising never to take those feelings for granted again.

However, for Kerian Denaris, the passing of the storm signalled one thing.

It meant that he had failed. Colette, the woman he loved, was sailing further away on the galleon *El Defensor*; unaware that Kerian remained alive and was searching so desperately for her.

Each of his previous attempts had begun with such renewed vigour, buoyed by false hope, only to be crushed into silence, as each expedition failed to locate a window of calm on the horizon, tinged by a sickly mustard yellow light and a skyline dotted with the skeletal remains of many ships.

The sea's surface was as flat as a millpond, barely a ripple marking the movement of the twenty-one-foot fishing boat *The Tulip* as she rocked gently from side to side. The paintwork on the vessel, once gleaming, was now worn and shabby and the hull leaked slowly in several places; testament to the punishment the valiant vessel had endured chasing storms up and down the coast over the last few months.

A splash shattered the silence, followed by another, this time accompanied with a string of expletives as the owner of *The Tulip* set to bailing out his vessel as it sat low in the water. There was a crash as something fell inside the boat, a further oath and then the pail used to bail out the vessel, flew out over the side, then skipped across the mirrored surface of the sea before sliding slowly under the surface.

Despairing sobs filled the air, heartfelt cries of agony in protest of failure and love lost. It signalled a momentary loss of control, a rare glimpse into the vulnerable side of the normally stoic man from which they came.

Kerian looked despondently about him with weary hazel eyes, cursing his own stupidity and lack of control in throwing away the only item left intact on his small boat with which he could try to remove the water slopping around his ankles. He stood up to his six-foot height, hands on hips, scanning the horizon for a sight of land or a passing ship from which he could hail assistance. However, he knew he was all alone out here. In fact he could be on the very edge of the world for all he knew.

No one would have been that stupid to dare set sail into the tropical storm that had just lashed this region. Its ferocity would feed the imaginations and tales of elders in taverns up and down the coast. Fishermen would only consider navigating these waters now the storm had passed. Help could be hours away.

He brushed back his salt and pepper hair from his weathered face, pulling the length tight and fastening it with a thin strip of leather. His mind wandered back, thinking of the path that had led him to this place; the curse cast on him by an evil sorceress now burnt at the stake, its enchantment aging him a year for every month he had lived. His time spent looking for a remedy, the desperate acts he had undertaken, before finding a slim clue in the dusty archives of a monastery in Catterick, where a faded manuscript detailed the location of a magical gemstone that could grant your heart's desire.

Kerian chuckled at the absurdity of it all. The jewel had granted his heart's desire but the results had been far from what he had expected. He sloshed across the waterlogged deck of his boat searching for a container to continue bailing. Although his trousers were folded up to his knees to try and keep them from dragging in the water they were still soaked through, as was his grubby grey linen shirt which hung on a frame verging on the gaunt.

He had to admit, that had been some storm. Practically everything not nailed down on *The Tulip* had been thrown about, with several items swept overboard. A fleeting sense of panic suddenly struck him and his hand quickly moved to his chest to touch his shirt and the shape of two pendants hanging from his neck, their presence reassuring the warrior and calming his tortured mind. He did not know what he would do if he were to ever lose these personal treasures.

Kerian took another deep breath to calm himself and considered his position carefully. Thomas Adams, the captain of the *El Defensor,* had once told him that sailing on the ocean was like being on the surface of a mirror and that whilst you sailed upon its surface there was plenty of time to reflect. It was true, he had endured another storm but this time his vessel was in urgent need of repair. The damage was quite severe and he knew with a despairing heart that it would take valuable time to make *The Tulip* seaworthy again.

On a brighter note, he was still alive, with no broken bones or serious injury. His aging was slowly reversing, making him feel stronger every day but it was a slow process and definitely not for someone with a low patience threshold.

He sank down on the edge of the boat and sat there thinking hard, chewing his lip nervously in thought. He needed to make for land, in whatever direction it lay. Get *the Tulip* repaired, take stock and ask himself several serious and searching questions. Why was he still doing this? Why was he out here, in the middle of nowhere, chasing storms and facing death like a lunatic?

Colette was slipping through his fingers and there appeared to be nothing he could do to change this, no matter how much he wished otherwise. He had even lost his birthright at some point in his adventures. The pale band of skin where his golden ring used to rest was yet another blow to his fragile psyche. He had lost so much, in such a short time.

Kerian sighed heavily, then looked over to where he had stored his saddlebags and suddenly had an idea. He reached up and carefully pulled out an object wrapped in the charred remains of a long black cloak. The mirrored shield gleamed brightly as he exposed it to the sunlight.

He looked down at his reflection in its surface, noticing the slow re-emergence of facial features he felt he had lost long ago. His hair was slowly changing back, even some of the lines were starting to smooth from his face. He stared at the image of the haunted man before him for a long time, realising that he had lost a lot of weight since he had last gazed upon his own features. Possibly too much! Had he been so focused in his pursuit that he had started to neglect himself?

His obsession was leading him into situations no sane individual would contemplate.

A forlorn flapping from above roused him from his thoughts and made him angle the shield to take in the image of the shredded sails on the main mast. The storm had ripped the canvas apart. Even if the wind returned, he would gain little speed with them in this sorry state! He flipped the mirrored shield over, banishing the image of the man within and then started to bail the water from the deck. With luck, he would find support when the fishermen arrived in the area to trawl in the hope the storm had disturbed the waters enough to make the fishing worthwhile, or if not, he would have to use the shield to paddle in a random direction and hope he found the shore.

He bent his back to the task and tried to ignore the voice in his head that told him to give up, find the mainland, settle down and rebuild a life for himself.

The problem with that thought was that giving up was something Kerian Denaris was not prepared to do.

He bailed some water over the side, sending ripples out from the boat and letting his mind wander, trying to imagine how his friends were on the *El Defensor*. If he knew Thomas, he was probably sitting in his cabin, boots up on the table, savouring the orange tang of his favourite alcohol, and soaking in the ambience of life at sea.

What he would give to be in Thomas's boots right now.

* * * * * *

Paranoia is a feeling you experience when you imagine people are out to get you; unfortunately, for Thomas Adams, captain of the Spanish Galleon *El Defensor,* this feeling was growing rapidly and he knew without doubt that they were.

The crimson flashing light blinking at his side confirmed his worst fears. The battered NV-07 handgun was nearly out of charge. There were maybe one or two blaster shots left, at best. The blue metal was cold against his sweating palm and his twitching finger nervously stroked the trigger looking for the reassurance the side arm could never give.

Thomas paused for breath beneath a spluttering lime green neon sign, advertising some type of futuristic drink and then checked behind him for the pursuit he knew was closing in.

At just under six-foot-tall and shy of his forty-eighth birthday, Thomas cut an imposing figure. His salt worn leather boots, trousers, loose cream shirt and braid waistcoat completed an outfit partially covered by a long dark trench coat that was soaked through by the persistent drizzle falling from the grey lifeless sky. His short dark hair swept back from a rugged face sculpted and tanned by his time spent at sea. An assortment of fading bruises completed his profile and his breathing came in gasps as he considered the limited options open to him.

He could always return the gemstone to the giant lizards tracking him and hope they would not kill him too slowly! Thomas shook his head, he did not consider that a viable option, they required the gemstone to power open another gate, the small stones Colette had remaining in her collection were not large enough to channel sufficient power to safely get the *El Defensor* through the archways between worlds, making any attempt dangerous for both ship and crew.

Without the stone, they could not continue their search for home and were at risk of being stranded either here in this futuristic nightmare world, or worse, marooned in the ship's graveyard.

Shouts and snarls sounded behind him, signalling his pursuers were closing. Thomas set off along the edge of the street, moving from one shadowy alleyway to the next, slipping from cover to cover as he had been taught all those years before in the academy. He kept his back to the wall, checked all corners, and when he was sure, ran across the street dodging the sweeping searchlights from a hover car running a frantic search pattern and zipping close by overhead.

How did he keep finding himself in these situations?

This urgent need for a gemstone had led Thomas to consider the one world where he knew he could find one. A world where for a price, or more importantly a risk, a stone could be found to secure passage to their goal. Inside the ship's graveyard there was only one archway out of the hundreds that ringed the derelict ships stranded there that had lost its keystone, setting it apart from the others. The broken arch was one of the few that Thomas had journeyed through several times in the past. It was just that he had failed to consider the bad feelings he had left in his wake the last time he had come this way.

It was at times like these that the captain wished he had listened to the advice of his crew. When they had arrived in Maraket, this place of gleaming skyscrapers, loud neon signs and futuristic technology, his friends had warned him to leave the scavenging to other crewmen with attributes more appropriate to the task but Thomas would not listen. He had things to sort out in his mind; he needed the distraction the landing would give to find his own self-worth. He slipped his hand into his coat pocket and felt the reassuring shape of a small toy *Matchbox* car police cruiser, his hand closing protectively around it.

Just by holding the toy, the image of a withered creature that preyed on lost souls and ate the bodies of the marooned sprang to mind; Images of a flaky skeletal face, hovering lights that danced around his body hypnotising the unwary and luring them to their doom. Thomas shook his head and turned a corner, finding himself arriving at the end of the street and a choice that made him wince at its absurdity.

Somehow, he had taken a wrong turn. He knew the docks were roughly in this direction but this was definitely not the waterfront. Instead, a graveyard lay ahead, complete with spectral mist which held an ominous foreboding. He could turn in there and hope to hide from the pursuit or turn back and meet the lizards head on. The weight of the nearly empty gun in his hand confirmed a full-frontal assault was suicide. A blaster shot ricocheted off the stone façade of the building beside him dropped an awning into the street with a crash of sparks deciding the matter for him.

The graveyard it was.

Thomas ran for the gateway, shouldering the railing and for once having something go his way. The gate swung open on squealing hinges and he found himself running up the gravel pathway. Rows of gravestones and neglected obelisks stretched away to either side, inscriptions worn away by the elements or slowly smothered by lichen. Plinths leaned over towards tilting grave markers as if engaged in secret conversations and mausoleums stood cold and aloof with warped doors opened in sinister invitation for the unwary to step inside.

The captain ducked behind a tall monument and dropped to his knees, facing back the way he came. The crying face of an angel loomed protectively over him, her wings sheltering the captain from the worst of the rain. The stonework was exquisite but Thomas had no time to critique the work, as his mind continued to think about the monster that stalked him in his nightmares and how it had taunted him with the miniature police cruiser.

The toy car was a trophy from a serial killer. Thomas had a fractured memory of his own past and knew the car had connections to himself but the images haunting him, whether hypnotically suggested by his nemesis, or real memories from his past, had shaken the captain to his core. He was no serial killer. Was he?

The gates to the graveyard squealed open as his hunters followed into the cemetery and slid between the monuments. Hisses and clicks signalled communication between the hunting party as they split and started to hunt him through the field of remembrance. Thomas clenched his gun tighter. He felt the damp start to seep through the material of his trousers and trickle down the inside of his leather boot.

Thomas raised his head and peered into the darkness beyond his cold marble shelter, his free hand touching the cool surface for a sense of reality as well as support. This marker was something real, something he could relate to, whilst somewhere out there, his enemies were seeking him.

A searchlight flickered across the graveyard, sending shadows slipping and sliding between the markers and putting Thomas further on edge. The lizards could be anywhere. The annoying hover car zoomed by on the right, its lights picking out the blackened ruins of a cathedral standing tall at the far end of the graves, a mere skeleton compared to the majestic building it once was. The drizzling rain, coupled with the briefness of the illumination made it difficult to make out the fine details of its crumbling structure, so Thomas turned back to the tombs around him and cursed how the grave markers gave cover to both himself and his pursuers.

Maybe he could hide in one of the crypts?

A flash of movement to the left caught his eye and he turned, focusing intently in the direction of the perceived threat. His gun hand swept up with a speed born from fear rather than professionalism as he balanced the muzzle of the weapon against the edge of the statue for stability and sighted through the luminescent twin v's along the top of the barrel.

Time stood still as the captain stared into the darkness, not daring to blink in case whatever he had seen moved again. His eyes strained hard to catch the smallest clue, the slightest hint of where his adversaries may be. They seemed to know his every move, huge reptilian creatures that walked on sturdy muscular hind legs that would kill him without mercy.

Sensing no further movement, Thomas began to slowly slide back down into the shadows, feeling the cool stone at his back despite the three layers of clothing he wore. He started to shiver, unsure if it was from the adrenaline coursing through his blood stream or the fact he was so cold. He had a momentary wish to know whom the erected angel immortalised, fleeting thoughts suggesting he could be sharing the same resting place before morning.

He tried to calm his breathing, collect himself, slowing his breaths until he started to make out the sounds around him. It was strange that in the confines of the graveyard his breathing appeared to have an echo. That was ridiculous! How could his breathing be echoing? Thomas took a deep breath and held it, his heart hammering loudly in his ears.

The breathing continued heavily from directly behind his marble sanctuary!

"I know where you are." A voice shouted from near the cemetery entrance. "Come now Thomas, we can be reasonable. Give me back the stone and I'll call off Cornelius and Horatio."

Thomas gritted his teeth and bit his tongue, he dared not reply in case one of the walking designer handbags Miguel Garcia used as his 'hired muscle' realised where he was and by the sounds of the sniffing and scrabbling behind him one of them was about to find out anyway. He edged slowly along the base of the statue, feeling the water flooding more steadily into his boot at the movement and drawing a surprised gasp before he could stop himself. His free hand slipped from the stone and landed heavily on a hard, cobbled tube. Thomas winced as he suddenly realised what it was. The lizard man's tail slipped out from under his hand and a rumbling growl rose above him. The captain looked up into the shadows between the angel's wings and took in the blunt snout and cold eyes of Horatio staring back at him.

It was time to move!

The NV-07 spat a crimson bolt of searing energy straight up, fired practically by reflex. Horatio bellowed in pain as the blaster scored a furrow across his reptilian nose and deflected from the spiny ridge of bone running from between his eyes all the way down his seven-foot-long height and out along a further three feet of reptilian tail.

Marble chips exploded into the air as the lizard returned fire, his own weapon sending a withering barrage of bolts down into the space Thomas had just vacated. The captain caught a glimpse of a long sleek laser rifle, before he ran blindly from cover out across the graveyard. The air filled with crimson streaks of sizzling light, headstones that had resisted the elements for years exploding into rubble as the two lizards mowed down everything in their path.

He ran up to a mausoleum, briefly considering trying the door and grabbing the handle, only for the door to disintegrate under another stray laser bolt. Thomas dodged left, sprinting beneath a monolith with an urn on the top. The urn went the way of the door; granite chips whistling across the captain's path like shrapnel.

Thomas held his arm above his head, protecting his face from the whistling debris and ran towards the cathedral. If he could get into the building, maybe, just maybe, he could shake the gruesome twosome from his trail. He turned around to see how close they were to catching him and the ground fell away from beneath him.

The breath crashed out of his body as he hit the floor and it took Thomas a few seconds to extricate himself from the mud that now plastered him from top to toe. He staggered back to his feet, sludge dripping heavily from his clothes and realised he had fallen into a freshly dug grave. He wiped the mud from his face then frantically looked about the ground for his gun that he had somehow dropped in the fall but it was nowhere to be found.

It appeared this night was getting better and better!

Hissing grunts from above signalled the arrival of Horatio and Cornelius and they stared down at him with their cold reptilian eyes, their tails flicking excitedly. Thomas blinked to clear the rain from his eyes and noted that both creatures were armed with 326-CZ laser carbines. Thick tongues squelched from between armour scaled lips as the reptiles regarded their cornered prey with a hungry look in their eyes. A lighter set of footsteps arrived and walked slowly around the edge of the grave before moving forwards to reveal a silhouette Thomas knew only too well.

"I see you are still dressing up for the occasion." Miguel Garcia commented, pausing to light up a cigar and puff on it several times until the end glowed red. "You never had good dress sense. Now, I believe you have something that belongs to me." The privateer, standing slightly smaller than Thomas, wore a long frock coat which had bandoliers over his chest. Large buckles on his belt and coat added to the look of a stereotypical pirate from the high seas, which was exactly the look Miguel was trying to convey. The fact that his flintlock pistols were blasters only served to reinforce his authority in this situation. Thomas frantically turned, checking both ends of the grave. Where was his damned handgun? He needed to put a shot right between the shifty man's eyes.

"Looking for this?" Miguel asked, holding up Thomas's gun. "Sloppy Thomas, real sloppy. Now hand it over."

Thomas reached into his coat and lifted out a fist-sized amethyst. Even in the dull light from the hover car searchlight wobbling about erratically overhead, facets gleamed alluringly. Thomas knew he had no choice but to comply. It was Miguel's gemstone after all. Maybe if he were lucky Miguel would just shoot him in the leg as a warning and spare his life.

"You know I'm going to have to kill you?" Miguel informed him, rolling the cigar backwards and forwards in his lips and blowing out a cloud of smoke as he beckoned Thomas to come closer to his end of the grave. "It's nothing personal."

"Sure it is." Thomas replied, considering his unpleasant fate. "It's always personal with you." So much for the blaster bolt in the leg theory!

"That's because you always make it so!" Miguel screamed down at him, his control slipping as it had countless times in the past. "Every time our paths cross you make me a laughing stock! Remember how you tricked me into marrying the Twinwood Ambassador's daughter?"

"Oh yes." Thomas replied, stopping as if a sudden thought had occurred to him and lowering the jewel gently back down by his side near to his coat pocket "What was her name again." He clicked his fingers. "I remember. Tess. How is the old battle-axe?"

Miguel ignored the jibe continuing to spout bile, pacing the edge of the grave in growing agitation as he remembered the slights against him.

"Remember when you sold me that treasure map? The sure thing? The legendary Eaglestone treasure? The map that led to that island of cannibal frogs?"

Thomas tried to hide the grin sliding across his face. Now that had been a funny one.

Miguel shook with rage, brushing his hand nervously through his dark greasy hair. "And then there was the DeParys incident."

"Oh yes." Thomas could not help but laugh this time. "The DeParys incident."

"Don't talk about the DeParys incident." Miguel snarled, pointing Thomas's gun straight at him. "No one must ever mention the DeParys incident again." Thomas observed the diode on the sidearm pointed at him and smiled to himself, even as he gently slid the amethyst back into his jacket. He also noticed that the hover car had swung around behind Miguel and his reptilian heavies and was now heading their way, wobbling unsteadily in flight as if the pilot was new to the machine. The captain suddenly had a sneaky suspicion who was at its controls.

"I guess you've got me." Thomas confessed, hoping to hold their attention for just a bit longer. "Just pull the trigger. Let's get this over with."

"I have been looking forward to this." Miguel smiled, stroking the end of his bushy moustache theatrically. He pulled the trigger...

...and nothing happened.

"It's empty." Thomas confessed. "I used the last shot when I re-fashioned Horatio's nose."

Thomas surprised everyone as he dove towards their end of the grave. The hover car suddenly accelerated directly towards the group at high speed. It clipped a monument, teetered unsteadily then flipped; a large figure dropping from the driving seat as the car crashed to the ground, rushing straight over them, practically knocking the three thugs off their feet before exploding in a ball of flame. Miguel found himself teetering unsteadily on the edge, only for Thomas to take advantage and grab his feet, pulling the buccaneer into the grave with him where they grappled fiercely, each desperate to gain the upper hand.

Thomas's remaining lizard captors turned as one, as a creature from mythology smashed straight into them. Eight-foot-tall, horns gleaming wickedly in the light, red hair stuck up in every direction and slobber foaming from the end of its nose.

Horatio met an uppercut that lifted the lizard off his back legs and rattled his brains. As the reptile fell senseless to the floor, his laser rifle was snatched up by the roaring hover car pilot, who set about brandishing the carbine with devastating effect. He pummelled Cornelius repeatedly about the body, microchips, circuit boards, sparks and smoke coming from the ruined weapon, as the massive Minotaur navigator from the *El Defensor* protected his captain the only way he knew how; by hitting things really hard.

Miguel went to draw a blaster as he grappled with Thomas in the mud but a right hook from the captain stopped him in his tracks, making his teeth clash painfully together and catching his lip, which bloomed crimson droplets of blood.

"Give me your weapons." Thomas snarled, dripping mud down on his opponent.

"Now, now!" Miguel held up his hands showing he was unarmed. "I wasn't really going to shoot you Thomas. Old buddy, old pal." He reluctantly passed over his two blasters, his dismay at doing so quite evident in his facial expression.

The Minotaur stomped over to the edge of the grave and looked down at the two men covered from head to foot in mud. It took him a few seconds to recognise the man he sought and he gripped Thomas's hand securely and hoisted the captain clear from what Thomas had fleetingly thought could have been his final resting place.

"In the nick of time Rauph." Thomas laughed, addressing his rescuer. "Just in the nick of time." He turned to look down at the bedraggled figure in the open grave and smiled, his confidence returning in a rush now the tables had turned.

"Come on Rauph, aren't you going to help me out too?" Miguel asked holding up his hand. The navigator glared, snorting angrily down at the man, staring him down. Thomas tried not to laugh as the Minotaur continued to appear menacing, despite the fact, Thomas had never known a more loyal and gentler companion. "So you want me to stay down in the grave?" Miguel gestured miserably. Rauph simply glared as intimidatingly as he could and turned away, his opinion on the matter clear to see.

"Thank you for your kind hospitality, and of course for the amethyst." Thomas bowed his head theatrically, his sodden clothes clinging to his skin. "We have to leave now. I suggest you stay down there until we are gone, otherwise Rauph may not be as understanding as I."

"I am going to get you for this." Miguel threatened.

"I will look forward to it." Thomas replied. "But it won't be here. I have a great dislike for science fiction. Put a sword in my hand, the wind at my back and the *El Defensor* beneath my feet and I am happy. Until another time then?" Thomas turned to leave, moving up alongside his massive rescuer.

"Let's get back to the ship as quickly as possible." Thomas suggested to his bovine friend. "Miguel has many friends. I would rather not be here when he gets out of that grave and gathers his hired muscle." Horatio started to stir on the floor, his tail curving out sinuously. Rauph responded by smashing the remainder of the laser rifle onto his head, knocking the lizard out cold.

Thomas slipped and slid along the path towards the exit of the graveyard and only when he felt they had put enough space between him and his adversary did he stop to consider his ruined wardrobe.

"You know Rowan is never going to let me in my cabin looking like this. I'm going to be in real trouble. I am glad you came after me Rauph, despite my telling you to stay on the ship. Come to think of it, where did you get the hover car from? You know if you had driven it properly, we could have saved ourselves this walk back to the ship."

Thomas flung Miguel's blasters away as far as he could, the weapons sailing off into the lengthening shadows amongst the gravestones. It was all well and good having such futuristic blasters, but once you passed beyond the ship's graveyard, they ceased to function as anything more exciting than a paperweight with an amusing story behind it.

"You know." Thomas turned to his companion, as an afterthought struck. "Those Laser rifles work so much better if you pull the trigger." Rauph wrinkled his snout in confusion and turned to his captain.

"Which part was the trigger?"

The Labyris Knight
-: Part One :-

New Adventures,
Old Foes.

What truly defines a hero? I inquire,
Perhaps it's their skill with a blade?
Charisma and cunning, do they require?
Yes! That is how heroes are made.

To lose this all, a dark twist of fate,
No treasures or tales to share,
Haggard souls, twisted by hate,
A saga of endless despair.

So, get on your feet, pick up your shield,
Grit your teeth then let out a cry!
Don your cloak, never yield,
And then on your blade rely!

So that's what defines a hero to be,
A stalwart who never gives in,
A knight who will face the tempestuous sea,
for his lover, his comrades, his kin.

The Bard of Hampton
(circa 1452)

Chapter One

The *Tulip* limped slowly into port, towed shamefully behind a kindly fishing boat like a bizarre trophy fish they had captured in their nets and were too embarrassed to display or too desperate to consign to the depths.

As Kerian sat, dejected, watching the shelter of the rough harbour walls slowly stretching around him and offering his vessel sanctuary, he found that instead of breathing a sigh of relief, he felt confined and crushed. As much by the weight of failure hammering down upon him as the thought of arranging repairs for his ship.

He looked around at the ships swaying gently in the waters, listened to the rigging clinking softly in the breeze and observed the crews polishing metal, applying fresh paint, off-loading fish or resupplying other vessels. Noticing the camaraderie shown amongst these people made him feel homesick for the *El Defensor* and her crew. Who would have thought that in such a short time they could have had such a lasting impact on him and become the family he desired?

Laughter rose from the anglers perched along the sea wall, nudging each other, waking others from afternoon slumbers as his sad vessel lurched through the waters beneath them. Bearded mouths opened in grins, pipes suspended from stilled lips, whilst others paused in mending nets or fashioning lobster pots to join in the mocking welcome of this unusual traveller of the seas. Kerian swallowed hard, then stood up straight, letting the ridicule wash over him, pretending the good-natured jibes had no effect at all, even though inside his rage burned as hot as the sun sinking slowly in the western sky.

The *Tulip* shuddered up to the dock and bumped forlornly against its pillars; allowing Kerian to throw her lines up so the dockhands could secure the boat in place. Grabbing his shield and throwing his saddlebags over his left shoulder, Kerian climbed up onto the jetty and thanked the men who had assisted in securing his ship. However, their raised eyes and smirks at seeing him with his saddlebags, led Kerian to believe there would be tales spun in taverns tonight about the idiot landlubber who went to sea in a boat and took saddlebags with him so he knew where to sit.

"Uh hum!" A throat cleared loudly behind him. The tone delivered in a fashion known worldwide as someone who felt that they were important, when clearly, they were not.

Kerian took in the old man standing there and tried to hide his irritation. Bushy sideburns and an impressive snowy beard framed his face, whilst upon his tanned forehead he had strands of white hair combed across to try to hide his receding hairline and a pair of spectacles pushed up on his forehead. His nose was red and swollen indicating a man who was happy with spirits as bedside companions after a day's work. The official wore a faded jerkin covered by a long flowing official coat of navy blue. Gold braid fraying in several areas denoted rank on his shoulders but Kerian was not interested in local decorum and simply wanted to move things along as swiftly as possible. He could see over to two guards standing at attention within easy distance of their commander's call but they looked bored and easy to overpower if the situation turned ugly.

"Welcome to Wellruff." The man opened. "I am the harbourmaster here. I need your name, where you hail from and more importantly your intended destination. I also need to know your business here, what cargo you carry and how long your stay will be." He cleared his throat again and lifted a ledger from his side, his quill hovering expectantly over the page as he intentionally furrowed his brow to allow his spectacles to slide down his forehead and perch business-like on the bridge of his nose. "So, do you have anything to declare?"

"Well rough? Seriously?" Kerian asked and then stopped himself. There was no need to cause trouble at this time if he could avoid it. "There is just myself, what I carry and my vessel."

The harbourmaster looked down off the edge of the jetty and frowned.

"I'm afraid you cannot leave your boat tied up here, especially if she needs repairs. It will need to be moved to the far end of the dock."

Kerian looked back at the man before him and raised an eyebrow.

"As you can see my vessel is in no condition to sail." He muttered, already realising where this was heading. "Let me save you some time. I need my boat repaired and restocked. How much do I need to give you to ensure this is done speedily and correctly?"

The harbourmaster shook his shoulders as if the very idea of asking for money was below him, before he chewed on the end of his quill and mentioned a sum that was as ludicrous as it was extortionate.

"Let me explain this to you." Kerian bristled. "I will pay you what the job is worth and no more."

"I'm sure this is how you do business Mr... Mr?"

"Denaris." Kerian shot back.

"Mr Denaris we only do things one way here. My way... Otherwise, you end up in the town jail. Kerian slid his hand into his saddlebags and felt for a few small gems then dropped them onto the open page of the harbourmaster's ledger, silencing the man in mid- conversation.

"...That will do nicely." The harbourmaster squeaked.

"I'll leave her care in your good hands then." Kerian nodded; confident his business with the man was over. He walked away, pushing his way through the guards with all intentions of heading for the nearest inn and having the largest drink offered. Then he looked up at the town before him, the sprawling mass of housing crammed tightly together, brickwork rust coloured in the light and paused, turning to one of the guards, clearly the more junior of the two, to size the youth up with his cool gaze.

"Where is the nearest decent inn?" he asked. The guard looked perturbed at being asked a direct question, more used to simply enforcing the harbourmaster's will.

"That will be the *Lusty Mermaid* sir." He spluttered. "Up Mill Street, then second left into Tanners Lane. You cannot miss it. There's a carved wooden mermaid nailed to the outside wall with large... err... umm."

"I think that I understand." Kerian smiled in reply, dropping a small gem into the man's hand to express his gratitude before walking on. He knew what he had just given the man was probably more than the guard earned in a year. In hindsight, it was probably a stupid thing to do and could lead to unnecessary questions and attention. However, Kerian already knew he would be the talk of the town and it was not as if he intended to hang around. He would be far away from here before any trouble would follow. He just needed time to get his boat repaired and he would be on his way.

He looked up at the rusty town of Wellruff that was going to be his home for the next few days and sighed inwardly. No matter what port he visited, they always looked the same, run down, shabby, smelling of fish and rotting produce. The main cobbled street led from the harbour up into ramshackle rows of houses that were dirty, stained and leaning so close to each other that if he were able to pick the middle one up all the others would fall over. Smoke rose from numerous crumbling chimneys leaving a haze that hung over the buildings like a suffocating shroud. Seagulls spiralled through the air, shrieking noisily as they searched for food, their cries competing with the calls of street sellers, curses of cart drivers and the gossip of housewives leaning on flaking cream coloured windowsills on both sides of the street.

This town was just another obstacle in a long line of such, its presence riling but ultimately something he could overcome. He settled his saddlebag more firmly on his shoulder and headed up the road. The *Lusty Mermaid* was waiting and Kerian was eager to meet her acquaintance.

* * * * * *

"I just don't get it!" Ashe Wolfsdale frowned. "What am I doing wrong? All your birds are flying beautifully. They look sleek, majestic, dangerous... But Sinders just looks like a swollen puff-puff fish, all roundish and well, kind of dumpy."

Austen gently hooded the sea falcon gripping his gloved hand and moved it safely onto a perch before turning towards his unhappy shipmate. He took in Ashe's exasperated posture, one hand on his hip, bottom lip sticking out in a pout and tried not to laugh. It was hard. Somehow, the four-foot high crewman before him tugged at the heart strings just as much as you wanted to throttle him sometimes. He sighed and sat down on the deck so that Ashe did not have to crane his neck up to see him.

"Maybe Cinders simply isn't ready to fly yet." Austen replied, his aged face gently showing the concern he felt for the little man before him, whilst trying not to smile at the joke everyone on board apart from Ashe seemed to get. "Give him some more time and maybe he will surprise you."

"Yes but look!" Ashe gestured, lifting his cage with the scruffy looking avian inside. "He doesn't even look like one of your birds. I'm starting to think he was adopted."

Austen found he had to agree, as he looked through the bars of the cage at the ball shaped creature within. Black and white plumage stuck out in no discernible order, making the bird appear anything but bird shaped, as if preening was something it felt only others of its ilk should do; an action far below its notice. A single beady eye watched the proceedings going on around it with some suspicion and as Austen looked on, one eye closed and another opened to complete the tour around the inside of the cage.

"It is a unique creature." Austen replied choosing his words carefully. "Are you handling him every day and letting him out of his cage in your cabin?"

"Well I try to handle him." Ashe replied solemnly. "But it's hard with this." Ashe held out his other hand exposing four normal fingers and the red stub for a thumb that was magically growing to replace the one Ashe had lost after his terrible torture.

"Marcus and Richard are working with me every day to try and get the thumb moving but it is really painful. What is worse, Sinders thinks it's a worm and keeps trying to snap at it with his beak." Austen nodded his head trying to show empathy, whilst secretly wishing someone, anyone, would call him away.

"And that's not all. I mean look what I'm dealing with." Ashe continued, pushing open the cage door and tilting it to see if he could tip his bird out onto the deck. "He...won't...come...out...of the cage." He shook the cage hard, but Sinders remained firmly wedged inside, using curved black talons to hold onto the bars. "See what I mean?"

He placed the cage back onto the deck and scowled down at the ball of feathers within, clearly disappointed at his charge. Realising that the cage was now free of danger, Sinders tentatively let go of the bars and stared up at the Halfling with a beady eye, then he hopped over to the open cage door, reached out his black and white feathered head, gripped the door and slammed it shut sealing himself safely inside.

"I think you just need to treat Cinders as a baby and be the mother it hasn't got." Austen stated carefully. "Love it, feed it, talk to it and show it by example what needs to be done."

Ashe stared down at his bird, hand on chin and tried to imagine what this information meant. Caring for a bird was not as easy or as glamorous as Ashe had first thought. He picked up the cage and wandered off across the foredeck towards the cabins at the stern of the galleon, his mind whirling with all the new information Austen had given him. The lack of attention shown by the Halfling towards the flying cars zipping around the glittering skyscrapers standing tall on the horizon behind him was a clear indication of how much his concern for Sinders was playing on his little mind.

When the idea of Sinders was first suggested, Ashe had dreamed of flying on the back of the bird and soaring through the heavens. The chances of that ever happening were about as real as his imaginary daydreams. He sighed heavily and trudged on, leaving Austen silently counting his blessings in his wake, not yet aware the little thief had pocketed the man's watch as they had spoken. Ashe intended to give the pocket watch back later, as Sticks, or as he seemed to be known now, Kerian, had told him it was bad to steal from his friends but practice was important if he was to keep his skills honed.

* * * * * *

The four sailors leaning against the starboard rail watched Ashe despondently shuffle off towards his cabin. The first of them adjusted the bow case across his back and turned to his colleagues, his quiver of black and gold arrows resting against his leg.

"That one has the weight of the world upon his shoulders." He observed.

"Is it any wonder Weyn Valdeze?" the young warrior known as Aradol responded. "If you had been subjected to the torture that one had, I do not believe you would be in any better mood. It was a wonder Rauph managed to find and rescue him in time." The young man, with short brown hair, wearing a white billowing shirt and tan trousers turned to follow Weyn's gaze and looked on with sorrow etched across his youthful face.

"That is true Aradol." The larger one of the four interrupted, his plump figure and patterned robes marking the man's calling as a salesman of exotic wares, rugs and a lover of fine foods. "But have you noticed his concern is never for himself but always others. He loves his bird so dearly and yearns to see it fly. It is a heart of gold I see in that one. Despite all of his pains and troubles he still tries to make light of his situation and shares his happiness and smiles to lighten the hearts of those around him."

"And their pockets." Voiced the last member of the group, gesturing with a thin pipe that sent aromatic smoke into the air. "That is probably why the two of you get on so well Ives. However, you take the money in a more open way, whilst Ashe has now deprived Austen of his pocket watch and no doubt several other crewmembers of whatever they had upon them." The brooding man swept back his long black hair, parted centrally and let his intense gaze scan the skyline and the specks of flying vehicles moving between the buildings. Then he gently lowered one hand and ensured the daggers he wore about his person, were all where they should be. You could never be too careful with regards to Ashe Wolfsdale.

"Now Mathius," Ives Mantuso replied, his face flustered at the warrior's suggestion of his merchant dishonesty. "In all my days I have never sold a defective item. What you see is what you get. I always charge a fair price and only add the smallest overhead for the shipping, storage, handling, security, heating, lighting and my personal upkeep and maintenance."

Mathius Blackraven tried not to laugh aloud as he noticed from the corner of his eye that Ives was also checking his pockets and belongings. Instead, he turned his attention back towards the view on the horizon. It was quite hypnotic and astounding at the same time. To think people could construct such enormous towers and live in them so high above the ground, the fact they had chariots that could magically fly like birds. The sights he had seen since joining this ship were incredible. The friends he had made priceless. For a man who once worked alone with only the shadows of night and the spectre of death as company, Mathius recognised how being aboard the *El Defensor* had transformed him for the better.

Aradol fidgeted uncomfortably, his youthful face looking at first one crewmate and then the other. Then he looked back at the small dingy skipping backwards and forwards across the waves about one hundred yards away, the boat turning in circles as if looking for something.

"I'm not really comfortable just sitting here doing nothing." He blurted out. "It's not right. We should let them know where we are."

Ives arched an eyebrow and 'tutted' sarcastically.

"And spoil the show?" He remarked. "You know as well as I that once he is back on board it will be do this, do that, fetch this..."

"...Go high!" Weyn muttered. "It's always 'Go High!' Just because I have eagle like vision doesn't mean I want to live in the crow's nest all the time."

"How long do you think it will be before they find us then?" Aradol asked, clearly still uncomfortable at watching their captain rushing backwards and forwards across the waves as Rauph pulled heartily on the oars. "How long does Colette's invisibility shield spell work for anyhow?"

"Well hopefully long enough for me to finish my pipe." Mathius replied, making smoke rings and sending them out one after the other into the air to make it look like the minotaur was rowing through hoops. "After all it is a beautiful day and my physician did say I needed to relax more."

* * * * * *

Kerian frowned as he stared at the large church standing before him. He could have sworn the guard had said go down Mill Lane and turn up Tanners Street. He had found a Mill Lane but this was definitely not Tanner's Street and there was no mermaid, lusty or otherwise, to be seen.

The imposing rust brick building towering before him consisted of a high bell tower reaching for the heavens, set upon a much wider, thick, squat, circular base that had stained glass windows at regular intervals around the circumference. Kerian's first thought was this could be a religious bastion of the St Fraiser monasteries all around the world, until he saw the freshly erected religious symbol raised high upon its walls. The flaming cross was there for all to see, but the sinister shape of a coiled serpent wrapping its sinuous length around the religious icon placed a disturbing image on this place of learning and worship. It appeared that the faith had undergone a change in senior management since Kerian had last encountered them.

He wondered what his friend Marcus would think of this. Maybe the monk was on a world where the teachings of St Fraiser were unknown. He could even be preaching to the newly converted right now, wherever he was. Kerian smiled to himself. He missed the worldly innocence of his travelling companion and his bouts of self-righteousness, even when the monk was clearly in the wrong. It was at times like these that Kerian realised how much he missed the company of others.

A loud hacking cough destroyed the warrior's sense of nostalgia, drawing his attention to a group of beggars huddled in a group up against a buttress at the base of the church wall. They were passing around smoke pipes and drinking from smeared bottles, swearing loudly and leering threateningly at passers-by before laughing together at their obvious discomfort. Others lounged on cover stones and leant against tombstones, some senseless, others hopefully just sleeping, although Kerian could not really tell for sure.

Kerian tried not to let his sorrow show at these unfortunate members of society, but he still frowned at the sight. It seemed ironic that these people had elected to gather around the church and the graves, as if subconsciously they had already given up on their lives and wanted to draw comfort from those who had gone before them. He debated placing a small donation onto a ragged blanket laid out to accept offerings from the charitable public, then reconsidered as he noticed one individual open a fresh bottle and start passing it around amongst his peer group. The money would only be used to drink and smoke themselves into further temporary stupor.

He went to move on and then noticed other headstones set along the base of the wall of the church, marking the resting places of several of the faithful interred into the foundations. Kerian found it unnerving to contemplate, the thought of having the weight of a church crushing down on your body, for all eternity. He shuddered and hunched his shoulders, moving on, whilst dreading the fact that at some point he would have to do the unthinkable.

Admit he was lost and ask for directions.

* * * * * *

The screams and wails of horror echoed the length of the dark dank corridor, some cursing those at work before them, others struggling against their bonds trying vainly to free themselves, whilst others pleaded and begged to be spared the grisly end that awaited them. The high priestess Justina stood silently attentive as she oversaw the masons at work, the horrified cries falling upon her slowly diminishing as the final stones were mortared into place to seal in, alive, those favoured members of the church elite that had supported her predecessor Abbot Brialin.

Tall, sultry, with long flowing black hair and skin as white as porcelain, the High Priestess's features were like those of a beautiful woman captured in a classic historical masterpiece. Her eyes were the iciest blue, promising depths to her person that could snare the unwary and destroy her enemies in an instant. At present, her cold gaze appeared immune to the suffering before her. This was just a task that had to be done and she intended to see it through.

The High Priestess was terrifying in her intensity and ruthless to the end. She was the new switch sweeping the religious sects clean. Brialin had ruled the cathedral at Catterick with an iron fist, using his position of power to manipulate people like implements, to be discarded once their usefulness was at an end. Justina bristled as she pondered this fact, recognising that her own manipulation, to overthrow the leader of the rival Serpent Cult in the town had been a similar successful ploy.

The serpent high priest, Pelune, was now dead, his power reliant on a cursed sacrificial dagger that bestowed health and vitality on its wielder. The dagger had been stolen in a bungled robbery and Justina had been witness to the slow lingering wasting the man had endured as his power had ebbed away. Abbot Brialin was also deceased, his end tied in to the same crew who had spirited the dagger away. This had left a power vacuum in Catterick that Justina had been all too willing to fill. She was now the high priestess of both the cult and the monastery and she was making very sure everyone knew who was in control.

Justina turned to the monk standing alongside her and gestured to the freshly completed mortar and bricks behind her.

"Is that everyone Brother Kalvin?" she asked, looking at the curly haired man beside her. "Is this all of those who supported Brialin?"

"Yes." Kalvin nodded enthusiastically. "...Everyone but Brother Anthony. He has disappeared and no one can find him. There are rumours he has fled to the Northern territories but his trail is cold." He turned to the last remaining opening in the wall and pointed towards it. "I presume this is for when you eventually catch him?"

"Not at all." Justina smiled cruelly. "It's for you." She gestured and the guards leapt forward to pin the struggling monk's arms at his sides.

"What? But you can't do this." Kalvin screamed. "I have helped you, given you advice. I have even shared your bed. I've shown nothing but loyalty towards you."

"Much like the loyalty you showed to Brialin's leadership?" Justina queried. "I don't think it would be wise to have someone so blatantly two-faced as a member of my staff. I mean you might even take it into your mind to betray me." She signalled to the guards to push Brother Kalvin into his tomb.

"I shall miss our nights together." She lowered her head, cutting off their eye-to-eye contact and ending their conversation coldly. "Brick him up."

Justina turned with a swirl of black cloak and headed back along the corridor. She had to give Brother Kalvin credit. He had an excellent set of lungs on him. The screams were clearly audible for the entire length of the corridor and only faded as she started to ascend the roughly hewn stone spiral staircase at the far end of the passage.

A pitter-patter of small scrabbling claws closed in from behind her but Justina did not pause in her walk or show surprise as something horrific caught up with her long skirts and swiftly clambered up her slender frame to sit chattering on her shoulder in a language only the priestess could understand. She stared down at the horrific skeletal creature, its skull too big for its small painfully twisted body beneath. The creature continued to clack its teeth together, its bony tail clicking as it moved about.

"Yes Hamnet, calm down!" she snapped, then, realising her impatience could cause offence, paused to stroke the exposed bony skull and raise a trill of pleasure from the ghoulish demon. "Vill is looking for me. He what? Where is he now?" The creature continued to impart the information its mistress required then sat back on her shoulder staring silently ahead, despite the fact its long dead eyes should have been unable to see anything.

Justina lifted her arm and touched a small agate gemstone set into a bracelet on her wrist. The gem cracked and smoked as the magic contained within rose to her command, conjuring an elliptic gateway into the shadows. The priestess stepped through and came out of a shadowy alcove just as her novice priest ran past, his wild red hair and wispy beard making the tall lanky man appear much more energetic than he actually was.

"You wanted to speak to me." Justina stated, in a voice that made the priest jump in his tracks.

"Yes high priestess." Vill replied. "I have been looking for you everyw…"

"Get on with it." Justina snapped. "Time is precious to me. Just make sure it is something worth my while, something interesting."

"Sorry." Vill stammered back, his eyes being drawn to the grinning monster sitting on her shoulder causing a shiver through his gaunt frame. "It's just that you wanted to know immediately if it happened." Justina's eyes widened at the implication of what Vill was suggesting. Could it possibly be?

"Is it the scrying bowl?" she asked eagerly, licking her lips in sweet anticipation. Vill nodded his head confirming her suspicions and making her heart beat faster.

"It started flickering on and off a short while ago. It shows rapid indistinct images of what looks like melting gold pieces but little else. I know you wanted to be informed straight away." Justina looked at Vill with her cold blue eyes and offered a smile that made the priest feel like he was staring into the face of a predator about to rip him limb from limb.

"You are in luck. I find that information very interesting. Very interesting indeed."

* * * * * *

The dingy was lifted clear of the sea, seawater dripping from her hull as it was swung up and over onto the deck, hoisted by a silent crew who realised their captain was not a happy man.

Thomas viewed the possible conspirators with his eyebrow raised in ire, looking at the crew one at a time to see who would crack first and reveal who had decided it would be amusing for him and Rauph to row backwards and forwards like idiots. Archer, merchant, young knave, assassin, Thomas had his suspicions but deep inside had to admire the camaraderie this group of individuals had built up during their time together.

He took his time, lingering on each crewman just enough to make his gaze uncomfortable then moved onto the next, using his training in interrogation skills to their limit, however none of the quartet owned up to anything. Maybe the fact that Thomas was covered in mud lessened his air of authority. He looked up above the four as if searching the heavens for inspiration, then looked down again with a strange smug look on his face.

"One of you did it. One of you decided it would be fun to leave us out there." Thomas snarled, in his best attempt at being stern. He walked slowly up and down in front of the group. "And mark my words, I shall find out who was responsible." He stopped on the last word and spun back to face his crew, already knowing all four had a hand in his prolonged voyage.

"Aradol slop and latrine duty for five days, Ives the dingy needs a new coat of paint. Mathius over the side, start scraping barnacles off the hull and use your blades for something useful for once. Weyn…"

"I know, I know." Weyn muttered. "Go high."

Thomas turned from them and walked away, smiling broadly. He knew he had the right ones because Abeline and Plano two acrobats from the Parisian circus that worked the rigging above had pointed them out when he had looked up into the sails. They had perched on the beam to the main sail, grinning like Cheshire cats from a Lewis Carroll story as they betrayed their companions with glee, probably because of their losses at cards a few nights ago. It was all good-natured fun and Thomas would never reveal the secret because he nurtured this good feeling aboard.

The captain took in a deep breath and soaked in his surroundings. His ship was back beneath his feet, the slow rise and fall lulling him with a sense of security. This was his temporary home and the people around him were his extended family that he cared for deeply. However, he also recognised that he was about to lead them back into danger. He retrieved the large gemstone from his pocket and hefted it in his hand. A heavy weight settling in the pit of his stomach. It was time to move on, time to gamble once again with the lives of everyone on board.

It was time to enter the ships graveyard!

* * * * * *

Kerian finally located the buxom figure of the Lusty Mermaid as the last light leached from the darkening sky above Wellruff. The building was taller than he expected having at least three floors, with wide balconies running around the upper floors to allow guests to sit out in the sultry evening air and take in the sights and sounds of the night around them.

The interior of the inn was boisterous, filled with smoke and a riot of sound and smell. Live music played on the stage, service staff weaved expertly through the dancing and swaying figures moving to the music. Several patrons leaned up against the bar sharing stories of their day and laughing at each other's shortcomings or amusing anecdotes. A card game occupied one corner, a palpable tension hanging over the table and its huddled occupants as they bet their income on a twist of fate and their ability to bluff what they held in their hands. Another man sat in the corner playing dice with some guards, an infectious smile on his face as he took the men for everything they had.

Kerian noticed with some sadness, that the guard he had tipped at the dock was standing there trying his luck and losing the gift Kerian had bestowed upon him. It was so sad that some people never recognised what they already had and always strove to get more, inevitably ending up with less.

He approached the bar and discussed his needs for a room whilst his boat received repairs. The innkeeper was only too happy to oblige and even managed to meet the extra request of having a balcony with a view of the rising sun. The innkeeper's joke about whether Kerian needed a stable for his horse, whilst gesturing to the worn saddlebags slung over his shoulder, drew a strained smile from his weary guest. It appeared the tale of Kerian Denaris and his arrival to this place had reached the man's ears faster than Kerian's lost footfalls had.

A gemstone retrieved from the saddlebag flashed in the candle light, securing the deal and trading itself for a worn key, hot food and a sanctuary for the rest of the week. Kerian asked if he could have his meal brought to his room. The inn was too loud, the colours and happiness too jarring after the harrowing experiences that had brought him here.

Eager to please his new tenant, the innkeeper poked his head through the serving doors to the kitchen, shouted a few orders before indicating that Kerian follow him up a sweeping staircase to the rooms leading off the balcony. He wandered along mumbling conversation that Kerian was too tired to listen to and finally halted before a door.

"This is it." He indicated. "If you want a bath, they are out the back in the bath house. Just talk to the girls and they will arrange hot water for you. Your meal will be up shortly." Kerian nodded his head and tried to smile but a wave of exhaustion was sweeping over him.

He entered the room alone and took in his surroundings, pleasantly surprised at how clean and light the room was. The bed was clean, the linen tight. The headboard not stained from previous occupants and the air in the room pleasantly scented with lavender. Kerian dropped his saddlebags on the bed and moved to the window, noticing that it opened wide as a door, allowing access onto the balcony and the night air, where a weather worn table and chair awaited him. He leaned on the balcony and looked out over the rooftops to the harbour and the sea, then turned back inside as a low knock came from the door.

His meal had arrived. He tipped the young serving maid with a tiny sapphire that matched the colour of her eyes and left her outside as he took the tray into the room. Tomorrow, he promised himself, he would seek a gem merchant who could exchange some of his small fortune into more suitable denominations. The stew was as inspiring as the room. Kerian could not believe how hungry he was; the gravy was rich and had a tingling spice that lingered on the tongue. The meat was so soft it could have been made from butter and even the vegetables had a taste and crunch to them that invigorated his weary frame.

Now that his stomach was full and warm, tiredness swept over him once again. He retrieved the chair from the balcony and wedged it fully under the door; a habit Kerian had utilised widely in his travels. No matter how civilised a place appeared he knew that sometimes the night came complete with nocturnal visitors that you did not want to catch you with your guard down.

He crashed down onto the bed, his head sinking into a pillow and closed his eyes, his hand holding tightly to the golden necklace that meant so much to him. Kerian knew he would see his love in the morning. He would check she was well, then make his plans for finding her and getting back to her side.

Chapter Two

As night inevitably gave way to the twilight period of dawn, Kerian found himself anxiously pacing on the balcony overlooking the city of Wellruff. His stomach churned nervously, turning somersaults, his pulse racing, waiting for the moment when the first rays of the sun would creep over the horizon and gently kiss the pendant he held in his hand, activating the magic deep within the pearl at its centre.

He completed another circuit of the small balcony, his brow creased in frustration, his mind willing the sun to rise into the sky and allow his few precious moments of time with Colette. Kerian knew this feeling of anticipation was childish but he could not deny his need to see her again, make sure she was safe and well. He had even brushed his hair and cleaned himself up, despite knowing that the amulet would not permit the young woman of his affections to know he was observing her from afar or hear the words he desperately wanted to tell her.

"I'm still alive. I am searching for you."

The sky brightened further, encouraged by a chorus of shrieking gulls and terns wheeling about the roof of the inn, fighting for food and scraps left over from the revelries of the night before. A golden line of light made the horizon glow, before the sun gently materialized, spilling light across the surface of the sea, its rays reaching towards the pendant Kerian held breathlessly before him.

The grey surface of the pearl shimmered, its luminescence increased by exposure to the brightness of the dawn. Then Kerian started to see a delicate shape form in the depths of the pearl, threatening to steal away what little remaining breath he had in his body.

She was beautiful.

Long blond hair, tumbled in loose tresses, violet ribbons attempting to tame the wildness of her loose style and draw the hair back from her face. Porcelain smooth skin, eyes of deepest blue. A delicate frame hiding a warrior's heart, she was reading a book of some kind and leaning against the wall behind her was... his sword.

Kerian's heart soared at the sight. This vision of Colette gave him purpose, the motivation to continue with his quest. He yearned to scream into the pendant, shout his love for her but he had tried this, many dawns before and knew it was a futile exercise, ultimately leading to dismay. He turned about, trying to improve the image and give an indication in what direction Colette lay but her profile remained the same no matter which way he faced, confirming in his heart that she was no longer on this world but had passed through the ship's graveyard and onto somewhere new.

The sun inched ever higher in the sky. Kerian noticed it out of the corner of his eye and now sent all of his will towards it to try to check its relentless motion, knowing that this was as much an impossibility as his love hearing him declare his feelings for her. He tried to angle the necklace and gain an inkling as to where she was, but it just looked like her cabin in the background and he was no clearer as to where he should venture next.

Colette's image started to fade as rapidly as it appeared. Kerian dared not blink in case he missed even one second of her face, trying to etch her features into his memory to sustain him through the coming day. Then she was gone, the pearl going back to its plain nondescript grey. Kerian sank to the floor of the balcony, his legs suddenly unable to hold his weight, his mouth dry, his heart breaking, clutching the pendant tightly in his hand as he quietly whispered that he missed her, over and over again.

* * * * * *

There it was again!

Colette paused in her studying, her finger hovering over the arcane script as a strange sensation of being watched made the hairs on her neck stand up. What was it? Her hand dropped to her belt, delving rapidly into a drawstring pouch to bring out a pinch of finely crushed gemstone, which she threw into the air, her fingers whipping through intricate gestures her long dead mentor had taught her.

"*Veritat!*" she shouted, watching the dust glisten and twinkle around her like a field of bright stars. There was definitely magic at work! Someone *was* watching her! Her hand moved towards the pouch for a replenishment of ground gemstone but already the sparkling air around her was fading and the dust slowly dropped to the floor. Whoever or whatever was watching her had stopped.

Colette took a deep breath and tried to calm her thoughts. Who could be doing this? Well whoever it was, she would be ready for them next time. A knock at her cabin door surprised her, jolting her from her thoughts.

"Come in." The door opened and Thomas stood in the doorway coated from head to foot in mud.

"On second thoughts..." Colette swiftly reconsidered. "Why don't you stay out in the gangway!" She walked over, trying to smooth the worried wrinkles from her face and smiled as bravely as she could.

"Is everything alright?" Thomas asked, his acute perception instantly picking up that something was wrong.

"I'm fine," Colette replied trying to hide her disquiet with a radiant smile, before turning to carefully place the book she was holding down on her bed. "Just losing my mind..." she whispered under her breath.

Thomas looked at her with his head tilted on one side, unconvinced with the reply but recognising that pushing the matter further could result in no information at all and risk alienating his mage.

"How did you get on?" Colette asked. "Did you get some?"

"Well Miguel was not quite as generous as I would have liked." Thomas confessed, frowning and shedding flakes of mud towards the floor. "I could only get one." He reached into his jacket and offered the flawless amethyst over.

"It's such a shame we have to destroy these gems each time we use the power within them." Colette stated, turning the beautiful stone over and over, staring into its depths. She looked up into Thomas's eyes and paused. "Did you say just the one? That is only enough for one gateway. What about the other one?"

Thomas shrugged his shoulders.

"It's the best I could do at the time." He confessed. "What about using some more of the smaller gems like we did to get here?" Colette's soft features transformed into a stern icy frown.

"We nearly lost the stern of the *El Defensor* when we came here to Maraket." She snapped. "It's too dangerous relying on several power sources at once. The spell can falter at an inopportune moment."

"We have no choice." Thomas shot back. "We cannot stay here. Miguel will set out in pursuit to get this gemstone back. We need to go through the gateway and the sooner the better." Colette felt a heaviness fall onto her small shoulders.

"What about the danger to the crew?" she asked. "I am not happy risking their lives in this way."

"That's not your decision to make." Thomas replied. "If this all goes pear shaped the blame lies squarely with me." He cracked a tired smile, trying to make light of the seriousness of the situation, sending a further shower of muddy flecks to the floor.

"Come on. I am about to summon the crew to their stations. The sooner we do this the sooner we can get to a safe new world and you can use all the leisure time we have there studying a way to solve our magical deficit."

Colette shrugged her shoulders and tried to smile back but the effort was forced as she considered the apparent danger to those she cared for. She had lost one man close to her and had no intention of losing others.

She stared into space, her mind thinking back to the magically aged features that had always held a warm smile for her. Kerian's long white hair tied back from his face like a lost Viking warrior but hiding a gentle heart. Thomas's arm came down around her shoulder.

"I miss him too you know?" he confessed quietly. "Come on, let's get this show on the road."

Colette carefully lifted his arm from her shoulder and brushed the muddy debris from her clothes.

"Really Thomas. Those mudpacks are only supposed to go on your face. Didn't you know that?"

Thomas laughed and bowed to the young sorceress, gesturing that she stepped out into the corridor ahead of him in an exaggerated and humorous attempt at gallantry.

"You never used to be like this." She commented back over her shoulder. "I think Rowan is quite happy with the rugged captain we all know. You do not need beauty treatments to win her over. She is yours already and you don't know how lucky you are."

Thomas smiled broadly as he followed Colette up towards the main deck, his mind split between the beguiling charms of the brunette-haired woman he had grown so close to after rescuing her and the dangers they were all about to face once he announced the call to *General Quarters.*

Colette concentrated on the steps she took, one foot falling after the other and felt like a condemned convict walking to the gallows. What Thomas was asking her to do was so dangerous. His happy go lucky response to her justified concerns vexed her. Whether the captain liked it or not, she was the one casting the spell. No matter how he tried to convince her otherwise, if a mistake was made it was on her head and not his.

* * * * * *

"Why is my boat up on stilts?" Kerian asked exasperated, his hands on his hips, his fists clenched tightly at his sides in frustration. "She is supposed to be in the water!"

"Well it's like this you see," confessed the shorter one of the two men before him. "We had to get the boat out of the water to plug the holes and check the rudder, which is completely shot and needs replacing by the way."

"That's when we found the other defects." The taller of the two interrupted. "We had to order in parts and they will take at least a week to arrive."

"A week!" Kerian felt his head would explode as he fought the feeling of wanting to grab both men and show them where he could insert the broken rudder parts within their anatomy. "That's too long!" He snapped. "Get the *Tulip* down from there; I'll take her somewhere else."

"Well you could take it to Horace's." The shorter plumper one commented, running his hand over his bald head. "It's three days by sea or five over land."

Kerian's mouth dropped.

"Are you telling me you are the only shipwrights in Wellruff? That's ridiculous!"

"Now, now!" The taller and thinner one replied. "Here at Gellions customer service always comes first. We can supply you with a courtesy kayak for the next few days if you want one."

Kerian spun on his heel and stormed from the boatyard fuming with barely controlled anger. A week! A whole week stuck here! His footsteps and thunderous appearance caused every cat and dog in the neighbourhood to run away with its tail between its legs as he stormed back towards the inn.

This place was so damned crooked! Even the gem merchant had tried to short change him. He had managed to change a few minor pieces but when he haggled on the price of a particularly impressive ruby Kerian had to stop and walk away. The man was going to pay him a tenth of what it was worth.

He was so incensed by what he had experienced in this port town. Everyone was looking to make a fast gold coin. They were all so rude and had an annoying habit of slipping into a local dialect that Kerian found particularly difficult to follow. This made him even angrier as he had a sneaking suspicion the people were talking about him but he could not prove it.

It was so hard to obey the rules instead of swinging a sword, splitting a few skulls and getting what you wanted without any problems at all. Being a hero was harder than it looked and it seemed to be getting him absolutely nowhere. His angry steps stopped in a smelly squelch and Kerian looked down to see the steaming pile of horse manure he had just stepped in. That was it; someone was definitely out to get him. He looked around to find a handy doorstep or raised kerb to wipe his boot on and noticed he was standing at the entrance to the Wellruff market. Maybe some retail therapy would help him clear his mind. He looked around at the stalls about him, his mind sizing up the selections and finding the choice somewhat depressing.

Costermongers selling assorted vegetables of various hues, balanced in precarious displays of geometric design, fought for space against platters of fresh fish, prawns, squid and swordfish. The rich aromas of exotic spices exposed to the air, piled in colours of crimson, mustard and green threatened to overpower the scent of sizzling meat prepared by vendors over charcoal burners then stuffed into pitta breads along with fresh chopped vegetables and creamy yoghurt dressings.

The hustle and bustle around these stands was somewhat staggering as prospective customers dressed in bright clothes buzzed around the stalls haggling prices and bartering sellers down to levels apparently so low that they were depriving food from the merchant children's mouths. It was like watching a swarm of bees around a hive and it instantly put Kerian on guard. Where crowds gathered, thieves also congregated.

His eyes scanned the crowd for shady individuals as he cautiously moved around the perimeter of the stalls. Walking slowly towards the end of the market, he watched women snatching up silks and holding them around their bodies before angrily dropping them back on the stalls and storming off when prices were disclosed, only to return moments later and haggle again. It seemed a market was a market wherever you were.

A vocal collection of men stood around a corral at the far end of the market, money exchanging hands over the livestock squealing, honking, mooing and clucking within. Kerian wrinkled his nose at the smell but moved closer to see one buyer walk off with three geese complete with rope leads and another with a cage stuffed full of chickens that were apparently the best egg layers in the kingdom. The horse paddock drew his attention, rekindling memories of his stalwart steed, Saybier, cut down in Catterick all those months ago. A lump formed in his throat as he moved closer to view the mares and stallions on display. One handler looked familiar and appeared to know his way around the animals he paraded for the buyers. Kerian looked more closely and confirmed it was the dice player he had noticed fleecing the guards at the inn the night before.

Kerian nodded as the man's eyes met his and after a moment's consideration the olive skinned, dark haired individual smiled nervously back, not yet sure how this man knew him. The handler completed his circuit of the ring before leading a prancing black and white horse swiftly back towards the stalls, checking over his shoulder in Kerian's direction as the observing buyers loudly shouted and waved assorted amounts of currency in the air as they bid for the ownership rights to the creature displayed.

The loud excited voices almost succeeded in hiding the arguing raised voices rising from the stalls, but a loud crash from behind the scenes and several expletives showed that all was not well in the world of horse sales. The end stall shook as the animal within rebelled at being paraded for all to see. The auctioneer shouted angrily demanding the next horse be brought forward, turning to the gathered onlookers and describing the mount as *Toledo*.

Kerian craned his neck and tried to see over the heads of the men anxious to buy and was quite surprised to see a fresh-faced youth with a swollen left eye backing out from the stalls tugging furiously on the rope around a cream coloured stallion with a jet-black mane and fire in its eyes. The horse stopped frequently, shaking its head, yanking the poor man backwards and forwards before charging, knocking the stable boy flat to the ground before bucking and rearing, hooves flashing through the air as the buyers swiftly backed away from the rails.

Kerian smiled to himself. That was some horse. Someone had obviously mistreated the beast and it was not happy to be near anyone, especially someone who it recognised was scared of it. The animal ran to the far end of the paddock, stopped in a swirl of dust then turned back and charged full pelt at its handler causing the youth to run back into the stalls, the horse charging after him.

The owner of the stall came out of hiding once he realised the horse was back in the stalls and started shouting at the bidders gesturing wildly in the direction the horse had gone. His vocal tone and agitation became louder and more pronounced, as the buyers refused to consider taking the magnificent animal, clearly deciding its rebellious nature was more trouble than it was worth.

Kerian turned away, satisfied that was as exciting as the sale was going to get, his eye now identifying a stall selling baked goods and pastries stuffed with fruits. Now this was more like it. He needed to put on some weight based on his last glimpse at his reflection. He gestured for two spirals of glistening pastry flecked with orange and browned sugar and paid the amount without haggling, much to the surprise of the seller.

As he bit into the sticky sweet treat and tasted the cinnamon spice laced through the delicate tart, he happened to look over at a stall selling lanterns. As the stallholder lowered a particularly large lantern for a woman to see, Kerian noticed the look of shock shown on the face of the man who had been observing him through the glass. It was the same olive complexion, the same shoulder length rebellious dark hair. Kerian noticed the dice man's eyes widen, as he realised that he had been spotted and he turned and ran off through the stalls, his passage marked by the curses and spilt merchandise he left in his wake.

Kerian took one more bite of his pastry and considered the pathway the man was taking. Clearly, he was worried about Kerian recognising him from the haphazard pathway he wove through the crowd. However, there appeared to be no logical reason why the man should feel this way. It was intriguing, the smallest of mysteries, the slightest hint of adventure.

Two tough looking figures moved through the crowd in pursuit of the fleeing dice man, making the unfolding scenario even more interesting. A little voice in Kerian's head warned him not to get involved but he simply smiled to himself. He had a week to kill in this city. What was the harm in getting to know the locals better?

He slowly moved through the bustling crowds, tackling his second pastry and drawing indignant glances from some passers-by who appeared to find it rude that he was eating his food in this way. Kerian shrugged apologetically and kept up the pace, watching a third figure join the pursuit. Now this man Kerian did recognise. It was the guard he had tipped so heavily at the harbour.

Now everything was starting to make sense. Kerian finished his last pastry, licked his lips and then picked up the pace. This was going to be fun.

* * * * * *

Justina stared down into the scrying bowl, her brow creased in concentration as she tried to decipher the jumble of images within. Golden coins bubbled and slid into each other. Cracked and shattered jewels lay in a pile on the floor like empty husks, signs of someone using magic in vast amounts. There was a sword with the emblem of St Frasier clear to see engraved on the hilt of its blood smeared blade. The images flickered and blurred as if someone was actively trying to make the headband that allowed such communication, to work. It was frantic, the actions of someone desperate to make a connection.

This selection of snapshot images... was that the remains of a dragon? Justina held her breath hoping for more information and noticing that the floor of the treasure vault appeared to be slanted over to one side. Lava bubbled at the far edge of the view. It appeared as if this treasure vault was slipping slowly into the volcano.

Justina tried to calm her thoughts for a moment could she teleport to this location now she could sense the headband? It seemed possible. Maybe with the advice from her familiar she could achieve this.

She turned in a swirl of cloak and headed away from the chamber anxious to collect the required items to manage the spell. There were several elements to consider including the distances involved and the heat when she arrived.

However, the prize, if it remained intact, would be well worth the risk.

* * * * * *

The alarm sounding general quarters rang through the *El Defensor* galvanising the crew into arming themselves and moving swiftly to their designated positions. Each one of them knew what this alarm meant and the thought of it chilled them to the bone.

Ashe looked out his cabin door and watched the crew moving with determined purpose. He sighed deeply and looked over at Sinders sitting in his cage cracking a nut with his beak.

"Thomas won't let me go to battle stations." He confessed to his pet. "He states I make too much noise." Sinders clicked its beak as if agreeing with the unfairness of it all, giving Ashe the excuse he needed to continue.

"You know we are going into the ship's graveyard, don't you?" Sinders trilled and fluffed its feathers as Ashe talked. "It's very scary in there. There are all these sad broken ships, all slowly being ground up filled with seaweed and treasure. I found a grey pearl on one of those ships you know and there are still so many left to explore. That's if the Scintarn hounds leave you alone long enough to look. They eat you or drag you to their master who slurps out your brains, but don't you worry I won't let anything eat your brains whilst I am around."

Sinders made another set of clicks and low whistles of encouragement.

"I know you missed the graveyard last time but you were asleep and Thomas made sure we sailed through very fast." Ashe replied. "Maybe if you are good, we can go out on deck and have a look together this time. If you are really lucky you might see some hounds or the killer giant eels!"

Ashe picked up the cage and set off after the other crew. Austen had told him to be more like Sinders parent. What better way than to share an experience with him!

Chapter Three

The sounds of heavy blows, groans and raised voices around the next corner indicated to Kerian that his pursuit of the olive-skinned dice player was near to an end. He stole a quick glance into the alleyway and confirmed his suspicions before easing back into cover and considering his options.

In the split second he had observed, he noticed the dice man up against the wall, receiving several blows to the face and a knee to the chest. Three against one were okay odds when armed but this man, despite his muscular arms and well-developed torso appeared to be allowing the three men to pummel him and was not putting up any attempt to defend himself. The alleyway itself, was a dead end, terminating in a tall fence covered in flyers and notices blocking the passage onwards. This fence was clearly an attempt by the authority of Wellruff to prevent shoppers entering or leaving the market district in any way other than by the main entrance and exit, helping to maintain the smooth flow of foot traffic and security, whilst focusing customer attention on the stalls and assorted wares sited along the thoroughfare behind him.

Kerian shook his head as his conscience pleaded for him to step in and save the day. His brain however, suggested that the dice man had probably brought this on himself and not to get involved. He sighed as he realised that he now had no weapons. His dagger was burnt to a crisp in Catterick, his sword was now in the care of Colette. The other dagger he had owned for just a short time was lost deep inside a dragon's treasure trove in an active volcano and he was glad to be rid of it. He had the reflective circular shield strapped to his back but it was useless in a situation such as this. The chances of hoping the three thugs were vain enough to stop and examine their reflections, whilst Kerian whisked their victim away, was a scenario as unlikely as the *Tulip* being repaired by the end of the week!

He looked around for inspiration and noticed the stall next to him had an awning along which the stallholder had hung row upon row of cooking pans, pots and utensils on display to his customers. Kerian reached out, grabbing the wooden brace supporting the main beam and snatched it away, sending the cooking implements clattering to the floor in a giant heap as they slid one by one off the end.

The shop seller yelled out in fury but Kerian decided he could always make good later and turned to the more important task at hand. The salesman would be too busy right now trying to stem the continuing flow of utensils from falling to consider pursuit.

With a deep breath and a twirl of the staff in his hand, Kerian walked calmly into the alleyway and leaned against the wall to watch the show. The burly attackers hardly noticed his arrival, intent on beating the man before them. One held up a mop of dark hair whilst the other threw a left hook that rattled Kerian's teeth, let alone the intended target. Kerian winced as another blow landed, then watched as the guard drew a dagger with a wicked gleaming edge, his angry face confirming he was about to resort to a more permanent resolution to the one-sided discussion he had been having with the man lying at his feet.

"Excuse me!" Kerian opened, deciding he had seen enough. "I don't suppose you know the directions to the *Lusty Mermaid*? Some kind soul gave me directions last night but I'll be damned if I can find it."

The guard turned towards Kerian's voice, his face a mask of anger that suddenly registered, then recognised, the man talking to him as his recent benefactor. The look on the thug's face spoke volumes. He knew who Kerian was and instantly knew that he could identify him for the crime he was about to commit. He gestured to one of his colleagues and pointed towards their unexpected witness, as his other associate piled in another round house blow, rocking the head of their dark-haired victim back into the wall with a grunt.

"Shut him up!" the guard snapped, before turning his attention back to the man at his feet and waving his dagger menacingly. "Give me back the money you stole from me last night."

Kerian moved away from the wall, setting his feet apart as he sized up the approaching threat advancing towards him. The man was heavy set and walked as if he were wading through water. His shoulders were wide and his biceps bulged beneath his tan tunic as he moved. Dark eyes peered menacingly from below a thick set brow. Kerian tried not to smile as the man huffed towards him fists clenched. He waited until the hired heavy closed in then snapped the staff in his hand up hard between the man's legs. Kerian tried not to laugh as the face before him transformed from someone wishing him harm into someone who looked deeply surprised.

As the air and the intention to do harm rushed out of the man, Kerian whipped the top end of his staff down between the man's bulging eyes rapping him hard on the forehead and sending him crashing to the floor. This was almost too easy. He stepped forwards towards the remaining two assailants battering the dark-haired man to the floor, intent on drawing another one of them away from their hapless victim. As he brought the staff down to tap the unknown bully on the shoulder Kerian glimpsed a flash of a bright blue eye from beneath the beaten dice man's bushy bloodied eyebrow. There was a low snarl as the wanton thug whirled to face him, just as a large meaty hand came down and grabbed the edge of the shield at Kerian's shoulder.

"What are you going to do about my brother's stall?" bellowed a deep voice.

Kerian rolled his eyes to the heavens, annoyed at the interruption and spun around on his toes, his staff whipping around, whistling through the air, intending to smack whoever this was around the head and silence his queries. Instead, it cracked soundly off a heavily muscled torso level with Kerian's face and then splintered apart. Kerian looked up in shock to face a large bald man with arms wider across than Kerian's legs!

"By Adden!" Kerian swore under his breath. The man facing him was taller than Rauph the minotaur! "Look let me just deal with this small matter and I will come back and..."

The floor disappeared from under his feet as Kerian was hoisted into the air by his tunic, skin pinching stitching stretching under the incredible strength of the man lifting him bodily from the floor.

"I take it you would like me to reconsider my order of priorities?" Kerian asked meekly before he found himself flying backwards out of the alleyway and straight into the bustling marketplace. He found himself skittering on the cobblestones, trying to stop his relentless backpedalling but the man holding him was refusing to let go. They crashed into a stall and Kerian's view was momentarily obscured by a cascading waterfall of over ripe oranges, vibrant lemons, purple kale and miniature green skinned pineapples. His breath crashed out of him as he landed, causing Kerian to open his mouth in shock, only for a stray strawberry to drop in the presented opening and choke him worse than the hulking brute attacking him.

Kerian struggled to see his foe through the tumbling citrus avalanche and lashed out blindly, punching several innocent bystanders before landing a good blow right on the end of his foe's large nose. It cracked as the blow landed, warm blood jetting from the man's face. Kerian twisted and turned like a wild thing as the stall creaked and groaned ominously beneath him, then it snapped in two, dropping him and his assailant to the floor in another explosion of free-falling vegetables. The brute loosened his grip at the shock of the drop and Kerian saw the opportunity, smashing his fist into the man's nose once more before trying to slip out from underneath him. Huge hands latched on as Kerian struggled. Several more stitches tore free and Kerian felt the front of his tunic come loose as the man lost his grip.

He slid through the crushed fruits beneath him, quickly rolling under a stall selling plants and cut flowers, coming out the far side with wilted daises hanging forlornly in his hair before ducking under a fishmonger's stall. Kerian crawled as quickly as his knees permitted, banging his shield along the underside of the stalls, making the fish jump and slither across the table top above him as if they had suddenly come back to life. He frantically scrambled away, determined to put as much space between himself and his pursuer as possible, barely avoiding the feet of the people scurrying around him.

An ear-piercing scream bellowed through the square, causing Kerian to pause in his crawling, wondering whatever this new problem was but before he could investigate something latched onto his ankle and dragged him back out into the open. He turned to find himself facing the burly shape of the second thug from the alley, clearly the guard's associate intended that Kerian not escape the clutches of the giant menace currently wrecking a rug merchant's stall looking for his elusive target.

"He's over here!" The man yelled, holding tightly to Kerian's leg and smiling as the enraged giant stopped his unruly carpet destruction and spun towards the shout.

Kerian did not hesitate, spinning over onto his back and kicking out hard with his right boot connecting just above the brute's knee. The joint popped with a sound like pulling a leg off a roast chicken and the man buckled to the ground in agony.

Kerian leapt to his feet, snatching a cooking pot off a stall and swung it with all his might, crashing the metal container into the side of the ruffian's head with a resounding clang. The man sank to the floor not sure if he should hold his head or his knee. Another blood-curdling scream sounded from back towards the alley, freezing the shoppers in the market who now realised something was very wrong. Fearing the worst, Kerian snatched the nearest thing to hand, cursing his lack of a weapon and ran to assist, only to find his huge adversary lumbering into his path once again.

"I shall make you pay for what you have done to my brother's stall." He roared, waving a wickedly curved blade in Kerian's direction.

"I really don't have time for this." Kerian muttered, bringing up the weapon he had blindly snatched from the stall to parry the attack, before looking on in dismay at the realisation he actually held a long stick of bread in his hand. This was not the item he had hoped for. Indeed, he would have considered anything else but the floury item he now held.

The hulk's blade flashed in the sunlight and Kerian's trusty stick shortened by six inches. The return swing shortening it by a similar amount as Kerian lunged forwards and watched the bread bend in his hand as he attempted to stab his assailant with what little remained. A backhand from the large figure wiped the look of dismay from Kerian's face and sent him flying into a group of onlookers, knocking several to the floor as stars filled his vision.

"I'm really sorry." He gasped, trying to stand and finding himself struggling to place his hands on something sturdy enough to support him. Instead, he found himself in the embarrassing position of pushing off a most indignant heavily endowed woman's posterior and dodging her deadly swipes with her shopping bag.

"Oh I really, really am sorry!" Kerian blustered, ducking again as the shopping bag whistled through the air where his head had just been. He struggled to untangle himself from the innocent shoppers with minimal damage only to find his neck grabbed once more by the hulking individual still roaring his demand for payment for his brother's damaged stall.

"Call the guards." Someone screamed.

"There's a wild animal loose." Yelled another onlooker, pointing dramatically back towards the alleyway. Kerian struggled to turn his head and see what the man was pointing at then realised to his horror he was being barrelled straight into a butcher's stall. He closed his eyes as he crashed into the display of chops, offal and ribs. The butcher chopping up a chicken for a waiting customer dropped his cleaver in shock and it landed straight across the splayed fingers of the brute pinning Kerian to the stall.

There was a startled scream as the man's index finger came away, blood jetting out across the meat on the stall. He straightened up in shock, grabbing his wounded hand and releasing the pressure on his captive. The uppercut Kerian delivered was fast and brutal, rocking the bald man's head back and setting him up on his heels. Kerian followed with another blow to the chin and then as the hulk staggered away, scrabbled up onto the butcher's counter and threw himself bodily at the man as he turned away, his arm wrapping tightly around the titan in an attempt to put him in a sleeper hold.

The reaction was instant, violent jerking and swinging, with Kerian's legs flying out behind him crashing off onlooker's heads, catching further stalls and creating yet more havoc. Pots crashed to the ground, fish slithered off plates, chickens escaped from crates running amok and causing further chaos. People ran screaming in every direction, whilst others chose to watch the epic battle going on before them, throwing coins thinking it was impromptu street entertainment.

Slowly but surely, Kerian's grip across his foe's windpipe began to win through. The man started turning crimson, sweat beading across his brow as he frantically attempted to tear Kerian from his back. Despite the weakening swipes, the man was still a force to be reckoned with. He staggered backwards smashing into some large vases, sending them to the floor, then turned another way crashing Kerian into a large pile of carpets, that sent a cloud of dust and assorted bugs up into the air all over the two wrestling men. Kerian wheezed and spluttered but refused to let go as his foe's actions continued to slow.

There was a final groan as the man finally dropped onto his knees, gasping and weakly clawing at his throat. Kerian squeezed harder, just to be sure and felt the titan go limp beneath him. Somehow, his attacker looked less threatening with his eyes closed, like a giant baby sleeping quietly, with all the energy taken out of him. Kerian staggered away, turning to take in the angry faces of the crowd, holding his hands up, trying to appear unthreatening and ward off any further attacks.

"Look I am really, really sorry about all of this." He confessed. "I never meant for any of this to happen." Over the heads of the people gathered around him, he could see the approach of several town guards. It was time to go.

Kerian turned, taking a step away from his foe, only to feel the man's hand crash down upon his neck once more, yanking him back and pulling tight. Kerian struggled to get his fingers under the constriction at his throat, his feet slipping on the cobbles as he struggled to set himself and step away but the strength of the huge man was astounding. He felt himself leaning over backwards, his shield digging into the back of his neck and the tops of his legs as his resilient foe snarled his impending victory to the crowd, despite being on his knees.

There was only one thing to do. Kerian smashed his head back as far as he could and felt it connect with the man's nose. It was like hitting a wall, making Kerian see stars but the surprise attack worked to his advantage, his foe releasing his grip at the impact and bellowing with rage. Kerian threw himself forwards, feeling the tightness at his neck increase before something gave and his linen tunic ripped free. He charged forward three steps, then turned to swing a kick at the man, catching the thug on the ear before Kerian surprisingly found himself falling to the ground as the titan grabbed his ankle.

Some of the crowd were actively clapping their appreciation at this acrobatic show, as Kerian's surprised facial expression displayed his clear amazement that it was him and not his foe who had fallen to the cobbles. He dusted himself off and closed again, a left and right smashing into the man's jaw, only for Kerian to end up shaking his hands at the pain rushing through his fingers. This brute was unstoppable! His large adversary laughed before slowly getting back to his feet, his movement stopping other stallholders from angrily rushing forward to complain about the damage to their stalls.

A quick glance past the hulk confirmed guards were closing on their position. Kerian needed to get away and realised he needed a swift diversion. He slipped his hand into his trousers and lifted out the handful of coins he had bartered for his gems. It appeared to be easy come, easy go, in Wellruff! He shrugged, mentally resigning himself to the fact that he would have to collect more gems from his saddlebags at the Inn and exchange them tomorrow!

Kerian eyed up his opponent, bowed and then with a dramatic flourish threw his hand up in the air sending golden coins spinning. The crowd took in the sight of the tumbling gold coins then surged forwards, greedy hands grasping at the unexpected bounty. Kerian ducked to the side as they came, noting the hulk losing his balance in the stampede and crashing to the floor as Kerian slipped away through the excited crowd. He angled between the stalls, making sure the guards were occupied with the unruly crowd, before he moved towards the alleyway where the dice man had been attacked. He felt sure that the olive-skinned man would be dead by now, Kerian's rescue mission now a case of tragic recovery.

He slipped through another crowd of shoppers, snatching a large hat and turning to admire some pots and pans as two more guards ran by. The reflection in one skillet showing a worried bystander having a heated discussion with the two men, waving his arms dramatically as he voiced his concern that he had lost his wife somewhere in the bustle of the market place. His frantic gestures pointed back in the direction of the alleyway and not the stalls where Kerian had been fighting. Kerian eased away, joining a group of shoppers gravitating in the right direction, then peeled away to pushing through a loud crowd now gathering across the alleyway and stepped forward into the shadowy passage beyond, temporarily leaving the chaotic sounds of the market behind him. The scene he beheld froze him to the spot.

Several bodies lay on the ground in congealing pools of blood, their corpses broken and torn apart. Blood was splattered everywhere, arterial crimson arcs painting a detailed tapestry of gore capturing the ferocity of the attacks. At the far end of the alley, the fence used to prevent passage to the market thoroughfare now lay in pieces, smashed and splintered timber lengths discarded as if a hurricane had recently devastated the area.

Kerian dropped to one knee turning the first victim over, catching a quick glimpse of wounds across the man's chest that could easily have been inflicted by a huge bear or equally ferocious wild animal. Here lay the thug Kerian had incapacitated earlier with the wooden prop from the stall, the man's days intimidating others now over. A female shopper lay nearby, her face ripped apart, one vacant eye staring blankly out into space. The next corpse belonged to the guard Kerian had tipped so heavily. The man's throat had been torn out; viscera and gleaming cartilage now exposed to the air. Kerian swiftly glanced around the alleyway, confused at initially not seeing the man he had intended to save.

He moved towards the ruined fence, peering anxiously through the splintered timbers into the alleyway beyond, before noticing a foot sticking out from behind a barrel near the far wall. His heart sank at the realisation the man he had tried so hard to save had also been attacked by whatever beast had killed the others. He ran over, pushing the barrel aside, only to spot the man's foot twitching faintly. The dice man was still alive. He had to have the luck of the gods!

The man's wounds looked severe; his clothes ripped to shreds, his body covered in bloody lacerations. His face was a mottled mess and his breathing ragged and unsteady.

"Oh dear lord." Kerian gasped, quickly staring around and rechecking the shadows of the alleyway just in case whatever did this was still be in the area. "What happened to you? What happened to those men?"

"You should have left me alone." The dice man groaned. "I could have handled it on my own. Now look what you have done." Rapid footsteps of approaching men made Kerian stop in his tracks.

"Stop right where you are!" A voice shouted. "You are under arrest for the murder of these people."

"Murder?" Kerian mouthed, turning slowly around to face the eight guards standing before him, his hands held up to show he meant no harm. "You have made a mistake. My friend and I had nothing to do with this."

"Of course you didn't" came a reply tinged with menace.

"Look my friend has been hurt, he needs medical attention." Kerian turned to gesture to the beaten figure on the floor as the guards closed in.

"So do you." Came the menacing reply.

"What?" Kerian replied incredulously, spinning back to the guards. "Can't you see we need hel…"

Kerian never even saw the blackjack blow that connected solidly with the side of his head. One minute he was standing in the ruined alleyway under the mid-morning sunlight, considering how he could escape, the next, someone had turned out the lights, the sights, the smells…

* * * * * *

The horizon ahead of the El Defensor glowed ominously as Colette commenced her gateway spell. She bit her lip in concentration as raw magical power slashed huge glowing runes across a doorway higher and wider than the billowing sails of the Spanish galleon on which she sailed. For a split second the crewmen observing this arcane display forgot the terror of what her actions meant for them, their mouths wide in amazement as the sky peeled back to expose the sickly mustard skies of their destination. Skeletal spars from wrecked ships reached for the heavens like brittle fingers of bone and a stench of decay washed over the deck as the *El Defensor* surged through the magical opening.

Colette looked at Thomas and waited for his signal that the ship had cleared the sorcerous opening before she held her breath and cancelled the magic rushing from the ruined amethyst in her lap. The magical portal slammed closed, leaving the ship and crew in the one place none of them wanted to be.

The waters beneath the ship continued to stream forward, rippling the thick mat of weed that circled the massive collection of maritime ghosts abandoned ahead. The whole flotilla of assorted wreckage creaked in an agonising slow spiral of movement that sent shrieks and groans of protest up from the derelict wrecks as they ground relentlessly against each other. Thomas held his finger to his lips confirming his orders of silence to the crew and signalled to Rauph asking the Minotaur to turn the helm sharply to starboard and start the slow skirt around the perimeter of this ominous place known despairingly by lost sailors as the ship's graveyard.

Huge archways of crumbling masonry soared to the heavens, running side to side to form a massive circle that reached out further than any of the crew could see, the far distant portals obscured by a heavy haze that reminded the captain of a New York smog. Thomas knew the archways completely encircled the slowly revolving island of wrecked vessels. Each towering construction offering those with the magical means to unlock them, access to thousands of different worlds.

Thomas licked his lips nervously, smelling a stench of rot emanating from the wreckage on the Port side that was so strong it lined the inside of his nostrils and coated the back of his throat. He turned to Abeline and Lubok, gesturing that they swiftly get aloft as the sails that initially billowed with the air of their passage now hung limp as if the life was sucked out of them. No winds blew here in the graveyard unless they came through open archways and Thomas had no intention of slowing their limited forward momentum with drag created from the massive areas of canvas.

A light touch at Thomas's elbow made him start and he turned to find his companion Rowan had appeared at his side. The captain felt instantly stronger in her presence, although he was surprised that she had managed to prize herself away from Commagin's crew and the Dwarven engineer's chaotic workshop below decks. It seemed whenever she had a free moment, she was in there tinkering and helping with the engineer's mad inventions. He took in her graceful figure, like a lost desert traveller being administered a long cool drink. Thomas loved how Rowan, despite her greasy overalls and mussed brunette hair, pulled back in a tight ponytail, always managed to appear elegant and exotic to his eyes. Fastened around her neck was a bright orange neckerchief, her tanned forehead and forearms had oil smudges across them and a battered wrench swung loosely in her hand, yet she still managed to look stunning as she stood taking in the sense of palpable tension around them. He nodded acknowledgement of her arrival and reinforced the quiet motions with his hand even as a smile warmed his nervous features.

He took a moment to take in the deck and the crew standing silently at the rails, still as statues, hands resting nervously on sword hilts, as the galleon beneath them rode out the swell generated from the closing gate and started to drift as the current nudged the vessel gently along its course. Thomas had to admire the dedication of these people. They clearly trusted him to make the right decisions and keep them safe. He only wished he felt as confident. The undeniable menace that was Malum Okubi would not take these trespasses through the ship's graveyard easily and Thomas knew the last time he had lingered here he had hurt the monster badly. It was only a matter of time before Malum found a way to fight back. He shook his head, trying to dispel the icy fingers of fear tracing up his spine and gazed up through the rigging and masts to the ship's lookout high above.

Perched high in the crow's nest, Weyn Valdeze scanned the mish-mash of decaying wreckage to his left, constantly looking for signs of life that indicated the enemy was aware of their presence. His gaze roved across huge derelict sea vessels, sloops, trawlers, packet boats, coasters, liberty ships and other transports he had no means to identify, scanning for the tell-tale movement of the large black Scintarn hounds that hunted for survivors from these wrecks then herded them back to be eaten alive by their master.

The archer turned one way then the other, then noticed something out of the corner of his eye and turned to gaze ahead in the direction the current was leading them. Something was different in the graveyard this time, you could feel it in the air. His eyes squinted into the murk, making out dark shapes dotted across the watery passage before them. There were objects in the water. Weyn frowned cursing the fact that he could not see any clearer. Was that the remains of a small sailing ship? What were the other shapes? He reached over and tugged hard on a rigging line set up specifically to register an alarm and send a silent signal down to the helm, warning of the trouble he had spotted.

Thomas looked up to see Weyn gesturing wildly ahead and turned to see where the archer was pointing but there was nothing to see from this low point to the sea. He ran over to the rigging climbed a few lines and reached into his waistcoat to draw out his spyglass extending the telescope and putting it to his right eye. The water ahead leapt into focus, first one dark shape came clear, then others initially shrouded by the murk became visible. The hairs on the back of the captain's neck prickled and his gut started to churn. What on earth? Were those wrecks out in the main channel? Had they somehow come free from the rest of the ruined hulks? Were they drifting like the *El Defensor* was?

He stared again, taking in first one shadowy seaweed draped ship then another, their shapes staggered out across the water. Dark vessels, ancient hulls, rusted prows and lance like masts sitting directly in the way of his galleon and it appeared that the *El Defensor* was closing on them. How could these vessels be staying in place? Even with no wind the *El Defensor* continued to drift forwards. Why were these vessels not doing the same? He stared harder, peering through the telescope and willing more detail to be apparent. Then Thomas noticed the lines pulled taut against the current, the loops of salvaged rusting anchor chain stringing the staggered wrecks together directly across their path. This was not a simple case of drifting vessels. This had been done intentionally.

They were sailing into a trap! Thomas dropped back down to the deck and ran across to Colette, bending close to her ear.

"Open a gate." He ordered. "Open a gate now!"

"Which one?" Colette whispered back, indicating the row of arches sliding silently past them.

"I don't care which one." Thomas snapped more sternly than he intended, his raised whisper sounding much louder than it actually was. "Just do it now."

Colette moved over to the rail and sank to her knees, spreading out a roll of cloth upon which several gemstones sparkled. There was a sapphire, a ruby, two orange agates and a diamond but none of them were big enough to power the opening of a gate on its own. She closed her eyes, visualising the arch, mouthing the words and forcing the ruby and one agate to snap as if they were made of glass, allowing the magical energy contained within them to spiral out. The twin tendrils wrapped around each other crackling, fizzing and even jumping apart from each other, before Colette gestured with her hands and sent them racing towards one of the distant gateways.

The supernatural power leapt across the water and clawed up the stone pillars, crackling and sparking across the opening. The dark swirling fog behind the archway disappeared as blue and orange power jumped from stone to stone, energising the ancient monument which flared brightly, as a mystical gateway split down the centre of the arch and parted in a bright flash of light. Water rushed into the ship's graveyard from a wide lazy river beyond the open gate, staining the waters ahead with a muddy hue, the weathered stone arch acting like a rustic picture frame, capturing a scene of vibrant grassland across which herds of startled grey and brown striped gazelles leapt and twisted like a living ribbon. A sun the colour of molasses slung low in the sky behind the fleeing creatures, giving the whole image a surreal appearance.

Thomas turned to Rauph and motioned towards the opening. His mouth shaping words he wanted to scream but knew he could not for fear of alerting his enemy of their position.

"Go! There! Now!" He gestured. The huge Minotaur acknowledged the request and adjusted the helm, muscles bulging as he set the *El Defensor* into a sweeping turn to bring it in line with their offered destination, the galleon banking under their feet in response. Thomas tried to relax the tightness in his shoulders as the ship headed for the archway and the promised sanctuary beyond. At least they would be away from this place quicker than he expected.

"Something is wrong!" Colette cursed making the crew gathered around her jump at the sound. "I can't hold it open." She closed her eyes, her brow furrowed as if in pain, hands held out gesturing towards the gateway, as she visibly strained to hold the passageway for them. The two magical energy streams sparked and jumped, the vista within moving out of focus then becoming clear again.

Thomas leaned forward, willing the *El Defensor* to pick up speed with all his heart and soul but it was not to be with no wind at their back and no oars with which to row. There was a crackling sound and then the archway went dark, their lush green destination disappearing, replaced with a swirling wall of dark grey fog.

"Turn to Port!" Thomas yelled at Rauph, only to discover his navigator was already ahead of him and wrestling with the helm, bringing the king spoke up from the deck and over to the other side as he spun the massive wheel. The whole galleon shuddered at the course direction, the crew stepping to one side and holding tightly onto whatever they could as the ship groaned in protest at the rough treatment.

The *El Defensor* peeled away from the archway in as tight a turn as she could but her forward momentum left the back end of the ship swinging dangerously out towards the ancient stone masonry. Aradol, Austen and Ives immediately snatched up boat hooks and ran to the starboard side of the stern, preparing to attempt the impossible and push off, if the boat collided with the arch. They held their breath as their vessel swung torturously around, putting her aft-castle in a direct line with the ancient masonry. The ship moved closer and closer, the faces of the crew wincing at the prospective collision everyone expected to hear. The galleon swung closer, the ship's hull inches from the crumbling masonry. Aradol closed his eyes expecting to feel the shudder and groan as the mighty ship collided, then got elbowed in the side by a grinning Ives as the stern missed the leading edge of the arch and swung into the now empty opening, the woodwork spared destruction by the slimmest of margins.

Austen turned towards Thomas to gesture that, incredibly, all was well, however the danger was not over. Crew members were gesturing wildly towards the prow of the ship, pointing out that the *El Defensor* was now heading directly for one of the anchored ships positioned in the water. Mathius led several other crew, armed with boathooks over to the port side of the ship, leaping up into the rigging to hang out over the side and view the ominous threat approaching. A large rotting trawler, draped with holed nets that hung heavy with slime, listed steeply in the churning waters, its prow pointed to starboard, stern to port, the exposed hull of the ship intentionally placed to block as much of the sluggish channel as possible.

Mathius turned towards Thomas and Rauph, gesturing that a turn to Starboard was required. The shaggy red-haired Minotaur acted without hesitation, turning the helm sharply, the whole ship shaking at the movement, the crew staggering to remain on their feet. The *El Defensor* swung out wide, only for her prow to rise up out of the water as a huge chain securing the trawler to the archways slid beneath her.

"That will clean off some barnacles!" Mathius muttered as the chain reverberated and scraped along the hull, putting his teeth on edge. So much for the quiet and quick exit Thomas had suggested!

As the chain found itself forced under the *El Defensor's* hull, it tightened, causing the ruined trawler to be suddenly dragged towards them, its rotting stern surging through the water.

"Over the side." Thomas ordered, "We need to stop that ship from making contact." Crewmen scrambled to act, setting their safety lines so they could climb down the rungs set into the hull and hang from the rigging, their cumbersome boat hooks small protection from the vessel swiftly approaching them. Every man wore a grim face set against a task that if mis-judged, would see them squashed between the *El Defensor's* hull and the approaching trawler.

"Brace!" Mathius warned, as the fishing vessel loomed ever closer. "We just need to ease the trawler along." The boathooks squealed in protest as they met the hull of the approaching ship, the crewmen setting the ends of their staves against the hull and angling them to try and deflect the trawler as if they were coming up alongside a jetty. One boathook snapped sending its owner scrabbling for higher ground as the trawler kissed the *El Defensor's* hull before bouncing back, leaving a slick green trail to mark the ship's unsolicited attentions. Other crewmen leapt to help, attaching safety lines and clambering down to help complete a line of volunteers eager to see their ship free of danger.

The rusted chain continued to rattle along the keel of the Spanish galleon, each crunch making Thomas wince anew. He risked a few stolen furtive glances over to the port side of the ship half expecting to see the appearance of the dark heads and flicking pointed ears of Scintarn hounds noting their passage but there was nothing to see. He made his way over to Colette and laid a steadying hand on her shoulder.

"Relax," he tried to reassure her, taking in the flustered look on her face and knowing that the words dancing unspoken on her lips probably involved something along the line of I told you so. "I know you can do this. Just gather your thoughts and try again."

Colette blew out a puff of air, her bottom lip extended to make her frustrated exhale lift a stray blonde lock of hair that had become stuck to her brow. Thomas stifled a laugh as the offending curl bounced back down into its original position, although Colette was in no position to notice. There was a sharp crack, followed by several others, and the remaining gemstones, suddenly rendered impossibly fragile by Colette's summoning of the magical forces held within, released their powers for the ship's mage to weave and manipulate as she desired.

She tried to ignore the noises around her, the rumble of the chain along the keel of the ship, the scramble of men grunting, swearing and struggling to nurse the fishing trawler along the hull and the palpable tension from the rest of the crew as they ran this terrifying gauntlet on their path to freedom, every one of them aware of what would happen should they fail.

The mage turned her attention back towards the prow of the *El Defensor* gazing along the row of available archways stretching out before them. What one should she choose, the fifth, the seventh or even the twentieth? What did it matter if they were far away from here? The mage took in the stonework, looking for some clue or sign to help her decide but each archway appeared identical to the one either side of it. No suggestions to indicate a safe port, no warning of what dangers may lie beyond. She gritted her teeth and prepared to cast her spell.

The *El Defensor* ground to a sudden stop, sending members of the crew tumbling across the deck and jolting Colette, breaking her concentration. What in the world was going on now? The mage impatiently gathered her magical power back, reeling in the crackling tendrils like a ball of errant twine and gathering them into her hand, unwilling to waste a single jot of power as they had precious little to spare.

Thomas was already racing across the deck, leaping up to stare over the Starboard side of his vessel and spot a sight that chilled him to the bone. The chain had almost completed its journey along the hull but had wound up entangled in the rudder. As he looked the chain twisted and turned, halting their progress as surely as if they were sailing through sand. He turned to the crew rushing up alongside him and pointed down at the obstacle pulled taut against the forward motion of the current.

"We need to break the chain!" He yelled, forgetting the silence he had ordered amongst the crew. The men gathered about him clearly agreed with his opinion but looked about amongst themselves, lost as to what exactly they would break the chain with. Thomas took in the stares about him and the looks of impotence, frustration and fear that mirrored his own feelings deep inside.

They were stuck fast! On one side the rusting anchor chain threatened to snap their rudder and leave them directionless and floundering in the water, on the other, the rotting trawler threatened to damage their hull. Thomas glanced towards Colette and watched her gathering the last remaining residue of magical power to her hand. The captain knew the energy would not last forever in its raw state and the longer they waited the less energy would be available to open the gateway for passage onwards. His mind raced to deal with the turmoil and sort out the indecision freezing him to the spot. At least the Scintarn hounds still seemed unaware of their presence. He had to be thankful for that!

"Awwwwaaarrrk ack ack!" The ear-splitting squawk cut through the air like fingernails being dragged down a blackboard. What in the seven hells? A long drawn out haunting howl rose in reply from the wrecked ships on the starboard side of the *El Defensor*, off towards the centre of the graveyard. The haunting dirge settled into silence, every member of the crew feeling the terror the unearthly sound instilled.

"Ack ack parp!" Another high-pitched squawk filled the air. Thomas turned towards the prow of the ship and gestured sharply to one of the crew to find and silence the source of the sudden outburst, despite a feeling growing inside that he already knew who was responsible. He lifted his spyglass to his eye and confirmed his feelings as he took in the sight of a diminutive figure talking to a caged bird with his usual high-speed enthusiasm and animated arm gestures.

"They are called Scintarn hounds!" Came a loud voice. "Don't their howls make you feel all spooky inside? No, I don't know why we have stopped moving. Rauph is steering the ship not me! I don't understand why you never listen to me!" The answering ear splitting cry from the Halfling's pet bird made Thomas roll his eyes to the heavens. Another loud mournful howl echoed from the wreckage; this time answered by several other hounds responding to the summons. Thomas gritted his teeth in anger.

When they got out of this a certain Ashe Wolfsdale was going to be in serious trouble.

Chapter Four

The bass tones of a sad lullaby were the first things Kerian became aware of as he struggled to regain consciousness. The second was the incredibly bad smells lingering about him and the hard surface on which he lay. He remained still, trying to gather his thoughts from a head that felt stuffed with cotton. Where had he ended up now? He remembered being in the alleyway trying to help the man who had been assaulted and then he recalled being hit on the head. The second he relived the incident, the pain flooded in and his fingers tentatively explored a raised egg-sized lump on the back of his neck confirming his memories.

Kerian groaned aloud before wincing, as the simple act of vocalising sent waves of discomfort through his skull. He licked his lips, feeling the dry cracked surface against the fuzzy carpet coating his tongue and tried to figure out how long he had been unconscious. The lullaby faded away and someone moved closer to him.

"At last my hero awakens." Came a voice tinged with sarcasm. "Maybe now you are conscious we can discuss the ramifications of interfering where you are not wanted eh?" Kerian cracked an eyelid and gazed up into the dark brown eyes and olive complexion of the man he had attempted to save.

"I notice you are still alive dice man." Kerian replied, swinging his feet from the bunk he was lying on, before holding his head in his hands as the world spun around him and threatened to make him vomit. "It appears my interference saved your life."

"That remains to be seen compadre." Came the sobering reply. "We appear to have moved from a place of commerce to a place with less than ideal future options." A loud rattling of metal being struck caused Kerian to open his eyes further and fully take in their present surroundings. Soiled straw strewn on a stone floor, dim light from outside the room. Stark iron bars on the small window set higher than needed to prevent anyone looking out. A slop bucket in the corner with stained flagstones adjacent. Clearly, previous residents had felt the bucket was a mere suggestion rather than a strict rule. The whole area measured ten feet by ten feet and if Kerian needed any further proof of his current predicament, the floor to ceiling bars across one end of the room answered his question.

"So what do you think of our new accommodation? Not as comfortable as the *Mermaid* eh?" Kerian took the opportunity to re-examine the man before him. He stood about five-foot-ten in height and had the dark looks of a gypsy. Curly jet-black hair, skin weathered by exposure to the elements, a shadow of beard growth and slight gauntness to his muscular frame. Dark trousers, scuffed leather boots which had seen better days and a blood-stained leather tunic completed his sparse wardrobe.

"Why did you run from me this morning?" Kerian asked. "I only saw you briefly last night so why flee from the horse stall?"

"I mistook you as a friend of the guard I beat at dice." His fellow prisoner confessed. "I see now that I misjudged you and for that Octavian Silvestri apologises from his heart. It was a simple mistake to make, kindness is something I have rarely experienced in life and when someone shows an interest in me, I am usually right to be suspicious." Octavian looked down at his feet as if reflecting on the truth of his own words.

"There is tragic sentiment in what you say." Kerian replied. "If our positions were reversed, I may have also felt that way."

"I also recognise that you remained near me when I lay helpless in the alleyway. Why would you do this for me?" Octavian asked, jumping to his feet and extending a hand. Kerian took his hand and shook it, accepting the thankful gesture for what it was.

"My name is Kerian Denaris." He offered. "I stepped in because the odds were not in your favour and that guard meant to kill you. I have done many wrongs in my life but after recent experiences I have decided I will not stand by and do nothing if someone is in need. However, I have a distinct feeling you did not win your dice game on luck alone." Kerian watched Octavian's face and the flush that came to the man's cheeks at the accusation, confirming the knight's suspicions.

"Octavian is no conman." He shook his head still looking sheepishly down at the floor. "I merely liberate funds from fools who do not understand their true value."

"So how do you do it?" Kerian asked. "Are the dice loaded?" Octavian reached into his trouser pocket and pulled out a pair of die shot through with blue and gold, rattling them loudly in his hand before handing them over for inspection. Kerian regarded the two cubes in his hand, the edges rounded by repeated use.

"May I?" He requested. A slight nod of his associate's head allowed Kerian to roll the dice on his bunk and they reacted like any dice would. A three and a five showed on the upper faces. Kerian rolled again, a one and a six. The rolls appeared random enough. He checked the sides. All present and correct. One to six represented on each. No side of the dice felt weighted to his scrutiny. He returned the dice to their owner none the wiser as to how this sleight of hand was being achieved.

Octavian winked with his mischievous brown eye.

"Lady luck be with me." He smiled slyly, then kissed the die in his hand. The cubes clattered across the bunk and landed six and six. Then the conman collected his dice kissed them and rolled again. Double six showed on the upper faces.

"Give me those." Kerian smiled leaning forwards and sweeping the dice up. He stared hard at Octavian' s face, then cast the dice. One and one.

"Snakes eyes." Octavian teased. "You lose."

"How?" Kerian asked, intrigued by the method to this man's good fortune.

"It's all in the wrist." The conman explained, sweeping up the die, kissing his hand then throwing them again. Double six showed as expected, accompanied by a devious smile.

"Where ever did you get these dice?" Kerian enquired, suddenly eager for the backstory.

"They were included in the dowry that I accepted when I married my wife." Octavian confessed. "Rumour has It that there are two sets of these dice and that my family used them to trick a devil out of a great treasure. Alas there is now only one pair. I know not where the other is. If I had both sets, the chaos I could cause." He stared down into his hand at the two cubes he held, shaking his head despondently at memories only he could relive. "I just fear that these dice are not enough to help me now."

Octavian looked up and met Kerian's intense gaze with his sad dark brown eyes, then turned his head away as if ashamed at discussing the matter with a relative stranger. He wiped his face on his sleeve, then cleared his throat before regaining his feet and started to pace within the small confines of the cell. After a moment or two of quiet reflection, Octavian turned to Kerian and attempted to change the subject.

"Enough about me," he muttered in a voice suddenly hoarse. "Tell me that tale of the man who sailed into Wellruff with saddlebags over his shoulder, yet no horse to go with them and is there any truth to the story those bags are filled with gold and jewels stolen from the back of a giant sea horse that took you to a city beneath the waves." Kerian rolled his eyes at the fabricated tale of his arrival.

"I'm sure you do not want to hear all about my dull adventures." Kerian smiled. "Indeed by the sound of things you have invented plenty of stories that make the truth definitely boring in comparison."

"Oh come now Sir Denaris. Why are you so secretive? Do you not wish to unburden your heart to Octavian? Why this unhealthy need to be so insular?" That devious smile reappeared as the con artist within his cell mate rose to the surface and attempted to disarm Kerian's guarded nature.

"Like yourself," Kerian bristled, not falling for the man's suave approach one bit. "I find it hard to trust people. Everyone I have ever trusted has betrayed me, so I tend to just say what needs to be said and no more. The pain is less that way. Do people really say I have treasure in my saddlebags?"

Octavian nodded, moving to elaborate further then stopped as he noticed the sudden agitation on Kerian's face. Kerian was clutching at his chest, pulling through the loose folds in his ripped shirt, untucking the material before removing his shirt entirely. Octavian looked on as Kerian dropped to the floor and started searching around in the straw beneath his bunk. Despite the disgusting mess he was digging through the man would not stop looking, making Octavian feel decidedly uncomfortable watching him.

"What is the matter?" He asked. Kerian ignored him, raising the discomfort Octavian felt at seeing the actions of the man. Kerian spun out from beneath the bunk and looked directly into Octavian' s wide eyes.

"Have you seen my pendants?" Kerian asked breathlessly, his face displaying a sense of panic that put the conman at considerable unease. Octavian shook his head, denying any involvement in his fellow prisoner' s loss.

"You must have." Kerian yelled. "One with an emerald off centre about this big." Kerian held up his thumb and forefinger to show the approximate size. Octavian shook his head; sure he had never seen this item of jewellery.

"The other one is gold, inlaid with pearls. It has a large grey pearl at the centre." His voice was becoming more frantic at the telling. Clearly the necklace meant a great deal to Kerian.

Octavian held up his hands trying to calm his cellmate down.

"When do you last remember having them?" He asked. "Try to calm down and think." Kerian furrowed his brow in concentration.

"I remember having them at the market." He confessed, images of the earlier skirmish rushing through his mind. Had he felt material ripping during the fight? He could not be sure. Had he lost them then? How could he have been so stupid not to check sooner? Kerian stood up and paced in agitation, checking the jail cell door, confirming it was locked fast.

"I need to get out of here and back to the market as fast as I can." Kerian confessed. "Is there a guard we can call. The longer we wait the greater the possibility my pendants and Colette are lost."

"No one is in a hurry to release us." Octavian confessed. "Don't you realise we are in here accused of murder. Until they recognise that we have no weapons on us that could have caused the wounds they have seen, they will be in no hurry to let us out."

"Murder! You can't be serious." Kerian snapped, banging hard on the bars. "I need to get out of here now! Guard! Guard!" As predicted his calls for assistance fell on deaf ears. Octavian placed a hand lightly on Kerian's shoulder.

"Please do not antagonise matters. They cannot hold us much longer." He looked up at the sky through the barred window and noticed the fading of the daylight. "They will let us go soon, otherwise they will have to feed us and if I have these guards down right, they will not want all the extra work." Octavian licked his lips nervously and sniffed the air as if this somehow confirmed his suspicions.

Kerian sank back down onto the bunk and cursed in frustration. His pendants could be anywhere, moving further away the longer he sat here powerless to pursue. He would not lose Colette this way, not after everything he had gone through but what could he do? He sat in silent frustration, his face grimly displaying a determination and quiet resolve to get his property back. However, deep inside his heart, there burned nothing but pure unadulterated rage.

Blinded by such emotion, Kerian had no idea that If he had taken a moment to calm down and consider his situation, he would have realised that when he had first seen Octavian in the alleyway, the conman's eyes had been blue and not brown.

* * * * * *

"Get a gate open now!" Thomas yelled, "and this time keep it open!" Colette spun her head around, magic energy spitting and dancing around her fist, her eyes blazing with anger.

"I warned you this could happen!" She snapped. "Don't you dare shout at me. We are in this position because of your recklessness not mine. If you think you can do better grab hold of this..." she gestured at the writhing energies crackling around her hand. "...and then let's see what you can do."

Thomas bit back a bitter reply as Rowan's hand came down on his shoulder. Her eyes warning him that this meaningless conflict would only cause further problems. He took a hard swallow then closed his eyes for a second to gather his thoughts, hearing the curses of his crew trying to hold back the trawler and free the chain from where it dragged against the hull. Howls continue to fill the air, much closer now as the Scintarns moved towards them eager for a feast. He opened his eyes, breathed in a deep lungful of fowl air, then turned back to Colette, his sense of control now recovered.

"Colette, please forgive me. I did not intend to shout at you. You know we need you to open the gate. Please pick one and do your best to hold it open. I have faith in you." He turned from the mage, aware he would still have to pay for his outburst later and looked at Rowan.

"Rowan please go and tell Commagin of our predicament. We need something to sever that chain as soon as possible." Rowan moved to action his request but Thomas laid a hand on her arm making her look at him once more.

"Thank you." He mouthed silently, acknowledging his loss of control and his thanks for her guidance. Rowan stood up on tiptoe and kissed him lightly on the cheek.

"I'll be back before you know it." she smiled, then she darted off heading for the lower decks where the engineer had his workshop. Thomas turned towards Austen as the sailor ran across the deck to assist the crew struggling against the trawler.

"Austen, take one other crewman, get down to the ballista and get a grappling hook secured to the end of the line, we may have to pull ourselves out of this."

The air crackled behind him as Colette chose an archway to open and threw her magical energies at the ancient stonework. The sky split with a shriek and water rushed into the graveyard, setting the boats and ships creaking and groaning in protest as the current moved them around. A huge cloud of mist poured from the opening accompanied by a perpetual roaring, as if a monstrous beast were in pain and Thomas tried to steal a look at their destination, but it appeared as if a bank of fog blocked the view. Despite the roaring and the likely danger, it represented, they had no further options. Colette had no more power. There was no other choice. It was through this archway or nowhere.

A scream snatched Thomas's attention back to the men struggling to fend off the trawler. He ran for the side and gazed down on an unfortunate sailor who had slipped after his safety line became tangled. It appeared that as he had struggled to free it from the ship, he had fallen and his leg had become trapped between the trawler and the *El Defensor's* hull. Mathius and several other crew were struggling to pull him free but he was securely pinned and his screams confirmed the severity of his pain. Thomas threw himself over the side, slipping and sliding on the deck of the slime covered trawler. He pushed vainly from its deck trying desperately to move the much larger galleon away as the man continued screaming in agony below him.

"Move damn you!" Thomas cursed, throwing all his might behind his push. Several other crew slipped down onto the trawler, taking their captain's lead, pushing with all their power and having as much effect as a mortal king trying to hold back a relentless tide.

"Please help me." the man begged, as the two ships ground agonisingly against each other. Thomas kept pushing ineffectively with the rest of the crew, his eyes darting about frantically looking for something to move the situation in their favour.

"It's okay…" Thomas paused, struggling to remember this man's name. He used to be so good at this and the fact the injured man's name did not readily spring to mind showed how poor his focus had been of late since leaving Stratholme behind them. "Don't worry Monahan. We will have you out of here soon." There was a loud twang as the grapple line shot out past where they struggled, trailing a line behind it as it sailed through the archway into the billowing cloud. The slack was swiftly taken up but the hook found no purchase and came back through the gateway without resistance. Thomas's heart sank as he knew it would take valuable time before they could re-prime and fire again.

A loud crunch and a jet of blood, followed by a much weaker scream of agony galvanised Thomas into pushing harder but his efforts seemed more for his own benefit and the struggling crew alongside him, rather than the poor man who was clearly going to lose his leg if they ever managed to free him. Monahan's eyes were glazed with pain and he was showing obvious signs of delirium. If they did not free him soon, losing his leg would be the least of the man's problems.

* * * * * *

Commagin, chief engineer for the *El Defensor* stomped up onto the deck with all the authority a four-foot-tall dwarf could muster, his white beard bristling beneath a strawberry red nose upon which balanced a set of wire rimmed spectacles set with lenses so thick you could use them as coasters. A set of rusty bolt cutters slung over the left shoulder of a stained brown work coat covered with pockets filled with blunt pencils, rulers and short candles. Around his tubby waist slung a belt with more pouches and tools that were probably never used but simply added to his senior technical appearance.

Rowan came up behind him and tapped Commagin on the shoulder, gesturing to the side of the ship where the taut chain holding them in place groaned and creaked, its large rusty links twisted and strained from the tension of holding the *El Defensor* in check.

The Dwarven engineer examined the problem with his poor eyesight as his little associate, a three-foot-tall Gnome with ragged clothes and holed boots staggered up on deck with a tool bag almost as heavy as himself. This assistant wore a stained apron with a couple of pencils stuck in the pocket in a direct copy of his senior colleague, his name spelt out in uneven mismatched embroidery over his right breast.

Barney was Commagin's apprentice, a thankless role for one so small, as often he was used as the analyte for all the engineer's mad experimental ideas. Recently he had been used as a test pilot for a risky diving suit apparatus and he knew there were other equally dangerous propositions lined up for the near future. These moments of sheer terror were interspersed with periods of tedium as Barney's other role consisted of cleaning up the results of the said failed experiments. He had often voiced his belief that his skills with a broom and dustpan were now as good as they would ever be.

The apprentice dragged the bag of tools over to his mentor and peered over the rail to take in the situation, trying to guess the solution his ingenious master would devise. The chain was huge. The links straining against the pull of the *El Defensor* so tightly that the air almost hummed with the tension in the line. His little mind raced at the challenge. Even if they managed to sever the links the tension was so high the chain could cause serious damage as it snapped back. The link would need to be removed at either the far pillar, or wherever the other end of the chain was attached.

Tutting heavily, as he was professionally trained to do, Barney ran back across the deck on his little feet and looked down onto the group of sailors struggling to free the trapped man wedged against the hull. Beyond them, on the deck of the ruined trawler lay links of chain wound repeatedly around an old mast. The answer was clearly simple. Grab a hacksaw and start sawing through the mast. He smiled to himself and ran back across the deck eager to hear his mentor's take on the situation.

"Ah, glad you finally had the need to arrive." Commagin chided, unaware his student had been weighing up the scene already. "See that pillar over there... I want you to climb down the side of the *El Defensor*, move along the chain hand over hand, then cut a link free when you get to the other side." Barney's eyes widened in horror as he took in the foaming water and the rushing current caused by Colette having opened the gateway. As he looked several large fish leapt from the water, then the sea exploded as a large silver eel leapt up after them, snatching the fresh meal from the air.

"Can't we simply cut the mast from the trawler and release the chain?" Barney asked. Commagin sighed heavily, shaking his head, despairing of his apprentice.

"Son," he opened. "There is no trawler over there, just the archways and a long chain. The chain has us stuck. We have no choice but to sever the chain. I am too old to do it. That leaves you. The crew are counting on you. I'm counting on you."

"But the trawler is over on the other side of the ship." Barney tried desperately to explain.

"Exactly," Commagin replied. "And the chain is over here!" He slapped the bolt cutters into Barney's hand. "Jump to it lad." The little apprentice swallowed hard, his head turning back to regard the rail behind him, where he knew the trawler lay and then ahead at the thick chain marked by flotsam and spume from the force of the current swirling by.

"But..." his voice was almost shrill this time.

"No more arguing." Commagin glared over his glasses, almost daring his apprentice to try his patience further. "The chain... now!"

Barney shrugged his shoulders in resignation, then handed over his apron to Rowan to prevent his tools getting wet. Hanging his head, he allowed Commagin to boost him up over the rail. The apprentice commenced slipping and sliding his way slowly down the side of the *El Defensor's* hull, picking his slick hand and footholds with care, determined to show his mentor that he was capable of the task at hand. As Barney neared the waterline and tried to figure out his way onwards, Commagin lowered the bolt cutters down to him on a line.

"Now don't mess this up." Commagin yelled down, peering over his glasses at his terrified apprentice. "Get it done quick and then hop back here sharpish."

The ballista fired again, the grappling line shooting through the arch into the swirling mist. This time when they drew in the slack the line held, fastened onto something the crew could not see. A roar of triumph arose from amidships as spare hands leapt to the task of pulling on the line to help the *El Defensor* inch forwards towards safety. The chain rose up out of the water as the tension upon it increased, bouncing Barney in and out of the foam and making him splutter as he proceeded to move hand over hand. At the helm Rauph continued to wrestle with the wheel, intent on freeing the chain with his firm movements but it steadfastly refused to turn, despite his best efforts.

Thomas battered the hull of his galleon in despair. His crewman was slipping away before his eyes, head lolling, drool hanging from his mouth, no longer showing his pain as the two vessels continued to grind against each other. The efforts of captain and crew were getting nowhere. Thomas turned to survey the trawler, considering accessing its helm as a means of freeing his wounded crewman. He left his sailors valiantly trying to save their friend's life, slipping and sliding across the slick deck, his passage made the more treacherous by the lengths of rotting netting strewn across his path.

The excited howls of the approaching Scintarns were becoming an annoyance now, in some respects Thomas just wished they would hurry up and get here so he could take out his frustration on the horrific creatures. He stepped over a length of rusting chain and started to make his way down the side of the fishing vessel intent on accessing the main cabin, one foot slipped from beneath, threatening to send him tumbling into the water but somehow, he regained his footing and slithered onto the main deck, finally examining the trawlers steering. The wheel was smashed to pieces, there was no way the helm could function from here.

A loud cackling taunt called out across the wrecks, freezing Thomas in mid-examination. He stuck his head out from the shelter on the main deck, trying to hear better and noted the flickering lights dancing across the wreckage towards his ship. Malum was coming. The captain could not help but shiver at the thought. They needed to get free and now.

Thomas moved back out onto the deck, suddenly wishing to return to his men, his hand dropping to the cutlass at his side. He knew the weapon held an enchanted edge and although it pained him to consider it, amputation may be the only option he now had available for his injured crewman. He moved to step over the chain then stopped. The chain... the solution had been staring him in the face all this time! He examined how the massive links were secured to the wooden remnants of the mast and considered trying to chop the chain or the mast. His sword was sharp enough to cut deeply into his desk, so why not through these? The mast was the thinner of the two making it the obvious candidate for his swing.

He spread his legs wide, trying to compensate for the movement of the ship and swung his blade as hard as he could. The trawler dropped suddenly sending the swing wide and it hit the coil of chain with a shower of sparks and cutting a bright groove in the thick metal. Thomas withdrew his cutlass, cursing loudly and moved to swing again, when a low growl froze him in his tracks. He spun towards the sound, coming face to face with the drooling mouth and glistening fangs of a Scintarn hound.

The creature was eight feet long, from the tip of its swaying barbed tail, along the bony armoured frill of black flint extending up its back running the entire length of the sleek ebony terror. The fur on the creature was short, accentuating the hackles currently raised upon its back. The hound's erect ears continually twitched, searching for the slightest of sounds. The paws of the creature were like those of a big cat, with claws allowing the monster to scale heights in search of prey, whilst its heavily muscled back legs permitted it to leap sizeable distances across the decks of the ships on which it hunted.

Further gleaming armoured frills ran above both of the creature's eyes, shadowing the pupils beneath, making them more terrifying and chilling to behold. Bared teeth allowed saliva to drip to the deck from a moist blood red maw.

"Where the hell did you come fro..."

The hound lunged, teeth snapping inches from Thomas's throat. The captain stepped back, his feet unsteady on the slick deck, swinging his cutlass up between the brute and himself purely to stop it from continuing forward and throwing him off balance. The steel of his blade sparked off the frill of the Scintarn, catching it on the tip of its snout, making the hound blink in surprise.

"Back off mutt!" Thomas snapped, trying to regain his bravado by slapping his cutlass first on one side of the creature's head and then the other. He stamped on the deck then lunged forward, the tip of the cutlass catching the hound on its ear. The Scintarn yelped in surprise then snarled menacingly before leaping forwards, pushing the cutlass up between them, this time allowing Thomas no chance to angle the blade and use it for his benefit. Teeth flashed and slobber flew as the beast contemplated a warm meal for the first time in days.

Thomas grunted under the weight of the hound as its snout angled in first one way and then another, desperate to sink its fangs into his flesh. He briefly considered asking himself what Malum was feeding his hounds, then realised with a cold finality that he already knew. Anyone sailing through these gateways suffered the same fate. All these ruined ships had been manned with food. All Malum had to do was sit, wait and let the food come to him, kicking, screaming, struggling and ultimately succumbing to his hunger, much like the prey of a bloated spider struggling in a silken web.

A wicked claw caught his trouser leg, as the hound dropped back down onto the deck, making the captain pull himself back shocked. His foot slipped again, dropping him onto his knee, forcing Thomas to parry furiously, slapping the wider edge of his blade backwards and forwards fiercely to prevent the Scintarn from gaining advantage as it charged forwards sensing his vulnerability. The beast jumped back, then lunged forward again maw open wide, teeth slicing through the air, only to come up short as Thomas met the lunge in kind, his cutlass thrusting right into the creature's mouth.

The Scintarn wailed in pain but could not stop its forward motion, the point and edge of the enchanted weapon slicing deeply into the roof of the hound's mouth before finally piercing its canine brain.

Several arrows streaked through the air from the crow's nest of the *El Defensor* slamming down into the hound making it quiver as the golden black shafts of Weyn's arrows hit home. Thomas breathed a sigh of relief as the creature dropped, its tail thrashing about on the green deck in its death throws but falling well short of its intended prey. More howls filled the air as several other Scintarns appeared along the decks of the closest wrecks, jumping excitedly along the rail, considering if they could make the jump from their vantage points over onto the slippery trawler like their canine brother.

The captain took the moment to check his leg where the Scintarn's claw had scored his flesh and rubbed the wound vigorously, noting the four stark marks on his pale leg and the wounds they had caused. He would need to see to this quickly, the last thing he wanted was infection to set in. He pushed his trouser back into his boot then withdrew his cutlass from the hound's mouth with a satisfying squelch.

Curses snatched Thomas back to his crew at the aft of the trawler and he set off back towards them, then caught himself, realising that he still had the chain to deal with. What was wrong with him today? He needed to focus! The chain needed to be cut free. His cutlass flashed through the air, once, twice and then again, wooden splinters raining on the deck as the cutlass edge bit deeply into the rotting mast without dulling the blade in the slightest. The wood split under his furious attentions, before parting with an audible crack, sending it crashing to the deck and then over the side.

"Thomas Adams!" screamed an ancient voice. "I'm coming for you!" The captain instinctively looked over onto the nearest shipwrecks, towards the source of the sound and noticed the flashing lights of his nemesis swiftly approaching. He knew that in moments he would hear the click clack of the barbed fans whirling around the monster's body, the colours of the fans flickering and flashing in complex visual patterns that hypnotised prey leaving them defenceless to attack.

"Not if I can help it!" Thomas replied. It was time to go. The corroded chain started to uncoil from the severed mast like a huge metallic snake, whipping across the deck and crashing over the side into the water. The trawler, suddenly free from its restraints, started to bob in the current, causing cries of rejoicing followed by further cursing and scrabbling as the crew realised the ships were starting to drift apart.

Thomas looked over at the men struggling to pull Monahan up, only to witness the unconscious man slipping further down between the parting ships. The captain sheathed his cutlass and ran to assist, struggling to remain balanced. He slid to a stop beside desperate men who were trying to hold the wounded sailor but every time that they lifted his limp frame, he slipped down again. Thomas struggled to assist but as every moment passed, fewer and fewer hands remained free to help as the distance between the ships grew greater. The crew found themselves with no option but to pull themselves up the side of the *El Defensor* or find themselves suffering the same watery fate as their injured colleague.

Ten hands became four, then two, with Thomas leaning far over the side of the trawler, frantically trying to grab Monahan's slick, blood-soaked form but he could not maintain his grip and the sailor dropped further down the hull of the trawler, his ruined leg dragging through the murky waters. The current, however weak, was enough to make the sailor's weight increase as he slipped up to his waist in the water.

"God damn you!" Thomas yelled at the unconscious man. "Don't you dare give up on me."

"Thomas grab my hand!" shouted a calm voice. The captain instantly knew it was Mathius but had no idea that the man was leaning out as far as he could on his safety line, his hands outstretched for Thomas to grab hold and be hauled to safety. The trawler continued slipping further away, making Thomas grunt with the effort of hanging on to Monahan. He instinctively knew he was seconds from overbalancing. Several thuds landed on the trawler behind him, the weight of the stalking hounds sending vibrations through the hull.

"Thomas, there are four hounds coming. I am tethered to the ship and cannot come to help you. You need to grab my hand now." The captain swallowed hard, facing a stark choice. Hold Monahan and face the hounds. Risk falling into the sea with his crewman and dealing with the monsters in the depths, or face the unthinkable. There was only one solution.

"I'm sorry." Thomas whispered, tears forming in his eyes. "I cannot hold you any longer." He let the man go, the very nature of the action a betrayal against everything the captain held dear. Monahan slipped into the water and was immediately snatched away.

Thomas felt Mathius grab his shoulder and arm and then he was swinging free, his own feet slipping into the waters. Other hands grabbed and assisted Thomas back onto the *El Defensor*, the captain's spirit broken. Another crewman lost. Each death an invisible weight that crushed Thomas more than he dared admit. The despondent looks from the men around him reinforcing his sense of failure.

The galleon shuddered as the huge chain snaked through the rudder, finally freeing the ship, allowing her to start a slow turn towards the open archway and the billowing mists as the crew below decks hauled hard on the ballista line. Rauph nursed the helm, directing the mighty ship away from the nightmare they were in. Roars from the crew suggested the relief felt by all as the *El Defensor* finally slid through the ancient stone arch, under the crackling magical energies wrapped around the pillars and on into the cloaking mists.

The captain felt his eyes torn towards the line of ship wrecks where a spidery form leapt on a figure caught in the water. Fans clicked and lunged repeatedly into the corpse, blood jetting into the air as the monster Malum took out his frustration on the sailor's still form, displaying his sense of failure in letting the *El Defensor* slip through his grasp.

Thomas turned from the scene with a sinking heart. He knew they now faced a potentially greater problem. When they had travelled through the graveyard previously, Malum had no idea where they had gone, or through which archway they had passed. By anchoring shipwrecks, he had reduced their choices to a few select gateways rather than the unlimited destinations the ship's graveyard normally offered. Malum now had an advantage. He knew where they were and Thomas realised that it was likely he would be waiting for them when they returned from wherever the fates took them this day.

The gateway shuddered then slammed shut, plunging the galleon and her crew into a world with no definition, no indicators, just the thin life line of the grappling hook securing the ship to something unseen in the mist. The continuous roaring sound surrounded them all, as the air, heavy with moisture, soaked them through to the skin. Thomas took a deep breath, not realising that he had been holding it. He needed to be a captain again, brush his insecurities away until he could examine them in the comfort of his own cabin. He turned from the gateway and looked towards his crew, trying to decide what needed to be done first.

"Drop anchor!" he shouted. There was no point in feeling their way blindly in this mist. They could be anywhere and could risk grounding again. "Take depth readings. Set a watch. Weyn, can you see anything up there."

"Not even my own hand!" came the disembodied reply.

Thomas listened as the anchor rattled through its port and dropped with a crash into the water beneath. The ship continued forward, then ground to a halt, this time at the wishes of the captain and her crew. A slight smile touched the corners of Thomas's mouth. They still lived, they had managed to sail through the graveyard with minimal losses. He stopped in mid-congratulation when he noticed Rowan holding Commagin tightly, Barney's apron hanging forlornly in her hand.

Chapter Five

The market place was still a hive of activity by the time Kerian made it out of the jail cell to relative freedom. Octavian had been right about the length of their temporary incarceration; with no evidence to hold them, the guards had finally elected to release the two bruised inmates with a stern warning that they would be under intense scrutiny over the next few days and in serious trouble if they caused any more disturbances. Octavian had slipped away into the shadows with a smile and a cocky wave, leaving Kerian free to chase his lost possessions.

His heart beat anxiously in his chest as he entered the cobbled market, his eyes darting about as the sights, sounds and smells of the commercial centre of Wellruff enveloped him. Lantern light gave the stalls a feeling of something from the pages of an illustrated fairy tale, enhancing or transforming the facial features of stall holders, casting flickering shadows over mysterious merchandise, heavily discounted now that the frantic trading of the day was drawing to a close. Smells appeared enhanced, the scent of sizzling meats and roasting nuts mixing with the heady scent of dried herbs left out in the heat of the earlier day.

Kerian noted the clientele had changed too. You had to look closely but the signs were there for a trained eye to see. The clothes worn by these nocturnal browsers appeared ragged, out of style by years, or ill fitting. Money was a luxury to these people and it showed in their faces when they managed to obtain a bargain, their eyes shining brightly as they turned with their prizes to scuttle off into the darkness and back to the hovels from which they came. Darker shadows lingered in the corners, intercepting food from the weaker bargain hunters as they tried to leave the market area, with passers-by ignoring the dull blows and frustrated tears that inevitably followed. Street urchins darted from stall to stall, little hands fishing for treats and unguarded coin.

Swiftly moving to the alleyway where he had first seen Octavian take his beating, Kerian took in the amounts of damp straw that had been scattered over the sluiced down cobbles and his heart sank. He thought back to the same scene earlier in the afternoon, remembering where the bodies had lain. His first thought was to move to where the guards had hit him but despite kicking the straw this way and that and then physically removing the debris scattered on the ground, there was no sign of his lost pendants. After wrestling with a large barrel to see if his pendants had fallen behind it, Kerian had to admit that his loss could not have occurred here. Not unless whoever cleaned the cobbles down had picked the pendants up. What if a random passer-by had found them? They could be anywhere by now! He did not intend to accept this scenario, because admitting this painful possibility meant giving in to his old enemy, despair.

He walked back out into the market square, catching some angry glances from a few stall keepers who, upon recognising his beaten features, rose nervously to their feet as he approached. One stall stood starkly empty, the remains of a few broken pots the only sign of the merchant whose brother had taken umbrage to Kerian's earlier actions and then lost a digit as a result. He turned to the candle maker's stall alongside the vacant space and plastered a fake smile across his face.

"Excuse me." He began. "I don't suppose you know where this man has gone." The candle maker appeared flustered at Kerian's question as if expecting another reaction, his hand openly reaching for a worn club to defend his belongings from a man who had earlier crashed through so many of his fellow merchant's livelihoods.

"Look," he replied nervously. "I never saw anything and I don't want any trouble." Something about the way the man acted raised suspicions in Kerian's mind. He moved forwards, making the trader take a cautious step back, despite the fact his whole stall remained between Kerian and himself.

"Well maybe you can help me." Kerian replied, dropping his arms down by his side and trying his best not to look threatening. "I appear to have lost something precious to me and I wonder if I could have dropped it during this afternoon's fracas." The stallholder flushed, his eyes looking away, confirming a guilty conscience.

"What do you know?" Kerian asked, his tone now turning decidedly chilly as he moved closer.

"I don't know anything." The hawker replied quickly. Too quickly for Kerian's liking.

"Where has the man and his brother gone?" Kerian pushed.

"Is everything alright over there, Turner?" shouted another vendor. "Do you need me to come over?" Kerian glared at the candle maker, then realised his blunt approach would not work in this case. He needed to change tact or he was going to end up back in the jail cell again.

"Look I just wanted to apologise to the two of them for the damage I caused and the misunderstanding. I mean you no harm." He paused, looking down at the floor. "I also really need to find the object I have mislaid." Footsteps approached from behind and Kerian looked over his shoulder to see several stallholders approaching, displaying a solidarity in the close-knit community of marketers that Kerian had not perceived would exist.

"Is this man bothering you Turner?" asked one.

"Look," Kerian turned. "I'm not here to cause trouble. I just need to find the two men that worked this stall and apologise to them for earlier. I mean no harm. I don't suppose any of you have found anything this afternoon. I appear to have lost…"

"There is nothing for you here." One trader stated, holding a large fish and trying to appear menacing. "I think you should leave before we call the watch."

"Okay." Kerian conceded, reluctantly stepping away. "I'm sorry, I'll just be on my way." He stepped away from the small group that had gathered, arms down by his sides, his mind racing. The candle maker knew something but as the stall holders seemed very loyal to each other. He was not sure what to do about it.

He wandered absentmindedly down one side of the market then turned and started back up the opposite side, his mind trying to conceive a plan for obtaining the information he needed. Clearly the trader and his brother had found something and had shut up shop and fled before Kerian had returned. However, the question remained, where had they fled to? He found himself standing at a random stall, perfume hanging heavy on the night air.

Kerian looked down at the tiny bottles of liquid laid out across the stall, all brightly coloured vials that shined and glinted in the lantern light. His eyes did not readily focus on the display itself but the miasma of different smells held unexpected consequences. Scent is a powerful trigger of memory and Kerian found his mind reminiscing with the association of the scents and the people and places of his past. Colette's smile filled his imagination, making his feelings of isolation more intense and a chill gloom to settle about him.

"For someone special?" came a voice at his side. "Is it vanilla you wish to woo the ladies with, or sandalwood to tantalise their senses? Maybe, lavender for restful sleep, you do look a little perky. Do you have anything particular in mind?" Kerian looked up to see a young woman standing beside him. She smiled sweetly, head tilted ever so slightly to one side, hair flowing like black ink, framing skin that appeared slightly luminous in the lights from the stall. Hoop earrings, eyes of smoky grey and intense ruby lips completed an image Kerian found difficult to turn away from.

"I'm sorry..." Kerian found himself taken aback at the unexpected attention, suppressing a shiver as the night air inexplicably turned cold. "Are you talking to me? Do you work here?"

"No. I am far away from here." came the mysterious reply. "Maybe Patchouli to relieve shyness?" Kerian could not help but find himself smiling in response, the attention from such a beautiful woman undeniably flattering to his aged form. He had forgotten what it was like to feel someone was interested in him. He found his smile widening, then realised that by doing so he was encouraging this exotic woman to continue.

"Definitely not needing Bergamot for depression then," she went on, reaching over to lift a bottle from the stall with a jangle of the bangles on her slim tanned arm. "Oh, no, I think not. This is for you, Causticum, Ignatia, a hint of seduction and a stolen kiss at midnight."

"What would that potion cure?" Kerian enquired, his eyebrow raised. "And who supplies the kiss?"

"Why, recovering from lost love." The woman replied mysteriously. "As for the kiss..." she licked her lip with a moist tip of her tongue. "...we will just have to wait and see."

"Can I help you?" asked the stallholder, shattering the moment the two were sharing.

"What? Oh..." Kerian stole a quick look at the young lady who appeared to be running the stall, then down at the small bottle he held in his hand. "Umm I'm not sure." He turned to address the mysterious woman who had been so entertaining, only to find she had moved away and was looking back at him over her shoulder with an enigmatic smile.

"Can I come back to you on this." He replied, placing the small vial carefully down on the stall. He turned to follow the alluring stranger, taking in the detail of her knee length plain white dress, how she wore it seductively off one shoulder, the way the bangles on her wrists sparkled in the light, the sway of her hips and the way she carried her slender frame.

This felt so wrong, looking at this woman in this way, especially with how Kerian felt about Colette but something about this woman and the chills she sent down his spine intoxicated him. He needed to know more, who knew, maybe she had the information he so desperately required? He licked his lips nervously and closed the distance eager to explore his irrational feelings further.

The object of his fascination ducked into a stall selling lengths of silks, exotic scarves and headwear. Kerian shook his head in wonder at his own naive actions and followed into the stall, only to find there was no one there but an elderly female trader, who took one look at the bruised and battered customer before turning away, suddenly intent on folding a length of silk already adequately folded.

"Excuse me." Kerian blustered. "But where is the young woman who just stepped in here?"

"As you can plainly see sir, there is no one else here but you and I." Replied the woman. Something about her answer made Kerian realise she was telling the truth. This made no sense. Where had his mysterious siren gone?

He stepped back out onto the main walkway and looked left and right, taking in the shadowy figures moving about their business but there was no sign of the young lady he had been admiring. This whole situation was bizarre. He smiled again, wondering if he had hallucinated the whole thing and whether the guards had been overzealous when they had hit him on the head. A rare chuckle escaped his lips. For just one fleeting moment, he had to admit to himself that the air of mystery had been fun!

"Do you feel alive now?" came a husky voice in his ear.

Kerian spun about, finding no sign of the mysterious woman. Customers stopped and looked at his bizarre behaviour and then stepped lightly aside. Another chill racked Kerian's form and he pulled his ruined tunic up around his neck, deciding for himself that there was nothing more he could do in the market tonight. The traders were all busy packing away and he knew his questions would only be treated with hostility and suspicion. He needed to find other sources for information. Maybe, the stallholders would seek shelter and a meal tonight rather than be on the road and risk attacks by bandits or wild animals in the darkness.

He realised it was time to go back to the *Lusty Mermaid*, have a stiff drink, something to eat and a long cold bath.

* * * * * *

The blistering air appeared to bow, then impossibly flex, akin to someone having dropped a pebble in water. Mystical energy crackled and sparked, threatening to ignite the volatile gases permeating the air within the crater of the volcano. An elliptical opening formed, sucking in the heat and surrounding air, as Justina stepped through the opening and out into the fiery abyss.

The sorceress staggered back as a wave of intense heat struck with the force of a blast furnace. Blue sparks rained down around her as the invisible protective field shielding her from the firestorm struggled to compensate for the sudden inferno she had walked into. Justina had known that there would be heat, expected it even, this was inside a volcano after all. However, planning for the impossible, then experiencing it first hand, were two entirely different things.

A small gem crumbled to dust between her fingers, adding more power to the shielding and reducing the blue sparks to only one or two every few seconds. The discharges now due to raining ash and soot colliding with the shield's surface rather than battling the holocaust. Justina took a faltering step forwards on the uneven surface, checked herself and her small travelling companion, then took a brief moment to look around and take in her surroundings.

She stood upon the steps of a once substantial temple, the entire structure now ruined, eroded by age and constant exposure to the elements. The whole building had settled on the left side, the foundations dipping to kiss a molten lava river bubbling and swirling below, giving the complete edifice a lopsided look. The stonework appeared ancient, the three long steps at her feet worn smooth from the passing of feet over the millennia.

A line of weathered pillars stretched for the heavens, supporting a roof that had terminal cracks throughout the masonry, caused by the temple's subsidence. The facia running beneath its skyline contained giant holes where murals had crumbled away. The whole building held a haunted and unnatural feel about it, as if something terrible lurked inside. Intense chattering rose from the creature perched on Justina's shoulder, forcing the sorceress to look across at her shrivelled skeletal demonic familiar and identify the nature of the problem.

"Hamnet what is it? I need you to quieten down. I am trying to think here!" She snapped before realising that her shrill companion was gesturing behind them.

Justina froze; readying a spell to hurl at whatever unseen threat awaited her, before she slowly turned to take in the sight of an incredible twisting and turning pathway of ruined steps leading up from the temple steps to a platform high above. The huge slabs of suspended stone hung lop-sided, some steps were missing entirely, creating a pathway now impossible to ascend.

The sorceress soon deduced that whatever magical enchantment had once held these gargantuan steps hovering steady in the air, now showed clear signs of failure, similar to the subsiding temple. However, it was not the stairs that were the cause of her demonic familiar's alarm but rather what rested on the bottom few slabs of smoking stone.

The crystalline skull of an immense dragon rested heavily on the step adjacent to the temple stairs. The teeth of the creature gleamed in the hellish light, reflecting back hints of russet and gold from the river of lava hissing and bubbling below. The sorceress tried to remain calm, taking in the sight of razor-sharp incisors, longer than she was tall, with only the slightest tremor to her slim frame.

What could possibly have brought down such a dragon? Justina looked to either side of the skull, trying to see the rest of the crystalline corpse and identify a cause of death but several of the next steps had succumbed to the loss of their enchantment and dropped away, taking most of the dragon's corpse with them into the bubbling lava. A partial back claw and a long sparkling tail glinted from steps far above her reach. Justina suddenly realised how thankful she was for her magical prowess and ability to teleport. No one could ever climb up from this temple, especially with these steps being so unstable and at risk of the forces of gravity. Anyone left down here would find themselves trapped and increasingly desperate.

The sorceress turned away, spinning in a swirl of cloak as she realised the meaning behind the images seen in the scrying bowl. Someone was trapped down here in the temple! Someone was actually inside there... waiting for her!

A patchy mosaic pathway snaked through the pillars into the temple's inner sanctum. Here and there, a glint of tantalising gold shone through, promising that riches beyond imagination lay within once the pathway reached its logical end.

"Stay alert!" Justina whispered to her eerie companion. Hamnet turned from the immense dragon skull towards the inner temple, her empty eye sockets appearing to see despite the fact her eyes had long decayed. She wrapped her skeletal tail around Justina's bicep and chattered in her demonic language, advising her mistress that she was indeed staying alert.

Justina moved cautiously along the crumbling path, nerves stretched taut as she stepped into the darkness. Friezes on the wall displayed scenes of idyllic life, farming, teaching, hunting and offering thanks to a king and queen of times long past but the sorceress had no time for such trivialities and quickly swept through the area, her long black robes whispering across the floor in her wake. Hamnet started chattering excitedly when they reached the end of the corridor and entered a semi-molten golden landscape. The treasure hoard beyond occupied an area measuring easily one hundred feet by eighty feet, with piles of plunder and offerings obscuring her field of view, making it impossible to see across to the far side of the building.

Coins from different realms lay scattered across the floor, piles of discarded currency now becoming soft and malleable in the intense heat from the volcano. Some coins had melted completely, forming shapeless mounds of molten gold, copper or silver, looking for all the world like huge melting candles, complete with slow moving blisters of slag impurities that bubbled and popped in pools dotted across the surface.

There was more wealth here than the sorceress had ever seen! This coin could finance her position for decades to come! Her eyes could not believe the depth of wealth she saw around her and it was all melting away! The very air of this temple reeked of old magic. Clearly, sometime in the past, powerful spells had been employed to protect the treasure. As in all things, when the magician died, their magic had faded with them.

A statue of horse and rider, half submerged in the puddled remains of a trove of silver coin looked for all the world as if the rider were trying to ford a priceless mirrored river slowly flowing across the floor. Ornate vases lay cracked in the heat, their contents spilled out onto the sloping floor. Gold leaf peeled away from a series of decorated wooden benches, the exposed wood charring in the high temperature as the thin metal covering dripped to the floor and smoke spiralled upwards through the hole in the temple ceiling above. Goblets lay forgotten on their sides as if revellers had just left the scene after drinking their fill and suits of warped and buckled armour lay on the ground as if ancient warriors had decided to take them off due to the heat from the roaring inferno.

Helmets, greaves and shields bearing insignia of armies from lands that had ceased to exist long before Justina's time lay forgotten and forlorn. Empty gilt picture frames marked heavily with soot jutted from piles of coin, the canvas of their absent masterpieces long since burnt away. Slow trickles of molten currency tracked across the floor and dripped over the edge of an open pit cut into the centre of the floor. Lava lapped hungrily at the edge of the pit, threatening to spill out across the horde and making the brickwork smoke as it seared the material away.

It took a while for the sorceress to realise that Hamnet was pulling frantically at her sleeve, as everywhere she looked there was something else to fascinate her roving eye. She looked at the mummified remains of the demon just as its skeletal hand scored the exposed flesh of her breast.

"What is it?" She snapped, knocking the creature's hand away and drawing two thin lines of blood across her bosom. Her demonic familiar chattered manically, gesturing to the far corner of the temple, the highest point in the slowly sinking structure and the side furthest from the conflagration.

"I know he's over there." She replied ominously. "He's been watching us ever since we walked in here..." Justina paused as a thought suddenly occurred to her and then looked more closely at the piles of molten gold. Everywhere she looked there were coins and metallic treasures but no gemstones. Not a single jewel anywhere. There had to have been jewels in this trove this treasure was simply too vast not to have... Justina paused as her eyes located the remains of a shattered gemstone.

"And he's been using magic..." she stated to herself. "I did not know Mathius could use magic." Justina paused, thinking back to the past and the man she believed to be hiding in the shadows. Mathius had been an elite assassin for the church she now ruled. Her predecessor Pelune, had used the Raven to kill targeted members of Catterick's high society, removing obstacles from his rise to power.

Justina recalled how she had transported the Raven aboard the *El Defensor* under Pelune's instructions; to retrieve a magical religious artefact; a golden serpent dagger that granted unholy powers to the one who used it, drawing life energy from the victims of its bite and restoring the vitality of the one who wielded the evil weapon. To hide his appearance from the crew, the sorceress had fashioned a headband rendering the Raven invisible, whilst at the same time allowing the sorceress to see everything the assassin observed.

However, something had gone wrong. Initially they had believed Mathius had been slain in combat by an aged traveller aboard the ship *El Defensor*. The headpiece had then somehow malfunctioned, the images it projected lost. When Pelune had all but given up on the possibility of finding his dagger, the headpiece had mysteriously come back to life. Flickering images had shown the treasure trove around her and a titanic battle, ending once again with the headband failing just as the same old man, complete with long white hair and a flowing moustache, had appeared to stab the wearer, ironically with his opponent's own sword. The remaining images had become confusing, revealing another figure in the treasure room but the last image Justina had identified was when the ancient warrior threw away the serpent artefact, somewhere in this very room. For all she knew the dagger could be bubbling gold beneath her feet but some inner instinct told the sorceress otherwise.

Mathius was still alive and he had the dagger hidden somewhere in this temple. The sorceress was sure of it. He was a man of darkness, cloaked in shadows, now armed with a cursed artefact of evil. Justina had to be cautious, even though it seemed fitting she would catch up with the assassin in this dark and treacherous place. Justina double checked all her magical protections were in place, then hitched up her robes and started to painstakingly work her way up the treacherous slope of coin and hoarded wealth. As her feet touched the liquid metal dripping across the floor, the magical shield instantly cooled it, leaving bright shining footprints that quickly melted and pooled moments after she passed.

The upper corner of the temple looked as if an explosion had occurred there. Several pillars having toppled to the ground, including part of a dividing wall, leaving a flight of naked stairs spiralling to nothing. There had been rooms here once, possibly for priests to get ready for service, maybe living quarters, or classrooms in which to teach or store items of value. Several appeared to have collapsed onto each other, forming a sheltered pit covered by the tumbled masonry.

The delicate remains of gemstones utilized for magical purpose lay scattered thickly at Justina's feet. Crisp empty shells, like discarded candy pieces, crunched loudly as the sorceress walked purposefully across them. Justina followed the trail, pausing just before the ruins, looking carefully, checking the shadows under the fallen masonry for threats, before she ducked under a huge slab of stone and became one with the darkness.

"*Komorabi*" Justina muttered, a small gemstone crumbling to dust within a setting on a bracelet at her wrist. A globe of pale light flared into being inches above the sorceress's palm, following her as she moved into the darkness, banishing the shadows to reveal a small room and a large gilded chair. Something sat slumped in the seat, a charred figure barely human, skin tight and blistered, a face heavily scarred, framed by scorched shoulder length hair. Charred boots burnt breeches and a cloak that actually looked as if it was physically smouldering.

Justina advanced towards the assassin. How could the Raven possibly have survived like this? She took one more inquisitive step, then froze as a warning hiss split the acrid air. Something golden slithered within the man's lap and it sensed her approach. She watched, fascinated, as the head of a golden snake raised up from the chair and focused its piercing gaze upon the sorceress from a pair of ruby red eyes. A gleaming golden fang eased from the snake's glittering mouth, dripping venom onto the arm of the chair.

The artefact was here! Practically within her grasp. The sorceress moved closer, fixated by the cursed serpent blade, considering the best approach to scoop the weapon up into her trembling hands. She could order Hamnet to collect the dagger but the power of the unholy relic and the risk of allowing it to fall into the demon minion's claws was too much of a risk to contemplate. If Justina wanted the relic, she would have to collect it herself. She moved within arm's reach, focusing intently on the flickering tongue of the animated evil before her, the snake's golden head swaying from side to side, clearly agitated and preparing to strike, its ruby eyes watching her every move. She was so focused on the cursed blade, she almost missed it when the charred figure holding the weapon moved.

The sorceress stepped back in surprise as the burnt figure turned to look at her with one brown eye open and an out of place cocky grin on his cracked and charred face. She suddenly realised that despite the burns and damaged skin, the face scrutinising her was not that of the Raven. The hair could have been the same length, where it had not burnt away; the headband she had crafted with her own magic clearly rested upon his troubled brow. The magical signature her own, all be it corrupted or broken in some manner she had yet to fathom but this was definitely not the Raven.

The ears gave it away first. Pointed bleeding ears, not human at all. Something from legend. Elven even. Could this be an Elf? The figure groaned as it repositioned itself, skin crackling painfully as the person moved. His hand tightened on the dagger, its coils slithering around his arm as he opened his other eye as if awakening from a long slumber. However, this second eye was not brown like it's twin. Instead, inside this socket, there glowed an eerie green mist that swirled and eddied. A voice, dry as dust and parched as if from long exposure to the sun suddenly rasped out, startling the sorceress further.

"It is about time you arrived…" the charred figure tried to lick his burnt lips, causing one end to split and bleed before he uttered a throaty laugh. His cracked voice echoed starkly throughout the darkened room, its meaning filled with menace and the promise of exquisite pain.

"Who are you?" Justina asked, her horror and confusion at the evil sitting before her clear. "What have you done with Mathius?"

"I think I'm about well done by now." the previous first mate of the *El Defensor* continued, sitting up slowly, as if the effort caused him great pain, before he let his gaze linger on the beautiful woman standing across from him. The golden serpent dagger continued slithering about his wrist, the hilt of the weapon settling comfortably in the palm of his raw blistered hand. Twin blades reflected the light source hovering over Justina's trembling hand, making the weapon appear cold despite its hellish surroundings.

"My name is Scrave…" the charred figure continued. "And if you had waited any longer, our romantic meal for two would have been spoiled."

Chapter Six

"We have to go back!" Commagin yelled at Thomas. "We have to go back for my boy!"

"We can't." Thomas mumbled, still shocked at discovering they had inadvertently left the Gnome apprentice behind. Thick mist continued to roll across the deck of the *El Defensor*, the constant roaring sound threatening to drown out every word. Commagin continued to huff and puff, pulling his beard in worry and shouting once again as condensation fogged up his glasses.

"We have to go back. I can't leave him alone there. Not the ship's graveyard of all places."

"I'm sorry but we can't go back." Thomas did not know what else to say. He did not know how to explain that they had no more power left to open the gate, let alone pass back through it or hold one open for a rescue attempt. They had no jewels left. Wherever they were now, they would remain here until they could find a more sustainable source of power.

"Get Colette to reopen the gate then, I'll go through in the dinghy, you need not risk the ship. I'll be in and out before you know it. No time at all." Commagin continued, as if he had not heard a word Thomas had told him. "Just give me a chance and I will make it right. I will bring him hom..."

"We can't!" Thomas shouted, bringing the engineer's ramblings to an abrupt and hurtful stop. "We just can't alright! We don't have the means." The whole ship appeared to freeze in place as the captain uttered the fateful words confirmed the apprentice's abandoned fate.

"We would have found a way for you!" The Dwarf replied. "No matter what the cost or risk... we would have found a way for you." His barbed words fell on Thomas with a venom that knocked the captain back on his heels. Commagin tore the apron from Rowan's hand and stomped away across the deck, his shoulders trembling as tears started to fall.

Thomas looked around at the silent crew, hands open wide, his posture trying to convey his innocence as water dripped from the end of his nose. The captain could not help but view the looks aimed at him as hostile, not only because of the loss of Barney but also the grisly end of Monahan.

"What are you all looking at?" he snapped, looking each crewman in the eye and daring them to find fault. One by one, the sodden crew dropped their gaze and moved away until Thomas found himself standing isolated, alone on the mid-deck. Rowan came over, her eyes sorrowful, brimming with understanding but Thomas wanted no pity.

"Please check on Commagin." He asked, waving her after the departing Dwarf. "He is the one that needs company at this time."

"And what about you?" Rowan questioned. "What about the mighty Thomas Adams?"

"The crew remain my priority." He bristled, turning on his heel to walk towards the stern of the ship, intent on checking on Rauph and determined to see if Weyn could cast a light on their situation from his high vantage point in the crow's nest.

Rowan watched Thomas set off through the drizzle and shook her head. Where had the fun-loving police officer she had known in Stratholme gone? It was as if she was looking at a different man, all stern, cold and stretched to absolute breaking point. His intensity was unsettling, as if violence brewed just beneath the surface. Something was wrong with him. Something had been clearly playing on his mind ever since he became upset in his cabin shortly after they left Stratholme. Was it her? Had she done something wrong?

Ever since she had found him distressed, staring blankly into his desk drawer at a collection of small mementos, gathered to remind him of lost members or departed crew, he had been distant. Maybe it was because she had witnessed him so vulnerable? Thomas had refused to explain what was causing his concerns, leaving her with nothing to do but hold and reassure him but from that watershed moment, he had spiralled into the troubled man she now saw before her. She needed to figure out what was going on before his dark unpredictable temperament tore them apart.

Rowan set off after the Dwarven engineer, her mind full of self-doubt and insecurity. Thomas did not seem to understand that she was still a stranger on this ship, often feeling the crew only permitted her presence because she was the captain's companion and not because she had won her right to be here. She bit her lip, holding her hands tightly in fists and marched off to do Thomas's bidding, cursing his lack of compassion and understanding towards her.

* * * * * *

Thomas reached the main mast and stared up into the waterlogged heavens where he knew Weyn would be scanning for dangers in... well, wherever they were.

"Weyn can you see anything up there." He shouted over the roar.

"I wish to lodge a complaint with your superior," replied a disembodied voice from the mist. "I simply must object to the fact that I am always interrupted when I am having a shower. Do you have no decency?"

"Pack it up Weyn!" Thomas shouted back, still feeling thunderous in mood, yet finding it hard to keep this sombre outlook when someone like Weyn still managed to find a way to bring a smile to his face. He took a deep breath recognising the need to calm his negative emotions and move forward. "Give it to me sensibly please!"

"Oh, well, it's either monsoon season, or we are docked under a waterfall." The archer replied, "I can't see anything, apart from billowing white clouds and something darker ahead slightly to starboard, over where the ballista fired."

Thomas turned to look towards the prow and just found himself facing a pale wall of rolling grey mist that appeared to stretch on forever. This was ridiculous! They needed more information on where they were and sitting here was not going to achieve this.

"Aradol," Thomas yelled. "Take Austen and the dinghy and retrieve that grappling line. Weyn states there is something out there. I want you tied to that line at all costs. Do you hear me? No heroics. I don't need you getting lost in the mist and adding to my problems." Aradol nodded, gesturing to Austen before they set about lowering the dinghy into the water and moved to do their captain's bidding.

Colette strolled over to Thomas, flipping her hair back, the blonde locks suddenly curly with all the moisture in the air. The mage met Thomas's troubled gaze and matched it with her own sad disheartened one.

"What have we done Thomas?" she asked. "What have we done?"

"What you had to do." Mathius replied for them both, walking up to the two conspirators and shrugging as he did so. "The rest of the crew always come first. No individual crewman is worth risking the lives of everyone else for. It may not be an easy idea to stomach but it was the right call to make."

"I was caught off guard." Thomas confessed. "Malum has never tried anything like this before."

"So, you were caught unprepared." Mathius continued. "Unprepared and not ready for the storm you sailed into. Just make sure it doesn't happen again."

"We need to get more gems." Colette added. "We cannot let ourselves be left without power again. Wherever we are, this must be our priority."

"No..." Thomas replied. "Our priority is taking the fight to Malum."

"It's a plan." Mathius replied but you must consider the fact he is currently one step ahead of us and when we travel back through that archway, the chances are, he will be waiting."

"The gemstones are our priority! Not some petty revenge on Malum." Colette shook her head angrily, blond curls bouncing.

"Oh, I guarantee you my revenge will be anything but petty." Thomas promised.

* * * * * *

Oars cut cleanly through the water as Aradol leant to the task of following the ballista line out into the mist. Austen stood at the back of the boat, legs wide, sliding a large looped safety line along the taut rope they followed.

"Where are we going?" he asked the young man rowing.

"To the end of the line." Aradol replied, grinning as he pulled the oars again, his muscles straining tightly against his shirt. "I must confess I have never been there myself but I understand that we all need a vacation from time to time."

"I thought we were already there," Austen replied, ignoring the feeble comedy attempt and gesturing back towards the ship, his grizzled seaman's face deep in thought. "For a moment there I thought we really were at the end of the line. I'm not cut out for this. I just want to look after my hawks and have a quiet life."

"Not with Thomas Adams at the helm." Aradol replied, full of confidence at his captain's ability to see them through any tough scrape. "I mean look at all the narrow escapes we have had in the past. We always make it through no... matter... what. What are you looking at?"

Austen gestured behind Aradol in the direction they were rowing, his eyes moving slowly upwards, then further as he took in the incredible image materialising behind the young rower.

"Stop rowing," he stated breathlessly. "You need to see this."

Aradol lifted the oars free from the water, letting the dinghy glide forward under its own momentum and turned to see what his fellow sailor was so fascinated with.

"Well would you look at that..." he said breathlessly.

* * * * * *

The *El Defensor* cleaved her way through the wall of mist like a shark through water, her prow breaching the cloudbank so suddenly, that her appearance startled a flock of purple flamingos into taking flight from a nearby sandbank, squawking their annoyance loudly for all to hear. The galleon emerged as a ghostly vision suddenly made real, her creamy white sails snapping tight as she picked up the wind moving across the crystal-clear dark blue water, launching her forwards like a stallion released to the wild, eager to race and gallop free.

The early morning sunshine warmed the wind as it whistled through the rigging, lifting the spirits of everyone aboard as they strained to see the object that had caused so much awe in Aradol and Austen's tale. As soon as their eyes lit upon the immense statue, everyone aboard could see why the two men had returned to the galleon so excited.

It was immense, soaring high into the sky, standing well in excess of two hundred feet tall. She stared out across the water in constant vigil, a sentinel guarding the waters from invaders. A huge waterfall backlit the statue, enhancing its majesty and reinforcing its powers of intimidation. The foaming water thundering down from a precipice easily half the size again of the towering construct at its base, the deluge creating the constant billowing cloud from which the *El Defensor* had appeared.

Skirts of cast bronze flowed down like a toga, clothing the tall regal form and leaving one shoulder bare. A large oval shield sat at her feet, set deep into the water with just the top half exposed above the waves crashing around its weathered surface. A spear rose to the heavens, the shaft wider than a tree trunk, the female guard holding the spear tightly in her left hand, whilst she shaded her eyes with the right, further reinforcing the guardian image the statue conveyed. A war helmet, complete with a raised feather crest and horns set on either side completed the immense structure, with small birds wheeling about her head from nests dotted on her brow, raised hand and shoulders.

Thomas took in the incredible sight, holding his breath without realising it. From his current vantage point the jaw of the statue looked too wide but it was difficult to make out details until the *El Defensor* had sailed further away. With this in mind, the captain's eyes started to trace the land either side of the waterfall, looking for signs of civilisation, a place to dock and resupply.

His gaze followed the cliffs down, both to the left and the right of the thundering waterfall, looking for breaks in the sheer natural walls and finding none. Dense jungles, thick with vines, creepers and no doubt, lots of wild animals, butted right up to the cliff edge helping to enhance the daunting appearance of this natural barrier. He turned, tracing the jungle, taking in small islands and outcroppings, caves and sheltered bays, as his visual journey tracked down the port side of the ship and out over the heads of his crew, all gathered on deck for the first glimpse of this new world.

On the starboard side of the ship, a similar picture presented itself; overhanging trees, long basking reptiles, splashing into the water from small inlets, their early morning lounge disturbed by the *El Defensor's* swift passing. Thomas reached into his waistcoat and pulled out his telescope to scan the coast, sweeping it around to the prow of the galleon, where he finally discovered what he had been searching for.

An island lay ahead of them, accessible from the coast by high, delicate arched walkways and bridges, under which flowed the deep blue waters they sailed upon. It was a walled city, with guard posts set at intervals along the dark stone barricade encircling a high mount covered in white and cream buildings featuring pillars and colonnades, topped with terracotta tiled roofs. Smoke spiralled to the heavens from numerous fires, confirming the city was inhabited and at the pinnacle of the mount there appeared to be a large state building, similar in style to the ancient Greek necropolis that Thomas had once studied in history books at school.

Such civilisation meant wealth. Wealth meant gemstones. Thomas felt a small weight lift from his shoulders. There was a thin glimmer of hope here. Maybe the fates were looking after them after all.

He continued his scan of the coastline, determined to come back to the island and noticed a strange sight in the jungle beyond the island. He swung the telescope back, squinting to gain better focus. There appeared to be a massive ziggurat sitting there, cresting from the jungle canopy, its cap stone gleaming golden in the morning sunlight, the pale stone steps of the pyramid dropping off into the dense undergrowth beneath. The structure had to be massive, for it to be seen from this far away.

Thomas filed this information away and continued his sweep with the lens, before realising something he should have noticed earlier. The coast continued back down the port side of the ship in an unbreakable barrier, out past his position then back over to the waterfall. The water they sailed upon was completely enclosed on all sides.

They were not sailing on the ocean anymore. The *El Defensor* was currently traversing a huge lake.

His mind recalled the numerous log entries back in his cabin, penned by the previous captain Rik Kavaliare. In all the hours Thomas had spent pouring over those old ledgers, reading of locations both fantastic and terrifying, he had never come across a lake being the final destination. The *El Defensor* had apparently never travelled to this world. He wondered what surprises lay in wait for them here and felt that familiar thrill of excitement rush through him.

Turning towards the helm, Thomas noted the eight-foot-tall shaggy figure of Rauph looking somewhat pensive and surprisingly insecure. The Minotaur appeared to be looking around him and licking his lips nervously. Thomas moved closer, then realised the possible cause. The Halfling Ashe Wolfsdale ran around the navigator's feet, throwing questions up at his huge companion and waving his birdcage around in the air. No wonder the Minotaur looked pensive. Having Ashe around your legs at the best of times made the heart beat faster and hands constantly pat pockets to check items remained where they should be. Thomas took a deep breath then decided to save his bovine friend from a fate worse than death and set off on an intercept course.

"So you see Rauph," Ashe shouted enthusiastically, "Sinders simply won't fly. No matter what I try to do, he won't come out of his cage. I mean how am I expected to get him to fly when he won't step outside. I have tried shaking the cage..." He shook the small cage for good measure rattling the bird around inside and causing Rauph to snort in shock at the rough treatment being shown.

"I've even tried to spin him out really fast." Ashe spun on the spot, cage outstretched, whizzing around on the open deck and flattening Sinders against the bottom of the cage with a protesting squawk. "...but it makes me feel really sick after... a... while." The Halfling confessed, stopping and staggering about, moving his head around and around in an exaggerated comic effect that had Rauph snorting with mirth.

"I mean what is a Halfling to do?" Ashe stood hand on hip, cage upside down, Sinders hanging resolutely to the bars at the back of the cage. "Look, even when I open the cage, he won't come out. I don't think he will ever do as he is told." He flipped open the door to show how true these words were and put the cage on the floor waving his arms wide.

"Much like someone we all know." Thomas added, arriving like the cavalry to save the day.

"Who's that then?" Ashe asked, open eyed, his innocent face like that of an angel. "Oh Thomas, I've been meaning to ask. Why is everyone so excited and up on deck? I mean we have seen places like this before, it's just a walled city, with a possible palace, likely unguarded precious jewels and a scary building in the deep, dark, jungle nearby." He battered his eyelashes sweetly, failing to notice how Thomas and Rauph were slowly stepping away from him and checking their pockets.

"Okay, not every place we go has a huge statue of a bronze minotaur guard but then..."

"What did you say?" Thomas asked.

"Scary building in a deep, dark jungle?" Ashe replied.

"No, the other bit..."

"Oh," Ashe shook his head remembering. "Palace and jewels maybe?"

"The Minotaur bit." Thomas pointed out. "What do you mean a statue of a Minotaur."

"Well it is, isn't it?" Ashe asked incredulously. "I mean from my vantage point that's what a Minotaur always looks." He walked closer to Rauph and stared up under the navigator's shaggy chin. "Yup, just like a Minotaur, see."

Thomas turned back towards the statue and looked again. He had automatically assumed the horns were part of a war helmet, not attached to the head underneath but now he thought about it, there was an uncanny likeness to Rauph's physique. Could it really be a Minotaur?

Thomas turned to Rauph, a questioning look across his features.

"Do you recognise her?" he asked. Rauph shrugged his huge shoulders.

"Why should I?" he replied. "I mean if I pointed out a human and asked if you recognised them, how would you answer? Just because I'm a Minotaur doesn't mean I know everyone. I mean do you know him?" Rauph pointed a finger over to the rail where two priests leant admiring the view, pale faded blue robes flapping in the breeze.

"Well that's Marcus and Brother Richard." Thomas answered without dropping a beat. "You know that as well as I do." Rauph looked over, squinted and then brushed the long chestnut hair from his eyes.

"Oh... so it is." He agreed, looking surprised as he recognised the two men. "Anyhow you know I cannot remember anything about where I come from." He lowered his head solemnly. "I don't even know if Rauph is my real name."

"I'm sure it is." Thomas replied, a lump in his throat. He knew full well where Rauph's name came from. It was the name of the stray cat the precinct had adopted after it was run over by a squad car. They had sent a rookie to get a collar and tag made for the mangy ginger tom and told him to label it 'Ralph' after the *Karate Kid* actor *Ralph Macchio* from the 1980's movies, because like the cat, Ralph managed to get up and keep swinging after being knocked down. Also, Thomas had to be honest, that knockout kick at the end of the film was simply awesome.

Thomas smiled at the thought, the rookie had only gone and spelt it wrong and the name Rauph, pronounced 'Rawlf' became the one that had stuck, christening the spitting, hissing, fur ball and unofficial mascot of the precinct. That was in better days, before the serial killer case, before the child's death, before the shotgun blast. Thomas shook his head angrily and tried to focus back on the lumbering giant before him.

The captain keenly remembered when they had found Rauph. The Minotaur had been floating, far out at sea, lying unconscious on the remains of a piece of wooden deck as sharks gently circled, nudging the wood at each pass to see if anything would fall into their predatory jaws. The crew had initially been terrified of considering dragging the Minotaur on board, worried about his immense size and scary appearance. Thomas had helped the crew hoist the gentle giant from the water and had noticed the huge haematoma and gash behind the creature's ear, the bruising and assorted wounds all over his body.

Someone had tried to kill Rauph and instead, by dumb luck or fate, he had ended up crossing paths with Thomas Adams and the *El Defensor* and they were now firm friends. It had taken some time for the crew to get used to the lumbering giant and to try and reassure him that they meant no harm. Rauph's mind, like his origins had remained a mysterious blank ever since.

Maybe Rauph knew of this place. That would be amazing... Then Thomas thought back to those horrific injuries and changed his mind. He shook his head and re-examined the statue. Maybe this was simply a mythological statue created in a semblance of a Minotaur?

The horns could be part of the figure's helmet after all and they could be making huge assumptions with no basis in fact whatsoever.

"Let's keep the sails trimmed." Thomas shouted to the brothers in the rigging. "Make the most of the wind we have." He turned back to Rauph and smiled warmly. "Keep her steady my friend. Let's do a sail once around the island, find the docks and ease into port. Just remember if they have no large ships the port may be shallow, so take it real slow." Thomas looked around at the crew lining the rails, their excited voices, faces brightened by glimpsing this apparent paradise, then turned back to Rauph smiling.

"Let's go around twice," he whispered. "We should fit under the bridges if you steer her straight. I want everyone in that city to see us coming." There would be no surprises this time, no sneaking under cover of night. Every time they tried to do that something went wrong. It was time to be open and honest. The change would be refreshing and who knew... it may just make things go their way for once.

* * * * * *

"Where has Thomas taken us now?" Brother Richard asked, his dark hair swept back from a face worn deep with worry lines. The monk turned to his colleague, a much younger acolyte called Marcus, who wore matching traditional blue robes of the Order of St Fraiser and the same flaming cross religious icon around his neck.

"It is quite incredible." Marcus replied. "Who would believe such beauty could even exist. I mean it was only a few months ago that I first left the cloisters in Catterick. Now..." he swept his arms wide at the sweeping vista before them. "...just look at the wonders we behold."

Brother Richard had to agree with the novice's wide-eyed assessment. The things they had seen since they had joined the crew were indeed inspiring. How could there not be a higher power when such places of exotic beauty existed especially alongside places of horror and decay such as the ships graveyard? It showed there was equilibrium in all things, just as the order promoted within its doctrine. If there was sky, there would be ground. If there was pain, there would be pleasure. Good always followed bad and everything had an opposite that balanced out in the end. Brother Richard had always believed things happen for a reason, no matter how terrible they were at the time.

At least he did, until he found Stratholme. Until he had found what he believed to be his own personal paradise before it was snatched away. Despite the beauty all around him Richard felt betrayed inside. Why had his heart's desire been so cruelly taken from him? He had no one to ask? His god appeared to have deserted him, had left him educating a novice who had ironically been sent to destroy him. The world was suddenly chaotic, balance non-existent. He stroked the chin of the only creature on board that understood him and it purred back loudly, before sliding its smoky fur along his arm leaving his robes covered in a coating of loose fur.

* * * * * *

Socks was Brother Richard's cat from Stratholme. At least it let Brother Richard think it was. The cat had become quite accustomed to life aboard ship, catching rats in the cargo holds and the bilges of the huge ship and growing quite content on a diet of fish that made its coat gleam. Pale green eyes blinked happily as Richard scratched diligently between the cat's ears making it stretch out with pleasure along the rail, claws digging into the paintwork as the cat received the affection it desired. Socks listened without understanding to the discussion held above it, then smelt something interesting and turned one lazy eye towards the helm and a certain cage left unattended on the floor.

There was a bird in that cage and Socks wanted to eat it.

* * * * * *

"I mean..." Marcus continued, "how could the creator have been so diverse in his imaginings? Everything here is so wondrous."

"Have you opened the book yet?" Richard asked, killing Marcus's enthusiasm with his carefully chosen words. Marcus reached down to pat a satchel hanging at his side, as if his hand would keep the book safe from prying eyes and fingers.

"Not yet." He confessed quietly. "I'm scared to do so after what happened. What if the knights get free again and I can't control them?" Richard looked over at the book and frowned at his young acolyte.

"If you do not take charge of the book you will never wield it with the power a bearer should control. I thought I explained that to you. Your fear is stopping you from becoming powerful, you should not fear power, you should embrace it before someone more deserving takes it away from you." Marcus hung his head, clearly unsure. Abbot Brialin, Marcus's previous mentor, had offered similar velvet coated persuasions but had been lying all along about the book and its contents, using them with devastating effect in Stratholme and nearly killing everyone.

"I'm just not sure I can control them." The young man swallowed hard, staring out over the water towards nothing, his eyes now glazed and unfocused. "I do not believe I am worthy." Brother Richard gritted his teeth as the words spilled from the acolyte's mouth. If only Marcus could hear himself! Here was a young man with the power to level mountains in his hands, yet he was afraid to use it. Why was he, of all people, cursed with such a responsibility? Maybe it was a test of faith. It had to be. Richard bit back the bile in his throat and forced a smile across his face.

"Let us discover your worth together." He smiled, turning back to stroke his cat only to find the animal had left its perch at some time during their conversation. "Power needs to be controlled if it is to be used effectively. I am sure we will find a way together."

* * * * * *

Socks skirted the legs of one sailor and slinked between the feet of another, almost sending the man falling onto his back. The cat's meandering course purposeful, almost reassuring, showing it was harmless and not a threat to be considered by the prey that this wandering path angled the cat closer and closer to. One pale green eye always kept the bird cage in view as Socks slipped behind a barrel and then under a tarpaulin. Claws dug into the ships deck as the cat crawled beneath the waterproof sheeting and wiggled itself nearer and nearer its unsuspecting meal.

The feral feline had been aware of Sinders for some time. It was the only bird kept separate from the aviary on the ship. Socks had tried his luck at the aviary but the birds always made such a ruckus and that human who nurtured the animals always shooed him away making any stalking in this area a waste of time and energy.

The cat licked its lips, exposing bright fangs to the air as its long pink tongue rasped across its button nose. Sure, life on board was good. Rats, fish and tit bits from the galley all supplemented its mealtimes but a fresh bird to eat. This was the meal it craved, to feel hot blood jet into its mouth, to hear light brittle bones crack. This bird was the ultimate treat and Socks had stalked the animal constantly always being foiled at the last minute.

The tarpaulin lifted slowly from Socks's head as he slithered across the deck, keeping a low profile and moving carefully, inch by inch, towards the bird who was still unaware of his presence. The cat stopped in mid stalk. The cage door was open. This was better and better. Socks wiggled closer, his green eyes taking in the shivering black and white bird in the far corner of the cage. The bird was clearly afraid of him and Socks liked his prey to be afraid. A prey's heart beat faster when the death blow came making the meal all that sweeter. Socks licked its lips again and slid closer still.

Socks had attempted to claim the life of Ashe's pet five times now, always watching and waiting for the moment that Sinders stepped out from the cage. Each time the bird had gained the confidence to step from its home Socks had been waiting but the bird had learnt that outside the cage meant danger and so it had stubbornly decided to remain safely in its home despite all the efforts of its owner to turf it out.

A leading white paw touched the open door of the cage and the cat changed tactic. There was no need to stalk now, the bird had nowhere to run. The cat slid its head into the bird's home and started to gather up its back legs to pounce inside and grab the trembling feast within. Muscles tensed, claws extended. Socks prepared for the meal to come and closed its eyes in a moment of sheer anticipation.

Sinders reacted instantly. Its sharp beak flashing out and pecking the cat squarely on the nose making it spit and moan, falling back through the door, just as a hand swept up the cage and swung off across the deck with it.

"No Socks!" Ashe scolded. "He is not allowed out to play with you. He has been a very bad bird and he is going back to his room. He is grounded!" Socks watched his gourmet delicacy swing off across the deck and sneezed in disappointment. He licked a white paw and dragged it across his bruised nose, watching carefully as the little Halfling headed off towards the cabins below decks. Dignity bruised, Socks turned and walked haughtily off across the deck looking for a sailor to trip or an unsuspecting crewman to sharpen his claws on. The bird may have escaped this time but it could not stay in that cage forever and when it came out Socks would be waiting.

Chapter Seven

Kerian stared despondently into his drink and took in the blurred image of the old man staring accusingly back at him. He noted the dishevelled white hair framing the aged face, knowing that even now, the magic spell cast upon him by the crystal dragon Rosalyine, was slowly transforming it into the jet-black hair he had in his youth. The furrowed brow, more from the frustration of his current predicament, rather than his curse inflicted ageing, appeared to frown sternly at Kerian, as if disappointed by his inaction and his abject failure to retrieve his lost pendants.

How could he have allowed himself to get into this mess? The answer was obvious. He had stuck his nose in someone else's business, got involved when not required. What was wrong with him? The old Styx would have laid waste, roughed up the stallholder, made him eat the damned candles from his stall, piece by piece, until he had begged to tell him the truth. He would have left the other market traders trembling on their knees as he stalked away, not caring about risking the wrath of such insignificant peasants.

Why was he so worried about upsetting a few locals? Was he mellowing in his old age? If so, he did not appreciate this sign of aging at all! Could travelling upon the *El Defensor* have changed him that much? It was not just the failed market scenario that irked him; something about Wellruff itself, now made him feel uneasy. There was a tension in the air, as if the storm he had been desperately chasing all these months was about to crash down upon him and maroon him battered and bruised here. He had already spent time under the care of the local authorities and Kerian knew that if he caused a scene and he found himself back in jail, he would find little possibility of early release, whilst the pendants slipped further from his grasp.

He clenched his fist in anger, wanting to lash out and punch something but knew such actions were ultimately self-defeating. His impulsive feelings were charging unchecked throughout his mind. He needed to stop, take time to gather the right information and then act, despite his need to charge off into the sunset and lay waste to every pot-selling stallholder on the mainland.

Then there was the strange, exotic woman who had whispered in his ear. He looked back at his elderly reflection and shook his head, chuckling despite himself. Quite clearly, in his present decrepit state, he was simply irresistible to all wandering damsels and mysterious single females. Whom was he kidding? A danger maybe? Maybe she had just felt sorry for him. It was time to get serious, put that pleasant distraction behind him and concentrate on getting back to the woman who *really* haunted his dreams. He just hoped Colette was safe sailing with Thomas Adams. There was an element of danger to travelling with Thomas on the *El Defensor*, as if the captain were a magnet to mayhem. Kerian knew Thomas tended to suck others into the whirlwind of chaos he danced around, leaving everyone immersed in the danger and excitement of the *El Defensor's* adventures.

Kerian sipped his drink, wetting his lips and allowing his eyes to scan the door of the *Lusty Mermaid* for what felt like the millionth time since he had settled down in the booth. Despite his vigilance on the coming and goings of several customers, no one from the market stalls had arrived to slake their thirst after a hard day selling turnips or ornate rugs to the discerning citizens of Wellruff. He nursed his drink a moment longer, his feet getting twitchy beneath, him adding to that growing sense he had misread the situation completely. No one from the market was coming in here. It was time to admit he had made a terrible mistake.

A burst of laughter alerted him to a larger alcove where several musicians sat tuning their instruments. Clearly, the evening entertainment had arrived. He watched the players adjusting lutes, blowing into piccolos, tooting flutes and tapping fingers on taut drums. Musical notes matched the frivolity and good nature of the band as they lit upon the evening air. As one man moved aside, shouldered good-naturedly by another band member clearing his throat, Kerian noticed a familiar face sitting against the wall staring at the group with his smiling dark eyes, his curly brown hair now clean and barely a bruise showing on his face.

Kerian moved slowly, trying not to draw attention to himself and settled gently back against the wall to observe the young man he had shared jail time with just a few hours before. More taunts and good-natured jibes followed from the musicians, before one band member offered his guitar over for Octavian to play, despite the obvious unwillingness of the gypsy to do so. Octavian closed his eyes and tentatively played the strings, his fingers lightly moving across the instrument, coaxing tunes from the battered guitar with a skill that suggested he had spent considerable time learning to play in his past. The melody was haunting and despite himself, Kerian became instantly enthralled.

Octavian appeared oblivious to the men and women around him, his fingers picking out notes, chords and harmonies that held his fellow musicians in awe. Then, after a slight pause, the gypsy launched into a melodious foot-tapping beat that prompted the other musicians to join in to the impromptu musical session, drawing yells of appreciation from many in the tavern.

Captivated by the moment and enjoying himself despite his woes, Kerian felt his spirits lifted and his problems lessened. The music cleansed him, soothed his fears and gave him a certain clarity that had been lost in the turmoil of his thoughts and feelings. The answer to his problems sat right in front of him. He needed someone who had knowledge of the market and its comings and goings. So what better individual to discuss this with than the very man who worked there? A slight but enigmatic smile lit Kerian's features as he settled back to enjoy the show.

* * * * * *

Octavian plucked the last string of the guitar and let the note hang in the air of the tavern. His eyes remained closed as he felt the music wash over him, opening old wounds and reminding him poignantly of his life on the road before coming to Wellruff. The bittersweet memories, the faces of those dear to him, threatened to bring tears to his eyes but he choked them back, promising himself he would soon return to those in need. He forced a smile onto his face before finally allowing himself to welcome reality again and opened his eyes to applause.

Kerian Denaris sat opposite him slowly clapping his musical performance. Octavian froze, a guilty conscious briefly flitting at the edge of his mind like a panicked bird in a cage. What was he doing here? Did he know Octavian's secret?

"Oh well done." The old man smiled. "Well done. Why don't you do this professionally? Surely, it pays better than mucking out stables at the market. Your music was beautiful, such a tragic tale of love. It almost moved me to tears."

Octavian had lived a long time on the road. He knew that in everyday life, people simply criticised you and the only reason for complements was if they wanted something. His guard instantly came up as he regarded the man before him, his mind debating if he should run or remain seated.

"I leave love to the wandering bards." Octavian replied cagily. "I get hurt less that way." He risked flashing his conman smile and tried to settle back against the wall in an effort to look casual. "So what can I do for the richest mad man in town?"

"I doubt you have left love to minstrels, your music has too much feeling for that." Kerian began, looking around conspiratorially before shuffling forward on the stool he had come by. "I need some information from you." Octavian's smile grew wider as relief swept over him. Maybe the old man did not suspect after all.

"Information is expensive." He teased, feeling his confidence return.

"Even to a fellow cellmate?" Kerian shot back, without missing a beat.

"Especially to one of those." The gypsy replied. "I mean an ex-convict is not to be trusted."

"And you are?" Kerian enquired, his verbal fencing skills honed razor sharp. "Look it's no big thing. I just need to know about a stall holder and his brother on the market. They have something of mine and I want it back but they have packed up and moved on."

Octavian watched Kerian's face darken as he said the latter part of the sentence and felt the temperature between the two men fall. It appeared Denaris was not a man to cross unless you were in a position of considerable advantage and as Octavian knew of only one stall manned by two brothers, he recognised the advantage was his.

"I have asked the other traders," Kerian continued, "but I have met with a wall of silence. I know they have something of mine and I need to know where they are so I can retrieve it. It is very important to me."

"Oops, that puts the price up." Octavian quipped, "especially now that I know how valuable it is to you." The gypsy smiled at Kerian's vulnerability and the conman in him now wanted to see if he could push his advantage further.

Kerian's face flushed with emotion and Octavian suddenly found himself reconsidering his actions. The conman warily observed his unexpected meal-ticket, noting the internal struggle playing itself out as Kerian's craggy features struggled to remain calm. Kerian reached into his pocket and withdrew a few small gems that gleamed tantalising in the tavern light.

"I don't know how much you want." He confessed but it is all yours if you help me get my belongings back." Octavian noted the edge to Kerian's words and weighed them against his own troublesome needs. The gems were worth a small fortune and would help with the ransom he desperately required, yet part of the gypsy conman viewed the old man's weakness as an opportunity to be even more ruthless. His rational mind said take what was offered and be content, this was a great unexpected haul, however, even as his mouth opened to say those very words, something else decided to edit the script.

"It's not enough."

Kerian choked and Octavian started in reaction.

"Not enough!" Kerian yelled, jumping to his feet and sending his stool spinning across the room. "Not enough. Why, I ought to take you outside and finish the job those thugs started.

"Better men have tried." Octavian jibed, his cocky persona now running fully unchecked. Kerian's hand shot out, grabbing a handful of tunic and hoisted the gypsy up into the air, leaving Octavian facing a decision. Maybe it was time to back off, take the gems and calm the old man down before someone got hurt? The problem was, he needed this money so badly and he could not risk losing this windfall now.

"If you hit me you get nothing." Octavian threatened, staring Kerian in the eye as he swung from the old man's clenched fist. Did he dare go for the big push, double or nothing? "Now put me down gently, laugh like it's a joke and get me a couple of those large gemstones I have been hearing about."

If Octavian had thought Kerian's countenance severe before, it now looked as if the old man was about to explode. The gypsy became aware of how the whole tavern had quietened around them and played on it. He motioned with his eyes, drawing Kerian's attention to the gathered onlookers and was rewarded as the old man lowered him back to the floor and roughly dusted him down. The laugh from Kerian's lips painted the picture of a mentally unstable patient stabbing someone and thoroughly enjoying the experience, rather than that of two old friends meeting and sharing a joke. Octavian could almost feel the threatened violence in the deathly gaze sent his way.

"Why don't you buy us both a drink." Kerian snarled in a low voice. "I'll be right back."

* * * * * *

"Where is Mathius?" Justina asked coolly, her gaze scrutinising the ragged figure sitting before her. The sorceress had no idea who this self-titled Scrave figure was but something about his nonchalant attitude made her believe he was a dangerous man to underestimate.

She took small calculated steps, turning her left side towards the Elf as her right hand moved to a pocket in her robes and carefully drew out an ornate silver wand beset with jewels. The gentle tugging of her robes at her back, also informed the sorceress that her demonic familiar was slowly sliding down her body to the floor. Hamnet was a loyal pet and quite a bonus in a close quarter fight so this was two against one before they even started.

Scrave remained seated, one hand slowly turning the hilt of a warped broadsword at his side, that was studded with small gems. The Elf observed the mage's pacing before him, his left eye missing nothing, understanding instinctively that this woman meant to attack him as soon as he dropped his guard. The vision from his right eye remained a constant frustration, shot through with annoying green swirls, that painted the vision of the woman's sultry figure and clinging dark robes with sparkling motes of emerald. To add to this concern, his right eyelid twitched uncontrollably, as if he had a stray eyelash he could not locate and it had been driving him mad for days.

He intuitively knew there was something wrong with his eye and had tried to poke and pry into the socket but the lack of resistance to his probing finger had made him stop in horror. He worried his right eye was missing but how could this be if he could still see?

The serpent dagger was agitated and constricted about his left wrist, its golden head arched; flickering golden tongue tasting the air for a scent of the prey it knew was within reach. Scrave allowed himself a dry rasping chuckle at the dagger's enthusiasm but he was facing a difficult situation. He knew he could destroy this woman in seconds but killing her was out of the question. Somehow, she had managed to get herself down here, so the likelihood was she also had the means to release him from this cursed place.

When he had awoken from his battle with Kerian Denaris, Scrave had spent days searching the piles of trove, discovering buried magical artefacts that did all manner of wondrous things to enhance his magical combat. Yet not one salvaged trinket bestowed the means to fly up over the ruined staircase and out to freedom. Instead, he found himself wasting valuable magical power trying to heal the toll that starvation, dehydration and constant exposure to the volcano's heat had levied upon his body.

His skin was constantly rebuilding itself, repairing the damage from his exposure to the incredible heat. Starting awake to find his heat shield failing, his clothing aflame and his skin blistering had become almost a daily battle of wills, leading to desperate spell casting and frayed nerves. At times Scrave had considered giving up and letting the volcanic fires consume him but his hatred burned brighter than the lava beneath him, fuelling his desire to live and gain revenge.

The Elf shuddered, brushing his charred arms to try to remove what felt like a mass of ants crawling across his flesh, biting and burrowing as they moved, his epithelial skin cells forming pink rafts across red sinuous muscle tissue and fat. He shifted slightly in the chair, trying to ignore the discomfort as he mentally plotted the means to bring this sorceress to her knees. Then he spotted the creature climbing down from the woman's shoulder and suddenly realised he had seen this beast before. Its skeletal tail had once wrapped around his neck awaking him from his sleep back on the *El Defensor*. Scrave knew he had managed to stab the magical monster with his dagger before it had teleported away. There was more going on here than he had realised.

"We don't need Mathius." Scrave rasped, forcing a smile that cracked his parched lips. "I feel I can manage a beautiful woman such as yourself well enough on my own. Mathius is where he belongs, on a ship full of losers. Now are you going to ask me any more stupid questions or can we just get on with it?" Justina smiled and readied her wand.

"I was hoping you would say that." She replied. A bolt of lightning exploded from her wand, the electrical power jumping and spiking across the space between them. There was a bright flash, an acrid smell of ozone and then, as her eyes cleared from the burst of energy, she noticed the charred figure sitting exactly as before.

Scrave tutted and slowly raised himself to his feet, groaning as he stretched and moved muscles he had not used in hours. He gripped the sword tightly in one hand, the hissing dagger wrapped about the other and took a step forward, the frown on his face saying more than the chilling words he uttered.

"That wasn't very nice." He snarled.

Justina replied with actions instead of words, sending another bolt of lightning arcing across the space and creating another flash of intense white light. Using the blast to hide her actions she cast another spell, manipulating the air around them, slowing time to gain insight into how the Elf had evaded her initial magic attack. The mage watched stunned, as Scrave motioned with his hand and snapped the sword up to intercept the crackling energy. The raw power of the lightning sped along the blade racing to touch the wire wrapped hilt of his gleaming weapon. However, instead of burning the Elf to a crisp and melting the sword, the energy impossibly reversed when it hit the gemstones, flowing back down to the tip of the blade as Scrave snapped the weapon to the floor, earthing it. Golden coins reacted from the electrical jolt to ricochet around the room. His speed was unbelievable!

The sorceress frowned and chose another form of attack. Miniature balls of fire leapt from her wand, crackling in towards her foe. Blistering orbs that would detonate, maim and incinerate the Elf. The fires collided with a protective barrier, their red heat dousing as cool magic leached the destructive power from within them. Scrave lunged towards her, shocking Justina because he appeared to move faster than humanly possible. He struck the sorceress across the face with the flat of his blade and retreated.

Justina staggered back, her teeth snapping in her head, long hair whirling a black curtain across her vision that parted just as golden scales flashed, red ruby eyes glinted and golden fangs snapped together inches from her face. The serpent dagger hissed in frustration as its attack missed, then recoiled and prepared to strike again.

"Really," Scrave yelled. "Really? I've been trapped in this volcano for months. Did you not think I would be used to fire by now? Show me some originality."

Justina stepped away, placing urgently needed space between herself and the Elf and felt something warm trickling down her face. Her tongue flicked out, tasting warm salt with a hint of copper. The mage wiped her hand across her nose noting the crimson trail upon her finger. The Elf had drawn blood when he had struck.

This was not what she had planned.

Scrave moved in again, his threatening manner making Justina adapt her magic for a more defensive approach. She gestured with her hands, sending a wall of golden coins up into the air, momentarily obscuring her assailant as the small golden circles spun up towards the ceiling in a dazzling wave. She slammed her hands back down, sending the treasure crashing down upon him, burying Scrave in a glittering deluge.

She wanted to run, wanted to teleport away but the Elf had the serpent dagger and she could not leave the weapon behind, knowing full well what the cursed blade could do. She took a deep breath, then cast another spell from her depleting wand as the coins continued to rain down around her.

Scrave screamed out his anger as the coins crashed over him, hundreds of individual hits that his magical shield could not hope to deflect. He felt every collision against his raw flesh and exposed muscle, wincing as each projectile impacted. Coins bounced and clattered against each other slipping and sliding across the floor until silence finally descended on the room.

The Elf looked around, blinking rapidly, only to realise that his foe had disappeared and worse that he had somehow managed to drop his sword underneath the mound of coins at his feet. The sorceress should have been directly in front of him however, yet the area held nothing but gold coins and shadows. He whirled on the spot, taking in the entire room and noted the little demon crouched behind his chair, hiding from the battle. That was one foe located.

Scrave entertained detonating a spell to see if he could make the mage reveal herself then smiled. There was something else he could do instead. He stood in place, then let his Elven heritage take hold before shrieking as if hurt and staggered towards the chair, moving closer to the spindly creature crouched in the shadows. He risked a quick look around, smiling at the tell-tale chink of coins behind him as something unseen but not unheard moved across the floor. The Elf continued feigning injury as he moved towards the chair, then threw himself at the creature hiding there. Hamnet shrieked and attempted to scarper across the coins and jewels as Scrave's hand clamped tightly on the familiar's tail.

"You don't get away that easily." Scrave snapped, whipping Hamnet's tail and causing the animal to bounce painfully on the floor before the Elf viciously smashed it sideways up against the chair. The demon shrieked then went unresponsive in his hand.

"I've got you." He hissed, then he swiftly turned, dropping the demon and reached out into thin air to tightly grab the throat of the woman who was stalking him.

"...and I've got you too.!" He smiled. The air shimmered to reveal Justina's struggling form, her arms ridged down by her sides, her feet kicking in thin air.

"How did you...?" she wheezed from her strangled throat.

"Find you? Oh that was easy." Scrave replied. "Elves can see body heat, or in the case of this room and your magical shield, a lack of it. Now let's stop fooling around and get serious." He held up the serpent dagger the twin points of the blades flashing in the light as the snake coiled about eager to thrust into her soft flesh.

"Can you see how my snake wants to bite you?" Scrave teased, pulling his wrist away as the snake aimed a strike at her cheek. "I could let my pet have its way...," he continued, staring deep into Justina's terrified eyes and noting the reflection of the glittering death awaiting her. "I think you have realised by now that I will have no problems killing you if you leave me no choice. However, there is something I need you to do."

Justina continued to squirm and struggle for air within his grasp, her feet straining to touch the floor. The sorceress's face flushed crimson with the effort to remain on tiptoes and ease the crushing grip on her throat and her eyelids fluttered rapidly as she fought to remain conscious.

"What do you want?" she wheezed.

Scrave took in the woman he held; her slight form, long hair and defiant blazing eyes. The way her breasts strained tightly against her silken robes as she struggled for breath. He undressed her with his eyes and had to admit that on some base level he found her to be quite attractive. He leaned in close and whispered into her ear.

"I want you to take me the hell out of here…"

* * * * * *

"Look it could have happened to anyone." Mathius confessed, trying to reassure the hulking Minotaur towering over him.

"I'm sure all it will need is a fresh lick of paint and no one will be the wiser." Ives added helpfully, staring up at the underside of the bridge above them, its pale soffit heavily scored and showing areas where some masonry had been knocked loose.

"And Weyn never holds a grudge for long." Aradol confessed. "Remember the incident when he mistook the… Or the time…" He shook his head and looked back down at Weyn's unconscious body lying on the deck and the huge purple egg-shaped lump protruding from his right temple. "Come to think of it, he's going to be mad for a while."

Thomas leaned over his injured lookout and sighed. Then he looked up at the top of the main mast and noted the splintered stays and the conspicuously absent crow's nest. He turned to Rauph and put his hand to his head, shading his eyes from the glare of the sun rising directly behind the huge navigator.

"I told you to sail through the left archway." He sighed. "The left… you know this side." He held up his left hand and waggled it in the Minotaur's direction. Rauph initially refused to look up from his feet and shuffled nervously in place, before his eye caught the movement of Thomas's hand.

"That's what I did." He rumbled. "I went through the archway on that side." He lifted his hand in a mirror of the captain's actions and instantly revealed the problem. His right hand was up, not his left.

"I meant my left." Thomas groaned. Why was everything so hard? This would never have happened if they had a low bridge clearance sign. Rauph remained looking confused, clearly not understanding what had happened. Thomas shook his head and declined to describe the yellow and black diamond signage of New York's road system. It was a waste of breath and he was simply too tired.

"Look at it this way." Mathius tried to keep his face from cracking a smile. "At least Weyn will never fall asleep in the crow's nest again!"

"We seem to have gained quite a crowd of admirers." Ives gestured towards the jetty and the assembled men in uniform bristling with assorted weapons, then to the upturned felucca-like wooden sailing boat and its floundering crew struggling to pull themselves and their sodden sails from the water after the Spanish galleon had crashed through them. "I hope everyone realises this was a genuine accident."

"Well why don't you explain it to them." Thomas snapped, walking to the rail and wincing at the damage the *El Defensor* had caused due to Rauph's mistake. "You keep telling me you are the only merchant among us who can... how did you put it? Sell snow to the huntsmen of the Tundra Wastes."

"I know I may have mentioned that in the past." Ives paled, looking aft. "However, I am sure that I had not just crashed my ship into one of their monuments and mown down their fishing fleet before I opened negotiations."

"So, it will be more of a challenge." Thomas shot back, watching as one man tried to balance on the upturned hull of his boat before crashing back into the water. "We all know how much you love a challenge." The captain turned back to Rauph and gestured with a curt hand signal grabbing the Minotaur's attention.

"Take us in gently." Thomas ordered. Then he paused for a second and held his finger up to stop the navigator from turning to his task. "Just for all our sakes, please don't crash into the pier!" Rauph lumbered off across the deck, eager to show his captain that he could be relied upon and took up his position at the ship's wheel. Thomas looked around the deck trying to calm his thoughts. The whole crew felt on edge. Or was it him? Everything was so confusing. He looked over at the less than friendly reception awaiting them on the jetty and meekly waved in their direction as the galleon cut across the water, churning up rich dark silt in her wake.

Red-headed gulls swooped down into the water, folding their wings and transforming their bodies into living arrows that plunged beneath the surface to retrieve bottom feeding fish disturbed by the *El Defensor's* passing. The wake from the ship rolled out lazily behind her, causing large swells that tore fishing nets from their hooks and lifted lobster pots from the floor, snapping the cane structures and allowing the suddenly liberated crustaceans a chance to live another day.

Thomas had to give Rauph credit as the Minotaur managed to skilfully steer the ship closer to the jetty, causing the assembled onlookers to step back in fear as the huge galleon relentlessly advanced. Lines were thrown from the ship to hands waiting ashore as the *El Defensor* nudged the side, causing the waiting people to stagger as several shudders and groans ran through the structure. The captain held his breath as the galleon settled beneath him and her motion ceased, signalling that the complicated docking manoeuvre was complete.

"The audience is all yours." Thomas gestured to Ives, noting how most of the onlookers had thunderous faces as they waited to see who would disembarked from the mysterious ship that had crashed into their bridge. "They look a little tense. May I suggest an ice breaker first?"

"An ice breaker?" Ives turned to the captain with a furrowed brow. "Whatever would I need an icebreaker for? There is no snow or ice for miles. The sun is high in the sky and there is barely a cloud in sight to mar the cornflower blue above. Sometimes Thomas I just don't understand you at all." He straightened his collar, pulled up the sleeves of his tunic, shrugged his shoulders and clicked his fingers before he walked to the gangway.

"I'll show you what a real salesman can do." Ives muttered, before setting off down the companionway towards the crowd of onlookers below.

* * * * * *

Kerian stood in the doorway of his room and took in the upturned bed, his ledger on the floor, his hand mirror smashed, clothes thrown about, his saddlebags flung to the side, the flaps up and the pockets now clearly empty.

Thoughts of peeling the smile from Octavian's face and then rubbing the raw flesh in sea salt, or impaling the man slowly on a very sharp stick whilst he begged and told Kerian the answers to everything he ever wanted to know faded from his mind as the reality sunk in.

He had been robbed!

Whilst he had been in jail his room had been ransacked. He walked slowly into the bedroom, lifting the saddlebags with the toe of his boot, confirming his worst fears. His jewels were gone. All of them.

What was he going to do? Without funds, paying for the repairs to the *Tulip* would be a struggle. Yes, he knew he had paid a considerable sum in advance but he also knew the likes of the men working on his vessel. The chances were that they would find something else wrong and the repair costs would continue to mount. It was a universal constant to anyone who had to have work carried out on something they did not have the skill to do themselves.

Without the Tulip he could not sail out into the storms looking for Colette. Colette... Oh no the pendant! How was he to set off after the pendant if he had no funds for transport and supplies? How was he to know where to go when Octavian wanted money for the information? How did everything spiral out of control so fast? How...

A sound behind him made Kerian spin, coming face to face with a serving maid who was nothing like the young girl he had seen before. Her uniform was ill fitting and her eyes were brown, not blue.

"Where's my normal maid?" he asked, as the young girl looked past him and saw the state of the room before sighing as she realised her workload had increased dramatically. She looked up at him with a frustrated look on her face, her bottom lip sticking out in disgust.

"She quit earlier today. Just took off and left. Said she was leaving town. Do you always leave your room in this state? If so, I am going to complain to my manager." Kerian sighed heavily, matching another sigh from the young maid as she bent to retrieve a pillow.

"Do you want me to fold your clothes or leave them as they are?" she asked. "If you do it will cost extra."

"Just leave them where they are." Kerian replied quietly. "Leave everything where it is."

"Oh, I forgot." The maid jumped as if poked by a sharp stick. "I haven't met you before. So on behalf of the *Lusty Mermaid* welcome to Wellruff." Kerian turned from the ruin of the room, pausing only to grab his empty saddlebags. He moved as if in a daze, shoulders slumped as he headed back towards the stairs and the drink that waited below.

Welcome to Wellruff indeed...

Chapter Eight

"I don't think they believe it was an accident." Aradol commented as the angry voices from the dock appeared to rise in volume. "They seem to be getting rather irate."

"Things do appear to be heating up down there." Mathius suggested, watching one member of the crowd yelling at Ives and waving his arms in animated motions whilst gesturing at the *El Defensor* and screaming his anger at their docking. "I think he wants us to move."

"What makes you say that?" Thomas asked moving closer to the side and peering over Mathius shoulder.

"Well he keeps pushing Ives away and making shooing motions with his hands." Mathius replied. "Oh… now he appears to have slapped Ives around the face."

"Maybe that's how they say hello around here." Aradol suggested. He cupped his hand to his face and shouted down at his colleague. "Hit him back!" Ives looked up at the ship, his face flush with anger and his eyes frowning at the instruction, just as the spokesman slapped him again, rocking Ives back on his heels.

"You really are not helping." Thomas turned to the younger sailor, his eyes suggesting it would be better if Aradol shut up. "Don't you have something better to do?" The captain studied the scene and the rising tension then reached out to touch Mathius on the arm.

"Put your daggers away." He stated calmly. "Just go and get Rauph over here. We may need him if things turn nasty. After all I don't think you could take the whole mob on with just two daggers." Mathius turned towards Thomas, his eyebrow raised as if insulted at the comment. Then he looked back and theatrically waggled a finger, counting the men before turning back and nodding slowly.

"The first nineteen should be no problem," he replied with a cold certainty. Then he smiled and nodded towards the back of the group. "It's the last guy I might have a problem with."

"That would be the old guy waving his walking stick at the back." Thomas grinned, realising the assassin was trying to lighten the oppressive mood.

"Of course." Mathius replied. "It's always the old ones you have to watch out for. After all, how do you think they got to be old?" Thomas nudged Mathius to remind him about Rauph and the sailor stepped away, flipping his daggers through his fingers as he went, leaving Thomas to consider the display of rampant male aggression below.

Another slap landed and the captain winced as Ives finally reacted and punched the representative firmly on the nose, drawing blood and several cries of protest from the assembled group. Spears rattled on the dock and swords were slid from scabbards. Thomas realised he could stand by and observe no longer. It was time to act before a full-scale riot developed. The last thing he wanted in a new world was to start a brawl before they had even made land. The captain loosened the cutlass at his side and stepped onto the gangway, raising concerned cries from the vocal mob as he descended from the *El Defensor*.

He held his hands at his sides and smiled to show he was not a threat, before marching down toward the jetty. The wooden beam gave beneath each footstep making Thomas feel as if he were bouncing down towards the ruckus, rather than calmly approaching it.

"Excuse me!" Thomas interrupted, drawing the wrath of everyone and leaving Ives valuable time to straighten his robes and repair his shattered self-confidence following his failed diplomatic sortie. "What seems to be the problem here?"

"You cannot dock here." The spokesperson spluttered, his cheeks as red as the blood streaming from his nose. "It is forbidden. I insist you move your vessel at once."

"Is there somewhere else you would like us to moor?" Thomas tried to reassure the flustered man by offering him an opening for diplomacy. "If you would like to point us to another location that would accommodate the *El Defensor's* deep draft, I am sure we can come to an amicable agreement." He fished into his pocket and withdrew some doubloons, clinking them loudly in his hands.

"You mean to bribe an official!" the man screamed. "I have never been so insulted!" Thomas stood mouth agape. Colour flushing his cheeks as the mob ranted and beckoned in his direction, pulling at their robes and rattling their spears against their shields in warning of imminent violence.

"I am sorry if we have offended you, we meant no harm." Thomas offered, trying to defuse the situation. "We are new here and are unaware of your customs. Surely, you can see we just need a place to repair our ship, purchase some supplies and then we shall be on our way."

A glob of spittle hit the quay near the captain's boot. Thomas responded with a glare that could melt steel plate before taking a breath and donning a fake smile. "Let's see if we can all calm down and sort this out like the gentlemen we are."

"You cannot dock here," came the stubborn reply. "If you do not remove your ship, I shall have it blown out of the water."

"With your mouth that should not be a problem." Ives butted in, earning another withering stare from Thomas's facial repertoire.

"I am done speaking with you." The harbourmaster stated coldly, averting his gaze from Ives to lock eyes firmly with Thomas. "You, I will talk to... You can't dock here." Thomas rolled his eyes to the heavens and held out a hand to prevent Ives pushing forwards again.

"You are to leave here immediately. You will not be granted refuge and if you resist you shall be thrown into jail. Have I made myself cle...?" The official's face paled and his eyes widened as he stared past Thomas to something over the captain's shoulder. Sweat appeared on the man's forehead and his tongue appeared to be stuck to the roof of his mouth, leaving Thomas wondering if the harbourmaster were having a kind of seizure. The crowd dropped to the floor, heads bowed, touching the jetty, their protest extinguished. Shields and spears clattered to the ground as all eyes were cast down to the floor in abject compliance.

"My lord..." squeaked the harbourmaster. "I am so sorry. I did not know. How could I know? I mean this is not even one of our ships. You must forgive me master." He threw up his arms in terror and sank to the floor, his hand grabbing Thomas's boot tightly. The captain looked down at the trembling man confused.

"Please save me." The man pleaded, begging as if his very life depended on it.

"From what?" Thomas asked, staring around blankly.

"What are they all looking for?" Rauph asked innocently from behind him.

"Defeats me." Thomas replied, shrugging his shoulders whilst trying to wriggle his boot out of the grasp of the harbourmaster, who held on as if he were sinking in quicksand.

"Do they need any help?" Rauph continued, moving from the gangway and kneeling down beside the cowering harbourmaster. "I am very good at finding things." The harbourmaster had his eyes closed now and was shivering all over. Rauph's nose snorted as he sniffed the ground, causing a low moan to escape the man's lips.

"You know if I didn't know better, I would suggest this man is about to throw up." The Minotaur commented. "Here let me help you up." There was a shriek of shock as Rauph hoisted the man to his feet then went to brush him down with his free hand, sending clouds of dust into the air as he did so and making the man wince at each touch.

Thomas took it all in, the cowering crowd, the terrified harbourmaster, the statue. This was not the normal reaction of seeing a Minotaur, this was the reaction of someone who saw them frequently and feared them.

"Look," he opened, tapping the harbourmaster on the cheek. "Just look... We know it's all a genuine mistake. Relax we won't hurt anyone. All of you, please stand up." No one moved. Thomas sighed then turned to his shaggy friend who was still holding the trembling spokesperson and uttered the words to confirm his suspicions.

"Please tell everyone to stand up Rauph."

"Stand up Rauph." The Minotaur snorted. The crowd slowly got to their feet, heads still bowed. The anger and outrage from earlier now long gone. Instead the assembled crowd looked pale and terrified as if they had only moments left to live.

"Please all of you relax," Thomas gestured, aware that Weyn and Mathius had now wandered down the gangway to check what was going on. He turned to the harbourmaster. "Look, do you know anywhere nearby that we can all go to have a drink? Then we can discuss how we can all help each other. I am sure this city, wherever we are, has a bar where honest men talk and trade."

The harbourmaster opened one eye, took in the grinning face of Ives clearly feeling superior at the recent turn of events and then looked over at the ginger coloured eight-foot tall creature holding him.

"You are in Taurean." He replied breathlessly. "Please put me down now." Rauph lowered the man carefully back to the dock and slapped him one more time to ensure that all the dust was off his shaking body.

"I...I think I know just the place." He muttered, appearing dazed, clearly surprised he was still alive. "Please master, if you would be so kind as to follow me." Rauph stood back as the man and moved off, then noticed Thomas urging him to follow.

"Who is this master he keeps talking about?" the navigator frowned at the captain.

"Just follow him," Thomas instructed. Ives, Weyn and Mathius moved to shadow the navigator, mingling with the crowd of supporters who now seemed overjoyed to have the Minotaur in their midst, all complaints of the *El Defensor's* docking fiasco now forgotten.

"Wait for me." A commotion at the top of the ramp had stopped Thomas in mid-step as he turned to see Ashe struggling to free himself from Aradol's firm grasp back on the *El Defensor*. The captain nodded his agreement at Aradol's actions before passing orders.

"Set a guard on the ship." Thomas ordered, before turning and fixing the Halfling with his intense stare. "Ashe... you are not to leave the ship. No matter what. If this ship sinks in the dock, I want your body found inside it when the ship is salvaged... Do you understand?" He glared in the Halfling's direction, lifting a threatening finger, making it clear that breaching this order would not be tolerated, then moved to follow the ever-increasing crowd that was tracking his shaggy navigator from the docks.

* * * * * *

The dazzling white marble facade of the luxurious royal palace stood perched high above the city of Taurean. Columns ran the entire length of the building, massive statues of Minotaur in various warrior poses sited between them. Large open spaces contained gardens, fountains and pastures where the hierarchy of the city could meet, discuss learning, politics and the intricate running of the populace below. Cool marble-floored hallways stretching for hundreds of yards, held planters densely packed with lush vegetation that could obscure secret meetings, sinister plots and passionate trysts. Shaded balconies offered incredible views out across the waters of the lake and safe glimpses of the dense jungles around. Despite the fact the huge pyramid temple always cast its shadow over the tightly packed homes of the workers below, its position was such that it never darkened the gleaming palace, a statement to those below of who was truly in charge.

Mora blew out her white cheeks, her green eyes bulging in anger. She ran her hands through her shoulder length long white hair, streaked with the odd stray length of rust orange, pushing it back from her bovine face as she paced up and down the marble floor of the balcony overlooking her sprawling city. A long blue dress enveloped her generous form and flowed out behind her as she walked, the deep royal colour hemmed with gold braid that matched the massive gilded horns on either side of her head.

She stopped at the balcony and placed her hands onto the warm carved marble surface, staring out over the city and docks that she ruled, not taking in any of the hustle and bustle before her but instead listening with growing ire to the rest of her preening entourage sitting around the table behind her.

"They want me to touch the children in the nursery." A blonde-haired Minotaur moaned to her associates. "Actually touch them. I mean what about my nails?"

"Oh, that's simply ghastly Karlar. Those human children carry diseases you know. Intestinal worms and head lice." A larger oak brown Minotaur added, her hair braided into a long ponytail that ran down over her right shoulder. "You should stop doing the charity work if you ask me."

She reached forward and lifted a palm sized mat of weaved grass studded with candied sweets.

"I never had that problem when I did charity work with the older ones." An emaciated, ebony black Minotaur replied, a gold earring flashing in her left ear. "Of course, all of my charity cases died Wanessa. It wasn't my fault no one fed them. I always managed to find time to feed myself."

"Oh Amnet you are simply a scream," butted in a plump black and white Minotaur wearing a pale chiffon dress that displayed her chest and hid nothing. "Speaking of a scream have you seen the new captain of the pyramid guard. He's simply dreamy. I would love to polish his horns."

"Shuesan I so know who you mean. He is so lush." A curly red-haired Minotaur fluttered her painted eyelashes. The Minotaur's tight-fitting toga wrapped around her body looked like the latest fashion from a distance but up close the seams were frayed and worn. "But he will probably never look at anyone like me. My life is so unfair."

Mora tapped her fingers angrily on the balcony. It seemed that no matter how often the most senior members of the matriarch society of Taurean got together, nothing positive ever seemed to get done. She grabbed a handful of grass and chewed on it in disgust. Pascol was so weak, the weakest of the group. Mora often considered replacing her.

"I need a flame." Shrieked a high-pitched voice. "Where is my servant girl." Mora turned back to the room to see another member of the group lounging on a padded bench gesturing a rolled-up tube of herbal grass. "I need someone to light this. Where is my servant when I need her?" A human child ran from the shadows, holding a small bowl of flame in her shaking hand.

The slim orange haired Minotaur sucked hard on her grass tube as the flame lit the end, then inhaled before releasing a fragrant smoke that she blew towards the servant powered fans swinging backwards and forwards on the ceiling. She looked down at the small child with distain.

"I think you were too slow." She hissed at the serving child, snatching the girl's arm before she could run away. "Next time you will be faster." She removed the roll of grass from her mouth and ground the glowing ember into the child's arm, raising a shriek of agony from the struggling infant, then released her so that she dropped to the floor sobbing.

"It is a privilege to serve one of us." She snapped, her orange hair remaining in a perfect style of sculpted coils upon her head. "Don't you ever forget it. Next time I want you, be here. You may go." The small child seized the chance to run for the safety of the shadows, tears streaming down her face, holding her burned limb to her side.

"Oh Chane, did you really have to do that?" Karlar moaned. "The rug is all singed now!" Titters of cruel laughter rang around the room. Mora turned away in disgust and continued her pacing. They all seemed to have forgotten why this meeting had been called.

"How are the plans for the midsummer ceremony progressing?" Mora enquired. "Do we have the gladiators, the sacrificial offerings, contestants selected for the Labyris contest?"

"Oh the gladiators are picked, the slaves purchased for the slaughter but we are still missing candidates for the main event. No one of royal blood dares to take the challenge so it looks like the pyramid will remain sealed this year." replied Wanessa. "It will be such a disappointment to the crowds."

"What about your son Drummon?" Shuesan asked, shouting out onto the balcony. "He is of age now. Surely, he would want a chance at the Labyris prize? Oh he is so dreamy."

"He is so dark and rugged, even his muscles have muscles." Amnet crooned. "I would let him take me for a ride any day. Maybe I should pop around and see him."

"Oh so true." oozed Wanessa.

"Excuse me! We do not pop anywhere." Mora snapped. "We are royalty, so we *visit*. I also expect you to remember that Drummon happens to be my son!" She tried to contain the smile threatening to cross her lips. She wanted them to nominate Drummon but she did not want to push the matter too strongly at this time.

"Your last surviving son." Chane laughed slyly, blowing another cloud of fragrant smoke towards the ceiling. "After what happened to Kristoph, I am surprised Drummon even dares to close his eyes and sleep at night."

"Kristoph was a mistake." Mora snapped back. "His death an accident."

"He was a mistake I would have liked to make." Shuesan bellowed. "He was so..."

"Dreamy." They all called out before bursting into laughter again.

Mora went to reply, caustic words on her lips, then she noticed something out of the corner of her eye. There appeared to be a crowd down by the dock. She squinted, cursing her aged vision and noticed the exotic ship at anchor.

"Why don't you all just... what is going on down at the docks?" she asked.

"Nothing to my knowledge." Wanessa mooed, shuffling out onto the balcony to join her leader. She rested her dark brown hands on the balcony and leant over. "You are right, there does appear to be something going on."

"Where?" Shuesan butted in. "I want to know the gossip as well." She stared over the rail and noted the people rushing to join the small procession winding up from the harbour.

"Well whatever it is they all seem rather excited." Pascol moped. "Maybe it's a party and no one invited me. My life is so unfair."

"If someone is having a party and I haven't been invited heads will roll." Chane glared.

"Why has everyone gone outside?" Karla moaned, still lounging back in the room. "It's all hot and sticky out there and I haven't finished putting on my makeup yet."

Amnet eased her painfully thin ebony hide between Wanessa and Shuesan. "Is there free food?"

"Why is it that you always want the free food." Shuesan moaned. "After you eat it you simply throw it up again. It's such a waste."

"Well that way I don't get fat." Amnet snapped back. "And as the food is free it doesn't matter what I do to it. Remember I do have two stomachs to fill." Wanessa nudged Amnet hard.

"We all have two stomachs to fill." She warned. "So from now on if there is free food you wait your turn and know your place."

Mora tried to ignore the catfight erupting alongside her and gazed intently at the gathering below. Something about this crowd worried her. Something niggled at the back of her mind. She did not know why exactly but a chill was running along her spine.

The Matriarch turned, barging the other Minotaur out of her way and walked back into the coolness of the fanned room, motioning to a hulking grey-haired guard with a twisted horn who stood silently against one wall.

"Aelius, please rouse my son. Tell him to go and find out what is going on down at the harbour. I want to know what all the fuss is about and if the slaves are getting rebellious, I want him to swat them down hard."

"Yes my queen." The guard snapped to attention then turned away, intent on getting as far from the room of females as possible. He tried to put a brave face on his reprieve then realised that he had to get Drummon and Drummon was nothing but a brainless idiot.

* * * * * *

"So my beneficiary returns." Octavian smiled. "I ordered you a drink, which you now owe me for. Have you secured the funds for my services?" Kerian sat down heavily, his saddlebags dropping to the floor at his side and looked across at the dark-haired youth, weighing up the man before him whilst trying to keep his own troubled thoughts from showing. He took a large gulp of his drink to boost his courage, grimaced at the taste, wiped the back of his hand across his lips and then leant forwards across the table.

"I don't like the way you spoke to me earlier." He said quietly. "Because of that, I think we should make things more interesting. I know you like to gamble, so let's set a wager for the information I require." Octavian's face fell, his expected payday now clearly somewhat resistant.

"What do you mean?" the gypsy asked suddenly suspicious. "Where is my money? Remember, information you don't have is expensive."

"I know," Kerian replied. "You already told me that but I have no idea how much your information is worth. What you know may not get me what I ultimately seek. I need reassurances. If you truly believe what you know is good enough, then you should be up for a spot of gambling. After all, life is not rich if there is no element of risk."

"I don't think so." Octavian snapped, clearly not liking the direction their conversation was going.

"Oh come on." Kerian goaded "I'll play any game of chance you like." A sly smile swept across Octavian's features.

"I believe dice are my forte?" he smirked.

"I thought you would never ask." Kerian replied, moving his stool closer. The hook was baited; the fish had nibbled, now it was time to reel the young man in.

"If I win," Kerian began, trying to keep his breathing slow and steady. "I want more than just information. I need transport, armour, a sword and a guide."

"Now that will not come cheap." Octavian replied. "So, what's in it for me?"

"If I lose, you can have every gem currently in my saddlebags and your information is yours to keep."

Octavian's dice suddenly clattered to rest across the table.

"So who rolls first?" the gypsy enquired grinning like a cat facing a bowl of fresh milk.

"Well I think you should throw first." Kerian replied, swiftly reaching forwards to scoop up the magical dice in his hand, clearly surprising the gypsy as his own hand closed over empty space.

"If you have my dice, how can I roll first?" Octavian asked, clearly confused.

"It's only fair that if you are going first, I should be able to choose what dice I use." Kerian replied.

"Then what dice do I use?" Octavian asked.

"Hang on a moment." Kerian got to his feet and moved over to the bar, leaving the gypsy sitting with his mouth open. He watched as the old man leaned over the bar and gathered something from the barman's hands. Octavian opened his mouth to protest as Kerian sat back down again, however this time it was the old man's unexpected smile that disarmed him.

The gypsy's eyes moved back down to linger on the worn and chipped ivory dice sitting before him, some of the dots were missing, there was a crack across one face and the six on one dice looked decidedly wonky.

"But this is not fair." Octavian began. "Why should I have to use these decrepit cuboids?"

"Because you have nothing to lose." Kerian replied. "And I have lost everything. Shall we begin?" Octavian sat for another moment, then leaned forwards and scooped up the chipped dies, shrugging.

"Okay then..." he said slowly. "The rules are simple. Highest throw wins. If we draw whoever rolled first wins." Octavian paused again. "You said you want a guide, a sword, transport and information. That's four throws, for four chances." Kerian nodded his head, he had no choice but to play and let luck guide his way.

Octavian rolled first, the chipped dice rattling across the table. The faces showed a five and a two. The gypsy shrugged his shoulders; not bad for a first roll. Kerian winced, then looked at the magical dice and tried to think. How did Octavian make these things work? He picked up the dice weighed them in his hand and threw them.

A two and a one stared back at him, making Octavian laugh aloud.

"Oh dear." The gypsy smirked. "Guess you are going out there on your own." Kerian mentally kicked himself. How did the smug youth make these damned dice dance?

"For the sword." Octavian laughed rattling the wonky battered dice across the table. A two and a four stared back. Kerian closed his eyes willing himself to roll a good score. If he had a good sword at least he could skewer the arrogant man to the wall.

A four and a two stared back at him.

"A draw. Too bad." Octavian winked. "First roll wins. Maybe if you ask the barman, he will lend you a butter knife to use on your travels? I believe it's the transport next." The dice clattered again. A five and a four this time, the four having three dots in black and one coloured in with blue ink. Kerian could not believe his eyes. What was with this man and dice. He felt himself flushing. Felt the heat rising beneath his clothes. Why was it so hot in here? He threw the magical blue dice watching the golden dots spinning on the utmost faces. A six and a two.

"Three for three." The gypsy taunted. "I hope you have a sturdy pair of boots, because by my reckoning wherever you are going to, it's going to be by foot. There is only one more roll to go. The important one. The information. It all rides on this one." The dice clattered on the table, the upper face showed a five and a six. Octavian's face broke into the widest grin possible.

Kerian looked at the dice that had betrayed him so badly and realised this was his last chance. He thought about the time they had spent in jail together. Tried to remember anything that gave him a clue as to how the man had made the dice respond to his wishes. He knew, whatever he did now would live with him forever. His life, his very future all depended on this roll. He went to open his hand then paused, a visible shake present in his fist.

"What's the delay?" Octavian joked, licking his lips in anticipation, his eyes moving towards the saddlebags imagining the wealth within.

What was it? What did Octavian do. Was it the way he held the dice when he threw them? Did he stroke the face he wanted to roll up? Could it be telepathy? This was his last chance. He closed his eyes trying to ignore the dryness in his mouth as his mind replayed the last dice roll that he had seen Octavian do. He replayed it in his mind; the gypsy sitting on his bunk in the jail cell, lifting his hand to roll the dice. What did he do? What was the secret of the dice?

"Come on Kerian. I don't have all night. There is wine song and women awaiting me now I have the funds to spare." Octavian moved to reach for the saddlebags causing Kerian to reach over and grab him tightly by the wrist.

"You haven't won yet." Kerian snapped. "You don't get as much as a crystal until I have rolled."

"Then get on with it!" Octavian replied. "The suspense is killing me." Kerian moved to throw the dice once again, then suddenly it came to him.

"If I throw my boat in as well would you let everything ride on this last roll."

"I thought your boat was being repaired." Octavian smirked.

"It is," Kerian replied. "But all the repairs are paid for; I understand the *Tulip* will be fully refitted when I collect her. As good as new." Octavian studied Kerian intently; looking for a sign the old man had the upper hand. A tick, a wandering eye, a sweating brow, any kind of tell or clue that would give the gypsy an inkling he was about to be ambushed by the desperate man before him but he could see no sign of anything suspicious.

"Okay." He nodded his head. "It's your funeral. Now cast the dice."

Kerian sat back on the stool. He offered a silent prayer to himself that he was right, promised any gods who wanted to listen a thousand things if they would simply guide his hand and help him be in Colette's arms once more. Then he threw a smile at the gypsy and rattled the dice in his hands, leaning forwards to make his roll. Octavian also leaned forwards; anxiously awaiting the roll that he hoped would change his future and release the funds he needed to return to his clan and save his family.

Kerian brought his closed fist up to his face then kissed the dice he held, before letting both of their futures fall from his hand.

Chapter Nine

Octavian brought his finger to his lips and motioned that Kerian remain quiet before he stepped out from the shadows and scanned the empty street ahead. He gestured for Kerian to join him and then turned to face the large set of closed gates that blocked their path back into Wellruff's market.

"What are we doing here?" Kerian hissed. "The people I need to catch left here hours ago."

"Don't you think I already know this?" Octavian turned with a frown across his features. "Just be quiet. There is a night watchman in the square and we need to avoid being seen."

"But why?"

Octavian ignored him, stepped over to the centre of the gates and pushed lightly on the wood, hoping against hope that the guard had not locked them. The thoughts of boosting the old man over the top of the obstruction did not bare thinking about. The gate creaked slightly, the sound amplified by the tension the gypsy felt inside him, then it swung ajar, revealing a dense darkness within. Octavian ducked his head inside, scanning for the lantern the watchman used to light his way and upon seeing no sign of it, beckoned for Kerian to follow him.

"Where are we going?" Kerian whispered. "If you work here why can't you just walk in as usual?"

"That's not going to work at this time of night." Octavian replied. Thinking to himself that was especially true with what he was planning to do. He continued muttering under his breath as he stepped lightly into the deserted marketplace, cursing the fact that Kerian had won the roll of the dice, tricking him into meeting his four demands.

The information on the market traders was not a problem; he knew their names, where they were going and how to catch up with them. The sword and armour were an issue that Octavian did not even want to consider. He had a few ideas where he could get a decent blade and a suit of chainmail but knew this would be an expense he could good ill afford. Acting as a guide also meant taking valuable time away from his own problems but at least he was a step closer to resolving these than a few days ago. He just had to lose his new shadow somehow. The gypsy patted his pocket and tried to calm himself, confident his dark secret remained close to his chest.

This just left transportation. A wry smile played across his lips. He knew just the transportation Kerian could use. If he were lucky, maybe the old man would break his neck, leaving Octavian guilt free to follow his own destiny. He paused in the shelter of an empty stall, listening out for a clink of keys or the fall of heavy footsteps to warn him of the man he knew would be patrolling the market somewhere in the darkness. He really needed to ensure no one saw him here.

Satisfied no one was near, he pulled Kerian after him and arrived at the doors to the equestrian and livestock stalls. A large padlock and chain frustratingly stared back at him.

"I don't suppose you know how to pick a lock?" he whispered.

"I'm afraid not." Kerian replied. "I do know... no, make that knew, someone who would have managed this in seconds." His mind flashed back to the time when he had travelled with Ashe and smiled. He remembered how he had once taken the Halfling to one side and scolded him about stealing from others, yet here he was now, wandering around a deserted market at the dead of night likely to do the same thing. If only Ashe could see him now! He could almost envisage him waving a little finger and tutting loudly.

Muted sounds from within the stables indicated that their proximity had been detected as animals shuffled and moved within. Octavian held the padlock in his hand then turned and set off along the outside of the building.

"Follow me," he whispered. "There's another way in around the back." The two unlikely figures slinked along the wall, trying to move inconspicuously from shadow to shadow, until they reached the paddock fence. Octavian placed his hands on the top bar then vaulted over the beam with ease, landing lightly on his feet and slipping silently under the awning to the back door.

Kerian looked at the fence and considered his options. He debated climbing over after the gypsy but then he reconsidered. The truth was that since he had lost the enchanted emerald pendant his joints had been aching terribly. He had recently discovered the necklace shielded him from extreme temperatures but it also helped stave off the effects of old age and protected its wearer from the more debilitating effects age could have. This was the initial reason why he had taken it so ruthlessly all those months ago.

Despite the fact the ageing curse was reversing on his body, making him look younger, the loss of the pendant had made all his aches, pains and stiffness in his joints return tenfold. He rolled his neck, feeling the creak of the bones in his spine and reconsidered the jump, pushing his hand against the fence to see if it would hold his weight and sending vibrations running along its length.

He swung up one leg, balancing precariously, preparing to hoist himself over and then noticed two fencing panels along, a gate slowly swinging open.

"Come on!" hissed Octavian from the shadows. "We don't have all night."

Kerian looked back at the fence, then over to the gate and decided to take the easy option, walking casually over to the gate, stepping through and then shutting it behind him, placing the latch back in place.

"Don't you think that was sloppy for your livestock staff to leave the gate open?" Kerian whispered as he crept over to join Octavian at the door to the stables. "Some of the animals could have escaped."

"What do you care?" Octavian snapped. "Just keep close and don't make a sound." Kerian nodded silently in agreement and stepped into the stables, the musky smell of animal hair, sweat and dusty straw, assaulting his nostrils and threatening to make him sneeze.

The stables were about thirty feet long and twenty feet wide, arranged with stalls either side of a central aisle. Each stall contained livestock of some kind. Octavian tinkered about in the darkness with something by the door and then a warm glow flickered to life within a shuttered lantern he held high in his hand.

Kerian allowed his eyes to adjust to the brightness of the lantern and gazed into the pens. Orange hued pigs lay curled together in one stall; the baby piglets all lined up in a row within the curled body of the mother sow, contented snuffles rising from the little creatures as they slept. Another stall held ewes and small lambs that bleated at being disturbed. One particularly vocal lamb issuing a protesting 'baa' when Kerian moved closer to take in the sight. Horses stood to attention alongside camels and birds roosted with heads tucked beneath wings. The low-lit scene appeared quite surreal in the shuttered light and Kerian found it even more haunting because of it.

Octavian walked into a nearby stall, lifting a blanket, saddle and tack from a stand before turning to the black and white stallion stabled there. With a skill clearly obtained from spending time with horses, the gypsy carefully applied the horse blanket and then slung the saddle over the horse's back, ensuring the pommel of the saddle was just in front of its withers. He slowly eased the saddle back into place, just behind its thick black mane, then cinched the straps tightly to keep the saddle secure and pulled the harness carefully over his mount's head, seating the bit in its mouth. Satisfied all was in place, Octavian turned to walk out of the stall, only to notice Kerian watching him.

"Your mount won't saddle itself." He gestured, pointing to a stall at the far end of the stable.

"Oh... sorry, yes of course." Kerian replied, walking to the rack and collecting a saddle, blanket and harness. "My horse is down there then?" Octavian nodded, barely containing his smile.

Kerian turned down the aisle and walked with the saddle slung on one hip. He had forgotten how cumbersome these things could be! He backed into the stall, securing the gate behind him and turned to come face to face with the pale forehead of the massive horse he had seen charging around the corral that morning. The stallion took one look at the intruder in its stall then head-butted him, sending Kerian crashing into the gate he had just closed. Not a stranger to obstinate steeds, Kerian knew he had to step right back in and show the cream and black horse who was boss. He shook his head, rolled up his sleeves and advanced with a steely look of determination in his eye.

Octavian chuckled as he collected some eggs from the chicken coops, carefully gathering them as the thuds and scuffles from the end stall reached his ears. A particularly colourful curse made him pause and look down the passage, expecting to see Kerian come flying out of the stall. A lone figure did stagger out of the darkness but it was from the opposite stall and the man held aloft a lantern, exposing a pale face with bleary eyes and ruffled hair complete with errant pieces of straw. A wicked wooden cudgel swung low to the ground from the man's right hand. Of all the luck! The night watchman had been sleeping in here! What if Octavian was recognised? He could not afford to be seen stealing horses. He was quite sure they hung people for that around here.

"What's going on?" the guard asked, staggering closer to the gypsy and completely ignoring the grunts and yelps coming from behind him. "Octavian, what are you doing with those eggs? Is it morning time already?"

So much for not being recognised!

Octavian plastered an innocent smile across his features, throwing his arms wide in greeting as if the two of them were long-lost brothers. The night watchman smiled in return, lowering his guard, presenting the opening Octavian wanted. The gypsy's right hand swung up, throwing the eggs he held in his hand straight at the guard's face, before following through with a clenched fist that cracked the man soundly against the side of his head. The lantern in the guard's hand fell to the floor and smouldered, momentarily forgotten amidst the straw.

The gypsy followed up with a shoulder charge, knocking the man off balance and onto his back, before Octavian landed hard on the man's chest, hearing the air grunt out of his body. Eggs exploded, showering them both with viscous egg white and golden runny yolk.

"I think my horse has a problem with authority." Kerian yelled from his stall, unaware of the wrestling match occurring mere feet away as he dodged vicious kicks and sharp bites from the stubborn mount. "He doesn't seem to want to have a saddle on him and won't stay still for a second."

Octavian lifted his head to reply, a long strip of egg dribble dangling from his chin and received a jarring blow to the jaw from the man beneath him. He staggered back enough for the guard to roll free and scoop up his cudgel. The club whistled through the air delivering a serious dent to the woodwork inches from where the gypsy's head had been, the bang echoing loudly throughout the stables awakening some of the sleeping animals. Octavian charged back in, punching lighting fast jabs to the guard's ribs and abdomen, desperate to keep the guard breathless and prevent him from calling out an alarm.

"I'm moving as fast as I can." Kerian replied angrily. "Banging the wood won't make me move any faster. It has been a while since I have saddled a horse."

The straw around the lantern sprang into flame.

The animals in the stalls reacted instinctively as a thin curl of smoke spiralled towards the rafters and warm flickering light multiplied. Birds shrieked, horses stamped and neighed, pigs squealed and lambs ran around madly trying to find a way to escape. A hobbled camel tried to lunge for the door in wide-eyed panic and instead found itself crashing through the gate of the stall, its leg unable to support it due to the length of cord that restricted movement. The camel's head landed heavily on the egg-soaked wrestlers rolling about in the straw, its huge stained teeth lashing out, biting down hard on the night watchman's exposed backside covering his breeches in thick slobber.

"Okay… okay! Give me a moment! Are there any apples out there I can bribe him with?" Kerian shouted growing frustrated at the impatient noises Octavian was making and the way his steed kept trying to push him to one side of the stall and squash him up against the wall. He stuck his head out of the gate and stood mouth ajar as he witnessed the surreal scene of wrestling figures, flailing camels, flames, smoke and penned animals going berserk.

Toledo took this opportunity to break for freedom, crashing out of his stall and knocking Kerian aside before coming up short at the scene, his nostrils flaring at the scent of the fire. The huge stallion turned about in the narrow confines of the walkway and ended up facing Kerian again.

"Get back you dumb horse!" Kerian snapped trying to force the stallion back into its stall. Toledo was having none of it and kept coming, its head crashing solidly into Kerian's chest, making him grab hold of the horse's reins in reflex as he was hoisted into the air and barrelled along the stalls. The knight's boots scrabbled across the ground, trying to find a grip as the stallion charged forward, its head pulled down under its uncooperative passenger's weight.

"Whoa!" Kerian shouted to no avail. There was nothing for it. He had to do something swiftly or risk being smashed into a beam or crushed into the wall. He let go with one hand and punched the horse as hard as he could on the nose. Toledo skidded to a stop, eyes rolling leaving Kerian hanging from one side of its neck gasping for breath.

A terrifying growl rose from the far end of the stalls where the fire was now really taking hold. Kerian felt his heart skip a beat as the bestial sound reached his ears. What manner of animal was that? He peered through the dazed stallion's legs and made out several large shapes thrashing about in the smoke, then one of them lifted the other and sent them flying through the air into a stall. A mass of panicked birds took flight at the intrusion, wings cutting through the smoke like scythes, tail feathers igniting as the flames kissed their plumage and marked their trails into the night.

Octavian clearly needed help. Kerian grabbed the reins firmly and turned to lead Toledo back towards the flames. The horse dug its hooves into the floor and resolutely refused to move, pulling him back around to face it once more.

"Now listen here horse!" Kerian snapped, waving his finger angrily. "Either you come with me now and behave yourself, or I will leave you here to burn. Do you understand me?" Toledo's dark eyes stared deeply into Kerian's hazel ones and some iota of understanding passed between them. The horse shivered and rolled its eyes, nose snorting as the thick smoke rolled across the ceiling towards them. "Just trust me." Kerian finished, using his hand to stroke the creature's cheek and try to reassure it all would be well. Kerian turned away and this time the horse followed, all be it hesitantly and with a visible tremor to the stallion's flanks.

"Octavian." Kerian shouted, struggling not to cough. "Octavian, where are you?" Damn, the smoke was getting too thick to see anything in here. Crashes and thumps arose from the stalls ahead and the frantic screams of terrified animals echoed around him as he tried to see what was going on. He pulled up the base of his tunic and tried to cover his face as he moved into the thick of things, only to find the large camel's body blocking his path, its neck snapped, head lolling to one side, flames licking its pelt.

The heat was growing more intense here and Kerian realised there was no way he could advance; the heat was simply too intense. He needed to find another way out. In a flash, he remembered the door they had encountered when they had first tried to gain access to the stables. It had to be here somewhere! He wheeled Toledo around, much to the relief of the stallion and headed back down the walkway, initially not noticing the door due to a row of harnesses hanging alongside it.

Toledo seemed to know what was required, pushing Kerian over into the door with a shove from its muscular shoulder and a snort that seemed almost derogatory in nature. Kerian lifted the latch and pushed against the wood only to hear the padlock and chain rattling on the far side. He had forgotten the door was locked! How could he have been so stupid? He coughed again as the thick acrid smoke continued to funnel along the walkway. The fumes were clouding his head, making it hard to concentrate. His eyes watering, Kerian turned looking for inspiration, then realised the stallion was the answer to his problem.

Toledo pivoted on the spot and in a response to Kerian touching his haunch, lashed out with his back legs, causing the doorway to splinter as his hooves smashed into the wooden door. The stallion kicked again, splintering the frame and leaving the top of the door hanging in the air.

"One more should do it." Kerian encouraged, touching the horse a final time to get the required kick. The door smashed to the ground, padlock still in place, smoke and fumes billowing through the opening out into the market area. Toledo did not hesitate, turning around and dragging his unexpected rider with him, almost wrenching Kerian's arm from its socket as the stallion ran clear.

"Whoa!" Kerian yelled as he bounced along the side of the horse, trying to keep up with the animal whilst avoiding its powerful hooves as they clattered across the market cobbles. He gritted his teeth, holding fast to the bridle, then timed his jump bouncing from the slick stone surface and lifting his foot up into the stirrup as his other hand reached out and grabbed the pommel of the saddle.

It was not the most graceful mount Kerian had ever done but he still found himself grinning as he finally seated himself on the powerful animal. He felt the muscles moving beneath him, the horse's sides breathing in and out between his boots. What an animal. He would never have believed he could feel this way about a horse again after Saybier. To think he was in control of such a magnificent steed.

Toledo stopped dead in its tracks, sparks rising from the market cobbles, throwing Kerian forward and unseating him. He flew over the stallion's head and smashed into some hay bales, the air blasting from his body as he crashed to the floor dazed. Okay, so maybe he was not in as much control as he would like to believe!

The far end of the stables exploded open, ash and glowing embers flying about the yard as Octavian, crouched low over the back of his black and white stallion, came crashing out of the inferno, his clothes and hair streaked with cooked egg. A menagerie of squealing pigs, bleating lambs, ponies and horses piled out pell-mell behind him and began to run riot around the yard adding to the overall confusion of the scene.

The gypsy pulled hard on the reins, his horse skidding to a stop as its rider turned in the saddle and gazed back towards the ruined building.

"Kerian, Kerian, where are you!" he yelled, squinting into the flames and trying to shade his eyes with a blood streaked hand. He moved the horse with his knees, adjusting his viewpoint, torn between finding his companion, not stamping on any of the roaming livestock and running from the scene before people arrived to catch him in the act of stealing a horse. His eyes darted about the area before identifying the saddled figure of Toledo through the smoke and a still form lying on the floor before the steed.

"Toledo?" The Gypsy nudged his horse over and looked down on the floor to where Kerian lay, secretly hoping that the old man was injured severely enough that this fools' quest would be over before it even started. His fallen companion's chest was still rising and falling but his eyes were closed. Maybe luck was on Octavian's side, maybe Kerian had a head injury or had lost consciousness? "Kerian what are you doing down there? We have to leave now before others come."

Kerian opened an eye and took in the ragged, soot, blood and egg streaked appearance of his reluctant guide, before groaning in pain.

"Octavian. Thank goodness." He began. "I want to ask you a question. Can we swap mounts? I think my horse is crazy."

* * * * * *

The *William O'Rielly* was lost at sea on the 18th April 1920, the doomed cargo ship said to have floundered in the Atlantic Ocean before issuing an S.O.S, answered by two British ships, the *Baltic Wanderer* and the *Minnesota*. No trace of the steamer was ever found and the fate of her crew was listed as casualties lost at sea in the Victorian Times newspaper later that same month. Alas, the real fate of her crew was grislier and more horrifying than simply drowning in heavy seas.

She was a sorry looking ship now, no longer a pride to the fleet that she had once belonged. Her decks appeared skeletal in nature; the gangways rotted and covered in moss, her masts splintered stumps that had become roosts for sea birds and wild grasses to inhabit. Brass fixtures were dulled and heavily coated in verdigris. Streaks of rust ran from the metal plate work like crimson tears. Warped doors and spider-webbed windows did little to alleviate the perpetual gloom that hung over the vessel like a shroud. As her stern swung slowly into the moving current beneath her hull, she exposed her vulnerable port side to the mass of wrecked vessels groaning and settling around her at the centre of the ships graveyard.

The O'Rielly's bow collided with another shipwrecked casualty of this cursed place, the impact splintering wood and sending the smaller vessel, it had struck, back the way it had come. All 66 tonnes of the schooner *Pioneer,* lost at sea in 1893, swung back into a swirling eddy from which she had spent months escaping, destined to repeat her destructive cycle all over again.

No more would crew or passengers wander the decks of either ship, although with a strong imagination, an observer would swear ghostly figures still paraded about their decks, their ethereal souls as lost as the ships about them. Until now that was, as a dark shadow, its movements as smooth as liquid ink, jumped onto the deck of the *O'Rielly*, huge paws extending claws to grip the slippery surface as surely as if it were walking a dry, level road. Hooded eyes stared intently about the deck; nostrils snorting seeking an elusive scent that the creature knew had to be hiding here somewhere, just out of sight.

The Scintarn hound whined in frustration, its pointed snout sniffing one way then the other. There was something here, it was sure of it, food for its master and if lucky a prize for itself. The beast became agitated, not sure where to turn, seeing only piles of rotting rubbish, discarded like flotsam on a beach when the tide begins to turn. The hound turned in a circle scanning for movement, expecting any cornered prey to run, scrabble to escape but nothing moved.

"What is it?" said a dry rasping voice next to the Scintarn's ear. "What do you smell?"

The hound jumped skittishly, quickly moving over to the side, its head down, terrified of its master as the creature known as Malum Okubi hauled himself over the side of the vessel to stand at the Scintarn's quivering side.

Malum's body appeared to be clothed in long robes that appeared solid one moment and almost transparent the next, cotton thin tendrils draped from the hem of these robes, the gossamer lengths twitching in the air, supporting barbed fans of bright colours that flickered and whirled around this horrific creature. The pattern of colours and movements changed at Malum's whim and could be hypnotic in nature, deadly to any foe foolish enough to draw near. His dry, husk-like skin appeared jaundice under the mustard sky of the graveyard, translucent veins pumping whatever the creature used for blood, around a body that was tall and powerful. What little hair remained on his head was thin and wispy, like a corpse from a long-forgotten tomb.

The Scintarn's armoured spine clicked loudly as it returned to sniffing around the deck. The scent was confusing but there was definitely prey here. It just needed to figure out where the source of the smell was hiding. It approached a small pile of rubbish and seaweed, its nostrils flaring.

Magic crackled, halting both master and hound as an archway activated nearby. Seawater surged through the opening as the gateway opened, the waves setting the *William O'Rielly* rocking to such an extent that Malum almost lost his balance. Several of his barbed fans flashed out and latched onto the side of the ship, holding the monster steady whilst his hound slid and scrabbled for footing.

A huge battle skiff came through the archway, its sleek one hundred and fifty-foot length and thirty-foot beam of deck bristling with pikes, laser cannons, trapping nets and twenty hardened crew. In the centre of the deck the two giant lizards, Cornelius and Horatio stood alongside their captain Miguel Garcia, the crests on their heads flattened, huge tongues tasting the air and clearly not liking what they scented.

"Thomas Adams, you sly bastard!" Miguel screamed, punching the air in triumph. "I would never have believed this possible. I knew you came from somewhere other than Maraket, I just could never prove it until now." He took in the dank depressing vista around him and then shivered. This place was horrible! "Although now I have seen where you came from, I can understand why you decided to visit." He muttered under his breath.

The skiff shuddered beneath him, the power cells maintaining its hover mode flickering as the vessel fully entered the ships graveyard. Miguel stared in amazement at the row of archways stretching off to either side. So many gateways, so many possibilities for an entrepreneur such as he. Then the privateer turned his attention towards the massive groaning wreckage of ships that lay sprawled before him as far as his eyes could see. What in the world was this place?

His vessel groaned beneath his boots, shudders running through the deck, making Miguel turn his attention back to his skiff and crew, unaware that his onboard technology would prove to be useless after prolonged exposure to the environment of the ships graveyard.

"What's going on Pheris?" Miguel asked, directing his questions to a dark robed man sitting on the deck before him. Pheris turned towards Miguel, his cybernetic eye automatically adjusting to bring the captain into focus. Several options for reply flickered across his vision and he ignored the more colourful ones for a simple honest reply.

"I'm not sure. This is all new to me. My powers are based on technology not mysticism. Something in this place appears to be interfering with our engines." He flexed his hand as digital readouts lit up across his palm, running an analysis on the ship's power before turning his attention to the large jewel he held in his other gloved hand. "Strangely enough, it does not appear to be interfering with the power stream coming from the gemstone."

"Well whatever the interference is, figure it out fast." Miguel hissed. "There is something strange about this place, something here is not right. Horatio, Cornelius, stay sharp, keep your weapons at hand." Pheris held up his hand, gesturing to one of his displays, even as it degraded and turned into glowing pixels of meaningless code.

"It's amazing how the structure of the gemstone has become so fragile." The cyborg confessed, taking a moment to tear his attention from the digital schematics flickering across his palm to observe the remains of the jewel in his hand and the thin tendril of power slipping through his fingers. "If you had not shown me the cloaked drone footage of the mage on that antique galleon opening the portal, I would never have believed magic could be drawn from a gemstone let alone open gateways to other worlds."

"Yes, it's fascinating." Miguel replied, not meaning one word of his reply, scanning the world around him with ever-increasing wariness.

"This mystical spell casting has incredible potential," Pheris continued, unaware of his captain's lack of interest in the topic. "However, the discipline is entirely different to what I am used to. I am literally feeling my way in the dark."

"Well, can you *please* feel your way to finding out what is wrong with the skiff first?" The ship shuddered again and Miguel found himself grabbing the arm of Cornelius to keep on his feet. As he staggered, he noticed something moving on the deck of a wrecked cargo ship ahead. There seemed to be an old man standing there, intently watching him, with a very large black dog standing at his side.

"Ahoy there!" Miguel shouted over, happy to see some sign of life in this depressing place. "Do you know where I can find Thomas Adams?"

The hovering ship suddenly floundered, then crashed down onto the water, all the power cells stuttering before going dead. Crewmen picked themselves up from the deck then started flicking switches and hitting buttons but It was as if someone had disconnected the controls from the mains. The ship did not sink as it landed; it was not designed that way; however, it was now nothing more than a floating raft, at the whim of the currents swirling about them.

Miguel got back to his feet and stared over at the man with the dog, noticing to his surprise that several other large dogs had materialised on the slanting decks of the shipwrecks all around them. The barge continued to float towards the wreckage, the rapidly shortening distance making Miguel suddenly understand just how large these growling animals were.

"I say sir." He called out to the strange man observing them. "I seem to be having a bit of a bother with my ship. Do you know of somewhere we can dock for repairs?" The crew started fidgeting with their weapons, clearly sensing the disquiet and overwhelming sensation something was horribly wrong.

The magical gate snapped shut behind them as the power from the spell failed, making Miguel jump at the sound and one sailor drop his pike in shock. The swell from the water rushing into the graveyard stopped, the forward momentum from the diminishing current just enough to push the barge ever closer to the derelict cargo ship and the strange man who appeared to be smiling, despite looking incredibly pale and unwell.

"You don't talk much do you?" the privateer muttered, as the skiff bumped up against the ruined craft. "Pheris, get this ship moving now. You can work magic with technology. So do some magic before you find yourself swimming home."

The cyborg cursed at his inability to make the barge function and dropped to the floor, wrenching open a console and looking inside at the wires as if they had betrayed him.

"I don't understand what is wrong." He replied. "It doesn't make any sense. The power seems to have simply disappeared."

One of the large hounds howled, then leapt across onto the skiff, jaws clamping down hard on a crewman's neck with a sickening crunch. Cornelius swung up his rifle, blasting the Scintarn with a hail of deadly fire. Horatio turned towards another of the creatures, perched on a nearby deck clearly ready to pounce and lifted his rifle, firing a spluttering bolt of crimson that hit the Scintarn in its chest, vaporising the monster. The lizard licked his chops in satisfaction, then brought his weapon to bear on the old man before them. The dogs started to whine and bark, clearly communicating their concern to their master.

"Stop!" The voice of the old man made the hairs stand up on Miguel's arms. The huge black animals watching them suddenly lowered their heads, turning towards their master, awaiting further commands. The privateer shook his head in dismay; he counted at least thirty of the animals now. What the hell did Thomas ever see in this place? It really quite terrifying. He needed to take control of the situation.

"We will not hesitate to shoot if you don't back down." Miguel warned, trying to sound more confident than he felt. "Call off your dogs. Or we will all start blasting."

"I don't think you will be fast enough to make a difference." The old man replied. "But by all means start blasting. I have plenty more Scintarns. I am sure you will run out of crew before I run out of hounds." Miguel drew his pistols and looked nervously at the diodes flickering on the barrels. Was the power going on the weapons too? This was going from bad to worse.

"Rather than kill you all." The old man said, lights suddenly flickering around him in staccato flashes. "I would like to invite you all to my ship so we can discuss your previous request. You see, like yourself, I too am searching for Thomas Adams. Just drop your weapons and then I can have you all for dinner."

"That sounds perfectly plausible." One crewmember said to another, as a loud clattering spread across the deck and weapons fell from open hands, making Miguel spin around in shock. What was everyone doing? Had they all gone mad? His crew were dropping their guns and pikes, walking away from the deck guns, leaving the nets and moving towards the old man and the flashing lights. Had they all lost their minds?

"What's going on with them? Why are they all acting so stupid?" He turned to Cornelius for answers, only to see the lizard shaking his huge head and flicking his massive tail in an agitated manner. "What's wrong with you? Snap out of it or I will make you into a pair of boots!" The huge reptile appeared unable to answer its captain's question, so Miguel turned to its huge brother who appeared to be scratching his nose as if a large bug had landed there and was biting him.

Malum leaned in closer, his fans whirring and clicking, licking his lips at the feast to come.

"That's right, you should all follow me now." He hissed his deadly command. "I am sure there is enough room around the dinner table for all of you and when I am full, we can discuss with those who remain just how you know Thomas Adams and then how you can all help me catch him."

Malum turned from the barge and started to pick his way across the wrecked ships, confident his clicking fans had the entire crew in their thrall. The Scintarn hounds moved to escort the mindless crew as they stepped one at a time off the skiff and started to wander unquestioningly towards their doom.

Miguel looked over at his lizard companions as his dazed crew walked past, gesturing that they grab Pheris as he dropped to the deck, sparks jumping from his cybernetic components.

"I'm really sorry Miguel but for some reason I don't feel at all well." The cyborg confessed before lapsing into silence. The buccaneer did not know what was going on but he had no intentions of leaving his cyborg companion behind.

A loud growl sounded from behind him, followed by several more from other huge hounds that had somehow managed to encircle them. Horatio turned offering his own deep-throated growl and an exaggerated thump of his tail, his earlier mesmerised state now apparently forgotten but Miguel stayed the lizard's hand.

"Let's just follow for now." He whispered. "Just pick up as many weapons as you can and then we can carefully assess the situation before we act. I do not want to show this creature how strong you and Cornelius are. Nobody messes with Miguel Garcia and lives to talk about it." The lizards, Miguel and the cyborg slowly moved across the deck, the two huge monsters picking up additional weapons as they walked, harried by drooling Scintarn hounds that snapped and growled menacingly at their heels.

Silence descended on the deck of the *William O'Rielly* as the straggling group slowly moved away. The silence stretched on for many minutes, allowing time for any imaginary shades of the dead to retake her rotting decks, before one small forgotten pile of refuse suddenly sprouted two small grubby hands and feet and detached itself from the deck where the Scintarn had stood. The rubbish pile shuffled and clanked across the ship then dropped onto the wallowing skiff and started eagerly digging through the contents of the ship's stores, foraging technological components and stuffing food into its pockets.

If there was one thing this moving pile of garbage could do... it was survive.

Chapter Ten

Kerian attempted to rein in Toledo on the hill overlooking the port town of Wellruff and ended up with the stubborn stallion turning in an agitated circle rather than do as his rider commanded. The horse snorted loudly in derision at such attempts to control his spirit and pawed the ground in protest as Kerian took in the predawn scene of the meandering path behind them.

Their rapid, if roundabout, departure from Wellruff had gone much easier than Kerian had expected. It appeared that the attentions of people focused more on the disaster of the market square and the hypnotic effect of the crackling flames consuming the stalls, than the two riders moving away from the scene. They had kept to the side streets, only stopping at the *Lusty Mermaid* to collect Kerian's saddlebags under much vocal protest from Octavian. This unexpected detour did have some merits, by heading back into town, before then moving out again, they avoided the crowds of people heading to witness the fire.

Octavian followed in Kerian's wake, his face tense, head down watching the ground in front of his mount, as if the weight of the world was upon his shoulders. Kerian was unsure what thoughts were passing through his travelling companion's mind but with the look of him, they did not appear to be happy ones. Maybe the thought of leaving Wellruff was preying on him. He clearly had no job to go back to; the thick column of billowing black smoke rising into the heavens from the market district was proof of that.

Kerian squinted and tried to note the small frantic shapes of people running around trying to put out the fire but the distance was too great. He tried to visualise in his mind where the *Tulip* was dry-docked, scanning the skyline trying to identify where she lay but he was unable to locate her. Then he tried to trace the cluttered rooftops for some sign of the *Lusty Mermaid* and finally gave the whole thing up as Octavian rode up alongside him.

"Why so glum?" Kerian quipped, trying to break the gypsy from his morose state. "The weather is with us; the sky looks clear. It is a perfect day to get out on the road. At least with this early start we will miss most of the other travellers upon this road."

Octavian looked up at Kerian and shrugged indifferently before continuing to push his horse past Toledo and advance along the trail.

"Oh yes this was a great idea," he mumbled as he passed. "No supplies, no water and a companion who leaves chaos in his wake."

"Who me?" Kerian replied, feigning insult. "I don't leave chaos; I create new opportunities. Your job was going nowhere, you were gambling most evenings trying to make money, gaining the wrong kind of friends. It was only a matter of time before you found yourself run out of town or strung up somewhere. Look at this as a liberation, a chance to wipe the slate clean and make an honest living."

"The only problem with an honest living is it doesn't pay the bills." Octavian responded. "How am I going to raise funds out here?"

"What debt do you owe?" Kerian enquired, his tone changing from jovial to concerned as he realised that he had hit a nerve.

"My debt is my own." Octavian shot back. "It is mine to carry, much like the one I now have with you."

"At least mine is getting you out in the fresh air, seeing the sites and living life." Kerian smiled.

"I was living life just fine in Wellruff." Octavian replied over his shoulder.

"Where are we heading?" Kerian shouted after him, struggling to make Toledo move and failing miserably.

"We shall strike towards the ferry at Lichfield." Octavian replied, ducking to avoid an overhanging branch. "If we hurry, we should catch the noon sailing. If we miss it there is a long wait and there is no other way to cross the Mereya, unless we head across the mountains into the Vaarseeti Desert..." he paused and muttered under his breath. "...and we don't want to be going that way."

Kerian nudged Toledo again trying to turn the stallion to follow Octavian's passage but a tasty tuft of grass was taking the horse's attention and he was not moving on until this morsel had been fully chewed and ingested. Kerian looked back over his shoulder at Octavian and then turned his attention back to his horse preparing to give the stallion a stern scolding.

As his head turned, he caught the rising sun just cresting the far horizon. Dawn was upon them. A sudden sharp pain of loss hit him, stabbing deeply into his heart and making breathing difficult. Colette! He was straying further and further away from Colette. The blow compounded by the thought he would not be able to see her beautiful face in the pendant. He had no idea if she was well, if she still loved him as much as his heart ached for her. He longed to be at her side, scenting her perfume, captivated by her enchanting smile and drowning in her deep blue eyes.

"I am coming for you." He whispered. "Keep safe until I can be with you again. I know you cannot hear me, I realise this is madness but I love you and I want to be with you forever. I promise this is only temporary. I will be back soon and I will sail to hell and back in the *Tulip* to find you. Just wait a little longer."

He choked back his emotions and turned angrily to the horse, unaware that his promise to return would become just empty words snatched away by the wind.

"If you don't get moving, I swear I'm going to have you cut up for steaks." He threatened the stubborn horse beneath him. Toledo swung his head up from the grasses and turned a baleful eye towards his rider, as if to say 'I would love to see you try' before dropping his attention back to the grass once more.

Kerian snatched the reins roughly on the right side, tugging Toledo's head up and over. The stallion snatched the reins back and turned to the left almost unseating his rider at the unexpected manoeuvre, before reluctantly picking up the pace and heading off after Octavian, making sure his path wove beneath every low hanging branch as he did so.

* * * * * *

The Monastery of St Fraiser was serene and calm, a place of worship and quiet reflection where scholars wandered the halls of the multi-tiered circular library, their shuttered lanterns casting mute light and flickering shadows along spines of books and rolls of faded dusty parchment that contained knowledge from the ages. The whisper of robes across the marble floor, complemented soft steps of sandaled feet, as hooded monks moved from shelf to shelf in pursuit of the elusive wisdom secreted within these hallowed halls. The library never closed to those who required its wealth of learning.

When Justina had assumed control of the library, the scholars decided not to notice. The new mistress removed no books, changed no access rights. Life for these monks, in whom the rustling page of a book and the curling cursive letters it contained were sacrosanct, continued as always, with another lead to chase, another story or enigma to pursue. What did it matter who was in charge as long as they were free to visit other worlds within the pages of the treasured tomes stored here?

The only change for those who paid attention, were a selection of newly appointed guards spaced evenly around the many floors of the library, their hourly patrols marching around the hub of the great hall at the centre of the ancient many storied building, an unspoken element of frustration. Studded leather armour clinked loudly against buckles and belts, heavy boots left marks across the marble floor and maces leant against bookcases tripped the unwary bookworm who failed to lift his nose from his obsessions in time.

If the scholars lifted their attention from their books, maybe taking a moment to consider the words illustrated within a book or scroll, they often turned to the centre of the library, where the great hall was located. The focal point of this airy space was the effigy of St Fraiser, the figurehead responsible for creating the order of monks' centuries before. The effigy rose up beyond fifty feet in height, with a dais beneath adding even more stature to the imposing powerful figure.

Numerous animals, frozen in time, stood all around the monk: A wren on his outstretched hand tweeting long silent tales observers could only guess at, a squirrel on his shoulder, nibbling on an acorn, whilst whispering into the saint's ear. Field mice slid down folds of his robes and a fox stood to silent attention at his feet, the carvings so lifelike that many a visitor stood awed. A hedgehog balanced on St Fraiser's sandaled foot, its little spines piercing the hem of the saint's robe. There was even a fowl standing slightly away from the sculpture, its front leg skilfully carved to flow into the traveller's robes, the tiny deer appearing to move in with no sign of fear in its posture, eyes wide, nose up as if sniffing the air. This attention to every minor detail, every nuance of the traveller, displaying the love and affection the order held towards their founder.

In the Saint's free hand rested a large ledger, known to all of the priests and monks studying within the halls. It was a larger than life copy of the very first volume added to the library, its pages detailing the journey and observations of the travelling scholar. The huge book hung open, a worn rosary draped across the page. On the end of the rosary, suspended from the beads hanging freely over the edge of the ledger, a pendant shaped as a flaming cross, the token of the order of St Fraiser.

The glass ceiling high above the statue displayed the grey clouds scudding across the crowded sky outside. On a day when the sun graced the heavens, the light would beam down into the hall, serving as further reminder that their learned founder was truly blessed but today everything was cloaked in foreboding shadow.

No one noticed the ripple that started to form in one of the darkened alcoves, the distortion of shadow, the wavering mirage created by heat on a summer's day. A solitary gold coin suddenly appeared from the distortion, dropping to the wooden floor of the library and bouncing on its ancient pitted edge, rolling and spinning past the shelves. One edge of the coin was slightly melted, the regal profile of a long distant king softened by heat, age and the passage of the currency from hand to hand.

The scowl from the nearest scholar, upset at the disruption from his studies fell sourly on the nearest innocent guard. The man stared down at his feet, shrugging his shoulders as the golden coin rolled past him heading for the balcony that opened out overlooking the statue of St Fraiser. With a skilful stamp of his foot, the guard's boot came down on the free rolling currency, stopping its movement and allowing silence to return to the room. The man bent down to pick up the coin, his eyes scanning for the possible owner to suddenly come crashing from the bookshelves in hot pursuit. The yellow metal felt uncomfortably hot in his hand.

A loud disapproving tut issued from the scholar as the monk returned to his books, his eyebrow raised in irritation. The guard shrugged his innocence before glancing at the treasure he tossed from hand to hand in disbelief. This was nearly a year's wages he held! His luck was in today. He took one quick look around, then popped the gold piece into his pocket and placed his singed hands behind his back, trying to look innocent.

The rattle of two more coins bouncing and spinning across the floor raised further disgust from the scholar whose quill skipped across the parchment before him at the disruption. The guard wiped his hand through his hair, pulled a strained face before marching towards the currency his booted feet coming down on the money and killing their motion dead with two loud stamps.

A wide smile spread across the guard's face as he bent down to collect the new coins, only to watch with disbelief as a sudden deluge of gold and silver pieces started to rain from out of thin air. He ran forwards, determined to pocket as much of the treasure that was suddenly coming to him before he skidded to a halt as two humanoid figures materialised before him and crashed onto the library floor.

Eyes wide, he took in the battered yet unmistakable figure of the high priestess as she struggled to regain her feet, tripping over the hem of her robes and staggering as if slightly disorientated. The male figure behind her groaned and vomited before trying to grab her leg with an outstretched arm that looked as if it had been skinned. Muscles lay bare to the air and for a second the guard wanted to believe the movement was an illusion, the figure had to be a corpse that had simply been caught up with Justina as she had teleported here from wherever the gold coins had come from. Until the corpse spoke in a rasping voice that sent chills up the man's spine.

"What have you done to me?" Scrave groaned, spittle dribbling from his lips. "Why do I feel so dizzy and sick? What twisted sorcery have you cast?"

"It's the side effects of teleporting such a long distance. Don't you know that spell?" Justina gasped, holding tightly onto one of the book cases for support as her demonic familiar ran up her arm and sought sanctuary in the shadows of the ceiling. Scrave retched heavily, before lifting his emaciated head and staring at her with undisguised venom in his eye.

"I would not have needed your assistance if I knew how to teleport!" he snapped, rolling onto his knees and attempting to pull himself up from the floor before crashing down onto his backside and lying there groaning as if the very ground beneath him were rolling about in high seas. At least he was away from the accursed temple. He was finally free. He lay back and closed his eyes, palpable relief flooding through his emaciated form.

The guard moved forward, slipping the wicked mace from his belt. The discussion between the two people clearly signifying his mistress was not friendly with her companion. Maybe if he assisted her there would be more gold coins as a reward? He lifted his weapon intent on smashing the hard-studded iron ball down onto the charred figure before him, only to find his eyes torn from the grisly creature by the sight of the elaborate double-bladed golden dagger wrapped tightly up the man's arm.

The golden scales winked in the little light that filtered into the bookshelves. It was so life-like as if the weapon was alive, which was impossible of course. He moved closer, determined to wrestle the dagger from the fallen figure. Ruby eyes blinked and a warning hiss rose from the blade just as his mace began its devastating downward swing.

Scrave's desiccated eyelids shot open at the sound. He saw the studded weapon hurtling down towards him and rolled away with inches to spare. The mace crashing onto the ground with an impact that jarred every scratching quill within fifty feet.

"Kill him!" Justina screamed, having recovered from the disorientation of her spell, galvanising the guards within ear shot to rush to her command. "I want his Elven head!" The exhausted Elf rolled again, coming up hard against a bookcase as the guard's enthusiastic attack brought the mace smashing down in an arc of destruction, catching the shelf inches above him and decimating the books stacked there. Manuscripts, errant paper pages, jagged splinters and a billow of disturbed dust filled the air, blocking the guard's view and allowing Scrave to scoot away from the man who found himself sneezing repeatedly. The Elf dived into the darkness between the shelves, the dagger writhing angrily on his arm.

This was madness! For the briefest of instances, Scrave had believed himself to be safe, finally away from the incredible heat, able to close his eyes and rest for the first time in months. Oh, how he wanted to rest! How he needed to sink down and close his eyes...

A hulking guard charged around the corner of the bookshelf swinging his weapon ineffectively in the close confines of the passageway, the weapon swinging up high only to get caught on an upper shelf. Scrave threw his arms up in shock, his actions permitting the sentient dagger to drag his raised weapon arm forward, plunging the twin golden blades deep into the guard's exposed chest. The man's scream of pain hung in the air as the blade fed.

Energy rushed up Scrave's arm as if he were struck by errant lightning, lifting the Elf up onto the balls of his feet as his body arched in spasm. The dagger pulsed in his grasp, coils writhing in morbid delight. It was as if the weapon was quenching a prolonged thirst and it would not deny itself this opportunity. Scrave was powerless to resist, too weak and out of control of his own functions to withdraw the crimson stained blades from the guard's chest. All he could do was hang on as the energy flowed through the gleaming serpent and further into his own battered form.

As he looked, the guard started to shrivel and sag before him, as if he were aging instead of simply dying. Before he could comprehend this further, he noticed his own exposed and charred arm where he clutched the dagger. The skin was starting to epithelise. Necrotic flesh was sloughing away and taut pink tissue, corded muscle and sinew were forming and knitting together under his gaze. He could scarcely believe what he was seeing!

With a final strangled gasp of expiring breath, the guard slid from the golden dagger and crashed to the floor, leaving Scrave standing dazed in the darkness, his heart racing, the dagger hissing contentedly on his arm.

What had just happened to him? What was this weapon doing? He felt younger, more vibrant than he had in days. This could not be real. Was he hallucinating and somehow still back in the inferno he believed he had left? The Elf reached out to touch the shelves beside him reassuring himself that he was really in the library and not dreaming. The clamour of guards following his route forced Scrave to focus on his chaotic current situation.

He needed to get out of here but he had no idea where here was, or more importantly where the exit lay. He needed to get up high and see more clearly. With a lightness and energy of body the Elf had not felt in months, he grabbed the edge of the massive bookshelf and started to climb up towards the ceiling, his feet lightly touching each shelf as he ascended into the shadows.

Guards entered the passageway from either end, cutting off any exit at ground level, drawn by the earlier screams from their demised associate, their arrival literally seconds after Scrave had disappeared into the darkness. They cautiously approached the fallen figure, gasping aloud and looking about fearfully when they realised the aged figure beneath them was once their colleague.

"Foul work is about here." Whispered one, gripping his mace tightly, his eyes darting about the dusty books looking for the being that had struck the fallen guard down.

"It's dark sorcery no doubt." agreed another equally on edge temple warrior.

Scrave watched silently from above, his arms and legs spread wide, the bookcases either side supporting his weight, chuckling silently to himself at the confusion of the people below and trying not to sneeze at the heavy amount of dust tickling his nostrils. He listened to their exclamations and thought back to a similar situation where he had been perched on a window ledge above an alleyway in Catterick over a similar amount of guards. He remembered the huge Minotaur Rauph teetering opposite him with a pink pair of lady's knickers hanging from one horn and felt a brief moment of nostalgia before he mentally brushed it away so he could start to focus on the matter at hand. He needed to get out of this library and figure out where he was. Ironically, the Elf had no idea he was actually in the same city he had been so fondly remembering.

Something ran over Scrave's hand making him twitch in reflex and almost lose his grip. What in the world was up here on top of the stacks with him? He hoped it wasn't a rat. Scrave had taken his fill of rats! The unseen threat chittered softly in the darkness. To Scrave the meaningless noise was filled with dangerous intent. The Elf tried to focus on the shadows, attempting to make out the details of whatever was out there, knowing instinctively that it meant him harm.

His imagination started to play tricks on him. Maybe it was a scorpion or something equally venomous. He tried to reposition himself aware that if he wasn't careful, he could dislodge something and give away his precarious position. A soft touch whispered across the back of his hand. The caress was anything but intimate, instead chills raced up the Elf's arm as he felt one of his finger's being lifted from its position despite his struggles to pull it away.

The raised voices of the guards arguing where their quarry had gone suddenly faded in importance as Scrave tried not to shriek as he felt what could only be teeth pressing at the top and bottom of his digit. The teeth clamped down hard and all pretence at stealth disappeared. Scrave shrieked, snatching his hand away and horrifyingly found himself dragging the creature that was biting him out of the darkness.

Haunting empty eye sockets glared at him as he snatched the sorceress's apprentice out from hiding. The creature knew Scrave had taken its tail in the past and now it was time for payback. Hamnet's skull like head filled Scrave's vision, it's evil nature and intent all too clear to see. The demon bit down sharply intent on causing its nemesis more pain.

Scrave tried to bring his other hand to bear, the golden serpent dagger hissing in frustration, knowing that this prey was not flesh and blood and would do nothing to boost its desire for ending life.

An unexpected tremor ran through Scrave's form as he tried to balance using just his outstretched legs. He realised with horror that he was weaker than he thought. Normally his balance and acrobatic skills were excellent. However, fighting with the monster hanging on to his hand and trying to use his other hand to assist in this fight without stabbing himself was easier said than done!

His left foot squeaked on the ledge informing the men below that the person, their priestess wished killed, hid in the shadows above them. Seizing the initiative two of the ignorant men, not bothering about the sanctity and precious nature of the items they walked amongst, shoved hard against the shelving making the bookcase creak ominously, unbalancing the Elf. Scrave tried to adjust his footing, still struggling with the snarling demon, only to find his foot slipping free. He fell clumsily, unable to bring his hands to bear and catch himself.

Hamnet twisted vainly in Scrave's grasp as they crashed down amongst the guards, sending the men sprawling, weapons crashing to the floor as books started to rain down, thumping on heads, arms and backs and sending clouds of cloying dust into the air. The demon released its grip on Scrave's finger and lunged for his exposed nose. Scrave saw the monster coming straight at him and was unable to move as the razor-sharp jaws snapped together. A large ledger crashed down onto the demon's head ending its vicious attack. Scrave lifted his free hand and on reflex, checked his nose, thanking his stars when he found it was still there.

He breathed a sigh of relief before realizing he was amongst a pile of men intent on killing him. Quick as a flash Scrave leapt to his feet, dagger in hand and ran for the far end of the passage, his feet coming down on loudly complaining heads and vulnerable areas of struggling flesh. The golden dagger hissed in frustration once more, this time at the missed opportunities behind it.

Scrave dashed to the far end of the shelves, having no idea where he was going but determined to get as far away from the fallen guards. He risked a quick look over his shoulder noting the fallen men gathered their feet and struggling to rise, one shrieking out in horror, trying to pummel Hamnet's flapping form with his mace. Clearly, the guard thought the demon was the terror that had dared attack them.

Guards crashed into Scrave from either side as he cleared the end of the shelves, bringing him down in a pile of breathless pounding bodies. Scrave fought scratched and bit at anything soft that came near, satisfying himself at the grunts and screams that arose from the chaos. He managed to get his head out from one guard's sweaty armpit only to see the dishevelled figure of Justina stalking towards him. Incredibly, despite all the chaos and thrashing, perspiring and cursing bodies piling on top of him throwing wild punches, the Elf had time for one bizarre thought.

She really was quite attractive to the eye. He tried to shake his head as a cocky smile slid across his face, however, he was in a headlock, making such a move slightly difficult. Besides, what was he thinking about! She hated him.

"Kill him slowly." She purred, leaning against one of the study tables and revealing a length of attractive leg from the slit side of her robes. The scream of the man to his side snatched Scrave back to the moment as a jolt of energy coursed into him. His mind may have been pleasantly distracted but his dagger had a single purpose!

Scrave staggered as the shock lifted him, his teeth snapping together as he convulsed. He lunged to one side and realised with amazement that the whole mass of men shifted with him as if he had suddenly gained the strength to shove them all. Scrave pushed a sweaty muscled arm from his face and ducked a haymaker punch that sailed into another guard. This was incredible was he this strong?

Another jolting shock, another scream. Scrave braced his feet, lowering his head back and pushing the scrum of people in the opposite direction, away from the woman who cared so hopefully about his untimely demise. If only the timing was better, he chuckled to himself amazed at the feeling of euphoria coursing through him.

The whole mass of bodies crashed into something hard, bringing Scrave's jubilant musings to a halt. What did these people think they were doing! He was mighty now unstoppable! He simply dug in and pushed harder, laughing at the fact other guards were now crashing into the mob behind him even as screams of terror sounded from the men before him.

He lowered his head and pushed once more, determined to thrust the guards out of the way and make his escape. Something snapped and the resistance let up as screams filled the air. Scrave kept stepping forward, ignoring the hands trying to hold him back and the wild punches bouncing harmlessly off his head as if he were being hit by a child.

People started to slide off around him, sweating hands started to clench clothes and the whole mass of bodies started to slip and slide across the floor before him. At last he was breaking free, he was finally making headway!

"Stop you fool!" screamed one man. "The balcony! You are pushing us over the edge!"

What balcony? Scrave discarded the thought, pushing harder, before he suddenly found himself staring eye to eye with a man who had sheer terror etched upon his face.

"Please I'm right on the edge." The man pleaded desperately. The Elf had no idea what the man was talking about and pushed harder, only to watch the guard drop away, screaming as he fell five stories to crash onto the cold marble floor below.

Scrave's blood turned to ice in his veins. His arms flailed at the suddenly open air before him, failing to locate anything to halt his momentum as other guards joined the side of the scrum at his back and continued pushing. If he wasn't careful, he too was going to fall! He tried to brace himself with his heels, then turned in place, his fingers outstretched pushing back but the mass of bodies was too much and he slipped relentlessly across the crumbling balcony. His boots squeaked in protest as the edge came closer and closer.

"Back up!" Scrave screamed. "Don't push anymore. We are all going to go over!" He turned again, putting his back against the scrum, his boots sliding an extra couple of inches towards the precipice as he struggled to place his feet and shove back as hard as the throng were pushing towards him. He bit down hard on a fumbling hand and grinned as it was pulled away but the mass of men continued shoving against him.

Justina walked slowly towards the hulking guards, her body swaying seductively as she assumed control.

"What are you all waiting for?" she asked the straining crowd. "Push him over!"

The grin slid from Scrave's face as if it were butter on a hot skillet. The force of the crowd surged forwards once more, Scrave's foot slipping over the edge. He tried to get his shoulder under the guards, hold his ground and push back, but it was hopeless. There was only one thing to do.

Scrave stepped away into nothing and smiled.

"Flossador!" he chanted, his spell snagging the wisps of energy from a crumbling gemstone in his earring and using them to make his command a reality. It was as if an invisible platform had suddenly emerged beneath Scrave's feet, buoying him up and preventing gravity from laying a claim to his previously tumbling form. He gathered himself and calmly moved to step away from the men staring at him in awe from the ruined balcony, their looks of amazement turning to one of horror as the push continued from behind them.

Scrave laughed as the guards started to slip over the edge and turned his back to walk away, intent on putting as much space between himself and the mob pursuing him. Screams rang out but the Elf did not care about the waste of life, shrill screams and wet thuds that filled the air. These people had tried to kill him, they deserved their fate!

A heavy weight crashed into his shoulder, another at his leg as two guards pushed from the balcony clutched eagerly at his body in an attempt to stop their fall. Scrave felt himself yanked to the side the spell struggling to support the extra weight putting him into a freefall. He tried to lash out with his hand, tried to force the men free but facing death can give a man reserves of strength he never knew he had.

The three men smashed down onto the massive open ledger held by the statue of St. Fraiser. Scrave groaned as his head slammed down onto the man beneath him, a sickening crack and sudden limpness of the man's form making it clear the guard had sustained a mortal injury as they had landed. The spell faltered then dispelled as the Elf's concentration lapsed.

He shook his head, trying to clear the stars dancing across his vision, hearing the screams of the men who continued to crash through the balcony and fall to their deaths. The rantings of Justina ordering the men to pursue him and the more sinister sound of footsteps approaching at a rush.

Scrave rolled as the mace came whistling down past him, bouncing up onto his feet as his right hand reached out, golden dagger hissing menacingly. The guard swung his weapon in low, causing the Elf to jump or get his legs swept from under him. He landed on the tips of his toes, the edge of the ledger creaking ominously beneath his feet. He risked a quick glance down and saw a long and painful fall below.

The mace whistled back across Scrave's vision, the guard clearly understanding that he needed to keep a distance from his magical foe. Scrave judged the swing then barged in, the golden dagger whipping out and scoring across the guard's side as the Elven fighter followed through to keep moving to the other side of the open book and much needed space.

As he paused, his left hand dropped to the sword scabbard at the guard's side, deftly drawing the steel blade held there. The gleaming steel glinted in his hand, the symbol of the flaming cross etched on the steel just below the hilt of the weapon.

The guard spun around finding himself facing a foe with a writhing golden dagger in one hand and his own sword in the other. This was now a different challenge. Originally, he had needed to keep his foe from getting close enough to use the dagger. Now the Elf had a sword, increasing his reach! He paused, the mace suddenly heavy in his hand, fear creeping into his mind.

Scrave noticed the hesitation and decided to capitalize on the man's indecision.

"What's keeping you?" he taunted, his tongue darting to his lip and tasting sweat. A thought ghosted into his mind. He really hoped it was his own sweat and not something from the disgusting armpit he had been buried in earlier. A shiver ran through his mind making his cocky grin waver slightly.

The guard looked around suddenly realising how high he was from the floor and the fact that an avenue of escape would be easier said than done. He knew he could not run, so he had a stark choice; kill the Elf before him or die. He had no intentions of dying this day.

Scrave lowered his blade and turned left side on, leaving himself with a narrow profile for the guard to attack. The sword felt good in his hand, an extension of his being that he controlled, in direct comparison to the writhing dagger wrapped about his right wrist. It was good to feel in control. He circled the tip of the blade and rolled his head working out the kinks his long incarceration had caused.

The guard lunged in, his cudgel swinging at Scrave's head. Rather than parry the swing, the Elf simply leaned backwards letting the heavy weapon pass harmlessly by, knowing the guard would have to stop the momentum of his mace before he could bring it back for another blow. However, his opponent was not as naive as Scrave surmised, dropping his arm to allow the wicked club's momentum to increase and swing back in from below.

Scrave suddenly realised the danger he was in, jumping back as the deadly weapon whistled bare inches from his leg. Before he could attack with the sword, the dagger on his right side yanked him around, pulling his arm directly into the path of the circling weapon, the golden serpent spitting as its length extended, fangs sinking into the guard's astonished face just as the mace slapped against Scrave's unprotected arm. Luckily, the shock of the serpent bite was enough for the guard to slow his attack, the power in the swing of the weapon decreased as the man tried to back away from the evil dagger. Instead of a broken arm Scrave just felt a wave of numbness race up his arm. If the golden weapon wrapped about his arm had been held in his hand, he would have dropped it to the floor in shock, instead it simply hissed and reared, preparing to strike once more, despite the numb arm it rested around.

The guard stepped back reaching for his face in horror, feeling that it was already numb. The poison of the serpent cult worked fast. Scrave yanked the dagger back and lunged with the sword, sinking the steel deep into the guard's chest, impaling the man in an act that was actually merciful given the terror shown on the guard's face as the blistering poison traced across his features. Scrave stared dispassionately as the man sank down lifeless at his feet, then looked up and took in his surroundings. He needed to get out of here fast. He quickly paced from one end of the open book he stood upon, to the other, aware that the chiselled gaze of the Saint above him was scrutinising his every move. Temple guards were arriving from all directions, blocking the exits from the hall and assembling on the balconies. He was cut off. He could not fly. His mind raced through the magic spells he knew but the art of invisibility was a spell that always eluded him.

"There is nowhere to run." Justina mocked from where she stood a floor above. "Give me the dagger and I will let you walk away from here."

"I'm afraid I don't get that intimate on my first date. I tend to just stick with flowers." Scrave replied, his thoughts worried despite the cocky banter he was attempting. "Maybe if we could have a second date, without…" he gestured at the guards all around. "… all of this company, I might consider some kind of trade."

"It's such a shame." Justina continued. "You show a great deal of promise. We could have had a future together."

"I knew you liked me." Scrave shot back, his sharp eyesight suddenly noticing a drain on the floor. His eye traced from the grill, up the sculpture, following the carved and polished folds representing the fabric of the Saint. They were like perfectly formed chutes in a child's playground. The ride would be rapid! It would take him past the carved form of an astonished dormouse and down under the flared tail of a hovering humming bird carved in exquisite detail. He just needed to shrink to a very small size… and Scrave had just the spell in his repertoire of magic. "I'll call you, I promise." He smiled. "But next time, lets meet at my place."

"Bring him down!" Justina screamed as guards moved to the railing armed with crossbows. Scrave winked, whispered something under his breath and then to all the assembled… he simply disappeared.

* * * * * *

The *Fickle Fish* tavern was every bit as quaint as the name suggested; with warm wooden beams, cream walls and a bar of polished walnut behind which bottles of exotic shapes and sizes promised oblivion to the adventurous and unwary alike. The outside seating flowed under arbours hanging lush with grapes and wisteria, the cool foliage dappling the area with much welcome shade. Cats lounged lazily in the sunshine, tails flicking away errant flies whilst narrow feline eyes scanned the caged songbirds swinging from the beams.

The harbourmaster ushered Rauph to a huge table set on a raised area above the main seating. Thomas noted the heavyset chairs around the table were solid, clearly not made for comfort and that there was not enough to seat all of the accompanying crew. He motioned to Weyn and between them, they picked up a bench and carefully lifted it up and placed it along the far side of the table. As one, they all crashed down onto the seat grinning as the calmness of the place settled around them.

"What, what are you doing?" the harbourmaster paled. "You can't sit here. It is not permitted."

"Sure it is," Weyn commented. "Come sit alongside us, we have lots to learn." The man stood clearly unsure what to do, before slowly lowering himself onto the bench as if the wooden surface would scald him.

"Relax," Thomas motioned, leaning across the table. "We are all friends here. There is nothing to worry about."

"But... you don't understand. This is highly irregular. We could be killed for this insult."

"What do you mean?" the captain enquired. "What should it matter where you sit?"

"It matters to them." He gulped, nodding towards the shaggy Minotaur. "It really matters to them."

"Rauph," Thomas opened. "You don't mind if we all sit here, do you?"

"Nope," Rauph replied turning his head first one way and then another, taking in the scenery and the buzzing bees bumbling from one flower to another. "He can sit with us if he likes. What can we have to eat here?"

As if on cue a flustered servant walked over placing a large tankard in front of Rauph, the lime green contents inside sending up an aroma much akin to a health shake. Then the man turned to walk away only to be caught by Mathius's outstretched hand.

"We have had our vegetables for the day." He remarked dryly. "We will settle for beers instead."

"Sitting here?" the stunned servant replied.

"Well I don't know about you but we would quite like it sitting here, so yes, right here will be fine." He turned to Thomas "What's wrong with these people? They all seem fascinated about our seating arrangements and we also seem to have gathered quite a crowd."

"I hadn't noticed, mumbled Ives, glancing at all the onlookers gathered on the street outside and entering the inn to witness the strange spectacle. "You know this place could be a gold mine back home. The caged birds are a nice twist. I wonder what the food is like?"

More servants came over to the table placing plates of food before the navigator and swapping nervous glances with the landlord who stood beside the bar, wringing his hands in concern.

A massive tureen of baked fish, garnished with exotic herbs and slathered in a rich tomato sauce steamed invitingly before Rauph, the smells making him close his eyes and moan softly under his breath. A platter of garlic flat bread followed, with a bowl of skilfully woven grass, oat and straw cakes, seaweed flavoured with cinnamon, a bowl of something that looked like crumbled chalk, mixed with grass and smelling faintly of lemon and finally several appetising desserts. The Minotaur attacked the food with glee, savouring eat bite as the textures and scents returned him to his distant veiled past. These tastes were all so familiar to him, yet he had no idea why. If only he could remember.

Ives borrowed a fork and leant far over to scoop out a tender morsel of fish from the tureen, which he balanced on the tines of the utensil with a skill that spoke volumes about how he managed to retain his wide girth. His face puckered as he chewed, making Weyn and Mathius chuckle.

"This fish needs more spice." The trader declared. "It is so bland!" He swallowed and the fork moved forwards again attempting to try some of the other delicacies on offer before his Minotaur shipmate ate them all.

"You know what." Mathius intoned, viewing the food with some distain. "This is all very nice but I don't suppose you have any steak on the menu?"

A plate dropped, shattering on the floor as the servant reacted in shock to the question. A hush descended on the gathering as horror spread throughout the crowd and people turned to pass on the words of sacrilege uttered from the stranger's mouth.

People standing outside on the street started to voice cries of alarm, their own calls rippling through to the people in the tavern like a ripple across a millpond, causing momentary confusion as to what gossip took precedent. The danger approaching from the street took on the form of a troop of Minotaur guards who barged their way through the crowd, dispersing the gathered onlookers with a threat of the brute strength they possessed.

The people inside the restaurant suddenly parted, shuffling back as fast as they could, desperate to find some space from the monstrous creatures bearing down on them, some suffering cuffs and shoves as several huge figures started barging through the crowd. Out in the street the cries of alarm were turning into wails of anguish and pain as the rest of the troops set about clearing the area.

Thomas immediately sensed something was wrong as the owner of the *Fickle Fish* and the harbourmaster went pale, as if someone had turned a tap on their feet and drained all the blood from their bodies.

"What is the meaning of this?" roared a deep bass voice. Thomas swivelled in his seat to see the largest, blackest, Minotaur he had ever seen stamping across the floor towards them, muscles rippling as if the creature had been working out in a gym with action movie stars from the 1980's cinema.

"How dare you pheasants even entertain sitting at our table." The Minotaur continued reaching out and lunging for the occupants of the table, unaware of his grammatical error.

Mathius was on his feet in a second, blades leaping into his hands even as the long bench was wrenched out from under the remaining crewmen and sent crashing into the bar, the bright alcohol bottles shattering under the devastating impact. Weyn dropped heavily onto his back; Thomas went sprawling and Ives found himself in the ridiculous position of leaning across the table with his fork sticking out of his mouth. The harbourmaster was not so lucky, falling first to the floor before finding himself hoisted up off his feet to dangle from the snorting Minotaur's hand.

"I will see you hanged for this, or possibly burnt aliv..." The monster snorted, his polished horns gleaming brightly, despite the dappled shade beneath the arbour, the vicious points inches from the suspended man. A grey haired, clearly older Minotaur guard leant forward and whispered something into the black Minotaur's ear, stopping the brute's comments in midsentence.

"What do you mean peasants, they are pheasants? That's what I said." The Minotaur retorted fiercely. "Birds have absolutely nothing to do with this." The grey guard continued to whisper making the black Minotaur angrier by the second as he tried to explain the mistake his prince had made.

"Pheasants, peasants, it matters little. My temper grows short Aelius. Remember who you are addressing. You may be the captain of the

Palace Guard but I assure you, you are wrong and I am right." He retaliated. "I am the Prince Regent Drummon. I am never wrong."

"You will be if you don't put my guest back on his feet." Rauph stated calmly.

Thomas slowly rose from the floor, moving his hand to his cutlass, sensing the growing atmosphere of violence about to erupt. The huge Minotaur grunted then threw the man in his hand physically out across the restaurant, sending the harbourmaster crashing across several tables before his left leg caught on one of the beams supporting the roof. There was a sickening snap as his unfortunate victim fell to the floor groaning in pain.

"Oh dear," Drummon stared directly down at Rauph, attempting to intimidate and goad the seated Minotaur into action. "His feet don't seem to be working too well. Now what poor manner of a Minotaur are you? Which clan do you come from and why would you ever allow humans to sit at the same table as we do?"

The Prince Regent stopped, his nostrils flaring as he scented the creature sitting calmly before him. There was something familiar about the chestnut brown, shaggy haired creature. Something... He moved his huge head closer, directly over the surface of the table, his nose inches from the navigator of the *El Defensor* then took a deep sniff.

The whole table flew up into the air, catching Drummon under the chin and sending him reeling with a snort, his immense horns catching one of the beams above as his head snapped back. The edge of the table crashed to the floor, the remains of the food slopping across the tiled surface and over the Minotaur's hooves. The Prince Regent roared in protest, snatching a spear from the older guard and turning with murderous intent to kill the unkempt shaggy upstart who had dared to challenge him so openly.

Rauph stood at his full eight-foot height, his two worn long swords unsheathed from the scabbards at his back and held with unwavering steady hands. Thomas stood to the left, his own cutlass out, the enchanted edge gleaming in the sunlight. Ives stepped to the right, his white sword, fashioned from the tooth of some enormous monster from bygone days faintly luminescent in the shadows.

Aelius moved forward to support his Prince, despite having had his spear taken from him, only to stop in mid-step as he found the points of two daggers pressing into his side between the breastplate and side plates of his armour.

"I can assure you my thrust will be fatal." Mathius whispered coldly. "Let's just keep calm and see what happens, yes?" Aelius nodded his head slowly; aware that his fellow Minotaur guards were too far away in the crowd to aid him before the mortal strike occurred. He was a veteran for a reason and knew his time would come to act if he bided it.

Drummon had no such sense and charged in with the spear held high. Thomas swung once, his cutlass whipping through the air, shortening the spear by two feet and leaving the charging creature with just a stick to fight with but the black Minotaur was too into his charge to notice.

Rauph brought his swords together, forming a cross shape to parry the thrust, pushing the staff of the spear up high. The Prince Regent kept advancing trying to use his bulk and speed to press the advantage, his majestic horns coming around either side of the parrying weapons, determined to pierce, gore and draw blood. Rauph instinctively recognised the ploy and brought his left sword down, striking the charging Minotaur's horn so hard the action yanked Drummon's head to one side and a large chip came away from its highly polished tip.

Drummon continued to charge, although his angle of attack was now lower, his head finally crashing into the Navigator's mid-section, lifting him from the floor. Ives stepped out to the side as the two creatures crashed past, powerless to intervene without stabbing Rauph by mistake.

The long swords clattered forgotten to the floor as the two titans wrestled amongst the tables. First one then the other appeared to get the upper hand as muscle and sinew fought and horns scraped and gouged.

Thomas smashed a chair onto the heavily muscled shoulder blade of the volatile Minotaur desperate to help Rauph get the upper hand and ended up holding just the leg of the chair, the rest of it smashing to splinters with no effect on the rampaging monster. Other Minotaur guards started to move into the inn forcibly ejecting some of the locals who could not believe what they were seeing. Gladiatorial contests of strength happened once a year when the Labyris contest occurred, not here in a tavern.

One Minotaur with a spiralled horn stepped forward, sword drawn, only to have two arrows slam into the wooden post next to him, the splintering force of the shots pausing the guard's advance in its tracks. The Minotaur looked across the room to see Weyn holding his bow at full stretch, another arrow already on the string, a smile on his face as if daring the creature to step closer.

Rauph threw the black Minotaur off him with a display of raw strength that was simply incredible. Drummon flew backwards through the seating area, chairs and table knocked from his path to career into the crowd. He hit a table hard, the legs snapping out from underneath it, the force of the fall dropping him to the ground.

The navigator quickly regained his feet, his shaggy chestnut pelt flecked with sweat and blood, snorting nostrils flaring for breath as he turned to follow through with his actions, now taking the initiative, charging himself, smashing Drummon back to the floor just as the black Minotaur got back to his feet.

A gasp rose from the crowd as Rauph's clenched fists rained down upon the dark pelt beneath him. Whispers started to pass from mouth to mouth; a strange Minotaur, who apparently held no animosity towards human kind, was fighting Drummon the Prince Regent and winning.

"I yield, I yield." Drummon cried, throwing his hands up trying desperately to protect his face and nose from Rauph's heavy blows. The navigator lifted his hand for one more punch when a silence fell over everyone in the tavern.

"What are you doing?" screamed a voice of authority. "Stop this at once." A large hand grabbed Rauph's raised wrist spinning him around to face an older female Minotaur in a blue dress. The navigator froze as he looked into her hate-filled eyes. Something deep inside him cracked open, like a forgotten treasure exposed to the sunlight after centuries hidden.

Her free hand struck his cheek, making Rauph start, the shock of the strike and his rush of memories enough to drop him to his knees. He instinctively lowered his head to the floor and uttered the words ingrained into him from birth.

"Forgive me Matriarch."

The words from the shaggy Minotaur caught Mora by surprise. Clearly whoever this Minotaur was, he knew the correct way to address her. She allowed her wrathful glare to wash over the occupants of the room, lingering on those who had allowed her son to be hurt in a common bar room brawl, only cut short due to Mora's firm command. She returned her gaze to the Minotaur who had dared to assault her son, taking in the huge shaggy creature, penitent before her: the unkempt chestnut hair, the worn swords, the battered, salt-stained armour and the dull horns devoid of decoration or mark of office. Who was this Minotaur?

"Who are you?" she demanded.

"Rauph," the kneeling creature replied, not daring to look up from the floor. "Chief navigator of the *El Defensor* under Captain Thomas Adams."

"Help my son back to his feet." Mora snapped at the surrounding guards. "Don't just stand there. Do it now!" The guards moved forwards in a rush, the terror on their faces clear, as they moved to assist the Prince Regent, helping him back onto his unsteady legs. Mathius and Weyn lowered their weapons, recognising the threat to the group was now no longer imminent, a nod from Thomas reinforcing the need to reduce the tension in the room.

"Aelius. How could you let this happen to my son? A public brawl. I shall ensure you will face a suitable punishment for this." Mora shouted angrily at the captain of the guard. He bowed his head resigned at whatever fate awaited him.

Mora looked back at the Minotaur who had dared lay a hand on her son, considering suitable punishments for such a treasonable act. However, something about this unkempt creature's voice was so familiar. Tingles ran along Mora's spine. It was like hearing a voice from a long-forgotten past. Something, some maternal instinct, made Mora lean forwards, brushing up the long hair at the back of Rauph's neck, lifting the rough chestnut braids to reveal a pale scar that she simply could not believe was there. Images of the ritualistic branding at his time of birth flooded her mind. It could not be.

"...Kristoph?" she uttered breathlessly.

Rauph dared to raise his eyes once more and met Mora's confused gaze.

"What are your wishes, Mother..." he replied.

The Labyris Knight
-: Part Two :-

Taurean Treachery and
Shifting Silver Sands

"They say that *Family* give you support,
care for you, nurture you,
rally around in times of trouble.
Yet in all my years as a healer,
I know that the worst physical,
mental, spiritual and financial harm
is done by *Family* too."

Overheard conversation
Albanee Ministry of Healing.

Chapter Eleven

The journey from Wellruff to the town of Lichfield ended up being a miserable and damp affair. The heavens opened with a rain shower that found Kerian's shoulders hunched and his collar turned up in a futile attempt to keep dry. Drops of water fell from the evergreen pines and deciduous trees bordering the trail with unerring accuracy, striking the shield on the warrior's back with metallic notes. Either the rain ran down the outside of the mirrored surface to soak his breeches, or trickled between the shield and its owner, soaking the shirt on his back and making it stick to his skin.

Before long, his wet clothes started rubbing and chaffing his tanned skin as he struggled to find some comfort and respite from the movement of the hostile stallion beneath him. His legs felt stiff and his bottom felt like it had been bouncing on a marble plinth.

There were some benefits to the weather. For one thing, the travellers sharing the road were few, most people seeking shelter and an open fire rather than suffer the discomfort the two travellers endured. This helped them maintain a good pace and allowed the odd scrumping of fruit from overhanging farmer's trees along the way.

The rain cleared just as they reached the top of a rise, the vantage point granting a view of Lichfield in all its glory as the sun came out to warm the earth. Kerian looked down upon the collection of inns and stores, munching a wrinkled apple as he took in the scene with a practiced military eye. The pleasant scent of petrichor improved his damp outlook, as he took in the rushing Mereya River, swollen from the recent rainfall. He noted the slight narrowing of the torrent where the ferryboat plied its monotonous trade and then groaned at the gathering of travellers waiting to cross. The river was running too fast for the ferry to operate. His heart sank. They could have a lengthy wait ahead of them.

"Ah, Lichfield." Octavian voiced aloud, breaking into Kerian's private contemplations. "In all my dreams I never thought I would be seeing you again so soon. You have not improved during my absence."

"How long has it been since you last came here?" Kerian asked, determined to show interest to the man who had remained so morose throughout their journey and intrigued at the opportunity of gaining some insight into his companion.

"About three months." The gypsy confessed. "I promised myself that the next time I passed through I would have made my fortune and have my own horse and servants." Kerian laughed aloud, drawing a scowl and a hurt look in response.

"Seriously...?" He tried to smooth over the slight. "You really expected to find your fortune in Wellruff?"

"It started out promising." Octavian shot back. "At least I was doing okay before I encountered the dreaded Kerian Denaris." Kerian thought about responding with something regarding the foolishness of gambling or joking about the livestock at the market laying golden eggs, then thought the better of it. He may be with the gypsy for some time and did not want to risk alienating him further.

"Well at least the road supplied us some food." He smiled, throwing his last apple across at his downcast guide who caught the fruit in mid air.

"Oh yes..." Octavian replied polishing the apple on his tunic. "How could I forget your positive attitude and opinion that the road will supply everything we need. Well I don't know about you but I would have preferred a stray deer or rabbit, or a chest of gold that had fallen off a wagon."

"Well it's still a possibility." Kerian grinned. He shaded his eyes trying to make out the ascending trail on the far side of the river. "In fact, I think I can see a loaded wagon with a wonky axle dropping a chest just at the top of that rise."

"We better head down and join the queue." Octavian remarked. "The sooner we cross over the Mereya the better. When it gets hot down by the river, the mosquitos start to bite and Lichfield's mosquitos are big!"

They dug their heels into their horses and Octavian cantered off down the trail, leaving a stationary Kerian behind, until Toledo looked up and realised it was time to go. Then with a sigh, the stallion clopped lazily down the road after the gypsy determined to take his own time, regardless what his impatient rider thought.

This was just Kerian's luck, having to rely on a depressed guide and a stubborn bad-tempered mount. He tried to smile, tried to see the good side in all of this but as yet the sun had not broken through the clouds in his mind. He needed to handle Octavian carefully. The man seemed duty bound to honour his loss with the dice but something told Kerian he could only push him so far.

* * * * * *

The Mereya churned muddy and brown, turbid with the run-off from upstream. Vegetation and debris swept past at a pace, making any ferry crossing fraught with peril. A thick rope trailed across the river, disappearing into a small building on the far side, its flat roof adorned with a series of signalling flags. The lowing of oxen from the building echoed faintly across the river, answered by another team of the large lumbering beasts located on this side of the swollen ford. The animals were housed in a twin of the wooden building on the far bank, the other end of the sodden rope coiled around a large winch visible through a slotted window.

The oxen walked in large circles, harnessed to a rotating capstan powered by their forward motion. The beasts were encouraged by an overseer with a switch and a bundle of food that dangled enticingly before them. The food was lowered when the ferry was stationary and then raised to encourage the beasts to walk towards their meal when the ferry was in use. As the capstan turned, it engaged a series of cogs that slowly turned the winch, gathering in the thick rope and moving its length across the river.

The ferry remained docked at the near bank, the heavy rope securely fixed to a mast at the centre of the vessel. It was easy for Kerian to imagine the ferry pulled across the water by one team of oxen as they turned the elaborate pulley system, before the other team of oxen dragged it back the other way when the return journey was required.

Despite the groans from the crowd, no amount of cajoling was going to make the ferryman attempt a crossing for at least an hour with the river running so high. He relied on his boat for his livelihood and was not about to risk this on the behest of impatient traders. As the sun heated up the land, the mosquitos came out just like Octavian promised and the ire of the crowd rose with the crimson swellings that marked banquets just had by the flying pests.

With nothing to do with his time, Kerian decided to take the opportunity to survey the sights that Lichfield had to offer. Octavian was quite happy for his charge to give him some space and smiled at the freedom offered.

"Will you be alright if I wander around?" Kerian checked, passing the reins of his stallion.

"Of course." The gypsy replied. "I need to get us some supplies for the rest of our journey."

"How will you afford it?" Kerian enquired suspiciously. Octavian looked over at a group of bored merchants and their guards sitting around a fire pit, then held up his hand and flashed his dice.

"I have a feeling the road is going to provide." He smiled slyly, before walking both his mount and Toledo over to the group and asking if he could join the travellers with a gleam in his eye and a smile on his lips.

Kerian shook his head and set off towards the stalls set up along the main street, determined to banish the images of chaos that ran through his mind, each scenario ending with the two of them fleeing a troop of irate merchants and guards who pursued them with revenge gleaming in their eyes. He hoped Octavian knew what he was doing. They only had the two horses to their name and could not afford to lose them. They were also stuck on this side of the river. If they caused trouble, they could find themselves not getting passage on the ferry.

Before long, he found himself swept up in the sights and sounds. There were people here with skin so dark it was almost tinged blue. Turbans and robes dyed in bright oranges, reds, blues and greens adorned men and women talking in strange tongues. Tattoos appeared to signify tribal identification of people and races of all kinds. The same colours gathered with each other, clearly travellers from strange lands passing through to exotic destinations limited only by Kerian's lack of imagination.

Stallholders appeared to be selling from transient spots. A spread blanket covered in little wooden carvings of animals with ivory horns, squat muscular forms, or creatures with long slender necks. Others sold small pots formed from bright coloured mosaic pieces or long pipes to smoke fragrant weed. A snake charmer weaved a golden snake backwards and forwards, catching Kerian's attention and a shudder as he noted the golden winking scales and remembered the deadly dagger left behind in the temple at Stratholme.

Kerian paused near an open fire where a woman turned kebabs on skewers over the glowing coals, the meat dripping fat and sizzling as she waved a fan to make the coals glow brighter. Kerian found his mouth watering; he was famished having only eaten a couple of apples on the road. The trader looked up at him and smiled inviting him to buy.

He put his hand into his pocket and felt the cold edge of one small coin. Pulling the currency out he looked at the end of his finances and debated whether he should spend his final money on the food. The seller waved the fan again, blowing the tantalising aroma in his direction. The temptation was too much. He flipped the coin towards her and sealed the deal; the guilt and self-reproach could come later.

The meat was sticky and chewy, each mouthful hot and succulent. The sliced onion still held crunch and wedges of charred peppers squirted hot juices as his teeth devoured the snack. For the briefest of moments, all of Kerian's worries fell away as he succumbed to the tastes in his mouth and sighed with delight.

Kerian flicked the wooden skewer towards a basket for waste and watched it bounce off the rim and fall to the floor. The young lady cooking the kebabs tried not to laugh as Kerian flushed with embarrassment, bent over to pick up the stick from the ground. As he moved to drop the stick into the basket a slender hand came from the other side and moved to drop her refuse into the basket causing Kerian's skewer to fall to the floor once more.

"Oh, I'm sorry," came the apologetic response.

"No, it's fine." Kerian replied lifting his head from the floor to come face to face with a pair of sapphire blue eyes that he instantly recognised.

"You!" stammered the maid from the *Lusty Mermaid*, her face going pale as she suddenly realised who the man was before her. "How did you find me so fast?"

"Give me back my money?" Kerian snarled, moving to come around the basket, even as the girl tried to dodge the opposite way. "I gave you a tip. I showed you kindness. Why did you take my property?" The look in the girl's eyes as she glanced anxiously around confirmed Kerian's assumption. She was guilty.

He lunged forward, hand outstretched to grab the girl's clothes, aiming to snag her shoulder but instead, he found himself missing her and stumbling over the wastebasket as the maid twisted away, her years of avoiding lecherous wandering hands at the *Lusty Mermaid* serving her well.

Kerian cursed as he struggled to remain on his feet, his legs tangling with the basket and threatening to drop him on the floor. He glimpsed the girl running into the crowd, the pack on her back bobbing up and down as she ran. He took up the chase without hesitation and was after her in seconds. That was his money, his future, running down the street and he wanted it back.

People in the crowd stared hard at the sight of the young girl fleeing along the road with Kerian in pursuit and he was surprised to see the concern on their faces. He never considered how it would look to these bystanders, a young girl, clearly terrified, pushing and shoving through the crowd as she fled from an older man. Several travellers seemed to be considering whether to leap to her aid, then took one look at Kerian's icy glare and opted to step out of his path just as quickly.

The maid took a running jump across a cloth on the ground covered in little nodding sculptures and polished stones but she landed badly, slipping over onto her back and crashing into some crates filled with chickens. The stallholders roared in outrage and started shouting and cursing at her, only to have Kerian charge over, kicking more of their produce aside as he closed on his quarry. He grabbed her roughly before she could regain her feet, holding her by the shoulder and shaking her violently.

"Hand over my money and I will let you go on your way." He growled. She looked at his angry face, then past him at the crowd of disgruntled traders and travellers and opened her mouth to scream as loudly as she could.

Kerian placed his hand over her mouth, reacting on instinct and only making his situation more damning for the onlookers. The maid bit down on his finger, making Kerian snatch his hand away and it appear that he was about to strike her. Several sets of rough hands latched onto him and dragged him roughly away.

"What are you doing?" Kerian yelled. "Get your hands off me!" He found himself spun around to face a group of people who yelled and shouted at him in a language he did not understand, clearly upset how he was treating the girl. Kerian tried to pull away, tried to turn back around and grab the maid but every time he tried, they spun him back again and started yelling and jabbering at him.

Kerian put his hands up in a motion to stop the man that was yelling the loudest and then glanced over his shoulder to see that his thief was already on her feet and escaping. The screaming and shouting continued, despite Kerian not paying attention and physical shoves followed to emphasis the anger in the words. There was only one thing to do.

He turned and smiled sweetly, causing the trader to cease his yelling and nervously smile back, then Kerian hit him as hard as he could, delivering a vicious uppercut that crunched as it landed. Kerian set off after his quarry, a roar of indignation and fury coming from the people behind left him.

The young woman now had a good lead and continued to dodge around obstacles, nipping between rows of brightly dyed robes, slipping past street performers, pushing people out of the way who balanced large packages on their heads or shoulders. As she ran towards the distant ferry she screamed out a name Kerian could not recognise.

"Stop thief!" he shouted after her, determined that there would be no more misunderstandings. She ran past a large cage containing several parrots who took up Kerian's call and mimicked 'stop thief' to anyone that cared to listen. People turned to watch and instead of leaping to assist, sent their hands searching for their own goods, patting pouches and pockets to ensure they had not been victims.

Their chase had now reached the rear of the queue waiting for the ferry. Kerian cursed as he tried to push through travellers who had waited so patiently and now saw his rushed passage as that of someone attempting to take the space they had spent most of the morning waiting for.

"Excuse me!" he shouted. "Coming through!"

"There's a line here!" one traveller shouted in a dialect Kerian understood. "Get to the back and wait your turn."

People were boarding the ferry at the far end, cattle, camels, horses, wagons and travellers with belongings perched upon their heads or backs. Kerian realised his target was aiming to get onto the ferry and put the river between them and he redoubled his efforts to close the distance. Twisting and turning, trying to slip through the crowd like liquid oil running down the keen edge of a sword, Kerian found that the irate people waiting in line and obstructing his passage turned his efforts into something more akin to lumpy porridge clinging to a wooden spoon!

He shoved one man aside, making the traveller drop the covered pot he held under his arm, allowing three red and black striped serpents to slither out and slither across the dry earth desperate for sanctuary from the screams of the crowd scampering desperately to get away from them. Kerian was oblivious to the fact, focusing intently on the young woman darting through the crowd ahead of him.

The pole marking access to the ferry suddenly lowered, indicating the vessel was full and setting off on the first crossing of the day. Kerian grinned, realising the young maid had left it too late and would now not make it, allowing him to slacken off his frantic pace.

He had her. There was no way she could escape.

Signal flags rose on the roof of the wheelhouse, answered by the observers on the far bank and the food was lifted from the oxen, making the beasts lumber forwards and start taking up the slack in the thick rope. Inch by inch the rope started to move around the wheel and the ferry eased from the shore.

The maid continued screaming for assistance and suddenly there was a young man with spiky black hair, a rash of acne and a tattoo on his neck standing at the rail, waving his arms about, gesturing for the young woman to jump from the ramp. He motioned with his broad arms that he would catch her. Kerian dug in his heels and pumped his arms furiously. This girl was not getting away. Not if he had his way! As she jumped, Kerian lunged for the pack on her shoulders, his fingers making purchase as she flung herself across the gap into her partner's arms. Kerian's teeth snapped together as he found himself pulled off the bank and into the muddy water. Vegetation slapped against his legs and water spray soaked him to the skin, the freezing temperature of the water sending needles of fire into his lower body as he held on resolutely to the prize in his grasp.

"Let go of me!" she screamed. "Let go."

"Not a hope!" Kerian yelled back, determined not to give up. His hazel eyes blazed defiantly at the couple as the young man struggled to pull his terrified companion into the ferry against the pull of both Kerian and the river.

"Help me Stefan!" she screamed anew. "Get him off me." There was a flash of steel and a dagger appeared in the young man's hand. Kerian stared up in horror, knowing he could not let go and parry any attack or he would risk falling fully into the rushing water below. The maid screamed as her companion lunged with the blade, the weapon slicing through her pack and making it come away from her shoulder, dropping Kerian lower into the churning river. He hung on desperately, the drag from his weight through the water putting strain on the already jeopardised integrity of his lifeline. Stefan grinned at Kerian's struggles then raised the dagger to cut the final tie.

"What are you doing?" the young woman wailed to her partner. "The gems are in my pack!" The smile melted from Stefan's face in an instant, instead of trying to cut the bag he now realised he needed to cut loose the man holding it. He adjusted his hold on the dagger and leaned out over the side. Kerian stared up helpless, realising he had no room to manoeuvre, whilst swinging from the maid's shoulder strap. He struggled to bring up his feet as the dagger flashed down, dragging the maid towards him and making the man's attack miss completely, drawing a scream from the girl. He took in the sight of other passengers on the barge observing the turmoil and starting towards him, presumably seeing the image of an old man grabbing at a defenceless young girl.

"Thief!" Kerian yelled, desperate to make his case clear. "Thie..."

The dagger flashed inches before his face as Stefan lunged again, the blade catching on the material of the pack and slicing the back of Kerian's clenched hand. Blood flowed from the wound but Kerian was determined to hang on as the waters beneath him churned and frothed.

People were yelling now, some confused, others amused by the entertaining event happening before their eyes. Kerian felt like his arms were ripping from his sockets but he refused to give in, determined not to let go. He swung up a leg, finally pulling it from the suction of the dragging water and tried to hook his arm around the maid's struggling form. If he could pull her over the side with him, he could obtain his belongings without the outside interference of her dagger-wielding lover.

He tried to dig deep with the reserves of strength that remained, only to hear a loud rip that seemed to be much louder than the turmoil around him. Kerian stared wide-eyed as the stitching on the pack start to loosen beneath his hand, one strand popping free at a time. His boot slipped from its perilous perch as Stefan's dagger slashed again, catching the material of the pack and finally severing it. Kerian found himself falling backwards into the brown water, the pack tearing open as he fell, a dazzling rainbow of tumbling multi-coloured gems twinkling after him.

The Mereya closed over Kerian's head in a rush, barely leaving him time to gasp a breath before he found himself tumbling in the current, his body dragged downstream as the might of the storm waters took hold. His skin felt on fire as the cold torrent thundered across his body. His heart pounded loudly in his chest as the current hammered him down, the shield at his back jarring against the riverbed before he was flung upwards back into the daylight.

Kerian gasped as his head broke the surface, then floundered, dropping below the water, allowing some of the river to pass into his open mouth. He surfaced again, coughing and retching, disorientated and completely at the mercy of the flood. Flailing about with his arms, he tried to turn onto his back and float but the shield seemed determined to drag him down in the water. He bounced and spun about, turning first one way then the other, flashes of little shanty huts and tall silver blue trees whipping past his vision. He was out of breath, exhausted and in no condition to swim for shore.

Something wet and dark brown barrelled through the water towards him, making Kerian splutter in horror, tales of carnivorous water lizards playing cruelly in his mind. As it closed he realised it was a log that had been lifted by the floods upstream and sent down the river with all the other detritus. Kerian reached out as it angled past, flinging his weary arms across his makeshift float and thanking his unlikely saviour as he was swept away.

From his position of relative stability, Kerian was able to look around and spot both sides of the river. He took a deep shuddering breath, then identified the nearest shore, not sure exactly which side of the Mereya it actually was but determined to get out of the water and back onto dry land before a real water lizard or hungry fish decided to nibble on his aged form.

He cursed his luck at losing the maid and his gems, then took stock on his destination. It looked miles away from this low vantage point! He lowered his head and began a slow stroke to shore.

* * * * * *

It seemed as if hours had passed before the muddy bottom of the riverbed struck Kerian's knee. He jerked initially, thinking something was attacking him, before looking up and seeing the tangled reed bed ahead of him. Dragging himself to his feet, slipping and sliding on the treacherous boggy ground at the edge of the river, he finally squelched free and crashed exhausted onto the grass. Time and place had no meaning. Kerian just wanted to close his eyes and sleep until he woke and then go to sleep some more.

"Uh hum!" came a familiar voice. "Are we disturbing you? Or are you still intent on chasing defenceless young women across the countryside?"

Kerian craned his neck and looked up to see its owner, complete with his ever-infectious smile sitting upon his horse, unfortunately the psychotic golden stallion followed close behind. Toledo whinnied as if laughing at his rider's moist state and picked a tuft of tasty grass to nibble on, one eye glaring in Kerian's direction. It snorted and shook its head, practically daring Kerian to consider getting on its back in his sodden condition.

"I see that whilst I have been obtaining supplies you have been taking a swim and getting some of the local beauty treatment." Octavian continued, gesturing firstly at the mud splattered all over Kerian's form and then behind him to where a small mule covered in supplies was trailing. "I thought the intention was to not cause problems and to keep a low profile?" he remarked rising one eyebrow. "The ferry is there for a reason. It is not a good idea to try and swim across otherwise everyone would be doing it."

With a groan that felt as loud as every ache and pain he had, Kerian pulled himself wearily to his knees.

"Where are we?" he asked, with a mouth that felt filled with half of the riverbed. "Where is the ferry?"

"We are about half a mile downstream from the crossing." Octavian replied. "There is no ferry anymore. The signal house is aflame, the oxen stampeded and the rope burned through. It appears whoever your elusive friends were; they are not keen on you being able to catch up with them again." The gypsy shook his head slowly from side to side.

"Why is it that you appear to bring out this trait in most of the people who know you?" Kerian bit back his response and flicked a glob of mud from his tunic, sending it spiralling into the bull rushes.

"So how long before the ferry is fixed?" he asked, stealing himself for the answer he guessed would be coming. "A few hours... a couple of days?"

"More like weeks." Octavian replied firmly, shaking his head again. "So I guess that sadly our journey is at an end. To think I worked so hard at getting Dorian the Donkey here. We will just have to return to Wellruff and think of some other way to pass the time."

"I'm not letting those tradesmen get away with my pendant." Kerian snarled, his ire starting to rise within him. He paced before the mounted gypsy, his mind churning in anger as the mud dribbled down from his clothes. "There must be a way. There just must be." Octavian flushed, knowing the only option available but not willing to offer the dangerous lifeline.

Kerian paused as his mind replayed what Octavian had told him about the region. Then he looked up at the young man and noticed the jovial nature had slid from his face, as if he had recognised Kerian had already concluded what he was dreading.

"Didn't you say we could travel through the Vaarseeti Desert?"

"I told you before." Octavian replied gritting his teeth. "There is nothing out there, nothing but miles and miles of shifting sand dunes. No settlements, no taverns, no ways to make money... nothing."

"Well surely there are other travellers considering the route? I mean, now the ferry has broken."

"They aren't that stupid." Octavian spat. "Besides, I did not agree to take you to such a place. You did not pay me enough for that."

Kerian picked at a stubborn lump of mud lodged between his tunic and his neck, only to discover something hard within the mess. He brushed it off then stared at it hard as his companion continued complaining loudly. A glimmer of red glowed through the mud. Kerian continued polishing it between his finger, confirming he held a small ruby. It was the last gemstone he owned from the dragon horde, the last connection he had with the island where he had sacrificed everything for Colette apart from the shield he wore secured on his back.

He turned back to Octavian and flicked the gemstone towards the gypsy, who fumbled the catch and bounced the gem from hand to hand before he finally caught it and secured the jewel.

"Consider yourself paid." Kerian smiled. "Just think of it this way. It's the ideal opportunity for us to get away from it all."

Chapter Twelve

Colette's brow creased into a frown as she trailed her fingertip along the spines of the dust covered books in Rauph's cabin. She knew what she was looking for had to be in one of these long undisturbed grimoires but the question was where? The mage reached forward and pushed a glass sphere to one side, the scarlet scorpion within, frozen in time, tail arched and pincers extended, in a pose it would retain forever.

The Anatomy of Magic, MacLeod's Ancient Lore, Protection Against Psionic Attack, Herbology and the Identification of plants that can eat you, Jay's Five Faces of Fear, Ye Monstrous Compendium, Grey's Spell Anatomy, Practical Skills and Magical Diagnosis. Colette brow puckered further. She needed to find something to protect the ship, a spell that would mask them from scent as well as sight. Maybe transmogrification held the key, or maybe even a complex illusion?

Her finger slid to a halt, a drift of grey dust marking her journey's end. *Davidson's Dark Arts.* It was a cumbersome volume and Colette grunted as she slid the leather-bound tome free and carried it over to the large table the Minotaur used for his navigation, wrinkling her nose as dust rose from the book and tickled her nostrils.

The book creaked open, the spine cracking from such a long period of disuse. Colette paused for a moment, feeling the richness of the parchment making up the pages, gazing at the handwriting, the elaborate cursive swirls and loops and the illustrations penned with such incredible artistry. She hoped secretly that one day she would create her own volume but these thoughts were for later. The fact that the Scintarn Hounds had tracked the ship so successfully had the mage concerned. She needed to find a way to travel undetected, to mask them all and keep the remaining crew safe when they travelled through the ship's graveyard.

They had lost too many. Thomas projected an image that was aloof and unfeeling but Colette could never act that way. The pressure of trying to protect everyone bore down on her like an invisible weight upon her shoulders.

The mage thought back, her mind remembering fellow travellers who had slipped away. Then she remembered hazel eyes and a weathered face that despite its sternness masked a heart of gold beneath. For a second her eyes watered before she brushed them sternly aside. A good mage always focuses on the task at hand, she could let her feelings show later.

Flipping the pages over to the index, Colette traced her finger down the page. There had to be something here. *Philosopher's Stone, Midas Touch, Wall of Force*... Oh, this was so frustrating!

"Why don't you help me?" she snapped, turning to the ruined chair in the corner of the cabin where a dark shape sat watching her silently. Her observer did not reply and simply stared out from his seated position because he was dead.

Colette stormed over to the chair, taking in the desiccated corpse sitting there, still attired in his magic robes, now coated in a thick layer of dust. Her blue eyes lingered on the mortal wound in the man's chest, the result of a ghastly spear wound that had taken her mentor from this world of the living, leaving his spirit trapped in ghostly limbo.

"How can you sit there so silently Master Sumnar?" she yelled. "Do you care nothing for this crew? Do you just intend to brood in silence, allow more good people to die?" The high mage's corpse remained silent, showing no signs of life, no movement of its head or bony gesture from its hands. Colette threw her arms up in frustration. It did no good trying to talk to her master when he apparently had no intentions of listening. The last time he had spoken was to shriek out the name of their Elven betrayer, Scrave, back at Stratholme.

"I don't know why Thomas still permits your presence aboard Lucas Sumnar!" Colette snapped, dropping the master title to emphasise her disappointment. "It's not as if you are holding the *Wizardseeker* any longer. If you don't care about anyone, be gone from here." She turned away heading for the door of the cabin. Her hand touched the handle of the door, intent on yanking it open and slamming it on her tutor when a dry rasping voice issued from the corner of the room.

"You cannot stop people from dying on the *El Defensor*..." the dead mage spoke, his voice little more than a whisper. "It is the curse of this vessel; you cannot prevent it any more than I could when I was alive. More are destined to die. Let them finally be at peace. Who are you to decide if this is right or wrong?" Colette moved to discuss the matter further, only to see that Lucas had lapsed back into silence. Her master just sat there, a dried husk, dead and unresponsive.

"It appears I was mistaken in believing you cared." Colette replied, leaving the cabin and shutting the door behind her.

Silence descended on the room like a thick blanket, every sound on the ship muffled beneath its weight. Nothing moved within the room, even the orb containing the red scorpion refused to rock, despite the gentle movement of the *El Defensor*. A heavy sigh filled the air, long, drawn out, filled with emotion, like the gasp from a fresh cadaver moved for the first time.

Despite the sigh, the high mage's corpse remained stationary, simply observing everything as if in quiet contemplation. Then in a slow, deliberate movement, one long bony digit twitched and the book of spells still lying open on the chart table flipped over a few more pages before falling open at a particular one.

Lucas Sumnar could do no more. He knew he had to conserve his strength. Dark times were coming for the crew of the El Defensor. He had seen them and he knew if he did not rest, he would not be able to help his friends when it really mattered.

* * * * * *

Thomas looked towards Rauph for some guidance, an indication that the Minotaur wanted them to break free from the troops boxing them in and preparing to march them away from the *Fickle Fish* but the navigator seemed in a daze, oblivious to the glances his captain was sending him.

What was wrong with the navigator? Why had he called the female Minotaur his mother? Was this where Rauph originally came from? Was this his home?

Thomas turned to check on his fellow crew members, Ives and Weyn, who were supporting the harbour master between them, the man's face pale and etched with the agony of his shattered leg. Mathius had somehow managed to disappear in the confusion, blending in with the shadows and becoming one with the crowd as the Minotaur had rudely ushered them from the Inn. Even now loud crashes and cries of dismay rose from the crowd as several of the troops set about destroying the quaint establishment.

"No please don't do that." Thomas turned to Aelius the captain of the guard, desperate to make a case for the innkeeper. "They did no harm. We went into the *Fickle Fish* and showed disrespect, not them." The aged Minotaur tried to appear stern and uncaring but even he flinched when a flaming brand twirled through the air to land in the thatch of the building.

"I'm sorry." He muttered so only Thomas could hear. "Examples have to be made to keep the population in line."

Thomas felt the accusing look from the innkeeper land on him like a lash, although no physical contact was made, the mental blow was pain enough for the captain. He watched as the man hugged his sobbing wife and held the hand of his child, his gaze unfaltering and unforgiving.

"I will make this right." Thomas shouted, as the Minotaur grouped together and commenced marching away, pushing the crew before them. "I swear I will make this right." The captain stumbled on the cobbled surface and found when he regained his feet the face of the innkeeper was lost amongst the crowd but he had seen enough and swore he would keep his word, whatever it took. Ives nodded at Weyn as they picked up the pace, supporting the harbour master between them.

"See I told you so." He grunted, gesturing to the smoke rising from the *Fickle Fish.* "Every time we find a nice place to eat it is always the same. Up it goes in smoke. I would really like to have an opportunity to eat somewhere twice!"

Weyn just kept his head down, taking swift glances at the crowd on either side of them and realising that their arrival was causing more than simple destruction. People were gesturing towards Rauph and appeared elated. He had seen this reaction from crowds once when a famous bard had come to sing, adoring fans, stretching and craning their necks for a glance of the famous singer and the opportunity to listen to his music. The thing was, as far as Weyn knew, Rauph was no singer. So why the adoration?

Ives turned his attention to the man they carried between them.

"You would think they would treat their harbourmaster with a little more respect." He remarked.

"I'm not really the harbour master." The injured man flushed. "I'm the harbourmaster's assistant. I run, fetch and stand in for him when he is asleep in his cabin."

"Who is this idle lout?" Ives demanded. "He doesn't seem much, especially as we arrived at the quayside after crashing into the bridge and yet he still never thought to raise his head and look out."

"I believe he is at the gambling pits." came the reply. "He likes to watch the gladiators and places bets on the side."

"Does he win?"

"Rarely, and when he loses, he is often in a foul mood and takes it out on others around him."

"I would like to have a word in his ear." Ives remarked. "You would think he would look after the welfare of his associates."

"His slaves you mean." Came the defeated reply. "I will be in so much trouble for this." Then his face spilt with a wide grin and he chuckled despite the pain.

"What is it?" Ives asked. "What's so funny?"

"You would need a step stool to reach my master's ear. He is eight-foot-tall just like your shaggy friend over there."

"He's a Minotaur?"

"Everyone of power is in Taurean. We all just do as our masters order us."

Weyn butted into the conversation.

"Has anyone noticed we have one missing from our party?"

Thomas moved closer, overhearing Weyn's innocent revelation.

"Keep it down!" he hissed. "Let's not draw attention to the fact."

The group continued to move slowly along the shop-lined street before entering a large open plaza with a curved colonnade around the perimeter. Fountains splashed elegantly into large ponds, miniature rainbows winking where the sun reflected on the water. Brightly coloured ornamental fish swam lazily about the lily pads, mouths gaping wide at the surface when anyone came near, eagerly sucking down the food thrown to them.

Statues of Minotaur on huge plinths were dotted around the area, their muscular physiques and fearsome weapons frozen in time for the people of Taurean to observe and wonder at the masters towering above them.

"What is this place?" Thomas asked.

"The *Plaza of the Fallen*." The harbour master's assistant replied. "It is here we remember the mighty, here we honour our previous masters."

"Who is that one?" Thomas asked, pointing out a large statue of a Minotaur standing proud, his face looking towards the sun. The sculptor had made every effort to ensure his subject appeared fearless, heavily muscled legs slightly parted, ornate armour and a huge double-headed axe at his side. The withered remains of flowers and offerings were spaced at the base of the statue, turning it into a shrine of remembrance.

"That's Kristoph, the prince." The injured assistant replied. "He went sailing with his brother Drummon and there was an accident on the lake. No one ever found his body."

"Kristoph?" Ives remarked. "Isn't that the name they were calling Rauph?"

The man struggled to turn his head, wincing in pain, taking in the long shaggy haired Minotaur walking behind them. "That Minotaur could never be the prince. Look at his matted hair, his dishevelled appearance. I mean looking like that, no one would recognise the prince unless they looked really closely at the shape of his horns..." His eyes widened suddenly, before turning to examine the statue. "By the Gods... could it be?"

Thomas tried to scan the crowds through the small gaps between the Minotaur troops as they led the group towards a bridge that rose in sweeping, graceful curves at the far end of the plaza before stretching off towards a large elaborate building that appeared more opulent than the other structures below it.

"I presume that is the palace." Thomas asked, trying to gain more information from Aelius.

"Don't talk unless you are spoken to... pet!" snarled Drummon, pushing past Aelius and towering over the captain. "Or I will take great delight in shutting you up permanently."

Thomas turned towards Rauph, expecting his colleague to say something in his defence, but his navigator appeared subdued, even beaten, walking along head held low, his thoughts, for once, not telegraphed on his bovine face. Rauph was not shackled physically, but mentally it appeared he was helpless to resist the path destiny had placed him upon.

Drummon's pelt shone midnight blue in the sunshine, emphasising his thick muscular frame. The only change in his colour was the top of his head between his horns where there was a thinning patch. A pale scar clearly showed above his left eye, a reminder of yet another example of Drummon diplomacy. Massive curled black horns, oiled until they gleamed, towered above Thomas, the symmetry of the lethal tips now ruined by the chip Rauph had taken out of the right one.

The prince regent stared intently down at the captain as if daring him to speak again, then, confident there would be no more noise, the Minotaur stalked off through the group towards Rauph, his sheer size and strength physically intimidating Thomas to the point that he only realised he was holding his breath once the massive beast had moved away.

This was not a good situation. Just one of these Minotaur was sufficiently powerful enough to bring the three of them down and ten such warriors surrounded them, all adorned with gleaming armour, axes and spears. Then there were the others carrying the female Minotaur in her brightly coloured palanquin. They were sorely outnumbered and in no position to escape. He bit his lip nervously looking this way and that, before noticing a shadowy figure at the base of one of the immense columns lining the plaza.

Thomas squinted to be sure and recognised the cloaked figure of Mathius smiling back at him. Where did he manage to find a cloak and how had he obscured his features to escape capture? As he watched, the assassin turned silently away, the cloak revealed as a tablecloth from the *Fickle Fish*.

"What do you think they want with us?" Ives asked sweating at the physical effort required to keep assisting their injured colleague along. "Thomas can you help us for a moment?" he pleaded. "My shoulder feels as if it is about to snap off. I need help or I fear I will never roll a carpet again."

Thomas shrugged and walked over, resigning himself to the fact they were practically prisoners until they reached their destination. He tried to grasp the injured man but the three of them were making it more difficult to walk with any speed. A large sadistic Minotaur purposefully bumped into the three of them and sent both them and their charge sprawling on the cobbles.

"Why did you do that?" Ives snapped, forgetting himself. A solid backhand from the guard sent the merchant sprawling. Thomas went for his sword, Weyn for his bow, only to be answered by a ring of glittering spear points and Drummon laughing in the background.

"I don't think your pets are house trained" he jibed at Rauph.

The navigator did not respond and simply stood there silently with his head bowed. The spear points glittered in the sunlight, tension visibly rising in the group. It would take just one false step to turn this into a situation where blood would fly and lives would be lost.

An explosion of red and purple parrots blasted over the group, feathers flapping like rolling thunder in a tremendous cacophony of surprised squawks and squeals as they took flight from the plaza floor, launching themselves into the air. Several well-timed deposits of bird dung struck across the group splattering all across Thomas's tunic. A young child screamed in laughter running around waving his arms having spooked the birds and pretended to squeal the same sound as the departing psittacines, before returning to the closest pillar in the colonnade and running into the shadows in a fit of giggles.

The Minotaur guards started snorting at the sight, none more so than Drummon, who slapped Rauph across the shoulders before snapping orders to the group to get everyone moving again. One guard turned to the injured harbour assistant and threw him physically over his shoulder despite the man's pain-filled protests and the group began traversing the bridge, revealing a truly magnificent view of the beauty of the city of Taurean.

As the Minotaur and their 'guests' crossed the bridge the young child held out his hand to a cloaked man squatting at the base of one of the pillars.

"I did wot you wanted now where's me reward?" He gestured, snot running from his right nostril, his cheeks flush from running. Mathius flipped a copper bit towards the child, then pulled his tablecloth cloak more tightly around him and moved to follow the distant party.

"That's one copper bit and a meal you owe me Thomas Adams!" he muttered under his breath, knowing that before this would end Thomas would owe him much more than that.

* * * * * *

"What is Ashe doing?" Rowan asked, nudging Commagin's arm and getting a dark scowl from the Dwarven engineer as amber liquid slopped from a test tube he was holding and dribbled down his arm.

"How would I know?" he snapped, wobbling dangerously on the tall stool he had used to get up to his work bench. The Dwarf furiously licked his arm, ensuring not a drop of his latest alcoholic experiment was wasted. "He's making a costume of some kind."

"But where did he get all of those feathers from?" Rowan asked, nudging Commagin again and getting another loud grunt of disapproval.

"Be careful lass this has taken a while to get just right." the engineer warned sternly. "If you knock my arm one more time, I swear I will bar you from my laboratory whether you are a keen engineer or not."

Rowan smiled at the gruff nature of her colleague. It had taken a while for Commagin to get back to his usual grumpy self and Rowan was glad to see him stabilizing from the loss of his lab assistant. The wounds were still there, a distant stare, a moment of unexpected silence but Commagin had found something to focus his distress onto. If only the same could be said for Thomas.

When that man finished acting like James Tiberius Kirk, heading off to who knows where with his 'landing party' she was going to have stern words with him. He needed to open up to her, divulge the secret gnawing at him, be honest with his feelings and tell her he loved her. This was not the USS Enterprise and her captain was not going to end up dating a green skinned woman if Rowan had anything to say about it!

"What else are you working on?" she asked, breaking her thoughts by lifting a mass of wires, dead circuits and springs from the workstation, even as one ear listened in to the furious banging and clashing of Ashe on another work station at the far side of the room.

"Are you sure he isn't doing anything dangerous?" Rowan asked, twirling a screwdriver in one hand. "He does appear to be tackling whatever it is with some gusto."

"Oh pickled walnuts!" Ashe cursed as he dropped something with a tremendous clatter, before falling to the floor as he tried to retrieve it, pulling what looked like strips of canvas, feathers and thin canes down on top of him.

"I'm sure he is harmless." Commagin replied, adjusting his spectacles as he held the test tube up to the light, licking his lips enthusiastically. "Why can't you leave me a moment to assess the success of my latest endeavour and come back in about three hours or so?"

Rowan gently placed the wires back down onto the bench and turned to take in the mish-mash that was Commagin's workshop. Pots, pans, wires, test tubes, flickering flames in glass lanterns and multi-coloured liquids shot around the place like some futuristic transport system. Piles of manuals and textbooks piled precariously on surfaces filled with clutter.

A rack shaped like a fish, stuffed with small pieces of paper swam alongside a calendar dated 3027. Silver discs hung spinning on wires, humming softly as they turned. Tools of every shape and size dotted the floor, hammers, chisels, spanners socket sets and jar upon jar of rusty screws and nails. Inventions from years past and times yet to be, lay alongside models of tanks and strange automobiles, whilst flying machines hung from the ceiling or were shoved, wings broken, onto shelves. Pieces of genius lay forgotten and forlorn, amidst disasters and debacles, everything coated in a thick layer of dust.

Small glass cabinets held figurines of little fairies and small models of dragons sniffing flowers and pulling hand carts. There were boxes with lids created from mosaic mother of pearl, dusty tumblers filled with mould, discarded lotions or potions. Assorted bottles in lots of different shapes and sizes. Come to think of it there were an awful lot of bottles!

Another crash followed, a nut related profanity its companion, before a loud rustling and crunching sound announced that Ashe was heading in their direction. Rowan backed herself into a corner, checking her pockets to ensure there was nothing of value to lose and was just placing a polite smile on her face when the Halfling squeezed between two stacks of newspapers that wobbled ominously at his passage.

"Hi Rowan." Ashe beamed cheerfully, his face beaming despite the feathers plastered to his grimy face. "I don't suppose you have any glue over here do you?" Rowan looked around and spotted a green pot filled with something runny and swiftly passed it to the miniature inventor.

"What are you doing?" she asked sweetly.

"I can't tell you. Its top secret." Ashe winked conspiratorially. "I'm going to amaze everyone and get Sinders to fly at the same time. It is going to be amazing and... this is honey."

"Uh..." Rowan took a second to understand what Ashe was talking about. "Honey?" she asked.

"I think so." Ashe replied, twisting the lid off the jar and sticking his finger into the gloopy liquid inside. "See!" He pulled his finger out and stuffed it into his mouth, sucking noisily. "hunneee."

"I can't see any other type of glue around." Rowan apologised, watching Ashe making the most hilarious set of facial expressions as he sucked on his finger. "Commagin do we have any glue around."

"It's in the green pot." The Dwarven engineer shot back from his high stool perch. "You can't miss it. It looks like..."

"Hunneee!" Ashe gurgled.

* * * * * *

Taurean was beautiful, even if the upper echelon of its inhabitants were not. Thomas found wherever he looked it was like seeing a colour brochure for a summer holiday made real. The island was roughly circular, with bridges spreading out across the huge crystal-clear lake. The party had walked from the previous plaza to an area higher than anywhere else on the island. The buildings perched upon this mount were mostly white with terracotta tiled roofs and statues as far as the eye could see.

Huge spacious buildings, large open balconies, pillared entrances enclosing manicured gardens and tinkling waterfalls. The other obvious change from the tightly packed streets below were the guards. The more guards seemingly standing at your door, the more powerful a position you had.

Passers-by stopped what they were doing and bowed, voices dropped away to be replaced by respectful silence as the procession of guards and prisoners passed by. The captain noted that the palanquin curtains did not move in acknowledgement. For all Thomas knew the female Minotaur could be asleep in there. It was quite clear to him who was senior overseer here.

Then there were the slaves. Everywhere you looked there were human slaves or the ever-present visual representation of them. Statues of overseers whipping the human population in the act of construction marked the architect guild. Friezes of slaves toiling in the fields marked the agriculture guild. Humans in sandals and for want of a better description, togas ran from place to place, coloured beads around their necks marking them as brightly as the tattoos down their arms marked their ownership.

"Are all these people slaves?" Thomas asked Aelius, watching the humans running around and bowing their heads in respect as the procession passed them by. "Surely they can't all be slaves. Are there some people that live their own lives, have their own properties and dreams?"

"Humans are never treated as equals here." Aelius whispered back. "It is not permitted. If humans are offered freedom, then they will want more rights, better pay, positions of power. The matriarch has ruled this can never be. Taurean's rule here. Humans serve us. This is the way it should be.

It is the way it will always be. Now be quiet before I am forced to silence you."

Thomas closed his mouth and turned away, realising the spans of the bridge forked ahead, with the procession going to the left, instead of to the right where the bridge led across from the island over to the mainland and the towering pyramid at its far end, surrounded by mile upon mile of thick dark rainforest. Something about the structure caused shivers to run down the captain's spine. The pyramid was ominous, a brooding presence that towered over everything. It was a majestic monument that made him realise just how small he was in comparison.

Was it a temple? Did they undertake sacrificial offerings to their gods like the Aztecs? He hoped he would never know. The fork continued to swing around to the left leading up to the final courtyard outside the marble steps of the palace. The procession stopped and the palanquin lowered gently to the ground.

The guards sprang to attention as the curtain was held aside and the female Minotaur stepped out onto the palace steps. A thousand questions sprang into Thomas's mind and he opened his mouth to ask but a stern look from Aelius stopped him in his tracks. Mora gathered her blue dress about her and turned to address the group.

"I have decided you shall all be invited to a banquet to celebrate the return of my dear son Kristoph." The matriarch decreed.

"What!" Drummon snarled in disbelief. "Celebrate the return of Kristoph! We do not even know this is Kristoph. Why should we celebrate it?"

"It will not take long to identify Kristoph's markings and confirm his heritage." Mora replied icily. "Summon the physicians. Let this question be answered to silence those with little faith at this miracle that has befallen us. After all, not everyone can have a mother's intuition." Mora towered above them all, radiating power and might. Thomas found himself slightly in awe of her presence.

"I don't believe this!" Drummon fumed. "What about his pets. Do they stay too?"

"If Kristoph wishes." Mora replied, leaving it clear in her tone there would be no argument in this. She turned to Rauph and offered the smile of an animal about to eat its young. "Let us get you and your slaves inside, get you cleaned up and then you can tell us where you have been these last few years." Rauph looked up, his eyes taking in the palace as if he were in a dream and he did not believe what he was seeing.

"Welcome home son." Mora announced. "Welcome home."

* * * * * *

Scrave stood at the outskirts of Catterick and looked around him in disgust. What in the world was he doing back here? He hadn't liked the place the last time he visited and definitely had no desire to stay. He swung his arms about to fight off the chill in the air and rolled his neck, trying to iron out the kinks from being shrunk so small and then reverting to normal size, much to the disappointment of a hungry rat that had stalked him for the length of the sewer tunnel he had taken to freedom.

So what was he going to do now? What way was he going to go? Scrave took in the shining palace at the centre of the city, then the docks far below and the harbour where boats gently bobbed on a surface silvered by the clouds above. He could try the docks, although he would need some funds to obtain passage but passage to where? He looked about, taking in the paths leading away and the milestones at the side of the road giving the distance to exotic locales that the Elf had no desire to see. The green tinge from his eye made everything look surreal as if he were in some nightmare from a fairy tale gone horribly wrong.

"Go North." Scrave felt the words like fire ants crawling across his brain. He looked about searching for the voice that had given him the instruction, knowing even as he did so that it was all in his mind. Go North. How ridiculous! What was North anyway? Something hopefully more exotic and warmer than Catterick at least... He paused, suddenly remembering the volcano he had been trapped in. Okay, maybe not too warm! The Elf wandered over to the worn milestone and pulled back the grass at its base to reveal the place furthest from the top. *Al Mashmaah.*

It sounded exotic alright. Maybe even a little bit warm. He shrugged his shoulders. Okay, he would head North and see what Al Mashmaah had to offer. He had nothing else pressing to do after all!

He would just follow the funny voice in his head and see where it took him and afterwards, he would consider if maybe, just maybe, he was going ever so slightly insane.

Chapter Thirteen

Kerian looked down at a weathered milestone sitting at a jaunty angle on the edge of the trail and tried to make out the eroded letters upon its surface. Failing to comprehend the names mounted on the back of Toledo, he swung himself from the saddle and dropped to the ground. Holding his back and stretching to ease the stiffness from his journey, the weary rider bent to brush the surface of the stone and tried to discern the faded words.

"Al Mashmaah." He shook his head, trying to visualise a map of the world and realised he had no idea where he was. Toledo nosed closer, checking to see if his rider was hiding anything edible and pushing him with his head, annoyed at the lack of attention shown.

"Just where are you taking me, oh knowledgeable guide?" Kerian asked. "And how far away is this Al Mashmaah?"

"Away from it all." Octavian snapped, his mood still sour, despite the time they had spent on the road together. "Just like you wanted. You will know when we get to our destination because at that point our arrangement will be at an end and I will be taking my leave."

Kerian looked at his guide's sulky demeanour and decided enough was enough. They were travelling into territory that was alien to him, a region of unknown dangers and he was not going to do this with someone whose loyalty was questionable at best. Dusk was drawing in and it was time to address Octavian's childish attitude so that future days on the road would not be as morose as this last one had been. He looked at the sky above, reckoning they had an hour before night fell, then cast his eye about for a defensive position where they could camp. A ruined watchtower on a nearby hill seemed to fit the bill perfectly.

"Okay," he opened, faking another stretch. "I'm getting tired and I'm hungry. Why don't we make camp for the night in that ruin over there? You take the horses and I will hunt down a feast fit for a king. No one ever goes hungry when Kerian Denaris oversees the menu." Octavian shrugged in a non-committal way and glanced towards the pale semi-circle of the moon appearing as light started to leach slowly from the sky.

"If that is your wish." He replied. "I'll get the fire started, see to the horses and prepare the area like the good little guide I am."

"I shouldn't be too long." Kerian smiled back, ignoring the sarcastic comment from his companion. "Just prepare yourself to be amazed."

* * * * * *

The tower turned out to be more ruined than Kerian had realised. The wall facing the road was largely intact, but the rear of the structure had crumbled away years before, exposing rotten beams and the skeletal remains of a spiral staircase that no sane individual would consider climbing. Tumbled examples of moss-covered stonework littered the ground, amidst spindly bushes and gnarled trees that had sprouted across the ruin as nature slowly reclaimed the site.

Despite these inherent difficulties, Octavian had done a masterful job of clearing an area for their sleeping rolls and had assembled a fire pit that cast flickering orange light up the inside of the derelict building. The hobbled horses stood near to hand, munching on a pile of undergrowth that their guide had pulled from the wreckage and Kerian had to admit he was quite satisfied at their choice of camp, despite the fact there was no roof to the building. As long as it did not rain, there could even be the opportunity for a good night's rest.

"You are absolutely correct." Octavian remarked, looking at the spit turning over the fire. "I am definitely amazed." Kerian felt his face flush as he continued rapidly turning the spit over the flickering flame as if his life depended on it. Smoke rose from the charred, emaciated rabbit he had managed to stun accidentally with a rock thrown at its head, it's spindly form a meagre mouthful for one grown man, let alone two.

"Was it already dying?" Octavian laughed. "I can only imagine it must have seen you coming and staggered out of the brush." He crossed his eyes and pretended to hop over to Kerian in a last gasp fashion. "Oh, please Mr Kerian sir, please bash my brains in and make it quick so I don't suffer." He collapsed onto the bedrolls rolling in laughter, jerking his legs in the air and sticking his tongue out in a comical way. Kerian found he laughed as well and discovered the sound a pleasing one. It had been a long time since he had heard anyone laugh, let alone himself?"

"I would be more worried about which part you get?" Kerian smiled. "And I think because I am the chef and the mighty hunter, I should have the top end."

"Luckily for you I thought to get some supplies." Octavian replied walking over to their belongings and rifling through a saddlebag. The gypsy pulled out a squashed loaf of bread and a couple of root vegetables, holding them aloft like prize treasures. Then he paused and returned to the pack and retrieved a wineskin.

"We can make a good stew and have a drink at the same time!" he smiled. A long, lingering howl cut the air, causing Kerian to pause in turning the spit, the smile melting from his face. His free hand reached for a sword, only to realise once again that he had no weapon to use.

"It's only wolves." Octavian remarked. "Haven't you ever heard wolves howling at the moon before?"

"Oh, I have heard wolves." Kerian replied. "I have also heard and seen much worse. When I travelled upon the *El Defensor* I saw Scintarns."

"What's a Scintarn?" Octavian asked, kneeling down beside the fire pit and dropping a pan over the flame as he deftly peeled and chopped the vegetables. Kerian stared into space remembering the huge black hounds that prowled the wreckage in the ship's graveyard.

"Trust me you never want to find out."

"You have never told me of this *El Defensor*. It is a grand name for a small fishing boat is it not?"

"The *El Defensor* is a Galleon, a huge ship." Kerian replied. "Not the little ship I sailed into Wellruff aboard. We became separated and I have been trying to catch up ever since."

"If such a vessel had been nearby, I would have heard of it." Octavian responded. "Wellruff is a hive of gossip. It would have been on everyone's lips if a ship that large had sailed through." He looked over at Kerian who was still gazing sadly into space.

"There is someone special to you on that ship, yes?" Octavian watched as Kerian slowly nodded his head. "Do you love her?"

"More than words can say." Kerian replied, a lump forming in his throat. "I would do anything for her and that is why I must catch up with those traders. They hold the means for me to track the ship and I will get it back." Kerian's face suddenly hardened as the warrior within him came to the fore. He blinked, then turned to Octavian, taking in the man's flushed face and realised he had probably embarrassed his companion by confessing something so personal.

"Enough about Me." He remarked, cutting the meat from the rabbit and dropping it into the pan with the sizzling vegetables. "What about my enigmatic travelling companion Octavian? Do you have any family to speak of and more importantly how do they put up with you?"

"I have a wife Ana and a four-year-old daughter Iolander. They are far away from here." Octavian forced a smile as he poured a generous portion of wine into the pan and threw in a handful of red and orange spices. "They put up with me because I am an incredible cook." He lifted the spoon and sniffed at the stew.

"When did you last see them?" Kerian questioned, interested in this turn of conversation.

"About a year ago." Octavian replied, a tinge of sadness to his voice. "I had to leave them for their own protection." He paused swallowing hard. "I have been trying to get enough money to go back to them but life is always putting obstacles in my way."

"Like my amazing rabbit stew." Kerian joked, taking the spoon away from Octavian and sniffing it himself before letting the lumpy mess slop back down. "I bet you would do anything for them too."

"I already have." Octavian replied, his hand drifting to his pocket and touching it for reassurance.

"Are they in the direction we are travelling? Maybe we could call and say hello?"

"I would not be welcome if they were." Octavian replied. "I have not secured enough funds yet and would only put them in jeopardy."

Kerian turned to his companion not sure how to take the reply and smiled.

"Maybe when this is all over, we can go and see them together." He remarked. "If all goes well maybe I can help you with your shortfall."

"I doubt it." Octavian replied. "You have nothing of value that would help."

"I don't know." Kerian smiled. "A minute ago, I had an anorexic rabbit on a stick. Now I have a stew. It is strange how life provides. You just have to have a little faith. Now whilst we wait for the stew, why don't you pour me some wine and tell me where we are going."

Wine in hand, the two men settled down nearer to the fire, the flickering flames casting shadows all around them. Another mournful howl echoed around the distant hills as Octavian leaned forward and poked at the fire with a stick.

"The whispering sands of the Vaarseeti desert are a perilous place to find yourself." Octavian began. "I have travelled three deserts in my lifetime and know the code that a traveller requesting aid is rarely turned away in such hostile environments but this is not true in the Vaarseeti." Kerian huddled a blanket around his shoulders suddenly feeling cold.

"The sands flow like liquid silver under the full moon and the winds ring trail bells topping poles set every five hundred yards to mark the caravan route that has been travelled for centuries. They say the route twists and turns, meandering like a slow river from one oasis to another, avoiding sinking sands and perilous wastelands. If someone asks for aid in this desert you need to turn away, for offering aid here is a weakness and it will ultimately cause your doom. You just have to stick to the trail, accept the rules and prepare to leave the Vaarseeti a changed man. The same can't be said for the Provan Legion."

"The Provan Legion." Kerian raised an eyebrow. "I have heard of them but I thought it was a fantasy, a legend?"

"Oh no, the story of the Legion is real enough." Octavian continued. "One thousand men went into the Vaarseeti and thought they could set off across the sands and cross the desert without following the trail. One thousand soldiers and all of their supplies disappeared without a trace searching for the lost city of Tahl Avan where they encase the dead in solid gold. Not a single survivor was found; the Legion lost, consumed by the whispering sands."

"Why whispering sands?" Kerian asked, trying to suppress the feeling of supernatural chills across his body.

"Well." Octavian hunched nearer to the fire. "They say when the winds blow just right the sand whispers the calls of the legion, still searching for each other to this day." He cracked a smile. "You will see soon enough. I would hate to spoil the surprise. The stew looks about ready now." They served the stew into bowls and ate slowly. Octavian grinning at the supernatural tale and Kerian thinking about a thousand troops lost in the desert. Kerian broke the silence first.

"Where did you learn to play music? I was impressed with your musical abilities back in Wellruff."

"I learnt it from my grandfather." Octavian replied waving a piece of bread in emphasis. "he had a violin that he played so beautifully it could make the hardest man cry, the stubbornest woman to tap her feet to dance and the most restless baby go to sleep. Some even said he could call up a storm with his playing." Kerian stopped eating, his eyes suddenly intense at the tale.

"What happened to your grandfather?"

"The same thing that happens to everyone eventually. He died." Octavian stated. "He stupidly picked a fight with a giant grizzly bear in the Forboding forest."

"And the violin?"

"Passed down from father to son."

"So your father has it?" Kerian pushed.

"No, he passed it down to his son as he had no skill with music."

"So you have it."

"Not anymore." Octavian revealed. "It's with my wife and daughter." He stood up and walked over to Kerian collecting his bowl. It did not take much in the way of perception for Kerian to realise he had pushed a little too far. Something he had said had touched a raw nerve.

"There is a stream a way over beyond the rise. I'm going to clean the bowls and fill our water skins for the long journey ahead. I suggest you settle down and get some rest. Where we are travelling, the going is hard. I would hate to have to leave you behind."

Kerian watched as Octavian disappeared into the shadows before settling back against his pack and closing his eyes, listening to the sounds of the night around him. The solitude descended upon him like a cloud, bringing dark thoughts at his temporary isolation. He missed the crew of the *El Defensor* and wondered what night sky they would be looking up at tonight. Closing his eyes, Kerian leaned back and let the sounds of the night embrace him. The hoot of an owl, the whistle of the wind through the gaps in the masonry, low neighs from the horses and the far-off howl of a wolf answered by another much closer to where he lay.

The howls came again closer; somehow more threatening now that he was alone. Kerian reached for a fist-sized stone and palmed it, then huddled down beneath his shield hoping it would serve to protect him if the worst were to happen. He suddenly felt cold and pulled the blanket tighter around him to try and ward off the chill as the sound of the wolves became more aggressive as the two animals located each other and lay claim to their disputed territory.

Kerian looked up at the ruined spiral staircase climbing towards the heavens and tried to visualize Colette's bright blue eyes and flirtatious smile looking back at him but even this failed to calm his jitters. He realised that the night was going to be a fitful one and he turned onto his side pulling the blanket up over his head, struggling to put out of his mind the image of one thousand soldiers marching to their doom, dying of thirst, their parched remains being swallowed by sands that whispered in the night. With a sigh he closed his eyes and tried to sleep.

A shadow moved on the staircase high above him, a slim delicate form with jet black inky hair, smoky grey eyes and ruby red lips. She lay on the steps, one hand gently cradling her cheek, listening to the wolves fighting in the darkness, a solitary tear tracking down her pale face.

* * * * * *

Miguel Garcia tried to suppress the overwhelming urge to vomit as he stared open-mouthed towards the host of this macabre and terrifying dinner party, he had found himself invited to. He sat within a ruined dining room, the long tables and chairs warped and covered in decades of filth. Vegetation and mould sprouted from the walls, rubbish had collected in the corners and at the far end of the room the ceiling appeared to have collapsed. The whole room sat at a tilt, leaning to starboard, adding a greater sense of surrealism to the nightmare predicament that Miguel, as yet, could see no escape from.

Another spasmodic jerk from crewman Gordon made Miguel wince. Although Gordon had been a mediocre member of the sailing team, he certainly did not deserve the fate befalling him. The buccaneer desperately wanted to shut out the sights and sounds around him but instead fought the need to turn away from the scene being played out before him that apparently none of his other crew appeared to see. He knew with certainty that allowing his disgust to show would seal his own fate, despite the fact that his two lizard henchmen squatted down on either side of him looking distinctly unhappy and as if they were sucking on lemons as the monster sitting before them worked his sorcerous magic.

The journey across the decks of the wrecked ships had been just the start of this menagerie of horror. Slipping and sliding, climbing and in some cases falling from one ruined hulk to another, following in the skittering steps of a creature that moved like a giant octopus or spider. Miguel had sailed many seas, seen many ships and vessels but even he had been stunned at the scores of ships designs he had witnessed on this journey. Modern collided with ancient. Planes, boats, ships, space capsules. It appeared if a vehicle sailed or flew it could be found somewhere within this conglomeration of decay. It was like a giant scrapyard but instead of hover cars it held ships. Then before Miguel could even begin making sense of the names around him, like the *El Gato, Saha Bank, George E Vreeland, Marine Sulphur Queen,* they had come upon the ruined cruise liner *Neptune.*

His crewman's foot slapped wetly on the floor, shudders and shivers running up and down Gordon's form. Miguel swallowed hard and tried to focus on the face of the demonic old man sitting at the head of the table, tried to focus on the soulless cataract-clouded eyes that rolled up in pleasure and found himself imagining the eyes of a great white shark as it was feeding. Indeed, the parallel drawn was intensely accurate, for this creature was feeding too.

Gordon's mouth was open wide, his eyes open and bulging in horror. A slim needle-like proboscis had been inserted into his mouth, piercing the palette and penetrating his brain. The attack had been so fast, so traumatic. Miguel replayed the sound of the deadly spear cracking through the bone and breaking whatever trance had been controlling his crewman, leaving Gordon with a split second of terror as he realised that he was being eaten alive. The proboscis was attached to a thin crimson tendril that pulsed at every noisy suck, the contents of Gordon's brain matter visibly being sucked up the tube to pass over their host's shoulder and disappear somewhere into the monstrous creature's back.

Miguel had wanted to fight back; his crew outnumbered this monster and they could surely have overpowered him but they all appeared to have no idea what was going on. To look at them, it appeared as if they were seated at some great party. They hoisted their hands as if holding invisible tankards, squabbled over imaginary meats and passed exotic dishes that simply did not exist, whilst hanging on every word of their host. When the monster decided to speak between mouthfuls that was!

The buccaneer had always been quick to fathom out a situation but this one confused him. The monster, now viewed up close, was like a giant jellyfish given human form. His body was indistinct, swirls of dirty white and streaks of smoky jelly made up his abdomen and torso, making it unclear and it was unclear if it was his body or some sort of strange translucent robe he wore. The monster had arms that appeared human, the skin all shrivelled and hanging limp like some of the old women that begged on the streets of Maraket. It also had an aged human head, wizened with tight eye slits as if squinting or if there were some oriental heritage. The gaze through milky white eyes appeared piercing despite looking as if the creature were blind. Slitted nostrils appeared to scent the air whilst the sparse hair upon the horror's head completed the image of a creature that had apparently been alive for centuries.

Around their host the air was filled with softly glowing fans that appeared to hover, their colours pulsing bright and dark in patterns Miguel could not follow. The fans opened and closed at various speeds, clicking and clacking, spinning and twirling. Only now that the buccaneer was up closer than he had intended, did Miguel notice each fan was attached to a thin tube that appeared to be growing from the monster's back. He also noticed how the fans had barbed edges which could be used independently, indeed several had pinned poor Gordon to the floor and to his seat as the monster fed.

It was like observing the tendrils of those fish that swam in the depths and used colours to lure unexpected prey. Miguel knew the colours had to be stunning, as they held the attention of every other person in the room. Even his lizards, viewing the display through heavily lidded eyes were having problems remaining in control and kept shaking their heads and snorting to clear their noses.

The only thing disappointing was that the display was lost on Miguel. He could not see what everyone else did because he had been colour blind since a child. Anything with red or green components was difficult to see with clarity. Colours appeared muted or confused, some shades not visible at all.

Gordon finally gasped his last, the resistance briefly witnessed now fled from the poor man's form. Miguel gripped the handle of one of his blasters, determined that if the creature came for him, he would give it a fight it wasn't expecting. However, instead of picking another crewman to feast upon, his host used several of his barbed fans to pick up Gordon's corpse and throw him to the side of the room, where a pack of ever-attentive black hounds sat waiting, heads up, ears twitching, clearly expecting the scraps of their master's meal. Miguel fought to contain the explosion of bile that rushed to his throat as the beasts dove on the corpse ripping it limb from limb.

Where the hell was Thomas when Miguel needed him? What kind of place was this? No wonder Thomas guarded his secrets so closely if this was the kind of person he lived alongside.

"I am so glad you are all enjoying yourselves in my humble home and partaking of this feast aboard the *Neptune*." The creature spoke, a thin smile spreading across his features as his fans continued to open and close.

Click clack, click clack.

The crew, still under the unexplained hold of this monster raised phantom flagons and toasted their generous host, cheering wildly.

"Now you have all eaten," the monster continued. "I need to ask who you all are and why you were looking for Thomas Adams." The crew looked lost at the request. Some smiled stupidly, others struggled to swallow mouthfuls of food they only tasted in their addled minds. One man started to cry unsure how to answer the question and apparently distraught he could not respond. Miguel tried not to smile. He never told his crew anything. When he ordered something, they did it, none of them needed to have the particulars. That was the kind of crew he liked.

"I know I heard one of you mention Thomas Adams name when you first came through the gate." their host continued, his fans now opening and closing faster, weaving and bobbing, picking up speed as the pastel colours flashed faster and faster along their barbed lengths. "The question remains which one of you was it?" The horror rose to its feet, fans slamming into the deck, giving it stability despite the list of the ship.

"Now then, someone here must know what I am talking about. Just tell Malum Okubi what he wants to know..."

Miguel swallowed hard as he watched the monster... Malum, stalk along the opposite length of the table, the fans flickering and swaying like serpents darting between the crew who stood silently, their hallucinatory feast suddenly over.

"Was it you?" Malum hissed, sniffing loudly, his head slanted to one side, milky eyes staring into space as he towered above one of the mercenaries Miguel had hired. "No... I don't think so."

"You see; Thomas Adams vexes me. I want him to suffer for what he did." Malum continued as he moved menacingly up to the far end of the table. "I want his ship, I want his crew and most of all I want Thomas, helpless and on his knees before me." There was a groan of pain as a limb detached from Malum's back, rising up over his shoulder. Judging by the size of its shattered diameter, this had once been a massive fan, now it was splintered and oozing ichor, clearly infected and causing the creature great pain.

"Thomas Adams maimed me and I mean to see him hurt as badly." Malum continued. "I need all of you fine men to help me right this wrong. You see I know where Thomas has gone, I know where he must return and when he does, I will be waiting to trap him. The *El Defensor* and all upon her shall be mine. I will have my revenge."

"We shall do our best to help." One crewman blubbed. "Just tell us what you want us to do."

"I need ropes and chains." Malum replied. "There are many lying all around us in the graveyard. I need to fashion a net. I am sure you sailors all understand the best way to catch fish is with a sturdy net and the *El Defensor* requires the largest net of all." Malum started his return down the side of the table where Miguel sat. Cornelius snarled in warning and started to draw a curved dagger from his belt. Miguel placed his hand on the creature's scaled hide and tried to calm him. It was not time to blow their cover yet. Horatio sat flicking his tail in agitation, his face looking as if he were suffering from a dental cavity that his tongue refused to stop probing.

"I think I should propose a toast." Malum hissed. "A toast to a successful fishing trip."

"Here, here!" shouted one over enthusiastic crewman as they all raised their arms in a toast. Miguel frowned. The man was acting as if he were intoxicated and all he had been consuming was fresh air for goodness sake! This was what he got for hiring cheap labour!

"If we are going fishing, what shall we use for bait?" another asked wiping his hand across his mouth to remove a spill from his invisible tankard.

"Oh, I don't know." Malum hissed, drawing up behind Miguel's chair and moving in closely to sniff at the horrified buccaneer. "Is there something wrong with your drink?"

Miguel froze in horror. He had forgotten to toast with the others! One false move had marked his undoing.

"Nothing." He whispered his throat suddenly dry. "I'm the designated driver." Miguel's eyes opened wide in horror as two fans slid slowly into his view opening and closing with clear menace.

Click clack, click clack.

"I don't think so." Malum snarled.

Miguel drew his blaster in a blur of motion, knowing he was the fastest man alive when it came to the quick draw.

Malum was faster. Fans whirled in snatching his bandolier and throwing him physically down onto the table causing the other crew to scurry swiftly out of the way. The blaster bolt scored the ceiling then fizzled and died in Miguel's hand as other barbed appendages whirled in spearing through his frock coat and pinning him. Malum reared up over the buccaneer like a monstrous spider, bringing his wrinkled head down to within inches of Miguel's face.

"How are you not affected?" Malum asked, his gaunt shrivelled head turning one way and then the other, his nostrils scenting his prey. "Why are you not like the others? Is it magic? Science? Sheer stupidity?"

"Less of the stupid." Miguel struggled to free his other hand, somehow trapped under him as he had landed on the table. "I'll have you know I'm a shrewd businessman."

Malum ignored the reply. Intent on trying to find the underlying cause of an enigma he had never encountered before. He moved closer, sniffing, strands of mucus seeping from his nose and eyes, dripping down onto the wriggling form pinned below him.

"Tell me how you did this?" Malum screamed. "Tell me now or I will extract the information from your brain."

Click clack, click clack.

Miguel's eyes went wide as he noticed the thin needle coming into view over Malum's shoulder, its end still dripping part of Gordon's brain matter. He had no doubts as to where this object was heading.

"Cornelius, Horatio…" he grunted, panic starting to set in as the needle edged closer to his left nostril. "For pity's sake boys, what do I pay you for? Get him!"

"Your lizards cannot help you." Malum's mouth split into a grin, rotten caramel coloured stumps of useless teeth serving as little boulders in front of the drool that oozed from the monster's mouth. "They are under my thrall like the rest of your pathetic crew. There is no escape."

"Please not the coat." Miguel moaned, as the drool dribbled across his shirt. "I only just got the thing cleaned after Thomas messed it up in Maraket. He owes me and I aim to collect!" The thin proboscis needle slid an inch up Miguel's left nostril preparing to punch forwards and plunge into his brain.

"So, it was you…" Malum hissed, his appendage suddenly pausing in its exploration of Miguel's moist body part. "You are the one seeking Thomas. This changes things. We have much to discuss you and I."

Miguel sucked in his breath as the fans suddenly stopped and the probe thankfully withdrew, lightly scratching the tip of his nose as it was extracted and drawing a drop of crimson blood. Malum sniffed, leaned in and licked the drop with a disgusting thin, fungus coated tongue.

"Take a seat and let us talk about old friends." Malum laughed, emitting a dry rasping sound that made Miguel shudder. "Maybe we can come to a mutual agreement that will benefit us both?"

Miguel sank back down into his chair, trying to quell the tremors running through his form as Malum moved back towards his seat at the head of the table.

"Where were you guys?" Miguel hissed, elbowing his two lizard henchmen. "Where were you when I needed you?" Horatio still sat in place snorting and swatting at invisible insects on his thick snout whilst Cornelius licked his nose, his eyelids clicking open and closed as if he had just been dazzled.

Malum lowered himself back into his chair, threw his head back and laughed before turning to face Miguel. His fans whirled out snatching the nearest crewman from his pleasant world of illusion as the monster prepared to feast.

"Now from the top." Malum hissed, ignoring the screams from the man pinned before him as the barbed fans plunged into his writhing form. "Tell me what you know of Thomas Adams."

Miguel looked on as the proboscis slammed into the poor crewman's right eyeball, puncturing the orb and squirting gore across the stained table top. The man thrashed and squealed in terror and pain, desperate to escape or find quarter from a creature that would grant him neither. A loud sucking noise started, reminding Miguel of a child sucking a thick milkshake up a straw and Malum rolled his eyes back in pleasure as he began to consume him.

The buccaneer turned to one side and was finally, violently sick.

Chapter Fourteen

"Well this is rather pleasant." Ives remarked, throwing his arms wide at the large airy room they had been ushered into. "Look at the marble, it is inlaid with gold. The drapes, so sheer and such vivid colours I could make a fortune selling these at home. Oh... And you just have to admire the view!"

Thomas took in the opulent surroundings of this tranquil scene; the plush furnishings, the pools of water with little fountains situated around the room to reduce the humidity that was building outside but a sense of unease increased within him. He stared at his human companions as he paced, Ives stood out on the balcony filling his face with fruit, sighing contentedly, whilst Weyn lay back on the couch, eyes closed in a rare moment of rest. The injured harbour assistant had been taken to receive medical treatment and Rauph had also been escorted to places unknown, leaving Thomas knowing he would not rest until the fate of his navigator was known.

"Calm down Thomas." Weyn said. "I can't relax with you pacing backwards and forwards."

"Come over here." Ives gestured. "Take in the view. The pyramid is breath-taking from here." Thomas walked over, hands in his pockets, his right hand nervously stroking the small police cruiser toy car he carried there. The humidity hit him like a solid wall, as he stepped out onto the balcony, instantly causing him to perspire. He stepped over to the marble balustrade and stared out over the magnificence that was Taurean.

The city spread out below him, elegant walkways radiating down from the upper, more opulent parts of the city, only to slowly deteriorate to narrower winding streets lined with ramshackle shanty shops and leaning homes of the poorer members of Taurean society. Several delicate spans ran out from the island across to the heavily jungled mainland where the ominous pyramid stood, it's stark silhouette silently brooding above a carpet of multi-coloured hues of green.

Thomas realised he had a much clearer view of the pyramid from here and an interesting feature had now become apparent from this elevated position. It appeared as if the pyramid was built over a massive maze that seemed to run up to its base and possibly under it. Several walls of the labyrinth appeared covered in thick foliage and had the appearance of having been standing for a long time.

"At least our captors are not philistines." Ives continued, juice running down his chin. "They seem to be looking after us well."

"A gilded cage is still a cage." Thomas replied. "We have guards at the door and looking at this view we seem to be in the only room in the palace with no apparent way to climb down. I mean look at the thick thorns climbing the wall, the jagged tops of those pillars, the really long drop to the ground where those guards patrol below. There is even a moat with something large slithering around in it."

"But the view Thomas!" Ives smiled, ignoring his obviously irritated friend. "Breathe in deep and take in the view."

A knock came at the door, causing Weyn to open his eyes and stare as if he expected, by the power of sight alone that the door would open. Ives put the bowl of fruit down on the balustrade, overbalancing a ripe fruit that slipped from the pile, rolled to the edge and plummeted to the ground, shredding its soft pulp on the thorns as it fell, hitting the path with a sickening squelch before something dark and sleek ran from the bushes and devoured it. Thomas followed the fruit's brutal demise and raised an eyebrow to his jolly colleague, his look saying more than words ever could about their fate if they tried to escape this way.

"Shall I get the door?" Thomas asked, finishing the conversation before it began. He crossed the room to open the door, just as the knocking started once again, more urgent this time, its intensity shaking the entire frame and vibrating the door wide open to reveal a large minotaur Thomas had never seen before.

"Um please come in." Thomas gestured, standing aside to let the hugely muscled short cropped chestnut beast into the room, before flashing a smile at the guards outside and closing the door after him. The Minotaur was impeccably groomed, gleaming horns polished and sharpened to deadly points, short close-cropped chestnut hair emphasising graceful yet strong facial features. Piercing dark brown eyes stared out over a silvery black nose damp with moisture. The Minotaur's hair between his horns was platted and combed to pass back over the top of his head and down his neck to hang free between his shoulder blades.

Thomas took in the stranger's clothes which looked like the uniform of a Roman legionnaire. Laminated black and gold strip cuirass armour with a Pteruges leather skirt, a light grey Sagum cloak fastened by a Fibula brooch in the shape of a pyramid also in black and gold. The only thing not gleaming on this magnificent creature was worn and battered scabbards strung across the Minotaur's shoulders which held some familiar looking long swords. The captain looked again, walking around the visitor, his eye noticing the tell-tale scar below the Minotaur's ear.

"Rauph?" Thomas asked, awe struck at the transformation of his friend from a scruffy shaggy monster into this sleek regal looking figure. "Is that really you?"

"I feel so stupid." Rauph replied.

"Rauph... Our mangy navigator? No way!" Weyn gasped, getting off the couch to walk around his colleague offering admiring comments. "Now I don't know who you are but I want our shaggy friend back please."

"I am Rauph." The navigator replied, clearly feeling a lack of confidence in his new attire.

"By all the gods. Our Rauph truly is a prince among these creatures." Ives commented from the balcony. Thomas took stock of the Minotaur, taking in Ives words. It was true, if there was ever a picture of a regal and elegant Minotaur prince, this was it.

"Rauph. This is incredible." Thomas said, relief flooding through him as he realised his friend was safe. "I have so many questions to ask you. They did not hurt you did they."

"They cut off all of my hair." Rauph replied, his eyes growing moist. "And they polished my horns!" he shook his head woefully, looking like a puppy that had just been given a reluctant bath. "I have never been so embarrassed."

A dull thump came from the balcony, causing Ives to turn and Weyn to reach for his bow. Low curses sounded as the mysterious figure tried to secure his perilous grip on the marble balcony.

"Any time you want to lend a hand." Mathius groaned, struggling to pull himself up over the edge. He collapsed onto the marble with a sigh. "I see that you are all coping badly with your captivity." He remarked, spotting Ives still holding the bowl of fruit and chewing merrily. "What's with the new guy?"

"Hello Mathius," Rauph waved cheerily. "Was there something wrong with the stairs?"

"Well you certainly brush up well." Mathius replied, rolling onto his back and gasping to catch his breath on the cool marble floor, deep scratches and grazes all over his weary features and hands. "You have no idea what I have gone through to get up here!"

"Why have you come to us Rauph?" Thomas asked, ignoring the groans from the assassin. "What plans do they have for us?"

"Everyone is really friendly," Rauph replied, before scrunching his forehead in deep thought. "They want us to have a great feast and are inviting everyone from the *El Defensor* to celebrate us rescuing a prince they thought was long dead. Oh, and they all keep calling me Kristoph and I told them so many times that my name is Rauph but they don't seem to listen."

"Everyone? The whole crew?" Thomas asked. "I'm not happy about that. There is no way I am leaving the ship unmanned. When is this feast?"

"Dusk tonight." Rauph stated. "Apparently I'm the guest of honour. We all have to witness the setting sun on the pyramid and be blessed."

"I don't like this and I certainly do not trust our benefactors" Thomas stated coldly. "Something is not right. We have all seen the brutality they initially showed towards us, yet now they all want to be nice. I need to get back to the ship and warn the crew."

"That isn't going to happen." Rauph replied. "They want to extend their friendship to you and offer you baths and pampering like they did to me. A phalanx of troops will be sent to the docks to extend the invitations to the crew and the serving girls are on their way here already. Just a word of advice. Don't let them take your hair." A knock sounded on the door, ending the discussion.

"That's probably them." Rauph warned.

"Ives, hide Mathius!" Thomas snapped. Ives ran out onto the balcony, pulling a throw from behind Weyn and dropping the archer heavily back into his couch. He threw the sheet over Mathius's prone form just as the door opened and several slave girls walked in with towels and fresh changes of clothes.

"We have come to take you all to the baths." The first petite slave informed them. "Please follow us."

"One moment." Thomas replied gently grabbing the young girl by the shoulders and easing her back towards the open door. "We need a private moment with our friend, can you please wait outside. Two minutes?" Thomas promised ushering her outside and closing the door.

"Oh I'm all for that!" Mathius smiled, pulling the throw off himself and making Ives catch the bowl of fruit that had served to complete his disguise as an occasional table. "Baths with the ladies."

"I'm afraid not." Thomas replied coldly, turning to Rauph. "When are the troops expected at the dock?"

"Within the hour." Rauph replied.

"Okay, Weyn, Ives, let's not ruffle any feathers and do what they want. Let's go with the serving girls."

"My plan exactly," Mathius replied limping towards the door.

"As I said before Mathius, I'm afraid not." Thomas restated.

"Why?" the assassin moaned. "They are just outside the door."

"And you are not supposed to be here!" Thomas shot back. "You are the one person they have no idea is with us. You need to get back to the ship and warn the crew."

"This is so unfair." Mathius groaned. "Okay I'll come with you all and slip out the door."

"No one must see you!" Thomas shot back. "You need to go back the way you came in." Mathius looked over towards the marble balcony and groaned anew.

"Over the balustrade?" he questioned.

"Off the balcony." Thomas confirmed.

"We must move faster." Rauph butted in looking slightly agitated. "Mother likes things done straight away. She doesn't like to wait."

"Is that really your mother?" Thomas asked, turning from the crestfallen assassin to regard his navigator once more.

"I do remember her." Rauph confessed. "But it is all really blurred. I can see images but nothing really makes sense."

"Okay let's go." Ives interrupted still holding his bowl of fruit and heading for the door. "I can't remember the last time I had a truly relaxing bath."

"Neither can we!" Weyn jibed.

Thomas turned back to Mathius and clicked his fingers to grab the man's attention. The scowl that returned showed the captain that his clicking fingers was one step too far but time was not on their side to argue rules of etiquette.

"I do not want the ship left unmanned for any reason. Feign sickness, important repairs, anything... but do not leave our ship unmanned for even a moment." Mathius looked at the two men eager to pass through the door to the baths and then back at the balcony and the perils that lay beneath it.

"Go back to the ship." He muttered. "Save the day again! Oh how I wish for those good old days when I simply killed someone and then went on my merry way."

* * * * * *

The shifting orange and white sands of the Vaarseeti Desert did not whisper as they were carried aloft by constant winds to wander and spin across seemingly endless dunes. Instead they either sounded like a persistent irritating hiss, or as Kerian was now experiencing, a fully-fledged roar.

Pulling the remains of his hastily fashioned keffiyeh headscarf tighter about his face, Kerian vainly attempted to prevent the coarse grains of sand from hitting areas of exposed skin and scorching them. Every step forward was unsteady, his weight causing the sands to slip beneath him, using all of his strength to simply stand let alone lead a horse through the shifting mountains of terracotta and cream. This was a torment like no other and the constant buffeting from the wind was depleting his energy supplies much quicker than he ever anticipated. After what seemed an eternity, he finally managed to lead Toledo down into the protective lee of a dune, offering some limited respite from the sandstorm.

Kerian finally began to make sense of his surroundings as the sound of the abrasive storm eased. It was a relief he could hear something other than the constant hissing of sand hitting the material of his cloak and scarf. He hung his head in exhaustion, gasping as the shrieking wind continued unabated above him, blown sand from the ridges of the surrounding dunes arcing off like crests of breaking orange waves before falling to the ground about him as an arid rain.

Octavian sat patiently ahead, sitting astride his own horse and wearing a smug grin on his face that instantly made Kerian consider walking over and removing it by force. His companion had been overly self-righteous during the last few days of hard travel and he appeared to be sadistically enjoying the assorted tortures he was putting Kerian through.

"That was really good." Octavian stated, slowly clapping his sand coated colleague, "You managed almost two dunes before you had to stop this time." Kerian gritted his teeth and choked down a venomous reply. He had to admit to himself he was in an alien world with strange savage rules and unfortunately, he needed to rely on Octavian more and more as they travelled further through this hostile desert.

They had slipped into a tedious routine since leaving the ruined watchtower, despite Kerian's attempts to smooth over their forced relationship. Octavian always took the lead, Kerian assuming the position of rear-guard, with discussion between them sparse and normally derogatory and at Kerian's expense, until they finally made camp each night. Although Kerian liked the time to think and observe the changing vegetation and wildlife on the trail, he found there was only so much cactus and dashing hares he could take.

Their journey continued this way for several days, observing the vegetation becoming sparser and the colour of the ground slowly changing from cracked soil to drier and more barren crumbling rock and sand. Kerian realised quite early on that Octavian was an excellent hunter. He often made excuses of checking the surrounding area after their evening meal and slipped away for a few hours, managing to bring back something worthwhile to cook for the following day.

His choice of supplies obtained by his less than honourable rolling of dice also appeared to be a blessing, not least of which the headscarf Kerian now wore and three large felt blankets that Octavian unrolled every evening for them to rest upon. Kerian soon found out that the desert, despite appearing lifeless, was far from it.

Crimson scorpions lay just under the surface of the sand and came out at night looking for places to hole up for the following day. Any rocky overhang, unattended saddlebag or a naive traveller's boot were all fair game to set up home. Octavian had almost let Kerian put on his boot with one inside, before appearing to reconsider and warning him to empty the boot out and reveal his nocturnal lodger. When the scorpion had fallen onto the blanket it had frozen in place not moving as if the soft surface upset it somehow, allowing Octavian to stab it in the back of its carapace with his dagger and hoist it up for Kerian to see.

"This is why we sleep on felt." He remarked. "The scorpions don't like it so they won't crawl onto this at night. Make sure you do not move too close to the edge whilst you sleep as the sting of a crimson scorpion can paralyse a limb and to be honest even with the four limbs you have, you are still having problems moving."

Another morning found Kerian awoken and informed by his gracious guide that he was lying on top of a shimmering sidewinder. When he had looked around the felt blanket there were small pieces of crimson scorpion scattered all around him, the external shells cracked open, as if something had eaten the creatures even as they had gathered around Kerian in the night. When he stood to his feet, boots firmly in place after his earlier scorpion experience, his blanket had moved as if alive. Carefully lifting the edge had revealed a silvery four-foot-long serpent that hissed disapprovingly at being disturbed before it slithered off across the hot sands to find another place to hide from the suns daytime heat leaving a tell-tale sinuous track behind it.

"The Sidewinder is a smart snake." Octavian had informed his shocked companion, with yet another smug look. "It finds warmth in the chill of the desert night and waits for the scorpions to come to it instead of wasting valuable energy hunting for them. You could learn something from this. It is not too late to return to Wellruff and if we wait maybe your belongings can come back to us as the market moves around."

The desert dunes took on a ghostly shimmering appearance at night and could easily be mistaken for waves at sea, heightening Kerian's sense of isolation from his friends back on the *El Defensor*. Sleep did not come easily with the crawling creatures of the desert threatening to share his bedroll. Black and purple coloured salamanders made strange 'pick pock' sounds as they raced across the sands using their widespread flat padded feet and whipping tails to traverse the soft surface beneath them. The whistling winds at these times created a haunting sound that echoed about the dunes, with Octavian joking it was the tormented dead making the noise, struggling to make their way free from the sands that entombed them. The guide post bells rang gently as the wind moved them, however finding each subsequent one marking the trail was another part of the frustration that travelling the Vaarseeti seemed to promote.

The desert constantly moved like something alive. Sometimes trail posts could be found high and free from the dunes, the tarnished bells ringing softly several feet above their heads. Others had either fallen over or been swallowed by the migrating dunes. The further they advanced into the desert the softer the sands became, engulfing heavy boots and pulling them deeply into the shifting material beneath. The relentless heat, seared down from the shimmering sun, drying mouths and making voices rasp...

"Did you hear a word I said?" Octavian shouted, nudging his horse closer. Kerian shook his head to clear it realising that his guide had been talking to him whilst he was reflecting on his experiences.

"I'm really sorry," Kerian replied, getting a mouthful of swirling sand for his trouble. "I'm absolutely exhausted walking up and down dunes. Why can't we go along the bottom of this one where there is some degree of shelter and pick up the trail when we get to the far end?"

"Have you any idea how far that could be?" Octavian replied, brushing drifting sand from his clothes. "It could add hours to our route... maybe even days at the rate you are travelling."

"I'm not as sprightly as you." Kerian replied. "You have to understand that my stamina is not as endless as yours." He frowned, more in frustration at himself, knowing that the missing amulet with the emerald inside would have made him at least Octavian's equal had he still worn it. He needed to catch up with those merchants and reclaim his treasures the faster the better.

Taking a drink from his water skin to clear his mouth, Kerian observed Octavian looking up at the next dune towering above them and then followed to the pinnacle with his eyes to see where their passage would take them if they moved off the trail. He seemed to be thinking long and hard before nodding his head and then said the words Kerian desperately wanted to hear.

"Okay then we will try it just for this dune but then it's back to the main trail. At least we can ride this part so maybe we will pick up some time if we are lucky." He tucked in his headscarf and turned his mount, dragging Dorian the donkey along with him.

Kerian turned to Toledo and met the cream stallion's stare head on.

"Don't even think of starting anything." He warned, before grabbing hold of the saddle to steady himself. "I'm just going to empty my boots and we can be on our..." If a stallion could display an evil smile, Toledo managed it, instantly moving sideways trying to tip Kerian from his one-legged stance but his rider was well experienced with stubborn animals and kept his balance, holding onto the pommel and pulling himself up. Kerian swung his leg over the saddle and gained his seat, before cracking the reins and digging in his heels to move his rebellious mount after Octavian, even as his guide slowly disappeared into the swirling sands.

His boots would have to wait until later.

* * * * * *

"Can you hear a trail bell now?" Octavian asked, perplexed and clearly annoyed.

"I thought I heard one over there!" Kerian shouted, pointing towards another orange and cream streaked dune that bore a clear resemblance to several other dunes they had passed in the last few hours.

"The trail has to be here somewhere." Octavian yelled back in exasperation. "We need to keep looking."

"Why not follow our footsteps back to where we came from." Kerian suggested, blinking his eyes and trying to dislodge the sand that had gathered around his face and upper torso. Octavian stormed over to him and for a second Kerian thought he was about to strike him, instead his guide snatched Toledo's bridle and turned the horse around before gesturing at the floor.

"What footsteps do you suggest we follow?" he asked over the howling wind.

Kerian unclenched the fist he had made to defend himself and looked down at the rippled sand, expecting to see the signs of their passage, only to realise that even the most recent tracks were already being obscured by the ever-moving sands.

"Oh by Adden!" Kerian cursed, his eyes meeting Octavian's and realising with sinking certainty that they should never have left the trail. He waited for the expletives and accusations that were bound to follow, but the gypsy had already turned his mount and was moving away, heading for the nearest dune in an attempt to get to the top, Dorian the donkey complaining loudly in his wake.

Kerian's mouth went dry at the prospect of being lost somewhere in this vast desert wasteland, so he nudged Toledo with his heels and urged the mount to catch up. Several laborious minutes later, with Toledo's legs sinking into the sand up to his hocks, they arrived at the crest of the dune to observe Octavian standing high on his stirrups, his headscarf removed, shading his eyes and looking first one way and then the other for any signs of a pole with a flashing silver bell on the top ringing in the storm.

"Any luck? Can you hear a bell?" Kerian asked, licking his lips nervously and realising how dry and cracked they had become.

"It will be you hearing bells in a moment if you don't shut up." Octavian warned angrily, turning about and repeating his actions, desperately trying to hear some sound to guide their way onwards.

Kerian moved to copy his associate, desperate to help in some way and assuage the guilt he felt for getting them into this predicament. However, Toledo was not having any of this and started off down the far side of the dune, roughly jostling Kerian along with him. Fumbling with his headscarf, Kerian tried to uncover his ears with his free hand whilst steadying himself using the pommel of the saddle with the other but all he could hear was the constant whistling of the wind and the rasping whisper of the mobile sand.

Toledo finally came to a violent stop at the base of the dune, almost unseating his rider, then started to paw and stomp the ground clearly agitated. Kerian looked around seeing nothing other than what appeared to be a never-ending wall of sand ahead of them.

They were lost! Lost in the Vaarseeti! The recognition of this fact sent a cold chill through Kerian's form despite the heat of the desert. They needed to backtrack, find their way to where they started but how many dunes had they traversed? had they turned left or right? Kerian had no idea and he felt the first tendrils of panic creeping into his mind. What were they going to do? How would he ever get back to the *El Defensor* if...

"It's this way." Octavian nudged Kerian's shoulder as he rode past, pulling his mount to the left and gesturing that Kerian follow him. "We need to get moving. There appears to be a sizeable storm coming."

"A sizeable storm?" Kerian opened his mouth in shock, instantly regretting it as sand blasted inside. "A sizeable storm... What have we just been riding through then?"

* * * * * *

The sandstorm hit with all the fury of a banshee, the force of the gusts slamming into the riders, making them bow their heads as if in prayer. The whirling sand tore into any exposed flesh, stripping skin and drawing blood in seconds. Despite Octavian's belief they were heading in the right direction, there had been no signs of any trail bells or marker posts for hours and the grim spectre of being lost started to encroach on Kerian's jumbled thoughts again. They moved together through a narrow pass between two dunes that gave some limited shelter, allowing Octavian to bring the horses to a stop whilst Kerian caught his breath and the gypsy tried to get his bearings.

Kerian took this opportunity to brush the sand from his clothes and adjust his headscarf. His toes ached inside his boots where the sand stubbornly kept managing to slip inside restricting space for movement and the opportunity to remedy this was too much to turn down. He tapped Octavian on the shoulder, signalling his wish to dismount before dropping from the saddle. The gypsy dismounted beside him and pulled a water skin from his saddlebag whilst he considered their next move.

"I need to empty my boots!" Kerian exclaimed. "Just give me a moment." Octavian nodded agreement but seemed preoccupied with the behaviour of his mount as it seemed to be shying away from him as he tried to secure his water skin.

Kerian sat on the ground, ignoring the sand particles whipping about him and tugged at his boot, pulling it away and tipping out a miniature version of the dunes through which they travelled. Oh, it felt so good to be able to wiggle his toes again! He pulled off the other boot and emptied this one as well, only to watch his first boot get picked up by the wind and thrown a few feet away in the direction the horses had no intention of travelling.

"Oh come on!" Kerian yelled, only to have his words snatched away by the wind. He pulled on his remaining boot and set off across the sand in pursuit of his absconding footwear. The weathered leather boot bounced across the floor before snagging on something that left it wiggling frantically in the wind. Kerian hopped up alongside it and moved to retrieve his boot only to find it was stuck fast to something metallic sticking out from the sand.

He knelt, scooping the soft sand away revealing the tip of what appeared to be an ancient spear. The forged metal still retained its sharp edge, despite appearing incredibly old. This was strange. Something appeared to be buried under here.

"Kerian we need to leave!" Octavian shouted. "Something is spooking the horses!" Kerian held his hand up, trying to prevent Octavian from moving away but his attention was focused on pulling at his boot to try and untangle it from a barb that curled out from the base of the spear head.

"I'll be just a moment. My boot is stuck on something!" He tugged hard, pulling this way and that before the spear head slid up out of the sand, still attached to the wooden shaft beneath it. A faded pennant appeared to be curled around the spear.

"Hang on a second!" Kerian yelled over his shoulder. "I've nearly got it free..." The boot suddenly came away tearing itself from the spear as the whole length of the weapon came out of the sand and fell free at his feet. Kerian fell backwards, landing on his backside and laughing at the unexpected jolt. He looked over to Octavian who was still struggling to control the horses and appeared oblivious to Kerian's undignified fall.

Shrugging his shoulders, Kerian pulled his boot back on and moved to get back to his feet. The offending spear remained on the sand, the faded pennant flicking in the wind that whistled across it. Kerian looked down at the small flag and wondered if he should take the spear. He had been unarmed for too long now and despite not having shown any skill with a spear during his military training he thought it would be good to be able to keep things at arm's length from now on.

As he leaned over to grab the spear, the sand near where the weapon had been located started to move, making Kerian jump and snatch back his outstretched arm. He moved cautiously to one side flicking the spear with the tip of his boot and moving it away from the disruption. Picking up the ancient weapon, Kerian moved over to the disturbance in the sand and poked at the area with the tip of the pitted steel.

The sand moved again, a scrabbling rapid motion under the surface that resulted in the level of the sand dropping and forming a small well. Kerian turned to ask Octavian if he knew what was going on but the storm seemed to have become worse in the few seconds he had been occupied and Octavian was fast being obscured by the airborne sand whipping about by the ever-present aggressive gusts of the wind.

He poked the moving sand again and was startled as something rose up out of the ground. It grabbed the tip of the spear, giving it a hard tug towards it. Kerian nearly overbalanced but just managed to avoid taking a second tumble by leaning his weight upon the spear and finding himself close enough to make out the bleached bone-like appendages holding the weapon tight. They appeared to be fingers, although there was no sign of human skin, it having been stripped clean by the desert storms long before.

"By Adden!" Kerian gasped, as the hand moved up the spear towards him, exposing a bony wrist and a yellowed radius and ulna that by rights should never have been able to move. Ragged pieces of uniform started to emerge from the sand, a leather bracer, rusted chain mail and an iron helmet slowly emerging from the ground. Kerian tried to move away, tried to free the spear but this just resulted in giving the creature the means to be able to pull itself from the soft sand.

An exposed set of ivory ribs, a ragged tabard with a clavicle showing through and a second hand now appeared, this one encased in a glove, but by no means any less horrifying than the rest of the ghastly monster appearing under Kerian's horrified gaze. This was once a soldier, of this there was no doubt, yet he appeared to be long dead and beyond such jerky movements as Kerian was witnessing. The helmet tilted slowly upwards, sand pouring from the rim to form a macabre veil that slowly parted to reveal the grinning skull beneath. Kerian forgot himself in terror, his hand finally dropping the spear which the undead creature still retained in its bony grasp.

"What are you?" he asked, not really convinced he wanted to know the answer.

The skeletal warrior had now pulled its feet from the sand and crouched, legs apart, spear held with the tip down towards the sand, its grinning visage suggesting unspoken horrors yet to come. Then it opened its mouth and impossibly issued a scream that seemed to still the air around it. Kerian back pedalled as fast as he could, acutely aware of his defenceless nature, even as he struggled to free the shield from his back.

The cadaver leapt forwards with a shriek, its spear darting out, glancing off the rim of the mirrored shield and sending vibrations up Kerian's arm with the supernatural strength delivered behind the blow. The spear flashed in again, this time low, causing Kerian to jump to avoid injury but his landing was unsteady, more of a stumble and he overbalanced, falling into a tumble that he exaggerated to roll clear of the creature.

It screamed again, sounding a ghostly clarion call to something Kerian had no intention of discovering, before lunging once more. Kerian dodged to the side allowing the spear to pass by on his left, then he spun on his heel, bringing the shield up under the monster's chin with a mighty blow. The exposed skeletal trachea crunched as the shield slammed in hard, a mortal wound to one of the living but to this creature it just seemed to be a mild annoyance.

Kerian slammed the warrior again, trying to take its head from its spine but its bony fingers were already painfully clutching at his flesh and attire. The skeleton gave a sudden jerk and its grip lessened as a water skin smashed into its skull, snapping its head over to an unnatural angle and showering both combatants with water. Kerian acted on the distraction and swung his shield in again, the mirrored edge shearing through the creature's spine and sending its grinning skull spinning off into the swirling sands.

The knight recognised his saviour holding the split water skin as the skeletal body toppled to the ground. Octavian was looking despondently at the bag and then he stared down at the creature lying on the sand at his feet.

"That was water we are going to need." He complained. "How have you ruined my day now? What exactly have you unearthed?"

"I have absolutely no idea." Kerian confessed nervously, brushing the sand from his face as he bent to lift the dropped spear from the ground. A piercing shriek froze him in his tracks and he turned back to where the creature had risen, noticing the agitated floor movement as several more spear points started to break through the surface. Octavian turned towards yet another scream, his eyes widened as he noticed two more of the skeletal creatures marching menacingly out of the swirling sandstorm, the desert sands cascading from their garb as they moved determinedly towards them.

"Come on!" Octavian shouted, grabbing Kerian by the arm and dragging him away from the spear. "We need to get out of here."

"Where are we going to go?" Kerian shouted back. "We don't know where we are."

"As long as it is away from here, I don't really care!" Octavian shot back, pulling himself up into the saddle just as several more creatures clawed and crawled out of the sand towards them. Kerian grabbed hold of Toledo's reins and swung himself up into the saddle noticing the decayed figure of a skeletal standard bearer marching towards him, a ragged pennant held aloft as he moved into battle.

Toledo snorted, stamping down hard on the bony fingers of a warrior extricating itself from the sand at the stallion's hooves, as Kerian dug in his heels and leant forward against Toledo's neck, following the charging example of his guide, as more shrieks and screams rose around them. Pulling sharply on his stallion's reins, Kerian turned the horse and charged towards the standard bearer, reaching out to snatch the faded pennant from the undead soldier's grasp, tearing its arm from its shoulder in the process, before whipping the staff around and taking the monster's head off with the solid blow.

"I'll take that!" he grunted, before digging his heels in hard and setting off after his guide. At least now he had something to keep these monsters at arm's length! The horses galloped from the relative shelter of the two dunes, out across the open desert landscape, the searing sand slamming into them and reducing visibility to less than ten feet as the horses charged away from the spear wielding horrors running swiftly across the sand behind them.

Kerian turned his head trying to make out the location of the skeletal troops and almost missed the sudden attack that came from the side. A large skeletal warrior wearing the same faded tabard and armed with a weathered scimitar stepped boldly into his path swinging its blade menacingly. Toledo jerked to the side, missing the swing by inches and almost unseating Kerian, throwing him to the left and directly into the path of the return swing. He dropped his head, pulling the shield up on reflex to deflect the blow with a resounding clang!

Clashes of weapons sounded from somewhere on his right, with Dorian the donkey braying loudly in distress but Kerian could not see where his partner had gone, the sandstorm obscured his vision. Shrieks and cries from beyond the grave echoed around him. This was ridiculous! He needed a weapon, fast! Luckily, he already knew where to get one. Kerian yanked hard on the reins, forcing Toledo to come around sharply and charged back towards the skeletal figure that had nearly decapitated him, lowering the pennant like a lance. Toledo neighed in protest, then dropped his head and charged as his rider commanded.

Kerian had seconds to take in the sight of this huge creature, wearing two sand coloured boots that flopped about its ankles, a warped scabbard and belt cinched around a faded tabard worn over rusted chainmail fallen long into disrepair. A conical helmet with a chainmail skirt hung down to protect its neck and a face guard that served only to emphasise the hole in the grinning skull where its nose should have been, before they crashed together with a sound like thunder. The lance knocked the creature back on its heels, permitting the knight to move in close and use his shield with deadly effect.

The shield slammed into the creature's head, snapping several of its teeth and knocking its helmet around as Toledo barrelled in, hitting the monster full on with its chest before launching swift kicks with its hooves that shattered the skeleton's femur, dropping the warrior to the floor. The scimitar tumbled away across the sand and Kerian nudged the stallion towards it, swapping the makeshift lance to his shield arm, before swinging down from the saddle, to scoop the blade from the desert floor in a graceful move that would have put side circus riders to shame.

Toledo wheeled again, nostrils flaring and headed back towards the bony warrior as it turned over and started to jerkily pull itself up onto its knees. The horse crashed down onto the supernatural warrior hard, shattering the monster's spine rendering it unable to move. It fell back into the sand and was finally still.

Kerian reined in Toledo, taking the opportunity to catch his breath and move his shield to his back, before clutching the standard and reins in one hand and the recovered blade in the other. Turning in the saddle, he struggled to identify where his guide had gone through the poor visibility of the storm. The shrieking came from all around now; the sandstorm obscuring the sun and any possible notion of identifying a landmark. Dark shapes were moaning and digging themselves out from the desert floor all around him. He had no idea where to go.

A large shadow lumbered towards him, bursting from the cover of the storm, nearly making Kerian jump from his skin. He swung the scimitar hard catching the grinning armoured skeleton in the ribs with a lunge that would have killed a mortal foe, before kicking off its round shield with his boot, only to watch the monster step back, then leap forwards again, its expressionless face all the more menacing for its exposed snapping teeth.

Kerian spurred his mount forwards, recognising the futility of fighting this dangerous foe and Toledo responded in kind, leaving the undead warrior in his wake, as it crashed down onto the desert floor, its ultimate fate swallowed by the storm as it rushed in behind them, leaving just its unearthly shrieks chasing his departure.

"Octavian!" Kerian screamed. "Octavian! Where are you?" He realised he might as well be miming the words over the tumultuous noises rising from the storm and the terrifying calls of the creatures around him. Kerian let Toledo go, praying they would not charge blindly into a ravine or the stallion catch its leg in a hole and fall. More shrieking skeletons charged out at them. Barbed arrows whistled past his head slamming into the desert sand. Horse and rider charged into a clearing where an emaciated archer was just putting an arrow to its bow. Kerian swung the scimitar hard, slicing the bow string and making the wooden bow jump in the creature's hand, smacking it hard on the temple.

Another skeletal figure charged in from the right, Kerian swung his makeshift lance as hard as he could, then followed through with a swing of the scimitar, only to watch in horror as the lance bounced off the monster's helm and the ancient blade wedged into the skeletal creature's shoulder joint before the weathered metal snapped at the punishment. The skeleton turned with slow menace and swung a club aimed right at Kerian's head, just as another shadowy figure came out of the storm swinging a mace that shattered the creature's arm and sent the monster spinning to the ground.

"There will be plenty of time to play with your flag and build sand castles later!" Octavian snapped, dropping the mace as if it's very touch offended him. "Follow me now. We don't have much time!" Kerian looked on amazed as the gypsy turned his horse and donkey about and charged off into the swirling sands. He shrugged in resignation, tugging the reins, urging Toledo into hard pursuit as the grounded skeletal warrior threw its club at his head with another frustrating scream, the weapon thankfully flying wide of its mark.

The swirling sandstorm rushed in around them, reducing visibility, making Kerian worry that he risked losing sight of Octavian again, when they suddenly burst out from under the storm and found themselves sliding down a sand dune towards what appeared to be an abandoned settlement. It lay half buried by the migrating sands, with only the odd weathered structure rising above the dunes, as if the desert were an endless blanket slowly smothering it. The storm raged behind them, sand cascading down in translucent orange and cream curtains.

The gypsy charged ahead, leading Kerian down between crumbling buildings that appeared to have been recently uncovered by the cyclone. On some sides sand piled higher than the buildings, pouring in through open windows and filling long abandoned cellars. Fallen pillars lay like dropped children's toys along the edge of a thoroughfare that led further into the partially buried city. It was along this route that they galloped, Kerian looked back frequently, checking the position of the skeletal horde chasing them against the backdrop of the screaming wall of sand. His face fell as he realised the number of ghostly troops charging down the dune numbered in the hundreds! They needed somewhere to hide, somewhere to defend themselves from these terrifying beings.

Octavian seemed to have the same idea, leading them confidently through an opening guarded by two immense statues of cloaked figures, their features eroded away by the desert sands. He turned down a shadowed passageway that opened into a wide courtyard piled with soft drifting sand and rows of indistinct statues, silent sentinels lining a pathway to a building on the far side. The riders charged along it without hesitation, arriving at an ominous squat building largely buried within the sand. However scary and foreboding the creepy crumbling ruin looked, it had one outstanding factor, it appeared to have a largely intact and intimidating stone door! His guide dropped from his horse and ran to the door, looking for a way to open the formidable gateway and secure them sanctuary inside.

Toledo skidded to a halt on the cobbles allowing Kerian to dismount and assist. Octavian was beckoning furiously, struggling to turn a wheel at the side of the entrance that had long seized from lack of use. They grabbed either side of the wheel and tried with all of their might, their faces red with the effort, grunting and groaning as they strived to get the wheel to turn, before Octavian noticed there was a lock on the wheel. He pulled out the bolt, bending to the task again and ever so slowly, the massive door started to rise with an ominous creaking and an outburst of ancient disturbed fetid air.

More shrieks and moans filled the air, angry sounds of the skeletal legion searching for the two travellers amid the ruins. Octavian nodded at Kerian, indicating he take the full strain of the wheel whilst the gypsy gathered the horses and ushered them through the entrance in a task that felt like it lasted a lifetime. The horses shied and neighed, clearly spooked by all the tension about them, with first one horse then another going inside the opening and then trying to get out again. Kerian grunted with the effort, his muscles shaking with the constant stress and weight, sweat running down his face and trickling down the small of his back, his leg muscles cramping from the effort before Octavian finally poked his head out of the opening.

"Why are you still out there?" he enquired. "There is a mechanism inside here that keeps the door open. I wedged it ages ago." Kerian looked daggers at his companion before carefully letting go of the wheel, only to find the door did indeed remain open. His look instantly changed to one of concern as shambling jerking skeletons started to enter the courtyard and run towards them across the open space, screaming for reinforcements as they came.

"Now! Now!" Octavian gestured, pulling Kerian through the doorway as ten of the monstrous creatures passed the centre of the courtyard and began to pick up speed, sensing their prey was cornered.

"The door! Shut the door!" Kerian screamed out. The creatures were getting closer, rusting armour hanging loosely from bony limbs, spiked weapons flashing through the air. "You better make this quick!" A pennant tipped spear came hurting through the air to clatter across the floor into the darkness, emphasising Kerian's earlier demand for haste.

Octavian flashed a cocky smile, waiting a few more agonising moments before pulling at something on the inside of the doorframe. The massive stone slab came crashing down, with a deafening rumble, crushing several of the skeletons flat, splintering bones, snapping spines and sending shattered metatarsals and limbs spinning across the floor at Kerian's feet. The two men and their horses were plunged into complete darkness that seemed filled with cloying dust and sand. Kerian tried to still his pounding heart, struggled to take in a full breath and then finally, started to nervously laugh, despite the fact he could see nothing at all and could only hear the horses jostling anxiously behind him and the muffled pounding of what could only be several skeleton warriors on the solid outside door.

"Well this is cosy!" Kerian joked, relief flooding through him. A scuffling sound came from over in Octavian's direction, before a flicker of light burst into being. The gypsy lifted a torch from a sconce by the door and soon had a flickering flame dancing from the end. Moments later another torch was discovered and both men stood looking at the blocked entranceway listening to the increasingly loud booming sounds without, as more and more monsters tried to gain access.

"I wonder how long the door will hold?" Kerian asked. "They do seem rather determined to get to us."

"We should be fine." Octavian replied walking back over to the door mechanism, a frown appearing on his face. "That's odd." He muttered, checking first his side and then glancing over to Kerian's. "There seems to be no means to open the door from this side. How strange. I guess we won't be leaving this way. The door creaked and shifted with a sudden snapping sound and lifted an inch from the floor, allowing billowing sand to rush in and causing the torches to flicker alarmingly before it smashed back down again. The skeletal warriors were indeed persistent. Kerian's hands shot out in a vain effort to try and hold the door down and imagined he could feel the vibrations of the stone through his palms.

"Can we at least wedge the door whilst it is shut?" He asked, suddenly aware of some rough grooves on the inner surface of the door. "I mean; we wouldn't want to make it easy for them, would we?"

"I think so, yes!" Octavian replied, stepping forward and slipping a bolt through the mechanism to firmly jam the device, keeping it tightly closed. "However, as you can see there are no handles to the wheel on this side of the door. We are definitely trapped in here."

Kerian's hand felt something sharp and jagged catch his palm as he reassuringly patted the locked door. He pulled his hand away and moved in closer with the torch to identify what it was. A jagged human nail hung there, adhered to the doorway by a dark sticky residue. The horses shifted nervously as a long drawn out moan echoed from out of the darkness behind them.

"You know it has just occurred to me that we might not be alone in here." Kerian stated, his face suddenly pale.

"You don't say." Octavian replied, his cocky smile noticeably missing from his face. "Why don't you tell me something I don't know."

Chapter Fifteen

"Now hold the book tightly, sense the power within." Brother Richard stated calmly. "You know that magic users take the energy from gemstones to create their spells, an act that is ultimately destructive, destroying beauty for what is basically short-term gain. We use our steadfast faith in our gods to know instinctively that the magic will be there when we need it to be. This is why we use artefacts such as this book to channel the forces that we need." He pulled up the sleeves of his pale blue robes and took in the younger kneeling monk beside him, eyes closed, an image of serenity, the book Richard desperately coveted held tightly in his arms.

"What if the magic isn't there when I need it?" Marcus asked opening his eyes and yawning before noticing the attention his mentor was showing to him. "What if when I release the power, I cannot control it?" Hesitation sounded clearly in the young monk's voice.

"Faith will guide you." Richard replied, his brow creasing as he tried to hide his frustration with Marcus's obvious weakness, behind a false mask. "Am I keeping you up?"

"No… it's just that I have been having trouble sleeping recently. My mind is a whirl with all these teachings and I lay awake at night tossing and turning on a bed that has become increasingly uncomfortable of late. It's as if my mattress has suddenly lost its stuffing and my pillow has become decidedly flat." Marcus confessed.

Richard moved to reply then paused. Funnily enough he had been experiencing a similar situation, he had just thought that the reduced movement of the ship was the reason for his insomnia. He stole a quick glance around the open deck of the *El Defensor* and then back down at the book held in Marcus's hands. No one was around, this was his chance.

"Why don't you let me try the book and show you?" he asked. The younger novice did not hesitate in passing the book over for Richard's eager hands to hold, making the monk feel like mocking Marcus's innocence, only for static electric sparks to jump from the cover causing Richard to almost drop it in pain.

"I'm so sorry." Marcus apologised, fumbling to catch the large blue leather book. "The book was matched to me back in Catterick. Only Abbot Brialin was able to hold it afterwards. I'm not sure how to undo his magic or I would hand this burden over in a second. You can wrap it in something to stop the shocks…"

"Yes but then because I am not in direct contact with the book the magic won't work!" Richard snapped, rubbing his hand to trying to return the circulation to it. His outward anger equally directed within. The damned book did not want him to hold it! Marcus was such a weak soul, with no vision as to the real power wielding the book could bring. Why did it refuse to match with him, someone so much stronger in character than this novice? He wanted this book to regain all he had lost at Stratholme. The book was right there for the taking but it might as well have been on another world for all the good he could do with it.

"Have you even opened the book?" Brother Richard snapped. "Conversed with the magical knights within?"

"I was told never to open the book unless asked to." Marcus replied, nervously rolling a bead on his rosary between his fingers, his body language clearly uncomfortable with the situation. "I am the *Bearer* of the book, not its master."

"Well how do you expect to understand the book; how do you expect to become proficient with its powers?" Richard asked. "Isn't it about time you took command of your fears for the better of the others, of this crew? You know you need to. They require all the help they can get. What happens if it's a matter of life and death and you sit there fiddling with your rosary? If you have no faith in your own abilities, you will never get the book to work as it should." Marcus hung his head in shame, the words delivered by Brother Richard like a lash to him. Richard realised he had maybe pushed too hard; it was time to change tact.

"I am right here to help you." He coaxed slyly. "Why don't you open the book now to check all is well with what it carries?"

"I can try." Marcus replied, changing his position to sit cross legged and place the book in his lap. He looked down at the worn blue cover, the design across it showing a series of holy knights and a solitary monk holding aloft a smaller representation of the book in his arms. Double locks prevented the book from opening and Richard's keen sight noticed there were some faint scratch marks around the actual lock openings, as if someone had tried to open the book in the past. Well he knew they would not have been successful in that undertaking. No one had ever picked a lock on a *Bearer's* tome.

Marcus took a deep breath then pressed his thumbs against the locks, closing his eyes and muttering a small incantation under his breath that Brother Richard, despite leaning closer, failed to hear correctly. The locks clicked softly open and the clasps yawned wide but the young monk paused as his hand moved to the edge of the cover, a slight tremor visible in his fingertips.

"What are you waiting for?" Brother Richard asked. "Get on with it, have faith in your ability to command what lies within."

Marcus steadied himself then flipped open the book to reveal what looked like a beautifully illustrated colour plate that filled the first page. It showed a darkened room, much like a drab prison cell, with damp stone slabs so cunningly illustrated you could almost reach out and touch the moisture with your fingertip. Mossy growth of vivid greens appeared almost luminous beneath the flickering torchlight from sconces attached to the walls. Bunkbeds, some occupied with sleeping forms whilst others had sheets drawn over the heads of those who had clearly fallen in battle were placed about the cell, armour and personal belongings could be seen in the shadows, hidden under the bunks, or perched on small intimate shelves but this was a barracks like no other Marcus had seen illustrated.

For one thing the illustration was so real! The attention to detail quite incredible. There was even a discarded playing piece from a board game lying on the floor that even as the two monks looked on began to gently rock backwards and forwards in rhythm with the movement of the *El Defensor*.

Movement at the far side of the illustrated room caught the novice's eye, as a knight suddenly appeared from between the line of a solid wall and a row of bunks, only by careful examination was it clear that the room must have continued off into the shadows and was much larger than the reader initially suspected, the illustration a clever optical illusion. The knight himself at first appeared to be a simple figure but as Marcus and Richard looked on the details in his armour and clothes began to sharpen into focus and become lifelike. The warrior suddenly looked up, shading his blue eyes as if impossibly blinded by the sunlight the open book had allowed to be directed into the darkened room.

"It's beautiful." Brother Richard whispered. "I could never have imagined it so." A cloud passed in front of the sun above their heads, creating a corresponding shadow to pass over the illustration in the book.

"*Bearer* Marcus." The knight addressed him. "Is it time? Are you in need of our service?" Marcus's mouth was dry, his response a parched squeak of a voice. He recognised this knight from his dealings with him in Stratholme.

"I don't need you at this time Bartholomew," he replied. "I am just checking on your welfare."

"Our fare is not well." The knight sank to one knee and gestured around at the still forms in the bunks about him. "Several of us are too ill to rise from our beds. Our wounds do not heal as they should. It is as if there is no godly power left to aid us, as if our very faith is being tested. *Bearer* you are a person of faith; in your hands we should be strong, instead this is happening. What have you done to us?"

"You see what happens when you have no faith?" Marcus jerked his head up from the page as Richard whispered the accusation into his ear.

"I have faith," Marcus replied, ashamed at having to defend his beliefs.

"Yes but your faith is not as strong as mine." Brother Richard advised. The knight remained silently on his knees, watching the conversation with a dark expression. A second knight walked around the corner and advanced to stand just behind his kneeling companion.

"Is it time for us to be called?" this fellow warrior asked.

"I am afraid not Tobias." Bartholomew replied. "It is as we feared. Brother Marcus remains the *Bearer*. This is the reason why we are not healing." The second knight looked up into Marcus's face, his features now set in an angry frown.

"I should have killed you when I had the chance." Tobias threatened, moving towards the front of the illustration, even as his hand reached for the sword at his belt. "Abbot Brialin should never have given you this position of trust. He should never have showed such faith in a man who obviously has so little of his own."

"I have faith." Richard stated from over Marcus's shoulder.

"What are you saying?" Marcus turned to Richard, initially forgetting the open book, his face seeking the meaning behind the monk's leading words. "What do you mean?"

"He means your time as a *Bearer* will be up when I finally stand before you." Tobias threatened from inside the book. "Release me from the book now. Let me put right what you have made so terribly wrong. Let me..."

"What are you looking at?" Colette asked.

"Nothing." Marcus stammered, slamming the book closed and hurriedly clicking the locks back into place. "Nothing at all... I'm sorry, I need to go now. I'll speak to you later." He swiftly got to his feet and tucked the blue book under his arm before heading towards his cabin.

Brother Richard let out an exasperated breath as he watched Marcus descend the companionway, leaving Richard suddenly alone with the young woman who had disrupted their session.

"Did I interrupt something important?" Colette asked, noting his glowering visage. Brother Richard took in the mage's petite form, her long flowing blonde hair, soft leather boots and rune patterned robes. She was dragging a rune etched long sword along the deck that was nearly as long as she was tall. Mages were so clumsy and over the top with their magic. If he had the power of the ledger, he would show people like her exactly where true power lay.

"Nothing important at all." Richard smiled. "Nothing we will not revisit at a later time when there is less chance of interruption." He turned away leaving Colette open mouthed at his rudeness. She stood there for a long time, standing by the starboard rail looking out across the water to the dense jungles on the far shore, her mind replaying the events and trying to fathom what she had inadvertently disrupted. Maybe, it would have been better to have simply moved towards the foredeck leaving the two men alone but she had wanted, no needed, some level of kinship with other members of the crew.

For some reason, since the strange feeling of being watched had ceased, she had felt more despondent, more alone, despite how irrational this feeling was. With her ghostly mentor being equally distant, she had just wanted some companionship. She stared down at the long sword in her hand and wondered why she was even bringing this weapon along with her. Maybe by keeping it at her side she could still feel a connection with the man who sacrificed his life to save her. She rubbed her eyes to ease the prickling she suddenly felt there. Colette found a comfortable place on the foredeck, away from the busy sections of the ship frequented by the crew and drew the gleaming weapon from its sheath.

Kerian's sword was beautiful, if such a word was appropriate for a weapon that had taken so many lives since its initial forging. Excluding the hilt, the actual blade was a little over four feet in length, the metal dulled, apart from the sharpened edges, central ridge and engraved runes running the length of the blood groove, that reflected the afternoon sunshine and painted rune shaped shadows across the mage's soft features.

The pommel was the size of her palm, carved in the shape of a roaring dragon, the deep-set emerald eyes emphasised using silver-plating set within the recesses below thickly scaled brows. The silvered teeth of the dragon helped to emphasis the artistry of the weapon; however, inside of the dragon's mouth was a solid piece of metal used to balance the weight of the sword. The grip consisted of a long strip of leather hide, spiralling down from the pommel to the cross guard, worn smooth from years of use, its length intertwined with black and gold wire. The cross guard had further roaring dragons at each end, the eyes beset with small emeralds.

Examining the blade closely, Colette noticed the signs of wear collected over the years, nicks along the sharpened edges, some peeling of the silver plate and dark stains on the leather grip testified that the owner of this sword had faced inherent dangers that always seemed to occur when men bore arms.

A rune beneath the rain guard caught Colette's eye. The mage thought she vaguely recognised the symbol, her mind trying to identify the hidden meaning of it but like the sword's absent owner, the connection with Colette was a fleeting one at best. It was possible that if she traced the runes out and returned to the reference books in Rauph's cabin she could understand exactly what this weapon's powers were. Maybe solving this mystery would help her to clear her mind and then leave her fresh to deal with the other problems that seemed to be building up around her.

Colette grasped the sword in two hands, feeling the weight of the blade and marvelling how anyone could ever use such weapons in a lengthy battle. The strain on a fighter's arms and shoulders must be immense. She stood legs apart and faced off against an imaginary foe. The weapon started to radiate a muted glow along the edges at the mage's touch however, in the afternoon light the colour was difficult to identify. Colette lifted the sword high, trying to swing it about her head, only for the weight of the weapon to bring the point of the sword crashing down to the deck where it scored heavily across two planks and stopped just short of Aradol's boot.

"Oh I'm so sorry." Colette blushed. "The sword is much heavier than it looks and I over balanced."

"Well I can only pity the foe who dares to cross such a proficient swordswoman." Aradol replied, with a deep sigh and wiped his brow to emphasise how close the weapon had come to wounding him. "I shall count my toes carefully when I remove my boots tonight."

"Oh don't make fun." Colette replied. "I am trying to better myself here. Instead of standing laughing why don't you come and show me what to do." Aradol moved in closer, putting his arms protectively around Colette's shoulders and helped her grip the sword again.

"I am afraid this weapon is too heavy for you." Aradol opened. "Have you ever considered a lighter blade?"

"It's this sword or nothing." Colette replied firmly, surprising herself with her assertive reply.

"As you wish." Aradol replied, moving in close behind her. "Just remember that if you gouge any more of the deck, I'm going to tell Thomas it was your own doing."

Colette bit her lip gently, trying to focus on holding the blade steadily out in front of her and realised it had a noticeable wobble.

"Spread your legs wider, set yourself a good base so you balance and then..."

"Shut up and help me steady the sword." Colette smiled.

"Aradol moved in closer, his arms encircling her own, his two hands gently cupping hers. She felt his breath on her shoulder, his firm muscles holding her safely. It had been a long time since anyone had shown her any tenderness in this way. She found her heart beating faster and discovered she was feeling giddy at his attentions, whilst her conscience questioned if it was wrong to feel this way?

The blade started to glow a bright white nimbus as Aradol's fingers touched the rain guard on the hilt, flaring brightly despite the bright afternoon sunshine.

"Why is it doing that?" Colette questioned under her breath, leaning back into Aradol's arms further and relishing the comfort it gave her. She found herself mentally pushing her protests aside. It no longer mattered what she did. She had no romantic ties to anyone. Kerian was gone and it was time to live again. The mage scolded herself to enjoy the moment and closed her eyes, finally giving in to the sensations washing through her body.

A loud tramping march broke through her reverie. The blade suddenly became heavy in her arms and before she realised it Aradol was lowering the tip to the floor.

"I'm sorry but I need to find out what that is." Aradol excused himself. "Thomas left me in charge of the ship so it is my duty to make sure all is well." He flashed a disarming smile.

"Maybe we can continue this at another time?"

"Another time then." Colette replied breathlessly, feeling like an embarrassed school girl all over again. She looked down at the blade in her hand and suddenly felt a surge of overwhelming guilt at betraying Kerian's memory in this way. Then she stopped herself, angrily holding back hot tears that had suddenly sprung to her eyes.

Kerian had died for her, this was true, there had been no way he could have escaped the hidden temple on Stratholme. Thinking fondly of him this way was fine but she was still a woman, still needed comfort, warmth, things this cold steel could never supply. She needed to take back control of her life and that would mean ultimately starting new relationships, no matter how hard and painful it would be to expose her heart again. If that was what she needed, then so be it. She would be strong, not only for herself but to ensure Kerian's sacrifice meant something.

Colette slid the sword back into its scabbard, sealing away the guilt as skilfully as she homed the blade and headed off after Aradol to see what all the noise was about.

It did not take long to find out.

A line of Minotaur troops had come down onto the jetty and were now standing to attention sunlight gleaming off their armour and weapons. What was going on now? Colette's mind focused as sharply as the tips of the spears the creatures carried. She swung the sword over her shoulder and placed her hands into the pockets of her robes, grabbing hold of a few key items she needed in case the situation became difficult, then moved over to the rail to see who Aradol was speaking to.

* * * * * *

Mathius ran down the cobbled street as if his boots and cape were on fire behind him. His heart pounded in his chest as if it would burst, making him regret the pipes he had smoked over the last few days. If he did not get to the dock soon, he was either going to pass out or cough up a lung! He skidded to a stop in front of a small crowd of people staring down towards the majestic silhouette of the *El Defensor* and froze.

The onlookers found themselves suddenly torn between the scene below where the Taurean guard were almost certainly about to storm the foreign ship in the harbour or the wild-eyed man with the psychotic look on his face, who's clothes looked torn to rags and who sported several impressive bleeding wounds on his hands and knees including a bite mark on his right shin. Several people shuffled nervously away, whilst others needed to be tapped on the shoulder to be made aware of what was happening right alongside them instead of down below.

"Damn it!" Mathius gasped, putting his head down and placing his bleeding hands on his knees. "What does an assassin need to do to get a break around here?" He took in a deep lungful of air, trying to calm the tremors in his arms and legs, then moved to the side of the thoroughfare, making several onlookers dart away, thinking he was about to have a heart attack or similar.

The assassin steadied himself against the warm masonry and took in the scene below. There were about twenty-five heavily armoured troops and a senior Minotaur who appeared to be in discussion with Aradol. Surprisingly the youth seemed to be standing his ground on the gangway refusing entry to the troops, despite the fact the grey-haired creature towered above him.

Mathius observed the Minotaur splitting into four groups of six, one set of six took up position at the stern of the ship, spear hafts slamming to the ground as they stood at attention, observing everything around them, whilst another six similarly positioned themselves for'ard of the Spanish galleon. The remaining twelve stood either side of the main gangway, their weapons presented to state their strength and power.

There was no way he was going to be able to approach the ship with these guards in place. That was, unless he approached from the water. If he could just lower himself into the lake and swim around to the anchor... The thought died in a second as the two perimeter sets of guards turned with parade ground precision, one guard from each group now looked out across the bay for that very same reason.

Think! Think! Mathius scolded himself. He needed a distraction. Some way of making the guards look away. He scanned the deck for inspiration. There had to be something that could get him past those guards.

* * * * * *

"Austen would you mind holding this?"

The crewman paused in amazement, his bucket and mop momentarily forgotten, as what could only be described as a child sized chicken handed him a gilded cage. He looked down at the shoes this creature was wearing and noticed they appeared to be a pair of stained work boots from Commagin's cabin. However, now they had been painted bright yellow and the paint was still wet and dripping across the deck. The trousers and tunic of this feathered creature were covered in what could only be described as fistfuls of feathers stuck in random clumps of gooey glue. This was not an aerodynamic creature, because in one clump of glue and feathers there also appeared to be a paintbrush, in another, a couple of spoons and a pencil that had somehow become caught up in this frenzy of feather and glue.

"Now when I say... I want you to open the cage door okay."

Austen nodded his head, momentarily lost for words as he stared down into the mouth of the soggy over-sized beak made from a piece of leather that still dripped yellow paint. The beaming eyes of Ashe shone out from within the contraption, wild with enthusiasm.

"Ashe what are you doing?" the crewman enquired as calmly as he could, looking down at the cage he was now holding and then back at the feathered Halfling once more, clearly pondering if this was some crazy dream.

"I'm going to teach Sinders to fly." Ashe replied breathlessly, wound up in the excitement of the moment. "Just remember release him when I say." Ashe stood back, stomped his boots, leaving a set of bright yellow footprints on the worn wooden surface, then set off running along the deck of the ship stopping every few feet to blow into a mangled trumpet and issue a loud 'Parp'. Movement on the ship froze as the feathered Halfling set off, squawking and stomping along in the yellow boots that were clearly several sizes too big for him.

The cartoon chicken charged around, completing a circuit of the area where the huge wind elemental used to be magically contained, then veered off to hit the companionway where the aft deck dropped down to the main. Ashe flung his arms wide, allowing a bed sheet, liberally covered in sticky feathers to suddenly spring open from a bundle on his back. The far ends of the stained sheet were cunningly attached to Ashe's wrists, making him appear to have a set of rather limp but nevertheless functioning wings.

"Tah Dah!" Ashe yelled, flapping his make-shift wings wide and jumping off the top of the ladder. His flight was short lived, dropping down to the main deck with a thump, barely missing crewmen who dodged away, hands reaching protectively for their pockets. The Halfling landed lightly, springing up with gusto, his wings billowing out behind him, several feathers whipping off and flying about as he ran breathlessly towards the foredeck and the climb that awaited him there. Ashe bounced enthusiastically up the ladder, then turned with his trumpet held high.

"Parp!"

Before anyone could stop him, he was off again, leaving another cloud of feathers fluttering in his wake. He charged around the foredeck, down the companionway on the far side, then back across the main to where Colette stood open-mouthed. Aradol turned on the gangway to observe the commotion, only to find himself pressed from behind and jostled back onto the ship by the grey minotaur who had seen the opportunity and was now taking it.

Ashe skidded to a stop before the astonished trio and held out his little hand to the ancient Minotaur halting the creature's planned invasion just before he gained a foothold. Down on the quay the other Minotaur troops moved closer to get a better view, not sure if this was livestock loose aboard the ship, or a threat to their captain.

"Hi, I'm Ashe!" the Halfling gasped. "Can't stop, I've got to learn to fly."

"Parp!"

The moulting chicken figure shot off again, feathers swirling about him, one boot flopping heavily to the side as his foot started to come free. The Halfling staggered to the base of the next companionway, a little less enthusiastic than his last time here and pulled himself to the top, just as one of his boots finally flew off to hit Abeline on the back of the head as the sailor was sitting patching one of the smaller sails.

"Oops, sorry!" Ashe grinned, in the infectious way only the diminutive thief could. "Can't stop I'm on a mission of great importance."

"Parp!"

Running hard, he snatched the boot back, leaving Abeline rubbing his head as he hopped around the corner where Austen was waiting with the cage.

"Open the door..." Ashe shouted panting, trying to cram his foot back into the yellow boot. "Open it now and tip Sinders out. Come on Sinders, it is time to fly..." The Halfling ran past, leaving Austen shaking the cage, desperately trying to tip the fuzzy white and black bird that was the centre of Ashe's attention out onto the deck. There was a soft flump and the ugly bird ended up dumped out, onto its posterior.

"Go." Austen shooed at the creature. "Follow your mad owner."

Sinders had no such intention of doing so and extended a thin neck from the mish-mash of plumage that was its body, stretching high, before quickly scanning the area for its feline nemesis and reaching out with its sharp beak to grab the cage that Austen held high out of reach.

"No!" Austen scolded, lifting the cage higher and placing it on a barrel. "After a show like this you will stay out of your cage."

Sinders stared with a blood shot eye that made Austen shiver. The bird was so strange; it went against everything the crewman knew of these birds. Its siblings all looked sleek like normal sea eagles. This thing looked like a cross between an ostrich and, well, one of those mythical Roc birds that terrorised sailors in the faded book of adventure stories Thomas had lent him. Even as Austen watched, the bird regarded the trail of yellow boot prints leading away and then attempted to pull itself into the tightest ball of plumage it could.

Ashe, meanwhile, was intent on continuing his laps of the ship. He had crashed down onto the main and was even now flapping his way back towards the foredeck. When he reached the ladder to climb up, he had to take a moment to lean on the bottom rung and wave his hand in front of his face to try to cool himself down. Sweat was soaking into the bill of his costume making it flap dangerously about and obscure parts of his vision. Who would have known that learning to fly was such hard work? He took another deep breath and continued on, staggering to climb ladders that now felt like small mountains.

Colette and Aradol found themselves feeling quite dizzy as the white and yellow feathered blob clumped noisily around the foredeck before reaching the top of the ladder leading back down to the main. From the look of things, Ashe's battle against gravity was not going well. The Halfling stood for a moment, taking the opportunity to gaze back down the length of the ship, shading his eyes looking for a sign of Sinders and not seeing him there. His enthusiasm clearly began to ebb as he realised his feathered friend was not following him.

"Parp!"

Never had a 'parp' been sounded with less enthusiasm. Ashe secured the trumpet at his waist and threw himself off the companionway, his boot catching on the top rung, tripping him on the ladder and sending him crashing face down onto the deck to land in a cloud of exploding feathers.

"Ow! Curly cashews!" Ashe cursed loudly, resorting to one of his nut similes he used in times of great exasperation. The feathered chicken shook his head and pulled himself to his feet, straightening his now seriously bent beak, before setting off with a determined scowl on his face, limping past the gangway and the party of astonished onlookers standing there. He reached the bottom of the next companionway, looked up at the steps reaching above him and felt his enthusiasm waning further. He paused and turned back towards the gangway and the tall grey Minotaur standing there.

"Excuse me…" Ashe gasped. "I… need a hand… to get up the ladder. This flying lark is… much harder than it looks. Can you give me a boost?" He beckoned at the grey-haired Minotaur, leading the creature out across the main deck from the gangway, much to Aradol's concern.

Aelius, captain of the Minotaur guard, looked down at the bedraggled Halfling and appeared torn between his current duty and the need to aid such a pathetic creature. Maybe he could put it out of its misery with a swift blow to the back of the head? The captain of the guard went to draw his sword but as he moved his hand, Ashe grabbed it and dragged the huge creature over to the companionway.

"If you could just boost me up?" Ashe asked gesturing enthusiastically. "That's great, now bend down a bit so I can get my boot in your hand and, oops, I'm sure that yellow paint comes right out if you rub it hard enough. Umm you seem to have some feathers stuck in your hair. I know just the thing that can help with that but no time right now." Ashe tore off around the aft deck, leaving the aged Minotaur looking in disbelief at the yellow paint dripping from his hands. The Halfling slid to a stop in front of Austen panting hard.

"Well, where is he?" Ashe gasped, his head turning this way and that, scanning the sky above for some sign of his feathered friend. Austen lightly tapped Ashe on the shoulder and gestured down to the ball of feathers on the floor.

"Why isn't Sinders following me?" Ashe asked, picking up his pet and cooing to it softly. "Why isn't he flying?" Austen tried to show compassion but had no idea how to respond to the Halfling's disappointed comments. Ashe scowled, pushing up his floppy leather beak and poking his head out from underneath it, streaking his nose with yellow paint.

"Well I'm not giving up!" Ashe snapped angrily. He took a deep breath and set off again, his hands cupping the jiggling form of Sinders as he headed for the companionway to restart his circuit again. The four-foot-high bedraggled chicken hit the top of the ladder and hopped down a few rungs, the trailing end of his feathered cape snagging on the top step to snap the Halfling around. Sinders shot into the air as Ashe's arms jerked upwards. The Halfling bounced off the rail, his feet slipping and sliding on the ladder. One boot flew off and then Sinders came crashing down onto his head knocking his beak completely over his eyes.

Ashe staggered backwards, blinded, wrapped up in his feathered cloak he had no idea where he was or where he was going. He felt a rail behind him, reached out to grab it and found himself falling over the side.

"Halfling overboard!" Plano shouted, reaching for a safety line even as he jumped to Ashe's rescue.

Austen walked back to his bucket and mop shaking his head at the sorry sight of the Halfling bobbing up and down in the harbour water, one yellow boot sticking up in the air. Plano soon swam up alongside and looped the safety line around the struggling thief before signalling to be pulled back aboard even as another strongly swimming crewman joined him and helped tow Ashe back towards the side of the ship. Despite Austen's concerns about Ashe's other more annoying habits the crewman could only shake his head at the spectacle he had just witnessed. He turned back to the gilded cage, just in time to see a bundle of feathers hop up onto the barrel, waddle back inside and pull the cage door tightly shut behind him.

The spluttering and cursing continued below as the safety line was drawn in and several wet figures ended up back on the deck, one of them a lot more bedraggled and upset than the others. Aradol and Colette rushed over to Ashe, Plano and the third bedraggled crewman.

"Ashe are you okay?" Colette asked with concern.

"Did he fly?" Ashe asked, spitting out a sodden feather. "Did Sinders fly far?" Colette's sad smile answered the question without words and Ashe slumped to the deck, all of his energy now ebbing from him.

"Don't worry." Colette tried to reassure the little Halfling. "Maybe he wasn't ready yet. I know If I wanted to fly, I would have been flapping after you in no time at all."

"Really?" Ashe smiled. "You really would have?"

"If I had feathers, I'd be circling the ship right now." Colette smiled back.

Aradol turned to look at Plano and noticed to his relief the man showed no cuts or bruises, then he turned to the third crewman who looked like he had been crawling across razor clams and scraping barnacles from the hull.

"Dear lord." Aradol whispered. "What in the world happened to you?" Mathius looked up from the deck, water dripping from his torn clothes and stared Aradol straight in the eye.

"Thomas has asked me to give you a message..."

* * * * * *

The King's Head was not glamorous or regal in any sense of the title, having been named after the legendary demise of a wayward king, who met his end dangling from the rotting gibbet just outside its ill-fitting door. Most traders on the road to Al Mashmaah would have avoided the place for better inns such as *The Globe* or *The Crimson Lion* and its latest customer was starting to understand why. Even now, Scrave found his gaze repeatedly drawn from the plate of congealing food upon his table, to a large glass jar displayed behind the bar, in which something vaguely skull-like floated in a curdled green solution with a cheap attempt at a crown wedged firmly upon its decaying brow.

Scrave knew he had eaten in worse places but this time his appetite seemed to be failing him completely. No matter how he tried, he could not force himself to eat even one mouthful of the greasy fare before him. He turned his attention to the goblet of wine accompanying his meal and raised it to his lips, only to feel his stomach curl and roll in disgust.

There was something wrong with him. He could not remember the last time he had eaten; the last time he had quenched his thirst. The dagger squirmed at his right hip and he placed his hand gently down upon it, ensuring his cloak was covering the exotic weapon. Could it be the dagger at work? He had felt infused with energy when it had killed. Could the weapon somehow be feeding him, making additional sustenance unnecessary?

Or alternatively, there was there something else going on? Something he had yet to comprehend? He raised his hand to his face, trying to ignore the slight tremor he felt and gently touched the eye patch now covering his right eye. The eyeball seemed to have disappeared completely, either shrivelled away in the heat from the volcanic temple or consumed by some unknown horror. Maybe Kerian Denaris had blinded him after their battle in the subterranean temple when Scrave had lost consciousness. That was a sick thing for the old man to do!

A shudder ran through him at the thought. How had Kerian won that sword fight? Somehow his mind refused to replay those last fateful moments, instead he felt an ache deep in his chest that held no logical meaning. Kerian Denaris... The Elf scowled, shaking his head, whatever had happened to Kerian Denaris? Something squirmed in agitation deep in Scrave's eye socket, making him pause in his dark thoughts to pursue even darker ones. Something sentient and menacing was moving about in his eye, something that probed his thoughts with a lascivious glee, promising impossible, unreachable things in fitful dreams and guiding his actions with ethereal suggestions he found hard to ignore. Whatever this entity was, Scrave felt better knowing the flickering green glow it gave off was safely secured and out of sight behind the patch. The less attention he drew to himself the better it would be, giving him valuable breathing time to try and figure out how he could remove and kill whatever it was.

Scrave closed his eye and leant back against the wall, allowing the sounds of the tavern to wash over him. A raised voice by the bar complaining at the lack of credit offered, the gruff, less than polite response. A group of men over to the right swapped tall tales, one telling the others he was taking his rod and moving to fish at the Mereya River where it was being reported an angler had landed several fish with precious gemstones in their gullets. The Elf smiled, despite his dark thoughts, now that was a fisherman's tale to be proud of. Obviously, the drink around here was very strong and there was clearly nothing else important to gossip about.

The bar door slammed and a new breathless voice arose from over by the bar. Scrave froze as he heard the unmistakeable words 'Elf' and 'green eye' mentioned. He opened his eye and took in the exhausted dispatch rider who wore the unmistakable livery of St Fraiser. It appeared Justina was searching for him and the dagger at his side, she clearly did not want him to get away.

"I've only seen one Elf." The barman replied. "He don't have no green eye though. He wears an eyepatch and he's right over... eh?" The dispatch rider turned to look in the direction the barman was gesturing, only to find an empty chair.

Chapter Sixteen

Kerian nervously licked his lips, struggling to calm the turmoil he felt within. He never liked to lose control, show weakness or give anyone around him cause to view him as anything less than the true warrior he aspired to be. However, recently his life had been nothing but one crisis after another. He slid slowly down the cool stone of the door and sat on the floor with a sigh, taking a mouthful of tepid water from his limited supply in a vain attempt to lubricate a parched mouth and cracked lips now coated in a thick layer of grit and sand.

The sounds of the screaming skeletons, sealed outside at the mercy of the storm, were slowly reducing in volume, although muffled thumps still echoed around the room as the monsters repeatedly tried to gain access to the two traveller's hiding place. Kerian tried to rationalise his fears, attempted to explain away the reduction in noise as the monsters simply losing interest in a quarry they could not catch, rather than the all too real rationale that they were slowly being buried alive beneath the whispering sands. The horses, clearly agitated at the sounds, paced nervously, tails flicking and eyes rolling as they picked up on the terrors without and the permeating sense of menace hanging thickly in the air within.

There had been no further ghostly wails, no obvious clues as to what creature stalked these darkened hallways but a sense of unease continued to hound Kerian. The knight looked at the ancient torch flickering above him, its yellow light a protective sphere that would keep him safe as long as he remained within its nurturing circle but he knew with certainty the torch would eventually burn out and he would then be plunged into complete darkness and an encounter with the monsters that awaited him there.

He looked over at Octavian searching for some signs his guide had a plan for getting them out of their predicament but the gypsy appeared as agitated as the horses, sniffing at the air and pacing out the entrance chamber they were in, leaving footprints in dust that had remained undisturbed for many years. Kerian had no idea what the man was smelling, his own nostrils were all clogged up with mucus and sand.

"So what do we do now?" Kerian asked quietly. Octavian started at the sound, his mind clearly miles away from their dusty tomb. The gypsy walked over and sank down alongside Kerian, holding the remains of the pennant tipped spear thrown by the skeletal warrior in his hand.

"I'm not sure." The gypsy confessed. "Do you mind if I look at your 'lance'?" Kerian shrugged indifference and walked over to Toledo, retrieving the standard he had used to keep the undead monsters at bay. Octavian was already unrolling the pennant from where it had tangled around the spear shaft and laughed aloud. He placed the spear to one side then took the standard from Kerian, unfurling it and angling the material so Kerian could see the faded symbol of a grey spider with a blue cross embroidered on its abdomen.

"Well what do you know." He smiled. "We appear to have solved an ancient mystery. We are the only two people who know what happened to the Provan Legion. Do you mind if I keep this?" He pushed the pennant aside and reached for the standard, his eyes sparkling in the flickering torchlight, bright with the excitement of the chase and the recognition of the treasure he had discovered.

"I don't know what it is about you Kerian..." The gypsy shook his head smiling and pushed his curly hair back from his face as he removed the standard from its shaft and started rolling it up. "... But It appears you are so irksome, that you even manage to annoy the dead!" Kerian offered a tired laugh in response but there was not much enthusiasm behind it. He kept thinking of the two light sources they had and what would happen when the torches died.

"Why would you ever want such a tired old thing? He gestured towards the banner as Octavian pushed it down into one of his saddlebags. The gypsy paused in his work and looked over, his mischievous smile beaming.

"I can hardly go into a tavern and spin a tale about the Provan legion without proof now, can I?" He smiled. "This insignia is going to get me many a free drink and who knows, maybe it's worth something?"

"So what happens now?" Kerian asked, returning his attention to their more immediate problem. "How do we get out of this place?"

"Well it won't be out of this door." Octavian stated. "So I guess we need to head further in."

Kerian looked around the area, the torchlight barely illuminating the hieroglyphics exquisitely painted and engraved on the walls around them. They appeared to be in a large chamber about twenty feet wide by twenty feet deep. Statues stood in niches along the walls, the humanoid figures wearing elaborate animal heads, jackals, eagles, cats and the like. His eyes searched for any kind of weapon but there was nothing suitable that he could employ to keep his feelings of unease at bay.

He slid the shield around onto his left arm, catching a blurred reflection of Octavian in the gleaming surface. The gypsy appeared dark in the shield, his outline indistinct and hazy, his eyes a piercing blue. Before

Kerian could study him closer, his guide got to his feet and walked over to a dark opening in the far wall, holding the burning torch aloft and peering through into the passageways beyond.

"We appear to be lucky," Octavian reported. "The corridors appear wide enough to get the horses down. I think we will need to extinguish one of the torches to conserve it. Kerian knew the request made sense and retrieved the second torch, reluctantly pushing its flame into a pile of drifted sand that had blown under the door. As the flames spluttered and died, something in Kerian's mind shivered and he suddenly felt very cold.

Octavian returned to the mounts, taking a moment to ensure his keepsake insignia was tightly secured, before he seized the reins of the horses and led them towards the gloomy corridor ahead. The animals appeared restless; Octavian's steed throwing its head about and the donkey kept baring its teeth and rolling its eyes. Kerian grabbed Toledo's reins and for once, the horse followed without question, realising that it had to place trust in its rider if it was to escape from this strange and unsettling place.

As they stepped into the corridor, Kerian became aware of the odour. It was a damp smell, slightly fusty, not the sort of aroma you would expect from a desert tomb. If disease had a stench, it was this. The acrid odour infiltrated the nostrils and coated the back of the mouth, making his saliva taste bitter and leaving a lingering after taste. Whatever it was, Kerian decided he did not want to find out the origin. Octavian slowed the horses and whispered back over his shoulder.

"The corridor branches ahead. Do you want to go left or right?" he asked.

"Right." Kerian whispered back. "Always follow the right wall then you won't get lost."

Octavian nodded and set off again, leading the horses down a slight incline and deeper into the darkness, their hooves striking loudly off the stone floor and echoing eerily about the corridor. Kerian observed his guide striving fearlessly ahead, the flickering torch illuminating the way for the guide and his steeds but leaving Kerian and Toledo partially obscured by menacing shadows. Something about this place was really starting to unsettle the knight and he had no idea why. There was also something different about Octavian but Kerian could not quite put his finger on it.

The gypsy halted again, allowing Kerian to catch up, holding the torch high to reveal a crossroads in the passageway, straight ahead had collapsed leaving just a left or right branch for them to choose. Octavian smiled and pointed to the right before pulling his horses along with him. Kerian led Toledo around the corner and noticed the ceiling now opening up above them, rising to approximately fifty feet. Sombre statues regarded the intruders with emotionless eyes from where they sat in alcoves set into the walls. Vertical lines of hieroglyphs soared upwards, telling tales in an alien language of pictographs and mysterious symbols that Kerian could not translate.

Octavian stopped again, considering a flight of stairs that led up along the left wall to a platform high above, or the dark passage straight ahead. He turned back to Kerian and handed the reins of his horses to him.

"Wait here. I'll just be a second." Octavian winked, offering his roguish smile before bounding up the stairs and taking the only light source they had with him. Kerian's eyes followed the light like a drowning man watching his only chance of safety floating away. The light caressed the wall motifs as it accompanied his guide up the stairs and then disappeared as Octavian explored the passage there. Kerian gasped as he was plunged into darkness once more. He froze in place, eyes straining to seek out a source of light, the breathing of the horses now incredibly loud to his ears, the click of a hoof tapping impatiently on the stone made his heart jump, whilst another sound, further away and less distinct snatched his attention. Somewhere in the darkness, something was being dragged across the floor.

Kerian looked back the way they had come, staring blindly into the darkness, his ears alert for more sounds, regarding whatever was out there and if it was coming closer. His hands started to sweat and he gripped the edge of his shield more tightly. Was that something moving up from behind? Were his senses playing tricks on him, or was an outstretched hand moving towards him in the darkness? Brittle, stick thin fingers probing the air inches from his face desperate to claw at his skin?

A trickle of light slowly started to illuminate the walls as Octavian returned from the passageway above, Kerian squinted, blinking hard to clear his nightmarish visions as the gypsy ran down the steps to rejoin him. He leapt the last few steps and smiled, holding out a dusty bundle in his arms.

"Consider this a down-payment on your sword." The gypsy beamed. "It is not a weapon, not even close to being a sword but it is armour and you have mentioned on the trail that you needed some." Octavian paused taking in Kerian's pale face and wide staring eyes.

"What's the matter with you? I thought you would be impressed; you look like you have seen a ghost." Octavian thrust the package into Kerian's hand as he took back his horse and donkey. "Don't thank me all at once, okay?" Kerian nodded his head and shook the dusty armour, holding it up in the air as the dust of ages settled about him in white luminous flecks. It was the sorriest looking armour he had ever seen. Some of the tunic was patched chainmail, one arm and some of the back consisted of larger metal links, there was a piece of leather breastplate over the heart and a row of blackened reptilian scales running around the tunic's skirt.

"Where did you get this from?" he asked, tearing his eyes from the ugly tunic and back to Octavian.

"Well go ahead, try it on." Octavian gestured enthusiastically, ignoring the question in his usual diplomatic way. Kerian slipped it over his head and found the armour hung off him like a sack. The length of the tunic came down to his knees and flapped around his waist. You could almost fit two Kerians inside it. Octavian stared hard, tilting his head to one side and 'tutting' to himself.

"It really needs something." The gypsy muttered to himself. He flipped open a saddlebag and delved inside, coming out with a thin leather strap, similar to the other fastenings used to secure all the supplies to Dorian the donkey. "Tie this around your waist and that will help pull it all in." Kerian did as he was asked, clumsily threading the belt around himself whilst holding onto Toledo's reins. Then he pulled the leather belt tight and cinched in the armour.

"So how do I look?" He asked, turning so Octavian could see the armour in all its patched-up glory.

"Oh it looks absolutely fine." His guide replied, barely holding in a smile. "I understand shabby chic is all the rage these days."

"So where did you find it?" Kerian probed, shrugging himself into the armour and stretching his arms out to make sure his movement was not impeded. "What's up there?"

"It's a crypt." Octavian replied. "There are three sarcophagi in a small room. The lid had come loose on one, probably when the side collapsed. I found this armour inside." Kerian's face fell as he realised what his companion's confession suggested.

"You didn't take this armour from a corpse?" he asked, suddenly realising he had shaken the remains of the previous occupant all over himself. "Don't you have any respect for the dead?"

"Well he didn't seem to be needing it anymore." The gypsy shot back. "Why can't you be grateful for once and stop moaning." The long drawn out moan echoing up the corridor froze the two men in mid-argument.

"I think we need to get out of here as quickly as possible." Octavian whispered with a sudden urgency in his voice. "Take the armour or don't take it, it means very little to me either way." He turned, holding the flickering torch up high towards the origin of the ghostly moan and hesitated, suddenly unclear if the group should continue the way they were going or back off and try the other way.

"Sounds can become distorted in places like this." Kerian whispered back. "We may as well head forward as backwards. Whatever that is, it could be anywhere in here."

"On we go then." The gypsy replied stoically. "Following the right wall."

"Let's hope it is." Kerian muttered to himself. "For all our sakes."

The flickering torch spluttered and smoked, bringing the pictograms on the wall into vivid colour then plunging them back into the shadows. The two men moved forwards into the unknown, their sense of dread rising at each step, senses on edge, eyes and ears alert for any signs of movement or further unsettling sounds. Two broken doorways on the right wall allowed glimpses into crypts long undisturbed, stone sarcophagi adorned with dried flowers and keepsakes or tapestries proudly displaying faded coats of arms to large spiders that showed appreciation with complex silken webs.

The left side of the corridor fell away from them, leaving the travellers feeling highly exposed and revealing a large courtyard that their flickering torch could not reveal the true extent of. The right wall ended just ahead, before also turning towards the courtyard, leaving the two no choice other than to move in this direction. The crumbling wall had numerous doorways along its length, stretching off into the shadows, entrances into yet further crypts and tombs.

"This place is a necropolis. A city for the dead." Kerian whispered. "Where in the name of Adden have you taken us Octavian?"

"Well if it's the lost city of Tahl Avan I'm asking for my money back." The gypsy paused, sniffing the air again. "All the bodies we have seen so far have just been old bones. No gold at all." He shook his head, holding the torch high; trying to cast its flickering light as far as it could reach, only to see the burning brand splutter at the sudden movement.

"We might need to consider fetching the other torch out." The gypsy announced, going back to his horse and retrieving the extinguished one. Kerian swallowed hard. Were they nearly down to their last torch already? A shudder ran through him.

"We are going to need to check every crypt." Octavian continued, still holding the unlit torch. "I apologise if it upsets your feelings regarding the dead but I have no intention of being left in the dark." Kerian stepped back, nudging Toledo, as Octavian headed for the nearest tomb and thrust his torch inside, taking a quick glimpse before shaking his head and heading to the next one.

"Nothing in here but corpses." The gypsy smiled, heading back over to the left side of the courtyard. Kerian wanted to yell at him to keep to the right wall but found the thought of speaking loudly in this eerie place intimidated him into silence.

Toledo lowered his head and shoved Kerian from behind, impatient to move forwards. The force of the push spun Kerian towards the wall. He swung his shield up to avoid it striking the stony surface and caught a glimpse of something dark and terrifying in its reflecting underside. A shadowy monster was purposefully stalking towards the same wide pillars Octavian had been heading for, its pelt shimmering in the light.

"Octavian..." Kerian yelled, spinning back towards the pillars. "Look out!" Octavian turned towards Kerian, torch held high, a confused expression on his face.

"Look out for what?" his guide asked. "There is absolutely nothing her... What is that?" Kerian moved forwards as fast as he could, towing the three horses with him, cursing his lack of a weapon and speed, as Octavian, unencumbered by the horses and oblivious to the danger of the hulking creature glimpsed in Kerian's shield, moved ahead, his shadow flitting from pillar to pillar as he moved to investigate his discovery.

Pulling the mounts along as fast as he could, Kerian led the trio of stubborn animals down the passageway to where the pillars finally stopped, the area before them opening out as the wall terminated with a ninety-degree turn to the left. A much wider courtyard now lay in front of them and what stood at its centre defied explanation.

"Is that a ship?" Octavian asked. Kerian blinked, not believing his eyes. It did appear to be a ship. However, the vessel was not important right now. He was more concerned about the monster he had glimpsed in his shield. Why had it not attacked Octavian when it had the chance and more importantly, where was it now?

"Octavian wait..." Kerian warned but his guide had no intention of listening and stepped out away from the shelter offered by the pillars, leaving himself completely in the open as he headed for the ship.

The ancient vessel was approximately twenty-five metres from prow to stern and about five metres wide. It was lifted up on a bed of stones, the keel clear of the floor, its ends tapering to points. Octavian moved closer, oblivious to Kerian's continuing concerns and reached out to touch the hull, brushing away the dust to find the woodwork had been painted yellow and white. He started to walk towards the prow, eager to examine the ornate figurehead there, when the torch, spluttered, smoked and then extinguished in his hand, plunging them into darkness once more.

"It's okay. Don't panic." Octavian joked from somewhere ahead. "Here's one I prepared earlier." There was a sound of flint striking, a dance of sparks and then a curse.

"Damn what's wrong with this thing?" Kerian bit his lip suddenly feeling very scared, isolated and highly aware of the sounds of the animals shifting nervously about him. There was a creature out there in the darkness, really close by. A single step followed by a long drawn out dragging noise came from the left. Then it repeated: step, drag.

"Oh for the love of Helena." The gypsy cursed again. "Light damn you!" A loud moan rose from far ahead, beyond the ship, clearly from a place they had yet to discover. A closer moan answered it from the left.

Kerian could not see a thing! The darkness was so complete. It was as if he were entombed in a block of solid black marble. He widened his eyes as far as he could, desperately trying to see something, anything that would explain the noises about him. Other than funny coloured blobs floating across his eye he could see nothing. An anxious shuffling headed right towards him, causing the mounts to shy and pull away but Kerian refused to let them go as they were the only protection he had right now and he was not going to leave himself exposed like his guide had just done. A warm breath on his cheek made Kerian jump and almost scream. Something was right in front of him, inches from his face.

"Hold this will you?" Octavian asked, thrusting something unseen into Kerian's trembling hand. "That's better. Now let there be light!" There was a spark and the whoosh of the torch finally igniting and catching.

"Now where were we…" The gypsy winked as he turned from Kerian and lifted the torch high, before setting off across the sand covered cobbles to check out the other corridors leading from the area. Kerian blinked rapidly, like a man waking from a dream and moved to follow, realising that he was trembling all over. What was it with this place that made him feel so on edge? It was like there was a supernatural chill about the necropolis and it was unnerving him. He had never been afraid of the dark before. Why should this place suddenly instil such dread in him now?

He shook his shoulders and paused a moment to take stock of his surroundings. There was no sign of the huge monster he had glimpsed earlier, no tracks on the soft sand floor, other than their own. Could he have been imagining it? Octavian appeared unaffected by the chilling miasma of the crypts and he had not seen anything that had caused him concern, yet Kerian could not shake the feeling there was something else here, something evil hiding in the darkness.

Kerian rubbed his eyes, maybe he was just over tired? Struggling to cross the Vaarseeti must have left him more drained than he had realised. He tugged on the reins and led the mounts away from the marooned craft with a bone-weary sigh, trailing Octavian's footsteps as the gypsy continued exploring the left wall around the larger courtyard, despite Kerian's earlier advice to stay on the right. Sometimes it felt as if Octavian was simply doing things to wind Kerian up. He gritted his teeth and reluctantly followed.

The gypsy suddenly paused in his exploring and gestured for Kerian to catch up. He was standing in the entrance to another passageway which led off into the darkness. Toledo's tail lashed from side to side, as if swatting unseen insects and the stallion started to nudge Kerian forward with clear impatience, encouraging him to catch up.

"This passageway leads down further underground. Shall we try it?" Octavian asked.

"Think about the torch." Kerian reminded him, stopping again only to have another impatient nudge from his feisty stallion. "We need light to see and that torch won't last forever. Why don't we go back to the vessel and see if there is anything there that we can use?"

"Aww come on." Octavian smiled. "We know the way back to the ship. Let's just go a little further and see what we can find. The craft isn't going anywhere. It hasn't gone anywhere for years. I'll put money on it that it will be right where we left it."

"Be careful betting." Kerian warned. "That's what got you into this situation in the first place." Octavian mocked a salute and grinned, before heading down the slope into the darkness, leaving Kerian standing by himself.

"Are you coming or what?" the gypsy's voice echoed back. Kerian shook his head, then took a deep breath and led the animal train down the passageway. Just grit your teeth, he reminded himself. You need this man. You need his skills. You need your head examining!

The corridor continued for about forty feet before opening up into a much larger circular area. The soft clinking of chains echoed through the darkness, indicating that some mechanism hung from the ceiling but it was too dark to see exactly what it did and in the centre of the floor there was what appeared to be a large well, with a stone cap secured on the top of it.

The sand beneath Kerian's feet crunched as he walked over the floor. The texture of the surface was different in here, somehow harder and more irregular as if pitted and exposed by extreme use. His foot came down on something hard and when Kerian looked, to his surprise he discovered he had stood on a shapeless blob of metal. He picked it up and tried to make out what the material was but Octavian was already around the far side of the well with the only source of illumination in the room and a troublesome look on his face.

"Wait up!" Kerian called, pocketing the piece of metal with the intention of examining it later. Octavian swung the torch about, taking in the hieroglyphics on the walls as he searched for faggots or braziers that he could use to replace the one remaining light source they had. He tried to ignore the fact that it was flickering alarmingly in his hand and continued his search, knowing in his heart there had to be other sources off illumination somewhere in the area.

The gypsy peered up into the darkness, listening to the chains softly clinking and rattling directly above him, then looked back at the capstone over the well. There were several grooves in the sides of the stone, as if the cap could be hoisted away with the right equipment. He placed his hand on the surface then withdrew it sharply when he discovered it was hot to touch. This place was becoming stranger and stranger.

Octavian checked Kerian was still leading the horses, then continued to walk around the well, noting the number of passageways leading from the area as he tried to create a map in his mind's eye. That was the third passageway leading in here. If they were not careful, they could easily get lost in this place.

Steps led up into the wall and Octavian took them three at a time to find himself standing behind what appeared to be a large desk or altar that tilted slightly over towards the central area. There were grooves set into the surface, roughly the size of a very tall human. Was this where the people of this place were embalmed? He didn't feel it was worth telling Kerian of his discovery because the old man was radiating an aura of pure fear that was almost palpable. He checked the surrounding area closely, noticing a series of levers set in the back wall, probably mechanisms for the chains above, before concluding there was nothing of use within reach. He jumped back down the steps and allowed Kerian to catch up. Noticing again how pale the man had become.

"I count three possible routes out of this area." Octavian reported. "Probably too many to search with this last torch. I have been thinking maybe you were right and we should head back to the ship after all. I mean they craft these vessels out of wood so maybe we can find something to build a fire and rest for a short while." Kerian's face brightened at the prospect and he started turning to head back out, then realised the choices available to him.

"Which one was it, Octavian?" he asked.

"That one." The gypsy indicated with authority.

"How do you know for sure?" Kerian asked. "I'm all confused."

"I'm the guide." Octavian quipped. "It's what you pay me for." He led the way without hesitation, the torch flickering alarmingly in his hand. Kerian closed in anxiously, the mounts started to act nervously as the light in Octavian's hand dimmed.

"Don't worry this is all under control." Octavian commented, heading up the passageway only to come to a portcullis that had not been there when they had ventured down this way.

"That's odd." The gypsy commented. "I could have sworn this was the way we came."

A low groan came from beyond the gate and something shuffled slowly towards them. Octavian turned back towards the larger area and suggested that Kerian keep up with him. Kerian struggled turning the animals around in the passageway and heard something banging against the portcullis. He turned, just as Toledo lunged forward, pushing him after Octavian and offering Kerian only a split-second glimpse of something dusty brown reaching a stained bandaged arm through the gateway, fingers outstretched, clawing at the air and the diminishing torchlight.

"What was that?" Kerian asked breathlessly when he finally drew up alongside his guide. "Did you see that."

"Hang on." Octavian warned. "Just be quiet. I'm trying to think. Now did we come in through there or... here!" Kerian stepped back kicking at the ground in impatience, only to find himself hitting several more fragments of cold metal on the ground. They seemed to be littered all over the floor and this room's function seemed to defy explanation.

"Follow me." Octavian motioned, "it's up here I'm sure this time." Kerian frowned and stared at the torch spluttering in his hand.

"It had better be." Kerian muttered, pushing past and giving Octavian a fearsome glare. The gypsy moved aside as the horses and donkey squeezed by, only to be flicked in the face by Toledo's agitated tail.

"It was a simple mistake." Octavian offered by way of an explanation. "Anyone could have made it."

Kerian reached the end of the passageway and found to his relief that he was back out in the wide courtyard again. He grabbed hold of Toledo's saddle and pulled himself up onto his horse. The courtyard roof was several tens of feet above them so he sat up straight and dug his heels into the stallion's side, spurring it into action and dragging the other animals behind.

Octavian jogged alongside, as Kerian manoeuvred the mounts, across the sand and back towards the marooned ship. Electing to explore the far side of the vessel, they discovered a wide gangway that allowed them to ascend to the deck. Kerian urged Toledo to make the climb, the horse's hooves clattering heavily upon the cedar wood planking that made up the deck. Dorian the donkey and Octavian's mount followed after him, with the gypsy coming up behind. Once they were all safely aboard, Kerian dropped from the saddle, crumbling the dried flowers scattered across the deck into pieces of dust as he walked to the far side of the ship and scanned what little of the area he could see.

"What are you doing?" Octavian asked coming up beside him.

"I'm just checking we are not being followed." Kerian replied seriously before turning back to the gangway.

"Help me with this." he urged, gesturing that his guide assist him with lifting the cumbersome ramp, thereby cutting off any slim chance of anything unwanted coming up onto the craft with them. The two men crashed the gangway down onto the deck, then sank to the floor, breathless but thankful to be safe for the time being.

Kerian closed his eyes for a second, whispering a silent prayer of thanks to his gods, then took in the vessel about him. There was a single mast in the centre of the deck, stretching high above them, the ragged main sail still remained in place, securely fixed to a spar off the mast. He noted that only the top of the sail was secured this way. Holes in the bulwark indicated where the bottom end of the rectangular sail would be located if the ship were under way.

Brushing away the dried flowers scattered about the deck, Kerian noted that the inner planks beneath were roped together with carved mortices and the gaps between these wooden beams were caulked with dusty reed bales. Assorted urns, items of furniture and dusty chests were secured under tarpaulins, evenly spaced about the deck. He turned towards the bow and took in the figurehead staring directly at him. It was carved in the likeness of a bird, much like a falcon, dried flowers hung in garlands around its neck and in discarded piles beneath, as if the creature had been worshipped in some way. Kerian then realised that the figurehead looked back over the ship and not out in the direction of travel, so the guardian could look out over the ship and crew, granting protection as they sailed.

"Well at least we have light for the moment." Octavian laughed, using the torch to light a lantern suspended above his head. Kerian grinned, despite himself, relief flooding through him as the lantern light flared brightly and gave out warmth and a feeling of security. He looked back at his companion who was now taking in the ship around them and then stopped smiling as a disturbing thought suddenly occurred to him.

"What colour are your eyes?" he asked carefully.

"Brown of course." Octavian pulled a funny face, using his finger to draw down his bottom lid and wiggled his right eye about showing lots of the surrounding white and a dark brown iris. "That's a rather personal question. Why do you ask?" The gypsy's tone had changed from happy to serious in a moment. Then after an uncomfortable pause, Octavian smiled again, jumping to his feet and moving across the deck to check the items secured there, purposefully not turning to look at his suspicious charge.

"We have some more torches!" he exclaimed, throwing a few in Kerian's direction from a pile stacked upon the deck. "Store these in our saddlebags please, whilst I get some others lit." Within moments four more brands were blazing from sconces evenly set about the mast and deck, finally pushing back the oppressive darkness that had lingered about them for so long.

Kerian looked thoughtfully at his guide, knowing there were more questions he needed to ask, more secrets he needed to discover but realising no more information was going to be forthcoming. He turned back towards the lantern, the hypnotic flame dancing before his eyes, allowing him to clear his mind and formulate his plan of interrogation.

"How ever did a boat get out here in the desert?" he asked, more to himself than to his guide. "Who do you think owned this vessel?"

"I have no idea." Octavian replied, moving over to some crates located near a hatchway in the deck that descended to a lower level. He drew aside the tarpaulin tied over them and opened the first crate, sending a cloud of dust into the air. Little golden statues glistened in the flickering torchlight. The gypsy reached in with a sigh and lifted one out, examining it with an eye to turning a profit.

"I'll tell you something." He gestured towards Kerian holding up the foot-high figure. "If this is one of the golden people from Tahl Avan, they were really, really small." The gypsy placed the little gold figurine to one side and continued to delve through the contents of the crate.

"How could you see me in the dark?" Kerian asked quietly. "How did you find me in the shadows?"

Octavian reached deeper into the crate and lifted out a long slender dagger and some golden scarab brooches.

"Now this is nice." He commented loudly, pretending he had not heard Kerian's last question. A heavy footstep reverberated throughout the ship, making Octavian freeze in his foraging and Kerian blink away from the lantern that now swung erratically on its hook.

"Was that you?" they both asked at once. Kerian shook his head, as another heavy step landed and something terrifying started to climb up from below decks. Its nightmare form becoming clearer with every step the lumbering figure took.

Octavian slowly, gently, placed the golden statues back into the crate and turned to face their latest threat, his head slowly angling up as the creature towered above him. It stood about seven feet tall, a terrifying mummy wrapped in bandages that had been applied with skill, dedication, ritualistic care and respect. Assorted treasures were wrapped about the creature's body, artefacts it was expected to take with it into the afterlife. The wrappings were only loose about its head, where the skin beneath glowed in the torchlight.

As Octavian stared in horror, he made out the face of the monster more clearly. It was frozen in a scream of pain, the attention to detail on its intricate death mask showing every piece of hair, every once pulsing vein and the blank expression of eyes that should no longer see. The golden head of the mummified fiend looked down with a creaking groan, appearing to focus intently on Octavian, where he knelt, afraid to move, at its feet.

"Look everything is just fine. It's just a simple misunderstanding. I've put everything back in place. Nothing is missing." The gypsy uttered breathlessly, holding his hands up to display the fact he was not hiding anything. The monster leant down, placing its face inches from Octavian's own, as its spindly gold fingers reached out to grab him roughly by the shoulders. By moving in closer, the creature revealed something even more terrifying than the malice radiating from its form, more disgusting than the smells wafting from its bandages and more horrifying than its open mouth frozen forever screaming in agony. The secret of Tahl Avan was suddenly revealed.

This creature wore no death mask. The agonised face preserved in gold was its own. The mummy had been encased in molten gold whilst very much alive.

Chapter Seventeen

Ashe laughed riotously, rocking backwards in the massive chair he sat in, almost dropping the goblet of milk he held in his little hand. The Halfling's face started to contort and go crimson and then he choked, blowing milk out of his nose and spraying it all over his plate. The harbourmaster's assistant sitting opposite him looked on in horror as droplets sprayed across the tablecloth, dotting his meticulous place setting. He reached for a napkin; slowly pulling the pristine linen from an elaborately engraved golden tube designed to keep the cloth in its shape before leaning forwards and wiping furiously to clean every trace of Ashe's outburst. It was now quite apparent to the injured man as to why his seat had been suspiciously vacant when they had all been ushered into the hall.

"This is the best bit..." Ashe grinned, wiping his mouth with the back of his hand and his nose with the back of his sleeve, before leaning forwards carefully balancing on the pile of teetering cushions beneath him. "So all that time we were looking for the sultan's treasure it was actually the flower on the pedestal behind us."

"Ashe! Please behave." Thomas glared at the Halfling, embarrassed at his lack of decorum and at how he always exaggerated tales about his past. As far as the captain was aware, the thief had never left Catterick in his entire life, so the chances he ever robbed a sultan's palace was highly unlikely, a proverbial shaggy dog's tale as it were. "We are honoured guests here and should act as such. Remember you are representing my crew."

Thomas watched Ashe bouncing about on the cushions as if it were a trampoline and tried not to laugh at the sombre pout that was now forming on the Halfling's lips. There was an innocence about the little crewman that warmed you to him, despite how angry he could sometimes make you feel. Ashe almost lost his balance and his hand landed on the table top allowing the captain a glimpse of his soiled bandage, a reminder of the injuries the little thief had suffered. Despite his pain, Ashe still managed to make light of things and smile, a trait they could all definitely benefit from.

"Please try and sit still." The captain warned, concern now colouring his tone.

"This chair is too big!" Ashe commented, wiggling forwards and trying to get comfortable. "When are they going to bring some food in? I am really hungry. Did Colette tell you I flew today? If I ask that Minotaur guard nicely, do you think he will swoosh me into the table?"

"I don't think so." Thomas replied, looking at the surly creature standing at attention to the rear of Ashe and briefly had the image of Ashe being smashed rather than swooshed into the heavy furniture. "We are all having the same issues; the chairs are too big even for me."

"But I'm much smaller than you." Ashe remarked. "It's much harder for m…" The Halfling suddenly dropped from sight with a crash, sending cushions up into the air and setting the wine goblets trembling.

Thomas rolled his eyes and tried to pretend everything was okay despite the fact his gut told him it clearly was not. He took a moment to look around and take in the great hall where they all sat. The hall, measuring thirty-foot square, was open on three sides, offering spectacular views across Taurean, the placid lake and the vibrant jungles around. A cultivated field was visible to the West dotted with manicured crops that grew in straight lines like an army on the march and trees clipped and shaped so that they appeared like giant olive grey mushrooms, whilst to the North the brooding pyramid commanded the vista. The sun was setting in a vibrant display of reds and oranges as if the sky were afire. The light colouring the whole feast and company in a warm ruddy glow.

Most of the crew sat about an immense dining table occupying the centre of the veined marble floor. Luckily, Mathius appeared to have got the message through to the ship and there were several noticeable vacancies; Commagin, Colette and Mathius among them. Around the edge of the hall stood at least thirty armed guards, standing to attention with an aura of strength radiating from them. Thomas also caught some sly aggressive looks that swiftly reverted to a neutral expression when they realised that he was paying attention to them.

The captain glanced over at the head table, set back and raised purposefully to aid in the feelings of superiority the Minotaur royalty portrayed. Numerous female Minotaur sat on the left side of the table, all pushing up towards Rauph, fluttering their eyelids at him and stopping just short of physically throwing themselves at the poor navigator, much to the chagrin of their slighted male escorts. Rauph sat oblivious to the unwanted attention looking totally miserable and dejected. He fidgeted and squirmed in his chair, his eyes staring longingly down at the table where all of his friends sat, telegraphing his clear desire to join them.

On the opposite end of the table sat more female Minotaur, some holding napkins to their faces as if to ward off a terrible stench or prevent themselves from catching something contagious from the humans seated before them. Servants ran about the table, pouring wine and serving food, trying to avoid the rough handling sent their way by two thuggish looking

Minotaur who sat, laughing and joking alongside their more darkly brooding drinking companion Drummon. However, the thuggish prince regent had no time for his loutish friends and instead spent his time glaring at Rauph as if he wanted to snap him in two.

Out of all the creatures seated at the high table, there was one figure that concerned Thomas the most. She sat regally at the centre of the table, polite smiles and whispered conversations shared with those sitting alongside her as if nothing were amiss. However, despite her body language portraying a calm exterior, the matriarch's eyes moved continuously, lingering on each member of the crew before her, judging them one by one, eliminating threats, calculating risks, much like Thomas from his position here on the floor.

The captain stared at her a moment too long, only for Mora's shrewd calculating gaze to meet his own straight on and stare unflinchingly back. There was an iciness to her that made Thomas feel cold, sitting there with her head held high, nose slightly tilted up into the air. In those split seconds Thomas realised that despite all this fake pomp and circumstance the matriarch clearly despised the group, visibly cringing when Ives laughed riotously and barely containing a look of cold contempt as the crew consumed the dainty starters and downed the wine from her personal store. As Thomas watched she leaned over to talk to Drummon and the Minotaur's dark visage turned to take in the captain as well. It was clear Thomas was starting to gain some unwanted admirers.

"How could you bring us here?" a voice stated at his side, breaking Thomas's thoughts. He turned to see the ship's cook Violetta, a plump and normally jolly member of his company who not only fed the crew but also worked wonders in healing their injuries. The captain looked at her angry face without understanding the ire directed his way.

"Everyone was invited." Thomas replied. "You are part of my crew; therefore, you were invited." He smiled only to find the smile dying on his lips. Violetta was clearly not satisfied with his answer.

"But they are slaves Thomas." Violetta replied indignantly, gesturing at the servants running around them. "How can you sit here and be served by slaves?" The captain flushed as he realised what his cook was saying. Violetta and her daughter were escaped slaves from a cotton plantation in 1815. They had found sanctuary on board the *El Defensor* when it appeared in the Mississippi delta after a tropical storm. Thomas had not realised how the humans attending them were a reminder of those dark times in their lives back in Louisiana. Even as he realised his error, a servant ran to refill Violetta's goblet.

"I can do it myself." Violetta snapped, snatching the jug away from the horrified young woman, then pouring herself and her daughter some milk and handing the vessel back. "Thank you for your kind hospitality." The servant went to bow her head and back away but Violetta stopped her with a click of her fingers.

"Don't you ever bow your head to me missy." She warned. "You are as much a human as me. You have every right to look me in the eye. I am not your better. You remember that now."

"Look I'm really sorry." Thomas replied, as the servant moved away looking confused. "I can't explain what's going on right now but the *El Defensor* is the last place you would want to be at the moment."

Violetta scowled, beginning to turn away, however a hand gently placed on her shoulder stopped her.

"Violetta, I am sorry for Thomas's insensitivity." Rowan interrupted calmly. "He is a man of deep thoughts, although often not about the people around him. He means no insult. Please be assured if Thomas feels you need to be here, he has a very good reason."

Violetta offered a sad smile in reply and turned to talk to her young daughter who was making short work of a plate of grapes.

"You do have a good reason, don't you?" Rowan asked, turning to Thomas and stroking his arm reassuringly. "What is the matter with you?"

The captain turned to his partner, taking in her look of concern, her beautiful hypnotic eyes, the curling wisps of dark hair hanging down to frame her face and felt his heart melt.

"I'm sorry." He whispered. "But I don't trust our hosts."

"Is it really that you don't trust them, or is it that you don't want to lose another one of your crew?" Rowan replied, leaving Thomas realising just how fortunate he was to have met such an intelligent and caring companion.

"Where's my napkin ring gone?" the harbourmaster's assistant asked aloud.

Several pairs of eyes immediately turned to a small Halfling who had just managed to climb back onto his pile of cushions. Ashe bounced up and down a few times to check his seating was just right, then realised everyone was looking at him.

"What?" he asked as innocently as a baby.

Thomas tried to hide his smile and looked away, only to find himself staring straight into the steely eyes of Mora the matriarch. Missing nothing, analysing, planning, plotting and making the captain instantly fear for the remaining crew on the *El Defensor*. As he watched she was whispering into the ear of a servant dressed in fine clothes, marking the man a more senior member of the servant class. Unsettlingly, her gaze never left Thomas's the entire time.

The captain met her gaze, held it and then despite the anxiety he felt inside, he lifted his goblet to spite his host and offered a toast in her direction.

* * * * * *

Aelius led his troops up onto the vacant mid-deck of the *El Defensor*, then held up his hand to signal silence as he stood and scanned the surrounding area with a military attention to detail. The ship appeared deserted just as his matriarch had planned. All of the human crew were now at the banquet, leaving the Captain of the Guard with the task of taking the galleon out into the middle of the great lake and sinking her there. All was peaceful on board. This would be a simple task; all be it a shame that such a magnificent vessel had to meet such an undignified end.

His tufted grey ears twitched as frantic banging noises arose from the stern of the ship. With a few practiced hand motions, Aelius selected six of his troops to follow him towards the sound as the remaining Minotaur troops split up and started to systematically search the ship from the prow. Something about this plan did not sit right with the grizzled veteran. He knew that he had to follow his orders but the behaviour of Prince Regent Drummon with his bullying attitude and Matriarch Mora's cold hatred of this strange crew had the captain asking himself questions he would never normally consider. The crew of the *El Defensor* appeared to co-exist peacefully with a Minotaur and there was no slavery or threats of punishment to keep them in line. They appeared almost as friends, working alongside each other for the greater good of the whole ship rather than an individual ruling class, a viewpoint so alien to Taurean that such behaviour could only be considered as a threat to society.

He stalked up the starboard companionway, hand on his sword, three guards moving stealthily up behind him, whilst the other three took the companionway on the port side of the ship. The Captain of the Guard took in the large open area before him and was initially confused for there seemed no signs of life here. The deck before him was patched up with mismatched timbers, recently by the looks of it. Clearly, this area of the ship had sustained considerable damage, possibly from a bad storm or maybe battle damage against unknown foes. He stared first one way then the other, his nose flaring, trying to locate a scent before noting the ship's helm shaking violently at every loud thump.

The Minotaur unit moved away from the companionway, advancing slowly over to the mahogany helm until they all noticed an opening in the deck, just below the ship's wheel, where a hatch had been removed to get into the steerage and rudder assembly. The loud noise appeared to be coming from there. Assorted tools lay scattered about the hatchway, vibrating across the deck in time with the blows from below.

Aelius knelt down and tapped loudly on the deck, then repeated his noise, until a balding head popped up from below, thick wire rim glasses over his eyes, white beard stuck up everywhere, sweat dripping from his forehead and behind his ears.

"Oh for the love of Maris, what do you want?" Commagin snapped, pushing his glasses up and taking in the seven armed Minotaur surrounding him, as if their very appearance was yet another annoying distraction to put him off his repairs. "Thomas needs this fixed urgently. I do not have time to talk. If you want the Captain, he's at a banquet, obviously I'm not such an important member of the crew or I would be there too. Pass me that wrench, will you?"

Aelius looked down at the scattering of tools and went to pick up a likely candidate.

"Nope not that one. That one." The Dwarven engineer gestured impatiently.

"I need you to come out of there and leave the ship." Aelius stated calmly passing the wrench over to Commagin's grubby hand.

"Oh I'd love to leave the ship." Commagin replied, dropping back down the hatchway and bashing away at the looped tiller chain that ran up to the helm and down into the depths of the ship, frantically trying to pull one of the links away to render the helm useless. "Yes good old Commagin can just go off and leave the ship when it's in this sorry state. Can't you see the steering is shot to hell? It is totally seized up!" Commagin started cursing and yelling at the chain but the links were sound. He threw the wrench back up out of the hole then grabbed the tiller chain in his bare hands and tried to physically rip the links apart, his muscles straining and his face turning crimson.

"Do you mean to say the ship has no means to steer?" Aelius frowned, carefully pushing his head down through the hatch, now the threat of low flying tools seemed to have passed.

"Come on you bastard, pop loose!" Commagin cursed under his breath, tugging and yanking for all he was worth, before gripping the chain in his teeth and giving it a good shake just for good measure.

"Maybe my troops can help you?" Aelius suggested, staring about the small space with interest. "What in the world are you doing?" Commagin stopped chewing on the chain and turned slightly embarrassed towards the aged Minotaur, one greasy hand reaching out to grab the chain and steady himself as his foot shot forwards to slide something on the floor further into the shadows leaving him teetering off balance. The chain link popped free with a sickening snap followed by a terminal 'clunk'. The tiller chain shot up towards the helm whipped several times over the spindle mechanism and then dropped back down past the engineer to clatter loudly into the bowels of the ship. The ship's helm immediately spun around, dropping the king spoke to the deck with a crack that made the assembled troops jump.

"You see." Commagin moaned, pointing despairingly towards the slots in the deck where the tiller chain had disappeared. "It is completely knackered. I'm not going anywhere. I'm afraid you will just have to leave me to get on with things." He wiped a hand across his face smearing it with the residue oil from the now missing chain.

Aelius pulled his head from the hatch and gestured to his troops to back away as loud sobs started coming out from the opening. One thing was for sure, the ship was going nowhere. He was surprised just how dedicated this engineer was. Clearly, he felt for this ship, although from the nose blowing and wailing that the Minotaur could overhear, this empathy seemed to be taking it a little far.

"Let us see how the others are doing." He ordered, gesturing for the troops to follow him below decks. The plan to steal away with the *El Defensor* had died, she was not going anywhere. They needed to round up everyone left on the ship so this was not a complete waste of time. The Dwarf could stay where he was until they had finished their sweep of the ship.

Commagin heard the Minotaur stomping away and sank down onto the floor in the hatch staring down into the hole and wishing he could slip down the small hole after the tiller chain and hide somewhere in the darkness. The engineer realised that Thomas was going to kill him for grounding the *El Defensor*. It was going to take weeks to fix this. Time the dwarf knew they no longer had. He reached into the darkness and lifted a gleaming crossbow from out of the shadows. The stock of the crossbow was polished silver, engraved with the scenes of a hunt taking place complete with a forest of warped and twisted trees, stags in flight and huntsmen with hounds. The arms of the crossbow were a deep matt black metal shaped by Dwarven hands to complete a weapon the like of which Commagin would never craft again.

The engineer had come prepared for a fight and fortunately for the Minotaur they had walked away from it, not realising how close they had come to death by way of a deadly crossbow. Commagin looked down at his weapon and patted it lovingly. This mess was not over yet and he had a feeling in his gouty toe that the *Lady Janet* would come into play before it was.

* * * * * *

"Don't those trees look funny?" Ashe pointed towards the orchard on the hillside where row upon row of olive-green trees appeared like giant mushrooms. "How come they all grow to exactly the same height from the ground?" The Halfling turned towards the harbour master assistant expecting his answer from the local man but he seemed to be preoccupied with something.

"Well?" Ashe asked, chewing a mouthful of grapes and soft white cheese.

"I'm sorry." the man replied, lifting up his plate and checking under his napkin. "I seem to have lost my knife."

"I can handle this." Ives replied, slipping up alongside Ashe and retrieving the missing knife from the Halfling's pocket and sliding it back across the table. "The trees are all that height because they are magic trees. We have something similar where I come from. The seeds float in the air and then when they have germinated, they slowly grow the trunks down to the ground, that's why they are always the same height from the floor."

"I too have seen these trees." Weyn winked, easing up on the other side of Ashe and removing a saltcellar from the Halfling's shirt pocket. "I think I know a friend who has a nursery maybe I can ask him to let you in and see them. You have to be very careful not to bump into any of the little floating seeds, or leave a door or window open otherwise they all blow away on the breeze."

"You would do that for me? Really? You are the best friends ever." Ashe threw his arms around Weyn deftly taking the archer's hunting knife from its sheath. Ives intercepted the snatched weapon and passed it back to Weyn, his face looking over at the trees and smiling innocently, as Ashe suddenly realised that he had lost yet another treasure. The merchant soon spotted what he was looking for, his keen eye noticing the real reason the trees appeared so meticulously pruned. Wild goats stretched up high on their back legs, reaching for the trees to bite the succulent leaves within reach, resulting in a straight line that any artist would have been proud to achieve.

Before Ashe could ask anything more about the magical plants, there was a loud noise from the head table. The Matriarch was getting to her feet. The noise in the hall died down to a low murmur. Servants ran over to the main table refilling goblets of wine for each guest, whilst the main course of assorted roasted game bird stuffed with nuts and accompanied by tureens of steaming vegetables started to arrive before the delighted diners. Thomas reached for his goblet and found a suspiciously empty spot on the table. He frowned in exasperation and immediately looked over towards Ashe, his annoyance plain for anyone watching. However, the Halfling was too busy struggling to get higher on his chair so that his view was not obscured and he was unaware of the mute accusation sent in his direction.

A flush of embarrassment rushed through Thomas as he realised that he would be expected to respond to a toast, yet he had no goblet with which to do so. A breech in etiquette was something he did not intend to do, especially whilst the prevailing atmosphere remained so hostile.

"Allow me sir." Thomas turned to see the senior servant offering him a polite smile and a filled goblet balanced on a silver tray. "We wouldn't want to miss the toast and risk upsetting the matriarch now, would we?" Thomas picked up the goblet and went to thank the servant, but the man was already backing away, lost in the hustle and bustle of the service around him. The captain turned back towards the head table just as another servant rang a small silver bell to bring respectful silence to the room.

The chatter of the crowd stilled as they awaited Mora's expectant speech, Thomas suddenly found himself irrationally on edge. The hairs on the back of his neck started prickling and alarm bells rang ominously in his mind. His instinct that had served him so well as a New York City cop kicked in. Something was about to happen, he could feel it as if the very air had been charged with electricity. The sort of feeling he used to get as a detective when he knew a criminal would reach for a gun, or when you knew someone was about to run for the door in an effort to escape the law. Thomas reached down with his open hand and gripped the hilt of his cutlass with two fingers, gently lifting the blade so that a centimetre of polished metal gleamed where the weapon stood slightly proud of its scabbard, ensuring a fast draw without the risk of the blade sticking.

"My honoured guests," Mora began. "It brings me great pleasure to offer this meal in thanks for the safe return of my missing son Kristoph, cruelly lost to me these five years past. Words cannot express my gratitude that he is safe at home amongst his family once more. Taurean would like to extend our arms in friendship to his saviours and offer you all a place in our hearts and homes forever."

"Here, here!" Drummon shouted, slamming his goblet on the table and causing wine to slop over the side.

"I propose a toast to the most valiant captain, Thomas Adams and his courageous crew who risked so much to bring our son home." Mora continued. She lifted her goblet high, the guests around her copying the gesture, much to Rauph's obvious embarrassment.

"To the *El Defensor*!" She toasted. The responding cry resonated throughout the room and everyone drank deeply from their goblet. Thomas found himself quite surprised at the tart gritty texture of the drink, like a claret wine that had not been filtered properly and heavy on sediment. He looked down into his goblet, licking his lips and not finding the aftertaste to his liking. This was nothing like the vintage he had been drinking earlier!

"To Thomas Adams!" Mora toasted. The cry was returned from the guests and further wine consumed. Thomas shook his head and went to take another swallow; secretly hoping this was a wine that improved, the more you drank. The captain paused with the crimson liquid lapping at his lips. The matriarch was staring right at him, a sly smile on her face.

Thomas froze, finding himself wondering about why the matriarch was acting so smug, then he lowered the goblet, nervously licking his lips, re-sampling the tart residue of the claret with a horrifying suspicion. Surely, the Matriarch would not be as bold as to...

"To Kristoph's little pets!" Drummon roared, interrupting the toasts and causing Mora's expression to darken. "I shall enjoy house training the ones he does not keep." The Prince Regent's two burly Minotaur lackeys seemed to find this comment amusing and burst out laughing, one of them slopping his wine over a servant and then cuffing her around the ear for making him waste it. The servant ran away, dodging the pawing of the other drunkard and ran out of the hallway crying, much to the further merriment of the jet-black Minotaur and his cronies.

"They are not my pets." Rauph said quietly. Several of the female Minotaur started to titter amongst themselves as Mora, her face furious at the interruption, walked slowly over towards Drummon and grabbed him firmly by the ear.

"I do not need your help in this matter." She snarled, cuffing him sharply on the back of the head and jolting him forward with the strength of the blow. "Know your place, or I shall delight in putting you in it." Drummon looked up wounded, his pride hurting more than the blow delivered, clearly aware of the other guests staring at him and laughing at his treatment.

Mora looked up at the people assembled before her and offered a curt nod as her mind raced. Aelius should be scuttling the *El Defensor* by now. When these disgusting creatures headed back to the ship there would be no sanctuary for them, her troops would be waiting at the quayside and then they could spend the rest of their days working in the mines, unless they were fit enough to be included in the Labyris celebrations. She thought on this long and hard, her smile growing wider. Certain people in the crew would need to be dispatched however, as they posed too much of a threat.

She looked over at Thomas Adams and her aloof features melted into a malicious smirk as she watched the captain sink slowly into his chair and struggle to place his goblet on the table with his shaking hand.

"To my son Kristoph!" she toasted. Nodding in satisfaction as goblets raised around the room for a third time. "It is so good to have him home."

* * * * * *

The sweep of the *El Defensor* was almost complete. Troops came over to report they had thoroughly searched the ship below decks and had found no other crew members. One Minotaur, exploring a disorganised workshop, was seriously injured when a tower of debris had fallen on him in a freak accident. The fighter was carried from the ship, groaning in pain, taken away for medical care and leaving the Minotaur captain's force reduced by three. He was not concerned, there could only be a handful of further cabins to explore on a ship this size and the remaining nine Minotaur would be sufficient to deal with any resistance.

He turned his attention topside to the opening into the cabins above decks and started walking down the corridor, gesturing that a fighter advance ahead of him and stand in front of the cabin doors to each room. Aelius was always systematic in his actions. He walked to the furthest door and opened it to take in the captain's cabin beyond.

The room contained a large desk with heavy gilt chairs set around the edge. A globe stood in the corner amid shelves of books and models of scaled ships similar in design if not shape presented in glass cabinets. The aged Minotaur took in the attention to detail and the intricate rigging at such a small scale and could not help but admire the craftsmanship and patience required in such an undertaking.

He walked around the desk, noting the battered tankard on its polished surface in which stood several worn quills, before turning his attention to the drawers. Aelius opened them one at a time, finding ink supplies, paper a ledger and then a drawer lined with a green felt sheet filled with small items that made no sense, much like a small child's collection of knick-knacks. The treasures included a wooden smoking pipe, golden buttons from a waistcoat, dice, a double-headed coin, a large sapphire that vibrated gently beneath his searching fingers. A small silver locket, a tankard, a senseless box with little silver balls that ran everywhere disappearing into little holes inside, a piece of slate with a drawing of a mouse on it, a petrified egg and a golden ring with writing on the inside.

Aelius moved to pick up the ring then paused when he noticed the golden badge sitting in the back of the drawer and lifted it out to sniff at it. The golden badge looked like a shield with numbers and letters engraved upon the surface. The pitted surface showed many small holes as if exposed to an explosion of some kind. NYPD and the numbers 3042 meant nothing to the Minotaur, so he sniffed the shield again, noting the unmistakable odour of old blood, before replacing the item back in the drawer once more.

A small door to one side led into the Captain's sleeping quarters and it was in here that Aelius noticed the distinct feminine touches that informed him this man had a mate. Cushions, throw rugs, potted plants in little cradles suspended beneath the portholes to ensure nothing spilled out in high seas. The Minotaur laughed to himself. This male would have a weakness if his mate was identified. He filed the information away and decided he would inform the Matriarch of his findings when he returned. He moved to leave the room and caught a glimpse of himself in the mirror made from an old ships wheel that hung alongside the door, causing him to start in surprise.

He looked so old. The thought stopped him dead, staring at the grey hairs about his face and ears. If he thought that he looked old, what did Mora think of him? Would he be replaced soon? The thought made him shudder. A guard came into the room gesturing towards the room next door.

"What is it?" Aelius snapped, annoyed at the interruption.

"There is a dead body in the other room. We don't want to go near it."

"I don't see why not." The captain snapped, pushing by and entering the room, taking in the chart table with the open books laid upon it and the ruined chair around which several guards stood warily. He stopped short, taking in the gaping mouth, the creases of the velvet robes heavily lined in dust, and the gaping hole in the figure's torso where the mortal wound had occurred. Then he noticed the magical symbols on the corpse's robes and the other runes and sigils on the chair in which the dead man sat. A shiver ran up Aelius's spine as he took in the scene. Somehow, he picked up on an atmosphere in the room. He felt as if he were being watched.

"It's magic sir." One guard reported. "I don't like the feel of this. We need to leave this place."

"I think you might be right." Aelius muttered. "This room is secure. Move on to the next one."

The next door opened into a small cabin. A birdcage hung from the ceiling and a small hammock was hanging from the wall. The Minotaur searching the room found there was very little space to turn and his horns caught in the cage.

There was a protesting squawk as the cage fell to the floor, jarring the black and white bird inside and springing the door, bending it back. The guard jumped back worried about what this creature was rolling about near its feet and it lashed out kicking the bird and sending it bouncing against the wall. Chuckles from the other guards turned the Minotaur's embarrassment into anger and he reached over and opened the porthole before roughly grabbing the black and white bird, swinging it sadistically by its leg. Several vicious pecks and squeals followed before the bird was hurled through the open porthole and the opening slammed shut. Leaving the guard with a bleeding hand and more chuckles of distain from his colleagues.

"I hope it can fly." The Minotaur smirked, trying to show he was in control of the situation. Aelius watched but did not find the situation amusing. He snapped an order, silencing the warriors and indicating the next room to enter. Without knocking, Aelius shoved the door open and stepped back as a stench wafted through the open door and into the corridor making several of the Minotaur place hands over their noses.

The room within had a large hole in the centre of the floor. A bed against the wall held a figure from which the stench was coming from and a young woman was sitting with him holding a flannel to the man's face and appearing to nurse him. Another figure lay on the floor with a sheet over his head. Aelius coughed several times before he was able to clear his throat enough to talk.

"What is going on in here?" he asked, trying hard not to be sick.

"Oh" Colette turned towards the open door appearing to have been caught by surprise and dropping her washcloth across the man's face lying in the bed, her hands shook and a small crystalline object fell to the floor.

"You can't be in here." Colette warned. "Please step outside in the corridor. These men are ill and under quarantine, if you come in here you need to stay with them."

"What's wrong with them?" Aelius choked at the foul smell. Colette wrinkled her forehead as if trying to remember something.

"Malignalitaloptereosis." Colette replied quickly. "It's extremely contagious. You get…" She wrinkled her nose again as if trying to remember the rest of the information. "You have giant pink spots, hot and cold shivers, violent sneezing, green gas and um, and purple hair."

"Purple hair!" exclaimed the man under the flannel.

"Let me see." Aelius moved forwards gesturing for Colette to remove the flannel.

"Don't say I didn't warn you." She remarked, pulling the flannel away to reveal a vision of horror.

The man beneath was barely recognisable as such. His pale skin had a greenish hue, mucus dribbled from his nose and his face was a mass of red oozing weals. The man's pallor was further emphasised by a shocking mat of wet purple hair.

"Hi," Mathius sneezed, causing everyone to step back. "Is it visiting hours already?" A wet farting sound issued from under the sheets making Aelius step back in disgust.

Colette covered Mathius face again before he spoilt the effect by laughing. She wiggled her hand down at her side, whispering words of a spell under her breath.

"What was that?" Aelius remarked, certain something else was going on here.

"I was just going to warn you how fast the disease spreads." Colette replied, trying hard to keep her face straight. "But it is already too late. You need to leave here and put yourselves into quarantine for at least a week. I have no idea how terrible the symptoms affect Minotaur."

"What?" Aelius asked clearly confused. Screams started out in the corridor. Confusion rippled through his troops. The captain turned to see one Minotaur pointing at another as red lesions started to boil and erupt from his skin whilst another screamed at a shock of purple hair sprouting from between his horns.

"Run!" Aelius shouted. "Get away from here. This is a plague ship." He ran for the door, pushing his way through the assembled troops, his nose wrinkling and becoming peppery before exploding in snot and mucus. The other Minotaur ran after him, some belching others shrieking in horror as the illness took hold.

Colette sat on the bed and smiled as she heard the screams running away. She pulled the flannel from Mathius's face and started to laugh as he laughed with her. On the floor the corpse under the blanket sat up and grinned as he took in the state of Mathius lying on the bed.

"Wherever did you get that idea from?" Aradol laughed as he watched the spots slowly start to fade from Mathius skin and his nose magically dry up. "I have never heard of Malignalitaloptereosis."

"Thomas told me a story once about a mighty magic duel that happened on his world." Colette began. "It was an epic battle wizard vs witch, where they polymorphed into different creatures in a bid to outsmart each other. The witch, I believe her name was Mim, cheated by changing into a purple dragon, so the wizard, Merlin, responded by transforming himself into a germ called Malignalitaloptereosis." Colette paused in her retelling.

"I wish I could have seen it. The mental strength needed to perform such spells must have been incredible to witness. I understand that a chronicler imparted the tale in a saga named *The Sword and the Stone*. You must ask Thomas to tell you the tale when he returns."

"I think I will." Aradol continued to laugh. "Although I fail to understand why anyone would put a sword inside a stone? That makes no sense."

"Will the symptoms last on the Minotaur?" Mathius enquired, picking at a scab on his nose.

"No more than an hour at most," Colette replied. "But it has given us breathing space and time to get the crew back from the banquet."

"I'm not so sure about the purple hair as a symptom." Mathius moaned, trying to grab tufts of his hair and check the colour.

"I remember now." Colette laughed as she put her hand over her mouth. "It was the witch who had the purple hair."

"Well can you change mine back please?" Mathius pleaded.

"Maybe later..." Aradol winked. "I think he looks kind of fetching."

* * * * * *

Mora nudged Drummon, leaning in close to conspire with him, as she watched the colour drain from Thomas's face.

"I don't know why you are so angry at Kristoph's return." she opened, not taking her eyes from the captain's trembling form. "You were supposed to have killed him five years ago. It is your fault you messed up. Now look at him cavorting with these humans. If the citizens of Taurean were to see this there would be an uproar. It cannot be allowed to continue." Drummon snarled as he looked over at where his long-lost brother now sat with his crew, after having removed himself from the head table and several disappointed courtesans. He was laughing, smiling and hoisting the smaller member of the crew high over his head and catching him again.

"He seems so happy with them." Drummon moaned. "Why can't I be as happy as that?"

"Oh you will be." Mora replied. "Kristoph has walked right into our hands. You can now legitimately challenge for the Labyris axe; you can finally be recognised as my replacement if you win the Labyris competition against another of royal blood." She broke into an evil malicious laugh, gripping Drummon tightly by the shoulder.

"I see…" The dark Minotaur offered an evil smile. "I really see." Mora's servant moved in close, placing Thomas's missing goblet on the table beside her, before whispering into Mora's ear, making her congratulatory smile at their joint subterfuge a short lived one. Her fingers tightened, digging into Drummon's flesh and making him yelp out in pain.

"Ow! Stop!" he complained, squirming beneath her brutal touch.

"It appears that I need to change my plans." Mora snapped, continuing to apply the pressure on her son's shoulder. She paused for a second, before meeting the black Minotaur's tear-filled gaze with her cold sadistic stare. "I want you to go out early tomorrow."

"Why?" Drummon replied, sinking lower in his seat in a vain effort to escape Mora's clutches.

"We need creatures for the Labyris tournament. I want you to take some of those crewmen. The archer, the fat one who eats too much and of course Kristoph into the jungle to help hunt some of them. Then I want you to make sure something unpleasant happens to them."

"What about the captain?" Drummon asked.

"Don't worry about him." Mora replied maliciously. "He is no longer a concern."

* * * * * *

"And then they all broke out in spots and started sprouting purple hair." Colette laughed trying to lift Commagin's spirits. The Dwarf tried to smile but at the back of his mind he was still trying to figure out how he was going to explain the broken steerage.

Torches flickered on the harbour side and Colette paused in her conversation and smiled as she saw the crew returning.

"Thank goodness they are back." She remarked getting to her feet.

"Colette!" Screamed a voice from the dock. "Colette! Run to the galley. Get the water boiling. We need towels and poultices." The mage was on her feet in seconds, dread turning her blood to ice.

Commagin was up in a second, snatching the Lady Janet into his hands and setting off suddenly all business-like towards the companionway. Rauph charged up onto the ship first, carrying the limp form of Thomas in his arms, closely followed by an almost frantic Rowan.

"What's happened?" Aradol stood open mouthed. "What's happened to Thomas." He took in the captain's blue tinged lips, his slack, unresponsive face and the bubble of blood oozing from his nose.

Violetta came up the companionway next, anger having set her face hard. She took in the oil streaked face of Commagin and the spiked hair of

Aradol slowly reverting back to normal from purple without letting her professional face waver.

"Rauph, get Thomas to his cabin!" she ordered, before turning to her young daughter. "Katarina get our Holy Saint, then help Colette get the herbs, water and towels we need. You two…" she gestured to Commagin and Aradol. "Get the armoury open, pass out the weapons and set the guard. No one gets on this ship without a fight!"

"Is Thomas going to be alright." Colette asked, taking in Rowan stroking Thomas's hand, tears rolling down her face. "What has happened to our dear Captain?" The rest of the crew were gathering on the deck behind them, streaming up the gangway from the dock, staring at the unfolding drama in dull eyed shock.

"Yes, Violetta." Commagin pressed, refusing to move until he understood the situation more clearly. "Tell us what has happened to Thomas."

"They've poisoned him." Violetta announced. "That Minotaur bitch and her court have poisoned Thomas!"

Chapter Eighteen

Kerian watched horrified, as the golden mummy lifted Octavian clear from the deck of the ship. The gypsy struggled in the monster's grasp, trying to wriggle and writhe out of its vice like grip, growling and snarling, clearly in considerable pain, his hands vainly reaching out to tear at the creature's ancient bandages and face. Kerian felt frozen to the spot, unable to move due to the fear and dread that radiated out from the creature. There were no weapons near at hand, no sword for him to slash at the monster, no mace, lance or hammer with which to bludgeon the creature and save his companion.

The mummy raised Octavian above its head, then threw him with incredible strength across the deck. The gypsy smashed into a stack of crates that splintered as he fell. The crash snapped Kerian out of his paralysis, forcing him to move, to seek an advantage against the supernatural creature before it turned its unwanted attentions in his direction.

Dorian the donkey brayed in protest, backing away and tugging Octavian's mount with him. The pack animal backed into Kerian's stallion and kicked out by reflex, making Toledo scream out in pain, rearing up high, hooves slamming against the deck as he landed, shaking loose a wide bladed oar from against the gunwales. Kerian turned from the source of the clatter just in time to duck as the mummy's outstretched hands clutched at his body.

He ducked, evading the creature, moving to clear space, its body brushing his arm as he rolled by, sending a numbing chill racing through his limb and releasing the scent of musty bandages from ages past. Ancient liniments and spices that had been involved in the preservation process along with mould spores and dust billowed into the air, leaving Kerian gasping for breath. The mounts continued pushing against each other, stamping and snorting, anxious to put as much space between themselves and the moaning creature that continued to pursue Kerian as possible.

The knight lifted the makeshift weapon from the deck and spun around, smashing the paddle hard into the advancing mummy's left side, before reversing the swing, whipping it back over his head and slamming the oar around towards the creature's other flank. A mummified hand reached out, faster than expected and caught the wooden blade before it made a second contact. Painful vibrations ran up Kerian's arm as the oar snapped in two. The fighter stared at the splintered oar in shock, before realising he needed to move again as the space between himself and the mummy shortened.

The creature was nimbler than its shrivelled form suggested, its relentless stalking across the deck, now becoming a clear ruse to back Kerian into a corner from which there was no escape. Bandaged arms outstretched, bony fingers clutching for Kerian's body, leaving the warrior no choice but to continue retreating. He took another step backwards, reaching the edge of the deck, the flaming torch in the sconce above him illuminating the preserved golden horror in blood curdling detail.

Octavian appeared out of nowhere, leaping from the ruined crates with a bestial snarl. The gypsy landed on the corpse's back, his arms grabbing around its neck, his head swinging in as if to bite the monster's throat. The mummy instantly concentrated on the new threat, leaving Kerian with valuable time to re-assess his position as both gypsy and mummy wrestled for dominance. Kerian lunged with the ruined oar, determined to help out, only to hear it clang off the monster's golden skin and raise Kerian's growing sense of inadequacy.

Where was a good sword when he needed one? This was ridiculous to feel so powerless! He looked up at the flickering torch in the sconce above him and snatched it down, hardly hesitating before shoving the burning brand into the monster's side and barely missing Octavian's flailing legs. The treated bandages caught instantly, flaring up and turning the monster's moans into shrieks of fear as it tried to smother the flames with its bandaged arms only to inadvertently spread and fan the fire to other areas of its body.

Octavian fell to the floor, rolling away, leaving the mummy wide open to attack. Kerian brought the torch and oar to bear like twin magical lances. He shoved hard into the monster's torso, pushing forward, edging the towering horror backwards towards the side of the ship. The mummy snarled in defiance, lashing out and grabbing for the splintered oar, tearing the remains from Kerian's hand and sending it spinning away into the shadows but not before the knight used the torch to push with one last gigantic effort, finally overbalancing the heavy undead creature and sending it over the edge of the ship.

There was a dull thud as the mummified corpse hit the ground. Kerian peeked over the edge of the ship, waving the torch backwards and forwards in front of him as if this would keep the nightmare at bay. He stared down at the flaming creature in morbid fascination, watching the bandages curl and char as the flames licked hungrily at the ceremonially prepared body, the corpse writhing and squirming as it vainly tried to get up off its back. Octavian came up alongside Kerian gasping and placed a hand on the knight's shoulder in thanks, before leaning over the side to observe the smoking pyre below.

"That was a surprise I could have done without." The gypsy remarked, his cocky smile slowly returning to his face. "I wonder how long it takes for a mummy to go out?"

"I don't think it was enough to stop it. I think we have only delayed it." Kerian replied, watching the corpse struggling to move in a more co-ordinated fashion as more and more of its gleaming golden body was exposed as the charred bandages fell away. "At that rate It won't be long before it is going to get up again."

"Well we can't have that can we?" Octavian replied. "Put the torch down and help me for a second."

The mummy finally managed to turn its heavy body, pulling itself to its knees, the last bandages falling away from its gleaming torso, religious icons and tributes dropping to the sand as the bindings keeping them in place succumbed to the ravages of the flames. Thick scented smoke rolled up from the monster as it started to moan aloud, calling out into the darkness, requesting aid from long dead servants buried in the crypts around it.

"Hello down there!" Octavian shouted, stopping the creature's ghostly oration as it turned to stare up towards the gypsy's call. "And now!" Octavian gestured and Kerian heaved with him, sending a crate of wares over the side to crash down heavily onto the monster's head, slamming the creature back to the ground. The discarded crate split open like an over ripe egg, spilling an assortment of golden statues and sacred offerings across the floor. Kerian stared in dis-belief as a slender sword still sheathed in its scabbard spilled from the debris and slid to the floor, just willing the knight to go and pick it up.

"A sword. Octavian, look. It's a real sword!" Kerian gasped. "I need that weapon." Octavian looked at the sword lying on the sand, the hilt gleaming as it reflected the flames from Kerian's burning brand.

"And your point." The gypsy replied, not sure what Kerian was getting at.

"Go down there and get it for me." His charge ordered.

"What? Are you serious?" Octavian shouted in disbelief.

"You owe me remember. If we are to get out of here, I need a sword. I am sick and tired of running all the time." Kerian replied seriously. "Retrieve the sword and that is one less thing you need to do for me. You will be one step closer to fulfilling our agreement."

"Can't I find you another one?" Octavian asked, as the contents of the crate suddenly moved. It appeared their gleaming monster was stirring despite the weight upon him. "Can't I get you a sword somewhere else, preferably one without a fearsome monster near it?" Kerian pulled himself up to his full height and stared at Octavian like a headmaster staring at a tardy child.

"No." he replied shaking his head firmly. "I want that one." Octavian moved to fire back another sarcastic reply then stopped himself. The look on the old man's face showed that this was an argument he could not win. The gypsy looked back at the little golden statues, bracelets and brooches in the pile then swiftly reconsidered. There was a small fortune down there. He shrugged his shoulders and moved to the skittish horses, laying a hand on Dorian's neck, settling the donkey back into a state where it no longer moved to escape but instead just stood there trembling, then reached into a pack on the donkey's back and drew out a cloth bag.

"I only need the sword." Kerian remarked, knowing full well what Octavian was going to do. "Let's get a move on shall we."

"I'll get your stupid sword Kerian, but I am not your lackey." Octavian replied. "You need to bring the mounts down from the ship so that we can move on before our friend manages to extricate himself from beneath that crate. I do not fancy facing him again and would prefer to be far from this place before he realises that we have escaped. Help me with the gangway please." The two men hauled the ramp back into place, dropping it down with a crash, before Octavian threw a mock salute in Kerian's direction.

"Permission to disembark." He mocked.

"Just get me the sword." Kerian reiterated, shaking his head and moving to gather the horses as Octavian quickly slipped over the side.

The gypsy hit the ground running, sack flapping in his hand as he headed towards the stern of the ship. The flickering torches on the ship's deck cast dancing shadows across the sand making the surface appear to ripple like water. Octavian charged around to the other side of the vessel and noted the shifting pile of treasure on the floor. He just hoped Kerian was as good with a sword as he implied, because spending time with this man was like moving from one unmitigated disaster scenario to another! Life was so much simpler when he had just been concentrating on getting the ransom.

Octavian slid to a graceful stop, then bent down and retrieved the blade and scabbard from the floor, easing the belt over his head and settling it on his shoulder even as his gaze took in the gold and jade covered items littering the floor. Glittering bracelets, sparkling brooches, golden clothes pins, small ornamental gilded statues and toys lay scattered across the sand.

He opened the sack and started to throw items in, his mind aware of the monster struggling to rise from the floor mere inches from him.

A loud clatter indicated that Kerian was getting their mounts down from the vessel, whilst the groans from the struggling mummy seemed to indicate the creature was becoming more agitated at its attempts to free itself from beneath the heavy crate.

"Are you coming any time soon?" Kerian shouted. "I can hear things moving around over here!" Octavian shook his head, wishing the man would stop complaining, for just one second, before reaching for a cloth bag made of lots of diamond shaped pieces of cream, red and black fabric that shimmered as if highly polished. There was a shoulder strap to the bag, so the gypsy scooped it up over his head and started shoving precious items into it as well; a short dagger, several necklaces, a facemask, a handful of rings, a bronze goblet and some small golden statues followed after but a brief glance.

Now this was a nice piece! Octavian held up the blue and green scarab beetle and whistled as he felt the weight of it. A golden circular brooch with tiny rows of sapphire and diamond rising up like a fountain of water on the front caught his eye as he scooped up yet more loot. This was a blessing in disguise! Maybe accompanying Kerian was a good idea after all.

The broken crate suddenly jumped up from the floor, rising several feet before tumbling down again, creating a cascade of artefacts and sand that made the gypsy start. He leapt to his feet, suddenly all too aware of the monster he had been foraging alongside. Octavian realised his concern as the debris settled, finding the creature now standing beside him, joints clicking and popping back into place. It turned towards him, mouth agape, its staring eyes even more terrifying to behold.

It was time to go!

Octavian snatched up the sack and ran, the weight dragging him down on the right side leaving him off balance, his gait awkward. The shoulder bag bounced up and down on his left hip and Kerian's sword smacked him soundly between the shoulder blades, like a jockey using a whip on a steed to gain every inch of speed that could be mustered. He stole a glance over his shoulder and noticed the mummy giving chase, the long golden legs of the creature swiftly eating up the distance between them. The gypsy faced forwards, then realised with a curse, that he was running in the wrong direction, as the prow of the ship came up alongside him.

The gypsy skidded to a halt, ducking just as the mummy's golden fingers closed where his head had been. The monster shot past, feet thumping into the ground as it tried to reduce the momentum it had just obtained. Octavian did not stop to check the creature's progress and immediately set off back down the hull of the ship, heading towards the stern as fast as his laden body could move.

The thumping of closing footsteps signalled that the monster had managed to turn about and was gaining on him again, making Octavian redouble his efforts. However, the stern of the ship looked so far away and doubt started to enter his mind. He was never going to make it. The mummy had to be only a few inches away, the wind blowing through his hair was not from his own running, it was those outstretched fingers clawing and scrabbling for his flesh!

Toledo burst out from the shadows at the front of the ship, Kerian guiding his mount with a skill that was instantly apparent. The knight cradled an oar in his right hand, wielding it as if it were a jousting lance. He kept his head down low and urged Toledo to give him all the speed it could. The stallion tore past Octavian, eyes rolling, foam flecks visible on its mouth the ground rolling with the thunder of his galloping hooves.

The oar whistled over the gypsy's head and smashed into the racing mummy with a crunch sending the golden creature flying backwards onto the hull of the ship and knocking Kerian clear from the saddle. Toledo reared, hooves flashing, stamping and snorting as it found itself without a rider to give it direction.

Kerian groaned from on the floor and rolled painfully over onto his side, his hand outstretched to Octavian. The gypsy ran over, eager to help Kerian to his feet only for the dismounted knight to push his hands roughly aside.

"The sword idiot!" he snapped. "Give me the sword!" Octavian lifted the sword from his shoulder but it appeared caught up in the shoulder bag strap and he could not free the weapon. Toledo started snorting and neighing in alarm, causing both men to stare over towards their opponent who was now slowly rising from the floor, the jagged end of the oar punched clear through its shoulder.

Kerian staggered to his feet as the mummy advanced towards the two men, its arms outstretched, a scream forever frozen on its features. He acted instinctively, shoving Octavian face first into the sand before grabbing the hilt of the sword and pulling it free from the scabbard. A lock of Octavian's dark curls flicked free, as the razor-sharp golden blade passed bare millimetres from his scalp. Kerian held the weapon in his palm, taking in its weight and balance before flipping the blade around and bringing it up above his head.

The mummy charged in and Kerian met the attack side on, his sword slicing in to clang off the creature's wrist, shoulder and face, raising sparks and making the monster veer aside. Kerian allowed the undead horror to run past, then turned on his heel and set himself again, this time with his feet slightly apart, the sword held down and to the left, ready for the return attack.

"Get up and grab the horses!" Kerian snapped, as Octavian sat up, holding the lock of hair in his hand, a glare set on his features. "Move, now!"

"What have you done to my hair?" Octavian wailed.

The mummy came in hard, reckless in its attack, despite Kerian's earlier response. The sword swept up, blade glittering, the monster's arm came down, fingers clutching. The clash of golden limb and ancient weapon was deafening. Kerian gritted his teeth, throwing every ounce of strength he had into the upward swing. The undead corpse groaned as its hand came away at the wrist and dropped to the floor.

Kerian spun about, bringing the weapon around to the left, completing a blazing circle of death that had the sword arching in once again. The mummy staggered as the blade smashed into its shoulder, cracking the golden veneer and chipping the fragile bone structure beneath.

"Go now!" Kerian snapped, as Octavian scurried to his feet. "We need to head deeper into the necropolis." The gypsy turned to flee, bag bouncing at his hip and the sack firmly clenched in his hand, actually taking those first few steps before finding himself cursing as his pace slowed.

"I can't leave him." Octavian confessed to himself, turning back as the mummy swung in with its remaining hand only to have the lunge parried by Kerian's expert swordsmanship. "My word is the only thing left that I have not ruined." He looked about for something to use as a weapon and flung his hand up in the air. There was nothing here!

Kerian feinted to the right, making the mummy adjust its attack accordingly, then reversed the blow, bringing the tip of the blade slashing across the monsters screaming maw. Teeth cracked as the blow landed and the mummy twisted its tall body, leaning down to smash the man that dared to hurt it in this way, it's turn bringing the creature's golden skull right down to the warrior's level. Kerian did not stop to gloat as the creature acted exactly as he had planned. He was already stepping away, whipping his blade around his head and smashing it down onto the weakened skull of his opponent with a deadly two-handed blow.

The warrior was in his element, skill and training honed for such a moment, knowing that one wrong step, one mis-timed parry could result in his own grisly end. Kerian had never felt so free, so unencumbered and oblivious to the worries about the future and the regrets of the past. He was firmly in the here and now; fighting and never more vibrantly alive.

Octavian watched in awe, his search for a weapon forgotten as he observed the swordsman pirouette and lunge with his blade. It was quite hypnotic to watch Kerian in action. He was actually quite good! The retrieved weapon now an extension of the man's arm, used with unerring accuracy to wear down the giant mummy. Each time the blade crashed against the golden trunk of the creature, an electric spark jumped between the monster and the weapon. It was like watching a play with two tragic figures dancing upon the stage against a backdrop of a humid lightning storm.

The mummy charged again, making Kerian dodge to the side as it charged past. He swung the sword in hard at the creature's leg, catching it behind the knee and dropping the horror to the floor. Before Octavian's astonished gaze, Kerian snapped the sword up, flipped it around his arm and smashed the blade down onto the already weakened skull, splitting the petrified golden skull with a hollow crunch.

Kerian took one look at the motionless creature, trying to confirm if it were dead, then turned about and walked over to Octavian, spinning the astonished gypsy around and tugging the scabbard free from around his neck, accidentally freeing the patterned shoulder bag from the gypsy's shoulder and letting it fall softly to the floor.

"The horses!" Kerian urged his companion as he slid the weapon back into its sheath. "Where are the horses?"

Octavian looked at the bag with a puzzled expression on his face. It should have landed with a loud thud when he considered how much treasure he had stuffed into it. He picked it up and squashed it between his hands. The satchel folded upon itself and went flat with no resistance. The gypsy shook the bag, then lifted the flap and stared inside, much to Kerian's annoyance at his poor choice of priority.

"Where's all my stuff gone?" Octavian asked in disbelief. "I know I put some things in here."

"We don't have time for this." Kerian said in frustration. "I told you I heard other noises. We need to go from here. Either leave the bag or bring it. No time to examine your ill-gotten gains here."

"But..." The golden mummy moaned and moved its damaged head towards them.

"We are leaving now." Kerian replied. He turned about until he discovered Toledo standing a safe distance away in the shadows. He ran over to the stallion and swung himself up into the saddle. "Come on!"

Octavian set off at a jog and ran around the side of the ship to find the pack donkey and his steed tethered to the rudder. He fastened the sack of treasure to Dorian's saddle then swung himself up onto his own horse and sniffed the air, tilting his head to one side. Kerian was right. There were a lot of creatures closing in. He reached into his pack and lifted one of the torches up above his head, standing on tip-toe in his stirrups so he could ignite it from a smoking brazier he had earlier set at the gunwale of the ship.

"This way!" he snapped, yanking the reins and turning his horse down a colonnade they were yet to explore. "We need to go this way."

The two riders cantered across the cobbles, heads down, Dorian voicing his reluctance with a loud bray as they set off into the shadows. The stonework showed more signs of weather here, ghostly statues set on plinths showed signs of wear, the pigment on the sculptures faded, some appearing faceless, the meanings of the scripture lost to the scouring ravages of time.

They came out of the tall corridor, hooves clattering loudly across the floor. Another courtyard opened out before them, a sequence of large ornamental fountains looming out of the darkness, their depths now filled with sand instead of life-giving water and ornamental fish. The two men guided their mounts around the spooky scene, their passage lit by the solitary flickering torch.

Ruined buildings stood silent witness as the men and their entourage moved further into the darkness. Shuffling within the shadows kept the travellers acutely aware they were no longer alone and that their passage was being monitored by unseen horrors. They dug in their spurs and urged their mounts to move faster as the haunting landscape unfolded before their torch.

Large steps led up to deserted temples, ominous passageways led off into the shadows. Kerian looked at several corridors, unsure which way Octavian would lead him, only to find the gypsy turning first one way and then the other before leading them on again. He settled back, in the saddle, hand holding steady to the reins, his other patting the sword now strapped to his side. He finally had a sword. Could his luck be about to change?

The howl from behind them almost made Kerian jump out of his saddle. He turned towards his guide and took in the scared look on Octavian's face. The gypsy faced forward, turning down a side passage, allowing Kerian the briefest glimpse of faded hieroglyphics and crumbling masonry before they emerged into another round courtyard with clinking chains rattling from the ceiling. Kerian felt his anxiety, so far kept in check, leap to the fore with a resounding shriek.

"Haven't we been here before." Kerian snapped sarcastically, his growing tension erupting in the only way he knew how.

"No, I don't think so, the ceiling is higher here and we did not have to dismount to get down the passageway. I'm sure this is the right way to go." His guide replied, turning first one way then the other, his stallion's hooves striking the hard metal droplets scattered on the floor to create a staccato sound as they bounced away into the darkness.

"That's what you said last time." Kerian replied caustically. Running steps echoed down the passages behind them. Their pursuit was closing in. "Where now?" he asked trying to keep the anger from his voice.

"This way." Octavian gestured, pointing up another corridor. The gypsy guided his horse up the passageway, Kerian following close behind. They came out into a large area with row upon row of small crypts set side by side, jostling for space along twisted pathways that wound through surely thousands of tombs. It was the biggest graveyard Kerian had ever seen. Each vault faced out onto a path, the openings dark voids in which unseen horrors lurked.

"Are you sure this is a safe choice?" Kerian asked, shivering despite the heat.

"We don't seem to have much choice." Octavian replied gesturing behind him where a stumbling figure of gleaming gold burst out of the passageway. "Our friend is not one for giving up."

"What do you mean?" Kerian turned to note the monster and then realised it was missing one hand. "By Adden how did he catch up so fast? That's impossible."

"Come on." Octavian gestured. "The quicker we get through here the better. I just better not make a wrong turn."

"What was that?" Kerian turned to ask his guide, but the gypsy was off, digging his heels into his horse, spurring the mount forward. The horses cantered along the pathway, Octavian's speed hampered by Dorian who brayed loudly in protest and who, in turn, blocked Kerian's forward gallop. The crypts stretched away into the darkness, far beyond the illumination of the torch. As they ran past each opening Kerian prepared to slash with his sword and urge his horse to move faster, waiting for the inky blackness within the crypts to spawn some unimaginable horror.

Kerian's imagination ran free and unfettered. Was that a ghostly hand? A glittering undead eye? His grip tightened on the blade as he risked a look behind him to see how fast his golden one-handed opponent was gaining on them. He looked again in disbelief. The creature had disappeared.

Now where had it gone?

The scream came from his left, as a heavily bandaged mummy shambled from its crypt, arms outstretched, the stench of death hanging from it. Kerian turned and swung his sword, feeling the satisfaction of watching the blade slice deep and sending the bandaged head spinning away along the path. He yanked the reins, bringing Toledo under control after its spooking from the undead creature only for another groan to come from the right, his stallion shying away and sending them in the other direction.

Kerian swung his blade up and brought it down in a chopping motion, splitting the creature's head like kindling. He turned to check on Octavian, only to find the gypsy was in a similar predicament but struggling to control two mounts to Kerian's one. He watched as Octavian swung his torch first to one side then the other igniting preserved bandages with a roar of triumph and causing other advancing mummies to back away as he swung the burning brand in their direction.

Several shambling figures approached from the rear, the stench of death radiating from the creatures in waves. Putrid bandages, stained grey and brown, encased each of the shuffling bodies from head to toe. Bony metatarsals poked from the ends of limbs wrapped in figure-eight strapping, whilst frayed dressings enveloped twisted torsos long deprived of their internal organs, or wrapped heads that no longer contained brains. One of the mummified creatures moved towards Kerian, a step then a long drag as it pulled its leg behind it. Another opened its mouth, parting bandages revealing an opening all dry and dusty, devoid of a tongue. A long moan issued from its mouth as it staggered towards him.

Octavian was already urging his stallion through the burning mummies, moving from one preserved creature to another, igniting the corpses with his torch as they struggled to escape the cleansing flame. The slowness of the creatures made it easy for the gypsy to dart in and light the bandaged corpses without difficulty. Even so, he found that the jerking paths of the monsters as they struggled with the flames were blocking off his options for escape and he had to turn the horses from the path they were following as the shambling dead relentlessly closed in around him.

Kerian urged Toledo forwards snapping the reins, trying to coax his horse through the flaming creatures. Toledo snorted in horror, pulling one way and then another its natural fear of fire making it roll its eyes and shake its head. Kerian kept a firm hand on the reins, looking for an opening then pushing his steed through.

Octavian shouted at Kerian, stepping forwards and plunging his torch into the nearest mummy, even as he gestured wildly in Kerian's direction. Flames licked hungrily at the corpse's bandages, turning the creature into a shambling pyre within seconds. Octavian attempted to shout over the groaning undead shuffling from the tombs about them but Kerian could not hear him clearly.

"What is it." Kerian shouted, trying desperately to understand what his companion was waving at.

"Behind you!" Octavian shrieked.

Kerian turned in the saddle and stared in horror as his golden nemesis lunged for him. He had the image of a golden screaming skull, now lopsided and all the more grotesque because of it, lunging for his face. He tried to parry the lunge, tried to swing up the sword and knock the monster away but it was just too fast and they collided with a crash. Kerian fell from the saddle landing badly and jarring his shoulder. He tried to roll, to get to his feet but the golden terror kept after him, batting him with its remaining hand, striking sparks from his armour and knocking the air from his frame.

He found himself slammed up against the opening of a tomb as his stallion screamed with terror and set off after Octavian, leaving Kerian deserted. The golden skull kept trying to bite him, forcing Kerian to use his blade as a shield, his actual shield impossible to get free as it was trapped between himself and the crypt wall.

A groan from behind made Kerian's eyes go wide. Brittle stick fingers reached over his shoulder, clutching at his armour, teeth snapping near his neck. The golden mummy moved back to swipe at Kerian with its golden hand and the knight saw his chance, ducking the swing, allowing the monster to tear the head from the animated corpse that had been clawing at him.

As the golden hand swept past, Kerian moved in, taking advantage and thrusting up with his blade. The weapon pierced the mummy's shoulder where it had been injured earlier and Kerian yanked down hard, tearing the ball of the shoulder joint free and slicing through the dried muscle and tissue like it was paper. The creature's arm dropped useless at its side and the change in weight distribution pulled the monster down to one side. Kerian dodged to the side and ran out onto the pathway, determined to put as much space as he could between himself and the golden monster which he knew in his heart of hearts was rising up yet again.

Burning mummies lay everywhere, thick pungent smoke snaking up from their bodies where they struggled to move across the floor. Kerian ran past them, slashing out at any creature unfortunate enough to cross his path. He ran around the corner, noting that some of the undead before him were still in the initial stages of incineration and staggered to a halt.

Octavian was on his knees, his hair grasped by the largest golden mummy yet, a tall pointed hat seated upon its head exaggerated the behemoth's height further. Ceremonial robes about its body suggested it was a creature of high rank. The gypsy's head snapped to one side as the monster swung him about like a child playing with a toy.

Hundreds of undead creatures shambled and shuffled from the shadows, groaning and moaning in a bizarre sounding dirge. Other golden mummies the same size as the one that had pursued them from the ship moved forward, armed with swords bigger than Kerian could even lift. He took in the surreal vista and felt despair. There was no way he could continue to fight this. He slid the sword back into its scabbard and held his arms up indicating his surrender.

The mummy turned his way with a rictus grin on its preserved face and although Kerian knew it was impossible, the creature appeared to chuckle. A shuffling form moved up behind the surrendering knight. He turned his face just in time to see a golden clawed hand sweep in towards his forehead and then darkness took him.

Chapter Nineteen

Miguel Garcia sank down onto the slanting ship's deck, his breath coming in searing gasps, his head held down in sheer exhaustion. If Malum's deranged and twisted mind decided to eat the buccaneer right now, Miguel knew that at this moment, his resistance would be so low he would actually embrace the grisly end. He knew, with a sinking heart, that he could not keep up this pace for much longer.

The buccaneer had eaten practically nothing since they had entered this hellish place, apart from some weevil-infested biscuits found in the galley of a holed tall ship, her stays and deck draped in curtains of twisted green creeper and sickly orchid blossom. The ship's perpetual motion only added to the pirate's feelings of nausea as the wreck twisted lazily in the slow current of the graveyard. Brackish water, alive with mosquito larvae, left his throat dry and barely quenched his thirst, but he preferred risking parasitic infection than going mad with dehydration. Miguel's clothes had transformed from their earlier finery, his coat now adorned with stinking slime, his shirt with streaks of sticky oil and stripes of terracotta rust were ingrained into the worn leather of his boots. The dandy of old would never have recognised the gaunt figure Garcia had become.

The length of heavy chain Miguel had been carrying across the wrecks started to grate, chink and clank, as the links slowly began to slip and tip from the haphazard pile they had made when he fell, the ever-present battle against gravity clearly one-sided as the links gathered momentum down the listing deck. A low growl at the pirate's ear reminded him that a pair of Malum's evil Scintarn hounds scrutinized every move he made. He turned to see a lip curled on one of his four legged guards, whilst hackles rose on another, clearly displaying the temperament of the creatures when a prisoner failed to comply with their master's wishes. With a weary sigh, Miguel stretched out and arrested the chain's movement.

"I'm going okay?" he snapped. "Just give me a chance to catch my breath and I will be on my way."

The nearest Scintarn hound snapped its jaws inches from Miguel's ear, making him shy away and stagger back to his feet. He stared sadly down at his boots, now streaked with an extra coat of excreta and grime from the neglected deck and sighed heavily. Would this torture never end? One exhausted footstep followed another, as the heavily laden man leant against the list of the ship, dragging the cumbersome chain behind him. The hounds jostled the buccaneer as he walked, nipping maliciously at his heels, or growling loudly to encourage Miguel to move more quickly or face becoming food for the terrifying watchdogs.

They reached the edge of the deck and Miguel noted the descending gangway swaying precariously between his current position and a row of wrecks lashed together far below. The derelicts, secured with rope and chain, reinforced with stay and spar, formed a crude rickety bridgework that took the pirate down and away from the graveyard hub and out across the water towards a truly incredible feat of engineering around one of the archways. Miguel took a deep breath and started down the swaying path, fighting to hold onto the chain and keep his balance on the creaking and groaning structure that moved more erratically with every step.

The current gurgled and bubbled as it flowed between the ships, floating debris nosed up against the wrecked vessels, putting extra strain on the flotilla of wrecks that practically hummed with the tension running through them. Miguel pondered what would happen if the supports should fail, sending him adrift and spiralling out along the main channel to be food for the giant eels that hunted there. As he watched from his vantage point, another wreck was added to the far end of the line as the inner hub of the graveyard continued its slow spiral to oblivion.

Two floating platforms served as the foundations for scaffolding now stretching up and obscuring the ancient masonry of one particular archway. Somehow, Malum believed that Thomas and the *El Defensor* lay beyond that particular gateway. He had used Miguel's hypnotised crew to set about erecting the skeletal framework up each side of the archway, securing the scaffolding to the ancient stonework in such a way that made it look as if they were insulating the stone. Even from here, Miguel could see the small figures of crewmen climbing up and down ladders built within the scaffolding, each one serving to carry sections of chain that were being strung across the archway and fashioned into a huge net that Malum planned to employ when the *El Defensor* next sailed through.

A scream echoed across the water as an unidentified crewman, probably weak from exhaustion, fell from the top of the left strut to the archway, his limbs windmilling uselessly as he tried to slow his fall before his body smashed into the floating barge at the base of the structure. Three black hounds leapt towards the body, ripping and tearing huge chunks of the man apart, before running away with their spoils to eat them at their leisure, leaving the remains of the carcass to slip into the muddy water. Almost instantly several jolts vibrated along the bridge, causing Miguel to stop his own journey and catch his balance or risk falling again. The bumping and jostling reduced as one of the giant sea eels completed its swim along the underside of the unsteady flotilla and arrowed across the water to the arch intent on recovering the discarded fleshy remains.

A warning growl from behind, reminded Miguel that despite this horror, the hounds still expected him to deliver his salvaged chain; he turned to say something to the two hounds, noting the dripping saliva from their jaws and then decided not to waste his wit on them. With a resigned shrug, he continued his weary slog along the undulating route.

The water continued churning, always in constant motion. Occasionally an explosive crack from behind Miguel signalled the death of a wreck deep within the mass of broken ships which made up the hub of the graveyard. The pirate had initially jumped at the sounds, now it was just another background sound, a characteristic of the ship's graveyard, like a wave crashing on a rocky beach. He had grown used to the death throes of the tortured vessels grinding themselves apart; they were an erosion of history and a constant reminder of the despair permeating this place. Oh how he would love to see a beach again!

Miguel finally arrived at the base of the scaffolding and stared up awestruck into the workings of the towering pieces of scavenged stay and mast, boom and rigging. His men moved about it like sluggish, struggling insects in a mighty web. The buccaneer craned his head up to see where the tower ended flush with the apex of the ancient stonework. You could almost step from the skeletal structure out onto the top of the stone archway, free to journey around the entire shipyard if you had the energy to do so.

The buccaneer gathered the length of chain he was dragging behind him before dropping it onto a pile of similar rusted and algae coated links waiting to be fashioned into massive lengths for the net. Alongside was a table with a set of bolt cutters, pliers and wielding apparatus and a pile of offensive refuse that even the Scintarns stayed away from. He took the opportunity to stare over to the other side of the archway where the second set of scaffolding rose towards the mustard coloured sky. Bright glowing lights flickered, bobbed and weaved amongst the struts indicating Malum's progress as the terrifying monster clambered up and down the structure like a voracious spider. Clearly, Malum was agitated; his flashing lights became more rapid when he was upset. Miguel did not want to see whom the poor unfortunate was that had caused the monster's ire to rise.

A sharp nudge against Miguel's thigh snapped him out of his thoughts; he looked at the sleek black creature snarling at him, its evil eyes showing a hunger barely disguised, the plates along its back clicking as it pushed against him, large paws padding about the deck in agitation. The message was clear, keep moving or be eaten.

Resolved there was no way to avoid his fate Miguel went to turn away, then realised the bolt cutters were missing from the table before him. That was strange! Where could they have gone? Before he could solve the mystery the impatient Scintarn nipped at his thigh, causing the pirate to yelp in surprise and move away as the creature desired. Its twin shadow loped over and took up sentry duty alongside its colleague, something grisly hanging from its jaws.

A wreck spiralled alongside, dazed crew members leaping from its decks onto the bridge to prepare for attaching the ship to the end of the line and extending the walkway as the hub of the graveyard slowly spiralled away. Miguel ignored the crew he once knew, knowing they were completely under the thrall of Malum and it was pointless to try to raise a mutiny of any kind. The walking firework display was simply too strong to tackle! The bridgework of ships bounced and jostled dangerously as the men prepared to tie on the latest extension.

The buccaneer began his treacherous walk back across the sloping decks, every footstep measured and tested in case of an accidental fall that could spill him into the water where the slithering giant eels awaited him. His hand slipped along a rail, gathering a handful of stringy wet seaweed as he went. After initially stinging from the salt content on the vegetation, the emerald seaweed soon cooled his hands from the rough abrasions caused by the chain links. He reached out to grab another handful, tugging it from an aged length of rope. One of the Scintarns growled menacingly and that was the end of Miguel's rest period.

"What about my coffee?" he joked feebly, the smile fading on his lips as swiftly as it had appeared.

The ship ahead bounced roughly up and down signalling to Miguel that something was heading in his direction. He looked and noticed Horatio and Cornelius stomping towards him, a massive length of chain links suspended between them, their forked tongues tasting the air. Oh if only he could rouse his two bodyguards from their trance. If only they would wake up and help him, he would not feel so helpless and alone.

The deck beneath his feet dropped as they arrived before him, the lizards seemingly oblivious of their master, both intent on simply dropping off their chains and thereby earning praise from Malum. Miguel wished he could just snap these two creatures out of their trance, he just needed a plan; needed some sort of...

Horatio shoulder charged Miguel as if he were not there, pushing the weakened buccaneer backwards right into one of the Scintarn's following him. The back of Miguel's legs hit the snarling hound, he fell over onto the deck, smashing the back of his head and seeing stars as the seaweed still in his hands flew up into the air and wetly slapped across Horatio's snout. Miguel found himself winded and gasped like a beached fish, trying to suck air into his lungs as the deck beneath him vibrated.

A loud snapping, splintering sound cut through the air and the whole deck shifted beneath the pirate, making him slide across the rotting wood beneath him. Horatio and Cornelius spread their legs wider to compensate for the movement, their tails reaching out instinctively to curl around the support posts of the ship they were on. The Scintarn hounds' claws skittered and scrabbled across the deck, one of them even slipping on the algae coated surface.

Miguel froze where he lay, waiting for the shaking and groaning reverberating through the wrecks to stop. He rolled onto his knees and slowly got to his feet, staring back along the bridge of wrecks to the scaffolding and noticed that one of the ships had moved out of line and was coming free. If the fragile bridge broke apart, the wrecks could all split away, sending ships crashing into each other or floating away from the hub completely. With a growing horror, he watched a mast explode, a chain snap and felt the tell-tale tremors rushing through the structure. He needed to get off this thing as soon as possible.

Turning to run, Miguel bumped back into his lizard bodyguards, who were still intent on walking down the bridge towards the archway, whether the ships threatened to tear apart or not.

"Come on!" Miguel snapped. "Get out of the way! This whole thing is going to go! We have to get back to the hub as fast as we can." He pushed against Horatio's scaly chest and realised he would have more luck trying to move a tower block! The lizard looked at him with cold eyes and allowed his long tongue to slip out of his tooth-filled maw and pull the seaweed into his mouth where he chewed it menacingly.

Another crack, loud as thunder signified something larger had broken free down the line and then, with a series of sickening lurches, the whole bridge of wrecks came apart. Miguel was thrown to one side, bashing his head again as the deck listed sharply beneath him, his feet slipped on the wet surface and he found himself sliding towards the edge. His hand reaching out, desperate to grab something to stop his slide but everything was slimy, slick and treacherous. Chains cracked and ropes snapped as the wreck swung free, sea spray flooding over the side and threatening to take the vessel under.

The swirling waters gurgled hungrily as the buccaneer slid uncontrollably towards them. He watched his approaching doom but was powerless to do anything. The surface of the water broke as a long grey eel slipped by, eyeing him with a deep black pupil the size of a dinner plate. It continued to circle, searching for a feeding opportunity just like the one now being offered. Miguel screamed out, terrified at the prospect of feeling the teeth of the creature slicing into his flesh, of seeing his life blood gush out to stain the water a murky crimson.

Something grabbed Miguel's foot. Stopping his slide and causing him to scream again, this time in surprise as much as in pain. Something sharp had pierced his boot, puncturing skin and causing needles of red-hot pain to rush up his leg. He tried to focus on his leg through the haze of pain and looked back up the deck to see one of the Scintarn hounds had grabbed him around the ankle, obviously now determined to eat him. The second Scintarn was jumping up and down, not sure if it should leap in, clearly excited at the thought of finally consuming something it had been following all day.

"Horatio! Cornelius! For pity's sake! Help Me!"

The second Scintarn decided to lunge forward, mouth open, strings of sticky saliva adorning its muzzle. Miguel closed his eyes, preparing for the worst, only to hear what sounded like an avalanche of chain sliding noisily across the deck and thundering past him. There was a yelp as the chain clattered by, then a mighty splash, as the rusty links slipped over the side of the ship taking the struggling Scintarn with it.

Miguel felt himself roughly dragged back up the deck, his leg shaken violently from side to side as the remaining Scintarn hound worried his foot. A loud crack sounded, like a sap filled log on an open fire, making the pirate assume the worst, that his ankle had been broken but the sound came again and again making him realise he could not be sustaining multiple fractures.

The shaking of his boot stopped and Miguel found himself wrenched further up the deck. He was hoisted into the air, then placed gently back onto his feet by a pair of huge scaled hands adorned with yellowed claws. The broken, battered and bloodied Scintarn hound slid slowly down the ship; its blood streaking the aged wood and marking its passage towards the water. It came to rest at the rail and whimpered pitifully, only to be violently snatched away by the voracious eel and dragged beneath the surface with a mighty splash.

Miguel tried to regain his composure, feebly attempting to brush himself down as he stared at his two lizard companions both testing the air beside him with their flickering tongues and hissing as if they had been asleep for a long time. Could they finally be free from Malum's evil influence?

The pirate looked back towards the archway as it slowly appeared to be moving away and noticed a sudden flurry of activity as the crew appeared to be running about as if suddenly aware of the horrors that they faced. Men screamed, Scintarns ran around dragging their prisoners to the deck and ripping apart those who dared to resist. Malum clambered down the outside of the scaffolding his tentacles writhing angrily as he sought to regain control of the people about him. One Scintarn leapt at a crewman and slammed him to the floor before raising its head and howling in excitement, gore dripping from its jaws.

Horatio snorted a greeting in Miguel's direction, the first genuine sound from the lizard he had heard in days.

"Thank you for saving me." The pirate stammered, still shocked at how close he had come to becoming the eel's entrée. He carefully placed his weight on his injured foot and tested how strong it was before realising his hench-lizards were looking at him with a clarity to their vision he had not seen in days.

"You both understand me?" he asked, as they hissed and nodded their heads. Horatio yawned before snapping his mouth closed with a sound like a heavy tea chest slamming shut, his teeth chewing on the stringy seaweed like it was chewing tobacco.

The wreck beneath them shuddered as it ran over something submerged in the channel, then started to spin lazily towards the hub. Miguel looked around, scanning the rusting hulks and rotting wrecks for signs of any Scintarns giving chase but they all seemed to be occupied over by the archway. For a brief second the buccaneer questioned how the ships had come to snap loose the way they had. He looked back over his shoulder towards the receding archways and scaffolding, wondering once again where the bolt cutters had disappeared to. After a moment pondering, he shook his head and took in their gently spinning trajectory, noting that it would make them pass under a decaying frigate who's ragged rigging dangled easily within reach.

"Walk with me." He ordered, gesturing that the lizards fall into place alongside him as the boom of the frigate moved closer. He took a tentative step, then another, expecting at any moment to hear the alarm, the rush of clawed feet across wooden decks, the howling and exciting pants of hounds closing on their prey.

"The hell with this!" Miguel remarked. "Run!"

* * * * * *

Thomas's body crashed down onto his bed, flecks of blood splashing from his mouth and nose, his eyes rolling up into his head showing the whites of his eyes. Violetta was instantly at his side, opening his blood shot eyes, holding a lantern near to check for pupil reaction, before parting his lips and noting the fresh bleeding coming from his mucosa and staining his teeth.

"Rauph, do you have any idea what this poison could be?" she snapped. Rauph stood powerless, slowly shaking his head in a daze, fighting his own internal battles, hearing that his mother had poisoned his friend, knowing in his heart there could be no other explanation but wanting it to be anything but true.

"Rauph!" Violetta yelled, trying to snap the Minotaur out of his musings. "I'll ask you again. Do you know what poison this could be?" Colette entered the cabin behind her, carrying fresh linen, Rowan following closely behind with hot water from the galley and Katarina at her side with a handful of herbs and a small metal pot of blackened sticks.

"I can't think of any." The Minotaur replied, his eyes filled with hurt. "What do you want me to do?"

"Hold him still for me whilst I examine him." The cook replied, trying to be calmer this time, her voice edged with authority as she realised that she needed to have the attention and trust of everyone if they were going to pull Thomas through.

"Oh Thomas!" Rowan cried, moving in and softly stroking his clammy hand. "Please come back to us." The captain started to jerk spasmodically on the bed, his twitching becoming more severe. Rauph leaned over and gently took Rowan's hand in his, before steering hers away and placing his own huge chestnut hand in its place to pin Thomas's hands to the bed whilst his other hand clamped down on the captain's forehead stilling his movements.

"Charcoal." Violetta gestured to Katarina. "Crush it up and mix it with something so he can drink it." The cook's daughter took to the task using a kitchen knife with the skill of someone who had spent a large portion of her life chopping and peeling. The charcoal reduced into smaller and smaller chunks before Katarina tipped the crumbling pieces into a Mortar and Pestle and finished grinding it into a powder. The little girl stuck her finger into the mixture to check it was fine enough then added some creamy goats' milk and stirred the mixture as fast as she could, turning the white liquid into a dark grey.

Colette looked on with concern and just a little respect in her eyes. She watched how the chef's daughter moved; selecting herbs with a calculating eye just like the mage would have for her own spell components. Katarina passed them to her mother almost before the chef asked for them.

Violetta crunched up some mint leaves and passed a few to everyone standing around the bed, before scattering lavender across the bed sheets and pillow, then she gestured for the charcoal drink.

"Chew the mint, it will help you." she remarked to everyone. "Rauph, hold Thomas's head we need to get him to drink the charcoal."

"Why are we supposed to chew this stuff?" Rauph asked suspiciously as Rowan popped some leaves into his mouth because he had no hands free. Violetta did not stop in her ministrations, gesturing that the Minotaur lift Thomas's head up slightly from the bed.

"When the smell gets bad, the mint will stop you feeling sick." Violetta replied as she moved the drink close to Thomas's blue tinged lips. "Rowan bring that bucket nearer. Rauph, hold Thomas still, we need to get him to drink. Katarina where is the saint I asked you to collect? Go and fetch it please."

"I can't get through the door there are too many people in the way." Katarina replied, heading towards the cabin door but clearly not sure what she was going to do when she got there. Violetta turned towards the door and realised there was a crowd of onlookers trying to catch a glimpse of what was unfolding within the cabin. Her face turned thunderous in an instant.

"Colette, for mercies sake please get the rest of the crew out of the cabin and let me do my work!" The cook exclaimed. "If they are not out of here in three seconds, I shall personally use my chopping knife to gouge out a few eyeballs." Colette turned with a nod, glad to have something to do and thankful she was not on the receiving end of the chef's warning. The mage whispered a few words and a jewel at her throat cracked, the energy from the stone flowing into her hand and wrapping around it to glow like fire.

"Get out!" Colette hissed, leaving no room for argument from the onlookers.

The crew moved back reluctantly and with some difficulty, having all edged into the narrow corridor to try to ascertain the state of their captain. Finding the wrath of Violetta and Colette aimed in their direction, they now found they all had to shuffle back against a stream of crew still trying to find a way in and get news! Ashe moved through the struggling flow like a salmon swimming upstream, angling in closer to the doorway, having wiggled between the legs of several onlookers before he finally popped out in front of the crowd only to come face to face with Colette's icy blue-eyed stare and flame wreathed hand.

"Violetta said to get out." She warned. "That means you need to leave too."

"But Colette," Ashe protested. "I won't be a problem. What if Rauph or Thomas need me? I can be good. You know I can. Why are you all chewing mint leaves? What in the world is Violetta giving to Thomas, because he appears to be turning a bit green?" A loud retching and a gush of fluid sounded from the captain's bedside but Ashe could not see what was going on because Colette was standing in the way.

"Just let me through and I..." The Halfling wrinkled his nose as he detected a sharp acrid odour wafting around the cabin. "On second thoughts..."

"Crack the porthole." Violetta ordered. "Rauph hold Thomas steady he's going to be sick again..."

"Leave now!" Colette snapped, instantly regretting her cold tone but also recognising the need for it, despite the hurt in her little friend's eyes. Ashe was already backing away as further vomiting sounds came from the bed, followed by dry heaving from Rauph that sounded like the Minotaur was coughing up something he had swallowed by mistake.

"You know, maybe I should go and feed Sinders. I have left him alone all night and he will be anxious to hear about the Minotaur and the food we had for our meal. I even saved him some seed cakes."

"That's a good idea." Colette replied, offering a tired smile. "You go and do that. Can you also check in with Commagin and ensure he has the watch stand throughout the night. I don't want us to have any problems atop ship as well as below. It's very important you tell him this message and that's why I am entrusting it only to you."

"A very important message." Ashe puffed out his chest and nodded his head, liking the sound of that. "I'm going to deliver an important message!" He turned and walked up to the crew still blocking the passageway.

"Excuse me, coming through. Bearer of a very important message here!" Colette couldn't help but smile as she watched Ashe shove his way through the crowd, his little hand held high before him like a badge of office, then she turned back into the cabin.

"Colette please check Thomas's pulse." Violetta instructed. "It was racing earlier but I am hoping it may have settled a bit now he has been sick." Katarina finally rushed back into the room, holding tightly to a small, carved figurine of the saint that Violetta held so dear.

"Thank you for being so fast child." She praised her daughter for her cool manner before moving closer and kneeling down at the side of the bed, placing the small carved saint in the captain's hand before closing her own tightly around his.

"Is there anything I can do?" Rowan asked Violetta as she moved up alongside Colette and touched Thomas gently on the shoulder. "Anything you need fetching... I just feel so useless."

"There are always things we can all do." The cook replied sternly. "The candles need maintaining, the bed linen needs changing, Thomas needs bathing and we all need drinks and hot water to hand. Above all, we need to hope that I managed to get as much of the poison out of him as possible before it really took hold."

"Is there anything else?" Rowan asked, tears running down her face as she stood wringing her hands.

"We pray!" Violetta replied solemnly. "We just pray."

* * * * * *

Ashe felt proud of himself. He had just delivered the very important message to Commagin. The curt response from the Dwarven engineer was a tad confusing however; Commagin had demanded to know exactly what Ashe thought he, Marcus, Mathius, and another half a dozen heavily armed men were doing out on the deck, in the dark, looking out over the dock. To be honest Ashe had no idea what they were up to, indeed, how was he to know. He wasn't a mind reader... although it would be a cool trick to learn!

The Halfling headed for the ladder, whistling innocently to himself as he went. Violetta would fix Thomas up in no time. After all, she was helping fix his thumb and it had been completely chopped off! Just having some bad food at the banquet was hardly a cause for concern. Although, he had to confess the sight of all the blood and vomit coming out of Thomas had been a tad disgusting. Well better out than in, as his mum had always said when he was ill. He skipped down the passageway and set off towards his cabin, a spring in his step, a song on his lips and a fist full of crumbled seed cake in his pocket. Sinders would be so pleased to have this tasty treat. He would...

The door to Ashe's cabin was ajar. That was odd. The Halfling popped his head around the doorjamb and realised no one was in the room and that there was a cool breeze blowing in through the porthole. This was stranger and stranger.

Ashe did not like leaving Sinders with the window open, he did not want the bird to catch a chill and Austen had explained that the bird was like a child and was his responsibility. He knew he had not left the porthole open. Then the Halfling noticed the bent and battered cage lying on the floor and his excitement at having a mystery to solve died.

"Sinders?" Ashe called out to the empty room. "Sinders where are you?" He dropped to the floor checking the corners of the room then picked up the cage and poked his face inside the opening; despite the fact he could have easily seen if the bird was there by looking through the bars.

Ashe shook his head, scratching his nose, before shuffling on his knees back out into the corridor and looking to the left and the right, just in case he could spot a ball of scruffy black and white feathers hopping along the floor. However, Sinders was not there.

The first fluttering's of panic started to rise in the Halfling's stomach. Where could Sinders have gone? He could not fly yet, so he would not have jumped out of the window… or would he? Maybe Sinders was that upset about his failure to fly earlier that he had gone out of the window to practice? Maybe the bird had been secretly living a double life, flying all along and waiting until he was good enough to surprise his master.

Ashe dragged a stool over to the porthole and clambered up onto it, standing on tiptoe to gaze out into the darkness, his nose just touching the bottom edge of the frame.

"Sinders I have some seed cake for you!" Ashe shouted through the opening. "Come back in here and have some." He stood balanced on the stool, head cocked to one side to hear the squeak or cry of his pet, then noticed the latch on the porthole and realised that there was simply no way Sinders could have got up through the opening unaided. So if Sinders didn't fly out of here, who had opened the window and where had his little black and white bird gone?"

Something bad was afoot. Someone had been in his cabin and his bird was missing. He needed more clues like in the detective tales Thomas told him, even if he did not understand what a squad car was and how ballistics and hair samples solved the crime. The captain always told him the smallest clues could bring a villain to justice. He would just need something to spot these small clues. He went to click his fingers and realised his thumb was not yet healed enough to do this. He needed a magnifying glass just like the one in Rauph's cabin. Rauph would not mind, he was too busy with Thomas to be using his magnifying glass. If he just borrowed it quickly, the Minotaur would never know.

Ashe dropped lightly to the floor and ran out of the door, skidding along the passageway towards Rauph's cabin. He lifted the latch and slipped inside as quietly as a mouse, intent on obtaining the glass and getting out again as quickly as possible. It was night time and the dead body in Rauph's room was scary enough during the daytime!

As Rauph's door closed, something detached itself from the shadows, its smoky form padded silently into Ashe's cabin. Slitted green eyes stared at the broken birdcage lying on the floor and a pink furred tongue licked sharp fangs in anticipation for the feast to come.

Socks looked back in the direction Ashe had gone and then turned its attention fully to the room. The cat stalked quietly over to the cage and dipped its head inside, its whiskers ensuring the entrance was wide enough for it to enter safely. However, the inside of the cage was empty and the tasty bird was gone! Socks wrinkled his nose in frustration before backing out of the cage, sniffing the air to try to find a trace of the absent, delectable feast that kept eluding him.

The cat stalked about the floor, turning in circles, head held high, then stopped, head tilted to one side, ears twitching to pick up sounds. Was that a faint tweeting it had heard over the sounds of lapping waves against the hull and the annoying voice of the Halfling in the room next door telling someone in there to not mind what he was doing and just stay dead quietly in the corner?

Socks stared at the open porthole far above, then crouched down before springing up and racing up the wall as only felines can, claws propelling the hunter up to the open porthole. The cat squeezed its head through the opening and looked about with its predatory gaze. Its quarry was out here somewhere. Sock's nose never lied. It looked to the left and the right and then stared down at the lapping waves below. There was a small ledge almost at the waterline. Huddled there, all cold and shivery, was the most bedraggled bird Socks had ever seen.

The smoky grey cat squeezed his whole body through the porthole like icing through a piping bag, his tail flicking from side to side helping to maintain the creature's precarious balance and allow it to consider its prey carefully. This was going to be a challenge, especially if the cat was going to keep dry himself. He would stalk the bird carefully, forcing the creature to move to an area where there would be no such hazards to consider and then, when he finally sank his claws into the bird and his razor-sharp teeth plunged into its flesh, Socks would finally feast well.

Chapter Twenty

"Can you tell me those symptoms one more time." The apothecary asked, rubbing his eyes and rolling his neck to try to wake up fully. "I'm not sure I understood them all." The old man yawned, giving Richard an unobstructed view down the doctor's gullet of enlarged tonsils, oral thrush and some serious dental decay.

Brother Richard struggled to hold his tongue, tired by the excitement of the evening and the interruption of his particular studies for this enforced nocturnal mission to Taurean old town. The chef Violetta had insisted Richard, being a learned man, should go and relay Thomas's symptoms to a local doctor, then report back his diagnosis, hopefully detailing the cure, both accurately and without elaboration.

The apothecary scratched his bottom through his nightgown and pulled his nightcap up slightly to free his ears, before gesturing that the monk repeated every ailment that had the captain of the *El Defensor* so close to death's door. A pregnant silence followed, with Richard watching the man furrow his brow and then stare off into space as if in deep thought.

"Are you absolutely sure of these?" the doctor asked, after what seemed like an eternity. "I mean absolutely sure?" He noted Richard's nod, confirming the symptoms from the notes compiled under Violetta's guidance.

"It's damned peculiar." The man muttered, tapping his toes and drawing attention to where one of his long stripy socks had a hole allowing his big toe to poke out. "He definitely ingested the poison? He wasn't bitten by a snake perhaps?"

"What can I say?" Richard replied impatiently. "We were at the palace eating and drinking one minute, the next we were all leaving, rushing for the ship and Thomas had lost consciousness, his pulse was rapid and he was cold and clammy to the touch."

"I need to see this patient to be sure." The apothecary replied. "But I would swear he is suffering from Nirschl poison."

"Nirschl poison?" Richard questioned. "I have not come across this Nirschl poison."

"It's not what." The doctor replied as he ran about the room stuffing assorted medicinal items into a worn leather bag. "It's who. The Nirschl lives in the jungle. Its poison is deadly. If I'm right, then your friend is already dead." He paused to check a small box filled with squirming leeches then slammed the lid and stared Richard right in the eye.

"If your captain never went into the jungle, I have no idea how he could have been poisoned this way but your description of the green veins raised across his skin make it too similar to discount. When did they start to appear?" Richard rechecked his notes.

"Shortly after he vomited." He confirmed.

"Clever woman, your chef." The apothecary commented, pulling a cloak around his shoulders and slipping some sandals on his feet. "I can't wait to meet her; she sounds very knowledgeable. Although, if she has given him willow bark to lower his temperature, she risks thinning his blood enough to make him bleed out before I even get to examine him."

* * * * * *

Kerian's head hurt! He knew this before recognising anything else in his current predicament. Then he felt a heat at his back and various other aches, pains and ills rushed in. Something was lying up against his back and his prone body was on a most uncomfortable surface. There was also a lot of noise, a low drone that rose in intensity then fell again, a bizarre chanting that battled for supremacy with the throbbing in his left temple. There was also something else; someone was talking to him urgently, telling him to wake up and calling him rather unflattering names.

The knight tried to smile and found himself grimacing as pain lanced through his jaw. Well it was not time to get up yet and until Kerian was satisfied that he had slept enough to deal with this infernal hangover he appeared to be experiencing, he was determined to keep his eyes shut. He tried to ignore the pain; at least he knew who was talking to him now. It was Octavian and he sounded close by. There was a strange smell in the air, much like sandalwood.

Whatever lay against his back was wriggling a lot and not in a provocative way. It was as if whoever lay behind him was having a bad dream and was struggling to get away. It was funny that Kerian had no recollection of where this person had come from and how they had met, especially as they were now lying together on what had to be the most intolerable bed he had ever lain.

"Wake up Kerian!" Octavian yelled again, causing a flash of crimson to cross the darkness that had been the knight's vista for so long. Kerian shook his head not wanting to wake up, but now concerned that Octavian may burst in and see whoever was laying at his back. He cracked open his eyes and awoke to a living nightmare.

Curling incense smoke filled the air around him, spiralling up from brands set about the large room. Flickering torches supplied illumination that danced energetic shadows across hieroglyphics and highlighted the profiles of statues that stared soullessly down towards where Kerian lay.

Kerian tried to groan as the light filled his eyes but his throat felt swollen and his tongue several sizes too large for his mouth. He took in the cold stone slab on which he lay, noted the heavy chain links wrapped around his body and then he noted the source of the chanting.

Shadowy figures moved through the smoke, some jolting and lurching, as if their stiffened limbs had suffered from long misuse, whilst others gleamed, their tall golden figures reflecting the torchlight set about the amphitheatre within which Kerian now lay. They moaned in unison, arms rose towards the heavens before bowing down towards the ground, the notes of the chant varied by volume rather than tone due to the lack of movement caused by the inflexibility of their throats. Kerian tried to move his head to take in more of the view and accidentally butted the person lying behind him.

"Ouch!" Octavian shouted. "Watch what you are doing?"

"Where the hell are we?" Kerian rasped. "What's going on?"

"We are in one of those rooms with the raised wells. I am not sure if we have been in here before. There appears to be some kind of ceremony going on. Hang on he's coming back again."

"Who's..." Kerian froze as the giant golden priest appeared in the corner of his eye, answering his question before he could utter it. The monster wore faded cream and scarlet robes, with an elaborate headdress that encompassed the shoulders with gold and blue beads that shimmered as it walked. The creature leaned over the two of them, its mouth frozen in a golden scream, its eyes examining the two intruders with a coldness that gave Kerian shivers despite the uncomfortable warmth in the room.

A guttural sound escaped the priest's throat and he gestured with his hand to someone below where the two captives lay. The chanting rose in volume, echoing around the chamber, rising in intensity as if the assembled creatures were reaching a state of rapture.

Kerian tore his eyes away from the monster looming above him and stared down at the chains around his torso and then he tried to follow the ancient links as they wound down across his body. For a second, he thought it was his imagination but the chain seemed to glimmer beneath its tarnished surface.

"Oh dear!" Octavian commented. "I don't like the look of that."

"Oh dear what? What don't you like the look of?" Kerian replied, "What haven't you told me?"

A loud creaking noise rose from down in the centre of the chamber. Kerian tried to twist and turn to see what was going on but could not see clearly, as the origin of the noise was below his feet. A loud clanking of chains vibrated through the stone on which they lay and Kerian suddenly felt the chain lengths grip tightly around him.

Stone grated loudly on stone as the chains slid across the stone surface. Kerian and Octavian suddenly found themselves dragged outwards and upwards into space, snatched away by the chains that tied the two adventurers together. Their legs went up into the air and Kerian barely avoided striking his head on the lip of the stone altar on which they had been lying; trading concussion for a sharp blow to his shoulder as he swung out, upside down into space, like a fish on the end of an angler's line.

The blood immediately rushed to Kerian's head as he swung backwards and forwards, the image of the golden giant mummy coming close and then moving away again as the two adventurers swung like a pendulum. Octavian started to curse loudly as everything loose in his pockets started to slide out and drop to the chamber floor, bouncing off the lid of the well that was being pushed aside as they swung.

Kerian looked down just as a rush of heat rose up and hit him, conjuring images of being back in the desert under the merciless sun. He squinted his eyes, trying to shield them from the golden glare below. Suddenly realising that the golden glint was liquid and moving. Suddenly the arid desert seemed a more favourable destination!

They were going to be lowered into the gold. Oh by Adden, they were going to be turned into two of these golden ghouls. Dipped slowly into the molten liquid and preserved with screams upon their faces for all eternity! He started to struggle, twisting one way and then the other, desperately trying to ignore the thudding, pounding headache that seemed so loud, over the chanting and the clanking of chains.

"Stop Kerian! Stop!" Octavian yelled. "Quit moving around, all of my treasure is dropping out of my pockets."

"Are you joking?" Kerian yelled back, trying to quell the rising gorge in his throat. "You are worrying about treasure, now of all times?" He looked back at the golden liquid bubbling below and watched golden brooches, coins, jewels and small items freefalling into the massive cauldron. The knight struggled again, trying to free his hands, slide a foot free but the chains were too tight! There was no way they were going to get out of this.

Something bounced off Kerian's head, making him close his eyes in reflex and then, when he realised that he was not going to be hit again he opened his eyes and blinked, not because of the heat but because he could not believe what he saw.

Colette's pendant dangled in front of his eyes, the grey pearl and golden setting dazzling in the torchlight. The exquisite workmanship, the delicate settings, the thin golden chain stretching up past his head to the neck of the man who had held it secretly all this time.

"Octavian! You bastard!" Kerian screamed, his blood boiling at the discovered betrayal. "You absolute bastard! You had my pendant all the time. You knew how much it meant to me." He struggled with the chains, swinging the two men first one way and then the other, causing more items to spin down to a fiery end.

"If we get out of this, I swear I will kill you."

"I'm sorry." Octavian replied. "I really am so sorry. I took it in the jail cell. You were asleep I hardly knew you then. I wanted to tell you when I realised how important it was to you but the time never seemed right..."

The chains shuddered and the chanting rose in volume. Kerian slowly gyrated, not daring to tear his eyes from the prize he had believed lost. The giant mummy rotated into view, operating a lever on the wall with slow deliberation. Its undead gaze staring in their direction as chain link after chain link slipped over the pulley in the ceiling and dropped the two men closer and closer to their doom.

Kerian felt the heat roll over him, reminding him of his perilous journey down into the temple beneath Stratholme, only this time Kerian did not want reminding of his past. He had been betrayed again. Taken for an idiot! Sent on a wild chase for nothing! How could he have left himself so vulnerable? His rage was all consuming, he wanted to lash out and kill the source of his pain.

"I am definitely going to kill you!" he hissed, his tone making it quite clear it was Octavian and not the mummy he was addressing. Another link slipped over the pulley, the molten gold inched closer and Kerian plotted impossible revenge!

* * * * * *

Sinders perched on a tiny algae-coated ledge just above the waterline, its bedraggled black and white form shivering with the cold. The thoroughly waterlogged bird's feathers and down were saturated, still heavy from the creature's earlier unexpected fall into the lake.

It had been sheer luck that in the bird's frenzied splashing and panicked flapping it managed to remain afloat long enough for the miserable avian to scrabble up onto the bottom rung of a ladder permanently fixed to the side of the galleon to allow boarding from one of two dinghies on board.

Sinders huddled here, cold and dejected, too small to reach up to the next rung and with no clear beak or claw holds to grab on to enable it to clamber up from its precarious resting place.

Every time Sinders tried to shake the moisture from its feathers or fluff itself up for preening, the bird found itself teetering and about to fall back into the gentle waves that rolled along the hull of the *El Defensor*. A light spray whipped up by the night winds from across the lake offered no warmth to the downcast bird and simply emphasised the chill that caused shivers throughout the creature's body. Sinders could not sleep or rest despite trying to huddle and curl itself into a tighter ball, resigned to the fact that any loss of consciousness could result in an equal loss of purchase on the slick wooden surface beneath its claws.

If only the excitable and annoying creature that came and fed it would attempt to rescue Sinders from its predicament? The bird had tried on numerous occasions to squawk for help but no one appeared to notice. It was as if the entire ship had emptied. The return of voices and movement on deck had come too late, by then Sinders was too weak to attempt further screeches for aid. Each squawk was lower than the one preceding it, leaving the black and white feathered ball with nothing to do but try and retain what little body heat remained until the sun shone from the heavens and took the chill from Sinders' bones.

A scrabbling from above barely registered with the bedraggled bird as it struggled to prevent its beak chattering, indeed, it was not until small pieces of debris started to rain down on the bird that it tilted its head and stared up the side of the galleon with one dark black eye from a nest of black and white plumage. The noises came again, louder, closer, as if something were coming down the ship towards it. Sinders felt a warmth bloom in its chest. The little person was coming to rescue it. Sinders would finally find freedom, warmth and something to eat: However, within moments it was clear this was not who the bird expected it to be.

A fearful squawk strangled off in Sinders' throat and the trembling of its form took on more urgency as the bird strained to make out the shadowy form advancing purposefully down the ladder towards it. Feline predatory eyes cut through the darkness, the deep green, almost luminous orbs, threatening death in a thousand, unspoken forms. White patches of fur appeared to float independent of a body, the sharp claws gripping firmly to each rung as the hunter made its slow descent. A maw filled with razor sharp teeth, yawned wide before setting in a sinister evil smile, the intention of its owner very clear.

Sinders watched nervously as Socks continued to advance towards it, the cat's smoky form becoming clearer as the gap between hunter and prey inevitably narrowed. The cat appeared confident in its approach, knowing the avenues for escape for its prey were slim but Sinders, although terrified, was more cunning and shrewd than Socks realised.

Socks scrunched up his body, preparing to drop down the last rung and pounce firmly down onto his meal. Claws flexed, tail flicked from side to side and then, with lightning speed, the cat dropped, his claws extended out in front of him.

Ashe's pet judged the timing perfectly, jumping up to meet the cat as it came down, beak extended to peck Socks firmly on the nose as the feline's claws brushed through his feathers, mere millimetres from catching on the bird's tender flesh. Socks closed his eyes in surprise, then meowed in pain as the bird that had seemed so meek and defenceless ran up his back gripping into the cat's smoky fur and pinching the skin beneath as it used the hunter as a ladder to race up and land on the rung that had been previously out of reach.

The hunter scrunched up as it hit the bottom rung, the elastic body bending with the force of the pounce and managing to balance perfectly as the cat pivoted with the grace of a trapeze artist to regard his dinner as it raced backwards and forwards on the upper rung looking for a way up.

A white sock whipped up towards the bird, only to meet Sinders' razor sharp beak pecking down hard onto it, making the cat withdraw and nurse its paw even as it lashed out with the other catching a lone feather and tearing it free.

Sinders squawked in protest and started to climb up a worn piece of hull, bird claws hooking into the wood as it used its beak to pull itself upwards towards the deck high above. Socks was up like a flash, realising that Sinders was in no position to attack if all of its defences were occupied. He leapt up onto the rung and raced to the edge where the bird was climbing, only for his jaws to snap shut on empty air as Sinders managed to drag himself just out of reach.

Socks snarled in frustration and leapt again reaching the higher rung Sinders had just managed to clamber onto. This ledge was wider, with a porthole situated in the centre wall. The cat scrunched up preparing to pounce, tail flicking from side to side with excitement. He pounced just as the porthole opened out towards him, slamming himself into the algae streaked glass and squealing down the outside of it. Socks hissed and spat shaking his head, before sliding under the porthole glass only to find the fledgling had disappeared from the far end of the ledge.

Voices raised from the crew quarters telling someone to close the window they had just opened, made Socks turn about to stretch half of his body through the porthole, emerald feline eyes stinging with the smoke and stench of these people living together. Someone laughed and pointed in the cat's direction but Socks was not interested in this recognition, he was looking to see where his black and white feathered feast had gone. However, no one inside showed signs of being startled by any bird-like intrusion, they all just lounged about or slept in hammocks whilst waiting their turn at watch.

The porthole slammed into the cat from behind and a mocking caw came from outside. In an instant Socks realised what his sly foe had done. Even as the cat had slid under the porthole Sinders must have jumped over the porthole landing on the side of the ladder rung the cat's slinky form had just vacated. The bird was behind him now and... Ow! Ow! was pecking his rump as hard as it could.

Socks jerked backwards, almost falling over the side of the ship as the porthole opened again. There was another squawk and a flutter of wings, droplets of water showering down onto Sock's head and making the cat wrinkle his face in disgust. Where was that damned bird?

Something black and white fluttered above him, dangling from the end of a rope, little spindly feet scrabbling to gain proper purchase on the one thing that could lead the bird up above decks after a successful jump from the rim of the open porthole.

The cat twirled about and lunged upwards, batting the bird with a claw and setting his prey swinging backwards and forwards as in a pendulum motion. Sinders held on grimly desperate to pull itself up beyond the reach of his foe. Little bird claws dug into the hemp rope as it struggled to pull itself up another inch, just as Socks claws swept through the air where it had just been. There was a flash of grey as the cat leapt up another rung, bypassing Sinders' flailing form and bringing himself to the ledge above, where he decided to sit licking his lips as Sinders continued to struggle up towards him unaware that it was inching towards it's doom rather than escaping from it.

* * * * * *

"It is a miracle he is still alive." the apothecary praised as he looked down at the dying man before him. He took in Thomas's clammy appearance, blood speckled lips, ragged breathing and wretched appearance, together with a dark spider web of veins throbbing just below the surface of his skin and wondered again how this man could even count himself amongst the living.

Thomas groaned as if in great pain, his eyes rolling; sweat soaked sheets pushed down from his torso by the captain's state of constant agitation. Rowan sat beside him, trying to reassure her lover that everything would be okay, wiping his brow, washing away the blood-stained saliva that dribbled from his mouth with a dedication just short of obsession, her fragility as clear as that of the man she nursed.

Violetta stood back, mopping the sweat from her brow, shaking with exhaustion from using her small saint to channel healing energy into the man who had rescued her from slavery. She knew Thomas's condition was grave. No matter how much she willed her saint to cure him, however much power she tried to force into Thomas's form, something dark and evil stubbornly pushed it away again. She could do nothing but watch patiently as the man they had sought for help carried out his examination with a quiet professionalism, despite the chef's inner wish to push the man aside and continue to invoke the powers of her holy relic in trying to save her captain.

"I don't understand it. It is impossible from what you have told me but this still looks like Nirschl poisoning. Tell me, he has not been tasting anything exotic in the market, wandered into the jungle and reported being bitten by anything?" The shaking heads around the room confirmed this was not the case. "Then this is damned peculiar." A knocking at the door stopped the discussion. Everyone turned to see Abilene standing in the doorway, his eyes heavy from lack of sleep.

"There's a troop of Minotaur at the gangway. They are asking if anyone wishes to join them in a hunt in the jungle today. The Matriarch has requested they offer this rare honour to hunt alongside them to capture creatures for the Labyris competition."

"Well tell them we refuse." Rowan snapped from Thomas's bedside. "No one is going anywhere with those murderers!"

"It is not wise to ignore a request from the queen." Rauph mumbled, ashamed he even had to say it.

"Well we don't care what the bloody queen thinks!" Rowan snapped back. "I think your mother has caused more than enough trouble already."

"We don't know that for a fact." Rauph replied, painfully aware he was defending someone against his dearest friends. "We have no proof."

"What further proof do you need?" Rowan snapped, pointing at Thomas who at that precise moment started to convulse. "Oh please not again. Rauph help me!"

"What's the cure?" Violetta asked, turning from the tragic scene of Rauph holding the captain down whilst Justina and Rowan rushed to assist him. She turned towards the apothecary, her weary features marked with concern. "I don't know what else I can do. How do we heal this?"

"I believe you can use extract from the crimson slipper orchid." The medic replied. "Also known as the death's head."

"So let's go get some." Colette stated, tilting her chair forwards from where she had been leaning near to the globe in the captain's cabin catching some much-needed sleep. "Which shop stocks it? I'll round up some of the crew and we shall have it back here for you in no time."

"I wish it were that easy." The apothecary shook his head sadly. "Nature is a funny thing. It always strives to create balance. You can find The Death's Head only near the lair of a Nirschl. The poison of the creature drips onto the floor and orchid seeds germinate where the acid falls. They thrive in these hostile conditions and nowhere else. Transplantation always fails. The local tribes say the sight of a Death's Head orchid is a warning from their gods, telling them to steer clear when they see the crimson blooms on the ground and trees."

"So where do we find the nearest Nirschl?" Abeline asked. "Let us know and we shall hunt one down."

"I think you will find it more difficult than simply going into the jungle and hunting one of the creatures down. The Nirschl are deadly creatures, they are the ultimate predator and their bite is often fatal. Ironically, your Minotaur guides may have all the information you require as to where the nearest Nirschl are. They go deeper into the jungles than most of us. Searching for the bigger and more dangerous creatures to hunt and return for the games. If anyone can lead you to this monster, they can." The doctor confirmed. "I'm afraid that if you cannot gather a Death's Head, your captain will never recover."

"Gather six crew." Colette ordered Abeline. "Volunteers only: ensure they are fully armed and tell them to, look out for each other, never wander off alone, never turn your backs on the Minotaur or trust any of them." She paused, gathering her breath.

"Hunt down this Nirschl and bring us back a crimson death's head orchid."

* * * * * *

Drummon sniffed the air wrinkling his nose in distaste as he made his way up the gangway onto the *El Defensor*, pushing his way past several crew who appeared unsure and uncomfortable as to how to handle the clearly unwanted intrusion. He was decked out in hunting garb, camouflage green and brown tunic over his armour, bow over his shoulder, arrows in a quiver at his side and his sword and dagger at his belt. So this was where his brother had been hiding all these years. He ran his hand along the rail, examining his hand afterwards as if he had been wearing white gloves and he had been checking the quality of the housekeeping. The ship was old, that was quite apparent and the lines were strange to him.

The Minotaur looked up at the mast and the furled sails, then checked the lines with his eye, before he began to impatiently pace the main deck, waiting for the group of men his mother had requested come hunting with him. People his brother clearly thought were above his own family. A sly smile spread across Drummon's lips as he considered the task the Matriarch had set him.

Several thoughts ran through his mind. Hunting was such a dangerous sport. All sorts of accidents could happen. People could fall into traps, the prey could turn on the hunter, people got shot all the time, mistaken for animals in the undergrowth by over-zealous and inexperienced hunters. He touched the red wood bow pre-strung over his shoulder and smiled, imagining the hum of the weapon as he loosed the string and sent a barbed shaft through the throat of one of these humans.

The huge Minotaur turned and leant against the far rail, toying with a wooden stave he found there, as a party of six crewmen began to assemble on the deck before him. An archer, a monk, a dwarf with a crossbow, a youth with the oldest armour and sword the Minotaur had ever seen, the pudgy man who had amazed Drummon with the amount of food he had been able to consume the night before, holding a sword that was bone white and another man who stood apart from them all, darker and more foreboding than the others, flipping a dagger backwards and forwards across the back of his hand.

Kristoph came out on deck, his face shadowed and heavily lined as if he had not slept.

"We are ready." He remarked.

"Is your captain not coming?" Drummon enquired slyly, tossing the smooth wooden peg from hand to hand and knowing full well the captain could not be joining them today.

"He is indisposed." Kristoph replied. "You know, captain stuff. Shall we get things started."

"Indeed." Drummon replied, laughing inside at the hurt shown in his brother's features as Kristoph tried to cover for the man he had clearly come to see as a dear friend. Drummon rolled his shoulders and flexed his arms before standing up and holding his arms wide, ushering the six men and his long-lost brother towards the gangway and the troops assembled below, signalling that everyone filed ahead of him so they could head to the shore.

"Excuse me." An older man who smelt heavily of birds stopped Drummon as he was about to step onto the companionway.

"What do you want?" Drummon snapped, incensed at the impudence of this mere human to address a prince regent in this way, forgetting himself in the moment and letting his role as the perfect host slip to reveal his true evil self.

"I believe that belongs to us?" Austen remarked, swallowing hard but refusing to back down, indicating the wooden stave still held in Drummon's hand.

"Oh of course." The Minotaur replied, tossing the peg up in the air and back across the deck, only for it to drop out of sight over the far rail. "Oops, oh how clumsy of me." Drummon turned to set off down the gangway, laughing to himself at his little petty act. Only to stop in his tracks as a loud yowl filled the air, followed by a raucous squawk. A scruffy bird took to flight, clearly disturbed from its roost by the falling stave, its erratic bobbing path leading it up into the air as if the bird had been drinking heavily the night before.

The Minotaur swiftly lifted his bow, setting a barbed hunting shaft to the string and pulled the weapon smoothly to full draw, sighting on the bird as it bobbed and bounced in the headwind from the lake. Drummon exhaled, concentrating on the creature estimating where it's flight path would take it then let fly, just as the sun came up over the mountains and flooded the area with light.

He dropped the bow from his line of sight, eager to watch his first kill of the day, his eyes straining against the light to mark the path of his arrow as it closed on the fluttering creature. It was moments like this that pleased Drummon, moments when he could prove his supcriority by crushing a weaker foe. Maybe, if he did a good job today, when the time came, his mother would let him be the one who burned this ship and everything that remained of Kristoph's previous life.

His eyes tracked the black silhouette of his arrow as it shot towards the bird, there was no escape for the creature, it was doomed. This was an excellent omen for the hunting that was yet to come.

The sunlight seared across the lake, the tip of the pyramid gleaming as the luminance of the dawn kissed the summit dazzling the crew and making Drummon squint, his eyes looked down by reflex, to note a surly cat slinking over the edge of the ships rail, its tail down, head also directed towards the departing bird.

Well only one of them could be the victor in the hunt today.

The arrow got closer and closer and then appeared to bounce into something in mid-air just short of the bird. Drummon rubbed his eyes in disbelief as it appeared that two arrows fell from the spot instead of one. How could that be? He rubbed his eyes again realising that the bird was now heading towards the shore, far beyond the range of his bow.

Drummon threaded his bow back over his shoulder and stormed from the ship, stomping his way down the gangway to where the troops and human crew from the *El Defensor* stood waiting. The crew seemed to be looking anywhere but in the Minotaur's direction and he failed to notice that the archer of the group appeared to be checking the string of his bow.

"Let's go." Drummon snapped. "We have prey waiting to be killed." Everyone fell in and started towards the path leading into the jungle.

"Good shot!" Mathius remarked under his breath.

"It was a piece of cake." Weyn replied as the arrow reappeared in his quiver. "And so worth it to wipe that smug look from his face!"

Chapter Twenty-One

The mummified citizens of the lost city of Tahl Avan continued to moan from their seats around the amphitheatre as the clanking chain rattled relentlessly over the pulley high above. Link after link rolled around the cog, lowering the chained captives suspended, closer and closer to their molten, glittering demise as the golden hued high priest looked on maliciously.

Despite the perilous nature of the situation, Kerian's attention remained transfixed on the one thing he yearned for more than life itself, or at least the tacit promise the object represented. He held his neck at an awkward angle, not daring to take his eyes from the pendant dangling from its golden chain, as the prize slipped agonisingly further and further down Octavian's neck. His one chance of finding Colette was inches from his nose, yet with his arms pinned, he was powerless to hold it one final time.

"Will you stop struggling?" Kerian snapped. "Because, if you lose my pendant, I promise that you will be so dead there will be nothing left to mourn at your funeral!"

"Do you ever stop moaning?" Octavian shot back, wriggling and shuffling against Kerian's back as if someone had dropped a poisonous centipede down his trousers. "You are giving me a headache. Why can't you be more positive? At least I am working on an escape. Oops" The pendant suddenly dropped several centimetres, to catch just behind the lobes of the gypsy's ears.

"Phew that was close." Octavian remarked, his cocky smile still present, despite the fact that they and the necklace were slowly inching towards their collective doom.

"Be positive!" Kerian shouted. "By Adden! How am I supposed to be positive whilst we are dangling like this? Am I supposed to be enthusiastic? The mighty Octavian is working on an escape plan huh? Well I feel safer already!" There was a pause. "Exactly what are you working on?"

"I wouldn't want to spoil the surprise." Octavian retaliated, continuing to wriggle fiercely as he tried to free his arm from his baggy tunic. The gypsy's mind raced. There was a way out of this but it was too dangerous to consider. If he lost control? No he could not risk it, even in these dire circumstances. He wrenched his arm around but his hand was stuck against the chain. It was so close but the chain was just too damn tight! If only he could free his hand and grab something useful at his belt.

"When I ask you old man, take a really big breath in."

"I get it." Kerian replied sarcastically. "And then I suppose if we both blow really hard; we can put out the flames? Oh be serious Octavian."

"I'm always serious." The gypsy replied. "On three then. One… Two… Three." There was a brief struggle as the two men tried to readjust themselves and the pendant wobbled erratically, then nothing but the slow clanking of the chain.

"Did you bother to breathe in?" Octavian asked. "Because if that was your best effort?" Kerian closed his eyes, fighting back a bitter retort. His head was spinning now, a combination of the earlier blow he had received, the fact he had been hanging upside down all this time and possibly the effects of breathing in the vapour given off by the bubbling gold below.

"Once again." Octavian prompted. "One… Two… Three." Kerian sucked in the biggest breath he could and instantly felt Octavian's arm wriggling frantically behind him in a desperate attempt to slip free. There was an increased tightness of the chain across the warrior's chest then an exclamation of joy from the gypsy.

"I'm not sure what you are planning to do next but before you do anything, I beg you, please don't lose Colette's pendant."

"I never got that far in the plan." Octavian confessed. "Hang on, I'll try and reach it." Kerian felt himself pushed this way and that as his companion tried to get into a position to catch the necklace before it fell. There were a lot of gasps and grunts then a despondent sigh. "It's no good! I just can't reach it."

"Don't… drop… that… pendant." Kerian warned, his tone edged with the implied threat of violence. He tried to angle his head again and made out Octavian's flush face, the man had his tongue out and appeared deeply in thought.

"Can't you just grab the chain with your teeth?" Kerian asked. Octavian stopped what he was doing and gave Kerian a dark stare before he resumed wriggling. The gold bubbled and gurgled in anticipation as the men descended ever closer.

"Hang on… Almost got it."

"Got what?" Kerian enquired. Octavian's new satchel slid into view, its movement jerking as the gypsy lowered it carefully between them. The lid of the satchel caught for the briefest of moments, giving a glimpse into the darkness of the bag as it moved past, allowing a scent of mulled spices and warm bread to rise towards them. Octavian's tongue reappeared as he tried to position the bag beneath the swaying pendant.

"Nearly… almost there."

A loud boom echoed through the amphitheatre causing the chanting to stop. The high priest pulled on the lever operating the pulley system, the chain halting its downward progress with a grinding jolt. The shock of the stop jerked the two captives as their descent halted. Octavian felt his neck flex and clenched his teeth in horror as the pendant slipped from his ears and fell out into space.

"No!" Both captives cried out, watching the necklace sparkle in the flames as it fell in slow motion before their eyes. Kerian's heart appeared to stop beating as he watched his future end, whilst Octavian groaned as a fortune in ransom slipped from his grasp.

The pendant bounced on the rim of the open bag, spinning like a pirouetting ballerina as it twirled around the opening. Both men held their breath as the necklace teetered, first one way and then the other, threatening to tip over, away from the bag, before the long golden chain following after it, slipped into the open satchel, its combined weight and downward momentum sufficient to drag the prized jewel in after it with a final seductive wink of reflected light.

The crash came again, making some of the audience stagger to their feet and turn towards one of several entrances leading into the auditorium. The huge priest moaned and gestured with his hands, requesting his undead supplicants investigate what had dared intrude on their ceremony. It watched as several moved to obey, then seemed to become confused as louder noises followed. The priest turned away from the lever in obvious agitation, stomping over towards the entrance, intent on making its demands clearer to the skeletal shrivelled creatures milling there, leaving the captives with little doubt that if the creature's features had not been set in gold, its face would have been a thunderous scowl.

"That's our chance." Octavian gestured, nodding towards where the priest had been standing.

"What do you mean?" Kerian replied still dazed at how close he had come to losing his precious gift.

"The lever is unattended. If we can get to it, maybe we can activate it and drop free." Kerian shook his head as louder sounds of disturbance came down the passageway.

"And fall free to where exactly?" the warrior asked. "Our destiny has merely been postponed. The source of our gilded overcoats still remains actively bubbling below us."

"But if we swing and build up enough impetus, hitting the lever should disengage it and release the chain, dropping us down past the rim of the well." Octavian replied.

"That's all well and good." Kerian said sarcastically. "But how do you intend to build up this said momentum? I don't think any of the walking dead below will volunteer to give us a push!"

"We have to swing together." The gypsy replied. "Like in a circus. But it will take team work." Kerian laughed aloud at the absurdity of the situation.

"I am well aware of your idea of team work." He snapped.

"Do you want to get out of here or not?" Octavian shot back, not waiting to receive an answer. "Now let's get this thing moving before the big ugly one comes back."

The two men wriggled and rocked, desperately trying to get the chain to swing. The thick links clanked and rattled and to any onlookers it must have appeared like the two men were struggling fish caught on a line. As they worked to move, both captives stared intently towards the entrance, where several more mummified creatures had now shambled over, including two large golden mummies that took up guard duty at either side of the entrance through which the priest had ventured, intent on discovering what was going on. The noise was getting louder, indicating that whatever the source was, it was heading their way and getting closer, despite the surge of monsters trying to leave the room.

"This is ridiculous." Kerian panted, beads of sweat dripping down his face and his heart pounding loudly in his chest at the exertion required so far. "We aren't getting anywhere."

"Don't give up now." Octavian replied. "Not now, we are too close."

More creatures shuffled by below them, arms outstretched as they tried to remain upright, some dragging shattered limbs, others trailing lengths of loose brown bandages behind them as they moaned and wailed to their shrivelled colleagues.

Kerian noticed a slight swing of movement and initially thought it was his imagination, the power of his mind suggesting that he had achieved the impossible when it was clear there was no way they were ever going to escape from this place. The chain swung the two men to the left and then in the action of a pendulum wobbled them back again.

"That's it!" Octavian shouted over the din from the mummified crowd below. "Keep swinging. It's working."

Kerian did not offer a reply; he was too amazed at the slight breeze washing across his skin, helping to cool his heat-exposed flesh. He tried to exaggerate the swing, gritting his teeth and bending his body in time with his companion as best as the chains allowed them to do, making the wobble into a more fluid swing.

Back and forward they swung, the arc getting longer and covering more distance at each motion. Unearthly screams started to rise from the passage and the unmistakable sounds of a skirmish echoed from down the corridor. One of the golden guards turned as if summoned by one of the groans coming from all around and headed off into the darkness after its master, followed by several shambling corpses.

"Push!" Octavian screamed. Kerian gritted his teeth trying to ignore the dizziness that was now washing over him as he put his body to the task, observing the lever moving closer and closer with each swing.

"How exactly are we going to grab the lever?" Kerian suddenly remarked. "I have no hands free and it is getting awfully close."

"I don't know!" Octavian replied, as the world tilted beneath him and the bubbling cauldron slid past their view. "Just use your head."

Two skeletal corpses shuffling along the far side of the well paused in their movements and gazed up at the swinging captives, following their arc with clicking brittle bones, their heads moving from side to side in grim parody. A stick thin arm, still encased in stained bandages pointed shakily at the prisoners and then issued a shrill call of alarm. The sacrificial two were attempting to escape.

"I think we have to hurry." Octavian warned, as the remaining guard looked up with its frozen face, eyes focusing on the clanking chain before slowly working down its length and locking on the swinging pair at its end. It reached up, screaming and drew the biggest sword Octavian had ever seen. A weapon clearly forged for the giant it belonged to.

The guard started to push through the crowd of shuffling mummies still mindlessly following their departed priest, pushing aside one so hard its spine snapped dropping its still wriggling body to the floor, lifting another free to throw it clear across the room to hit the edge of the well and drop in to the bubbling gold beneath, still fighting the oncoming tide of dead.

"Yes..." Octavian confirmed as the swing took the golden guard back into view, just as he cleaved a brittle skull with his gleaming weapon and smashed another mummy into quivering pieces for daring to block his path. "...We definitely have to hurry."

"Almost there." Kerian replied, as the end of their latest swing resulted in him having to turn his head or risk smacking his face against the lever. "One more swing should do it." The two men flew back across the room, their heads missing a wild swing made by the guard's sword before they reversed their direction, dicing with death for a second time as the guard leapt up making a futile grab at their mode of travel.

Kerian closed his eyes as they crashed into the lever, freeing the mechanism. Lengths of chain started clattering loudly through the pulley, resulting in an avalanche of metal falling from the ceiling, moving backwards and forwards as it plummeted towards them. Octavian prepared for the drop to the floor, thinking in his mind that they only had one chance to fall safely, when the chain snagged on the lever snapping the two men to an instant stop that left them hanging painfully, still wrapped in the chain.

"Well that's not exactly how I planned it." Octavian confessed.

"I think I'm going to be sick." Kerian replied meekly.

The gypsy started to pull at the slack chain, yanking it through with his free hand, link by link, all too aware of the monster bearing down on them. The golden giant seemed to know its prey was in no position to flee or defend itself and dragged its sword along the stone floor, raising sparks that matched the ones now rising from the golden cauldron as length upon length of chain snaked directly into the molten pot.

"Hurry, hurry, hurry!" Octavian repeated to himself, still pulling desperately at the chain to feed himself more slack and loosen their bindings, but the chain he was pulling was hot from landing near the bubbling gold.

The giant mummy clambered up onto the platform on which they had landed and charged across the stone with a scream, intent on dismembering them. Kerian looked up towards the face, frozen forever in agony and felt his resolve drain from his body. He could not free himself and the creature was swinging its sword with a determination that could result in only one possible ending. The sword lifted up high then swung in, edge glittering, cutting through the air straight towards Kerian's vulnerable form. He closed his eyes tightly and felt himself drop to the floor just as the sword smashed the lever they had been suspended from into jagged pieces.

Kerian threw himself clear, scrabbling to regain his feet as the monster slashed the air with its blade, gouging chunks from the floor and walls as it tried to turn its weapon on the small creatures at its feet. An overhead swing smashed into the floor as Octavian and Kerian leapt aside, both men running in opposite directions, determined to confuse the giant as they weaved between its golden stomping feet.

"This way." Octavian yelled, indicating a darkened passageway behind them that appeared quiet in comparison to the milling monsters. "I think the horses are down here." Kerian turned trying to understand how the gypsy knew to head that way, could he smell the horses or something? Then he spotted the fresh hoof prints on the floor and nodded in agreement. It made sense! He ducked as the guard's sword swung in again, so close he felt the air from the blade on his face. Darting to the left, then the right, directly into the path of a smaller mummy, missing its outstretched clawing hands and open mouth, only to watch the creature explode as the guard's deadly backswing obliterated it.

Octavian faced similar opposition as more shuffling monsters closed from the other end of the platform, some ghouls even dropping from seats high above in their manic attempts to recapture the escaping sacrifices, risking shattering their fragile forms on the hard stone as they landed. He shoved one of the mummies, sending it into the path of another, then grabbed the loose bandages of a third to loop around the neck of a fourth shuffling corpse, resulting in the mummy dragging the protesting undead creature behind it.

The scent of musty spices rose thickly from the corpses, making the gypsy sneeze at the cloying smell. He darted to the side, moving ever closer to the passageway and tripping another mummy as he went. The giant sword swept in low causing the gypsy to jump or risk being chopped clean in half. He staggered and fell into the shadowy corridor, just as Kerian ran in alongside him, the reverse swing of the monster's sword missing them by inches. They both stumbled into the darkness, Kerian cursing his lack of vision whilst acutely aware of the sounds of the lumbering monster pursuing them.

Octavian ran into the portcullis first, crashing into the iron gate with a grunt and a curse, too busy looking back at the gigantic shadow chasing, to note what was right before him. Kerian shuffled up alongside, running his hands along the wall like a blind man.

"Find the lever." Octavian ordered. "We need to get through the gate." The heavy sounds of footsteps crashing to the ground behind them made the two men search faster despite the low light.

"Ah Ha!" Octavian shouted aloud. "I've got it." A clanking noise sounded as the portcullis started to rise. Not waiting for the gate to open fully, Octavian dropped and rolled under the portcullis, Kerian swiftly following him. The gate continued to open as they hurriedly backed away from it into a narrow corridor that was even darker than the last. Heavy snorting rose behind them.

"Toledo? Is that you?" Kerian asked. The horse snorted in response, pawing the ground impatiently. "We really do need a light in here."

Sounds of shuffling in the darkness and further movement on the other side of the corridor appeared to indicate that Octavian had found his horse too. Within moments, a spark was splitting the darkness, followed by another that caught on one of the torches they had secured earlier, allowing a pale light to flicker feebly into life.

"Our supplies." Kerian remarked with a smile as soft illumination revealed their passageway was actually a long narrow alcove where both the horses and Dorian the donkey were hobbled near an old water fountain that babbled lazily. A pile of items on the floor also held a surprise. "And my sword! Our luck is finally turning. Quickly, untie the mounts, we need to be far away from here." Louder snorting sounded behind them, followed by the rasp of metal on stone, as Kerian bent to retrieve his blade.

"Steady Toledo." Kerian put his left hand back into the shadows behind him to reassure the stallion and found himself touching something cold and hard. His horse added further confusion by bolting past him on the right, spooked; knocking the other mounts and getting them snorting and agitated within the confines of the passage. Octavian dropped his torch in the confusion, plunging the whole area into darkness again. Meanwhile, Kerian's hand still remained resting on the cold hard object behind him which appeared to be inching steadily closer, snuffling heavily as it did so.

"Hang on." The gypsy tried to reassure his colleague, unaware of the horrors running through Kerian's mind. "All I can say is I am glad you shut that portcullis. Imagine what it would be like if we had left the gate open?"

"Octavian. You found the mechanism. Therefore, you were the one who needed to shut the portcullis." The breathing came louder, the cold object beneath Kerian's hand shifted again, as if trying to squeeze towards him down the narrow confines of the passage.

Octavian nursed the torch back into health and swung around from his two mounts, raising the burning brand high, only to come face to face with a pale faced Kerian and the looming horror of the giant golden mummy squashed into the passageway behind him, its mouth agape and its sword raised high as it tried to ease sideways towards them. Kerian's companion dropped the torch in shock, retreating in surprise, astonished at how quickly the mummy had crept up on them.

"Kerian, look out!" he whispered in warning, gesturing with a shaking hand.

Kerian was already acting, spinning and bringing the blade he now wielded straight up to parry the restricted downward swing of the monster. The two weapons smashed together, the sheer ferocity of the attack forcing Kerian back down the passageway towards Octavian and the horses.

The creature was so strong! The force of the restricted blows from the mummy's ancient blade rang loud as it met Kerian's own defensive movements. To the left and the right, the monster jabbed and prodded, looking for ways past Kerian's defence but the knight was resolute the giant guard's attacks would not best him.

Kerian lunged forward, scoring the giant's hand and making it jerk back, before he lashed downward with his blade, catching the giant in the leg, scoring deeply into the golden surface. On the offensive, he pushed his advantage, parrying high, deflecting the giant's weapon away and up high every time it tried to land a blow. Then he changed tactic, stepping to the side, allowing the supernatural guard's sword arm to crash down, its blade scraping along the wall, only for Kerian to run up the monster's arm and slam his blade home into the undead monster's eye socket.

The creature let out a mournful cry before slumping down in the corridor, its undead corpse lifeless. Kerian slithered down the golden creature and walked over to where the mounts and the gypsy waited.

"Oh so well done." Octavian clapped sarcastically. "How are we supposed to get the horses over that? That golden monstrosity has completely blocked the corridor back into the city." Kerian walked straight by, leaving Octavian still moaning behind him. He had no time for the gypsy. There was something odd about this corridor.

Why leave the horses in a dead end? It made no sense. Why was there running water and places for the horses to be tied? It was not a stable, that much was clear but something had made the undead bring these animals here for some reason, almost as if they were just waiting for someone to take them for a ride.

He placed his hand on his hips thinking aloud. Then he walked back towards Octavian who still stood there holding the torch high. Kerian flashed a disarming smile.

"Do you mind if I borrow your torch?" He asked, taking the burning brand in his left hand even as his right curled into a fist and smashed the hilt of his sword into Octavian's forehead. The gypsy's head snapped back, then rocked forward only for Kerian to slam an uppercut under his jaw, rocking the man up on his feet, before dropping him to the floor.

"That was for stealing from me!" Kerian snarled down at the groaning gypsy. "And this..." He delivered another stunning blow to Octavian's skull, splitting the skin and drawing blood, this time finally robbing the gypsy of his consciousness.

"...is for making me believe I could trust you."

* * * * * *

Thomas indicated then pulled the police cruiser up to the kerb in a controlled skid, the strobe of the police light joining those of the emergency services already at the crime scene. He turned off the ignition, letting the air conditioning unit whine to a stop, took a deep breath and then climbed out of the battered pool car, allowing the sultry night air to wash over him.

You had to be mad to work in New York in the summer: Hot and humid during the day, uncomfortable and sticky in the evening. The roof of the car felt hot under his fingers as he locked the door and placed the car keys carefully into his pocket. His work colleagues teased him about securing the car at the best of times but Thomas knew that the only reason he had survived so long on these crime-ridden streets was because he was careful and never took chances.

As in all crime scenes, Thomas took a moment to take in the orderly chaos of the area; a team of paramedics were attending to one poor soul, clearly dead on the floor, his life dripping out of him like a leaky faucet. Blood stained packets of gauze, discarded nitrile gloves, hissing oxygen lines, cracked drug vials and a humming defibrillator; medical detritus marking a battlefield where the outcome had not been favourable.

Over in the open back of an ambulance, two other medics comforted a mother, clearly in shock, her pale face peering forlornly from a wrapped foil blanket, her eyes red rimmed, cheeks streaked with tears, her body visibly trembling. Uniformed police milled about, unrolling yellow police tape and pushing back the crowd of vultures who had come to gawk at the proceedings whilst filming everything with their mobile phones to upload on social media sites in an attempt to gain momentary fame.

Thomas checked his police shield was prominently displayed at his belt and patted his right hip to confirm his side arm was secure before he headed purposefully through the crowd. He knew his fellow detectives were already at the scene. He could see the tall figure of MacMichael wrapped in a shroud of cigarette smoke and his shorter side kick Eede flirting with one of the female cops even now.

"Nice night for it." Thomas opened. "So what have we got guys."

Eede looked over with a goofy grin. "Hiya Thomas. Where's Jerry?" MacMichael started to laugh at the traditional greeting, even though it had grown tiresome for Thomas, and then ended up coughing heavily before spitting some phlegm on the sidewalk.

"Littering is an offense. Write him up Eede." Thomas jibed.

"Get your own secretary." MacMichael fired back. "I don't pay him by the hour for nothing."

"I get paid?" Eede replied, arching an eyebrow and crossing his arms, his grey trench coat flaring out behind him like a cape. Thomas took in the shorter man, his denim shirt, beige trousers and cowboy boots completing an outfit that would not have looked out of place on a pop star.

Thomas shot out his hand to ruffle Eede's spiky strawberry blonde hair and got a scowl that would have scorched him to the ground with its intensity. The shorter detective stared up at Thomas with a look of horror. "Never touch the hair man!"

"Uniform code on a day off today?" Thomas joked. "Or is it wash day and you have nothing clean."

"That's a good one." MacMichael replied, exhaling more cigarette smoke, whilst staring at a pretty onlooker through his shades, his outfit of a denim shirt with the loudest waistcoat Thomas had ever seen, finishing off a look that only MacMichael could pull off and still be taken seriously. The man had jeans with designer holes in them that looked as if moths had been having a feast at the wearer's expense. He even had his long black hair slicked back and tied with an elastic band. Thomas wasn't sure if this was a hippy thing or what but if anyone could pull off the look it was MacMichael.

"So what have we got?" Thomas prodded again, impatient to get in out of the heat.

"Umm." MacMichael cleared his throat and pulled a pencil from behind his ear to tap it on his notepad. "Child abduction. Johnny Datchler. Disappeared about two hours ago. Mum states he was playing in his room. No signs of forced entry, no signs of a struggle. It's as if the child just opened his bedroom window and flew away."

"Johnny Datchler?" Why did that name sound familiar and why was it suddenly so hot?

"Yep, Mums the hot dame in the back of the ambulance." Eede shot back. "Forensics should be wrapping up by now. Why don't we go and take a look at the crime scene?"

Thomas allowed Eede to lead, MacMichael following behind, as the three men headed across the road and took in the house for the first time. It was a detached property, living room and kitchen on the ground floor, bathroom and bedrooms above. Garage on the left. Pretty well-kept garden. Wonky number six on the door. Thomas walked up onto the porch, took in the football, the red racing bike and the swing. It was almost as if he had been here before.

They walked into the hall, Eede laughing and teasing the forensic team by offering 'high fives' they could not return due to the fact they were all bedecked in gloves and gowns.

"It's up here." MacMichael gestured. A potted plant sat on the landing window, all shrivelled and dry. Out of place in a house that was so orderly and neat. Thomas moved into the bedroom, his throat suddenly dry. He knew this room. The bed with the Star Wars duvet and the Highlander movie poster on the wall, displaying Christopher Lambert proclaiming to the world 'there can be only one'.

"Hey, he's wearing your clothes." MacMichael gestured, ribbing his partner at Christopher Lambert's look.

"His coats the wrong colour." Eede laughed. "What do you think Thomas?"

Thomas tried to laugh, attempted to join in with the banter of his colleagues but something drew him to the open window where forensics had dusted heavily. The net curtains rippled into the room despite Thomas feeling no breeze. He moved closer, noting something was bizarre about this scene. He ducked his head through the curtain to take in the rooftop outside.

Moss had been scrapped away from the tiles in a few places, whether from the boys exit, the assailant's entry or the forensic team. He leaned out further, ignoring Eede's joke that he did not need to jump, especially when he had friends like them.

"Hurry up and jump Thomas." MacMichael joked.

Thomas felt a compulsion to run his gloved hand around the frame and felt something cold and metallic wedged under the sill. He leaned over, further out than before and tried to grab the object, still unsure what he had touched but knowing in his mind that there was a sense of déjà vu to this entire scene.

The object suddenly popped out from where it had become stuck and almost slipped from Thomas's grasp. He caught the cold metal toy and carefully brought it back into the room before he dared open his eyes and stare at what he held in his hand.

"Thomas has a new set of wheels." Eede joked.

Thomas stared at what lay in his hand in shock, not understanding how he could be here. Not comprehending the replay of events or how he could be holding what was now in his hand. He had to be dreaming, there was no other possible explanation.

How else could he explain how he came to be holding a matchbox police cruiser with G12 stencilled on the roof?

Chapter Twenty-Two

"Now I know why they are all wearing green." Ives moaned wiping his hand down the front of his cream tunic and leaving an emerald smear across his rotund stomach. "Everything here is wet, dripping or oozing slime."

"Much like yourself..." Weyn replied, indicating the sweat patches beneath Ives arms and around his neck, where buzzing mosquitos dive bombed and plunged their proboscises deep into the merchant's skin, gorging on blood enriched by the exotic banquet from the evening before.

"I find it fascinating." Marcus confessed, flipping over to another page in his journal and sketching furiously in his attempt to document his discoveries. The monk regarded his small ledger with thought, seriously considering if he would need a larger one. He had always imagined documenting his adventures as a member of the St Fraiser monastery; copying the actions of the founding saint, gathering knowledge for others to read. Now, here he was, worlds away from the cloisters, with so many things to document he did not know where to begin.

Rauph stood silently alongside the men, his eyes closed, his nostrils flaring, taking in the deep loamy smell of the tropical jungle where the Minotaur had decided to establish their base camp. Haunting animal howls and bird cries echoed throughout the forest canopy, awakening memories the navigator never even knew he had. Gnarled and bulbous trees stretched up to create the roof of this natural cathedral, their trunks covered in strangling vines, exotic orchids and creatures that slithered amongst the shadows.

"What's up Rauph?" Aradol asked, clunking over in his father's ancient ill-fitting armour and ruining the Minotaur's reflection. "You appear to be leagues away." The navigator cracked open an eye and regarded his colleague with a look of confusion.

"I am right here alongside you, mere feet, not leagues away," he tutted. "I do not understand you sometimes Aradol." Something shrieked out a challenge from the darkness of the forest, setting off a cacophony of sounds from the lesser beasts that lived in the jungle.

"Well I for one am glad you are here." Aradol confessed, supressing a shiver before turning to look around the clearing at all the Minotaur assembled there. The huge animals moved about the area with purpose, passing through emerald green and vibrant lemon columns of light where the sun pierced the canopy above. Some were loading creatures into cages, the animals stunned from toxins set within the traps that subdued them. Others poked spears at the more violent creatures, laughing as the monsters reacted with hisses, roars and in one unfortunate Minotaur's case, a face full of barbs from the tail of the enraged creature that he teased. Other Minotaur headed off down game trails, determined to win a prize declared by Drummon for the most ferocious and deadly monster to be captured alive for the games.

Although the ground was largely clear here, with only sparse, low growing spiky shrubs and a rich layer of leaf mulch, it still moved. Insects crawled, wriggled and jumped, eager for food scraps dropped by the party, or the rich nectar from the occasional flower, lazily spinning down to the ground from its mother plant high above in the sunlight. Blue ants gathered leaves, marching in lines, waving their prizes as if miniature flags in a parade the crew were too large to appreciate. The trails heading further into the jungle looked narrow, claustrophobic and extremely hostile in nature. This was a world away from the city of Taurean, which lay somewhere off to the West, several hours' trek from where the hunting party had moored shallow barges that they had employed to get here.

Commagin paced restlessly near the entrance to one of the tunnels, eager to move on with the search and find the death's head orchid. However, no one had informed the crew where they were meant to hunt or given them the approval to go, leaving the Dwarven engineer with nothing to do but walk around in ever widening circles muttering impatiently under his breath, his crossbow slung over his shoulder.

"We are wasting valuable time." Mathius commented, as he closed to the far side of Rauph, flicking a large spider from Aradol's shoulder as he passed. "You need to talk to Drummon and get some idea where we can find this plant so we can get back to the ship. I have no doubt that whilst we tarry, Thomas is getting worse."

"Don't you think I know this?" Rauph replied, his eyes adopting a haunted look as the weight of their problem crashed about his shoulders.

"I will go with you." Weyn announced. "I want another chance to annoy our host and to have a look at his regal longbow. Maybe if I ask nicely, he will let me have a go."

"I would not count on it." Mathius replied. "Marcus please don't put your hand on that tree branch."

"Why?" Marcus enquired, leaning forward, pushing aside glossy leaves bigger that his hand as he moved further into the foliage to get a better glimpse of a particularly impressive red and yellow patterned butterfly.

"Because it's a snake!"

* * * * * *

"Drummon, we want to get involved in this hunt as well." Rauph opened in a rush; worried his courage would desert him if he did not say what was needed as quickly as possible. His outburst drew the Prince's attention away from a team of Minotaur that were dragging a large sack from one trail entrance, the creature inside thrashing and rolling about in a vain attempt to escape. "Where would you like us to go?" The huge black Minotaur turned menacingly towards Rauph and Weyn, agitated, before he suddenly appeared to calm himself, flexing his hands and breathing deeply.

"There is jungle all around you, teeming with creatures." He replied, throwing his arms wide. "Pick a trail, explore, find a monster worthy of the Labyris competition and bring it back. You do not need me to show you where to go. You have been here many times." Rauph looked about taking in each trail and finding nothing in his memories that agreed with Drummon's suggestions. He wrinkled his nose in frustration and turned back to the Prince Regent wanting to say something but unable to form the words.

"We did not wish to assume or break protocol." Weyn butted in, upon seeing the difficulty Rauph was having in formulating his response. "After all we did not want to be rude and felt it only fair to give your men a head start, before we win the competition and bring back the most dangerous animal for your tournament."

"Do you always let your pets speak for you?" Drummon snarled, moving in closer and towering over Weyn. "I'm starting to dislike this one immensely."

"I like them to show a degree of free will." Rauph replied. "They are more productive that way."

"What did you say?" Weyn turned to look at Rauph in surprise at the derogatory comment, only to be cuffed violently across the back of the head by Drummon, the force of the blow dropping the archer heavily to the ground.

"Stay down, hold your tongue and know your place human." Drummon growled. "Or I shall remove your tongue for you." Weyn shook his head in shock, spitting soil from his mouth, wincing with pain as his lip started to swell from hitting the ground. The archer's face flushed red at the insult and he started to get back to his feet, his hand reaching for a hunting knife at his belt.

"How dare you touch me!" Weyn snapped, tensing his whole body to leap up and tackle the Minotaur, his common-sense evaporating in a haze of anger.

"Stay down or I will have you flogged, servant." The sound of the warning was unmistakable, yet what struck and wounded the archer, more than the tone of the words, was the source of the order. As the archer looked up from his sprawled position, he saw Rauph clench his fist and raise it towards him, threatening violence if Weyn dared to challenge the command.

Confident Weyn would remain grounded, the navigator turned from his fallen companion and moved over to Drummon, slinging an arm around the Prince Regent as if they were the best of friends, ushering the thuggish creature away from Weyn and acting as if he had no concern about the crewman.

"Kristoph, you really must learn to control your humans better." Drummon remarked as they walked away. "How can you rule them, if they continue to act in this way? Independent thought should not be encouraged; it should be crushed."

"I understand you are only trying to be helpful." Rauph replied, knowing just how close Weyn had come to physical harm as Drummon's hand eased away from the hilt of a dagger at his waist. "It is just that where I have been, they do not treat humans this way. There will need to be a period of..."

"Adjustment..." The Prince Regent confirmed. "You just need to show them who is in charge. Set an example from time to time. Now you are home again Kristoph you shall need to address your bad habits."

"Please stop calling me Kristoph." Rauph mumbled. "My name is Rauph. I do not remember ever being called by any other name." Drummon threw his head back and laughed.

"Whoever hit you on the head must have done so really hard." The Prince Regent smiled, knowing that in fact, he was the one, who had delivered the near fatal blow. "Now let's talk about getting involved in this hunt."

The rest of the *El Defensor's* crew ran over to aid their fallen comrade and lifted him gently from the floor.

"What just happened?" Aradol asked.

"That black thug hit me." Weyn replied. He stared over in the direction of the departing Minotaur as they nodded and talked to each other. "I swear I'm going to kill him."

"I think there may be a line forming... Once we get Thomas back to fighting fit." Ives replied, brushing some crushed leaves from Weyn's knee.

"Just give me the word and the *Lady Janet* will give him a steel tipped enema that will have him shitting through a straw for the rest of his days." Commagin growled. "Just one word." Weyn shook his head, the Dwarven engineer's threat not even drawing a smile.

"I still can't believe it. Rauph just let him hit me. He never stood up for me. In fact, he threatened to have me flogged. After all we have been through together."

"Really?" Aradol asked, looking over at Rauph and then back to Weyn in disbelief. "That doesn't sound like Rauph."

"There are many things Rauph has been doing that are foreign to him." Ives confessed darkly.

"I should just shoot the bastard between the horns." Weyn continued to rant, moving to retrieve his bow.

"Let's not do that right now." Mathius lay a calming hand on Weyn's shoulder taking in the Minotaur troops all looking in their direction. "Your chances of getting away with the assassination of the Prince Regent are slim at best. You may be the best archer I know but none of us is spear, sword and Minotaur proof.

"I can work with those odds." Weyn spat blood from his split lip at the ground in disgust, even as he knew the assassin was right. "I know I can defeat him."

"It's the others you need to think about." Mathius replied trying to calm the man further but knowing Weyn would remain hurt and angry until the heat of the exchange had abated. "You need to pick your moment."

"Deep breaths now." Ives commented. "Let's finish brushing you down and then we can go and find out what is going on in a calm and rational way."

* * * * * *

"Sinders where are you?" Ashe yelled, cupping a hand to try to enhance the sound and send it echoing through the darkness of the ship's hold. The return call sounded lonely and full of poignant loss, matching the feelings blooming in Ashe's stomach.

The Halfling held up Rauph's magnifying glass, making his nose appear twice as large to any onlooker, before bringing the implement up to his right eye and examining the black and white feather he held there. There had to be more clues than this, there just had to be but the longer Ashe had sought his black and white pet the more despondent the normally enthusiastic Halfling became.

Ashe knew deep inside that the longer he went without finding Sinders the more chance there was that something horrible had happened to him. Maybe he had been sold into bird slavery, press ganged into service on another ship, or even bird-napped? Maybe he would get sinister packages with a ransom demand, or even feathers like the one he held in his hand, with more feathers being sent until the Halfling paid up and got a bald Sinders back.

That would be exciting...

The Halfling plunged his hand into his pocket and retrieved a silver bit and a candy sweet from the banquet now covered in lint from his pocket. If they requested a ransom any funding might be a bit of an issue. He would have to get a loan from Thomas to ensure Sinders' return.

What if whoever had Sinders actually hurt him, making it impossible for the bird to come back? What if... Terrible scenarios flashed through the Halfling's mind as he sank down onto the deck, his eyes trying to focus on the feather in his hand, despite the fact it appeared to be trembling. He considered the unthinkable. Ashe held his chest, feeling his heart pounding inside as if desperate to escape from beneath his rib cage. Tight bands ran around his torso crushing him and leaving him gasping for breath.

What if Sinders were dead?

The Halfling suddenly found he could not breathe. Spots danced before his eyes. He tried to suck in air and yet was powerless to do so. The air down here in the cargo hold felt hot and thick. Oh, why did his heart hurt so much?

"Are you okay?" Ashe looked up at the face of Abeline, who for some inexplicable reason appeared all blurred.

"Umm... What's that?" Ashe replied, his mind racing to make sense of what was going on.

"You appear to be crying." The acrobat stated in his Parisian accent. "I do not like to see my friends crying. What is up little man?"

"I have lost Sinders." Ashe sobbed. "I went to the banquet and when I returned his cage was on the floor, the porthole was open and he had disappeared. I have searched everywhere but he is nowhere to be found. I don't know where else to look, and I have no idea where he has gone."

"Oh dear Ashe." Abeline replied holding his hand out to help the little Halfling to his feet. "I am sure your bird is fine."

"How do you know that?" Ashe gulped, wiping his sleeve across his tear streaked face.

"Because you still love your bird so much. How can anything be truly gone when you hold it so close to your heart, eh?" The crewman who normally spent his day either in the crow's nest or swinging about the rigging letting out the sails or gathering them again, scooped Ashe up and took him to the ladder leading from the hold, sitting him on a step so he was level with the crewman's nose.

"If I were you, I would talk to Austen. He knows all of the birds on this ship. If anyone has seen where your Sinders has gone, it will be him."

"Are you sure?" Ashe smiled, his mind filling with fresh hope. "Oh that is such great advice. I wish I had thought of it." The Halfling turned to scamper up the stairs, only to find Abeline refusing to let go of his shoulder.

"What?" Ashe demanded. "I need to go and see Austen right now, just like you said. Why are you not letting me go?" Abeline tutted and shook his head, holding out his free hand, palm up.

"Oh of course." Ashe slapped himself on the forehead. "How foolish am I?" He reached into his pocket and drew out a drawstring bag that chinked as he weighed it in his hand. With careful deliberation, he started slowly counting out coins into the Frenchman's hand.

"I have to be honest..." Ashe commented, as he continued piling the coins up in the acrobat's hand and noting that the frown on the crewman's face had yet to fade. "Most of my friends don't charge this much for information. Oh what the heck! Have the whole bag."

Abeline released Ashe and watched the little man shoot off towards the main deck before he opened the drawstring bag and slipped all of the coins back inside. He secured the pouch back in his jerkin and only then did he take the time to climb up the ladder himself.

"Most friends don't end up paying for their information with the informant's money." He chuckled.

* * * * * *

"So tell me Drummon. You know it has been a while since I hunted here. What is the deadliest creature in these parts? Panther, Tiger, Wild Boar, Lurker Beast or what about the Nirschl?

"Nirschl?" Drummon almost choked on his water skin, dripping water down his chin. "What do you know of the Nirschl?"

"I know it's dangerous." Rauph replied. "More than a challenge for my slaves."

"It will be suicide." Drummon replied. "There is only one in this jungle and she is really unhappy since Mother decided to keep her baby."

"If the creature is so dangerous, what is there to lose? Just point us in the right direction." Drummon turned about the clearing to get his bearings.

"That way." He pointed to a dark trail, which still had heavy growth, signifying the path had been disused for some time. It's about one hour away. Heavy going, but you will know when you get there because..."

"Of all the Death's Head orchids." Rauph replied. Drummon stared at Rauph in surprise and then let a smile crease his face.

"See, you are remembering things already." The Prince Regent beamed. "It's almost like you never left. May the gods bless your spears."

Rauph turned and headed back across the clearing to his troops and Drummon watched closely as voices raised and accusing fingers pointed within the group. He stood arms crossed until the group headed for the trail, then gestured for three of his troops to come over.

"Follow them. Let them get a distance from here, then I want you to kill them."

"Any particular order?" the younger Minotaur of the group asked, barely containing his excitement.

"Start with the archer. I want him to die first. Then it is totally up to you."

"It will be done Prince Regent." The squad leader promised, snapping a smart salute before gesturing to his fellow hunters and heading down the trail the crew of the *El Defensor* had just taken.

* * * * * *

The noises of animals, loud and threatening enough within the clearing, now became more sinister as the group hacked their way along the darkened trail. Ominous rustlings signalled that creatures were near but when the crew looked in the direction of the sound, they only caught the briefest of glimpses of dark creatures scurrying over the forest floor, slithering up the twisting branches or rapidly swimming away across forest pools of stagnant algae coated water. Larger creatures stared back at them with dark emotionless eyes as if daring the crew to attack, whilst others waited until the party had passed before breaking cover and climbing up into the forest canopy.

"This whole place is alive." Marcus whispered. "I feel as if a thousand eyes are on me right now, watching my every move."

"That's because they are." Commagin replied, turning slowly, the *Lady Janet* cradled in his arms. "And I will put good money on it that all but twelve of those eyes want to eat you."

The monk came to a stop as the Dwarven engineer moved past and looked about him before realising that the six creatures who did not want to kill him were his own party. It did little to reassure the nervous cleric whose wide-eyed innocence had somehow become smothered in the oppressive atmosphere.

"Careful now." Mathius warned, holding Marcus back as Aradol slashed relentlessly ahead with his father's long sword, clearing a path through the thick vegetation. "How much further now Rauph?"

"I was told it was about an hour away. However, I have no idea how much time has passed." The navigator shrugged, unable to check the sun in the sky and therefore calculate an accurate passage of time.

"Surely we should have seen the red orchids by now?" Ives commented. "We must have gone wrong somewhere. Let's turn around and go back."

"We stay together as a team and move forwards," Mathius stated calmly. "If we separate in here, we may never find our way out." The assassin suddenly turned around and stared back down the hacked tunnel they had travelled, his breathing calm, movements paused as his eyes searched for something to confirm the feeling he had in the pit of his stomach. He gestured to the engineer and suggested they move away from the others slightly back down the trail.

"You feel it too?" Commagin confirmed.

"Since the start." Mathius replied. "We are being followed."

"Three of them, maybe four." The Dwarven engineer stated calmly. "Shall I wait for them here and introduce them to my mistress." He patted the stock of the silver crossbow leaving no misunderstanding as to what the trackers would be acquainted with.

"Not yet." Mathius replied. "I meant what I said. If we split up here, we may never see the *El Defensor* again."

"Is that the orchid?" Marcus yelled, drawing the attention of the two men back to the rest of the group. "It looks beautiful but how are we ever going to get up to it?"

They had stopped at a fallen tree lying across the trail and were staring over its creeper-strewn bark towards an open area just ahead. Pools of still water mirrored the thick foliage above and emphasised the height of several tall, swollen trees, making them appear to drop far into the earth as well as soar upwards, their trunks strangled with thick vines and heavy mosses.

"Is that a Death's Head orchid?" Aradol asked in wonder, lifting himself up and over the tree trunk and slipping down the other side only to sink inches into dark slippery mud that released a pungent odour of decay as he broke the thin surface.

"Where is the stupid flower?" Commagin enquired, finding it hard to see over the deadfall. "Help me up so I can see." Rauph grabbed the engineer by the back of his tunic and hoisted him up onto the fallen tree so the Dwarf could stare out over the area and take in the vibrant blues, greens and purples in the thick vegetation bordering the clearing.

"I'm sorry," Commagin continued. "But I can't see it for looking." Ives tapped him on the shoulder and pointed up the nearest gnarled trunk to where the tree appeared to have warped and twisted about thirty feet up from the floor, the thickened growth seemed to have created a platform similar in size to the stock they had all gathered around. Thick curtains of vegetation draped over the strange tree crown and right on the very edge, a solitary red orchid flower bloomed.

Rauph swung himself over the tree trunk and sank into the mud alongside Aradol, splashing the ancient armour and drawing a look of disbelief from the young warrior.

"This could be a problem." The navigator muttered.

"It will be if I have to polish this armour by myself." Aradol murmured under his breath.

"I thought the apothecary said they just grew on the ground." Weyn remarked, slipping over the tree to land in the sticky mud alongside his crewmates, splashing Aradol's armour for a second time.

"Really?" Aradol remarked at the extra splattering of sludge. "Please can we be more careful."

"There's another one over there!" Ives added from the far side of the fallen tree. "But I don't think it is going to be any easier to get to."

"Oh I see it." Marcus pointed, gesturing to another strange tree crown further back into the clearing where a splash of crimson swung from the underside, the grey finger-like roots of the plant interwoven into the bark of the strange tree. "Let me see what I can do." The monk jumped up and ran along the top of the dead trunk, his feet lightly placed and his balance perfect. He leapt from the end, grabbing a sapling that quivered under his weight and used it to flip himself across one of the mirrored ponds where he landed on some ragged clumps of grass before easing himself around behind one of the tall trunks and coming up fast when he saw what lay on the floor before him.

"Umm Mathius can you come and look at this?" Marcus shouted over his shoulder.

"Not really." The assassin replied, trying to keep an eye on everyone and also keep his line of sight back along the trail. "I'm a little bit busy." Weyn ignored them all, slogging across the mud and staring up the tree at his lofty goal.

"This doesn't look too bad?" he commented, pulling firmly on one of the vines. "I think I can get up there without a problem." He made sure his bow was firm at his back and started to climb up hand over hand, his legs swinging as he ascended.

Ives huffed and puffed as he pulled himself over the deadfall before dropping down the other side to watch Weyn climb up into the shadows. This was all too energetic for the merchant. He was simply not built for scrambling around in trees. He looked for a likely place to sit and noted a similar fallen tree set back into the vegetation. That would be a perfect place to watch the show. The merchant slithered and slid across the ground and finally arrived at the huge log. He spun about, placed his hands on the log and vaulted himself up to sit on the top. Something cracked as he sat down.

"Mathius I really think you should see this." Marcus called again, with more urgency in his voice.

"Commagin?" Mathius turned to the Dwarf and signalled back the way they had come.

"Oh don't worry." The engineer replied, slipping down the side of the tree he had been standing on and placing it between himself and their pursuers. "The *Lady Janet* and I have got it covered."

Mathius nodded then set off across the mud, his mind trying to process the threats in the area. There was something wrong about this place, something that did not seem right. He pulled his boot free from the mud and suddenly realised what it was. There were no wildlife sounds, no bird cries, no hooting, shrieking and braying. It was as if the whole jungle were holding its breath waiting for something to explode. Intuition made the assassin reach for his blades, even as he rounded the corner and slipped between the tree trunks to take in what Marcus was looking at.

There was a large depression in the ground, devoid of water but filled with something much more alarming. Jagged bones and shattered skulls littered the ground, interspersed between clumps of old foliage and dried moss. Ivory tusks from huge beasts lay discarded, along with ragged pelts stained dark with dried blood and wriggling with maggots. The heavy stench further emphasised that the two of them were staring down into what appeared to be a huge nest. Some leathery pieces of shell still lay at the bottom, cracked open, the sticky yolk within, a veritable feast for the buzzing flies that flew about in clear agitation at the disturbance caused by the two men.

"What kind of a creature has a nest like this?" Marcus asked.

"I'm not entirely sure." Mathius replied. "I'm starting to think we need to get back over to the trail as quickly as possible." A scream from across the clearing snapped Mathius attention to where Ives had been sitting but the merchant had disappeared.

"Where did Ives go?" Mathius shouted, gesturing towards the tree, an unexplainable sense of panic rising in his chest. "Aradol go and check where he is. Marcus…" The assassin turned only to find Marcus was no longer at his side.

"Marcus?"

"Up here." The monk replied, drawing Mathius's gaze upwards to where the monk was picking his way up one of the gnarled tree trunks. "You know these trees look all wet and slimy but they are actually quite dry when you touch them."

"Marcus, please get down from there."

"I will in a minute, just let me get the orchid. It's just above my head."

* * * * * *

Aradol arrived at the tree where Ives had sat, cursing the mud now splattered liberally across his armour. This was going to take ages to clean. He looked at the seat and noted the dust motes twinkling in the air around the edge of a hole shaped exactly like the rear end of the merchant he knew so well.

"I knew you were putting on weight." The young warrior laughed. "But I never thought you would be able to break a tree with your mighty backside!"

"Please help me up." Ives spluttered from down inside the trunk of the tree. "The wood must have been rotten or something." The merchant struggled to turn around and finally got up to poke his head back through the hole where he grabbed the edge only for it to crumble away in his hands, causing more hilarity from Aradol.

"It's not funny." Ives snapped. "This wood is completely brittle. Its…" The merchant paused, looking at the piece of tree trunk in his hand and noting the unmistakable shape of scales that made up the material he held in his hand. This did not make sense. If the merchant did not know better, he would have assumed that he was holding the sloughed skin of some huge sn…"

* * * * * *

Commagin narrowed his eyes, setting his sights along the barrel of his crossbow as he noticed the unmistakable shape of several Minotaur silhouettes back along the trail, drawing their weapons and advancing swiftly in his direction. It appeared they were no longer content just to follow the party, their intent for harm was now clear.

"Come to Daddy." he purred. "Just one step closer…" The Dwarf waited as one Minotaur trooper moved into the line of fire, then gently pulled the trigger and felt the satisfying thwack of the crossbow as it jumped in his grasp, the quarrel slicing through the air only to miss its intended target completely.

"What?" The engineer could not believe it. His aim had been perfect. How could he have possibly missed? He peered back along his sight and lined up the grooves to ensure his next shot would be true. The Minotaur were so stupid they had not even noticed his missed shot. This should have been like shooting chickens in a henhouse.

He breathed in and then let it out slowly, preparing to pull the trigger once again. The tree shuddered beneath him, sending a second quarrel whistling off into the foliage but this time the troops noticed and immediately dived for cover, returning fire as they advanced towards the Dwarf, arrows slamming into the trembling deadfall. Commagin flinched in surprise, stepping away from the moving tree only to crash into Rauph's legs.

"Careful." Rauph warned, lightly pushing the Dwarven engineer back towards the fallen tree, unaware of his colleague's worrying discovery. Commagin dug in his heels, pushing back into his friend as the tree they had been using for cover slowly rose from the floor, showering the area with mud and wriggling bugs.

* * * * * *

Leaping up for the platform, Weyn was aware of the shouts of concern raised behind him but remained confident his colleagues would manage to deal with whatever it was. His fingers gripped inside a natural crevice in the trunk of the tree as he struggled to pull himself up towards the top of the unusual tree crown. The archer had never felt so alive! He was going to show everyone just how good he was. The Death's Head orchid was almost in his grasp. He gazed at the bright red flower, the bulbous slipper shape of the strange alien bloom, the reservoir of collected nectar inside the folds of the exotic plant and the wiry antenna that rose from its tips.

Weyn never saw where the arrow came from that slammed into his outstretched arm. One minute he was reaching for the orchid, the next he was screaming in pain and his right arm was pinned to the trunk of the tree. His legs shot from underneath him in shock, dropping his full weight onto the arrow, causing the archer to scream even louder. The tree moved with an ominous creak and a part of the tree bark opened to reveal a large reptilian eye that stared at him with undisguised malice.

The archer could not believe what he was seeing. It had to be the pain causing him to hallucinate. He struggled to grab a firmer handhold deeper in the crevice, desperate to take some of the strain from his arm, only to feel the crack inexplicably widen and a waft of fetid air escape. Weyn looked on in horror as a huge mouth split apart, revealing row upon row of razor-sharp teeth and a flickering tongue.

Yells of alarm rose from the ground as the entire copse of trees began to shake and sway. Arrows pierced the air, slamming into the moving trees and peppering the ground around the heroes.

Weyn's grip slipped and he found himself crying out as agonising pain coursed through his arm. The archer found himself thrown about like a rag doll, as the creature he was attached to, shook its head, trying to dislodge him from his position and flip him up into its open mouth. A long tongue flickered out and licked the archer, probing him as if he were a crumb of food waiting to be consumed. Weyn was unable to fall free, due to the hunting arrow pinning him to the monster's jaw. He could only scream as the wet tongue slipped across his skin, raising welts on his face where it touched.

A loud roar resounded through the air as more of the undergrowth started tearing up all around the clearing, showering muck and filth as several areas of foliage animated and the Nirschl became fully awake.

Rauph stood in the middle of it all, watching in disbelief as each tree trunk opened reptilian eyes initially mistaken as simple knots in the wood. What they had assumed as dangling vines proved to be the shaggy manes of the creatures and the deep cracks in the trunks transmuted into open maws dripping with venom. As the monsters extricated themselves from the mire, the Navigator had just enough time to understand that every trunk was connected and all of these swaying heads were one gigantic beast, before he set his feet, drew his swords and prepared to do what Rauph did best:

Slay monsters.

Chapter Twenty-Three

It was the constant sound of moaning that first alerted Octavian that he was still alive. He opened his mouth, inhaled, sucking in some loose sand and set off a coughing fit that made his head ring. The gypsy sat up carefully, allowing the corridor in his view to slowly level out before he gently touched his head and found his hand coming away sticky from the congealed blood of a wound.

What in the hell had just happened?

Did he dream this or did Kerian actually attack him when his guard was down? Octavian furrowed his brow in confusion and felt a dull throb at his temple. He supposed Kerian had every right to get upset when he had found out about the pendant but that was all water under the proverbial bridge by now. They had moved on, saved each other's lives more times than he could count. Surely, Kerian would not throw their friendship away on one simple piece of jewellery?

Realisation flooded in. The pendant... It had dropped into the satchel he had been wearing around his neck. Fighting a wave of nausea, he looked down over his travel-stained clothing and confirmed that his bag was absent.

Kerian had stolen his satchel and the ransom contained within. Octavian's heart sank. After all this time, all the efforts required to try to gain the riches needed to rescue his family, he was left with nothing.

No, not nothing! There was still the treasure packed away in Dorian's packs. Octavian lifted his head and stared around the corridor, taking in the restless shape of his stallion and nothing else, no Dorian the donkey, or for that matter Kerian or Toledo. Where had they gone?

The constant moaning reminded Octavian of where the corridor remained blocked with the corpse of the golden sentinel. There was no way Kerian could have ever got both animals over the corpse, so he had to have left by another way. The giant's body shifted slightly, causing the gypsy to step back, before he noted another shift equally as small. Whatever creatures were groaning on the far side, they were attempting to remove the obstacle and come after him.

The gypsy staggered towards his mount, patting the creature to reassure it that he was near before realising that his saddlebags had gained a few extra items. Water skins and food, Kerian had not left him high and dry after all. He found a note tucked into the saddle, and pulled it free, struggling to read the angry charcoal strokes in the low light.

'I have left you some supplies, so you have a chance of getting back to civilization alive. It is more than you deserve. Look after yourself Octavian for It appears this is what you are best at.'

"He never even signed the note." Octavian muttered to himself.

The giant corpse shifted a few more inches, easier this time, signifying the creatures on the other side were literally getting to grips with the situation. Octavian found his head spinning again. He felt quite sick.

The gypsy turned his attention to his mount and untied the creature before carefully examining the corridor. A thin stream of light appeared to be coming in through the wall at the far end. Octavian walked his stallion over to investigate and noted a cleverly disguised doorway that would have been almost impossible to see unless you had an inkling it was there. He pushed against the stone, feeling it grate across the floor, opening it wider to permit a small drift of sand to slide into the corridor, along with a blast of heat and a spear of blazing sunlight that flooded the passageway with painful illumination.

All Octavian could do was close his eyes tightly and allow the feelings of nausea to pass as his eyes slowly adjusted to the sunlight. It felt like he had been underground for an eternity. The gypsy shaded his eyes with his hand and stared down at the shifting sands at his feet, noting the slowly filling depressions marking where Kerian and the two animals had passed. His eyes followed the trail, marking how it weaved between two lop-sided stone obelisks before passing over a small rise and out of sight.

To his left, two large crimson scorpions darted backwards and forwards across the facial features of a fallen statue, their claws locked in combat, tails held high dripping with venom. High above, an eagle soared across a faultless sky of cornflower blue, crying out to let the world know of its passing. The terrible sandstorm that had earlier threatened their lives now appeared to be nothing but a faded memory.

Octavian fought the impulse to simply follow the trail, his mind undecided as to whether he should pursue Kerian and regain the bag, or simply strike out on his own but with the sun high in the sky it was hard to get his bearings and decide in which direction it was best to go. He looked behind him at the cool shadowy corridor and noticed the unmistakable shape of shuffling corpses staggering towards him. Somehow, the creatures had managed to move the giant's corpse aside and were now in active, if somewhat shambolic pursuit.

The gypsy put his shoulder to the stone door and started to push, grunting under the effort as it pushed up the sand along its bottom edge and added stubborn resistance to his efforts. He dug his feet in, feeling the sand sliding away beneath his boots as he struggled to close the opening. The door inched ever closer and Octavian breathed a sigh of relief, when several gnarled and bandaged hands pushed through, clutching at the air, the moans of their owners made all the louder due to the closeness of Octavian's head to the door.

It took a moment of sinking dread for Octavian to realise that there appeared to be no way of holding the door closed. He knew then he had no choice but to run, or simply be overwhelmed by the weight of bodies pushing from the other side.

He pushed one last time, noting the satisfying crunch as several brittle fingers sheared off in the gap, then ran for his horse, gripping the reins and swinging himself up into the saddle, just as the first few decaying mummies stumbled out onto the searing sand. Octavian felt his stallion leap forwards beneath him, as he dug in his heels, picking up speed to first canter, then gallop across the desert. He rode beneath the two obelisks before cresting the rise to reveal the sight of hundreds of deserted ruins partially engulfed in sand, stretching away as far as the gypsy could see. Kerian's tracks led off ahead and Octavian gave a resigned shrug of his shoulders when he realised his horse was already following them.

A mournful sound came from behind the rider, making him pull back sharply on the reins, turning his mount to stare back over the desert, to locate the source of the cry. Shifting dunes formed the horizon below the blazing orb of the sun that shone down onto the half-buried lost city of Tahl Avan. Husks of buildings, some worn down to skeletal structures, rose from the sands like ghosts, their beauty eroded by time and weather. For a second Octavian wondered what it would have been like to live in this wondrous place all those years ago, a moment shattered as two mummies staggered over in his direction.

His mount shifted beneath him, anxiously pacing as it noted the monsters shuffling towards it but Octavian ignored the horse's agitation, focusing on a disturbance far away across the ruins. He stood up in his stirrups to gain a better view. A battalion of soldiers appeared to be streaming down the dunes and attacking something within the lost city.

Skirmishes appeared to have broken out in several places, with golden figures fighting the soldiers to stop them gaining entry to the sacred halls of Tahl Avan. However, from his vantage point, Octavian could see the legion had managed to breech the defences in several places and gained entry despite the fierce opposition they faced. There were so many soldiers, which, from a distance, looked like thousands of little ants scurrying madly about.

It suddenly occurred to Octavian just how far he and Kerian had wandered through the buried ruins and then he realised there was still so much further to go. He turned his horse about, his mind now decided as to what to do. Staying here, near the entrance to the catacombs, was folly at best. The mummies still pursued him, there were four now heading in his direction, all be it at a speed that would be easily outpaced by his horse. No firm travel plans could be taken until night fell and the stars revealed the direction he could take. There seemed little left to do but follow Kerian's trail and hope that in his haste the warrior either dropped the bag or ran into trouble long enough for Octavian to repossess it.

He dug in his heels, took a deep breath and then cantered down into the desolate, ruined landscape, leaving the moaning mummies skirmishing the Provan legion and the golden giant warriors of Tahl Avan behind him.

* * * * * *

"Sinders is about this big." Ashe indicated by cupping his hands to explain. "Black and white feathers that are, well kind of scruffy. Oh and a very sharp beak."

The large green and red wading bird tilted its head to take in the strange creature wading out towards it, one eye rolling to keep an eye on a tasty fish morsel it had wedged between its webbed feet and the other watching warily in case the Halfling got too close and it needed to take to the skies.

"Sinders has the saddest eyes and is probably feeling very scared. We are new here and Sinders doesn't have many bird friends. I have also been told Sinders only just learned to fly so is probably very tired…" Ashe noticed his voice was starting to catch in his throat as the bird shivered its body, fluffing up its feathers and clicking its long beak in warning at his approach through the dark silt of the harbour. "My friend is lost, lonely… and I really need to find Sinders as soon as I can."

The wading bird speared its beak into the water, snatching up another unsuspecting fish, then threw its head back and launched into the air with a mighty flap of its wings that nearly knocked Ashe from his feet.

"Just let me know if you find anything." Ashe shouted after the departing bird, stepping sharply back as it deposited a foul-smelling dollop of excreta into the water right before him.

"Well that's just charming." Ashe muttered as he watched the flight path of the creature as it angled around and flapped lazily towards the palace. He looked around the area for another feathered creature to interrogate, then shook his head and paddled out of the water, taking his time to dry his slimy toes on Commagin's face towel before popping his boots back on. The Halfling walked up past the gangway of the *El Defensor,* pausing to hang the towel out to dry, before turning his attention to the long trudge up the path towards the city of Taurean. He kicked loose a stone and started passing it backwards and forwards between his feet as he wandered up the cobbled street, his mind full of possibilities and questions.

Taurean was a large place for a bird to hide in and Ashe found that wherever he looked feathered creatures tweeted, swooped, pecked and pooed as they travelled around their home. The wading birds were keeping tight lipped about what happened to Sinders, the gulls just hopped away whenever he came near and mocked him with triple cries that rang like 'Ha! Ha! Ha!' to Ashe's little ears.

Parrots flew in military formations, greens, reds, oranges and yellows all vibrant and bright against the emerald hues of the trees under which Ashe had earlier discovered several of the ship's crew had gone adventuring without asking him. The parrots seemed to love talking, chattering incessantly as they swooped overhead but they never seemed to stop for a talk as they were always in such a hurry. Smaller fawn coloured birds bibbed and bobbed for grain and seed in the streets, pursued by thuggish crows that hopped about like crotchety old men, breaking up the feeding birds with raucous caws and sharp nips of the beak. A bird could go to just so many places here.

Ashe adjusted his *bycocket* hat, making sure that Thomas's quill remained secure in the band and tilted it at a jaunty angle on his head, before setting off up the hill, leaving the *El Defensor* at his back. He had grown very fond of this hat, even though Thomas kept singing a silly song about someone called Robin Hood who was always riding through a glen, every time he saw him wearing it. It never made sense to Ashe, well he had to be honest, not much of what Thomas said ever made sense to him!

The Halfling stared at his reflection in a window, pulled his jerkin straight and sauntered up the cobbled street, his eyes scanning the skies, rooftops and eaves for signs of his black and white feathered pet. If Ashe had been on top form, the sights and sounds of the city would have easily distracted him but the information he had gathered from Austen kept playing through his mind so much that he failed to notice the poverty of those about him.

Sinders had flown! Austen swore he had witnessed the bird's maiden flight. Now, how was that fair? Especially after he had worked so hard to get Sinders to fly! He was so incensed that he missed several small purses that people were just asking to have filched.

The Halfling bit down on an apple that had somehow worked its way into his hand and chewed thoughtfully as he walked, threading his way through the crowd. He bowed theatrically to the young ladies wearing thread worn and tired dresses, often patched and taken in, touching the tip of his hat as he acknowledged them, making them smile, titter and blush as he skipped and jumped past boots with holes in the soles and cloaks with multiple patches upon them. Others stopped their chores, hammers held in mid-strike, brooms stilled in mid-sweep to observe the diminutive figure's strange actions and found themselves smiling. Despite the deep lines of weariness etched upon their faces and the tediousness of their tasks, they all found Ashe's antics amusing.

Ashe continued his wandering, noting a small purple bird with a long curled tail and a cream breast, darting about under the stall and shop awnings; it's beak, like a silver rapier, dispatching insects and swallowing them up. A smile broke across the Halfling's face and he started to laugh aloud as he chased the bird, his eyes drawn to the way the plumage of the tail formed an inverted 'w' and the way it appeared to float after the bird as if it were a kite rather than an extension of the delicate avian.

"Excuse me!" Ashe giggled, swerving around one man and ducking under a stall to avoid walking into another. He looked up into the wooden beams of one covered walkway and noted the beautiful bird swooping up and down around the obstacles there and out the other side.

Oh if only Ashe could fly! He would love to be as delicate and graceful as this creature.

The arcade of shops ended suddenly, leaving Ashe running out into a large plaza where huge statues of Minotaur stood around. His rapid footsteps slowly padded to a halt as he took in all of the heroic poses around him. Ashe had seen these statues before, once on the way to the feast, when he had been warned sternly if he had wandered off, he would not be let in to have the food and secondly on the way back, when everyone was really too worried about Thomas for any sight-seeing.

"Wow!" Ashe looked about him and instantly noticed there was something different about the people about him. The humans wore smarter clothes but they appeared colour coded as if they were in a sports team. Huge Minotaur walked about the area with their families and everything appeared so refined. One stood before a large fountain and flipped something from his hand into the water before walking off.

Such behaviour needed further investigation! Whatever was the creature doing throwing something into the pond? Ashe ran over and pulled himself up onto the edge of the elegant structure, noting the tinkling of the fountains just before he realised there were huge orange fish swimming lazily about the pool. The Minotaur was throwing rubbish in the fountain and there were fish in here! What did he think he was doing? They could eat whatever it was and become unwell.

Ashe looked into the reflective surface and noticed something metallic at the bottom of the pond. Was that...? Could it be...? The Halfling rubbed his eyes in surprise, then rolled up his sleeve and plunged his hand into the water causing several exclamations from passers-by.

Ashe leant over as far as he could, his fingers brushing the bottom of the pond until he located the item and pulled it to the surface.

"I'll be..." Ashe remarked, checking the coin he held in his hand and biting down on the edge. Nope, there was nothing wrong with it. The Minotaur was throwing away perfectly good money! Would wonders ever cease?

Ashe slipped the coin in his pocket, thanking his luck and balanced on the edge of the fountain before holding out his arms and running lightly along the edge, swooping and rising, pretending to be Sinders and happy he had saved the ornamental fish from becoming unwell. Then stopped in surprise; from his raised vantage point there appeared to be several more coins dotted on the bottom of the pool. The Halfling rubbed his eyes in disbelief. There seemed to be loads of them! Why would someone do this?

He sat down on the edge of the pool and quickly pulled off his boots before starting to roll up his trousers.

"What are you doing?" a young voice asked. "Don't you know you are not allowed in the fountains?"

Ashe paused to take in a scruffy looking youth with spiky black hair and an infectious smile that appeared to be talking to him.

"Are you serious?" the Halfling replied, noting the youth's poor quality of clothing and the malnourished look about him. "They are throwing good money away here. It could hurt the fish and if they don't want their money then I know several people who do, including me!"

"You will get in trouble." The youth warned. "Don't say I didn't warn you."

Ashe sighed, noting once again how ragged the child looked and pushed his hand into his pocket, digging out the coin he had just retrieved. He flipped it over and stared open mouthed as the child caught the coin then quickly flipped it back into the fountain as if the coin's very touch was scalding him.

"Why did you do that?" Ashe asked, quite hurt that his gift had been sent to the bottom of the fountain with a loud plop.

"That coin is more trouble than it is worth." The urchin replied. "I'm sorry but I have to go."

Ashe watched as the boy turned away, shrugged his shoulders and then waded out into the pool. Get in trouble for wading in the pool. That was what pools were for! He plunged his arm under the water sending several ornamental fish darting away in terror and retrieved another coin. It did not make sense. If there was money to waste why were people in the lower city wearing rags. He plunged his arm in again, gathering several more coins before popping them into his pockets.

This was a crime! One of the worst imaginable! Wasting perfectly good money when people around were so poor! He bent his back to the task more enthusiastically, not believing his good luck as a huge shadow fell over the Halfling whilst he foraged enthusiastically between some lily flowers.

Ashe looked up at two massive Minotaur who did not appear very happy to see him.

"Oh hello!" he beamed. "Isn't it a beautiful morning for a paddle?"

* * * * * *

Kerian carefully led Toledo and Dorian into a ruined house that still had a functioning door and pushed it closed behind him, shutting out the darkness and the nightmarish creatures that shambled about within it. He was absolutely exhausted and truth be told terrified, with no idea how much further he had to travel to leave this sprawling city of the dead.

Several stones had fallen from the stairwell, so Kerian pushed them over to the door and formed a blockade to ensure that only the most determined creature would gain access and not without making a great deal of noise. After seeing to the animals and offering them the meagre remains of dried grasses he found sprouting from the door and poking tentatively through the holes dotted across the faded mosaic tiles, Kerian set about exploring the house, looking for supplies and anything he could use to start a fire to warm the room from the descending chill that seemed to be particularly focused within his make-shift shelter.

A ruined chair and some old paper scrolls served as a base for the fire which Kerian carefully built at the base of the stairs so that the opening to the floor above would serve as a makeshift chimney. After further scavenging, he soon had enough fuel to ensure the fire would last until the early morning without sacrificing the torches he still held in his supplies.

Kerian spread out his blanket and felt a moment of regret for leaving Octavian behind, then angrily brushed the feeling aside. The man deserved worse for deceiving him. He was lucky he was still alive! He had killed people for less in the past.

The fire crackled merrily, in a direct opposite of Kerian's mood as he huddled closer to the warmth offered, rubbing his hands, before pulling over his saddlebags and making a support for his back so he could sit with some comfort. Only when everything was secure and the fundamental tasks were complete, did the warrior sit back and allow his exhaustion to wash over him. His nerves were shredded; all he wanted to do was sleep until the sun rose.

Mummified creatures had stalked him relentlessly through the sand filled streets all day, their shambling and shuffling masking a greater intelligence than he initially thought they possessed.

One time they had herded him into a street where the road had collapsed into the catacombs beneath and he had faced a lengthy battle before he had fought his way free, narrowly avoiding the cold brittle touch of the creatures and the risk of disease that it could bring. Others lay in wait underneath piles of sand that only shifted when he wandered near, whilst sounds of skirmishes moved ever closer, although Kerian had no idea who was fighting who.

He broke some hard bread and started chewing on the crust, working the bread to ensure he produced saliva to moisten his mouth as well as make his dry meal edible. Although there was a temptation to drink plenty of water, the warrior kept his consumption limited. He would look for more water tomorrow but knew his horse and donkey needed the fluid more than he did if he was going to escape this harsh environment and rediscover civilization, wherever that was.

Kerian leant back and grabbed Octavian's satchel, wanting to hold something in his hands that would put all of this terror at bay. It was time to hold Colette in his arms once again. He looked at the design of the satchel, diamonds of material stitched carefully together and a flap that stretched across the top to secure items carefully inside.

The design was simple; he would not have given it as much as a second glance before. Now it was priceless as it held the one thing that mattered the most to him.

He threw open the flap and stared inside, only to find an emptiness before him. What? How could this be? Kerian upended the satchel, shaking it in case the pendant had somehow lodged on the shimmering fabric inside. Nothing fell out. He ran his hand around the inside of the bag and then repeated the action around the outside, knowing there could not be another pocket but checking anyway. His search came up empty. This made no sense, there had to be a pocket. He had seen the pendant fall in here with his own eyes.

Kerian repeated the moments in his mind. Had the necklace fallen out again? No, it was impossible. He had guarded the satchel with his life. Could Octavian have removed the pendant after they escaped? No, this was equally ridiculous, they had had no time whilst they were busy trying to escape.

The knight shook the bag harder, rage building inside him. This was all so wrong. Why was all of this happening to him? He crunched the bag up; feeling the lack of resistance to his actions and knowing this meant the bag had to be empty.

"By Adden! Am I cursed? Is bad luck persistently haunting me?" He threw the satchel away in disappointment, sending it flying into the shadows. He wanted the bag as far away from him as possible. A sharp exclamation came from its destination.

"Come out from there." Kerian warned, drawing his sword and regaining his feet in alarm. "I will not ask you again."

"I mean you no harm." The shadows replied with a voice that felt familiar and made Kerian's heart suddenly beat faster. He knew who she was, even before she walked out into the light, her white dress as spotlessly clean as if it had been recently laundered, worn in the same way, provocatively off one shoulder, the bangles on her wrists clicking as she walked hesitantly towards him. Kerian took in her smoky grey eyes, ruby lips and long black hair and thought back to when he had first met this enigmatic woman in the market place at Wellruff.

"How… How can you be here?" he asked, unsure whether to let his guard down. "What are you doing in the middle of the desert?"

"I won't hurt you." She promised, moving a step closer despite Kerian's edged blade. "Just let me share your fire. I will not trouble you."

Kerian couldn't help but move backwards, her gentle smile disarming him and making him lower his weapon! Seeing this exotic woman here was an impossibility. He could not think straight, something about her turned his thoughts into a fog, making it hard to concentrate and focus on what was before him.

She walked past him, her hands held up, moving dangerously close to the fire, the material of her dress translucent as she placed herself between Kerian and the flickering light, revealing a body of graceful curves that made the warrior's breath catch in his throat.

This woman was intoxicating, enchanting in every way and yet something about her manner warned him to be vigilant.

Kerian moved cautiously to the side, wanting to place the fire between himself and his exotic visitor, creating a natural barrier until her intentions were known.

"Have you been following me?" he asked. Smouldering grey eyes held his gaze as he moved, the woman kneeling on his blanket, hands still held near the flames, so close that Kerian could not understand why her palms were not blistering or turning red.

"I had to..." she replied. "You are the only one who can help me get a message through."

"What message would that be?" Kerian enquired, now more confident that the fire was between them. A sad smile passed across his mysterious visitor's face and her head bowed momentarily before she looked up at him again, her eyes now moist with tears.

"He cannot see me!" she exclaimed. "No matter how hard I try; he does not heed my call. He is becoming more animal by the day."

"Who?"

"Octavian. Where is he by the way? Oh of course. He is probably out hunting, providing for his charge as he always does."

"No, he's..." Kerian started.

"He was always good at providing. I can never fault him for that." Her gown slipped further from her right shoulder, revealing a tantalizing glimpse of the curve of breast but as Kerian tore his gaze away he noticed an ugly scar on her flawless skin. It was a sinful defacing of perfection, leaving her branded forever.

"What is that?" he asked, not able to help himself. His visitor swiftly pulled her dress back up as if ashamed by the revelation and stared at him intently through a curtain of ink black curls.

"It is nothing." She stated, suddenly much colder, her smile now removed from her intoxicating features. "It is a mark of ownership."

"That is terrible. Who would dare to mar such beauty in this way? Wait a moment... You know Octavian?"

"Of course. I have known him all of my life." His visitor confessed, raising a hand to brush her hair back from her face, her cheeks suddenly flushed. Kerian waited for more information but his unexpected guest remained silent clearly not intending to divulge any more secrets.

"When will you arrive at the petrified forests of Blackthorn?" She asked. Kerian started at the question, initially not sure what was meant by such an unusual query and caught by surprise at the change of topic.

"I'm sorry. What do you mean? What petrified forest? I am going to Al Mashmaah." He threw his arms up in the air, rolling his eyes to the heavens. "That is, if I knew where Al Mashmaah was."

"What?" the look of surprise and hurt that washed across the woman's face was almost painful to observe. "But you have to be coming. The cards foretold you would bring Octavian back to me."

"I don't know who's cards you have been reading." Kerian replied. "But they surely were not mine. The last time I had my fortune told I was informed I would die and I am still here to tell the tale."

"You lead a blessed life." She replied in a voice now husky with emotion.

"Well I think your assessment is over generous." Kerian replied. "My life is one catalogue of disasters after another. I can't even find a damned necklace."

"The pendant you seek is right there in that bag." She gestured, bangles clicking. "And despite your thoughts otherwise, you will see your love again."

"How would you know about my love, or if I will ever see her again." Kerian snapped, his ire rising. He stormed across the room, forgetting he was using the fire to protect himself and retrieved the satchel from the shadows, shaking it angrily in her face. "There is nothing in the bag and I have already informed you as to my low opinion of seers and fortune telling. My path is my own, my future what I choose it to be. I am not a character in a book where my destiny is plotted out for me."

He threw the satchel across the room where it landed upside down at her knees with a thump. Kerian froze, his arm still outstretched from the throw, his face showing surprise at the loud sound. He slowly walked back towards her, stunned at the unexpected development and got down on his knees to examine the satchel with inquisitive eyes. His mysterious guest allowed a smile to cross her features, before she sat back quietly allowing Kerian to discover something she already knew.

Kerian lifted the satchel carefully from the ground and instantly felt how heavy it had become, almost dropping it, as a suit of exquisitely made leather armour slid out from the open pouch and cascaded across the floor. Greaves, bracers, cuisses, a set of rerebrace, jerkin, undershirt, breeches, boots, underclothes, all in hues of subtle reds, beiges, browns, yellows, creams and dulled metal links. Kerian continued to lift the bag, noting a dagger, sheath, belt and hooded cloak also tumbling to the floor.

This made no sense! It was clear there were more items on the floor than could have possibly fitted within the bag. Kerian dropped to his knees and lifted the satchel up, staring into its depths but if he was expecting to see a massive interior, he was disappointed. The satchel looked just the same as it had before.

"Where did all of this come from?" he asked. "Did you do this?" A slight shake of the head denied any involvement.

"But that's impossible!"

"Nothing is impossible if you let yourself believe." His mysterious visitor whispered, licking her ruby red lips. "You need to find Octavian. Time is running out. I don't know how much longer I can go on."

"Octavian is gone." Kerian confessed. "I left him back in the catacombs."

Grey eyes turned flint cold.

"You did what?"

"I left him. He stole from me."

"The cards are never wrong." She whispered. "How can this be?" Kerian looked down at the armour scattered about his feet and started lifting the items up, examining them one at a time.

"The pendant is not here." He stated. "Where is it. You told me it was in the satchel."

"Kerian, you need to shut up."

"I will do no such thing." He replied, moving to get back to his feet.

"You have made a big mistake." His guest stated coldly. "You need to find Octavian, you must travel to Blackthorn and the next time you argue with me..." she leaned forward and lightly caressed Kerian's forehead, paralysing him with her deathly cold touch. "Keep on the right side of the fire."

Kerian's arms felt like lead. He could still breathe, still hear, still blink but all other motion was alien to him, as if he were a marionette in a show awaiting the puppet master to pull his strings. Coldness flooded through him, a coldness that burned, setting his nerves ablaze. He fell back across the blanket, his body landing in a heap across his saddlebags.

His guest paced about the room in agitation, her white dress flicking up at every turn as she walked the floor, her hoop earrings golden halos in the reflected firelight.

"Oh Octavian what have you done now, you stupid man?" She wailed. "You managed to alienate the only man who could help you. Trust an obstinate man to make such a damned foolish mistake. This could cost Iolander her life. Don't you realise what you have done?"

Kerian watched her movement with mixed emotion, terrified that he was dying in some way and would never recover from whatever paralysis this woman had inflicted on him whilst another part of his mind tried to understand how such a beautiful woman could know Octavian. As if she knew he was thinking about her, his visitor stopped pacing and came back over to sit alongside his still form, tracing a freezing cold finger up the bare skin of his arm and setting his nerves afire. She leaned in close and whispered huskily into his ear.

"You will sleep now. Then tomorrow you will find Octavian and you will bring him to Glowme Castle. My daughter's time is too short to be ended by a stupid argument between two men who are too proud to see that the only way for them to get what they want is to both work together." She paused, moving around in front of Kerian, her lips inches from his, her hair brushing seductively against his cheek.

"Somehow, you look younger Kerian." She whispered, moving forwards to brush his forehead with her ruby red lips causing agony to surge through his body and arch his back from the floor. "As to how I know Octavian..." she smiled, her eyes losing focus as she reminisced.

"He's my husband."

Chapter Twenty-Four

The walled fortress city of Al Mashmaah was a sprawling metropolis, constructed, as legend would have it, surrounding a magical oasis that saved the life of a nomadic prince who had staggered, half-insane with dehydration from out of the whispering sands of the Vaarseeti desert and almost expired on the spot. The tale described how a glowing vision had led the prince to a life-saving, magical well in the middle of the desert and its healing waters had saved his life and made him the leader of the settlement that had grown from this miraculous occurrence.

No one knew exactly where this once magical well was situated, its location lost in history and buried somewhere under the sprawling mass of humanity that now called Al Mashmaah their home. Several shrewd entrepreneurs swore that they were the custodians of the original site, where, upon visiting their genuine 'holy well' people could taste the waters and witness the life-saving properties of the elixir for themselves (all for a mere silver coin or two). People being what they are, they flocked to the city and as all traders know, where there are people, there is profit.

Merchants, far and wide, knew that if you wanted to buy or sell exotic wares, dabble in the slave trade, strike shady deals in a dark back alleyway, barter for goods in the bazaar, or wager away your life savings in the gladiatorial pits, Al Mashmaah was the place to be.

Scrave had to confess that he had seen larger cities, indeed, several more futuristic than this one, during his time serving aboard the *El Defensor*. However, the exotic skyline to Al Mashmaah, adorned with minarets and vast golden domes, around which falcons circled shrieking their haunting calls, appealed to the adventurer deep inside him.

The travel weary Elf moved to the side of the caravan trail, taking in the sights and smells of the city, including the guards riding giant armoured salamanders up and down the side of the road. These intimidating escorts ensured the long snaking queue of traders working their way towards the main gates did nothing to impede the flow of produce and the subsequent taxes that swelled the city coffers.

Scrave asked himself, for what felt like the thousandth time, exactly what he was doing in this place. There seemed no logical reason for his strange compulsion to head away from the coast and the life he had known as a sailor. No sense in accompanying a caravan of traders several weeks across the most inhospitable terrain the Elf had ever experienced, where half of the caravan viewed him suspiciously as if he were about to rob the merchant train, whilst the remaining members looked at him assessing if he had anything valuable for them in turn to steal.

Maybe it was the damned eye patch. However, Scrave knew it was foolhardy to take the patch off. His eye socket glowed like a fire worm in the darkness and there was that accursed itching sensation in the open socket that just begged him to scratch and scratch and...

The Elf took a long draft of stagnant water from his flaccid water skin and spat into the sand, moistening his lips and relieving the parched sensation in his throat. He shrugged his shoulders, repositioning his pack, before pulling a wide brimmed hat further down on his forehead to mask his appearance from watching eyes.

A mounted guard charged up the route, rushing to assist with a problem that Scrave could not identify from his position down the trail, the salamander sticking its legs out in a comical dance as its giant padded feet swiftly and powerfully propelled it across the sand in time to an undulating muscular tail.

There had been a lot of prying eyes of late.

Wherever Scrave had travelled, the temple guards had not been far behind. He knew that staying in Catterick was pointless with the exotic priestess so intent on catching him. The serpent dagger secured within his robes had always been a troublesome weapon, generating more interest than it should have but this woman would give mercenaries a bad name with her resolute pursuit and Scrave was equally as stubborn to not give up possessions that belonged to him.

Okay, he could have taken to the mountains, become a hermit and hid in a cave hoping she would lose interest and give up her search. On the other hand, maybe he could have entered the jungles and joined a long-lost tribe or become a farmer on some desolate patch of land that nobody could ever grow anything on. Somehow, he could not see it. He could have run off to sea, but the voice in his head told him that with the possibility of becoming the captain of the *El Defensor* now firmly lost, to join any other ship would have simply been unbearable.

There had to be something else, something that would lift his spirits and take his mind away from the infernal itching of his eye. His gut instinct was telling him that that very something lay within the walled city of Al Mashmaah. The question was exactly where within the walls his quest would end? From his viewpoint, walking down the trail he noted at least five defensive walls signifying how the city had continued to expand past the ramparts and defences. Even now, with a fifth wall towering fifty feet high, murder holes, watch towers and battlements manned with alert guards and signal fires, people had elected to set up a shanty town to the right of the city, and one or two had set up buildings that looked a lot more permanent in nature, clearly expecting the city to grow yet again and take them under its protective wing in years to come.

The serpent dagger in his robes coiled in warning, making Scrave step back just as a merchant charged past with an irate camel train, the huge pad like feet of the creatures touching down in the sand just where he was going to tread.

"Watch it idiot!" shouted the driver. "Are you blind? Maybe you are with just one eye?" He spat a wad of something disgusting in the Elf's direction and whipped his camels harder wanting to get a prime place in the bazaar from where to sell his wares.

Scrave fought the impulse to run up to the man and slash his throat with his golden dagger, despite the fact the weapon clearly wanted him to do so and instead whispered a few words under his breath, wriggling his fingers and asking his magic to undo the saddle where it passed under the camel's belly. The last gemstone in his left earring crumbled to dust and the saddle and all of its wares slipped off the plodding creature and crashed to the floor, spilling pots, pans and rolls of silks into the sand and sending the camel galloping free in fright.

The merchant cursed aloud, infuriated at the delay, pulling his other camels to a halt as he struggled to round up his errant beast and collect his goods from the floor, much to the loud complaints of those directly behind him, who slowed to a halt with oaths and raised fists.

Salamander mounted guards raced to assist as the domino effect of the train stopping abruptly caused minor collisions further back up the trail, with traders behind finding themselves coming to a rapid stop also. Horses bolted and wagons swerved from the trail to avoid running into the people in front, only to find themselves mired in the drifting sands.

Scrave chuckled to himself as he walked past, doffing his hat as he did so and whistling a little tune under his breath to drown out the man's cries of outrage. He knew it was petty and that he now would have to pay for an extra gemstone to his magical arsenal but the Elf was not the one to let somebody get the better of him and this 'idiot' deserved all he got. Besides, if this place had as good a market as he had been led to believe, he would have no problems finding a decent gem merchant.

The Elf pulled his hat down further and continued along the trail, his whistle gaining in tempo the more his spirits lifted.

* * * * * *

Twelve knights stood in a circle chanting, their swords interlocked in a circular pattern on the floor. Sharpened steel tips pointing inwards towards the centre whilst the hilts circled around. The air above the blades appeared to pulse, once, twice then impossibly flared open wide, creating a portal through which the sultry form of Justina stepped, dressed in her tight black robes, her demonic pet perched on her shoulder. Her tall gangly acolyte Vill, with his bobbing head and goatee beard followed after her and finally eight temple knights stepped through before the portal snapped shut with a resounding crack.

Justina lifted her head high and took in her bleak surroundings. The first thing she noticed was the state of the alleyway she stood in. Refuse piled high on both sides, unimaginable decomposing fluids seeping from the piles and running sluggishly down gutters past large rats that squeaked in noisy protest at the intrusion of so many feet in such a small space.

"What in the world is the Elf doing here?" she muttered aloud, gathering up her robes to prevent them dragging through the slime and flashing a tantalising length of toned ankle. "And what is that god awful smell?"

"I think I just stepped in something." Vill confessed, wiping his sandal across the cobbles and smearing something brown and sticky in his wake.

"High Priestess is it wise to bring temple guards to Al Mashmaah?" said a voice from the shadows. "We are not a dominant religion here. This may cause undue scrutiny." A portly acolyte shuffled forwards a large blue book under his arm.

"Kaplain please don't hide in the darkness." Justina gestured. "A *Bearer* should have more presence, especially with the power at your disposal." She turned to watch the twelve magical holy knights gathering their blades from the floor before they stood back at attention awaiting their next command. "Besides, there was no need to create a gate such as this. I am more than capable of teleporting under my own power. I am not as weak as my predecessor."

"I meant no slight High Priestess. I was merely offering you the respect that your position deserves." The *Bearer* dabbed a cloth to his perspiring forehead and offered a nervous smile. Justina walked over and let her eyes roam down the man's chest and lingered there.

"You need to rethink your understanding of respect." She whispered, reaching down and lifting up a pendant of a black phoenix that hung at the man's breast. "Really, Kaplain, an obsidian phoenix? Why it's almost blasphemy. I hope for your sake you have not converted?"

"I still worship the order." The acolyte stammered, reaching into his robes and pulling out a pendant with the flaming cross upon it. "The church has regular meetings but they are not actively encouraged by the local sects."

"I would have hoped that as a *Bearer* you would have remedied the lack of knowledge these heathens and their charlatan preachers displayed." Justina replied sternly. "How many loyal followers do we have?"

"Not enough to take on the Obsidian Phoenix." The Kaplain confessed.

"Well we can discuss the politics of religion later." Justina smiled, in a way that seemed to drop the temperature of the alleyway by several degrees. "Where is our most magnificent church?"

Kaplain turned away, clearly uncomfortable and gently laid his blue book open on the floor before ordering his twelve knights to go back inside the pages. Once the last knight had stepped inside and reverted into a vivid illustration, the bearer closed the book and stared up into the high priestess's eyes.

"You are standing behind it." He confessed.

The high priestess took in the squat one-story building. Noting where the mud packed walls had crumbled, the paint had pealed and the shutters had rotted away. A pigeon flew in and waddled into a hole in the roof where loud coos informed her it had taken up residence. A mangy tomcat sauntered along the alleyway and ran its body along her leg making Justina jump. Hamnet responded instantly, her spindly demonic form dropping down from the high priestess's shoulder to pounce onto the feline, before tearing it limb from limb in a frenzy of squeals sending chunks of blood stained, quivering flesh skittering about the alley.

Justina studied her familiar as it tore the cat apart, her mind struggling to come to terms with the situation she now found herself in. She noted the rats running down the alley towards the carnage, noses twitching, tails flicking, eager for an opportunistic meal. It was then that Justina realised the skyline.

"We are not even within the city walls, are we?" she stated coldly.

"Well, not exactly." The acolyte quivered. "But we are first in line for when they start building the sixth battlements."

"I would hope the inside of this church looks better than the outside." She threatened, stepping gingerly around the remains of the cat. "What of the Elf? I trust we have better news on that front?"

"He is in the city. I have my spies watching him. He appears harmless enough. Why are we so interested in him? I can have him killed if you like. Accidents happen around here all the time."

"I believe I'm looking at one waiting to happen right now." Justina stated calmly. She paused as her thoughts moved back to the burnt man that she had found in the subterranean temple beneath Stratholme, the way he held himself, so sure despite his predicament and his cocky debonair smile.

"No." she ordered, a smile touching her lips. "I want to see him captured alive."

* * * * * *

"That will do fine." Scrave confirmed, as he pushed back his long black hair and inserted the newly mounted earrings where they belonged. He tossed a golden coin onto the table where it wobbled on an uneven edge before keeling over, the regal face of the coin all distorted as if exposed to unbearable heat. The jeweller initially pleased at receiving praise for their workmanship looked down at the coin, before pushing back his headscarf and frowning.

"I do not recognise this currency." He confessed, picking up the melted coin and examining it on both sides before biting it with his teeth. "Is this real gold? It looks very old? Maybe you would like to tell me how you came by it?" The smile was as fake as the sincerity in the question.

"I'm sure it is very old. You could even say it is an antique." Scrave smiled, thinking of the horde of the remaining coins that were no doubt melted by now, back in the heat of the subterranean temple. He finished fastening his earrings in place and mentally calculated the fact he had the power for six spells readily available about his person. Two stones in each ear and another two strategically disguised as the eyes for an owl brooch on his lapel that he had also managed to save from a fiery oblivion.

"Are you sure you would not like to have some tea to discuss this further?" The jeweller asked. Scrave drew his dagger in a smooth motion, the twin golden blades pointing at the jeweller's throat as the serpent coiled tightly about his arm hissing threateningly.

"Quite sure." He replied in a quiet, yet intensely threatening tone. "You have been adequately rewarded for your services. Do not force me to reconsider the deal." The jeweller looked on in wide-eyed horror, taking in the hypnotic movements of the glittering snake, the ruby eyes, the needle-sharp curved fangs.

"I have never seen it's like. The workmanship is exquisite." He whispered. "May I examine it further?"

"I am walking away so you don't have to." Scrave warned. "Good day to you, dear sir. Let us hope for your sake that our paths never cross again."

The Elf stepped from the small shop and swiftly mingled with the crowd, immersing himself in the ambience of the bazaar that Al Mashmaah was famous for. The market place was simply staggering in size and spectacle, consisting of an ancient paved square surrounded on all sides by a thirty-foot wall, that ran nearly half a mile on each side. The sights and sounds washed over him, assaulting his senses, everything from traders haggling and yelling, to the rich scents of herbs and spices infused upon the air.

Scrave currently stood by the south wall, having just exited the jeweller's shop, which was one of the more permanent fixtures of the market, having been constructed within the second wall of the city. He allowed his gaze to take in the rows of visiting stalls stretching out before him, the sky above them shaded by massive sails of dyed silk that stretched out from the walls to huge poles set about the square. The sails flapped and snapped as the breeze passed through them, a rainbow of hues, protecting the shopping public from the rays of the sun and spaced so that the majestic palm trees set about wells throughout the area were able to show their glossy green leaves through and bask in the hot morning air, adding additional shade to the delight of many shoppers.

The Elf set off at random, strolling up one aisle, taking in the sights, content that his dagger would warn him of any danger and deter the most tenacious pickpockets with its terminal kiss. Slave traders displayed their wares, from heavy labourers, to exotic serving girls, pleasure slaves and even gladiators stood on open display, muscles oiled to show off their attributes to the passing buyer. Freak shows offered tantalising glimpses of multi-limbed mutations, whilst other more heavily curtained areas catered for the more exotic and erotic needs of clientele.

Vivid fruits, enormous vegetables, sacks of brightly coloured and fragrant spices, weapon smiths, blacksmiths, basket weavers, potters, bakers and butchers all within yards of each other, selling their wares and shouting to attract customers. Auctioneers sold curios, vendors sold food, Ironmongers banged pots and pans. Potions for hair loss, lotions for supple skin, tonics for strength, colonics for... well it just went on and on. Scrave found it all rather overwhelming following the length of time spent on his own, struggling to survive just a few months prior.

The Elf moved to walk past a stall selling terracotta pots, serving dishes and other household goods and suddenly found his legs were not responding as they should. There seemed to be a resistance in the air, slowing his walk to a crawl and then to a complete stop. Instead of walking past as he intended, he found he was being drawn to the stall, despite having no interest in the wares on sale at all.

Scrave passed under the awning and found himself wearing a stupefied expression that made one or two shoppers view him with some suspicion. He went to shrug and found his arms refused to obey him. What was going on? This behaviour made absolutely no sense. He needed to get control of himself and walk away, he had to…

The pain that lanced through his head dropped him to his knees, like a spear stabbing through his brain. He gasped in shock, only realising he had regained the use of his hands when he felt them holding the sides of his head as he rocked to try and stop the agony he had to endure.

"Are you okay?" A woman asked cautiously, gathering her items and slowly edging away without waiting for a response. Scrave gasped aloud, moving his hand to his eye and feeling something squirming and burrowing in his socket. He let out a low moan as the pain slowly began to ease.

"Do I look alright to you?" he snapped, staggering back to his feet and reaching out for the stall, nearly knocking several urns onto the floor. His head spun for several seconds more, leaving him only vaguely aware that the woman had now hurriedly taken her leave and that the purveyor of the stall now had a giant bald man standing alongside him, holding a very large cudgel in one hand, his face a mass of fading bruises. As Scrave focused on the particulars of the hulking figure, he noticed with some interest, that the man appeared to be missing one of his fingers.

"Can we help you?" The stall holder enquired, clearly not intending to sell anything to this strange one-eyed man who was either clearly insane or intoxicated. Scrave tried to focus, struggled to concentrate on the stall and let his eyes roam over the ironmongery before him. He had no need for pots and pans. What could he possibly find of interest on this stall?

"As I said before…" the shorter stall owner stood up and leaned over his goods to emphasis his statement, now confident that his backup was near. "Can I help you? Or should I ask my brother to help you instead?"

Scrave found himself suddenly leaning forwards and sniffing the man. Sniffing! His mind was horrified at the repugnant actions of his body! A similar expression of disgust was being displayed by the shop keeper, who moved to pull back, only for Scrave's hand to shoot out and grab him around the throat, putting him off balance and leaning forwards.

The Elf's other hand moved in fast, reaching for something at the purveyor's neck. He pulled hard and found himself drawing a pendant out of the trader's robes. A shout of alarm rose from the man's mouth and his muscle-bound brother moved to rush around the stall. Scrave noticed he was now holding a small pendant in his hand, with a glowing emerald at the centre.

Before he could apologise for his uncontrollable actions the insult was further compounded by the Elf licking the jewellery. He simply could not believe what he was doing! A pleading thought in his mind hoped that this was all some sort of hallucination, it had to be a mistake!

"Where is Kerian Denaris?" he asked in a gravelly voice nothing like his own.

"I know of no Kerian Denaris," the shopkeeper gasped, even though Scrave was half strangling him.

"If you do not know Kerian Denaris, why are you wearing his pendant?" The gravelly voice continued. Scrave swallowed, his mind rushing in panic. Why had his voice changed? What was...

His hand dropped to his side, the pendant slipping inside his pocket and the serpent dagger slipping eagerly around his wrist.

"The pendant came from Wellruff market." The seller choked.

Scrave felt himself moving again, his body not his own. He dragged the man physically over the stall, sending pots and pans crashing to the floor and dropping him bodily to the ground, just as his brother charged in, his arms extended, hands outstretched eager to grab the drunkard who dared to place a hand on his brother.

The dagger shot out, once, twice, hissing in delight as the blade struck with unerring accuracy, taking an ear with the first lunge and slicing deeply across the man's bicep with the second. Blood oozed from the wounds, as the ear flopped wetly down onto the pavement. The fight instantly disappeared from the huge man; he sank to the floor, screaming in horror, trying to grab his ear before any passers-by trod on it.

Scrave moved to apologise, still mortified at what was going on and found himself reaching down to grab the original stall owner and hoist him to his feet.

"Are you sure you do not know where Kerian Denarissss is?" The man shook his head in terror. Similar thoughts raced through Scrave's mind. Dear lord was he hissing now?

"No I swear that I have no idea."

Scrave watched in disbelief as his hands smashed the seller about the face, breaking his nose and causing blood to jet across Scrave's tunic. Then as suddenly as it started, he found he was himself again. He almost overbalanced as his motor senses returned and the trader dropped to the ground. The background noises from the bazaar had dropped to a murmur. Scrave spun, the serpent dagger writhing on his arm. Every eye on every stall seemed to be staring at him.

"I'm sorry." Scrave confessed to anyone bothering to listen, despite the carnage at his back. "It wasn't my fault."

"Thief!" someone shouted to the left. "That man has stolen from the stall. Call the guards."

"No that's not true." Scrave stammered, even as his mind shouted to him. Run you fool. No one will believe you. You need to run now! His feet seemed attached to legs made of jelly but he somehow managed to place one foot in front of the other, running for the closest aisle desperate to put some distance between himself and whatever had just happened behind him.

* * * * * *

"There appears to have been a slight disturbance in the bazaar." Kaplain reported. "I believe your Elf is responsible and he is trying to escape as we speak."

Justina looked up from the ledger Kaplain had recorded about his observations in the city and pushed it to one side.

"Right now?" she asked.

"My sources tell me he has stabbed two stall holders and fought with several guards. Stalls are overturned and it is by all accounts a chaotic but also extremely fluid situation."

"How sure are you of this information?" Justina asked, checking her wand and pulling her cloak about her. She remembered when she had seen Scrave in action back in the library. Chaos seemed to be a staple partner to the cocky character.

"Well he may not have stabbed as many people as said. This is hearsay after all but I think we can be confident that whatever is going on it is happening now."

"Then let us go and help stop this menace to trade." She smiled. "You never know, maybe if we do a good job, we will gain a few more followers to our church."

* * * * * *

Thomas stared at the toy car in his hand, his world upside down and now paused as if a movie on his DVD player. Where was the *El Defensor*? Why was he in this room when he knew this tragic scenario had played out long, long ago. He knew they would leave the house. Knew they would get a report of a child's body found tomorrow, buried in a shallow grave with his head staved in.

He could not stop this from happening. It was history. In the past. Thomas Adams had no DeLorean time machine fitted with a flux capacitor, that he could jump into, drive at 88 miles an hour and go back in time to prevent this tragedy from occurring. At the moment as far as he knew he was at a banquet with a load of bovine characters and was the captain of a Spanish Galleon that could sail to different worlds.

Now he thought about it, both scenarios were equally ridiculous, yet he knew in his heart the ship was real. He had a beautiful woman there and was going to ask her to marry him. Once he got his head straight and his crew safe that was...

"What's up Thomas. Jerry hit your head too hard." Eede enquired. "Put the toy down and let's get out of here."

"Last one back to the station buys the doughnuts." MacMichael grinned, always ready to see the light in any dark situation with typical practicality. Thomas placed the car onto the windowsill and moved to leave the room, turning around and taking in the scene for one final time. Everything was how he remembered it. The books on the locker, the milk and half eaten cookie on the saucer and the toy police cruiser sitting on the windowsill.

He followed the two detectives down the stairs, tracing his finger down the bannister and feeling the pile of the carpet crushing under his feet. This felt so real. The only thing he didn't recognise from the situation was the heat. He touched the door and pulled his hand away from the handle. It was as if a fire were burning outside.

"Allow me." Eede laughed, opening the door and offering a theatrical bow. "Don't ever let it be said chivalry is dead." He laughed. "We have all just been taking a well-earned rest. After you my dear." he gestured. Thomas stepped out into the night and looked across at the frail woman whose world had already ended, knowing that tomorrow she would spiral into screaming chaos.

Then it hit him. The toy car was still on the windowsill. Yet he knew in his future he had the car. It had been given to him by Malum Okubi, who in turn had gained it from Thomas when he had been washed into the graveyard. So where did Thomas get the car from? He wracked his brains, his mind not focusing on the car he was heading to.

The damned heat was making it difficult to think. The toy police car had been evidence in the case when they had tried to discover the serial killer. It was suggested that whoever had killed the boy had also been collecting trophies of his victims and then the toy had been discovered in Thomas's locker at the precinct placing him as the number one suspect. He knew this as fact, a nightmare made real, yet he had just seen that he had left the car in the boy's bedroom. How did it end up in his locker? He had not put it there. So who had?

This made no sense! He reached down for the car door handle and noted with surprise that the wheels of the car had melted like toffee and that the wing mirror was dripping like candle wax. Now he knew that had not happened before! He turned to ask his fellow detectives if they were having any vehicle malfunctions only to find that the road was bubbling and dripping into a crevasse that had apparently opened up as he had walked over. The crime scene was on fire, the ambulance emergency light popping with the heat. This had to be a dream… It just had to be!

He started to turn one way and then the other, his mind a whirl, not knowing what was real or make believe. He found himself moaning, his throat suddenly parched and sore. This whole situation was prompting more questions than answers. He needed to lie down. Needed to sleep.

* * * * * *

The cell door slammed shut with a depressing clang. Ashe noted the key turning in the lock and with a resigned shrug, moved to sit on the bunk, only to find it was somewhat higher than ones he had seen in your normal everyday jail.

"Oh that's just great!" he exclaimed, taking in the Minotaur scaled furniture towering above him. "I'm not that tall, I'm sure there is a discrimination law being broken here somewhere." He jumped up, grabbing the edge with both hands before struggling to pull his little legs up over the edge. Breathless, he rolled onto the hard surface and took in his temporary lodgings.

A bunk and a bucket. Damp walls and resident rodents. He shrugged again and grabbed the thread bare blanket he found there, wrinkling his nose at the unmistakable smell of damp Minotaur.

He had really messed up this time. Thomas was going to kill him. Well how was he to know that throwing away good money was allowed but then collecting it for yourself was not, even if the first person clearly did not want it anymore? The laws in this place were crazy!

Ashe looked at the wall where the only source of light entered the cell. The bars were a long way above his head. He did not think it worth the effort to see if the cell had a good view. He was not planning on staying here. This was a miscarriage of justice!

The Halfling slid off the edge of the bunk and ran back over to the door, staring up at the keyhole about two foot above his head. He put his hands on his hips, tilting his head one way and then the other, before he reached up to his hat and pulled out a slender lock pick. This scenario was what Ashe lived for. He would have the door open in a jiffy!

He turned back into the room and looked for a chair. It didn't take long to realise there wasn't one available. He ran over to the bucket, tipped it out in the far corner whilst trying not to gag at the appalling smell, before upending it and clambering on top. The door lock teased him from a foot beyond his reach, even with his arm fully outstretched and standing on tiptoes. The bucket suddenly cracked, dropping Ashe to the floor. He looked at the ruined pail despairingly. Trust him to be given a cell with a normal sized bucket! His little feet pattered about the cell, checking for something he could use to get up to the door lock. It did not take very long to give the damp cell a thorough search.

Ashe climbed back onto the bunk, struggling to swing his legs up again, before he finally lay there staring at the sunlight creeping slowly across the stone wall. There was no way he was going to get out through the door unless he suddenly grew sharply over night. The window was far above his head, further than the door lock. He was cold, tired and suddenly very lonely.

Thomas would have to come and get him. He was sure the captain would get this all sorted out. He would put things right. He was a sheriff where he came from. He had told Ashe this several times in the past. Thomas would...

Thomas was ill. Thomas was going to do nothing! The implications of this hit Ashe with the force of a sledgehammer, smashing his hopes into tiny fragments. The Halfling prided himself with never swearing, his mother having told him that only crass unintelligent men resorted to base profanity. Several colourful nut adjectives ran through his mind but this was a more serious situation than normal and no one was within earshot.

"Oh bugger!"

* * * * * *

"Get more water and towels." Violetta yelled. "He's burning up again." Colette and Rowan looked on powerless as Thomas thrashed about the bed, wrestling with his delirium, the poison tracks across his skin darker than ever.

"What can we do? What do you need?" Rowan asked, holding Thomas's hand so tight her fingers were going white. Violetta turned towards her, her own face dripping with perspiration, her eyes sunken and haggard from using the saint in her hand.

"This illness that has him is so strong. Violetta confirmed. "I am barely keeping him from slipping away. Every time I try to heal him, his illness attacks him from somewhere else. It is like a snake with many heads. I never know where the next threat is coming from."

"Is there any way we can find out how our shipmates are doing in the jungle?" Rowan turned to Colette.

"I simply don't know what we can do." Colette confessed shaking her head slowly, "but maybe there is something in my master's spell books that could help."

"Anything!" Rowan pleaded. "...Anything!"

Colette ran for the door, fighting back her own tears, determined to stay strong and resisting the urge to scream her frustrations at the world, unaware that deep within the jungles of Taurean her friends were screaming too!

The Labyris Knight

-: Part Three :-

Of Twisting Labyrinths, Deadly Pyramids, Petrified Forests and Haunted Castles.

"Nos morituri te salutamus"

'We who are about to die, salute you.'

De Vita Caesarum (121 AD)

Chapter Twenty-Five

"Grab the Orchid! Grab the Orchid!" Marcus yelled, as the world appeared to explode around him, one of the huge Nirschl heads lunging for his darting body, razor sharp teeth snapping shut inches from his heels.

"You grab the flower!" Mathius shot back, stabbing furiously with his twin daggers and scoring direct hits on the dense hide of another striking head, only to grimace as his blades bounced off, the attacks completely ineffective. "I'm a little bit busy over here!"

The assassin tried to gauge where everyone was, aware they were all separated but the air was full of spinning leaves, showering mud and the thrashing limbs of the awakened monster, making it difficult to see clearly in any direction. An arrow whistled by, plunging into the serpentine body snaking past him, making the Nirschl writhe in agitation, its movements snapping the arrow shaft clean off with one rapid ripple of its massive coils.

Mathius counted off the moving heads, one, two, swaying over by Ives and Aradol, the two men fighting side by side trying to hold the Nirschl's snapping jaws at bay. Three, another head passed by overhead blotting out the light as its serpentine form nearly rolled right over him, dragging the bloodied and battered form of Weyn, pinned to the side of its jaw. Four, five, both over by Rauph who bellowed out a challenge, swinging his long swords to the left and the right as the monster tried to crush him in its immense coils. The sixth head slid past Commagin who had dived to the side as the

Nirschl slithered by, the Dwarven engineer firing crossbow bolts as fast as he could load them but not towards the monster; instead, he appeared to be taking on the group of Minotaur that had been shadowing them.

Another terrifying snakehead glided through the raining debris, orange eyes not blinking, its body slinking rapidly from side to side as it arrowed across the ground towards Mathius. That made it seven heads, there was only one creature that met this description: Hydra but this was the biggest hydra Mathius had ever heard of, just one head was the size of a small wagon!

He shoved Marcus roughly to one side as the creature struck, aware the monk was pre-occupied by an attack from another front. Marcus used the unexpected propulsion to dodge beneath the Nirschl's snapping jaws and grab hold of the vines, creepers and lengths of stringy hair that dangled from its head, before resolutely starting to climb.

Mathius dodged the other way, timing his move almost to perfection as the seventh serpent head opened its jaws wide, exposing a moist pink fleshy glottis with a flickering tongue and razor-sharp fangs. The Nirschl struck with great speed, darting forward so fast that Mathius nearly missed his step on the slick ground, the edge of the creature's snout catching him hard on the back and knocking him flat into a puddle as it barrelled past.

* * * * * *

Ives screamed out in horror, his wailing tones matching the metronomic waving of his white sword, used like some kind of natural repellent towards the creature attacking him. The huge scaly head swayed backwards and forwards in time to his panicked gestures, its heavy lids slowly sliding closed and then opening again, to reveal deep orange reptilian eyes that intently studied its prey before it prepared to lunge. The Nirschl slowly pulled back, forked tongue flicking out from its mouth, lightly caressing the tip of its snout, then it attacked, rushing forward, intent on ripping the merchant in two.

Aradol moved up alongside Ives, swinging his ancient blade and splitting the underside of the monster's snout with his first swing. The Nirschl angled its head up defensively, attempting to slither over them both as Aradol continued turning with the momentum of his swing, snatching up Ives's white blade with his free hand, before forcing it up into the soft underside of the creature's jaw, shoving the weapon all the way to the hilt. Blood and gore showered down onto the young warrior as the snake writhed and jerked in pain, frantically trying to pull its head away from the source of its agony.

The Nirschl reared up into the air, before slamming down again, trying to crush the creature's that had dared to injure it. However, Aradol was already moving away, dragging Ives clear as the snake's head hit the ground with such force that both men found themselves struggling to remain on their feet as the ground trembled beneath them.

* * * * * *

Weyn groaned aloud, finding himself dropping rapidly towards the floor as the Nirschl head he was pinned to slammed into the muddy ground, knocking the breath from the archer and sickeningly wrenching his right arm. Weyn snatched the quickest of glances, noting that the creature was rapidly slithering towards the cause of the grievous wound Aradol had just delivered. The archer reluctantly released his grip on the slick scales beneath him, letting his whole weight hang from his injured arm and through gritted teeth, struggled to use his left hand to pull the hunting knife from its sheath at his side. Weyn screamed anew as he found himself roughly dragged across the churned jungle floor, his clothing snagging on low shrubs and catching on sharp protruding branches that sliced painfully across his skin.

Cold mud and dead vegetation rapidly swept up before him, making the archer gasp as if drowning. The Nirschl's head surged rapidly forwards as it slid across the ground, turning first left, then right, battering and shaking Weyn's ragged body, until the archer felt it would almost be better to amputate his own arm, than experience any more of this excruciating pain.

He finally wrapped his left hand around the hunting knife's hilt and yanked the blade free, only to find himself almost lose it as he roughly collided with yet another low shrub. Sheer determination kept the blade from falling free from his grasp as he swung the weapon up and slashed repeatedly at the hydra's mandible, trying to work free the arrow that held him pinned so resolutely to the monster.

Dark blood welled from the creature's lip and the snake's slithering course across the ground slowed as it noted the fresh pains from its jaw. The Nirschl lifted its head up from the forest floor leaving Weyn to swing freely and scream anew, its eyes blinking slowly as it took in the sight of the numerous figures of warm prey running about, before it turned and dived towards where one of its own, long, sinuous necks coiled about in a tight circle.

Weyn saw the impact coming and hacked even more furiously, desperate to free his arm before it ripped from his socket. The archer hacked blindly, the pain in his limb so intense he now had no idea if it was his bloodied arm, the arrow shaft or the creature that he was attacking. He dropped free with inches to spare, the arrow shaft suddenly snapping under the frantic sawing, causing another wave of white-hot agony to lance down the archer's arm as he crashed into the Nirschl's trunk with a sickening thud. The archer found himself thrown across the jungle floor, his body limp, as if he were a puppet suddenly cut free from its strings, just as the Nirschl squeezed through the narrow, scale-lined orifice it had been aiming for, in its determined effort to rip free the source of the agitation at its jaw.

* * * * * *

Rauph noted his bloodied companion falling apparently senseless to the ground and roared a furious challenge to the Nirschl as two of its heads slid hungrily towards him. The Minotaur's swords hacked and slashed at the coils about his feet, cutting great fleshy gashes into the monster's quivering flesh as the twin open maws, filled with needle sharp venomous fangs, arrowed in towards the battling navigator from either side.

The Minotaur judged which head was the closest, then jumped up, using the wounded body of the monster at his feet as an impromptu step to give him the extra height to launch himself at the nearest hydra's open mouth. One long sword swung in overhand from the left, catching the creature's nostril and ripping through it, slicing down through flesh and scale, through the moveable maxillary lip to gouge across the roof of its fleshy pink mouth before Rauph pushed up hard with the weapon, wedging the blade between the hydra's palatine and ectopterygoid. His other sword swung in low, severing the end of the hydra's flickering black forked tongue and sending the tip sailing out into the jungle.

Somehow, the navigator managed to find a footing on the Nirschl's bottom jaw and literally stepped inside the snake's mouth, his feet struggling to find purchase on the slippery surface just behind the hydra's twitching tongue. The injured tongue continued to jet dark viscous fluid about its mouth, adding to the precariousness of Rauph's footing. The Minotaur tensed his body, muscles bulging as he strained to force the creature's mouth wide to prevent it from snapping its jaw closed and piercing his body with its gleaming fangs. Fetid breath rushed from its throat, washing over the navigator and making him gag at the putrid smell but Rauph held on, using the handhold of his wedged sword to keep standing upright as the snake continued to try to close its jaws and crush him.

A second rubbery tongue flicked across the back of Rauph's tunic, causing the Minotaur to risk a backwards glance over his shoulder, eyes widening as the second hydra head crashed in, its jaws open as widely as the maw the navigator was forcing apart, its angle of attack at ninety-degrees to the mouth in which Rauph stood. Fangs as long as broad swords and as curved as scimitars, stabbed in from either side, missing the Minotaur's tensed frame by inches. Deadly poison sprayed from the venom channels of the two sets of fangs as they locked together, creating an illusion that both Nirschl heads were locked in an obscene parody of a passionate kiss with the Minotaur trapped helplessly between them.

The fumes from the venom made Rauph's eyes water but he refused to panic, locking his legs and arms, pushing back as hard as he could, forcing the mouth of the hydra wider still, despite the horrific nature of his predicament. With the two heads locked together, neither snake could bite or swallow him, no matter how hard they squirmed or wriggled but the Minotaur instinctively knew that he could harm them.

* * * * * *

Commagin noted the two hydra heads collide together and tried to shout a warning to his navigator friend but the collision came so fast he was not sure if the Minotaur heard him. The Dwarven engineer, cursed aloud, finding himself torn between firing his crossbow at the writhing heads and risking hitting his swallowed crewmate; or to continue with his holding action at keeping the Minotaur troops at bay from his position on the jungle floor.

An arrow ploughed into the dirt at his feet, a second whistling past his ear, causing the engineer to duck his head, before he calmly pushed up his glasses, lined up the sight of his trusty crossbow and let the *Lady Janet* roar. Crossbow quarrels stitched through the jungle foliage, tearing holes in leaves, splintering saplings and sending the three Minotaur harrying him diving for cover. A sharp bellow informed the dwarf that at least one of his quarrels had hit home and he allowed himself a smile as he reached to reload, a length of immense snake slithering in front of him, temporarily obscuring his view.

A Minotaur warrior charged from the undergrowth, issuing a challenge to the Dwarf as he vaulted across the mottled scales of the Nirschl, a wicked halberd glinting in his hands. Commagin turned towards his huge adversary and moved to bring his crossbow in line but the warrior was too fast, skilfully swinging his weapon down low, snatching the crossbow clean from the Dwarf's hands and sending it spinning off into the undergrowth. Commagin opened his mouth to voice his anger at the creature, only to find the haft of the halberd sweeping up across his chin, splitting his lip and snapping his teeth together. The Minotaur continued to whip his halberd about, a superior smirk across his bovine features.

"So that's the way it's going to be eh?" Commagin snarled, wiping his lip and noting his hand had come away red. He scrambled to his feet, devoid of his favourite weapon, before setting his feet and pushing up his sleeves to expose his muscular arms. "Come on then let's be having you." He charged forward, completely unfazed by the fact he was about to take on a creature nearly twice his size and oblivious to the fact that a snapping hydra head had just swept through the area he had vacated.

The Minotaur snorted in surprise and tried to bring his halberd in close but Commagin was quicker despite his age, barrelling in with his head down to crash into the warrior's abdomen. The Minotaur grunted at the collision, amazed at the force of the impact and the fact that he found himself pushed back across the mud by nearly a metre. However, his astonishment quickly turned to pain as the Dwarven Engineer slammed a clenched fist right between the Minotaur's legs, once, twice, each time bringing the creature's horned head lower as he doubled over with the force of the blows.

"I'll... teach... you... to lay hands... on the *Lady Janet*." Commagin snarled, landing a punch at each syllable and spitting blood from his ruined lip. "You over grown bulls think you are so tough. Well we Dwarves are made of sterner stuff laddie." The Minotaur shook his head trying to clear his pain glazed eyes, presenting a target to the Dwarf that the engineer found irresistible. Commagin pounced, grabbing hold of one large floppy Minotaur ear that had dangled invitingly close, before biting down on it as hard as he could.

The Minotaur bellowed in pain, eyes watering, nostrils flaring as he tried to shake Commagin free. The halberd fell forgotten to the floor as the guard reached up with his huge arms to grab Commagin by either side of his head, desperate to prize the Dwarf from his body. Every time the Minotaur tried to squeeze, Commagin bit harder, shaking his head like an enraged terrier and dropping the warrior to his knees in agony.

In an act of sheer desperation, the Minotaur flung his head to one side, managing to catch the Dwarven engineer with his curved horn, sending him skidding away across the muddy ground. Minotaur hands reached out to touch a bloodied stump where an ear should have been, bovine eyes stared through a haze of maddening pain to watch the dwarf pick himself up from the ground, strands of jungle foliage tangled in his hair, mud smeared across his face and body, the ragged Minotaur ear still dangling from his mouth. His appearance, enhanced by the muddy war paint, looked every bit that of a Dwarven warrior from legend. That was, apart from the glasses hanging lopsided across his face! Commagin tugged hard at the remains of the flesh hanging from his mouth, tearing a chunk off the leathery appendage before spitting it away into the bushes.

"You won't be sewing that bit back on." He taunted. "Do you want your ear back? If you do, why don't you come and get it?" He worried at the ragged remains ripping another chunk free. "It's getting smaller the longer you hesitate."

The Minotaur charged blindly towards the Dwarf, his raw power and speed surprising Commagin and making the engineer realise that maybe he should not have been so anxious to antagonise the beast. Horns came down, lining up to gore the Dwarf, the points just as sharp and dangerous as the halberd discarded on the ground. For just a second, Commagin considered whether he should have spent more time trying to find the *Lady Janet*, than having this dust up. The shape of another Minotaur warrior coming out of the jungle passage, this one armed with a bow and determinedly heading in his direction, further reinforced the need for a weapon of any kind. However, by now the first Minotaur was upon him.

The charging Minotaur crashed into Commagin full tilt, only to find itself hitting an immovable wall of Dwarven muscle. Commagin set himself firmly, his boots only sliding a short distance in the mud before gaining purchase and then he grabbed the gleaming horns as they came either side of him. Instead of attempting to stop the creature in full charge, Commagin had considered the forward motion and power presented by the charging creature and instead of resisting completely, he pushed the Minotaur's head down with all his might, letting its own enraged momentum slam it face first into the ground. The engineer added further insult by placing his boot firmly upon the creature's forehead, pushing its snout further down into the filth and muck.

"Stay down if you know what is good for you." Commagin warned but the Minotaur was now completely enraged. Heavily muscled arms pushed up from the mud, staggering the Dwarf, forcing him to step backwards, only to lose his footing in the slime as the Minotaur lurched upwards, lifting Commagin from the ground and dropping the Dwarf heavily onto his back. The Minotaur seized the initiative, kicking out, catching Commagin in the ribs and pushing him through the slime with the force of the blow. The Dwarf rolled about gasping for air, as the bovine warrior grabbed a splintered sapling from the ground, pulling the miniature tree and a good-sized root ball from the mud before swinging it down in an attempt to flatten the Dwarf where he lay.

Commagin twisted one way then the other, as clods of mud cascaded down about him, the plant smashing into the ground scarce inches from him. The engineer thought he could second guess his attacker, feinting a roll to the left, only to instead roll further to the right but his enemy was so angered, so enraged, that he just followed through his strike, kicking out at the same time and knocking the Dwarf back within striking range.

There was a roar of triumph as the Minotaur swung the ragged sapling down, dead centre. Commagin threw up his arms in a feeble attempt to block the blow, groaning in pain as a huge shadow slid by overhead. The sapling dropped limply to the ground, splattering the Dwarf with more mud and slime. He opened his eyes in surprise, then blinked several times, unable to believe his eyes. The warrior remained where he had been standing, his muscles twitching the veins in his legs fluttering beneath the skin but as the Dwarf moved his eyes upwards, he realised that the top half of his attacker was missing!

Commagin continued to raise his eyes, only to encounter the sight of one giant Nirschl head hovering above him, gore dripping from its jaws as it chewed away on the foolish morsel that had strayed too near to it. The Dwarf started to cautiously edge away, moving as slowly as he could in the slick mud without drawing attention to himself, as the monster chewed steadily above him, his actions carefully measured to prevent the Nirschl from displaying the same fatal attraction towards the engineer as it was showing to its current meal. Commagin placed a hand carefully down into the mud only for an arrow to slam into the ground alongside him. Another arrow ploughed the earth on the other side, clearly indicating that the shooter was sighting his weapon and gauging the distances. The next shaft would be directly in the middle, right where Commagin lay.

The Dwarf locked gazes with the smug Minotaur, who was even now drawing his bow on him for this third and final time and realised there was nowhere to go. If he ran, the hydra would no doubt spot him, scoop him up and serve him the same fate that had befallen his first foe. If he stayed where he was, he was completely at the mercy of the Minotaur. The archer nodded his head in mock salute as he prepared to deliver the fatal blow, letting Commagin know he had him dead in his sights as he brought his bow up to full draw.

A gleaming dagger blurred through the air, slicing through the bowstring and making the weapon snap back against the bowman. Commagin took in the surprised look on the Minotaur archer's face then followed the arrow as it arched through the sky, spinning erratically, only to slam into the Nirschl head that Marcus was climbing high above.

* * * * * *

"Oh for heaven's sake keep still." Marcus swore, finding himself swung this way and that as the Nirschl glided itself around several swaying necks and slunk around spiky bushes and clumps of vegetation, sending the young man smacking roughly into its scales for what felt like the hundredth time. The monk grabbed hold of a long length of hair and vine and tried to clamber over towards the blood red orchid that was sprouting from a gap in the creature's scales just under its chin but every time he tried to pick up momentum, the hydra changed direction as it slithered about the jungle clearing throwing him off balance. This was ridiculous!

Marcus snarled in frustration, gritting his teeth and refashioning his grip on the length of creeper, hair and vegetation, a plan forming in his mind. The makeshift rope certainly appeared sturdy enough! He took the length of Nirschl mane, pulled it tight, then leant out away from the Nirschl, planting his feet firmly beneath him, before using the vines to pendulum rappel himself around the neck of the creature, his feet running lightly across the snake's scales, trailing the length of matted plant matter behind him.

The monk's outstretched fingertips just brushed the blood orchid as he stretched out to try to retrieve it but the Nirschl chose that moment to dive towards the ground, leaving Marcus cursing in frustration as the plant's stalk bounced and the blooms nodded at his failed attempt at capture. The monk cursed again, then considered what the Order of St Fraiser would think of his colourful language. This was obviously what resulted from mixing with the colourful crew of the *El Defensor*! Knowing that he could not stop his momentum and reverse easily, he found himself completing the circuit of the Nirschl's head, the vine pulling tight across the hydra's throat. The snakehead dipped, trying to free itself, further slowing the monk's momentum.

Marcus found himself scrabbling for stability, reaching out to grab another handful of thick vine and hair with his free hand, to prevent the return swing, only to realise he now had a set of makeshift reins in his hands. He pulled back hard, drawing the loop tight and forcing the hydra's head up, the monk gasping as the view changed. The snake shooting up towards the trees high ahead, an astonished marmoset sitting on a low branch shrieking in horror as the huge snout rushed towards it. Marcus eased up on his pull and found the Nirschl dropping back down towards the jungle floor again, making the monk's heart leap to his throat at the sudden feeling of weightlessness at the instant drop.

The serpent's head swooped towards the ground, dodging several other hissing and snapping Nirschl maws by inches, slithering over piles of squirming coils and offering Marcus a glimpse of the chaos below. His friends ran about hacking and slashing, pursued by snakeheads, snapping teeth and rolling coils of reptilian monster. One person caught his eye. Mathius broke from the undergrowth, dropping to pick up a dagger from the ground before turning to tackle a Minotaur who held the remains of a broken bow. They clashed head on, the assassin's dagger flashing out, the Minotaur responding with a mighty sweep of the broken bow, sweeping Mathius legs from beneath him but the assassin was just as fast, grabbing the front of the Minotaur's tunic and dragging him down as well.

Mathius rolled on the ground, wrestling with the brutish creature, slipping and sliding, trying to land punches that failed to cause damage due to the oozing slime coating both of them. Even as they struggled in the mud, the huge Minotaur's superior strength started to show through, allowing it to land several teeth rattling blows, despite Mathius's deadly hand-to-hand skills.

The assassin attempted to employ his dagger, striking out intent on plunging the blade into the beast's breast but found himself overpowered by the monster, his weapon slipping from his grasp and dropping to the ground. The Minotaur landed another blow, making the assassin see stars, then used its bulk to push Mathius down, forcing the assassin's face into the stinking morass they had churned up beneath them.

Marcus struggled to control the Nirschl, making the serpent head veer to the right and circle back towards his struggling shipmate, before pulling back hard. He now knew that the hydra would move upwards as a result, slowing its forward momentum, before the monk slackened back on the reins, fully aware the creature would then dive down towards the ground. The monster responded as expected, dropping to the floor, its snout grazing the ground as it crashed through the two fighters, knocking the Minotaur over and rolling the creature through the mud, even as its rippling neck shoved Mathius roughly off to one side, leaving the assassin gasping and scrabbling in the mud.

The monk turned his head to follow the action, his eyes searching for and finding Mathius, who somehow managed to stagger to his feet from the tumble and then started to scan the ground, clearly looking for his dagger. He offered a prayer of thanks to St Fraiser for his friend's safety, then realised with a start that he was still steering the Nirschl! He looked up just in time to see another hydra head slither directly across his path, this one snapping and striking at Aradol.

Marcus's hydra head crashed into the side of the other's snout with an angry hiss, coming to a sudden stop before backing away, only for Aradol's serpent head to open its jaws and spit a stream of venom at its attacker, not realising it was retaliating against itself. Razor fangs plunged into either side of the creature's face, the teeth missing Marcus's reins by inches, causing the monster to buck defensively, knocking Marcus from his footing behind its head and dropping him down to swing helplessly from the reins.

Aradol noted the advantage offered and swung his blade at the exposed throat of the Nirschl head that until seconds ago had been attacking him, his ancient blade slicing deep into the monster, parting muscle, flesh and shearing through the snake's gullet. The serpent reared away, releasing its grip on the snout of Marcus's snakehead, only to find that once it released its grip, its own head was now strangely loose and floppy. It dropped down to the jungle floor, knowing it was wounded and protectively nursing the vulnerable area, allowing the Nirschl head with Marcus still swinging helplessly from it, to silently glide away and nurse the smarting wounds inflicted upon its snout.

As the huge Nirschl crashed to the ground, snapping vegetation and sending up showers of dirt and slime, Aradol charged back in, swinging his sword with all the force he could muster. The brutal attack sheared through rippling scales and exposed a pulsating pink fleshy stump behind the snake's head as the huge jaw slowly separated from the hydra's neck with a squelch. Gore sprayed all over the young knight, thick viscous fluid pumping from the decapitated creature as the neck writhed about on the ground.

"And that's two." Aradol gasped, his breath coming in exhausted gasps as he staggered away from the hydra head and stepped over to the first one still twitching feebly on the floor. He swung his blade up high and slammed it down into the creature's skull, piercing the monster's brain and hearing its death rattle as he did so.

"Come on Ives." Aradol gestured. "Help me roll this thing over. Your sword is still under here." He stepped into the puddle of blood and gore slowly draining from the monster and started to shove hard in time with the spasmodic jerks of the creature's twitching body. The rest of the massive creature was still up and fighting, struggling to drag the dead part of itself around the clearing as it responded to the other ship mates attacking it. The head slid several feet across the ground, gouging up mud and debris as the Nirschl gave a determined jerk and Aradol took advantage of the movement to roll the limp head over, bringing Ives white blade into view.

"Here we are!" Aradol grinned, reaching into the slime and lifting the weapon from the sticky slime. "Here Ives, catch!" The sword arched through the air, drops of gore splattering the ground as it flew straight towards Ives, only for the blade to slip straight through the merchant's hands, crashing into a bush and landing out of sight.

"Oh come on Ives. I threw it right at you!" Aradol shouted, exasperated at his friend's inability to catch the simple throw. "What's wrong with you?" Ives tried to reply but found that what he was looking at defied description, he gestured wildly with his hand, pointing behind the young warrior, trying to warn him of the horrors occurring at the fighter's back.

Aradol spun around, sword held steadily before him and stopped in confusion. He stared at the pink fleshy stump that had once been a snapping and snarling Nirschl head. Instead of the stump simply quivering or lying limp and flaccid, the wound pulsed, bulged and stretched as if something lay just beneath the surface. Flesh puckered and expanded, protruding then snapping back as if something were pushing outwards from inside the moist stump.

An ungodly shrieking rose from the wound, then two separate lumps appeared to push to the surface. The skin cracked, splitting open like a rotten vegetable, oozing out pus, gore and two shiny squealing hydra heads that uncurled from the single stump, scenting the air, tongues touching each other before they hissed loudly, turning as one to face their attacker.

Aradol could not believe what he was seeing. How could this part of the creature still be alive? He had just removed its head and now it had grown two more! What did it take to kill one of these things? He twirled his blade, whipping it around in his right hand, before bringing it in front of him and holding it with two hands.

"Ives. Please go and get your sword." Aradol shouted, not daring to take his eyes of the twin serpents twining and swaying before him. "I think I'm going to need your help." He dared not look to see if the merchant was carrying out his order, his attention fully focused by the slimy baby monster heads swaying before him.

"Just hurry up back." Aradol muttered to himself, his gaze darting beyond the hissing Nirschl heads for signs of any other assistance that could be coming his way, only to note several snapping swaying heads and trunks of glistening scales crushing and flattening the jungle around him.

Was that Marcus swinging from a Nirschl head high above? Where was Commagin? Mathius and his blades? The unstoppable force that was Rauph? He really did need some help and fresh ideas here. What he would give for the archer right now. His gaze snapped back to the twin heads, which suddenly shot forwards, one high, and the other low, jaws open, fangs still stained with the pink flesh they had torn apart to be born.

Aradol rolled his neck, took a deep breath, then stepped forwards into the fray, hoping against hope that enough of his friends would notice his predicament and come to his aid.

...before it was too late.

Chapter Twenty-Six

Ashe lay with his eyes closed, arms behind his head, trying to put it out of his mind just how bored he was. The cell held no obvious way to escape, there were no loose bricks, secret tunnels, enchanted rings or magical portals to whisk him away, despite a lengthy fruitless search. With nothing left to occupy his time, the Halfling had to content himself with imagining life once he managed to escape, in the hope that the method of this jail break would somehow reveal itself when the time was right.

At this moment, Ashe was painting a rose-tinted tapestry in his mind, hiding from the law, an outlaw on the run, living hand to mouth, visiting exotic locales, from mysterious castles to dusty tombs, ice fortresses to desert oasis, each stop adding further legend to his own personal heroic saga. Ashe the adventurer always saved the day, his trusty friend Sinders always perched on his shoulder. The Halfling rescued damsels in distress, liberated treasures for the 'Keep Ashe Happy Fund' and of course, vanquished the monsters and villains that all heroes dealt with on a day to day basis.

Whom was he kidding! Ashe sighed deeply. He could just see himself living in a tent; the reality would be nothing like what he imagined, getting wet and soggy when it rained, baked and dusty when it was not. Finding himself at risk of being eaten by grizzly bears or other monsters as he tried to eke out a pitiful existence in the woods, eating slugs and bugs. No hero of any kind would be so boring as to spend half of his saga hiding out in the woods camping!

A fluttering sound from above made Ashe frown and open his eyes, annoyed at the intrusion into his reverie. What could possibly be causing the noise?

"Aak, Squawk!"

"Sinders?" Ashe sat up on his bunk, staring around the cell. "Is that you?" Another loud cry sounded from the barred window and then a feathered blob crashed down from above, bouncing onto the bunk in the most undignified landing. Wings wide, feathers akimbo, clawed feet sticking out in odd directions. Ashe squealed with delight, making the strange bird try to pull itself into an even tighter ball.

"You found me Sinders! You found me! Oh I have some seedcakes for you in my pocket. I'm afraid they are rather crumbly now and this one has some fuzz on the edges but I saved them for you." Sinders opened one mad rolling eye and started looking about at the mention of the food. Ashe offered some on his hand and laughed as his pet swiftly gobbled it up.

"You have to tell me where you have been." Ashe gushed. "You have missed so much! Someone tried to poison Thomas, Rauph and the others have gone into the jungle to find an anti-goat. At least I think that's what they said." Ashe tried to remove the image from his mind of a goat that could heal people. He had no idea exactly how the goat did this and to be honest was not particularly interested. He was more concerned about the fact he had not been invited to go off and explore the jungle. Then again, Sinders had been missing at the time, so he had been rather preoccupied. He watched Sinders finish the first seedcake with pure adoration in his eyes.

"Then I found a place where they throw perfectly good money away." Ashe continued, barely taking the time to breathe. "Only, just because they throw it away does not mean you are allowed to keep any of it. No matter how much you think otherwise. So here I am locked up for a huge misunderstanding. I'm expecting someone to come along any time now and tell me this is all just some big mistake."

The door to the cell rattled as a key was inserted.

"See, there you go!" Ashe smiled and then a frown swiftly crossed his face. He had forgotten to ask if there was a policy about keeping pets in the cell. He did not want to get in trouble yet again. He swiftly looked around the room, not seeing anywhere Sinders could hide, then he slid over the edge of the bunk and ran towards the door, wanting to stop the gaoler from coming in and discovering the uninvited guest. Sinders waddled to the edge of the bunk then dropped to the floor with a squeak and rolled towards the Halfling.

"No stupid bird. You have to hide you have to..." The door creaked open.

Ashe's eyes went wide. He looked to the door then down at the bird, then grabbed the only other item of furniture in the room and upended the broken bucket over the bird, only to look down and find Sinder's beak poking out through the hole he had made earlier. The Halfling cursed, staring around frantically, looking for anything else he could use to cover the bird, before realising his time was up and planting his bottom on the broken bucket with a barely contained squeak. The door creaked open revealing two large Minotaur guards who came into the cell, took a quick look around to check the room was empty and then started to back away again.

"It's about time you let me out of here." Ashe stated sternly, the effect somewhat tempered by the fact he was sitting on the bucket. "Hey where are you going?" Ashe wanted to run for the door but he could not leave Sinders after just finding his pet again. He moved to stand up, only to find the doorway filling with the large female Minotaur that had been in charge of the feast from the other night. What was her name? Mora or something?

"Do you not stand when a lady enters a room?" Mora asked, as she walked into the cell, her long blue gown swooshing about her.

Ashe looked up at the leader of the Minotaur, taking in the long soft scarf she wore about her neck, the delicate golden tips of jewellery on her horns and the look of sheer distain worn on her face. In that moment the Halfling realised he did not like this lady cow very much. He moved to stand with the sternness of her voice, then felt his bucket jolt beneath him and sat down again as fast as he could.

"I'm sorry but I can't stand." Ashe replied, suddenly rubbing his hip. "I have some umm arthritis in my hip and the bunk here is so hard."

The guards snarled out in the passageway, clearly unhappy about the lack of respect shown to their matriarch but a swift wave of Mora's hand stopped the two burly bodyguards from coming into the cell and turning Ashe into a strawberry smudge on the wall.

Mora clicked her fingers and a stool was ushered into the small cell by the gaoler, allowing her to sit and bring her hands together bridging her fingers.

"What is your name?" she asked coldly. Ashe stared hypnotised at the gleaming rings on her fingers, noting the sparkling gems and formulating the value of the hand, rather than view it in the intimidating way Mora intended.

"What is your name?" Mora shouted, leaning forwards to tower over her prisoner.

"Um, Oh… Ashe Wolfsdale." He replied, holding out his hand and gripping Mora's, only for the Matriarch to snatch her hand away as if the Halfling was something disgusting that she had accidentally touched.

"The arrival of the *El Defensor* has been nothing but an irritation to me." Mora confessed. "Why did you decide to come here of all times, just as Drummon was about to be sworn in as my replacement?"

"Well I'm not in charge of the ship so you need to ask Thomas that question." Ashe replied. "Oh, but you can't, can you? Because I heard you tried to poison him."

"What do you mean tried?" Mora smiled with no warmth at all. "No one recovers from Nirschl venom, absolutely no one. Oh, I am very much afraid that your captain is quite dead by now. Some of Kristoph's friends are about to follow him, if I am not very much mistaken. Their trip to the jungle was bound to be filled with hidden perils; there are so many wild animals out there. I know Drummon would have tried his best to help these sad unfortunates but tragic unexpected incidents happen all the time."

"That's horrible." Ashe snapped, moving to stand and yet again feeling the bucket nudge beneath him, forcing him to sit again. "You can't get away with this. The crew of the *El Defensor* simply will not sit and let you do this to our friends. If you harm anyone, you will be making a very big mistake."

"The concerns of your crew do not disturb me." The Matriarch hissed. "Your ship will be impounded, your remaining crew sent to the mines or sold as slaves. Kristoph will take part in the Labyris competition and once a terrible accident has befallen him, my troops shall act with ruthless efficiency. Drummon will be crowned as I previously planned and all will be as it should be. It will be such a shame about Kristoph but sacrifices have to be made for the greater good."

"Don't you think it's a little careless of you to confess such information to me?" Ashe replied, his stern look returning to his little features. "When I get out of here and tell the crew what you are planning, they will be really angry with you."

"What makes you think you are getting out of here?" Mora replied with a glacial laugh. "You have been found guilty of stealing from the fountains. The penalty is death by hanging."

"Don't I have the benefit of a trial?" the Halfling gulped.

"Oh." Mora brought her hand to her head in a mock pretence at forgetting. "Did I not tell you? We had the trial a few moments ago. Of course I did all I could for Kristoph's friend, tried to plead for mercy from the magistrate but the crime was simply too severe."

"I only picked up some coins someone threw away!" Ashe exclaimed. "I did not know I was doing wrong."

"Of course you didn't." Mora agreed. "This is why I have scheduled your hanging for noon today. We did not want you to suffer too much and the magistrate felt it was better to put you out of your misery as soon as possible so that you don't upset yourself by dwelling on the matter. We can clearly see that you are disturbed."

Ashe sat there open mouthed. Hung! This was not good. This was not good at all! Hang on a moment... what did she mean disturbed?

"What's the time now?" he asked his mouth suddenly dry.

"You have about an hour to get ready to meet your maker." Mora replied. "Shall I arrange for a last meal for you? You must be really hungry after spending all this time in here."

Ashe went to voice his reply, tempted to ask for something that took more than an hour to cook but he knew the Matriarch did not intend to get anything cooked for him.

"Well. I do appreciate all you have done for me." Ashe stated. "Don't hit your head on the door frame on the way out."

Mora stood up and brushed her dress down before letting out a deep evil laugh.

"Goodbye Ashe Wolfsdale." She smiled. "I shall make sure to let the hangman know to make you suffer before he finally throws the lever to snap your neck. It's a shame I will not be there to see it but I have a competition to arrange. I am sure Kristoph will be heart broken when he hears the news of your unfortunate indiscretion and fate."

"His name is Rauph!" Ashe snapped as Mora turned to leave. "He has always been Rauph and will always be Rauph to his friends."

"Yes so you say." Mora responded. "However, as I am sure you can see. Being Rauph's friend can have terminal consequences." She walked from the cell, the door slamming shut behind her and the key grating as it turned in the lock.

Ashe stood up, moved the bucket and looked down at Sinders who stared back at him with a crazy rolling eye.

"Well that's a turn up for the books!" he remarked to the bird. "They are going to hang me for collecting some coins that no one wanted. Whatever next? I suppose they would really have a fit if they knew I had one of the cow lady's rings then!" He held up the palmed ring and angled it to take in the light from the deep red ruby set into the golden band.

"I guess I've still got it." He smiled. "Now if it is alright with you, I feel we have just about outstayed our welcome here and it is time for us to leave. I had faith that a means of escape would arrive and true to form..." he turned towards the now vacant stool, already knowing the increased height would allow him to reach the lock that until now had eluded him.

"...something has."

* * * * * *

Kerian pulled back into the shadows as a huge golden guard stalked by, menacingly swinging its massive sword from side to side, scattering scarlet scorpions and disrupting sand drifts that had collected within the ruined shell of the city. The knight held his breath as the giant sentinel passed, struggling to contain his frustration at how agonisingly slow his departure from this accursed place was.

Toledo pushed his snout over Kerian's right shoulder and sniffed the air and then shoulder barged the concealed warrior out into the open.

Clearly, his stallion was as desperate to leave Tahl Avan as he was! Kerian wiped his shoulder with his left hand, checking there was no horse saliva marring the beautiful workmanship of his new armour, then considered his situation.

There was no doubt he wanted to get away from this city as fast as possible, leave the horrors he had witnessed far behind him and banish from his mind the hauntingly beautiful woman who had paralysed him with the coldest of touches. However, despite his best efforts, the going had been painful, with Kerian finding himself constantly playing cat and mouse with the ten-foot-tall golden mummies that haunted these ruins and seemed determined to stalk him wherever he went.

A shiver ran up his spine at the thought of Octavian's mysterious wife. She had disappeared when he had finally recovered from his paralysis. There had been no sign of the woman, no indication she had even been in the room with him; no signs of tracks on the floor or indents in the soft sand to show where she had walked or knelt. It was as if the woman had not existed. Could it all have been some kind of a strange erotic dream?

No, the armour was proof that something had happened in the run-down hovel he had used as his nocturnal base. Kerian remembered he had grunted at the effort when he came to remove the barricade from the door. Either Octavian's wife was a lot stronger than she looked; or she had not left the dwelling that way. The sun hung high in the sky when he had first cracked the door of his sanctuary, making it clear there was a significant period he had no account for. The flawless red-streaked sand outside confirmed nothing had drawn near during the hours of darkness or left for that matter. This whole situation had the stench of sorcery about it.

Kerian gathered the reins for Toledo in his hand and led the stallion out from beneath the shelter of a collapsed roof that had served as cover from the undead eyes of the golden sentinel. Dorian the donkey reluctantly followed at the end of the train, dragging his hooves and showing a distinct dislike to being out under the hammering strength of the sun's rays.

The knight licked his lips, feeling the hardened ridges of skin rasp against his tongue and considered another mouthful from his water supplies before declining it. The longer he could conserve his water, the better his chances of getting to Al Mashmaah and crossing the Vaarseeti desert. All he needed to do was find some of the markers with the bells on, just like Octavian had shown him and then hope these would lead him back to civilisation. It was clear he was never going to find any markers whilst he remained in this haunted place. He needed to travel to the outskirts of the city and get his bearings. It all sounded so simple in theory but it was anything but in practice.

He led the two mounts down a narrow alleyway passing between several tall weather-eroded granaries and out across a plaza where a squat temple took centre stage, its roof slanted in such a way as to leave one side of the building completely sheltered from the whispering sands. The preserved side of the building consisted of a polished marble facade that had miraculously survived the scouring elements and reflected back a ghostly image of Kerian, making the knight pause in his walk as he took in the full effect of his new armour.

Knee high boots of soft brown leather protected his feet and shielded his legs from the blowing sands. Cream breeches disappeared beneath a chainmail undercoat of small golden metal links. A tunic of padded leather, highly polished in such a way as to enhance the shades of golden brown and sandstone quilting upon its surface, completed the breastplate and shoulder pads. Warmer cherry brown colours used on the bracers and rerebrace protected the upper arms and the cuisses on the top of his thighs. A beige hooded cloak hung almost to the ground, the hem engraved with a string of mysterious hieroglyphs and tiny cobalt blue gemstones.

A gilded belt at Kerian's waist held a foot-long dagger at his right hip and the sword recovered from the subterranean boat threaded through on his left. The knight was a little concerned about how loose the sword felt in the makeshift sheath. It was as if the belt expected a different weapon; one he was apparently yet to discover. He shrugged his shoulders, ensuring his mirrored shield remained secure on his back and then turned to swirl the cloak about him, noting how the blue stones flashed brightly as it moved.

There was something comforting about this armour. It had looked too large to start with, yet when he tried it on; the material fitted him as if tailored specifically. It had been a long time since Kerian had felt such confidence in a uniform. Somehow, wearing this armour, he felt like a true hero, that he could take on any challenge and stand a good chance of succeeding against it. He just wondered how the clothing had managed to appear in the satchel, especially when he had checked the bag carefully and found nothing inside at all.

His left hand reached down to reassuringly pat the aforementioned satchel. As before, it felt flat and empty. Kerian carefully lifted the lip of the bag and noted the silvery material inside, just as when he had previously examined it. There were no signs of any hidden compartments, no signs of a sword that would accompany his new armour and most importantly, no signs of Colette's missing necklace.

Octavian's wife had promised him that the pendant remained inside the bag. She had also promised he would see Colette again. There had been a confidence about her comments that made him believe she was not lying to him, after all 'the cards had told her so'.

The cards! Kerian chuckled to himself. It was nothing but superstition! If he had believed in the cards, he would have given up on his quest months ago. After all, he was supposed to be dead. He had to admit that sometimes life did take strange, unexpected turns. I mean, here he was, staring at a mirrored surface, admiring his reflection in a city that had been buried under the sand for hundreds of years!

He went to move away from his mirror image and then stopped himself. What was that comment she had made; the one about him looking younger? He walked closer to the marble surface and stared at his reflection carefully. His hair was definitely looking darker. His temples not as grey and his facial features not as deeply etched.

Could she be right? Was he getting younger, or was it down to the poor quality of the mirror he was using? Toledo nudged him again, eager to be off and across the desert. Kerian swung himself up into the saddle and pulled the hood of the cloak down over his head before giving Toledo free rein to head in any direction the stallion chose. Maybe the horse would strike lucky and they would end up finding a short cut to the edge of the metropolis. To be honest any suggestion would be good now. He felt he had been wandering aimlessly around these ruins too long!

Kerian looked up to try to get his bearings and noted an ominous bank of clouds steadily building on the far horizon. It looked as if they held the potential for yet another storm. What was it with the Vaarseeti desert and storms? The sun shone hazily from its position in the sky, making Kerian start when he realised how low it was; how could so much time have passed already? How many hours had he lost wandering aimlessly about this sprawling ruined city?

The wind whistled hauntingly through a tall minaret and whispering grains of sand started to dance in little agitated swirls at his feet. Maybe the storm was closer than it looked? Kerian scanned the buildings around him, looking for some sign as to what direction to take. An alleyway to the left had an exquisite arched bridge built between the two buildings signifying that another roadway existed above but there were no obvious signs of how to get up there. Another exit from the square led down to a dried canal bed, the skeletal grasses of the waterway reaching up to the heavens, their brittle stalks clicking a warning note of the approaching storm.

Toledo surprised Kerian by taking another route entirely. Nostrils flaring, the stallion angled across a plaza where an eroded horned statue kept silent guard, before plodding into a passageway that led back underground. Kerian felt the hairs rise on his arms as soon as Toledo moved away from the sunlight. He remained acutely aware of what horrors lurked beneath these shifting desert sands, however, the relative silence after being in the winds outside, was deafening and Kerian thankfully drew his hood back as the cool stone of the chamber closed about him.

Wonderful pictographs on the pillars and walls documented life in this great city before the wrath of the gods had razed it from the face of the known world. Kerian's eye roamed over these illustrations, marvelling at the rich colours and the cityscapes displayed, noting that most depicted traders and caravans setting off across the desert.

Dorian brayed, the sound echoing loudly in the confines of the passage, making Kerian jump and reach for his sword. The donkey incredibly picked up the pace and drew alongside Toledo the supplies on its back jostling loudly as the impatient donkey rushed to get ahead. They exited the passageway in a disorganised group and entered a sheltered courtyard with an intact ceiling of stained glass, that permitted a multi-coloured view of clouds scudding impatiently across the sky.

Kerian dropped from Toledo's back and advanced cautiously, noting that the entrance to the room was gated and could be closed behind him to keep the creatures of Tahl Avan safely outside. The stone slabs angled down towards a large hole in the floor but Kerian could not see what was in there from his position. Stone seats lined the walls with stand-alone charcoal burners placed every few yards. Gutters in the floor suggested this area required good drainage but he was unclear as to what the purpose of the room was. His eyes continued scanning the courtyard, searching for dangers, despite the fact Dorian had spoiled any chance of surprise by announcing their presence so loudly.

The donkey lunged forwards, pulling tight against his line, leaving the knight with no choice but to release the animal or risk injury to both the obstinate creature and his mount. Kerian knew he could not afford to lose either! Dorian's hooves clattered to the edge of the hole and then the animal moved down a ramp that remained out of view. Toledo looked towards Kerian, as if asking for permission to follow and then independently set off after its smaller companion.

Kerian quickly followed the beasts, hand on the hilt of his sword, only to discover that the courtyard held a greater discovery than he had expected. Not only was this a place of sanctuary from the storm, it also held two deep pools that gleamed turquoise. Dorian and Toledo were gulping down water at one pool, whilst the other steamed gently as if heated in some way. He appeared to be in a bathhouse of some kind.

Dorian brayed loudly in delight and then dropped its head to continue drinking its fill. Toledo appeared more reserved but still lapped at the water as if he had not taken a good draught of fluid in several days. Kerian found himself smiling at the obvious delight the mounts showed, knowing this was indeed a lucky find.

The knight moved away from the pool, leaving the two creatures to slake their thirsts as he continued his exploration of the area, checking the walls and cupboards in the courtyard, ensuring the security of his position and noting that more hieroglyphics and pictograms covered the walls. Finally, he returned to the main entranceway and secured the gate with a thankful sigh.

He saw to the mounts, releasing the saddles from both horse and donkey, only for Dorian to wade further into the pool and splash about like a particularly excitable child. The light from through the coloured roof dimmed rapidly as the cloud cover finally obscured any trace of sunlight that remained. Kerian moved to retrieve some charcoal and kindling from a stockpile he had discovered during his earlier reconnaissance and delighted as a small flickering fire soon rose from one of the burner stands.

With all of the housekeeping out of the way, he looked again at the steaming blue pool and shrugged his shoulders. If he was to spend another night in the lost city, he might as well relax in a warm bath whilst he did so. The soak was luxurious, easing away the aches and pains of the journey, relieving his itching scalp and making his hair feel like something other than greasy straw. It was a good while later before he reluctantly climbed from the pool and got dressed again.

A frown creased his brow as he realised there was still one more concern to eliminate. Octavian's wife had demanded he find her husband and take him to some strange and foreboding castle. If there was one thing Kerian disliked intently, it was being told what to do! He had no intention of tracking down Octavian. The man was a jinx!

He gathered up some more fuel and added it to the fire, letting the flames rise up to cast more illumination across the darker walls of the room. He loved the fact these murals showed merchants at work plying their trade and could almost imagine that people of wealth met in these very chambers and conducted important business deals within these opulent settings. One thing was for sure, they would have had something more appetising than dried bread and hard tack to eat. He lifted the bread to his mouth and let his eyes linger on the mural illustrated on the wall across from him.

"Well I'll be…" Kerian muttered, his attention all but taken away from the stale bread he was chewing in his mouth. The picture showed the city of Tahl Avan when it was a thriving trade centre. Illustrated Caravans moved along trails from distance towns and cities, some carrying goods to trade, others leaving the city with purchases. He took in the vivid colours, the small nuances emphasising different races and exotic trade items. Here someone was buying a bird in a cage, there a travelling circus, high in the sky a griffon flew amongst the clouds.

Kerian held up a makeshift torch and gently traced his finger along a northern route showing travellers crossing the desert. He smiled at the illustrated camels, monkeys and amphorae painted there, before his finger arrived at the destination. It was a walled city patrolled by men on lizards waving a banner between them. Kerian squinted annoyed at his eyesight being so poor in the darkness and brought the light closer. The writing on the banner was impossible to misread. His eyes went instantly wide in recognition. This was not just a wall mural. Neither was it just an artist's impression of the lifestyle of the city, this was so much more! He lifted the brand in his hand and mouthed the words on the banner, feeling the way they rolled from his tongue as he smiled.

Octavian could go to hell as far as Kerian was concerned. He had just found a map to Al Mashmaah!

Chapter Twenty-Seven

Weyn opened his eyes and tried not to be sick. The archer knew his right arm was ruined. It felt numb and about three sizes too large. His fingers felt like cold sausages, pins and needles stabbing aggressively. He tried to raise his hand and found himself screaming with pain. There was no way he could lift it. He pulled himself to his knees and took in the massive hissing multi-headed monster still snapping, spitting and lunging around him. Severed limbs wriggled about the clearing, Nirschl snakeheads swooped and glided about searching for prey to rip asunder.

He reached for his bow, slipping it awkwardly from his shoulder and unsteadily nocked one of his magical arrows to the string using his left hand. A wave of dizziness swept over him, forcing the archer to close his eyes, then slowly open them again, in an attempt to stop blacking out. Where was Rauph? He could not see the Minotaur. A figure rose from the muck and mire about twenty feet away, dripping gore and slime, making Weyn start before he realised it was actually Mathius, bleeding from assorted lacerations and abrasions, a dagger clutched firmly in his hand.

A shadow fell over the assassin, another Nirschl head dropping silently down towards him, fangs dripping venom that hissed as it hit the jungle floor. Mathius appeared completely unaware of the impending danger and indeed appeared to be more distressed about the state of his dagger by the way he was staring at the blade.

Weyn reacted on instinct, his left arm bringing up his bow, right hand clawing ineffectively at the bowstring as if he were suddenly a child with no power at all. The archer's right arm screamed in protest, the strength in his limb gone. There was no way he could manage to draw his bow, the resistant poundage in the sturdy weapon simply too much for the wounded man to handle. There was only one other thing he could do as the hypnotic hydra head slithered closer.

"Mathius!" Weyn screamed. "Above you!"

The assassin looked over at the archer with apparent confusion, noting Weyn's cry but clearly not understanding him. He lifted a muddy hand as if to wave back in acknowledgement, causing the archer to curse at the absurdity of it all. Did Mathius not realise the danger he was in? Weyn started to take a step towards Mathius, not sure exactly what he would actually do to stop the approaching Nirschl. Another massive figure rose from the mud and charged towards Mathius drawing a sword.

Was that Rauph? It was so difficult to tell. It was clearly an angry Minotaur but the creature was coated in so much muck and filth that there was no way for Weyn to tell for sure if it was the navigator. So why was he attacking Mathius? None of this made any sense at all. Everything was moving much too fast. A fresh spasm of pain ran up the archer's right arm and he looked down and noted, with horror, the jagged remains of an arrow jutting from his fleshy forearm. Bile rose in Weyn's throat, the bitter taste making the likelihood of vomiting that much greater. At least he now knew why he could not draw his bow, the splintered shaft appeared to run right through!

Weyn tore his gaze away from the horrific wound and looked pleadingly back over to his shipmate, realising that he needed as much assistance, if not more than his colleague did. Mathius had stopped in place as the Minotaur charged towards him, assuming a defensive position despite his battered look, still apparently unaware that death was stealthily approaching from above. Weyn watched powerless as the Nirschl opened its jaws wide and lunged straight down at the assassin and the mud caked Minotaur.

The Nirschl's head swiftly extended, then snapped tight at full stretch, bringing the monster up, just short of its prey, fangs smashing together above the assassin, who incredibly appeared to duck down just at the last second, the deadly maw clamping shut inches above his head. The Nirschl drew back and then lunged again, still coming up short, clearly frustrated and pulling with all its might. It strained against the main trunk of the hydra body behind it but failed to reach its goal, due to having its neck entangled with all the swaying heads and slithering coils across the clearing.

Mathius smiled at the reflected image in his dagger blade and then struck out at the Minotaur alongside him, only to find that this foe was no longer there. Although the hydra's maw had closed inches from Mathius's head, his horned foe had been taller, much taller. When the jaws had snapped closed, they had taken the Minotaur with them. Even now, its muscular legs wriggled urgently as it hung above him; despite the fact that the Nirschl's jaws had pierced the Minotaur's body in at least a dozen places.

The assassin limped cautiously away, one eye watching the Nirschl as it commenced swallowing the poor Minotaur, spasmodically gulping as it pulled the creature further into its mouth with each immense swallow. Mathius reached Weyn, who moved to hold the assassin tightly by the shoulders; however, his right arm failed him, making the friendly attempt of reassurance a decidedly ungracious and awkward affair.

"I thought you were dead that time for sure." Weyn stated in concern. "Did you not see the snake?" Mathius grinned, as the two fighters staggered apart again, both showing signs of utter exhaustion, the chaos of their surroundings forgotten.

"Of course I saw the snake." He smiled, not daring to admit how close the strike had come. "Why did you not use your bow? I thought you were supposed to be a dead shot?"

"I can't draw my weapon." Weyn confessed, pointing down at his arm and shaking his head. Mathius stared at the splintered arrow sticking from the archer's arm and held his tongue, deciding to forego the obvious jokes about the archer shooting himself. Instead, he opted for a subtler attempt at humour.

"Trust our archer to complain about a splinter." He grinned. "A little scratch like that! Huh, I don't know what all the fuss is about. My granny would still be able to fire your bow with five of those."

"I'd like to see how." Weyn remarked, failing to see the funny side and gesturing towards the Nirschl. "I am totally useless down here when all the snake heads are up there without the use of my bow."

"Oh I don't know about that." Mathius replied cryptically. "Just let me show you."

* * * * * *

Marcus lifted his legs up just as a jagged tree stump came within inches of permanently removing him from his precarious perch. He swung about at the end of his makeshift set of reins, banging and smashing against the shimmering scales of the hydra's neck, desperately trying to get his feet up under him. He needed to lunge for the crimson plant dangling just beyond his reach. This was insane; the Nirschl was not slowing for an instant, clearly agitated about the injuries inflicted on its other heads by the crew of the *El Defensor*.

The hydra angled to one side just as another length of the giant serpent shot past, heading straight towards the others. Marcus barely had time to focus on the multi-coloured projectile, before he realised this was not another head but instead a vicious barbed tail. The appendage slammed into an ancient tree trunk at the edge of the clearing, almost disintegrating the rotten wood with the force of the blow. The ancient sentinel groaned loudly before crashing to the ground, directly across the path of the hissing head that the monk was hanging from.

The Nirschl reacted instantly, defensively spiralling straight up into the sky to avoid the collision, dragging the monk up along with it. Marcus found his grip slipping and frantically struggled to hold on, before the beast dropped again, swinging him around in front of the creature's nose. Marcus found his boots suddenly scrabbling on the curved fangs, desperate to maintain purchase or end up eaten alive. The monk grabbed the reins tighter and slowly began to pull himself up; over one of the monster's flaring nostrils, past a slowly blinking eye. Every inch climbed was a gargantuan effort as Marcus tried to position himself where he could make a play for the elusive lifesaving plant, acutely aware that just one slip would spell his doom.

* * * * * *

The remains of the crumbling tree trunk bounced and rolled across the ground, picking up speed as it twisted, before catching on the edge of a depression in the ground that flipped it end over end, before finally crashing down onto the extended neck of one of the 'kissing' Nirschl heads. The injured snake jerked back in reflex, fangs retracting, pulling away and breaking its macabre kiss, just as the navigator pushed up as hard as he could from inside the other Nirschl mouth, snapping the lower mandible of the serpent with an audible crack and leaving its bottom jaw hanging useless.

The hydra went wild, writhing and jerking about on the jungle floor, thrashing its head from side to side; aware its jaw was broken, yet refusing to stop trying to bite the prey that had dared harm it in this way. Rauph dropped away, leaving the monster flailing as he moved towards the second Nirschl head now pinned by the fallen tree and without pausing for breath plunged one of his huge swords into the creature's orbit, levering the blade right behind its dark orange eye. The Nirschl head appeared to go rigid and then slumped to the floor unmoving. Rauph spun away, intent on returning to the head with the broken jaw, only for the Nirschl's massive tail to slam into the ground next to him, barbs spreading out as four razor-like fingers.

The navigator jumped backwards, noting how the barbs clicked together as they slowly reverted into a wicked point. The massive tail slowly lifted from the ground barbs extending and then surged to the left, slicing a devastating path through the undergrowth, cutting through even the thickest vegetation and laying waste to everything therein.

Rauph ran in the other direction, turning back to his earlier task, intent on despatching the Nirschl with the broken jaw, only to find it dragging itself through the muck towards him. The air suddenly filled with crossbow quarrels, stitching a line up across the creature's broken jaw, ricocheting from a large upper fang and then running down the Nirschl's scaled neck. One quarrel punched clean through an umber eye, piercing the eyeball with an audible pop and dropping the Nirschl head lifeless to the ground.

"Seems I'm always here saving your hairy arse." Commagin grinned, stepping out from behind a boulder, reloading his retrieved crossbow as he came. Rauph lowered his weapons and tried looking over his shoulder, turning first one way and then the other.

"What are you looking at?" Commagin laughed.

"How did you know my bottom was hairy?" Rauph pondered aloud. "There are no tears in my garments."

"Your whole body is hairy, oaf!" The Dwarven engineer replied, plucking some errant leaves from his bushy beard. "It's therefore a good bet that your butt would be just as hairy as the rest of you! Now let's get moving, you can examine your hairy bottom in your own time." The dwarf raised his crossbow stock to his shoulder and squeezed off another couple of shots at a slithering shape nearby.

Rauph moved up alongside his smaller friend, knowing all too well the dangers of being in front of Commagin when he let loose with his favourite weapon. The Dwarf drew a bead on a Nirschl head rushing towards them, the creature moving so fast it churned up a bow wave of plants and soil as it carved its way across the ground.

"I've got this one." The engineer announced, lining up the monster in his sights. "There is no need for your input dear navigator." Commagin cracked a smile and pulled the trigger only for his crossbow to misfire.

"What?" The Dwarf spluttered. "Not now Janet of all times!"

Rauph pushed the agitated engineer to one side and lifted his swords out wide as if welcoming the Nirschl to come and take him. He gritted his teeth and prepared for the crash to come as the hydra head lunged.

An arrow sliced through the air, slamming into the side of the monster's snout, a second arrow piercing its eye sending the Nirschl veering away and missing the navigator and engineer by inches. The wake of jungle debris thrown up by the creature washed over them, leaving the two characters dripping in slime and muck.

The Nirschl squirmed and thrashed, hissing in agony as it tried to remove the arrow sticking from its eye. It recoiled, turned back on itself and tried to twist into a knot at the pain, its remaining good eye turning to stare with undisguised hatred at the two dripping figures. Another arrow streaked through the air slamming into the second eye, popping the gleaming surface causing the monster to shriek in agony and writhe even more.

"Oh good shot!" Mathius grinned, "Do you want me to shuffle to the left or the right?"

"Right." The archer replied. "The sooner we finish this up the sooner I can go home. Do you know how uncomfortable it is lying on the floor?"

Mathius looked back over his shoulder and smiled at the archer, who was lying in the mud with his legs in the air, the bow balanced on the base of his feet. Weyn was already nocking another arrow, leaning back to pull with his left hand and complete the draw. Mathius shuffled slightly to the right, feeling the tension of the bow lying across his shoulders where he supported it, along with the weight of the archer's legs.

"Now if you could just move upwards a fraction." Weyn asked.

"Just don't forget to miss my ear!" Mathius replied as he pushed up from the mud. "I'm rather attached to it."

"Then make sure you duck!" Weyn replied, releasing the string and sending another enchanted arrow spinning out towards the writhing mass of hydra. "Where next?" the archer prompted, as the arrow slammed into the serpent's eye just behind the last missile he had sent out "I think that Nirschl head has had the fight knocked out of it."

"Aradol is to the left." Mathius replied shuffling around on his knees and dragging Weyn through the muck after him. "I have no idea where Ives is."

"What about Marcus?" Weyn joked as another massive hydra head swooped by overhead, the monk dangling from his neck. "Whatever do you think he is trying to do?"

"Oh you know Marcus. He's always hanging around with the wrong type of monster and causing trouble." Mathius joked. "You never know, if we hurry and sort out Aradol's problems we might still have time to take a couple of pot shots at him."

* * * * * *

"That's it, just a little…" Marcus muttered under his breath, swinging backwards and forwards with the movement of the hydra head and inching ever closer to the prize of the crimson orchid. "And I've got it!" The monk leapt for the delicate bloom, just as the Nirschl swung its head away. Marcus's hand snatched at the bloom, inadvertently crushing the flower and snapping the stem off.

"Okay, so I haven't got it!" Marcus moaned his disappointment, only for the reins he was holding in his other hand to finally part with an audible snap sending the monk slipping and sliding down the creature's neck, bumping and scraping over every scale as he fell towards the ground.

The monk hit the floor at a run, deftly dodging two strikes from the Nirschl as it attempted to swallow the prey that had eluded it all this time. Marcus threw himself behind a tree trunk and ducked down low before daring to look at the mess he now held in his hands. The Death's Head orchid was ruined, the petals disintegrated and smeared across his palm like the desiccated remains of a gossamer butterfly wing he had once found wedged in the corner of a forgotten dusty window frame at the monastery in Catterick. Sticky sap smeared his fingertips and seemed to make his fingertips tingle and feel slightly numb.

Marcus shook his head. He had no idea what part of the flower they required for the antidote but it was clear that what he held in his hands would never do! They only knew where one other bloom existed. It was on the head of the Nirschl Weyn had become pinned to.

A massive hydra head angled in from the left snapping its fangs as it tried to flush the monk from his cover. Marcus took a step to the right leaving the creature to close its jaws on nothing but air, then dodged back again as another monstrous maw snapped and hissed from the right, this one sporting an injury on its jaw from where thick blood welled. Marcus stared intently, noting the splintered arrow shaft jutting from the wound. It had to be the head he was looking for. The creature slithered past hissing angrily, only to reveal, as it turned, the ragged remains of the death's head orchid that had once bloomed there.

Marcus's heart sank, both blooms were shredded. There was no way they could make an antidote now. The thought hit hard. Because of their failure, their captain was dead! Something huge slammed into the tree trunk just above the monk's head, showering Marcus in an explosion of debris and wooden splinters, completely obscuring his vision. He coughed and spluttered, staggering about blinking his eyes, trying to clear his vision as he felt behind him for the cover of the tree, only to discover it was no longer there. What could have hit with such devastating power?

The dust cloud settled revealing two Nirschl heads waiting patiently just outside of the area of devastation, hissing gently and nuzzling each other, tongues flicking as they waited for their prey to stagger into their killing range.

"This doesn't look good." Marcus muttered, feeling his legs turn weak and rubbery beneath him. One of the Nirschl heads coughed then slowly blinked a soulless eye before it slithered silently off to the left. The other head tilted to one side, then slunk off in the other direction, the intention of the two creatures clear as they slowly circled their prey cutting off his escape.

"This doesn't look good at all."

* * * * * *

Ives pushed his way through the undergrowth, still on the trail of his elusive sword. It had to be here somewhere. He needed to find it and get back to help Aradol, although secretly Ives knew any assistance given would be limited at best. He knew he was no good with a sword. His father had always found him a disappointment. It was only after the other male heirs of the family had died that he was bequeathed the family sword and his record in wielding it had been poor at best.

The merchant shook his head remembering his failure against the wind elemental when he had dropped his blade and had almost lost it in a storm several months before. He had ended up shuffling along a beam with his robes all hitched up around him, trying to get his sword back, it was hardly the stuff of heroes.

The undergrowth was so dense and resistant to Ives attempts of penetrating it that he found himself uttering curses normally reserved for only the most insulting barterers. He pushed at a large palm shaped leaf, then fell through, his foot sliding forwards, only to come down on nothing as he stepped into a depression. Ives crashed through the undergrowth, slipping and sliding down a slope, barrelling through low bushes, snapping twigs and ending up flat on his face in an undignified heap.

It took a few painful moments, with the air whistling in and out of his lungs before Ives managed to pull himself unsteadily to his feet, only to find his hands sinking into the mud and his boots filling with stagnant water. The merchant staggered to his feet, his boots sinking deeper into the mire. He flapped his arms, windmilling comically, mud and debris dripping from his garb, before he finally managed to get his balance and wipe his eyes clear.

His errant blade lay a few feet ahead, the hilt sticking proudly up from the swampy ground, offering itself to him. Ives stretched out his hand then realised he was unable to reach the blade without moving closer. He cursed loudly, dragging one foot free of the clinging mud before plunging it back into the bog a foot further ahead, then turned to his other leg to repeat the ridiculous motion. The swamp slurped, sucked and belched as Ives moved inch by inch towards regaining his family treasure. The titanic battle back in the clearing was soon a distant memory, as the merchant threw everything that he had into dragging himself towards his sword.

With a final satisfying squelch, Ives finally managed to extend his arm enough to curl his fingers around the hilt and begin to ease the weapon from the silt. As he did so, the merchant allowed his gaze to relax and finally focus on the boggy landscape beyond and the blazing crimson banner of bobbing blooms that dominated.

"Well I never." The merchant froze with his arm still extended, not believing what he was seeing. He scrunched up his eyes then took a moment to examine what he had literally stumbled upon. He was standing in a swampy depression slightly lower than the main battlefield. The area measured roughly twenty feet by thirty feet and Ives stood at the bottom end of the clearing. A small, sluggish waterfall fed the swampy morass in which he stood and entered from his right. Shattered pieces of leathery debris dotted the base of the waterfall and even as Ives watched another wet sloppy lump of something unrecognisable plopped from the rim of the fall and dribbled into the mass of scarlet flowers.

The whole area had a serenity to it, as if Ives had found himself in a place of tranquillity, a world removed from the terrors literally feet away. The carpet of death's head orchids stretched from the fall and smothered two thirds of the clearing. The blooms nodded and bounced as if caressed by a gentle breeze, the flower stalks jostling for space with what appeared to be a mass of black, spindly, immature ferns. The bristling stalks terminating as tightly curled fiddleheads or curled over clumps that clung to the end of the swaying stalks, masking the potential to explode into blades of growth as they matured.

Ives could not believe his luck. Here was the bounty they required. The answer to all their prayers, the motherlode of treasures and this time it was not an expert swordsman or stalwart hulking adventurer that was going to save the day. No, it was going to be a humble shopkeeper who had fled his arranged marriage to the ugliest woman he had ever known. A gentle merchant of the exotic who had left his debts behind and signed up for a life of adventure on the mysterious galleon, *El Defensor*.

With a grunt of effort, the merchant started to slog painfully towards the orchids, grimacing with the effort of each step, one man fighting against the suction of the bog as he moved closer to the gently swaying blooms. Ives found himself breaking into a broad smile as he edged closer to his prize. Sweat was dripping from his face, muck and slime coated his robes from his armpits down to the bubbling swamp but the merchant was beyond caring. He was going to be the hero for a change. He would finally prove his position and worth to the crew he called his friends.

Ives could not wait to show Aradol his spoils.

* * * * * *

Aradol spun around, his weapon glinting in the diffused shafts of light filtering through the jungle canopy. The smaller hydra heads were fast, attacking in rapid lunges and strikes. One head snatched forward, teeth latching onto his shoulder guard, the snake wriggling from side to side as it attempted to pump venom into this metal-coated prey. The young warrior bashed down hard with his sword, prizing the serpent's grip away and smacking the head down, only for its twin to arrow in from the other side, forcing Aradol to retreat several hasty steps.

An acrid smell rose from his shoulder plate, causing the young man to pause as he realised that his ancient plate mail was smoking. What kind of venom did these creatures have? It was like acid!

Aradol slashed his blade in from up high, only to have one of the supple Nirschl heads coil along the blade, wrapping itself around his outstretched arm, the snapping head slithering rapidly up towards his face. The warrior could not bring his ancient weapon to bear as the second head darted in, as it tried to grip onto the ornate filigree engraved across the borders of his ancient breast plate. Venom started to ooze from the hydra's mouth scoring deeply into the forged metal.

The first butterflies of panic started to tickle the back of Aradol's mind as he wrestled with the creature. He could not concentrate on the foe before him. Ives was out there somewhere and he was alone. Aradol had needed to save the merchant's neck several times already. The man was a solid friend, someone you always wanted at your back in a bar fight but he simply could not use a sword with any degree of skill. He was probably bumbling into some other disaster even as Aradol wrestled with this monster.

The Nirschl attacking his breastplate pulled back and then shot forward angling straight towards Aradol's exposed face. The warrior threw up his left arm in reflex, only to watch the snake coil around this arm as well and then the whole body drag him physically towards the stump that he had earlier decapitated.

A face of delicate porcelain flashed across the young man's vision. A flash of blonde curls tied with violet ribbons, a flirtatious smile. Aradol gritted his teeth and bashed one arm repeatedly against the other, his gauntlet squeezing the neck of the Nirschl as hard as he could, in the hope the creature would loosen its constricting grip. The creature was having none of it, coils tightening in response and turning into what felt like bands of iron, crushing his limbs.

No this could not happen! Aradol screamed his defiance to the world. He was not going to die this way! One Nirschl head lunged forward; fangs extended striking for Aradol's face. He closed his eyes and saw Colette's face.

A wet thwack sounded, splattering Aradol's face with slime, making him open his eyes in time to witness his own grisly fate. The Nirschl on his sword arm, failed about headless, blood and gore spurting from the stump. The coils about his right arm slackened off and the monster fell writhing to the floor. A huge long sword swung in, cutting the Nirschl down and sending a chunk of serpent sailing into the bushes.

"Can we join in?" Rauph asked, reaching over to grab the second juvenile head and throttling it, making the monster release Aradol and constrict itself around the navigator's massive muscular arm. "You looked like you were having fun and I did not really want to intrude but Commagin said he did not think you would mind."

"Please knock yourself out." Aradol replied before dropping to the floor his legs feeling like rubber.

"Why would I knock myself out and miss all of this." Rauph grinned, pulling the snake neck straight before artfully tying it into a knot. The Nirschl head struggled to breathe, tried to pull itself apart but the Minotaur yanked the monster harder, causing a bulge behind the knot where the creature desperately tried to disentangle itself.

"Watch out for the other neck!" Aradol warned, rolling his shoulders and opening and shutting his hands as the blood supply started to return with a flood of accompanying pins and needles. "They regrow if you chop the ends off. Oh hell, what about Ives?"

"Really?" Rauph grinned swinging his sword left and right before artfully cutting the knotted length of Nirschl off and laughing as it bounced on the floor. "No one told me that. We have missed out on so much fun! How long do they take to grow again?"

"Don't be a donkey." Commagin remarked, putting a quarrel through the eye of another much larger Nirschl head crashing in their direction. "Just kill the damned thing so we can go home."

"Ives!" Aradol shouted, turning about then repeating the call. "Ives, where are you?"

"I haven't seen him." Commagin confessed, clomping nearer and bringing up his crossbow. "Where did you last see him?"

"Over in the bushes." Aradol pointed, getting to his feet and scouring the floor trying to identify the merchant's trail. "He went in there looking for his sword."

"Ives!" the warrior shouted again. Oh where was the man?

* * * * * *

Ives heard someone calling his name and paused in his slog through the mud.

"Aradol is that you?" he shouted back, turning from the crimson orchids to direct his enquiry back towards his friend, unaware that the black fronds of the ferns had all turned in his direction. "Don't worry I'm fine."

Aradol paused in his crashing through the undergrowth, hearing his friend's voice coming back through the jungle somewhere to his left. He turned to Commagin gesturing that they head towards the noise.

"What are you doing? Have you found your stupid sword yet? All the fighting is going to be over before you get back here."

"My sword is not important." Ives shouted back. "I've found a whole garden of the orchids we need to cure Thomas."

Aradol paused once again in his noisy passage. "What did you say? I thought you said you have found a whole garden of orchids." What did Ives mean, a whole garden of orchids? They had only seen one or two. Why would there be a whole garden of them? Something dark and sinister in Aradol's gut squirmed. Why did the statement a whole garden of orchids fill him with sudden unnerving dread?

Ives turned back towards the blazing display of crimson and waded forward another step, his hand reaching out to grab the nearest bloom.

"Hang on a second." Ives shouted back. "I'm just going to get one of the flowers."

Aradol continued to push through the foliage, suddenly feeling an urgency to get to his friend. What was it the doctor had said about the orchids? Something about if the natives saw the blood red blooms they knew to stay away.

"Wait Ives. Just stop what you are doing. I'll be there in just a second to help you. Don't move!"

"Don't move." Ives laughed looking back over his shoulder as he stretched out his hand. "You are only saying that because you want to say you found the orchids first. How stupid do you think I am. Aargh!"

Ives snatched his head back around and looked at the tip of his outstretched hand. Blood was welling from the fingertip. What had just happened? How had he managed to cut himself? Did these orchids have thorns?

He leant forward, hand outstretched again, then shook his head as the tiny fern heads stretched out towards his hand. The swamp suddenly lurched. Ives steadied himself shaking his head but this seemed to make the whole area move again. The merchant blinked hard, licking his lips with a tongue that felt numb. What was going on? He looked back at his finger and noticed it had swollen.

"Ives stop what you are doing!" The shout of warning seemed echoing as if far away. There was a new sound now, a mewling like loads of baby kittens waiting for food. Where was the sound coming from? The swamp appeared to tilt again and Ives found himself crashing down into the orchids. Mud splattered everywhere but the merchant was strangely beyond caring. He tried to regain his feet, pushing up from the mud only to feel several more of the stinging strikes on his hands and arms.

He fell onto his side, the blood pounding in his ears, his eyes open wide as a spasm surged through his body. Ives blinked again bringing into focus one of the black ferns that bobbed up and down inches from his face. It was strange but up this close the fern looked like a miniature... the thought remained unsaid, Ives eyes looked out unfocused, his heart fluttering one last beat before it stopped forever.

The baby Nirschl lashed out with its tiny heads, venom striking Ives face in several places, the fangs of the monster digging in deep and ripping bloodied pieces from the paralysed merchant's cheek. Other baby Nirschl surged forwards eager to join the feast, whilst all around the orchids bobbed and nodded in silent reverence.

Chapter Twenty-Eight

The cabin door creaked gently open, to reveal a neat, tidy berth that instantly put Richard's bunk to shame. The priest eased inside, lightly clicking the door closed behind him before nervously scanning the room. The bookshelf was too obvious; Marcus would never leave his prize on open display. Under the bunk appeared to be an equally risible idea, so where exactly would the novice hide his magical blue tome?

The room was so small that Richard could barely turn around without brushing against the walls. Scanning the room was taking mere moments, yet nothing seemed out of place, nothing seemed unusual. Brother Richard dropped to his knees and shuffled around on the floor, cursing his stained blue robes for getting in the way and obscuring his inspection. There was not even a speck of dust in the far corners; not a single clue to identify a hiding place where Marcus had secured the book that was his devout responsibility.

Richard placed his hand on the bunk and started to get up, only to freeze as he heard footsteps approaching along the corridor. Could it be? Had Marcus returned from the jungle already? How would he possibly explain his presence in the monk's room? Beads of sweat dotted the priest's brow as the footsteps moved closer. His breathing sounded loud to his ears and his heart felt like it would just jump out of his chest with its constant pounding. His discovery was inevitable; Richard knew he would have to face the genuine accusations and go from there...

The footsteps passed the cabin door and continued on, leaving Richard dizzy with relief. The cabin suddenly felt uncomfortably hot to the priest and he placed a finger down the neckline of his robe and pulled it forward, waving his free hand to pass some cooler air onto his skin. He needed to regain control of himself and calm down, needed to focus on the task, no matter how uncomfortable it made him feel.

He threw his head back, closing his eyes, trying not to let the feelings of guilt wash heavily over him. Did he really have a right to do this? Was it his duty to take the book and use his past experiences to command the volume to do his bidding instead of Marcus who he thought inept? Richard licked his lips nervously, could he ever hope to be a *Bearer* again and wield all of the mysterious powers that came with it?

Staccato Images flickered through Richard's mind of another magical ledger from times before, granted to a *Bearer* who spent three thankless years exploring icy godforsaken tundra, three years evading frostbite and obsessively counting his toes in the morning to check they had not turned white, or worse, black and necrotic. It had been a time of terrors, avoiding giant wolves and bears that prowled the wilderness looking for their next meal; or running for your life from grey and white striped sabre-toothed tigers that relentlessly stalked their prey. A period where a *Bearer* and his magical ledger were revered and respected; where heavy browed natives shared magical secrets using little figurines woven from sticks and grasses. Richard sighed longingly. Why should he be the one without such magic, when acolytes like Marcus misused and neglected it?

Brother Richard opened his eyes with a start, realising he had been lingering too long thinking of those days. It seemed that he was always destined to lose the power given to him: the role of a *Bearer*, the power of a magical wish, a congregation that revered him, his beautiful church on Stratholme. Well this time it was going to be different. Marcus had a power he was incapable of using, a power that was languishing somewhere in this room. As the only senior figure from the order, it fell to Richard to liberate the tome and restore the blessed religious icon to its former glory.

He pulled himself back to his feet and looked around the cabin once again; trying to get into the mind of the youth that he was spending so much time with, a mind he had spent so long trying to impart knowledge and insight to. Prayer beads suspended from a hook in the wall gently rolled backwards and forwards to the lulling movement of the galleon, their hand polished surfaces testament to the dedication of Marcus to his religion. The sound was almost hypnotic, slide, bump, slide, bump; Richard turned away and then stopped. Why did the beads bump?

The priest moved closer, watching the beads roll and then jump, as if bouncing out from a depression in the wood. He pushed the jewellery aside, running his finger across the depression before pressing down hard into the worn knot in the plank. Could it be this easy? Secretly in his heart, he hoped it was so. The wooden panel squeaked loudly in protest then popped out, revealing a dark space hidden behind.

Richard's heart rate quickened as he blindly reached inside, not daring to believe he had been so successful, only to snatch his hand back in pain as an electrical shock burnt his probing fingers. He sucked angrily at his singed skin then scooted up his robe to cover his hand as he delved into the shadows, this time successfully bringing Marcus's prized book out into the open. He lay the volume down with reverence on top of the bunk and took a moment to take in the battered tome. The book had clearly seen better days, the blue cover scuffed and stained, the imprint of the monk and knights travelling across the leather surface now ingrained with dirt and grease. The locking clasps encircling the volume appeared tarnished and at one lock, there appeared to be a deep scratch as if someone had tried to tamper with the mechanism.

The priest tutted to himself; his eyes moist with tears at seeing the beautiful book mistreated in this way, it was a desecration of the worst kind. All books impart knowledge to the reader and as such, they deserved treatment of the utmost respect. Marcus clearly appeared to show no respect to the magical gift bestowed upon him. Indeed, whenever Richard had pushed Marcus to use his powers to control the volume, he had regarded the book with unmistakeable fear and loathing. The priest knew all too well the beauty and power this book contained, nestled between the battered façade of its scuffed and worn covers. He also knew that with care and devotion, all of the damage to its surface would begin to repair. It just needed to be in the right hands, wielded by someone who rightfully belonged as *Bearer.*

Using his stained robe to protect his fingers, Richard turned the book over examining the damage and wincing as if witnessing gaping wounds on an injured charge. He tried to open the book, testing the locking clasps only to find they resisted his attempts at entry. The priest was not disappointed, he expected Marcus would protect his book, preventing access to its pages by keeping it locked. However, what Marcus failed to know was that locking the book only prevented entry from people who had no idea how the magical tome was constructed.

Flipping the book up so the spine stood uppermost, Richard traced his fingers along the faded lettering to locate two small metal studs at either end. Several *Bearers* had refused to open their tomes when they returned to the monastery following journeys of discovery, addicted to the power and comfort their charges bestowed but Richard knew exactly how to access them.

Abbot Brialin had opened one once in a fit of rage, after caving in the skull of an acolyte who no longer wished to be part of the order, only to find after the novice was dead that the volume remained locked and the key lost. Consumed in his fury, the Abbot had dismantled the book as Richard had looked on, rage dulling the Abbots awareness of those around him until after the deed was complete. Richard furrowed his brow as he remembered. If he was right, he had to press just about here.

The priest pushed down hard and felt the studs beneath his fingertips depress with a click, then he slid one finger across the spine to push lightly at the edge of the uppermost locking clasp, before lightly tracing his finger down to the bottom clasp and repeating the same action. There was another soft click as something disengaged out of sight beneath the spine.

Richard smiled as memories returned to him, tapping the recessed edges of the spine where the pages met, before turning the book onto its side and pushing the original two metal studs again. The locking bars suddenly detached from the surface of the book, releasing a small cloud of dust before sliding down the ledger to clink together on the bunk, allowing the priest to lift the pages completely free from the clasps as a loose folio of work that was no longer secured and now available to open at the priest's whim.

With feelings of great trepidation, Richard eased open the front cover and stared into the darkness of the cell painstakingly illustrated across the front page. He held his breath, waiting for the magic of the book to transform the painting into reality, his eyes absorbing every detail, every nuance of the stone cell; the discarded game pieces left on the floor, the sparse orange lichen patches growing on the stonework in the top left corner of the page, even the glistening patches of moisture on the walls under the bunk at the bottom right corner. Richard was mesmerised by the magical book, the artwork within intoxicating him with the magical and destructive power it contained. How different it was to his own volume all those years ago?

His own *Bearer's* tome had depicted a large tent rather than a cell, with creamy billowing canvas rustling in the background, rich opulent rugs on the ground with fine grains of desert sand tracked in across the deep pile, leaving footprints that could be dispelled with the slightest breeze. His holy knights slept together on bedrolls placed around a smoking fire pit, over which a roasting animal was slowly being turned on a spit. When the priest was cold from exploring the tundra, he used to open the book to not only feel the warmth from the fire but to also share tales with his knights and dispel his feelings of isolation.

As far as Richard knew, there were other magical books in existence with illustrations as varied as a ship hold, a cave and even a back room in a tavern, although Richard had never been fortunate enough to glimpse them all and was sure these were but a select few of the powerful icons out there.

A pungent smell wafted up into his face as his eyes scanned the shadows looking for the knights that should have been waiting attentively within. Richard wrinkled his face with disgust, it was a smell of rotting, a stench of disease. A shuffling figure moved slowly forwards from a bunk at the back of the cell, coughing heavily and gasping loudly for breath at each step.

As the shape drew closer, the magic of the book transformed the illustration into reality, allowing Richard to hear the unmistakable rattling wheeze of a person with serious respiratory problems. The priest could not prevent himself drawing back from the book as the stench of decay washed out over him. It was foul, leaving a taste that coated the tongue and inflamed the nostrils, almost making Richard gag with its intensity.

The shadowy shape moved into the pool of light beaming down into the illustration from the open book cover and slowly lifted his head to regard the reader. Richard gasped in shock, barely recognising the face of Bartholomew as the emaciated knight blinked up at him. He looked like a corpse, his eyes sunk, hair matted, canker sores oozing across his face and neck. His tabard stained and holed, chain and plate mail spotted with corrosion.

"Bartholomew what has happened to you?" Richard groaned in horror. "How could Marcus neglect you so?"

"Is it time Brother Richard? I stand ready for my *Bearer's* instructions" Bartholomew rasped, his voice gravelly and gasping, his eyes rapidly blinking in the brightness before opening wider when he realised there was only one member of the order standing before him. "Where is the *Bearer*? Where is Brother Marcus? I am sorry but he is the only one entrusted to open this book. Please explain how it can be that you are here without him? I must warn you the book will defend itself if you wish us harm."

"Brother Marcus has deserted you." Richard said calmly. "I am afraid he has neglected you and left you all to perish. I am here to save you." Bartholomew shook his head sadly, his matted hair crawling with what appeared to be lice.

"No one but Abbot Brialin can break the sacred bond we hold with our *Bearer*." Bartholomew stated darkly, licking his lips and scratching at a sore on his unshaven cheek. "I wish it were not so but this is the way of things. So it is written, so it is done. We must adhere to Brother Marcus's orders unless we consider them counter to the aims and dictates of the order or if Abbot Brialin commands it so."

"I bring sad news Bartholomew." Richard replied, pausing as a wracking cough sounded and a feeble hand raised from one of the bunks behind the illustrated knight. He waited, weighing the words in his mind, carefully considering the consequences before continuing. "Abbot Brialin is dead. I… I am in charge now. How else do you think I could open this book and talk to you as I am."

Bartholomew's eyes widened and for a second, he appeared like a cornered animal, anxious for a way out of his predicament but unsure that the way offered was something much worse. Richard tried to contain his elation at the sight. The knight was clearly desperate for help; it would only take the smallest of nudges but the priest knew he had to be very careful for his plan to work.

"Marcus is off exploring the jungle miles from here, no doubt drawing his little pictures and scribbling notes in his ledger. It pains me to say this but I believe he has forsaken you and gone off in search of an exotic plant. I am as disturbed by this as yourself. He has left no instruction as to your care, neither has he dictated a route of succession if he were to fail to return."

"No succession?" the diseased knight wobbled, putting his hand out to steady himself. "Then what happens if something unexpected were to befall him?" He looked up at Richard, his face pleading. The priest sat quietly, allowing the knight to make his own assumptions, his face moving through a series of distraught emotions. "If he has abandoned us to our fate then we are doomed."

"I am afraid that the Abbot may have been naive in choosing Marcus as your *Bearer*. I understand he had been unwell at the end." The priest stated calmly, his face a mask hiding the deceit beneath.

"I was not aware the Abbot was ill." Bartholomew commented. "He appeared well enough when we razed the village of Stratholme." Richard paused with his mouth open, cursing his stupidity at elaborating the tale with such foolish fantasy. How easy it had been to forget that the knights had been present during the battle at the windmill, the sacking of Stratholme and the arson of his previous home, with the Abbot at their side.

"I... I mean, he was not thinking clearly." The priest stated, his words coming out in a rush. "The village and the church were both mine, filled with dedicated worshippers who were adding strength to our order. Clearly Marcus fed falsehoods to the Abbot's ear to make him act in that destructive and wasteful manner."

"I do not understand this." The knight frowned, appearing confused and began to pace about the floor. "Did Marcus say why he has left us? I know he is a weak *Bearer* but he is no threat to the order and certainly not someone Brialin would have allowed to easily sway his opinion. You must be mistaken."

Richard realised that his attempts at swaying the opinion of the knight were failing. He needed something to push his point. He looked into the book, his eyes taking in the groaning figures in the shadows, the restless emaciated figures on the bunks. All of this power wasting away, all of this magic failing! If he did not tread carefully yet another opportunity to claw back what was rightfully his, would literally slip through his fingers. He started to fidget with the hem of his robe, feeling the crackling energy of the book beneath his fingers threatening to shock him through the material. It was building in intensity as the distrust of the knight grew. He needed something, anything. Then it hit him.

"I do not believe Marcus is weak." Richard began, a shake evident in his voice as he fought to control his emotions. "I believe he is a deceiver, a charlatan. He has been against us all from the beginning. Is it possible he was a spy sent amongst our ranks? Look at how he mistreats you. No true *Bearer* would ever betray the bond of trust between himself and his book. I mean, how can you fight for the order in such a pitiful condition? You face certain destruction within days, sooner if you were summoned to fight. How can you win glory for the church in this sorry condition? I am incandescent with rage at our betrayal, at how easily we have been duped. This has to stop now."

Bartholomew stopped pacing and stared back up at Richard, still clearly unconvinced by the priest's tale. This was infuriating! What did it take to sway this damned book and the holy knights within? Time was passing by; The party could return at any moment and Marcus would discover his underhand desperate actions. He needed the book secured and joined to him swiftly before it was too late.

"I cannot spend much longer talking to you, for I am needed elsewhere." Richard stated, deciding that the only other option would be to feign an element of disinterest. "You need to make a decision on behalf of your men, Sir knight. Either you accept my leadership, or I will have no choice but to leave you to die. My time is limited."

"It will mean breaking my word and my bond." Bartholomew replied, still clearly conflicted. "Without the direct orders of Abbot Brialin I cannot remove Marcus as *Bearer* for there is no one that can replace him."

"Abbot Brialin is dead!" Richard shouted, his patience at an end. "You will all be dead if you continue to delay in this pointless manner. I admire your dedication to your role but to do so at the risk to your colleagues, to cause the death of your friends. I have spent long enough talking to you, I am offering myself as Marcus's replacement but you must act fast. I cannot linger."

Richard grabbed the front cover of the book, feeling the angry sparks racing across the surface and smelt the scent of burning as the defensive energies of the book charred the fibres of his robe. He looked down at the illustration one more time, then moved to close the cover, the sunlight from the portal in the cabin wall slowly moving across the bottom of the page, trailing permanent darkness behind it.

"I'm so sorry." Richard whispered, although it was not clear exactly if the priest was sorry about what he was about to do, or that he was sorry he had failed in securing the book for himself.

"Wait!" Bartholomew screamed as the shadows engulfed him. "Wait, Brother Richard. Just a moment longer I beg of you." Richard gasped, surprising himself when he realised that he had been holding his breath. He opened the page again, carefully guarding his hands as he allowed the sunlight to stream into the book and illuminate the cell.

"If Abbot Brialin is dead and you are his successor I suppose we must arrive at some arrangement for the good of the church and the order." The knight stated desperately. "In these exceptional circumstances, when the *Bearer* is absent, or in imminent danger and has not taken steps to arrange for succession the good of the order must come first." Richard tried to hide his smile at the success of his manipulation. This was exactly what he wanted to hear.

"This is what I have been trying to tell you." the priest replied, "I have been a *Bearer* in the past. I am already well versed in the care and attention you need to return this volume to its former glory. The sacred bond of *Bearer* must be maintained by swiftly appointing a replacement. I humbly offer myself for this position. I solemnly swear that no harm shall come to your pages. I shall pledge my time in repairing this ledger and that none shall gaze upon the image of your holy illustrations unless it is for the glory of the order. I shall sacrifice my life before I allow anyone unworthy to observe your brilliance."

Richard looked around the room, knowing what was needed next but not seeing the means to do it. Damn! He was so close. He was not going to let this opportunity pass due to a technicality. He placed his little finger into his own mouth and bit down hard, tasting the coppery tang of blood welling from the wound, even as he cried out in pain.

"I offer my blood to seal the bond." Richard promised through a crimson smile. "My oath is made before you all." He held his finger over the portrait and let it drip blood slowly into the picture from the tip of his macerated digit.

Bartholomew nodded his head solemnly, observing the priest's actions and satisfied they were correct and true. "Then let it be shown in these pages that the book has passed, the *Bearer* replaced. May St Fraiser watch over us, may his words protect us and his glory guide our path."

Richard could not believe this was happening, it was like a dream. Power and meaning were coming back into his life. He could not, would not, risk losing it.

"I am proud of your dedication Sir Knight." Brother Richard stated calmly. "May it remain so following the orders I shall give you." Bartholomew dropped to the floor, his head held down as the words of praise fell about him. "Now let us heal your wounds, calm your souls and make this order great again." The illustrated knight raised his head, looking up towards his saviour with relief upon his face.

"I am ready *Bearer*!" He replied with due reverence. "My knights are here awaiting your command." Richard took a deep breath of relief, then pulled his robe aside, grabbing the leaves of the damaged volume with his bare hands, half expecting the powerful shock to slam him across the small cabin, only to find, much to his relief, a warm trickle of power running up his arms instead.

"Then what are we waiting for?" he replied menacingly. "Come, take my hand."

* * * * * *

Although the banquet hall at the palace was one of open air and light, some said even a delight to the senses in how it imparted a beautiful view of the Taurean city and its surroundings; the main throne room was intentionally designed to be its opposite, a place of darkness, built to intimidate any who entered its space. The walls, hung with dark tapestries, which muted sound and instilled disquiet upon visitors who found they gazed upon scenes of bloodletting and torture, conquest and gladiatorial sport, undertaken by the fiercest of Minotaur, painstakingly embroidered in vivid threads of colour.

Torches flickered in sconces set around the walls, creating pale islands of sickly yellow upon a wooden herringbone patterned floor, that amplified each footstep upon its surface with an ominous sound. The only natural light came through a stained-glass window set high above the throne in the ceiling, making it appear as if this seat of power sat in a tight beam of light whilst the subjects around it lingered in shadow.

The throne was set back and raised on a dais, it was an imposing piece of hacked marble that was all hard angles, functional but not attractive in any way and as cold and stern as the rulers who spent time sitting upon its surface. The thought of embellishment, carvings or an elaborate headrest were clearly considered unimportant when faced with the imposing nature of the monsters that ruled Taurean from here.

Mora sat on the throne, trying to ignore the numbing sensation spreading across her buttocks, listening with half an ear to the rambling skinny Minotaur pacing nervously before her and wishing that she had had the foresight to bring a cushion to sit on. She had several pressing things to attend to but knew it was important to at least show some attention to the creature gushing pleasantries before her. After all, this tournament would allow her to abdicate gracefully once Drummon took his rightful place here, living out her final years pampered on one of the more pleasant islands nearby, her every whim catered for, her every desire met.

"The labyrinth has been cleared as instructed Matriarch." The games master reported. "Any human vagrants using it as a home have been rounded up and I am sure you will be delighted with the ideas I have for using them to light up the celebrations. We have assembled the viewing stations along the top walls of the labyrinth and are already selling tickets to the wealthier members of Taurean society. The killing areas are being populated with the jungle creatures supplied by the Prince Regent and may I say there are some excellent specimens that are sure to keep the crowd entertained."

Mora shuffled on the throne, making the underweight Minotaur pause in his report. He looked nervously towards his ruler and then, after realising that no displeasure was directed his way cleared his throat and continued his handover.

"May I say that this celebration looks to be unmatched by any other in living memory. The populous will be talking of this day for years to come."

The matriarch looked down over her nose at the snivelling games master and attempted to smile but this slimy creature showing her homage was so far below her station that she decided it was not worth the effort.

"Are the traps prepared inside the pyramid? There must be no malfunctions, and the ways to bypass them must be exactly as I have specified." The Matriarch stated. "The people will want our new ruler to be cunning as well as strong. He must show intelligence as well as ruthlessness."

"Everything will be as you command Matriarch. If you like I can use some of the vagrants to test the mechanisms? I personally guarantee you shall not be disappointed."

"Make sure that I am not." Mora warned. "Or it will be you who tests the traps... although I would ensure you have your eyes gouged out before you do, after all we want the test to be fair and you already know the answers to the riddles." The Matriarch finally allowed herself to smile as the games master gulped, his Minotaur eyes rolling in worry.

Movement from across the room caught Mora's eye and she stared out into the shadows over to the huge double doors where Aelius stood guard. Drummon burst into the room, his black pelt flecked with sweat stains and grime, his boots trailing thick mud from the jungle across the wooden floor. He had a ridiculous grin on his face which instantly put her on guard. It could only mean one thing. He had done something stupid.

"You may leave." Mora gestured with the back of her hand at the games master, not wanting him to be around to witness what was bound to be something she would need to sort out. "You may kiss my ring."

The Minotaur moved forwards to offer his allegiance, however the Matriarch had no interest in watching him and was instead trying to imagine what her son had done this time. The games master cleared his throat nervously, drawing Mora's attention back to the Minotaur.

"Why have you not left my presence?" she snarled. The games master paled and began to shake.

"You don't appear to be wearing your ceremonial ring." He stammered. The Matriarch looked down at her offered hand and noticed that her official ring was missing from her finger. How had that happened? Her brow creased in concern, making the Minotaur visibly quake in his boots.

"Just go you fool, before I lose my patience." Drummon arrived at the throne bubbling with enthusiasm and dropped to his knees to offer his dedication for the shortest length of time before rising enthusiastically back to his feet.

"What brings my son into my presence this afternoon?" Mora asked, her mind still trying to fathom out where she had lost her jewellery. She knew she had put it on her finger before she left her bedroom and was starting to retrace the day in her mind. "I hear your expedition went well. It appears the games master is thrilled with the exotic specimens you have captured and brought from the jungle."

"That's not all." Drummon gushed. "I've solved our problem regarding Kristoph. He won't be coming back." Mora paused in her recollection of her journey through the palace in her mind's eye. What did he just say?

"Excuse me? What do you mean he will not be coming back?"

"Well I gave him directions to the Nirschl's lair, then I sent three of my crack troops to finish off whatever crew manage to survive, if any." Drummon beamed, clearly extremely pleased with himself. The Matriarch took a deep breath and raised her hand to her forehead, rubbing the skin just above her right eye and below her curled horn. Mora suddenly felt she could feel a migraine coming on. It was at times like this that she seriously questioned what she had seen in the bull that had fathered her two sons. Clearly the pedigree had not been as pure as the papers had suggested.

"Drummon you do realise how hard I have been working to build up your standing amongst the people of Taurean, despite the fact they all think of you as a lout who is stupid and does not care anything for them."

"Well that's because I don't." Drummon replied. "Hang on a minute, who said I was stupid? I'll pound them." His face turned thunderous in a second.

"Come on tell me who says all of these things?" he roared. "Let me crush them and break their legs."

"Yes of course you will." Mora shook her head, then instantly regretted the action. Her head hurt so much whenever her son was near. An image of the Halfling from the jail cell entered her mind, of him holding her hand.

"Ashe Wolfsdale." She whispered. "That damned thieving Halfling!"

"I shall crush Ashe Wolfsdale." Drummon announced loudly. "I shall make him rue the day he was born. I will make him suffer so much. Umm, who is Ashe Wolfsdale?" He looked about confused as if expecting this slanderer to be near at hand so the punishment could be instant and devastating.

"Everyone says you are stupid!" The Matriarch snapped. "Because it happens to be true! You are stupid and thoughtless. You are a brute who worries more about where the next ale is coming from rather than what is going on around you. This is why I have been unable to abdicate earlier because if you were to assume the throne as a right of bloodline the citizens of Taurean would rebel and the Minotaur could feasibly be overthrown. If only I had birthed a cow rather than an imbecilic bull." Drummon looked at his mother in horror, shocked by the outburst.

"Kristoph is needed to give you legitimacy." The Matriarch continued. "With him here you have a worthy opponent to beat. No one can dispute the fact you are the rightful heir. No one can doubt your right of accession. We need Kristoph alive to make this happen and you have just instructed him to journey into the deadliest area of the jungle. I told you to arrange for an accident to happen to his friends, not to him. We need to isolate him from the support of the crew of the *El Defensor* and weaken his resolve so that his family are his only confidants before we arrange for his demise at the Labyris tournament. You truly are as stupid as they say." Drummon felt the words falling on his body like lashes from a barbed whip. He flinched at his mother's displeasure as the words rained down on him.

"Take a platoon of troops and go back into the jungle. Find your brother and bring him back here safe and sound. Make up any excuse, throw yourself upon his mercy but I want you to convince him this was all a huge mistake and that no harm was meant to come upon him. Your regency depends on him believing this. You had better pray that he is still alive and well."

"Mother I promise I shall try to do better." Drummon replied head hung low in supplication. "Just tell me where that Ashe Wolfsdale is and I shall start to set things right." Mora ignored her posturing child and looked up at the stained-glass window above her, noting where the sun appeared to be shining through the glass. Noon was fast approaching.

"Aelius, come here swiftly." The Halfling had but moments to live but she did not want to find her ring falling into the wrong hands. The guard ran over as fast as his aged legs would allow.

"Matriarch what is your bidding?"

"The Halfling prisoner is about to be executed. I believe I have inadvertently left my ring in his cell. Please be kind enough to retrieve it, so that the royal seal does not fall into the wrong hands."

"As you command." Aelius replied turning sharply and marching back across the hall, signalling to two guards from the shadows to join him. Mora watched the captain of the guard leave the room and thought about the Halfling dangling from the end of a rope. She imagined his little legs kicking out, his neck snapping like dry kindling and his face going blue as the body beneath him failed to draw in enough air through his crushed larynx.

"What is it with people in this throne room." The Matriarch stated with an icy undertone. Drummon looked up at her, holding his hands together much like he used to do as a baby calf. "Why are you still here? Get back to the jungle and find your brother!" Drummon physically jumped before turning and marching swiftly for the door, bellowing out for a runner to send word to assemble the troops ready to accompany him in his search. She watched until her son had left the throne room then rubbed at her finger where her missing ring normally rested. The Halfling would be dangling from the rope at any moment. Those little legs kicking about now.

This time her smile came swiftly.

Chapter Twenty-Nine

Aradol crashed through the vegetation, slipping and sliding down the slope and out into the clearing, just in time to witness Ives drop face first into the crimson orchid bed. The merchant appeared to twitch as the blooms shook violently around him, then stilled, confirming Aradol's worst fears that something terrible had befallen his friend. He took his first step towards Ives and immediately sank to mid-calf in the mud, his ornate armour adding extra weight and dragging him down into the engulfing morass.

"No Ives, no not you!" the young warrior gasped, struggling to fight his way through the noxious mire, blinking back the tears. Aradol offered silent prayers to any gods who would listen, that he would reach his friend in time, despite knowing that the violent jerking of Ives body signified that no matter how hard he tried to push through the mud, it would never be enough. "Oh damn this armour!" Aradol yelled, struggling with his ornate breastplate, before wrenching it free and snapping one of the leather ties in the process. He flung the armour back towards the muddy bank behind him and started to wriggle out of his chainmail vest, leaving him wearing just a rust-stained undershirt.

"I am coming Ives, I am coming! Hold on!" Aradol turned around and shouted, almost losing his balance in the slick mud. "Commagin, Rauph I need help down here!" He resumed his slog through the mud, turning one way and then the other, wrestling with his gauntlets and bracers and flinging them back towards the dry ground. The discarded armour clanked onto the slope, just in front of Rauph, as the navigator blundered down the slope in response to Aradol's call.

The Minotaur was initially annoyed he had needed to leave the battle with the Nirschl behind him and then became confused, as he took in the form of Aradol appearing to go for a swim in the swamp, clad only in his undershirt. Rauph's soft brown eyes quickly scanned the area ahead of the young warrior and at first noted the sweep of scarlet orchids, before his gaze fell upon the body of Ives lying half-submerged within the flowers.

Aradol continued to push ahead, calling Ives' name as he waded through the mud. The merchant's body jerked again, as if something were attempting to pull it further into the vivid display of blooms, eliciting another cry of anguish from the young man at the hopelessness of his cause.

Commagin slithered to a stop beside Rauph and groaned aloud at what he observed. The dwarf had witnessed too many corpses in his life not to recognise that Ives had breathed his last. He sadly pushed his glasses back up his nose and took in the area, then rapidly swung the *Lady Janet* back up against his shoulder, peering along the sights of the weapon, his body instantly alert. The dwarf swept the crossbow from left to right, drawing a bead on everything that moved, his lips mouthing the question no one had yet asked. If Ives was dead, where was the creature that had killed him?

The swamp lay churned up near the dead merchant, with one clear set of tracks leading back from his corpse towards the floundering figure of Aradol who was ploughing his way through the swamp towards his friend, yet there appeared to be no sign of any other tracks. That meant whatever had killed their shipmate was either airborne, in which case it should have been on top of Ives body right now or circling above, or it was hiding somewhere in the nodding orchid blooms or even below the clinging surface of the swamp. Aradol had stupidly discarded much of his armour to speed his passage through the mud, unaware of the danger he could be heading towards. He needed to warn him!

Aradol remained totally focused on his desperate slog towards Ives, aware in the back of his mind that Commagin was yelling at him but too immersed in his grief at his friend's fate to care. Pushing through the swamp was rapidly sapping the young man's strength. His lungs gasped with each breath, as if inhaling liquid fire, yet he refused to give in and resolutely carried on. He finally drew level with Ives' leg, noting the pale skin was already starting to turn mottled from lack of circulation, a death's shadow of bruising forming where the blood was now settling in his corpse without his heart's beat to pump it.

The knight reached out, grabbing Ives soiled tunic with his free hand in an attempt to turn him over and release his face from the muck. As he did so, the scarlet orchids shook violently, spewing forth hundreds of miniature darting and snapping baby Nirschl heads, their strikes focused on the warm flesh of a prey that had foolishly wandered too close. The warrior snatched his hand back in horror, the immature hydrae attacks spitting out sticky venom that missed Aradol's exposed skin by inches, yet still set his arms stinging.

Aradol's antique sword swung in, decapitating several small heads and setting the miniature monsters squealing in pain. Other juvenile hydrae darted in from the sides, eager for fresh flesh to feast upon, their open jaws striking out towards the young man, straining for a tantalising bite. The knight tried to backpedal away from the monstrous mass of snakes but the clinging mud stopped him in his tracks, leaving him mired like a fly in a spider's web. He suddenly found himself fighting a defensive battle, parrying lunges, darting heads and snapping fangs, his exhausted actions those of a desperate man who faced one choice: Fight... or die.

Something smashed past Aradol's head, scything through the nearest orchid blooms, sending bright blood red petals spinning up into the air and barrelling several baby Nirschl over. A roaring Minotaur followed closely behind, charging past the immobilised fighter, pushing him over to one side with such force that Aradol crashed into the mud with a wet splash. Rauph paused only to snatch up the venom streaked metal object he had just used as a makeshift missile before he charged ahead, smashing, slicing and crushing everything within reach.

Stunned by his heroic friend's actions, Aradol looked on in awe as the Minotaur laid waste with the makeshift weapon in his hands, filling the air with ever louder distressed sounds of wailing baby Nirschl. Rauph roared in anger, adding his own voice to the discordant choir, daring his foes to face him and receive a reckoning for hurting his friends.

The Minotaur's eyes blazed with fury as he slashed and chopped at the creatures squealing in terror within the orchids, his muscles rippling with every strike, his armour and hair hissing and smoking in several places where Nirschl venom had been spat across his torso. Rauph seemed unfazed by the injuries he had suffered and continued on his rampage regardless. He truly looked the hero the tales rumoured him to be.

This was Kristoph reborn, caring compassionate and terrible to behold, facing overwhelming odds with what looked like a badly dented tea tray.

Aradol desperately tried to pull himself out of the sticky mud, struggling to stand properly to help defend his fallen friend's body without falling over but he was simply too exhausted to help. He had fought so hard and now found himself openly weeping at the frustration of futilely battling an emotionless swamp that sapped his strength and used the knight's crippling grief as its ally. A sturdy hand came down on Aradol's arm, gripping him firmly before helping to ease him from the swamp's cloying embrace.

"Come on lad; let's get you out of here." Commagin shouted in Aradol's ear as he struggled to ease his friend back towards the shallows but the young warrior refused to retreat, vainly tugging at the corpse of his dead friend with mud-slicked exhausted arms.

"I won't leave him here!" He screamed. "I'm not leaving him here to be eaten!" Commagin's eyes shone as he took in the resolute stubbornness of the distraught young man and instantly knew it was pointless to argue with him. He swallowed hard, trying to dislodge the lump that he felt in his throat and pushed his way forward through the sludge to stand alongside him and help.

"Here let me help." The engineer gently offered, noting that Aradol was staring intently at the bloodied mess of wounds upon Ives' body where his corpse had been pulled free of the orchid patch. A mighty roar sounded behind them, from back up the slope where they had originally fought with the mother Nirschl, causing Commagin to turn and see the trees and bushes snapping and cracking as something huge slithered their way.

Rauph appeared oblivious to the approaching danger, lost in his battle rage, he continued to crash through the mud, sending baby Nirschl slithering away as fast as they could wriggle, his ferocious battle cry finally making Aradol blink as if he were coming out of a trance.

"What are you staring at Aradol?" Commagin probed, realising shock was setting in and trying to remain calm for his shipmate. The Dwarf tugged as hard as he could to free Ives from the clinging swamp, grunting with the effort but he needed Aradol's help or he would never succeed. As he struggled, Rauph struck a baby Nirschl with his metal tray, a resounding crash rang out as the infant serpent was sent spinning through the air, hissing in pain.

"Come on there is no time for daydreaming son; we need to get out of here." The engineer prompted. "Let's do this together. On three, okay? Then we can get our friend out of this mess and back to dry land. People are going to pay for this you mark my words."

"I just can't help thinking that tray looks familiar." Aradol gasped, clearly not comprehending a word Commagin had uttered as he floundered through the bog.

"It should do." Commagin shouted over the tumultuous noise of the approaching terror. "It's your breastplate!"

* * * * * *

Marcus darted left and right, Nirschl jaws snapping shut all about him, each one hissing in frustration as the young monk used every trick that he could, to avoid the slimy creatures trying to eat him. Where was everyone? Each time he tried to get a glimpse across the swamp to find his friends, he ended up seeing flattened jungle foliage, rolling coils of hydra and yet more stagnant swamp. Was he fighting this damned monster just by himself? Why was no one coming to help him?

The monk pivoted on one foot and kicked out at a snapping jaw, catching the surprised hydra right on the nostril, making it snort and shake its head as it backed up sharply. Marcus followed through, dropping under the shocked Nirschl's jaw as it drew back, just as another hydra head slammed into the ground behind him biting and nosing at the mud in search of its elusive prey.

A mass of slime-coated coils rolled above Marcus as he continued to dodge backwards and forwards beneath the Nirschl's body, the girth of the monster blotting out the sky as the monk twisted and turned, matching his move with the undulating body of the serpent above him. A loud angry hissing sounded from behind, revealing yet another hydra head flattening itself down to slither under itself and skim along the ground, tongue flickering in and out rapidly as it tasted the air and arrowed towards the young novice.

Marcus knew he had seconds to spare as his hiding place rapidly shrunk in size as the two Nirschl heads rubbed against each other in passing. He dodged right, then holding his hands over his head dashed left, out into the open, mud and slime kicking up behind him as he ran across the debris littered ground.

A low wail echoed hauntingly through the jungle, its origin from somewhere ahead of the monk. Marcus found himself running from a known terror behind, towards an unknown terror ahead. He leapt over a fallen tree trunk and found himself sliding down into the large nest he had spotted earlier, pieces of fragile shell and gnawed bone snapping and spinning away from his feet as he slid to the bottom. His eyes darted rapidly about the depression, seeking some sort of refuge from the rampaging Nirschl. Should he keep running and risk discovery, or take his chances and hide hoping the monster, by some miracle, would pass him by and keep moving?

The massive tail of the creature thudded down in front of him, directly into the centre of the nest, blade-like spikes quivering as it started to tighten and flex upon itself, helping to draw the rest of the huge Nirschl's gigantic body along the ground. Marcus retreated back towards the edge of the depression and started scrabbling back up the slope towards the terrifying rumble of the approaching monster. He threw himself over the lip of the nest and rolled under the tree trunk, just as the first flickering tongue nosed over the top of the fallen log.

The monk held his breath as the immense monster started to slither right over him. Scales rasped noisily against the trunk as the Nirschl dragged itself inch by inch over the tree. Swamp muck and slime dripped off the underbelly of the hydra as it slithered past, showering down onto Marcus's hiding place in a rotting deluge that made the monk want to gag. The daylight disappearing above him as more and more of the immense serpent slithered across his hiding place.

The novice took a deep breath, not daring to make a sound as the full weight of the Nirschl crushed down upon the fallen tree. The huge constricting coils of the serpent touched the ground, plunging Marcus into a terrifying darkness that amplified every sound of the hydra's advance.

Marcus had never experienced the paralysing fear of claustrophobia until that moment; the terrifying thought that the monster could smother him, crush him to a pulp or simply pause in its travels long enough for him to run out of air, almost paralyzed the monk. He fought back the unsettlingly image of clawing at the scaled body of the creature with bloodied nails until he expired from asphyxiation and instead struggled to remain calm and face his fears. Despite his resolve, he suddenly found himself gasping for breath as his anxiety threatened to smother him.

The tree trunk cracked like dry kindling, the explosiveness of the clear sound making Marcus flinch and scream in terror. He lifted up his hand in reflex, searching in the darkness for some sign to reassure himself the tree would remain true and shelter him from the monster, only to find his hands hitting the trunk a lot sooner than he had expected. Even as his fingertips explored the rough bark, he could feel the undeniable pressure upon his hands as the tree continued to bear down.

He was going to be crushed alive! The weight of the Nirschl was going to push the tree down into the soft ground of the swamp and squash him like a bug! Marcus tried to move one way and found himself up against the embankment but the trunk had already grounded on this side and was creating a small avalanche of slime that cascaded down against his shoulder and face, making the monk spit and cough. He tried to move the other way and found himself coming up against the rough scales of the Nirschl as it slowly slithered by, causing him to recoil in revulsion.

The monk kicked out screaming but in the midnight darkness, he had no target to hit, no foe to slay. Marcus felt his elbows hitting the mud at either side of him as the trunk pushed ever lower. The panic was all encompassing, the blood-curdling sound of the monster moving over him making it impossible to remain calm, the very presence of the Nirschl threatening to unravel his delicate psyche.

The tree groaned again, further cracks sounding through the darkness as it shifted above him. Although he could not see it, Marcus knew the rough bark was mere inches from his face. He turned his head to one side willing the tree to stop its descent, praying to St Fraiser for mercy as debris rained upon his skin, his breath now coming in ragged gasps. He was losing control! The rough bark of the tree trunk touched his ear. Marcus could not contain himself any longer. He opened his mouth and screamed.

* * * * * *

"Where do you think it's going?" Weyn asked, as Mathius pulled him to his feet. "Come to think of it, where has everyone else gone? Did they all get invited to a party and forget to tell us?"

Mathius ignored Weyn's pitiful attempt at humour and set to brushing what mud and debris he could from his clothes as he surveyed the battlefield. The Nirschl was slithering away, clearly badly injured from the fight, its gigantic form oozing over the lip of the nest he had discovered earlier.

Although the Nirschl heads were quick and lithe, the main bulk of the monster's body was so big and bulky that it appeared to be using its spiked tail to gain leverage in the floor of the swamp to propel itself through the muck. Even as he watched, the tail reared up into the air and shot forwards, slamming into the ground with such force that Mathius felt it through the soles of his sodden boots.

Several of the hydra heads were badly injured a few oozing stumps sporting tiny sprouting hydra heads that snapped and squealed at each other whilst the bigger intact heads did their best to ignore them. Other heads lay on the ground clearly dead, one with a broken jaw, another with an eye hanging free from its orbit, the necks dragging through the mud like unwanted anchors making it difficult for the Nirschl to advance.

"Could it be retreating?" Mathius offered. "It doesn't look like it has fared too well against us." Weyn looked down at his arm, then gazed across the debris-strewn swamp and watched fascinated as the monster slid further into the nest and prepared to throw its tail out again.

"I don't think we fared too well either." The archer admitted. Another strange cry came from the wall of trees beyond the Nirschl and the hydra heads began to snap in clear frustration as the creature struggled to move its bulk towards the sound.

"Well I for one want to know where it's going, just in case it is gathering reinforcements." Mathius replied. "I can't see any of the others either, so we need to find them quickly and get away from here." A stray red petal danced across the assassin's vision, spinning gently towards the ground. This whole expedition had been a gigantic waste of time!

"Do we really need to follow it?" Weyn asked, frankly horrified at the thought. "Why can't we just let it be?" An unmistakeable roar rose from ahead, a sound both men instantly recognised.

"I might have known Rauph was in the thick of it." Mathius muttered. Weyn laid a hand on the assassin's arm.

"We really should wait here." The archer said. "You know how Rauph doesn't like to be disturbed when he is having fun."

"I think this is too much fun even for our Minotaur." Mathius shook his head and set off in pursuit of the slithering nightmare, moving easily in the Nirschl's wake where the foliage had been flattened. He looked back over his shoulder at Weyn and noticed the archer's crestfallen face.

"Come on!" Mathius grinned, trying to make light of the situation. "Keep up! We make a great team. I'm sure the others will need us again before we know it." Weyn shook his head in wonder at the stupidity of his own actions and then placed one soggy boot in front of the other and started to follow his shipmate.

"That's what bothers me." Weyn mumbled in reply.

* * * * * *

Rauph roared again, his angry bellow competing with the wails and squeals of the baby Nirschl slithering away from the rampaging Minotaur as fast as they could wriggle. The navigator charged up behind one, kicking the hissing mass of little heads with his boot, sending the serpent somersaulting through the air to crash into a puddle of stagnant swamp water.

The Minotaur looked about the clearing for fresh enemies to confront, his nostrils flaring, eyes wide and staring, prepared to attack anything that drew close. The baby hydrae were literally falling over themselves, to race across the mire, forging a way back towards where the mother Nirschl's lair was located. Commagin and Aradol had taken the initiative to drag Ives away from danger to the closest edge of the clearing, luckily out of the way of the slithering tide of venomous monsters scurrying rapidly away from Rauph's destructive wrath.

The trees at the edge of the clearing swung angrily from side to side, thunderous crashes and cracks, accompanied by exploding clouds of debris, rose to the heavens as the mother Nirschl finally smashed its way through. Rauph snorted loudly and heaved Aradol's breastplate after its owner, sending the battered armour skipping across the ground like a warped discus before it bounced up the slope after the men and crashed into the undergrowth. With a slow roll of his neck, the Navigator reached behind his back and drew forth his swords, hefting the weight of the blades in his hands and whipping them about as he prepared for the titanic battle he knew had yet to occur.

The Nirschl tail crashed down into the mud, sending spouts of muck rocketing into the air. Its extended spikes gouging deeply through the cloying matter before gripping firmly and flexing. It contracted in a series of ripples, the Hydra finally pulling itself through the remaining undergrowth like a living avalanche, lengths of coil flopping and sliding upon itself as the monster hissed its defiance, it's bulk crushing everything foolish enough to stand in its way.

Juvenile hydrae wriggled desperately towards their mother, cutting 'S' shaped trails across the swamp floor as they squealed for protection. Massive Nirschl heads dropped down to nudge affectionately at the distressed infants, their size making such gentle actions seem impossible. Nostrils flared at the heavy scent of blood permeating the swamp, before hard orange eyes identified their fallen brood lying broken and scattered across the ground.

A roar of anguish rocked Aradol and Commagin as they struggled up the far bank but the anger was not directed at the fleeing men, instead several sets of orange eyes narrowed in hatred on the solitary Minotaur who dared to stand his ground against them.

Rauph offered a salute with his swords, then stood with his feet apart, mud bubbling gently beneath him. He was ready for this battle. His mind was clear. There would be only one outcome. He turned side on and prepared for the strikes to come, only to hear the cry of a juvenile Nirschl from right next to his feet. The navigator took in the bobbing crimson orchids that still remained intact and used the edge of his blade to lift up a leaf and expose a small Nirschl quaking in fear beneath the nodding blooms.

The hissing of the Hydra amplified tenfold. Several Nirschl heads darted forwards, venom dripping from their jaws, fangs bared, coils bunching up behind them as they prepared to strike, yet the creature did not attack, clearly fearing for its young. Rauph pushed forward with his sword nudging the baby and registering the rage directed towards him as the Nirschl heads angled in, surrounding the Minotaur with a wall of hissing and snapping snouts.

Rauph looked from one set of eyes to the other, turning slowly and showing no fear as he regarded each one in turn, his sword never wavering from the baby at his feet. His threat was clear, the implications obvious to both parties. Yet doubts were slowly entering the Minotaur's mind. How could a monster so huge and so destructive have the potential to be so gentle and caring? It was so protective of it's young, displaying an intelligence that was unexpected. The thought sobered the Minotaur, raising yet more questions.

Moving with great care, every move exaggerated, Rauph carefully slid one of his swords back into its sheath. A blast of air ruffled Rauph's chestnut fur as one Nirschl head moved in closer, its nostrils flaring in warning. The Minotaur turned his gaze fully upon the swaying head, saying nothing with words but letting his slow actions portray what he wished to do. He held up his empty hand to show it contained no threat, then reached down towards the blood orchid under which the infant hid.

The risk to life and limb was obvious but Rauph suddenly realised he did not wish to kill this magnificent creature. He took in the destruction about him, the mangled and shattered bodies of the baby serpents, the hideous wounds inflicted on the mother Nirschl. What had this creature ever done to them apart from react in defence to their unwanted intrusion?

Hisses and snarls increased in volume but the navigator refused to acknowledge them, as the embers of his explosive rage finally extinguished, he carefully reached under the delicate bloom, gripped it firmly by the stem and lifted the plant clear from the swamp, exposing the unharmed quivering baby Nirschl beneath. Then he slowly took a step back and closed his eyes.

The Nirschl lowered one head and opened its mouth, gently scooping up its offspring, before withdrawing back through the wall of angry serpent heads that remained sentinel around Rauph. Each head hissed in warning, venom dripping from bared fangs.

Hoping that his intention was now clear for the monster to see, Rauph remained stationary; his remaining sword held down at his side, his head lowered in respect. A large Nirschl head nosed forward, sniffed at the Minotaur and then opened its jaws wide, revealing its razor-sharp fangs, complete with a flickering tongue. Rauph remained standing, not flinching as the open mouth moved closer, its fetid breath washing over him in waves. Somehow, the Navigator knew that if he so much as flinched the creature would swallow him completely without a second's hesitation.

The jaws remained wide for what seemed like an eternity and then ever so slowly, the creature withdrew, its deadly fangs clicking gently together, lips merging as one as it retreated. The monster turned its head to one side, regarding the Minotaur with an unblinking orange eye, as if the creature were memorising this intruder, remembering his scent, focusing on his appearance and making it expressly clear that if their paths were to cross again the outcome would not be as favourable.

Rauph watched the Nirschl slowly slither back across the swamp, tens of baby offspring herded before its coils. It slid through murky pools of stagnant water and merged with the jungle foliage, camouflaging itself. Wisps of mist appeared, rising like wraiths from the water and it took the Minotaur a concerted effort to identify the monster as it eerily disappeared, piece by piece.

Only when the last head pulled back into the shadows did the navigator dare let out a sigh of relief. He took one shaking step, then another, barely believing that he had dared to face the creature down. Rauph slogged his way back to the shore and climbed up to where Commagin was comforting Aradol and helping him fashion a makeshift stretcher so they could carry their fallen crewmate away from the area.

The foliage snapped and cracked to their left, causing Commagin to swing up his crossbow in alarm, fearing that the Nirschl had decided to change its mind and finish them off, only for Weyn and Mathius to burst through the foliage, dragging an exhausted and dazed Marcus between them. All three were covered head to foot in thick foul-smelling mud and slime that dripped from their clothes.

"What happened to all of you?" Commagin gasped, releasing the trigger and lowering his weapon.

"Oh you know Marcus." Mathius replied flicking some mud away from his clothes in an action as pointless as it was laughable. "Always wanting to experience things and have fun. Whilst we were all struggling with the Nirschl, he stopped to play in the mud and nearly suffocated. It was lucky I recognised his boot or we might never have found him." The smile on Mathius' face fell as his eyes took in the still form of Ives lying on the stretcher, his white sword alongside him. He instantly realised that his friend had fallen in battle and regretted his poor attempt at levity. Weyn physically winced at the sight and Marcus let out a gasp of horror, sinking to his knees in shock as the cost of their ill-fated expedition struck home.

Rauph gently placed the orchid bloom at Ives feet then turned towards the sun and stared silently off into the distance. The others took up the weight of the stretcher and began a slow sombre trek back towards the trail that had brought them to this godforsaken place, leaving the Minotaur alone with his thoughts.

The navigator appeared to stare at nothing for a long time but Rauph was not staring into the unknown; his instincts told him Taurean lay over in that direction and this was exactly where he wanted to direct his anger. For it was back in the city that he needed to go, to supply the antidote that had cost so much this day, to save his ship and his crewmates, to root out the evil that festered in the palace that rose above the downtrodden populace. He knew he could no longer make excuses on behalf of his powerful family; they were tyrants and dictators and he had to set things right.

No, Rauph was not looking at nothing; he was staring at the enemy.

Chapter Thirty

She lay on her side as if sleeping; the seductive curve of her body draped in a drifting blanket of reds and creams that constantly moved with the caressing touch of the winds from the Vaarseeti desert. Her haunting face, painstakingly sculptured from blocks of granite, once stared out towards Al Mashmaah, her expression as chilling and inanimate as the massive stone sword on which she once rested her hand.

It was rumoured you could see all the way to the ocean from the watch platform constructed behind her headband and that the beacon burning there was a guide that lifted the hearts and spirits of many a trade caravan. An ever-present flickering light that pierced the darkest veil of night, signalling to any weary traveller that their crossing of this harsh unforgiving landscape was soon to be over and that the exotic delights of Tahl Avan's mighty city awaited them. She was a symbol of hope, a statement of power, an icon of a forgotten age that guarded the trade route bringing commerce and life to a city of many splendours.

Now she lay forgotten, sleeping at the side of the trail, the passage of time and the constant erosion of the winds tumbling the sentinel from her lofty position in the heights, to now stare wide-eyed into nothing, her lips frozen open, as if in shock at her unforeseen downfall. Broken slabs of stone lay scattered across the sand, remnants of the shattered sword, stunted fingers from an outstretched hand, segments of a shapely thigh, all forming miniature dunes where the wind had swept up the desert and delivered it as an offering to the fallen titan.

Even now, her exotic face retained a poignant beauty, lying gently cushioned upon a dune, creating the illusion that the statue was merely taking a well-earned rest and that she would awaken to resume her duties when summoned. A powerful, fairy-tale image that would cause even the most hardened of travellers to pause and consider the wonders she may have gazed upon in her days of glory. Not that Octavian had taken the time to notice, seeing as he was so preoccupied following the meandering trail of a man, who, along with two horses, seemed to have no idea that the fastest way to cross the desert was to travel in a straight line!

"Where are you going now?" Octavian muttered under his breath, guiding his stallion around a mound almost as tall as himself that appeared to have once been the heel of a large boot. "Why are you going this way?"

He reached up and scratched furiously at the back of his neck, trying to quell an itch just behind his ear that was as infuriating as the old man he was following. If only he did not need to find shelter nightly to keep his horse safe from predators whilst he wandered the ruined city hunting for food. If it had been any time other than now, he would have caught up with Kerian long ago, resolved their differences and moved on to his real quest; raising the ransom for his wife and child. If only he had been more careful and not been bitten escaping from Glowme castle as he ran through the petrified Blackthorn forest fearful for his life, if only...

Octavian shook his head in frustration. That was a lot of 'ifs' and he needed to address these problems methodically, one at a time rather than try to solve them all in one go. The very thought of the impossible things he needed to achieve was almost paralysing and he could not allow himself to become despondent when his family needed him! If he really thought about it this was the reason why he was still following Kerian's meandering trail. Octavian's gut instinct told him that Kerian still had a significant part to play in his life. The man was a great fighter; apparently loyal, as he did leave supplies so the gypsy would not perish crossing the desert. He could have just left him with nothing, all alone, at the mercy of the shambling undead citizens of Tahl Avan.

He still felt bad about stealing from the knight and felt a compulsive need to make amends. There was something undeniably charismatic about Kerian's gruff voice; his moody brooding frown and the explosive temper that often grated on the gypsy's nerves. However, the man also had a softer romantic side that tempered this, a side that Kerian appeared to view as a weakness and rarely exposed, despite it being his most endearing quality. He was a companion you would want by your side when times were at their darkest. Something, Octavian was beginning to realise more and more with each passing lunar cycle.

The gypsy sighed heavily and nudged his stallion forwards, taking his eyes from the meandering trail for a moment just to check behind him and make sure there were no mummified creatures shuffling towards him from the outskirts of the necropolis. It was definitely a relief to be free from the claustrophobic haunted ruins, to be away from the constant risk of surprise attacks from bandaged corpses with screaming golden faces, or giant sentinels with swords that could slice you in two with one swing.

There was also something to be said for feeling the wind in your face, even if it was filled with tiny missiles of whistling sand. At least it did not smell of embalming spices or musty rotten spores! A smile formed on Octavian's lips. Kerian had smelt like that when he had donned the armour the gypsy had found. That had been a cruel trick to play on the fighter but it was amusing!

Octavian's ears picked up the faint sound of swordplay and he turned back towards the city expecting the volume to increase as he turned. However, as he moved, he realised the sound was ahead of him, over the next rise. He nudged his stallion with his knees, urging the mount to move faster across the desert and canter up the leeward side of the dune.

He reached the summit in moments, riding through a vertical curtain of sand that blew up from the windward side of the dune, that resulted in the gypsy blinking rapidly, as he tried to ward off the blast with his open hand and shield his face from the gritty onslaught. He turned his stallion side on, to angle the mount away from the buffeting and took in the unfolding scene below.

An oasis lay ahead, a small pool of water surrounded by towering palms and scrub worn ragged by sustained winds and neglect. A derelict watchtower lay toppled on its side, blocks of stone scattered across the sand.

Octavian blinked back tears from the wind and noted Toledo and Dorian pulling anxiously at their reins where they were tied to one of the palm trees. A giant scarlet scorpion ran about the oasis, its tail arched high, its claws held up and opened wide, worrying the mounts. However, every time the scorpion closed in to kill the two animals, it was met by a solitary figure that attacked its crimson body, slashing away with a sword and making a general nuisance of themselves before dodging back to safety amongst the palms.

Kerian Denaris, the only man Octavian knew who could find adventure, excitement and danger, miles from civilization, in the middle of the desert, had managed to do it again! Giant scorpions were exceedingly rare, yet Kerian had not only managed to find one, he had managed to make it extremely angry!

The scorpion's tail slammed down into the sand, inches from Kerian's feet as the knight turned and slashed with his sword, the blade clearly bouncing off the bulbous vesicle from which the cruel aculeus stinger emerged. Octavian found himself chuckling at the sight and the absurdity of it all. He had travelled all this way to offer his apologies to the warrior, rehearsing how he would open the painful subject, only to find he was instead going to have to leap into a fight and rescue his accident-prone companion!

He checked the dagger at his belt, then dug in his heels to ease his stallion down the dune towards the oasis. Sand tumbled away from its legs as the mount began its descent; causing the animal to rear up and almost touch its rump to the shifting landscape. The gypsy struggled to control his horse, tried to reassure it, even as he observed the developing scene ahead.

Octavian could not believe he was riding to the rescue! He needed to be careful or he was going to gain a reputation for himself; a vagabond gypsy who kept rescuing an old man! The smile turned sour as thoughts of his family entered his mind. Those were the people who needed saving! No hero would abandon his family in the way he had.

"Steady, steady!" Octavian warned as the horse neighed nervously beneath him. "Everything is going to be just fine..." The hairs rose on his arms and his nose detected the slightest of scents, as the dune face that he had just slid down exploded above him, showering sand across the gypsy as another giant scorpion, disturbed by their passage, clawed its way out of the dune, huge pincers snapping at the space his horse had just vacated.

Two scorpions! Two! Kerian was an absolute loadstone for danger! Octavian lowered his head and kicked in his heels urging his stallion forward. With a powerful leap and whinny of terror, his mount bounded away from the dune, legs thrusting down, propelling the gypsy out from under the curtain of falling sand and into the clear, just as a huge claw swept in and sliced at the air behind him.

How his stallion never broke a leg, Octavian could not say but the resilient and loyal animal scrambled down the sand dune as if its tail was on fire. Violently jostled and jolted about in the saddle, it was only by sheer determination that Octavian managed to stay on board his mount and not lose his seat to tumble to the scorching sands flying by beneath its flashing hooves.

The oasis and its confused geography moved nearer as the horse desperately closed the distance, sweat rising from its flanks as it charged. Octavian could sense the rising terror in the beast; feel the way its flanks vibrated beneath him as it struggled to breathe under the strain. The gypsy snatched a quick look behind him and noted the scorpion charging across the sand in pursuit.

By the gods, this was going to be close! He needed somewhere to hide, somewhere to get his horse out from the reach of those gigantic claws. He looked back towards the oasis, took in the broken watchtower and the way its shattered structure lay upon its side. There! That was where he needed to go! He tugged furiously on the reins, forcing the stallion into a tight left turn, ignoring its frustrated snorts and cries as he dug his heels in.

"Come on you can do it." The gypsy shouted encouragement as he gave the horse its head, allowing the stallion to fly across the sand. He risked another glance over his shoulder only to be horrified with the speed the scorpion was pounding across the sand after him, the menacing bulbous claws held high as it arrowed towards his position.

The ruin loomed ever closer, its slanted opening leading to a darkened interior masked by the shadows from the sun. He could not tell how deep the room was he was charging into, or if it had any depth at all. He had no idea if he was steering himself and his horse into relative safety or was charging straight into a solid brick wall. The panting from his mount signified it was too fatigued for any fancier evasive movements and was more likely to collapse from exhaustion if he tried. Octavian had no choice but to commit to his course or face losing his horse to the ravenous creature charging after them. It was all or nothing!

Octavian noticed Kerian dispatching the stinger of his scorpion out of the corner of his eye, sending it flying across the sand and making the monster curl up in defence of its injury, claws slashing in from the left and the right as it tried to retaliate. He had the briefest of seconds to recognise the fact that Kerian was somehow dressed in different armour, before the image of the struggle was lost behind tumbled masonry, waving grasses and bedraggled palms before the gypsy found himself charging headlong into darkness.

The stallion slid across the stone floor, shoes sending up sparks as it struggled to gain purchase and slow its momentum. Octavian swung himself from the saddle and urged his horse in as far as it could go, up against the far wall, which in years past was the floor of one level of the tower. Luck was not with them as the stairwell leading to the lower levels was not on the ground but rather up in the air and there was no physical way that he could raise the horse high enough to allow passage through to safety.

This was quite literally the end of the road. Octavian turned back towards the entrance and gasped as the scorpion barrelled in after them, legs straining to push its large body inside to grasp the succulent prey that had tried to run from its embrace. It shoved in again, causing dust and sand to drift down from the 'ceiling' in an alarming manner and causing cracking noises to echo throughout the masonry.

The scorpion backed up then thrust a large claw into the entrance, pincers clicking together mere inches from the cowering gypsy and his horse, the sound so loud it was as if the very air was being sliced. The scorpion withdrew again and approached from another angle, claw extended into the opening as if fishing, turning the bulbous chela first one way then another to try to grab the morsel it knew was there. Claws snapped closed on thin air, although this time Octavian did find he had to suck in his gut or risk being half the man he used to be!

Clearly frustrated, the scorpion backed away, its beady black eyes scanning the entrance as it flexed its legs and dug its tarsal claws into the sand.

"Ha! I out foxed you." Octavian taunted. "You can't get to me or my horse, no matter how hard you try. Why don't you go off and eat Kerian? He's got more meat on him than I have and will probably moan incessantly whilst you do it." The scorpion scuttled a few steps to the left, then a few more to the right.

"Yes that's it. You just go away!" Octavian yelled. "There is nothing here for yo... Oh hell!" The monster lunged forwards, throwing itself physically into the opening, claws slashing the air as its legs dug in hard, scrabbling determinedly over the baked sandy ground. Octavian parried frantically with his dagger but his reach with the weapon was so poor he could not do any significant damage. Dust from ages past started to fall from the ceiling and the masonry creaked and groaned ominously at the strain put upon it.

A pincer scored across the rump of his horse, causing it to stamp angrily and add yet another danger to the close quarter battle. The stallion shoved hard against him, trying to worm its way behind his form and into safety, with a strength the gypsy could not hope to match. Octavian knew he could not stay here and do nothing and as the claw retreated in preparation for another attack, he followed it and plunged one dagger right into the scorpion's eye.

The crimson giant threw its head up, crashing into the ceiling and sending fractures coursing across the stonework as if an earthquake had struck. Octavian had mere moments to look up in shock at the sunlight streaming into his hiding place, before blocks of stone rained down about him. He threw up his arms, only to have one knocked away by a tumbling block, then tried to step back just as a pincer shot out of the dust and gripped him firmly about the waist, yanking him from his feet.

More stone fell, crushing the scorpion as it squeezed tightly at its prey. Octavian threw his head back as agony shot through his body, only for another tumbling block of masonry to strike a glancing blow to his brow, before crashing down onto the grasping claw and plunging his world into darkness.

* * * * * *

"He's at the end." The gaoler replied, leading Aelius along the dank corridor to the cell where the incarcerated Ashe resided. "He talked so much when I brought him down that I felt it was a good idea to place him as far away from the other prisoners as possible in case they complained. What does the matriarch believe she has lost? I certainly have not seen anything anywhere." The hunched Minotaur picked his nose with a dirty fingernail and flicked the residue away into the shadows.

"It's personal." Aelius replied, eager to simply collect the ring and get away from the disgusting smells that permeated the air of the dungeon.

"I don't know why there is such a rush to find it. Whatever it is, I'm sure we will find it after the hanging." the crippled Minotaur continued, his other nostril now getting equal exploration time. "I promise I will thoroughly clean the cell out afterwards, just in case someone else needs to be locked away."

"I am under the impression it is rather more urgent than that." The captain of the guard replied coolly, regarding the broken horn of the Minotaur and wondering how he had managed to sustain the injury that had twisted his spine and sent him to the very bottom of the palace pecking order; maybe it was a games injury or an expedition that had gone terribly wrong? Certainly, looking at the creature's dirty armour and having already witnessed his unpleasant personal habits, it was not convincing when the guard had said he would give the place a good clean. The Gaoler clutched at his back frequently, straining as he shuffled along, it was unlikely he ever bent down to clean anything in his restricted state.

"If it is in there, I will find it, you can assure the matriarch of that but I've never missed an execution yet and I'm not going to clean out the cell and miss the main show today." The gaoler sniffed. "I love watching the legs kick whilst they dangle at the end of the rope, it's like they are trying to run on air and then when the neck snaps..." The gaoler stopped in mid-sentence and stared open mouthed at the open door before him. "How?"

"Why is the door open?" Aelius remarked, a feeling of dread swelling in the pit of his stomach. "I was of the understanding that most jail cells had locked doors to keep the prisoners in."

"But it was locked." The guard replied pushing hard against the cell door to dislodge an obstacle behind it and step into the room, staring around it as if expecting to see the prisoner exactly where he had left him. Aelius looked over his shoulder noting a chair lying on its side on the floor, clearly the obstacle that had partially blocked the door, an upended slop bucket in the far corner, its bottom cracked and staved in, the bed with the bundle of rags scrunched up in one corner and some seeds scattered across the floor. The window high up on the far wall was solidly barred, too small to squeeze through and well out of the reach of a tiny prisoner.

The maimed Minotaur pulled the door back and stared behind it, noting the damp walls and accumulated mould growth but alas no hidden

Halfling. Then he looked up towards the ceiling, way too high for a Halfling to scale and again realised there was no miniature convict to find.

"This makes no sense. Where could he have gone?" the gaoler wailed. "What am I going to do. The matriarch will be very unhappy. No one has ever escaped from her dungeons."

Aelius did not know what to say. Part of him wanted to comfort the Minotaur who was about to become a permanent fixture to his own dungeon, if the Matriarch let him live after his mistake, whilst another part of him wanted to shake the creature as hard as he could. He stared around the room as the gaoler threw the blanket from the stone bed up into the air, just in case the Halfling had shrunk to half his size and was somehow hiding there.

There was nowhere to hide. There was the chair, the broken bucket under the bed and nothing else. He spun from the room walking out into the corridor his eyes scanning the floor and walls for clues as to where the fugitive had gone. The corridor ended at a blank wall, no windows where he could have squeezed out of, no other doors he could have entered.

Aelius started back the way he came, pushing at each cell door on reflex, searching for the slightest give to indicate the cell was empty and a viable hiding place. Instead he got curses, abuse and maniacal laughter from behind the doors. He looked into another cell and saw the gaunt starving faces of humans who had somehow upset the Minotaur ruling class. A skeletal child, its stomach swollen from malnutrition, lay on the dirty straw floor, clearly too weak to move, her parents too emaciated to help.

The captain fought back the pity he felt, trying to maintain his professional standing, he was Aelius, captain of the matriarch's guard after all. All of these people had threatened his ruler, somehow, although in his heart he knew there was no way a child such as he had seen in the last cell could have done anything to offend his queen and deserve such an appalling punishment. It occurred to the Minotaur that his queen had rather a large number of 'criminals' in her cells.

Aelius shook his head angrily, embarrassed that he was even considering such treasonous thoughts. He looked down on the floor, trying to focus his mind, his eyes searching for tracks through the puddles as the passageway headed away from the cell. The only footprints still gleaming in the damp appeared to belong to Aelius and the crippled guard. There was nowhere the Halfling could have gone, accept this way but if the lack of tracks indicated anything it meant the little thief had escaped quite some time earlier.

The corridor turned left and opened into a chamber where the gaoler had a table and chair. The remains of a meal lay on the surface alongside a suspicious half-empty amphora of wine. Aelius turned his accusing gaze fully on the gaoler, who immediately held his hands up in protest.

"I swear I never had any." He stated. "The amphora has been with me for several days."

"Then you must have been asleep at your post." Aelius snapped, his frustration at the Halfling's escape and the inner conflict in his mind finding an outlet. "The matriarch will not be pleased at your negligence of duty."

"I have neither left my post or slept, nor have I drunk anything."

"Then where has your prisoner gone?" Aelius demanded. "Answer me that." The gaoler lowered his head in submission, meekly averting his eyes as he looked around the floor of the chamber before his gaze drew him to the only exit from the room, a flight of stairs leading upwards and out from the dungeon.

"There is only one place he could have gone but I cannot explain how." The gaoler wailed. He hobbled for the stairs, grunting and swearing as he tried to manoeuvre his twisted body up the steps. Aelius moved to follow, checking the chamber with his keen eyes, noting nothing amiss, no signs of a fleeing refugee; it was as if the little thief had disappeared into thin air.

It seemed to take an eternity to climb the stairs following the crippled Minotaur but eventually they reached the first landing that offered an open door out onto a courtyard where the scaffold awaited Ashe Wolfsdale, or the option of stairs to a higher level in the tower. The morbid image of the noose hanging from a crossbeam momentarily caught Aelius off guard. He observed the barrel placed under the rope to enable the condemned prisoner's head to reach the noose and realised that such forethought indicated similar executions of small people, maybe children, had taken place before. His mind turned to the image of the emaciated child back in the cell.

Why were they hanging the Halfling? All he had done was collect coins that people had thrown away. Even to a seasoned soldier such as Aelius, used to following his matriarch's orders without question, the sentence seemed grossly out of proportion to the crime. He looked around the courtyard. The portcullis was down, guards stood to attention on either side and other guards patrolled the walls high above. All was as it should be, as if the Halfling had never left his room.

Aelius marched across the courtyard, stepping through the shadow of the gallows and beneath the snapping brightly coloured pennants of

Taurean hanging above the portcullis, his attention directed towards one such guard who visibly straightened as he approached before throwing a sharp salute.

"Have you seen any sign of a Halfling passing through this courtyard?" The captain questioned. The guard looked confused, trying to peer around his captain and see if there was any sign of a small creature walking about.

"Not right now sir." The guard replied. "Although I understand there is a Halfling prisoner of some importance below. The matriarch even came to see him. Although as I understand, he must have done something treasonous as they are going to hang him in a few minutes. I presume this is the prisoner you are talking about." Aelius smiled despite himself.

"You are a sharp soldier." He replied. "You seem to have your ear to the ground but are your eyes as good as your ear for gossip? Have you seen the prisoner since the Matriarch visited?"

"No sir." The guard shook his head. "If the Halfling had come out here, I would have seen him." Aelius had a feeling this would be the response he would get and was not surprised at the guard's attempt to confirm his diligence. It appeared that Ashe Wolfsdale had literally disappeared into thin air! Mora was going to be extremely angry at this setback, especially as it appeared the ring had gone with him.

The weary captain looked beyond the guard and through the portcullis, watching the servants going about their duties. One serving girl was feeding a flock of chickens, throwing seed from a bucket at her side. The chickens squawked and scratched at the grain energetically, a bright blue bird with a long flowing tail darted between their pecking forms, snatching seed from their beaks and flitting from one side of the pen to the other. The chickens started to jostle and one pecked out at the servant making her shriek and drop the bucket to the floor spilling the grain and creating a miniature riot at her feet. The bucket rolled about as she turned and fled, leaving the poultry to fight it out amongst themselves.

The gaoler came up alongside him gasping for breath and breaking Aelius's train of thought. There was something about that serving girl, tugging at his mind but it was fleeting like a dream and as difficult to remember upon awaking, especially with the crippled Minotaur wheezing at his shoulder.

"Maybe he kept going up." The gaoler gestured, pointing back to the tower they had just exited. Aelius let his eyes roam up the outside of the oppressive stone structure, there were at least four floors to the thing and it did have an opening out onto the ramparts above.

"Well he never got out here that's for sure." Aelius snapped, spinning about and heading for the open door, gesturing to the guards on either side of the portcullis to follow him. He went back onto the landing and turned to the ascending stairs, taking them two at a time. The first landing had two locked doors and the stairway spiralling upwards. He took another step and set off up the only logical way left open to an elusive prisoner.

The next landing had two exits leading off to a long corridor, which had several doors leading to guard quarters but with the extra two guards to assist in the search, this escape route was swiftly dismissed, as the passage led back around to the landing in a loop, leaving no other exit. They took the stairs again, armour clattering as they climbed the steps, before arriving at the top to push open the door and access the battlements.

The wind on the exposed ramparts blew away any fog remaining in Aelius mind. He gasped at the shocking chill after the shelter of the palace walls but remained alert enough to send the two guards heading off in separate directions to scope the walls and ask the sentries already patrolling if they had seen any sign of the escaped Halfling.

He leant against the crenulations nearest to him and stared down to the courtyard far below, catching his breath and allowing his mind to focus on the problem at hand. His eyes scanned the view searching for a little figure running away, only to find his eyes drawn back to the serving girl who was back in the chicken pen finally reclaiming her dropped pail now that the chickens had sated their appetite.

What was it about this scene that kept drawing him back? It could not be the serving girl; they were all fully vetted and knew the punishment for failing to do as their masters wished. Betrayal was very unlikely. The chickens? Poultry was poultry as far as Aelius was concerned. He watched as the girl finally shooed away the last aggressive chicken and scooped up her bucket to return to her chores.

It was so odd; the fact there had been no attempt to take the gaoler's food especially by an escaping prisoner deprived of nourishment. The watery tracks in the corridor belonged to the gaoler and himself, as if no one else had walked along the passage. The fact the chair had been blocking the cell door from opening as if it had tumbled recently. Then there was the bucket. What was it about the bucket?

One minute it was in the corner of the room, the next, impossibly, it was nearly under the bed. How did a bucket move by itself? The realisation hit the Minotaur hard. The reason the tracks in the corridor showed footprints going one way only, with no sign of an escaping Halfling was that the Halfling had not escaped! He had still been in the cell in the one place

Aelius had been unable to check because the gaoler had been in the way and the gaoler could not check, because his spine was bent and twisted.

The damned Halfling had been under the bed the whole time! What was more, something had been in the jail cell with him, hiding in the remains of the broken bucket. Aelius was sure of it. He turned to whistle to the guards, summoning them back to him as he made for the stairs. He reached the first landing in a rush, heart beating fast and peered down over the handrail to the flight of steps below. Was that a noise of little footsteps running up the stairs towards him? He charged for the next flight leaping down them his armour sparking on the metal runners marking the edge of the steps.

A loud raucous tweeting from an animal clearly being tortured rose up from the base of the tower. Aelius had heard that sound before when he had been on the *El Defensor,* back when the Halfling had been trying to teach his mangy bird to fly. The bird! Damn it was so obvious now he had all the facts. The bird was under the bucket.

Aelius tore across the next landing charging down the steps two at a time, he turned the corner, the younger guards charging down the steps behind him. He roared aloud, announcing his charge as he practically flew around the corner, only to collide with the crippled gaoler working up the stairs towards him. The two Minotaur smashed into each other, Aelius unable to slow his momentum and carrying both of them bouncing down the steps.

They crashed into a heap at the bottom, Aelius shaking his head and looking up to notice the unmistakable figure of Ashe Wolfsdale slipping through the open door and out into the courtyard, a bundle of scruffy black and white plumage perched on his shoulder. Aelius shoved the gaoler off him and struggled to his feet, crashing through the door just in time to see the Halfling balancing on the barrel under the gallows. Ashe clambered up the very rope meant to hang him, then pulled himself up onto the cross beam before leaping like a swashbuckling hero for the pennants hanging above the portcullis. The captain of the guard could only watch in amazement as the Halfling went up hand over hand to the top of the archway. His little legs kicked once, before he was up and over the top, taking time to pause and give a little wave before he was away.

Chapter Thirty-One

Scrave pulled the ragged keffiyeh closer around his face and huddled down in a shadowy corner at a small table he had managed to procure in a very busy bar. To any casual observer he was a tired merchant amongst similar traders, travel weary from a long day in the desert. His company consisted of excited men haggling business transactions and whispering rumours of fortunes to be made, punctuated by swirling plumes of fragrant smoke from hookah pipes and mouthfuls of exotic food. He regarded his own plate and fought the urge to push it away. He was not hungry, neither was he thirsty, despite the fact he had been running and dodging the guards in Al Mashmaah for the better part of a day. He tried to push the worrying thought from his head that he had not been hungry for a long time.

What was wrong with him? Why had he acted so strangely when he had found Kerian Denaris's locket? Sure, the old man was a bastard, who had stabbed him through with his own sword and left him to die in a temple that was slowly sinking into a volcanic abyss but why hold that against him? He simply did not believe he could ever be obsessed with an item of jewellery the man had supposedly worn!

He reached up and felt the shape of the emerald pendant through his tunic, where it now hung at his neck and pondered. He certainly never remembered seeing the necklace when they had spent time travelling together, although something instinctively told him it was indeed Kerian's and now this niggling thought was telling him to get outside the city walls and find the man it belonged to. An action that Scrave knew was ridiculous and a completely pointless exercise, as Kerian was aboard the *El Defensor* and likely worlds away by now.

Scrave also believed himself a cautious Elf who had not lived this long, by undertaking irrational actions, no matter where the prompting for such rash acts came from. He was a fugitive now, especially after the disturbance he had caused in the market place. If he ran from Al Mashmaah, he risked discovery. What was more, it seemed wherever he had run today the guards had always managed to cut him off or appear ahead as if whoever was directing them was using magic to do so. If he made for the desert, the salamander-mounted guards would run him down in a matter of hours. As such, despite his compulsion to flee, he needed to do the opposite, mingle with the crowds and be invisible by staying in plain sight.

Even now, he felt his feet itching in his boots, wanting to feel the ground passing beneath them instead of just sitting here surrounded by intoxicated traders, in a dreary inn, with lacklustre food and tepid ale. He looked around at the assembly of faces in the crowd, the shifty glances of people doing secretive deals, the camaraderie raised by travelling together. It was the stark opposite of how Scrave felt. Here he was surrounded by people but had never felt so hopelessly alone.

Scrave ran his finger nervously across his right cheek, feeling the scaring disfigurement he had received at the hands of an invisible 'assassin' when the assailant had pierced his cheek with the very dagger the Elf now carried at his waist. He knew that the ornate diamond tattoo that lay there was no longer a fluid and beautiful work of art. Instead, it had become a visible target emphasising the wound at its centre, a puckered misshapen scar that should have been healed, if Violetta had acted on it quickly enough.

His sensitive fingertip traced across the raised skin, expecting the same ragged feel he had experienced on multiple previous occasions but instead he found himself stroking a much smoother scar than he remembered. It mattered little; his delicate Elven heritage was a joke. He was hideous now, unable to return to that world, his missing right eye adding further horrors to his visage. He was like a monster in a tragic play, expected to wail his lament from the shadows where no one could glimpse his horrific image.

Scrave turned his attention to his food and picked at the congealed spiced lamb on his plate, its herb encrusted, charred skin, half submerged under a pile of steaming aromatic lentils. The meat had definitely seen better days, especially if it actually was lamb. He thought back to the name of this dreary tavern, 'The Cranky Camel', if he remembered right. Maybe this plate before him was the final resting place of such creatures that had outlived their usefulness, served up on a lentil bed with cucumber yoghurt for dressing!

It was time to leave. He had to find Kerian, he needed to return the necklace to him. He moved to stand then checked himself. Actually, no he did not need to go anywhere! He was going to sit down and play with his herby camel until the coast was clear! He moved his body as if signifying he was trying to free his trousers from riding up and crushing his groin, noting the hands of several nearby merchants slowly returning to their tables and meals, away from the sheathed weapons they had automatically reached for. Oh yes, the Cranky Camel had its fair share of cranky customers too!

"Crossbow at the ready!" A voice shouted from behind a nearby partition. Scrave froze, had they found him again? Were the guards surrounding him as he spoke? His eye darted about the bar but strangely, no one reacted, no hand reached for a weapon, no eye cast a worried glance.

Instead, the customers acted as if nothing was happening. A rattling sound emanated from the screen indicated dice being thrown.

"We shall guard the door." Muttered another disembodied voice.

"Speak for yourself." Came the reply. "I'm picking the lock on that chest and taking the treasure."

Treasure? Scrave thought, looking about and trying to identify the aforementioned chest. There was no obvious treasure here and they were definitely not talking about the food.

"You always want the treasure for yourself." Someone stated indignantly. "One of these days that will backfire on you."

"As a Prince I'm entitled to all the treasure. It's only fair it all comes to me." Shot back another voice.

"Allow me to congratulate you, sir. You have the most totally closed mind that I've ever encountered." came a much deeper voice. "This is becoming predictable and I'm getting hungry. Where is our dinner?"

Scrave found himself shaking his legs, continuing the rucked up trouser routine, as he slowly walked over towards the partition to find out what was going on.

"The chest opens to reveal a combination locked box." Stated someone else, followed by a roll of more dice, but you fail to open it."

"What?" came the cry of disbelief! "Of course I can open it I am a master thief."

"Not this time. Oh and behind you a dragon crashes through the door."

"Oh come on!" A youth stood up, his spiky blond hair making him look like an inverted brush, a set of spectacles balanced on his nose. "A dragon. How can a dragon fit through the door?"

'Sideways,' Scrave thought to himself breaking out in a grin.

"Sideways" came the reply, without missing a beat.

"Why does it always have to be a dragon. Why can't it be a stegosaurus?" A massive man stood up towering over the group. He was wearing a velvet cloak and by the size of him, looked as if he could take on Rauph, his voice matching the deep one heard earlier. "I'm going to ask where our food has got to. Anyone fancy a drink?"

"I've already ordered and it's on its way. Fireball chilli, spiced potatoes and ales all round." A youth stood up, all cocky smile and quiffed brown hair, he gestured for the tall man to sit down then stared across the table at the person who had announced the arrival of the dragon as a sly smile slid across his face. "I think you are going to tell us the combination."

"No I don't think so." The faceless voice replied. "The dice have spoken." As if on cue, another throw of rattling dice sounded.

"Get him." The voice was filled with pretend menace and all of a sudden, the partition rocked violently as a rush of people seemed to descend on the end of the table still hidden behind the screen. An octagonal dice slid across the floor and ended at Scrave's boot, he bent down and picked it up.

"Right I know the combination now." Another voice sounded, amid the grunts and scuffles. "The treasure is mine by right! I shall keep it under lock and key as is my right as ruler of the world!"

A serving maid, petite, all blond hair and a winning smile, came over to the table with several platters filled with steaming potato cubes and bowls of spiced meat and beans. The sound behind the screen stopped with the clearings of throats and chairs being scraped across the floor.

"No really, he's fine." The cocky youth stated to the maid, explaining away something only she could see. "We are going to let him out of the head lock now." The young woman laughed, placing the plates down before stepping nimbly out of the way of the sprawling mass of legs and arms on the floor. She walked back past Scrave who raised his eyebrows questioningly and placed the recovered dice in her hand.

"I think they dropped this." He whispered. "What in the world is going on behind there?"

"Oh I don't know." Her smile wavered as she noted Scrave's face but when the Elf showed no sign of threat she relaxed." They come in once a week and play at some mad game. Apparently, the last place they were at, a windmill I think, burnt down." She shrugged her shoulder and patted down her dress as if uncomfortable at having her passage back to the bar blocked by the Elven trader.

"A game?" Scrave asked. "What kind of game?"

"Don't ask me. It is all rather confusing. All I see is them arguing all the time and setting fire to things but they seem to be having fun." She replied, "The owner is quite happy for them to play, as long as they drink plenty and eat lots of food." She smiled politely, not sure how to voice her need to get by, then gestured towards Scrave's table. "Your food is getting cold."

"Oh, so it is." Scrave muttered, forgetting the disturbance behind the screen and moving over to sit down, thereby allowing her to walk past. He noted her backwards thoughtful glance as she weaved through the crowd, then she was gone and he was alone once more with his tepid meal and his depressed state of mind.

"Excuse me?" Scrave looked up to see a young man standing before him; his hair all messed up, his face a mass of acne and his throat all red as if he had been held in a headlock. The youth seemed really uncomfortable and unsure of himself. "I don't suppose you have seen my dice? Someone said you picked it up."

Scrave took a moment to take in the young man's hazel eyes and noted intelligence and wariness in there, the look of someone who had experienced a life of disappointments and betrayals. The Elf smiled and gestured towards the bar.

"I gave it to the serving maid, I'm sorry I thought she was going to give it back to you." The answer clearly upset the boy, as he became even more red in the face.

"What's the problem?" Scrave asked. "I'm sure she will return it if you ask."

"I'm sure she won't even talk to me!" came the nervous reply.

"Why not?" The Elf asked. He watched as the young man anxiously fiddled with the hair behind his right ear. The maid in question was back to serving, delivering another plate of 'cranky camel' to another unsuspecting customer.

"It's so much easier in my stories, the heroes always know what to say." The boy replied. "Always so much more confident than I can ever be. I don't think I can."

Scrave grinned and raised his arm, signalling for the maid to return. She appeared more nervous this time, glancing over her shoulder towards the bar as if hoping the barman would call her back. Scrave gestured to the young man standing beside him and she immediately reached for her pocket, fumbling for the dice secreted there but her face revealed something else was going on.

"Well here's your chance." Scrave smiled. "Short of locking the two of you in a store cupboard and not letting you out, there is no better way to get to meet someone than over a lost dice. I promise, you will have a lot more stories to tell living in the real world, than just playing your games."

The Elf watched the youth turn an even brighter hue of crimson as he shuffled towards the petite blond waitress, then he turned his gaze away, secretly hoping the two would hit it off, even as the serpent dagger at his waist writhed in warning. His gaze glanced over to the entrance of the inn and he noted the four heavily armed guards entering.

Unbelievable! The maid had betrayed him! Here he was trying to do something nice for someone and she turns him in! He stood up again, pushing his lamb to one side and started to slide through the crowd, jostling against other customers who glanced at him both suspiciously and aggressively. He turned to avoid another collision and backed into a large merchant upsetting the man's drink all down his robes.

"I'm terribly sorry." Scrave offered. "Let me buy you another one." The man snarled and threw a punch, which the Elf nimbly ducked, allowing the clenched fist to slam into the face of another seated customer. The man stood up swearing, his associates sitting about him also getting to their feet, reaching for anything they could use as weapons. The man with the spilt drink tried to apologise but his pleas for understanding fell on deaf ears. He backed up towards his own group of travellers who also leapt to their feet in defence of their friend. Within seconds violence exploded as one set of traders jumped at the other and the air was filled with flying chairs, tossed tables, beer tankards and congealed lumps of lentil coated lamb.

Scrave ducked and dived, avoiding shards of shattered crockery, limbs of broken furniture and the odd bloodied tooth spinning across the floor. He ducked into the kitchen, pushing past a protesting chef and confused serving staff before slipping out the back door, leaving the ruckus and mayhem behind him to ease into the velvet darkness of the alley behind the inn.

Of all the luck! He thought about where he had to go, out across the desert. No! Not that way he had to avoid doing what his mind was telling him it was just going to lead him into more trouble.

"Elf!" came a sultry voice from the shadows. "Fancy meeting you here."

"Huh!" Scrave spun towards the sound, only to find himself facing a blistering orb of fire magically flung from the owner of the voice. He threw his arms up instinctively, with no time to dodge the fireball, when thrown with such deadly accuracy. The magical missile slammed into him, flames flickering hungrily around his body, searching for something to sear and feed its fire.

There was a surprising flash of green from Kerian's pendant and a blessed cool wave of magical protection rushed over Scrave in response to the blistering attack, deflecting the heat of the fiery blast mere inches from his skin. The fireball swept hungrily past, igniting litter, searing the brickwork of the inn, catching some of the thatch on the roof and turning the squealing rodents that resided in the shadows into four-legged charcoal biscuits.

A second fireball roared in, washing over Scrave's stunned form before he could even draw a breath, the orb of magical power angrily crackling as it swept past him to impact on the side of the inn and throw his steaming silhouette up against the wall.

"I'm impressed. Not many people can block a fireball, let alone two." Justina stated, stepping out into the light thrown by the flickering flames of her attack, her dark robe parting to reveal a tantalising glimpse of the smooth curve of her left leg, her right hand holding a smoking jewelled wand. "Your magical powers are stronger than I would have believed."

Scrave lowered his hands and tried to regain his shaken composure, gently checking his body, ensuring nothing vital had been incinerated. The serpent dagger hissed angrily at his waist, urging him to draw it and strike back at his enemy now that she was revealed. He reached down and allowed the enchanted blade to coil comfortingly about his wrist, the scales gently rasping against his flesh. He had no idea how he had avoided the blasts but realised he could not allow her to catch him by surprise again.

"I guess being so mysterious makes me more of a catch." He laughed nervously, trying to portray a confident manner, even if his legs felt like jelly. "I would never seek to be predictable for the likes of an exotic beauty such as yourself."

Justina stepped nearer, the light from the flickering flames lovingly caressing her body and highlighting her captivating face. Scrave found himself wondering what it would be like to hold such a beauty in his arms, feel the soft curve of her breast crushed against his chest. A hungry crackle arose from behind him as the thatch of the inn firmly ignited.

"As if I would ever be interested in the likes of you." Justina replied arching an eyebrow and offering the Elf a heart stopping coltish smile. "You did well with the warm up, now let us see how you deal with the main event."

"So much for foreplay." Scrave muttered, his mind reaching for the magical words in his limited magical repertoire. "If you want unpredictable, then I'm your Elf."

An earring shattered, magical energies flowed and a shroud of darkness dropped over Justina. She took a deep breath, refusing to panic and stepped to the side, recognising the limits to the spell from her own arcane studies and the fact that it would only affect a specific area of the alleyway. The light was initially blinding as she stepped from the shadows making her squint, seeing double images of the flames racing across the roof and two smirking eye-patch wearing targets. Justina blinked and waited for her vision to clear only to find herself still facing two Elven foes as her eyes adjusted.

Scrave smiled warmly and tilted his head, his mirror image did the same. He offered a wave and as his right hand lifted on one Scrave, the left hand lifted on the other.

"Now what a handsome chap I am!" both images said as they looked themselves up and down. "Surely, dating two of me leaves all kinds of options in the bedroom. How unpredictable is that?" Justina's brow furrowed in concentration. Which one was the real Elf? Which one illusion? She gripped her wand tightly, there was only one way to find out.

Fireball after fireball burst from the end of her wand, the blistering orbs roaring across the narrow space, tongues of flame hungrily consuming everything they touched. Both Elves threw their hands up in mock horror as the magical missiles slammed into them, burning searing holes straight through Scrave's torso on the left image and taking the head off the Scrave on the right, before both disappeared into wisps of smoke like the illusions they were.

Justina walked forwards, her wand sweeping the alleyway, searching for any clue as to the Elf's whereabouts. She was not stupid enough to believe that she had killed the cocky magician. He was still here somewhere. Angry and scared voices were filling the air, guards were entering the alleyway now, looking at the sultry mage standing there with her wand in her hand and then at the roaring fire behind her, the roof of the inn now consumed by the inferno.

"Stop right there!" one guard shouted.

"Or what?" Justina snapped, flicking her wrist and sending out a bolt of magical force in his direction. There was a clatter of armour and the other guards slid to a stop, staring down in horror at the giant warty toad now pulling itself from the guard's armour with a frustrated 'ribbit'.

The sorceress turned away from the guards, her eyes sweeping the alleyway in the other direction as she carefully retraced her steps to where the supernatural area of darkness still remained, looking like a foreboding tunnel leading to nowhere. Her sandal came down with an unexpected crack and she moved her foot to find a small slither of glass on the floor. Her splintered image reflected back at her. Justina could not help but smile. The Elf was not stupid; he'd used the distraction of the darkness to move behind her whilst she was blinded, then used this mirrored glass to cast an illusion in front of her and distract her whilst he made his escape.

She scanned the alleyway warily, eyes flashing with renewed interest. Then a thought occurred to her that initially made her feel very cold. If he had been behind her when she had stepped out of the darkness, why had he not plunged his dagger into her unguarded back? Loud voices came from the end of the alley, breaking her concentration. The guards had reinforcements now and were heading towards her with renewed confidence.

Justina smiled as she remembered the Elf's cocky smile and the way he held himself. She was going to enjoy catching him and she knew she would manage it. Scrave had not seen the last of her, she promised herself that. She was determined more than ever to apprehend him. She raised her wand threateningly, then stepped backwards into the very darkness that had been used against her, triggering her own spell at the same time and causing a stench of brimstone to fill the air as she teleported away.

* * * * * *

Colette sat in the shadows of Rauph's cabin feeling worthless. She had checked every one of the spell books on the shelves until her eyes ached. There were spells for every occasion written lovingly and precisely within the aged pages, yet not a single one offered help or a means to ease the burden placed upon Violetta. There was nothing here that could be used to help the chef arrest the poison coursing through Thomas's veins. It was a complete dead end. There was nothing she could do and it was driving her insane.

All of this immense power collected in priceless ancient volumes, spidery words of script that made your eyes hurt to read them, arcane alien phrases that made the tongue twist with pronunciation and the hairs on your arms stand up with the anticipation of shaping the supernatural energies contained within but nothing that would serve her in this hour of need. Colette ran a frustrated hand through her hair. She was surrounded by all of this power and she still found herself impotent.

The ghostly image of her mentor sitting silently in the corner, further infuriated her. She needed his guidance more now than ever and yet he sat there as silent as the corpse he was. She stood up, feeling adrift and headed towards the door, failure laying heavy upon her shoulders. Then she noticed the open tome on the cartographer's table. How had she missed that one?

She changed direction, her finger tracing the edge of the table, her eyes dancing across the spidery script. The spell on the page did not offer the answer to her problem but it still grabbed her attention, bringing her to a standstill. She knew she had never read this spell before, had never even known of its existence. Someone slipped past the doorway behind her but Colette was too occupied to notice or she would have seen Brother Richard's deceitful glance as he passed, a large and cumbersome blue book tucked under his arm.

Colette's gaze consumed each word hungrily, her lips silently mouthed the strange words. Time for the young mage stood still as the world moved on around her. Hours passed but Colette found she had no hunger other than her insatiable need to consume the knowledge the arcane text revealed, no thirst to quench other than her desire to absorb the ancient magical secrets illuminated before her.

"Colette! Colette!" The intimate moment between mage and magic was shattered, Colette found herself gasping as if surfacing from the depths of the ocean upon which they sailed. She looked around in a daze and noticed Abilene leaning through the door, his face flushed with excitement.

"What is it?" She asked, still gasping as reality rushed in around her.

"They are back!" He shouted. "Rauph and the others, they are back!"

* * * * * *

Octavian felt as if his body was covered in fire ants, scorpions were stinging his arms and there was a marching band playing in his head. His fingers felt tender, the itch on his neck was intense and unrelenting and his mouth felt dry, his teeth sharp. He turned his head from side to side, groaning, feeling the rough texture of the ground blanket between his head and the desert sands.

"Stay still. I've sorted everything out. Just relax, you really hit your head hard. Everything is going to be fine."

Was that Kerian? He cracked open an eye that felt swollen and misshapen. The sky above looked bruised, clouds scudding across its surface as if in a hurry to be somewhere. Octavian felt his heart beating faster. It was late, too late. Everything was not going to be okay. He tried to rise up on his elbows, tried to brush the cool cloth bandage from his forehead but he felt so weak, it was so difficult to think clearly. A spasm of pain shot through him making his body arch up off the blanket. Kerian's hand came down onto his chest trying to hold him down.

"Look Just relax." Kerian said. "I've laid out the blankets, we have a fire going, the horses are safe and secure on one blanket, we are on the other. Nothing under the sand is going to get us." Octavian tried to croak a response, tried to warn his friend that he needed to be scared of what was above the sand. It was too late, he had no time to get away, he could feel the hunger rising in him.

The need to hunt, the need to kill.

"W...What the?" The stammer in Kerian's voice portrayed the horror in what Octavian knew he was witnessing. The beast was coming to the fore. He had been so careful, always securing the horses and making sure Kerian was settled before he moved far enough away so he was not a danger to his friend when the change came over him.

Cramped fingernails scratched at the fabric of the blanket, the ends thickening, elongating becoming yellowed talons, his feet stretching out, the boots splitting, his trousers tearing as the monster within transformed him from the gypsy traveller into a hideous terror.

Octavian opened his eyes again, watching Kerian's shocked face as the fighter backed across the blanket, trying to give as much space as he could to the transforming nightmare before him. He tried to shout, tried to tell Kerian to run but his mouth was changing shape, the fangs sprouting from his gums, the words of warning coming out as a strangled growl.

The gypsy's body spasmed, thick fur sprouting from the backs of his hands in dark brown tufts. He tried to scream, tried to voice the agony coursing through his soul. Octavian jerked violently, flipping over onto his front, his back twisting and reshaping into the wild animal he was becoming. The animal he was cursed to transform into when the moon blessed the world with its luminance and bathed everything in its platinum light.

Trespassing through Blackthorn forest had left Octavian with a terrible price to be paid, its petrified forests held monsters that fought with tooth and talon, their bite so infectious that they had the power to warp the body and place you under the thrall of a master even more evil than the horrors he controlled. An evil twisted being, ruling from a ruined castle as terrible as it was foreboding. Castle Glowme was where his poor wife and daughter were still held hostage, suffering who knew what at the monster's hands.

Octavian wailed his lament to the stars, roaring with anger and frustration at the pale lunar globe suspended in the sky, as its rays gently bathed the blanket and illuminated the awful transformation thereon completed.

The creature opened its stark blue eyes and turned towards Kerian with a snarl, tail flicking behind it, a long pink tongue running down one gleaming incisor, huge paws pushing the blanket deeply into the sand, before its claws snagged on the material, crushing the smooth surface into rucked peaks that exposed the deadly sands beneath.

It stared at the man standing at the far end of the blanket, then at the three mounts snorting in terror, trying to pull their reins free from stakes pounded into the sand. There was no gleam of recognition, no association with those with which it had travelled.

Instead, it saw prey and it was hungry.

Chapter Thirty-Two

Thomas slammed the door of his apartment shut, feeling the heat through the steel-clad door as he sank to the floor exhausted. The humidity was intense; it was as if something was repeatedly pounding his head. His clothing was drenched and sticking to his skin as if he had been swimming. His mind was a concoction of confused images; he had no recollection of his journey home, everything was just a jumbled blur, yet he knew that here of all places, he would be safe.

He tried to stand on legs of jelly, feeling a terrible weakness coursing through his exhausted frame. His left hand clutched at the small table near the coat stand, only to upend a wooden bowl on its surface, spilling a set of house keys onto the floor where they slowly melted into shiny puddles of liquid metal. Thomas staggered along the hallway, fatigue rolling over him in waves. All he wanted to do was give up, sleep and let whatever illness this was pass him.

The captain wandered by the open kitchen door, noting the full-sized stuffed Disney tiger that hung upside down from the ceiling where MacMichael had nail gunned it during their last movie night. One of these days he really needed to get it down but right now it was an effort he simply could not sustain. Steadied by the furniture, Thomas lurched across the living room where the television screen was slowly melting. His autographed *Raiders of the Lost Ark* poster ignited like the opening of the old *Bonanza* Western TV show.

The bedroom was cool and dark, a blessing after such heat, a refuge from the searing assault relentlessly pursuing him. Thomas crashed down onto the bed, his body beyond caring as his unorthodox landing knocked his latest *Peter Swift* mystery novel, *Bullets Never Forget* from his bedside table. The paperback dropped onto its front, revealing the black and white cheesy photograph of author Philip Blackwood, complete with his bushy moustache and lady-killer smile to the world.

Thomas tried to make himself comfortable on the bed but something was not right, something nagged him that his sanctuary was not as safe as he had first believed. There was a smell in the room like a spoilt barbecue. He started as something moved beside him, something that crunched as it turned. Thomas shivered as a stick-like arm draped over his shoulder and its owner nestled in close, crackling with every movement of its body.

"Come back to me Thomas. Come back." Came the desperate voice at his shoulder. The captain knew he should resist the urge to turn but this whole scenario was like a nightmare he could not awaken from, the decisions already scripted and pre-ordained. He turned towards the husky voice, the stench of burning flesh getting stronger as he rolled.

"Thomas, hear me, we have the cure, Violetta is giving it to you now but you have to fight, you have to come back to us. The *El Defensor* needs you... I need you."

"Rowan, is that you?" He had to be hallucinating! None of this could be real. It was all in his mind! The smell was becoming more intense, like the unmistakeable smell of a body from a fire scene or a particularly bad road traffic accident; it was so strong. An acrid bitter taste rolled across his tongue, making the captain almost retch. Thomas reached out blindly in the darkness, one hand vainly searching for the source of the infusion, to push whatever it was away from his face, to stop it from choking him but there was nothing there. His other hand flailed for the bedside lamp, his body inadvertently brushing closer to the smoky figure lying alongside him.

"I love you Thomas."

The light snapped on and Thomas screamed. Rowan lay beside him on the bed, her body completely charred, the skin blackened and cracked, raw pink flesh showing through horrendous wounds where the meat of her body was sliding from her bones. Her hair was a dull charcoal instead of auburn and curled into tight blackened spirals that crumbled to dust as she turned her head towards him. Her eyes gleamed in the artificial light, strangely the only parts of her horrific visage not consumed by the deadly kiss of the flames.

"There you are." She smiled, her teeth stark against a mask of oozing cracked flesh.

Thomas lashed out horrified, pushing her away, feeling his fingers sink into molten fat and seared tissue. He fell from the bed; his head hitting the floor, making him see stars and threatening to make him vomit with the force of the impact. He crawled as swiftly as his aching head would let him, buoyed by the terror induced panic of what he had seen, scurrying across the carpet on his hands and knees, moaning his terror through clenched lips as he headed for the en-suite bathroom and the gun he knew was hidden there.

Something slid from the bed behind him and dragged itself across the floor in pursuit, leaving a greasy, blood streaked carbon stain behind it.

"Thomas! Stop fighting us."

Terror maintained an unrelenting grip around the captain's throat. His head hit the bathroom door, he turned over, scrabbling for the handle, the warm metal yielding to his touch, popping the latch and pushing it open. He retreated across the tiled floor, the opening door rebounding from the wall and catching his shoulder as he slid further into the room. His terrified eyes noted the charred corpse clawing its way across the floor after him and he renewed his efforts to put distance between himself and it.

His right hand came down on the tiled floor, only to feel the surface transform beneath his touch, reaching out and wrapping around his wrist like a hand. Thomas reacted with a scream, his left hand struggling to free his trapped limb only to feel other tiles moving about his body, clutching at his legs, his ankles, his waist, pinning him to the ground and restricting his ability to move. Something clutched at his head, dragging him down just as he noticed the shape of Rowan's charred body coming through the doorway after him.

Thomas reached blindly for the pedestal under the hand basin, knowing there was a matt black Ruger LCR .38 calibre special taped there in case of home invasion. His fingers brushed the grip, his sweat-slick fingers slipping from the weapon as he found himself physically dragged back across the floor. His left hand hit the tiles as he slid away, only for the surface to immediately morph into an impossible claw that completely encapsulated his only free limb.

The nightmare in the doorway crawled closer, scabbed skin falling away at each movement. She moved closer, one stick-like hand closing on his upper thigh, the other on his left shoulder.

"Thomas don't fight it. Let the antidote do its work." Rowan whispered as her charred skull moved closer. She leaned in, lips cracking as they became a macabre smile. "Just remember I love you." Rowan leaned in closer to kiss him and Thomas screamed aloud in terror as her smoky skin finally touched his parched lips. He felt the cooked skin rupture as they touched, pus and blood smearing across his own lips. He struggled, pulling to the left and the right, yet the hold on him remained tight. He was helpless, could only look on in horror as the blackened creature before him moved away, her brow furrowing in disappointment at his revulsion.

"Please." Thomas pleaded through tears. "Please, just leave me alone." He kicked out; struggling to escape but the fatigue he had been experiencing stole the energy from his effort. He lay soaked in sweat, unable to fight any longer, completely spent and beaten. His eyes closed on the horrors of the bathroom and the burnt caricature of the woman he loved, hoping that if he held them tightly closed for long enough, he could somehow escape from the horrors now deeply etched into his mind.

"Open your eyes Thomas." Violetta's voice cut across the darkness. "Come on captain it's time to wake up now." Thomas clenched his eyes tighter, dreading what he would see if he dared to open them. Someone pushed his eyelids up, revealing flickering torchlight so bright it felt as if it were searing his retinas.

"No let me go!" he shouted. "Leave me in peace!" he scrunched his eyes shut again, to the chagrin of the person trying to force his eyes open.

"I don't think so! Not after what this cure has cost us!" Thomas had a second to consider that the voice he heard was Commagin's before someone slapped him hard across the cheek then grabbed hold of his earlobe and squeezed hard.

"Goddamit! Get off me!" Thomas yelled, opening his eyes again to take in the familiar surroundings of his cabin. He noted the people holding him, Commagin, all smeared with dried mud and spotted with blood, Colette, her eyes bright with relief and rimmed with weariness. Violetta looked exhausted, her icon in her hand, a man he had never seen before standing beside her and across the room Rowan, with tear streaked cheeks and a hurt look upon her face.

"Welcome back Captain." Commagin sighed in relief. "We have a lot to talk about."

* * * * * *

Kerian pushed back against the animals shifting nervously behind him, determined to place as much space between himself and the monster that Octavian had become. He remembered all too clearly, the warning about the sidewinders and the scorpions Octavian had given him and how dangerous it was to inadvertently step off the blankets onto the desert sands at night.

He could not believe his eyes, the creature evolving before him bared little resemblance to the gypsy he knew. Kerian held his sword out in front of him and could not help but notice the slight tremor running along the blade, causing the tip to waver ever so slightly.

The thing before him defied description. It was as if someone had grabbed several exotic animals, mixed them up in a bowl and created the snarling monster standing erect in front of him. Its head was similar in shape to a leopard but with a thick black shaggy pelt marked with camouflage stripes of blue and grey instead of spots, a little like a tiger. Under the lunar light, the markings appeared to shimmer and move with a life of their own. The torso was more difficult to decipher, due to the shredded remains of

Octavian's clothes hanging from its frame, where the monster had literally exploded out of them. It was thick and finely-muscled, with ridges running down its curved spine where the remains of Octavian's tunic appeared to stretch from the skin as if something were protruding from his body.

It's tail was like that of a wolf and the hind legs, upon which the monster currently stood also appeared of that nature, yet thicker, more powerful, ending in claws that remained extended several inches from the paw, their use clearly meant to disembowel and rend prey. The remains of one of Octavian's boots hung from the right claw and flopped about the blanket as the creature turned towards him.

The abomination had wide shoulders and long muscular arms that ended in splayed hands. Yellowed talons extended down from thickset fingers that flexed as the transformed gypsy made fists from his hands then opened them wide again, as if he were experiencing an attack of pins and needles. A maw bristled with huge teeth, razor-like incisors and the upper set of canines extending down past the lower jaw.

Bright blue eyes had replaced Octavian's brown, the dark irises slit like those of a feline, stared hungrily over towards Kerian as the figure twisted on the blanket in preparation of attack, rucking up the material and revealing areas of treacherous sand beneath. His mind flashed back to the market place in Wellruff when Octavian was being assaulted by the guards and then considered the remains of the people in the alleyway. Was this the fate that awaited himself?

The beast's tail flicked from side to side, as if the horror was excited at the prospect of such readily available food. Clear drool dripped from the side of its mouth, making Kerian feel even more unsettled. The monster was clearly visualising Kerian's grisly demise. Meanwhile the knight's mind raced trying to think of a way of defeating this thing without harming Octavian. His eyes surveyed the beast, searching for possible weakness and coming up short. With a start, Kerian realised he had seen this monster before, back in the tombs, reflected in the mirrored image of his shield.

"Octavian?" Kerian began gently, not willing to strike out at the man if he could avoid it. "Are you in there?" The monster snarled in response and dropped down onto its front hands, shoulders hunching up as it stared at Kerian with its mesmerising blue eyes. The bushy tail flicked from side to side, the creature's rear legs scrunching down preparing to pounce.

"By Adden, what have I got myself into now?" Kerian whispered to himself, watching the tail sweep from side to side before it came to an ominous halt. The blade in his hand suddenly felt woefully inadequate. "Octavian you have to sto..."

The creature attacked, jaws opening wide, talons outstretched, propelled forward with incredible power from back legs that launched it like a quarrel from a crossbow. Kerian could not hope to parry such an attack within the limited space he had to manoeuvre, yet he tried his utmost to meet it, hoping somewhere beneath the surface Octavian would be alert enough to snap out of this and metamorphose back into the annoying gypsy he now knew so well.

The collision almost knocked Kerian clear off his feet. He brought his blade up to meet the charge, only to find it knocked back towards him with such force that if he had not been wearing his new armour, he would have ended up injuring himself. He turned sideways as the creature continued to push, parrying the clawing talons and snapping jaw that attacked with a ferocity that found the knight sliding back across the blanket, despite his best efforts to hold his ground.

Steel blue eyes stared into his own with no sign of recognition, just a cold determination to bring down prey no matter what the cost. The mounts behind Kerian snorted in terror stamping furiously, pulling at their ties, making Kerian realise that if he let the monster past, he risked losing much more than his own life. He could not let this creature injure the horses. They were literally life and death out in this desert.

Kerian parried a vicious swipe from the left, then shouldered forwards, closing the distance between them, pushing back at Octavian's snarling form with his right side as he tried to get beneath its vicious jaws. Teeth snapped inches from his face, then lunged down to bite deeply into the shoulder guard of his armour. The warrior felt the vice-like grip bear down sending a numbing pain through his right arm, nearly making him drop his sword.

He struggled to release his pinned blade, only to find Octavian's hind leg kicking out towards his midriff, the claw sparking off his blade, more by luck than design, before tangling in the loop of his mysterious satchel. Kerian found himself pushed away by the force of the kick, the grip on his shoulder mercifully ceasing as the creature released its bite in preparation of another attack, the satchel slapped back to hang at Kerian's side as the beast's claw released its grip. The respite was instant, feeling rushing back into his right hand as his sword came up just in time to flick out the blade and score a glancing hit across the monster's snout as it swiped at Kerian, knocking him backwards across the blanket.

Desperate to miss colliding with the horses, Kerian took a step onto his left heel trying to use the backward momentum to angle his body, pivoting himself so he could bring his right foot down to stop his movement, only to feel it sinking into the soft sand. He reacted as if scalded, vivid images of the creatures Octavian had told him about forming in his mind. His boot pulled free from the clutching sand just as Octavian leapt at him again, talons outstretched.

His sword swept through the air, the blade glittering in the chill moonlight, its keen edge catching one outstretched claw before the warrior reversed the strike, bringing it back to slice across Octavian's chest, causing the beast to roar in outrage. It pounced again but this time Kerian was ready. He turned in towards it, allowing the creature to slam into his back and hit the shield slung there. Talons curled around the edge of the shield as the monster's rear claws scrabbled against the metal surface and Kerian suddenly realised his error. The monster was simply too heavy to hold and he felt the power go from his legs as the weight of the creature dropped him to his knees.

Kerian felt hot breath panting at the base of his neck as he was crushed down towards the blanket. His hands pushed back against the shifting material as he desperately tried to support the weight of the beast upon his back. The knight scrambled for purchase of some kind but it was impossible, with one hand gripping the hilt of his sword and the other struggling not to get tangled up in the satchel. Kerian tried to heave himself up and push against his attacker, only to inadvertently pull the blanket away beneath him, leaving his face now hanging out over the edge, where something silver slithered just under the surface. He suddenly realised this was the moment.

"Sorry Octavian." He gasped. "It's either you or me." Despite his instincts screaming not to do so, Kerian threw himself forward, his face coming within inches of the squirming sands, before he pushed off with his feet and dropped into a roll, using the weight of Octavian to pull him forwards and allow him to flip over, leaving the snarling monster suddenly beneath him.

Snarls of fury turned to yelps of pain as something under the sand attacked the exposed back of the beast. The monster bucked Kerian up into the air, before pushing him off to the side, its actions violent but not directed towards the knight; instead, it focused on getting itself up off the treacherous sand as swiftly as possible. Kerian tucked and rolled with the action desperately hoping that this motion would move him back towards the safety of the blanket but he was not sure where he had landed, all he knew was that he needed to keep moving if he wished to avoid the venomous creatures hunting beneath the desert surface.

Sand exploded up around Kerian as he rolled, silver serpents striking out from beneath, their seeking jaws missing him by the narrowest of margins. He slammed up against something hard, jarring himself with the collision but continued to roll up and over the resistance to find he was perching unsteadily on a slab of fallen masonry half buried in the sand.

He drew up one knee, turning towards the snarls and roars on the left, where Octavian continued to roll across the ground, snatching at lengths of silvery coiled serpent that appeared to be burrowing up through the sand and striking at its form. The beast snatched snakes from his ragged vest, yanked others from his thick bushy hide and got to his feet, tearing several snakes apart and showering the sand with gore before he ran off into the deepening shadows. The sand appeared to boil as other serpents, hungry for flesh, cannibalistically devoured the remains.

Kerian uttered a sigh of relief. It appeared that for now at least, Octavian was still alive. He noted the creature's path of travel, then swiftly continued his reconnaissance, noting the flickering fire pit around which he had set camp was now somehow way over to the right. A large, open expanse, of rippling sand lay between himself and the relative safety of the blankets. Kerian had no idea how he had managed to roll so far. Panic was clearly a great motivator!

He listened to the growls and snarls growing fainter as Octavian loped off across the desert, knowing this respite would only be a brief one; Kerian knew he could not hope to fend off Octavian in his current bestial form. The creature was simply too strong, too full of fury and hunger to ever pause in its attacks. Whilst prey stood unguarded on the rucked-up blankets, it was a foregone conclusion that the beast would circle around and come back for another try. Everything would be fine as long as he managed to figure out a way to get back across the sand and prepare. At least he had managed to keep the beast from killing any of the animals.

His self-congratulation and smile for getting to the relative safety of the rock slid from his face as his eyes locked on the form of a sword lying in the middle of the sand. Disbelieving, Kerian looked down at his hands and confirmed his worst fears. It appeared panic made you also do stupid, thoughtless things as well!

He had managed to maroon himself on a little island of stone, surrounded by an ocean of treacherous sand, with a terrifying monster loose somewhere in the darkness. What was more, he was unarmed, with no way to defend himself against Octavian's beastly nature.

"Well I suppose it could be worse." Kerian muttered. "I could have been stuck on this rock with Ashe Wolfsdale."

* * * * * *

"So where is Ashe Wolfsdale?" Thomas asked, rubbing his forehead and wishing there was something he could do to make his growing headache go away. He looked down at his toes, ten little bald people poking out from the bottom of the blankets and wriggled them to check they were working and that the pins and needles were lessening.

"No one has seen him." Mathius confessed. "Apparently, he went off looking for his bird after it flew away. Where he is now is anyone's guess."

"This whole situation sucks!" Thomas shook his head unaware the other crew around him were looking confused at his use of slang. "Ives is dead, Ashe is missing and the helm was sabotaged by the Minotaur boarding party."

Colette risked a quick glance over at Commagin's blushing face but refused to elaborate on the slight untruth. There was enough to worry about without considering the veracity of how they happened.

"Aradol? What about him." Thomas asked, his mind struggling to locate where everyone was.

"He's taken a small party to a cove we noted on our row back to the ship. He's taken Ives's body so they can bury him properly. He was determined to do it himself but I convinced him to take others to help. Marcus will keep an eye on him I'm sure." Weyn stated, his head bowed, exhaustion on his face, his arm held up in a crude sling.

"Weyn get your arm seen to by Violetta. I need you to be back in fighting form." Thomas ordered.

"I'm not sure I can." Violetta confessed. "I used all of my energy trying to save you."

"I need him fighting fit!" Thomas snapped. "Whatever it takes. Get it done!" He turned to Commagin trying to distance himself from the negative emotions he knew he was creating. The ship was in trouble. He could worry about apologies later.

"Your priority is to get the helm responding. I want you on it now. Take as many people as you need."

"It's not that." Commagin confessed. "It's the small space we need to ease the mechanism through to get it working again. Barney is not available for such work and I can't fit."

"I don't need excuses. I need it fixed. Can you at least do that?" Thomas replied. "Rowan is good with machines. See what she can do to help. Colette, surely you can help in some way as well?"

"I'll see what I can do." She replied cagily, wanting more than anything else to be back in Rauph's cabin going over the spell she had discovered there.

"How did we get in this mess?" Thomas shook his head.

"Thomas don't you think you should be resting and leave the running of the ship to the others?" Rowan asked from across the room, her fingers nervously dancing across the globe.

"That's how we got into this situation in the first place. I do not have time to rest. One of my crew is dead, one is missing and my ship is to all intent and purpose landlocked."

"There are two people missing." Commagin stated under his breath.

"What?" Thomas tried to calculate what the engineer meant, his mind going over the facts. Surely, he could not mean... "Look I know Barney is missing, I meant no disrespect but I have other more pressing matters at hand. Do you know the damage Ashe can cause if he is allowed to run around Taurean unchecked?"

"It's not Barney." Commagin replied through gritted teeth, "Although he is still as important as any other member of the crew. No, it is Rauph who has gone off. When we got back, he left us at the dock and set off towards the palace. I'm afraid there was no stopping him."

"Well did you at least try?" Thomas could not believe what he was hearing.

"Have you seen Rauph when he has set his mind to something?" Mathius replied. "I'd rather fight two Nirschl than have to step in front of him."

"And I for one did not feel that suicidal." Commagin confessed. "He seemed intent on explaining to everyone up there what it was to harm his friends. It appears our navigator is more loyal to his shipmates than his captain." Thomas sighed, as the words struck home, delivered in a level voice, the barbs were no less sharp or wounding.

"Look I'm so..." Thomas cut himself off. He could not afford to be sorry. He swallowed hard and moved to sit up, only for the cabin to swim about him. His hand reached out to grab the edge of the bunk so he could steady himself.

"Get the ship repaired and move us away from the dock. This is your priority. Nothing else matters. Are we clear on this?" Thomas turned towards Weyn and Mathius. "As soon as Weyn's arm is tended I want the two of you to go into the city to find Ashe and Rauph. Do this as quickly and as quietly as you can. Then get back to the ship. We need to be out of here as fast as possible."

The crew started to disperse from the cabin, one after another glancing towards Thomas, some relief on faces that the burden of command was back in its proper place, whilst others looked on with a mixture of anger and disbelief.

Thomas closed his eyes until the cabin door clicked closed, cursing his headache and the way he had needed to take control. His old Korean mentor sprang to mind, explaining to him that he could not be in charge and be a friend to everyone. Sometimes, in moments of danger, things just needed doing; you could not worry about feelings at such times. His mind flitted back to when he had once had to push the broken-down squad car through a poorly timed gangland shootout, with Chiou at the steering wheel and hot lead whizzing through the air. Chiou always told him hurt feelings could be ironed out later. It sounded great in principle but Thomas still felt awful about how he had had to act.

He opened his eyes and noted that he was not as alone as he had thought. Rowan still sat by the globe, her eyes red rimmed from lack of sleep and weeping. He tried to offer a tired smile and struggled to sit on the edge of the bed.

"Oh Rowan, how has this all happened?" She stood up and moved nervously towards him, her hands by her side. Thomas took her into his arms and felt the sobs racking her form.

"I thought I had lost you." She cried. "When I've only just found you." She held him tightly as his hands stroked her hair and he breathed in the scent of her. Honeysuckle and oranges, it was funny how these little things only served to intoxicate him further.

"You know I'm not going to leave you." Thomas comforted her. "I'll never leave you. You are the best thing that has ever happened to me. Whilst I was poisoned, I dreamt something terrible had happened to you. It almost made me lose my mind. If anything were to happen to you, I'd hunt down whoever was responsible to the ends of the earth."

"And extract terrible vengeance." Rowan gulped, as her sobs eased and slight tremors ran through her. "I would expect at the least, terrible vengeance but you don't look strong enough to avenge anyone."

"Your wish is my command." Thomas replied, pushing her away from his chest to take in her beautiful eyes and her tear-streaked cheeks. "You know me, I may look a little rough around the edges right now, but I'll be back on top form before you know it. Just give me a sword to swing and a ship to sail."

"I have another command as well." Rowan replied; her voice hoarse with emotion.

"And what is that my lady."

"Well before you apologise to everyone for being a thoroughly nasty person, I want you to do two things for me." Rowan's eyes sparkled with more than just the moisture of her tears.

"Name them." The captain replied, pushing a stray lock of hair from her face.

"Well you need to have a bath and get dressed as befits a captain of the *El Defensor*."

"And then I get to kick arse and chew bubble gum?" Thomas butted in, quoting from the 1988 movie *They Live*.

"Where are you going to get bubble gum from?" Rowan laughed.

"That's the point of the quote." Thomas joked, using his thumb to dry an errant tear. "You know, 'Kick arse and chew bubble gum, and I'm fresh out of bubble gum.'"

"No, that's not what I wanted you to do." Rowan smiled back, her trembling now easing beneath his warm caress.

"Then what?" Thomas asked. "I need a clue here."

Rowan looked up into Thomas's drawn face, the bruising from the poison still etched on his gaunt features. In that unguarded moment he looked vulnerable and unsure, his sweat-stained clothing hanging from his form, his bed sheets rucked up about his body. She took his head gently in her hands and angled it down towards her face.

"Kiss me stupid." She replied huskily.

Chapter Thirty-Three

"If I eat another piece of raw eel, I swear I shall just die!" Miguel groaned, spitting out what felt like the thousandth bone from the bloodied raw fish he held in his fist. The pirate turned to the huge lizard lounging alongside him and waved the slimy eel at him. "I mean you could have at least attempted to fillet it first!"

Huge jaws opened wide to display a pale gullet and Miguel found his meal snatched from his hand and swallowed completely, bones and all, with a mighty crunch of the creature's massive jaws. Miguel snatched his hand back in shock, quickly checking the fingers on his hand as his armoured companion licked its snout with its long, forked tongue. A loud snort and a belch showed the giant lizard's displeasure at having its offering refused.

"Look I didn't mean it that way!" The pirate replied defensively. "It's just that I've had enough of just sitting around here. We need to get out of this place; we need to take back what was ours." He stood up unsteadily on the slanted deck to emphasise his point and immediately regretted it. The musty curtain he had rolled up beneath him as a cushion to save his clothing from the dampness, slid off the bench and down the slope to flop into a puddle of stagnant water.

"I just don't have any idea how I'm going to do it." Miguel muttered to himself, dejectedly sitting back down on the damp bench. "I don't suppose you have any ideas?" The lizard man slowly blinked a yellow eye in response, its movements sluggish due to the lack of sunshine available within the ship's graveyard. "At least I still have you Horatio, old buddy." The pirate sighed, patting the monster's scaly shoulder, despite knowing that his gratitude would only stretch so far if the mercenary reptile ever ran out of food.

Miguel sighed deeply as he took in his dismal surroundings. It was hardly what one would call palatial. They had holed up in a decaying riverboat paddle steamer, complete with a rotting paddle wheel at the stern of the ship. The blades stood proud of the water where the riverboat had settled nose down, due to a rusted cargo ship having crashed through her bow, leaving the boat at permanent 35-degree list. The whole vessel creaked incessantly, shivers vibrating through her timbers as she groaned and moaned at her undignified end.

The '*Timour Dream*' measuring 155 feet by 33 feet may have been an opulent passenger vessel in her time but you would never have thought that to look at her now. Even without the listing deck and pervading stench of rot, the walls dripped with damp, elaborate patterned wallpaper either peeled near the roof or bulged near the base. Patches of pale grey mould crawled across the shadier places and assorted fungi grew in the corners of the room far from the pale shafts of green light that filtered through seaweed-coated portholes.

The sloping deck, warped and in places rotted through, made any rapid progress about her decks treacherous. Discarded casino furniture lay shattered, card tables and roulette wheels smashed to pieces by the collision of the two vessels. Indeed, the only furniture to survive the accident were benches fixed to the deck, of which only a few seemed in good enough condition to bear any weight placed upon them.

An ornate mirror hung askew on the wall, its reflective surface drawing the eye from the dreariness of the room. Half of the silvered backing had flaked away giving an appearance of pubescent acne to anyone foolish enough to gaze into its depths. As Miguel's eyes focused on the glass, the main door of the lounge bumped open, making his reflection appear to shiver within the frame as Cornelius staggered through. The lizard's huge scaled arms carried items of salvage collected from the hold of the ruined riverboat.

Miguel stared at the detritus deposited before him, as if the items might offer insight to his clouded mind. A fine china teapot and cup, several bottles of fruits and vegetables pickled in a clear liquid and sealed tightly. A leather beaver hat, a rusted sabre, a pair of men's boots, too small to wear. A long coat unfortunately torn, a fistful of patterned porcelain buttons from dresses long rotted away, a bottle of French perfume in a cut-glass bottle and a wooden keg. Clearly, there was not much inspiration amongst these items.

He leaned over and placed the beaver pelt hat on Horatio's head then rolled the keg towards himself. The seal seemed fine, the wood of the keg not showing signs of deterioration, sweating or rotting. He tapped the keg with the hilt of the rusted sabre and sloshed some of the nutty liquid from inside into the salvaged teapot then had a sniff. His eyebrows raised in surprise when he recognised the liquid was ale. Maybe his luck was improving after all!

The lizard's long tail curled around and dropped a further item on the table, a sack, containing a roll of oilcloth with something hard wrapped inside and some sort of dog-eared logbook. Miguel raised an eyebrow in surprise. Why would the lizard have brought this to him? He took a long draught from the ale and moved to adjust the flame inside the spluttering lantern mounted on the wall beside him, before lifting up the book to investigate its curling cursive text.

He flipped through the pages, weary eyes scanning the words before him without taking much of it in. Slaves collected in one port, cotton at another. Trades and deals made, profits and losses recorded, dodging the ice, sand banks and submerged tree roots and the treacherous weather that plagued the ship as she plied the Mississippi river. The pirate's eyes narrowed when he noticed a particular passage near the end of the ledger, written in a less refined hand than the previous entries.

'It has fallen upon myself, Robert Atkins first officer of the 'Timour Dream' to document this tale of woe, in lieu of our Captain Shamus Hennasy, taken before his time by the midnight hounds we have all come to fear.

We spotted a strange vessel late on the evening of April 14th, 1856 after a night of terrible storms. She had dropped anchor near Swallow's Turn, almost completely obscured by a veil of thick yellow fog. Lanterns on her starboard side alerted us to her presence and helped us avoid a collision. Captain Hennasy ordered full stop whilst we took in her profile. The cabin boy Jenkins swore it was a Spanish galleon straight from history class but with two tall masts where there should have been three; occupying our river space in a time period she had no right to be.

Captain Hennasy ordered that we advance with caution, rumours of ships carrying cholera were rife on the river and as First Mate, I was also concerned for our welfare and suggested the captain allow the men to bear arms. I confess I feared that if what Jenkins stated was true, she could only be a ghost ship, somehow marooned between worlds. We advanced in silence, using the current of the river to power our momentum and as we drew ever nearer, we heard strange voices upon her decks. Jenkins swore he spotted a column of smoke on the aft castle with red demon eyes floating inside but we just thought he had taken too much ale from the captain's table.

A disturbance drew our attention to a man floundering in the river. None from the huge galleon moved to help him or voiced the call 'man over board' so as good Christian men we moved to assist the 'drowned rat' from a drifting log as we passed; indeed, once we fished him from the river, he introduced himself as Plantation owner Miles Downey. The Galleon had apparently abducted two of his slaves without due payment and he meant to have them back.

With a promise of much reward and future rights to exclusivity in transporting Mr Downey's goods, the men took up arms and prepared to board the strange ship when the strangest of happenings occurred. The mighty sails of the galleon afore us appeared to billow and crack, before filling when I swear no wind did blow. I followed the Captain's orders, observing that the engine room stoked the boilers as we set out in pursuit, only for the mighty galleon to part the very air before her, opening some sort of gateway into a world that smelt of brimstone and had a sky the colour of mustard.

The men were afraid to follow, believing the ship we followed to be cursed, steered as it was by a horned devil seen by Jenkins's very eyes. Yet the captain had his mind on the profits he was yet to make and would not listen to the warnings given, instead he threatened to put us all off ship at the next dock, without work or profit, if we did not do his bidding. Therefore, with no choice, we pursued the galleon of the name 'El Defensor' into hell and soon wished we had not.

That was nine days ago. Our ship now lies mired in the wreckage of other crumbling hulks, the paddles snared with a thick weed that appears to grow almost as fast as we slice it from the hull. Some vessels about us are of strange design, others appear ancient, their function as mysterious as the facts that their decks are empty of crew or purpose. Every time we send men to try and free the ship they fail to return, despite being armed with musket and powder. The Captain Hennasy was taken yesterday. The men debated a rescue effort but were afraid. May god forgive our cowardly souls.

The hounds that took him are ravenous beasts, sleek, black and possessed with a single-minded purpose. They are like devils hunting the ruins for offerings to their satanic master. Jenkins states he has seen glowing coloured lights amid the ruins yet he swears he has taken no more of the Captain's ale.

The demon dogs are becoming more confident in their attacks. I fear it will not be long before they attack in numbers and in our own weakened state, I fear the outcome will not be a positive one. I record this passage so that others searching for our remains will know of our fate and enclose the Captain's prize possessions so they can be passed down to his rightful family as is only fit and proper.

Robert Atkins First Mate
Timour Dream
23rd April in the year of our Lord 1856.'

Miguel closed the book with a thud.

"It apparently did not end well for the crew of the *Timour Dream*." He muttered to himself. Things were starting to make more sense. Thomas Adams and the crew of the *El Defensor* had lured others to this godforsaken place in the past. It was as if his nemesis were some kind of siren, paying his way in souls for rites of passage through this scrapyard of floating hulks. Just how long had he been doing this? What kind of a monster was the man? Well he knew one thing for sure. When they got out of here, he was going to make Thomas Adams pay.

He picked up a porcelain button and rolled it between his fingers, deep in thought. They needed to find a way out of this place. If only they could get their hover skiff back and working, it was the best transport available but he needed to get the repulsor engines functioning again and there was only one person he knew who could do that; Pheris.

A smile slid across his face as other elements of the plan started to form in his mind. Of course, he needed the cyborg as he had computed the complex mathematics necessary to open the gateways. The problem was that Pheris lay somewhere back on the huge passenger liner *The Neptune*. Once Malum, he with the glowing lights and sharp claws, realised there was very little meat on the cyborg and that his powers had faded leaving him inert, Pheris was discarded, left in the corner, a mass of broken circuit boards and body parts. The thought made Miguel's blood run cold.

The Neptune was Malum Okubi's lair. What if the monster found him there as he tried to salvage Pheris? What if he used his annoying mind trick and took over the will of his lizard again? There had to be a way of making sure the monster was far away from them before they dashed for the liner. No, it was all too dangerous! He had no means of defending himself if caught and had a feeling Malum was not one who liked his prey to escape. So, how was he going to manage this apparently impossible task? It was all so damned frustrating. He brought his fist down on the table with such force that the button popped from his grasp and bounced down the front of his coat, leaving Miguel fumbling to recover it amidst the useless empty holsters and bandoliers he had strapped there. The button fell free, despite his efforts and bounced onto the soggy curtain roll.

Scowling at the lost button, Miguel reached out and dragged the oilcloth over, parting the roll of material to discover a long slim box carved from warm mahogany. He lifted the latch and opened the lid, then gasped at what he beheld. The plan Miguel had been forming in his mind suddenly became more achievable.

He tapped his finger on the table and looked across at Cornelius who was busy sticking his forked tongue into one of the glass jars and hooking out some of the pale looking preserved fruits from inside.

"Hey Cornelius, were there any other kegs in the hold, smaller ones with black powder inside or maybe little balls?" The lizard gulped down the fruit and licked its snout before tilting its head to one side as if thinking carefully.

"Hello!" the pirate shouted. "Small kegs, black powder, balls?"

The huge lizard nodded his head in confirmation before returning its total attention to the glass jar. Miguel closed his eyes, working out the timings and the complications that could occur. It would be difficult and not without risk but if they could re-float the skiff and power open a gate... he could put this nightmare long behind him." He staggered to his feet and tried not to wobble too much on his ale infused legs, before reaching into the walnut box and pulling out the two beautiful flintlock duelling pistols that lay within.

"Boys, I really do believe I have a plan."

* * * * * *

Kerian stared out across the striped desert dunes, his eyes straining to catch sight of any hint of Octavian, or the beast he had become. The dunes had turned black and white under the light of the full moon, giving the whole setting a stark and surreal feel. The winds had dropped to a low hiss, amplifying the snorting and jostling sounds of both the horses and donkey as the animals jockeyed nervously for position upon their blanket.

Ripples of movement zigzagged across the sand, emphasising the movement of the sleek silver serpents just beneath the surface. As Kerian watched another 'v' shaped ridge slithered towards his sanctuary of stone then disappeared as the creature dropped lower and waited patiently for its prey to step from the stone and reveal itself.

The dropped sword mocked Kerian from fifteen feet away, its blade reflecting the moonlight and gleaming invitingly, its location so tantalisingly close, yet frustratingly out of reach. The knight recognised he had no other weapon to defend himself, no way to respond to the creature when it returned and he knew with a grim certainty that the creature would indeed be back.

Toledo snorted loudly and pawed at the ground, turning about in concern, eyes rolling, head shaking from side to side, as the stallion tried to free itself from the stakes in the ground. Dorian began to bray loudly in protest and Octavian's horse leant back against its stake jerking its head anxiously from side to side, haunches trembling with the effort. Kerian realised the actions for what they were. The mounts had scented something bad was coming towards them and that could only mean Octavian.

A supernatural chill raced up Kerian's spine causing him to tremble and lick his lips nervously. He reached behind and freed the circular shield from his back, slipping one arm through the straps, before pulling his cloak closer around himself and stamping his boots to ward off the penetrating cold that came from more than just the desert night.

Kerian slowly turned, putting the horses at his back as he looked out over the tumbled stonework slabs and back towards the ruined watchtower. It was possible he could jump from slab to slab and get to relative safety, hold up until morning but this would mean abandoning the horses and he was not willing to do this. It was also possible that he might find a makeshift weapon somewhere in the ruins but it was a longshot at best and more likely wishful thinking on his part.

The sand shimmered at the edge of the stone slab, the surface becoming more agitated as the creatures below grew in numbers. Kerian's hand itched for the sword abandoned on the sand but to even consider attempting a rush for the weapon was tantamount to suicide and he had worked too hard and too long to give up on living now.

The beast struck as Kerian turned away. He had a split second of warning, barely enough to raise his shield. A scream from one of the horses, a flash of movement from the side, a harsh guttural cough and then Octavian was upon him.

Sparks lit the night as the creature's claws scored across Kerian's shield. The knight ducked instinctively as the monster hit him, the force of the collision spinning Kerian around, his boots skidding across the stone slab as he tried to halt his unexpected motion, the loose grains of sand upon its surface making his footing precarious as if he were on ice. One boot came down on soft, yielding sand and Kerian felt something squirm violently beneath his sole before he snatched his foot back in horror.

On reflex, the knight lashed out with his shield, hoping to force the beast back, halt its attack and give him space to brace and prepare for further assaults that were bound to follow but there was nothing to hit. Octavian had disappeared.

Kerian tried to calm his racing heart, the shock of the encounter making his pulse boom loudly in his ears and his breathing come in ragged gasps. His hazel eyes nervously scanned the desert landscape as he peeked out from behind the limited protection of his shield, his breath fogging the mirrored surface within. He knew he had to quell his panic, needed to focus on the situation and not succumb to the temptation to rush for the dropped sword.

By Adden! Where was he? Sinister shadows flitted about the eerie landscape, distracting the eye, fooling Kerian's perception and making it impossible to spot the creature that had attacked him. Alien shapes of blue and grey rippled over the dunes as the clouds danced to a private symphony that only they were at liberty to hear, their joyous passage unaware of the tense drama unfolding beneath them. Even the persistent wind had dropped to a low murmur, as if holding its breath for the terrors yet to unfold.

"Come on, show yourself." Kerian muttered, continuing to turn, straining every sense for a clue to the monster's location. His eyes scanned the dunes, the scattered stonework, the ragged palms and straggly clumps of grass struggling for life around the star speckled oasis. The knight paused, taking in two pale blue spots of light within the shadow of one of the clumps of tall grass. Was it the eyes of the creature, a glimpse of the oasis beyond? He could not be sure.

The horses started to shift again, nostrils flaring, nervous shakings of their heads, a rising tension that Kerian felt deep within his chest. Was that Octavian lying in the shadows by the ruins? Could he be the strange silhouette up high upon the toppled watchtower?

With a blood-curdling roar, Octavian launched out from the shadow of a sagging palm tree, his pelt adapting to the light and dark of his backdrop, shimmering as its colours blended to an almost perfect camouflage. The beast's movement was so fast, that the serpents beneath the sand had no chance of striking it.

Kerian spotted the sleek explosion of movement and instantly decided that his current position was no good for staging any kind of defence against such a charge. He judged the distance between the slab beneath his feet and the next partially submerged block of stone over towards the ruin and leapt across the gap, throwing himself through the air with his heart in his throat. He landed on tiptoes, teetering, windmilling with his arms to make himself fall down and hug the cooling ground.

The scream behind him sounded almost human. Kerian spun about from his prone position, bringing his shield up, only to realise that he was never the intended target of this attack. Octavian tore into the horses on the blanket, claws slashing to inflict a vicious laceration to his own stallion's rump, splashing its black and white hide with crimson droplets, before turning to lunge at Toledo.

"No!" Kerian screamed, powerless to assist the stallion as the monster leapt forwards, snarling and spitting and Toledo pulled back heavily against his tether. "Over here. I'm over here you bastard!" He needed something to throw, something to distract the beast; a stone, a piece of bleached wood, a clump of soil and grass, anything to divert the creature's attention back towards him and away from his terrified steed. However, this was a desert, hammered on the anvil by the sun during the day and frozen solid during the night. There was nothing to throw.

Kerian briefly considered his shield, then disregarded it just as swiftly. It was the only thing likely to save him this night and he had no intention of throwing it away! He moved towards the edge of the stone slab, determined to leap back towards the horses only to note the sands shifting inches from his boot and a silvery serpent head emerge, its cold black eyes emphasised by its glowing skin. The snake hissed in warning, its head gently swaying as several other small mounds of sand parted to reveal other slender snouts with flickering tongues as the sand between the stones undulated before him. There was no way he was going to make the jump. His starting stone was higher than the one he now occupied so he was doomed to fall short.

The knight clenched his right fist in frustration, then lowered it to his side where it brushed against the satchel at his hip. This was all pointless there was nothing he could do. Kerian looked back over towards Toledo and watched as Octavian toyed with the stallion, goading it first one way, then the other, snarling and slashing at it with his claws as it snorted in terror.

The satchel, of course! He could throw that! Kerian slapped at his side, fumbling with the strap as he tried to pull the bag free from beneath his cloak but it was all entangled and as he struggled with the bag his hand brushed against the flap lifting it free and opening it. As soon as he lifted the flap the satchel took on a firmer feel as if it was growing heavier. Kerian found himself dragged down to the right as the bag strap tightened around his neck and took on the weight of the contents inside.

The shadowy opening of the bag beckoned, offering up its contents for Kerian's use. He plunged his hand in blindly, to discover a smooth fist sized object atop a jumble of other items. The knight hefted it up and threw it as hard as he could, without looking at what he had actually held in his hand.

A golden statue arced through the air and crashed onto the centre of Octavian's back, making him spin around to face the threat, allowing Toledo to rear up as and lash out with a flashing hoof, catching the monster on its shoulder with a heavy crack. The beast turned, snarling in rage, its mouth opened wide, baring its fangs. Toledo slammed down another hoof, scoring a glancing blow across the creature's snout and making it leap backwards in surprise.

Another priceless statuette spun through the air, crashing into the back of Octavian's twisted knee. He crashed down onto the blanket, then with a snarl sprang back up and leapt just as Toledo stepped aside. Dorian was not as lucky. The beast dropped down on the terrified animal, its teeth plunging into the donkey's neck and savaged the ass in a spray of gore. The leash holding the donkey secure snapped as the monster bore down upon it. Dorian brayed in terror then sank down onto the sand, kicking weakly.

The ground appeared to boil as several silver serpents slithered from below and sank their fangs into the struggling donkey, injecting their venom and wrapping around the doomed animal's legs and body, making Octavian leap clear, frustrated at his lost victim.

Kerian watched in horror as the monster retreated across the sand, his body blending in with the shadows in moments, making the creature practically invisible again. The knight looked towards the jerking body of Dorian, the pitiful brays from the creature now nothing but its own death knell, then towards Toledo who paced in agitation backwards and forwards on the blanket, threatening to churn the flimsy protection up and leave the two horses at the mercy of the same creatures squirming all over the poor donkey.

Octavian would be back in moments; his hunger had not been sated. Kerian stood to dust himself down and as he did so, the flap dropped back over the satchel. The bag instantly became lighter at his side, almost making the knight lose his balance. He reached down cursing, his hand fumbling with the flap, lifting it up only to find himself staring into an empty bag once more.

"Oh not now!" Kerian complained aloud, bringing his shield back around to guard himself as he focused his attention on the search of the bag. The silvery lining remained inert, the location of the contents of the bag once more a mystery. Kerian let the flap fall again and found himself staring at his own reflection in the mirrored surface of his shield.

A much younger Kerian stared back at him. One with jet black hair, a flushed face and hazel eyes tinged with sadness. The image froze Kerian in his tracks. It was as if he had never been cursed, never aged. How could this be? He lifted his right hand to his hair and grabbed a lock of ebony in the reflective surface, pulling it forward so he could see out of the corner of his eye and watched as the face in the mirror pulled the same contorted face that he knew he was making. The lock of hair in Kerian's hand remained grey with age, unlike the one in the mirror.

What was going on? What powers did this shield have? What did the youthful image before him mean? Something shimmered in the glass, reflected back over Kerian's shoulder. Octavian was back, purposefully stalking across the sand towards him, down on all fours, hackles up, piercing blue eyes not focusing on anything but the prey in front of him. His pelt still shimmered in the moonlight but in the surface of the mirror it took on a translucence that showed something below the surface of the monster's skin.

Kerian angled the shield to get a better picture and gasped. Octavian, the real Octavian, was clearly seen in the picture, trapped and struggling to get out from within the monster, clawing at the skin trying to fight his way free, fingers splayed as if he were trying to part the hide and pull himself from the beast that controlled his body and haunted the desert that night. The gypsy's face contorted, screaming at Kerian, clearly trying to warn him of the stealthily approaching danger.

As if on cue, the two stallions began to snort again and stamp their feet. Kerian reached down to the satchel again, fumbling with the pouch, his eyes not daring to move from the terrifying image of the snarling monster stalking towards him. It had worked when he needed it last time, maybe it would again. The flap lifted and his hand plunged into the bag only to feel the same lack of weight, the same feeling of emptiness. His time was up, there would be no salvation from the satchel this time. It was all down to him.

Octavian leapt across the sand, his body arrowing in towards Kerian, unaware the knight was intently watching his every move. The beast picked up speed then pounced; claws outstretched.

Kerian waited as long as he dared then turned to face the charge, swinging the shield around as hard as he could, intercepting the beast in mid-air. The shock of the shield slamming into the monster sent vibrations racing along Kerian's arm and he knew if the weapon had not been strapped on, he would have dropped it. The edge of the shield knocked away Octavian's outstretched claws and slammed into the side of his snarling snout.

The knight tried to follow through, to flip the monster over himself or at least knock him harmlessly off to the side but Octavian's rear claw snagged the edge of the shield then became tangled in his cloak, snatching Kerian around and dragging him after the lunging monster. The two of them collided, Kerian desperately trying to avoid the creature's snapping jaws and vicious claws by hanging on tightly and trying desperately not to let go. The two of them crashed down upon the stone slab, Kerian's right hand clutching Octavian about the throat, trying to force the beast's jaw upwards, whilst the monster's claws slashed across the bracers and shoulder pads of Kerian's armour determined to find a vulnerable spot.

Foul breath washed across Kerian's face as he struggled to pin the creature but it was simply too strong and determined, it's growls and snarls echoing around the dunes, emphasising the victory it felt sure it would achieve. The beast was just so strong! So full of energy!

Kerian pushed up his shield trying to knock the monster away, realising as he did so, that he was exposing his lower limbs to the kicking back claws. He tried to draw his legs up under the pitifully small shelter the shield offered but realised it was leaving him with less ability to fight back. He grunted as the horror pounded hard against his stomach and rolled. A hind claw punched him in the side, snagging on the satchel strap.

The knight pulled away as far as he could, trying to save himself from the slashing claw, struggling to free the strap from the monster's foot. The shield smacked off Kerian's forehead making him see stars and groan aloud. He tried to focus, tried to shake the double vision from his eyes and pulled at the strap as hard as he could.

The satchel suddenly snapped free, dropping to the floor and flopping open. Kerian's hand flailed for the bag, trying to keep it safe. Colette's necklace was still in there. He was not going to relinquish the satchel ever! His shield slipped down as he turned his attention to the satchel. His right hand slipped inside the bag and wrapped around an unmistakable shape. Something any warrior, especially with Kerian's training could recognise with their eyes closed.

Octavian's maw opened wide, lunging for Kerian's exposed neck. The knight pulled his hand from the bag, dragging an ornate sword from its depths. As the blade left the satchel the metal exploded into blinding light, a crystal set at the hilt of the blade appeared to sense it was finally freed from years being kept in the darkness and drew upon its enchanted powers, celebrating its release.

Then for the first time in a thousand years, the desert night was bathed with the light of the sun.

Chapter Thirty-Four

Kerian closed his eyes in shock, the burst of light from the magical sword searing his vision, causing explosions of vivid red to flare across his closed lids. He knew he needed to be doing something, needed to parry Octavian's assault but he was completely blind! He felt claws frantically scratching at his clothes, heard screams of pain as the monster thrashed beside him and all he could do was flail about with the incandescent weapon in his hand and hope that he hit something vital.

His vision had failed him, shadows and flares of light adding to his confusion as he struggled to push across the stone. The knight's mind started playing tricks on him, was he the one screaming or was it Octavian? The last thing he had glimpsed was the beast's jaws coming down towards his neck, now he was struggling to slide out from beneath the creatures pressing weight, striking out desperately to prevent his grisly demise.

All of his senses were amplified, the scuffling and screaming so loud, the scent of sweat and animal musk overpowering. He jerked away from a flailing limb and tried to get to his knees, feeling the satchel flopping down at his side and the warmth of the desert stone beneath his hands. He had to get away, needed to move from the monster thrashing about alongside him to give his eyes a chance to recover. Kerian started to crawl, oblivious to the direction he was heading, the hilt of the magical blade striking the stone as he moved, flaring brightly at each jarring motion.

A warning hiss froze Kerian in place, his hand raised in mid-air. Hell, he had forgotten about the damned snakes! His breath caught in his throat, could he move to the right, to the left? Had he inadvertently crawled into a corner? He dared not back up, for he knew Octavian was still screaming in pain behind him, a sound like knuckles cracking prompting each agonised vocal outburst. Kerian blinked away the tears, desperately trying to see more clearly but everything was just a great big red blur. He had to chance it, had to move either one way, or the other.

Something sounded on the rock behind him. A footstep heavily followed by another, breathing coming in ragged gasps, signals that the monster was pursuing him again. A hand came down on Kerian's shoulder making him start in surprise and move to dodge away.

"Kerian, don't!" Octavian warned; his voice edged in pain. "For both our sakes, stay exactly where you are."

* * * * * *

"So when she asked how much Taurean Elite Guard stock I had in me, I replied I have it in me most nights, sometimes twice!" Karlar laughed, checking her reflection in her vanity mirror and teasing one of her blonde curls.

Squeals of laughter filled the fan-cooled atrium as the herd of aristocratic female Minotaur sprawled about on their loungers, the punchline to the story causing the larger Wanessa to choke on a seedcake she was gorging and several of the others to pass wind. Pascol wrinkled her nose at the odour, pulling a handful of red hair across her nose as if somehow this act would filter the pungent smell, only for her shoulder seam to part as she moved. She gestured to the small serving child standing behind her, ordering her to spray perfume to sweeten the air. Shuesan put down a manuscript she was reading, allowing the parchment to curl back upon itself and obscure the hand drawn sketch of the local strolling players who were stealing hearts in the town's public houses and sneezed loudly.

Wanessa rolled her eyes wildly, her slaves battling to dislodge the seedcake from her throat by hitting her on the back and offering sweet drinks, which the choking Minotaur angrily tossed aside. Chane stepped in, pushing the servants away with heavy blows, her tufted orange hair formed into a fan as subtle as her volatile actions. She slammed a fist down hard behind Wanessa's neck forcing the seedcake to rocket from her maw and skid across the marble floor. Wanessa sucked in a huge gasp of air and moved to sit down, her hands incredibly reaching out for more food to replace the fragment of slobber covered seedcake just lost.

Mora sighed heavily at the wanton display of vulgarity and gluttony. These were the ruling elite, the people destined to replace her, the matriarchs of choice to rule the populace. Tradition decreed it, Mora had spent hours checking and rechecking the laws, trying to find a loophole, something to allow her to rule until the day she died but the rules were clear. At the time of her next birthday, she would be forced from power and one of these spoilt cows would be stepping literally into her robes as she was put out to pasture! The very thought of it made Mora bristle with rage. She had to find a way; some means to maintain her hold on the lifestyle she had come to enjoy but the texts revealed nothing. No way to justify more years on the throne, no way to extend a role that Mora had literally been born to. It was her birthright and she had no intentions of giving it up before she was ready to.

Then she had discovered a clause in the rules of the ancient Labyris contest, an antiquated and brutal means to succession for rulers of the past, to ensure only the strongest Minotaur sat upon the throne. Today it was more of a theatrical contest with contestants' content to risk their lives simply navigating the deadly maze at the base of the pyramid, in a massive spectacle of colour and violence that kept the populace entertained, enthralled and therefore controlled. No one was brave or insane enough to attempt the second and most dangerous part of the challenge ascending inside the pyramid for the actual Labyris axe.

Mora smiled to herself, she knew that in the past anyone seizing the axe could claim the throne, something unheard of in present generations. This year a true prince would be competing, Drummon would be taking part and through Mora's manipulation, he was going to win and therefore secure his right to rule.

The Matriarch was sure none of the group lounging before her had the intelligence or foresight to realise her plans; that her champion would dare to undertake the second deadlier challenge and risk going for the Labyris and then seize the throne. The very thought of it made Mora grin. Threatening to turn the female led Taurean society into a male led one. It was so ridiculous and therefore equally unexpected!

Mora believed it would go one of two ways, either Drummon became the ruler of Taurean, shaking the very foundation on which modern Taurean was built, whilst becoming a puppet king for Mora to pull his strings and manipulate whoever she chose. Alternatively, the winner could declare a favour from the ruling party, instead of accepting his chance upon the throne, Drummon could plead that the ruling party continue to offer protection over the populace and Mora as that humbled ruler, was more than happy to accept such an onerous task. Either outcome was acceptable to her; she just needed Kristoph to be a legitimate challenger to make the ceremony more impressive, more spectacular and more binding than any challenge that had gone before.

There was just one problem. No one knew where Kristoph was.

Mora moved to stroke the royal ring and realised a second too late that it was still missing. Why had Aelius not returned with the jewel? Surely, the Halfling was swinging in the breeze by now, his eyes food for the crows, the ring safely back in the captain's hands. It was a troublesome feeling that lurked in the back of her mind, like an itch she could not scratch.

Something was not right and the thought of losing control and her throne made Mora feel the pressure rising. She turned her attention back to the master of ceremonies for the games who had been talking continuously about all of the wonderful exhibits and surprises he had in store. The matriarch tried to concentrate on the enthusiastic presentation, noting that with all the spectacle this Minotaur was including, the cost would be astronomical. Taxes would have to rise next year.

"So all is ready?" she asked. "The tournament can now go ahead as planned."

"I await your command your majesty." The games master bowed. "All I need is a date."

A loud clatter came from outside of the double doors leading into the chamber. The clattering of plate mail crashing to the floor, cries of outrage swiftly silenced with dull thuds and grunts.

"What in the world is going on?" Mora asked, indicating with her hand that the guards best investigate and swiftly. Could it be Aelius returning with her ring? Had Drummon made it back from the jungle with Kristoph in tow? Or was it something else? Mora's hand slipped into the sash of her robe and felt for the stiletto dagger she had secreted there.

The doors crashed open, sending the guard nearest the entrance spinning away to smash into a brazier of hot coals that crashed to the floor, scattering burning embers across the rugs. Ammet thrust two serving children towards the coals and started screaming for them to pick the embers up with their bare hands, as smoke started to spiral up from the rugs. Chane leapt up, snatching a serving tray from in front of Wanessa and sending finger food all over the astonished rotund Minotaur. The stern Minotaur scooped the tray across the floor, batting the coals off the rugs and onto the cool marble where their heat could harm no one.

Karlar, meanwhile, was on her knees, flashing a sizeable amount of cleavage into the fallen guard's face as he struggled to regain his feet but as she knelt a shadow fell across the room, stifling her forward advances as the huge figure of an enraged Minotaur smashed his way into the room.

Rauph roared his anger to the world, his eyes blazing, chestnut hair matted, covered in the detritus of the swamp and dried blood. He looked around the room, his chest rising and falling with the effort of fighting his way this deep into the palace, before his eyes fell on the figurehead of his mother.

"Poisoner!" he snarled, stepping threateningly towards her. A guard rushed in from the left, only to have his helmet crushed by a vicious swing of Rauph's sword, leaving the unfortunate Minotaur to drop senseless to the floor. Karlar sighed deeply from her position on the floor, dropping the head of the guard she was comforting to gaze at the raw unbridled strength of Kristoph, Prince of the Taureans.

"He's so dreamy!" Shuesan gasped from her lounger, drawing a look of sheer venom from Karlar.

"Kristoph, how wonderful to see you here." Mora stated, as if a crazed Minotaur bursting in to her private chambers was an everyday occurrence. "What can I do for you?"

"Ives is dead because of you." Rauph shouted, stepping closer, shoving an ornate urn decorated with griffons out of his way, its delicate shape shattering into a thousand pieces on the tiled floor. "Weyn is badly injured and you even tried to poison my captain."

"I don't even know who Ives was, let alone had anything to do with killing him." Mora stated calmly, her hand gripping the hilt of her stiletto tightly for reassurance. "The name of Weyn means nothing to me either. All I know is that you class them as your friends and therefore I must protect you from them and remove you from their corrupting influence." Mora paused in mid speech.

"What do you mean *tried* to poison your captain? He's dead; no one can escape the kiss of the Nirschl."

Rauph parried a halberd strike and smashed the guard to the floor before the Minotaur had space to draw breath, then strode forwards purposefully, one of his long swords held firmly in his massive hand.

"You have no right to interfere in my life. No right to choose who I can and cannot have as my friends. They are more a family to me than you have ever been." Rauph snarled. "How dare you try to hurt them."

"Oh I will do more than hurt them." Mora replied quietly. "I intend to kill all of them."

Rauph roared in anger, swinging up his sword, preparing to bring the blade down upon his mother's head, only for his blade to be stopped in mid-swing by a blade of darkened worn steel. The force of the blow vibrated up the blade, as Rauph turned towards the interloper determined to inflict his wrath upon them.

Aelius stood his ground, his apparent age hiding a strength created by will alone.

"I cannot allow you to do this." The captain of the guard grunted, the muscles of his arms bulging at the force it required to stop Rauph's blow from landing. "The matriarch is under my protection."

"Then you have chosen your side and I respect you for it." Rauph groaned. "I shall try and kill you quickly."

"Better Minotaur than you have tried." Aelius replied. "Yet you forget, I am the one who trained you." The captain performed a *Moulinet* parry followed by a circular cut, twisting his blade around Rauph's weapon and lunging forwards, smashing the hilt of his weapon up under Rauph's jaw, knocking the navigator back and away from his mother with a cry of pain.

"Mother I could not find Kristoph or Ashe Wolfsdale." Drummon shouted from the doorway of the room, his voice dropping away when he saw the dazed guards lying about the floor. "What is this?"

The black Minotaur charged into the room with a roar, knocking servants and guards alike from his path as he moved to defend the Matriarch from his brother.

"Kristoph what are you doing?" He screamed. Slamming into Rauph and knocking the dazed Minotaur further away from his goal.

Rauph pivoted, swinging his sword in a deadly arc that shaved the top of Chane's orange mane and decapitated several gilded lilies in an ornate display. There was a shriek of shock from Chane, followed by the titter of several members of the female ruling elite who witnessed what had happened.

Aelius stepped back, dropping his guard, his personal honour not permitting him to continue to fight the young prince now that Drummon had joined the fray. Weapons clashed together as the two brothers turned on each other. The deafening sounds echoed throughout the room as the Minotaur thrust and parried, feinted and disengaged, trying to find an opening in each other's defences.

"Why were you looking for Ashe Wolfsdale?" Rauph snarled, snapping his blade hard against Drummon's forcing the weapon out to one side. "You stay away from my friend."

"Ashe Wolfsdale is no longer a concern." Mora stated as the two brothers clashed, causing Rauph to pause in his attack and allow Drummon to bring his sword back in line again. "He was hung an hour ago."

"What?" Rauph turned in shock, without thinking, leaving his side dangerously exposed. "What do you mean hung." Mora smiled slyly, noting Drummon drawing back his weapon to deliver a crushing blow.

"Hung by the neck until dead." The Matriarch gloated. "A suitable end to a disgusting little thief."

An urn crashed into Drummon's back, making him stagger and miss his opening, the lunging blade of his weapon glancing off Rauph's horn with a shriek that set everyone's teeth on edge.

"Your little thief is hung high; Ives and your captain are dead and your Weyn is injured. How many more of your friends do I need to kill before you realise you have no choice but to obey me?" Mora continued, trying to hide her confusion that her son's attack had failed. Her eyes scanned the dazed figure of Drummon who had turned in anger to look at a high pedestal behind him as if it had become animate and suddenly attacked him. The urn had apparently fallen from its peak, something that was impossible without a violent earth tremor and Mora knew no such tremor had occurred.

All of the fight had left Rauph, he stood dazed. Drummon shoved him hard in the back, sending the navigator down upon his knees to sprawl before his mother.

"Now that is so much better." Mora stated. "You are back where you belong at last, penitent before me repenting your sins."

"Listen carefully Kristoph as I do not like wasting my breath." She continued with a voice as sharp as the dagger she held within her robes. "I will take great delight in killing every one of your friends, every member of the *El Defensor's* crew unless you toe the line and do as I command. Do you understand me?" each word of her final sentence delivered with the finality of a coffin lid being nailed shut. Rauph moved to lift his head only to have it pushed back down towards the floor by Drummon.

"I'm going to kill you in the maze." Drummon wheezed in his ear. Rauph looked up dazed not sure what his deranged brother was on about.

Mora turned to the games master cowering in the corner.

"Two days and the celebrations start." The Matriarch ordered. "Do not fail me." The games master swallowed hard and paled as she rose from her throne and walked about the room taking in the destruction about her. Her robes swept about her as she turned to offer her thunderous gaze towards Kristoph.

"In two days you shall take part in the Labyris tournament and fight to the death in the labyrinth. If you do this, I shall spare your crew until after the contest and then we shall see where we stand. You no longer have leave to depart the palace. You shall live here, locked away from your friends and their corrupting influence. Any attempt to contact them will result in serious penalties for your friends. I have given you a two-day reprieve for those friends that remain living. My generosity will not last for long." The Matriarch moved towards the exit her hand finally coming out of her robes, holding the slender dagger.

"Two days then I can kill you." Drummon laughed getting to his feet and pushing Rauph's head back to the floor again, bouncing the navigator's horns painfully on the marble. "This time I'll do it right and you shall stay dead."

Mora turned at the doorway and gestured to the servants hiding in numerous places about the room.

"Make sure this is all cleaned up before I return." She ordered, taking in the shocked faces. "I'm moving to my bed chambers to rest, all this excitement is simply draining. So keep the noise down." Mora swept from the room in a rustle of material. Drummon sauntered after her, chuckling to himself, snatching up a delicate cake as he walked by and taking a large bite before laughing through a mouthful of food.

"Two days, brother." He laughed. "It's all over in two days."

Rauph remained prone on the floor for what seemed like an eternity, his mind churning with the revelations just made to him. Ashe and Ives were dead, Thomas poisoned. How many more of the crew would suffer from being able to call him friend?

The navigator staggered to his feet and collected his blade from the floor before he made a slow exit from the room and turned towards his lodgings in the west wing. As soon as he left the room erupted in gossip behind him as the female Minotaur judged the raw animal strength they had just seen.

As the excited discussion rose and the servants started rushing about the room tidying up the damage from the fight, Aelius walked out from behind the pedestal, looking perplexed as if he were busy investigating the mysterious toppling urn,

* * * * * *

"Now are you sure you are up to this?" Thomas asked, staring into the inky darkness where the steerage chain had dropped into the bowels of the ship. "It's going to be a long way down."

"I could ask you the same question about your ability to be up and about captaining the *El Defensor* when you were near death's door with a fever a few hours ago." Rowan replied, her hands frantically tying her hair back with a headscarf and pulling it clear from her glowing face. "Commagin tells me he sends Barney into the workings of the ship all the time to make repairs where he can't reach. I work in engineering so it is my job to step up and do something to earn my keep on this ship. I trust Colette and will be back before you know it."

Commagin huffed and puffed behind her, clearly upset about the mention of his lost friend as he set about sorting through a huge sack of tools.

"That will do it," he grumbled, hefting a huge wrench over towards her as if it were as light as a feather.

"What am I expected to do with this?" Rowan asked, grunting as she took the weight of the wrench.

"You need something to protect yourself with if there is a problem and you might need a lever of some sort if the chain is snagged." The engineer replied, removing his thick glasses and polishing them on a dirty rag.

"Problem... What sort of problem?" Thomas spluttered.

"He's only kidding." Rowan replied, determined to show she was not as anxious as she actually felt. It was just like going on her first solo flight, where she had to depend on her own ability rather than that of her instructor. She swallowed hard; come to think of it her first flight was not her greatest. Maybe it would be better if she did not recall this situation.

"It's just the magic I'm worried about." Thomas confessed. "I don't understand it and I can't control it. What if something goes wrong?"

"Thomas Adams you have never worried about my magic wielding abilities before, so why would you worry about them now?" Colette teased. "Why don't you just admit it's different when you have a personal interest in the item being magicked."

"I don't feel this way about it when you cast magic upon the ship." Thomas blurted in response. "And I have a personal interest in her."

"Is he comparing me to this barnacle coated antique?" Rowan winked at Colette, pretending to be insulted. "I should be the only woman in your life and don't you forget it buster, especially after what we just did in your cabin." Thomas turned scarlet and ran his hand across his forehead.

"That's not what I mean. It's... You know..."

"I am touched you are concerned. Now let me do my job." Rowan stood on tiptoe and kissed Thomas lightly on the cheek. "Besides if it does go wrong, I'm not worried. I always wanted to lose some weight; I will be just like James Barrie's Tinkerbell and you can be my Peter Pan. You never know you might look good in green tights."

Thomas turned, scanning the deck for something to focus on to stop his concerns from showing and ruin his image as a gruff captain. He noted Commagin untangling a long spool of thin chain across the deck, the engineer's hands feeling each link, checking for damage and leaving it positioned so he could feed it down into the hole. It was a job that Thomas knew he could not help with, even though he wished to intrude and double check the Dwarf's meticulous work. There was so much at stake here.

He looked over to Colette noticing her fishing in her pouch for a gemstone to cast her spell and scowling at the small stones she held in her hand. What if the jewel Colette used did not hold enough power within its clear core, making the spell fizzle out whilst Rowan was still trapped in a space too small to regrow? This whole situation was nightmarish!

"Everyone stand well back." Colette warned; her scowl still clear on her tired face. The ship's mage closed her eyes in concentration, muttering under her breath as she concentrated and prepared to cast her spell. A cold wind blew across the harbour, lifting her golden curls creating an illusion that

Colette was using her skills to tame the very elements swirling around the ship, as the pulsating energy from the shattered gemstone snaked up her arm.

"Hang on a moment! She needs a storm lantern." Commagin spluttered. The dwarf shuffled over and placed the lantern in Rowan's hand. "To light your way in the dark and find your way back." Rowan paled and Thomas noticed a slight tremor in her hand.

Colette gritted her teeth, her mind struggling to hold the spell in check, her hand appearing to pulsate with the energies harvested from the depths of the topaz she had used to energise her spell.

"Can we get on with this now?" she growled. Rowan looked more apprehensive, her complexion paling, her cheeks flushed at the unexpected wait, allowing the anxieties within her to surface.

"I love you." Thomas stated calmly. "I will be right here waiting for your return."

"You tell me this now?" Rowan choked. "How is that supposed to make me…"

Arcane energies rippled across the deck appearing to wrap around Rowan's form and then she appeared to vanish with a barely detectible popping sound. Colette carefully walked over and leant down, picking up something from the deck before turning towards Commagin with the delicate treasure secured safely in her palm.

Thomas rushed over, his heart in his throat and stared over the mage's shoulder to see a tiny miniaturised Rowan standing in the middle of Colette's hand. Rowan now stood about five centimetres tall, the lantern and the wrench shrunk in perfect scale to her. Commagin shuffled over and held up a long rope that had a small cage securely tied to the end. Threaded through the bars to one side of the door was a large safety pin, the type used in old-fashioned diapers, with a clip that fitted snugly over the end to prevent accidental injury. Fastened onto the safety pin through one of its fine links was the end of the thin chain that Commagin had laid out across the deck.

The engineer eased open the small door of the cage with his stubby finger and rested it against Colette's hand so Rowan could step inside. Rowan jumped across the narrow gap and then, just before she swung the door closed, she turned and blew a kiss in Thomas's direction. The captain smiled and offered a smart salute in return, trying not to openly show his emotions and growing sense of pride, as he stared lovingly at the woman that he now realised he wanted to make his wife.

"Now lass, remember when you get down there in the depths of the ship, I want you to locate the end of the large chain that has come free. Then I want you to carefully thread this safety pin and chain through a link near the break and then open the pin and clip it around the thin chain to form a loop. Make sure it securely fastened and then I can pull the whole chain back up above decks to make the repairs to the helm. I know the slim chain looks as if it will snap but it is enchanted and much stronger than it looks. So cheer up, I know you can do this." Commagin pushed his glasses up onto the end of his nose. "There's no time like the present. So let's get to it."

Before Thomas could say anything, Rowan backed fully into the cage and Commagin pushed the door closed then moved over to the hole in the deck. The Dwarven engineer carefully lowered the rope into the darkness, taking his time to feed both the rope and chain into the hole and ensuring that the thin chain did not snag or knot as it snaked across the deck.

"Well there's nothing more for me to do here." Colette smiled, brushing her hands together to remove the debris of her spell.

"What do you mean?" Thomas remarked. "You need to stay here until she comes back up."

"No I don't." the ship's mage smiled. "Rowan is quite capable of taking care of herself and I have things to do."

"Like what?" Thomas demanded, quite angry at the thought Colette was effectively abandoning Rowan.

"Sword fighting lessons with Aradol." The mage smiled, winking a suggestive coral blue eye. "After all, Aradol doesn't have a large cabin to play in!"

* * * * * *

"What is the point of having a magical sword that glows like the sun, if it does not produce heat as well? Octavian asked, trying to stop his teeth chattering together. "I don't know about you but I could really use some warmth, or at least a blanket and a roaring fire right about now." He stared hungrily at the light bathing his legs and desperately wished the illumination could be as comforting as it looked.

"Be my guest." Kerian replied stiffly, gesturing across the sands to where their supplies lay, the two stallions now quietly standing as silent sentries above the scattered bags and belongings. "I'm sure as long as you run fast enough you might make it over there without being bitten more than six or seven times!"

"Now that's the Kerian I remember, all warm and fuzzy." Octavian replied, cracking a strained smile. "I had no idea how much I had missed your eternal optimism. The gypsy shivered, pulling the tattered remains of his clothes about his shoulders and abdomen and inched towards the glowing weapon.

"Just stay over there." Kerian warned, his hand lightly resting on the hilt of the magical blade, in preparation to use it again at a moment's notice. Octavian swallowed hard, his smile fading as his eyes noted the threat Kerian's tone implied.

"At least you could offer me some clothes." Octavian shivered. "I mean you must have some to spare because I distinctly remember you were not wearing that outfit the last time that I saw you." The desert wind suddenly whipped through the dunes, wailing its haunting lament, making the gypsy tremble intensely. Kerian lifted the flap on the satchel at his side and shook his head before tipping the bag upside down and showing the barren insides to his companion.

"Sorry, I seem to have left my other set of clothes on my horse, which is..." he clicked his fingers and shrugged his shoulders before rolling his eyes. "Oh yes, across on the blankets, with the food, the firewood and the water. You will just have to suffer like I am."

"But..."

"I prefer to suffer in silence." Kerian warned.

"Can I at least share your cloak?" the gypsy pleaded. "After all, I did stop you from putting your hand directly down onto a snake!"

"Excuse me if I am a little reluctant to get too close to someone who has the propensity to sprout claws, fangs and is clearly in need of a barber." Kerian replied, still weary of his now strangely serene and mellow companion. Octavian looked up at the full moon as if in deep thought, his lips tinged blue in the nocturnal light. Wisps of cotton cloud stretched to breaking point across the star-spangled sky, as the gypsy's mind pondered the strange phenomena he was experiencing.

"I must confess I am a little confused at the moment." Octavian muttered. "I should still be in my animal state right now, with the moon so full and high in the sky. I never have control at such times and yet here I am sitting in the glow of your sword and I am not inclined to change, no need to run free. My blood is not pounding in my veins and my body is pain free. It is most confusing."

"Your bestial side is an interesting quirk to your personality but I can assure you I am in no hurry to see it again any time soon." Kerian confirmed, his finger tracing an absent-minded circle in the loose grains of sand on the surface of the stone beside him. "I take from this that you have changed before, back in the market place in Wellruff. You killed the guards, you were the wild animal."

"They got what they deserved." Octavian snapped. "You saw what they were doing to me!"

"I'm not arguing with you." Kerian stated calmly, his expression thoughtful. "However, if I remember rightly it was not evening when the change occurred. There was no moon in the sky. Are you telling me you can change into that monster at whim?"

"Yes, I can change in moments of stress, when the beast recognises that I am in danger and wishes to protect me from harm." Octavian confirmed. "I have no control over the animal's reactions once I change but after the danger is past, I revert back to my normal self quite quickly. However, my control is not as well defined at times of the full moon. Then the monster has to come out whether I wish it to or not."

"This makes no sense. The moon has been full several times on the road. I never saw you change and your wardrobe has never looked quite so threadbare as it does this evening."

"I always take the time to undress before I change form. I hide my clothes then collect them again as dawn arrives. How was I to know you were going to leave me lying under the stars to bathe in the full moonlight? I am always so careful, always making sure you were resting and the horses were secured before I metamorphosed and hunted the surrounding areas for food. I always found you snoring soundly when I returned, never realising I was anything but the reluctant guide you had conned into taking this godforsaken trip." Kerian shrugged his shoulders, smirking at the mention of his subterfuge and then looked up sharply.

"What do you mean snoring?"

"Like a hog with sinusitis." Octavian smiled before continuing. "I have no choice, I have to change, if not I become irrational, easier to provoke, more prone to violent outbursts. Somehow, letting the beast out calms the animal urges within me."

"This evening was not calm, anything but!" Kerian snorted. "Your calmness has cost us poor Dorian and possibly more, although we won't know exactly how much until daylight."

Octavian shivered again, hanging his head in shame. A long-eared owl shrieked in triumph as it swooped down to pluck a silver serpent from the dunes. Monstrous wings cut the air, lifting the nocturnal creature away to consume its nocturnal feast, leaving the gypsy wishing he could leave as easily.

"Damn, I'm so cold." He tried to steady his chattering teeth.

"It serves you right for not dressing for the weather conditions." Kerian joked, shuffling over with the magical sword in hand. He lifted his cloak to drop part of it over his shivering companion's naked shoulders.

"Thank you." Octavian nodded, pulling the cloth close about his body.

"I said you could share it, not take it all!" Kerian stated, tugging back. "I'm cold too!"

"Are we snuggling?" The gypsy chuckled, laughing as Kerian pretence to jerk away. "What would my wife think?"

"I think you should consider that it is still a long way until the dawn." Kerian replied calmly, as his mind recalled the revelation whispered into his ear by the exotic woman, he now knew was Octavian's partner. "Also remember that I am the one still holding the sword!"

Octavian tilted his head and fluttered his eyes.

"You know if you snuggle well, I might reward you with a love bite!"

Chapter Thirty-Five

The small cage descended slowly into the bowels of the ship, the chain controlling the descent paying out in fits and starts as inky darkness closed in around Rowan like the grip of a giant fist. Whilst Commagin tried to lower Rowan as smoothly as he could, the unavoidable jerks as he fed out the chain turned her clockwise, then anti-clockwise, leaving Rowan with the choice of looking up towards the light above, or feeling sick with the constant spinning of the cage. She closed her eyes to calm the butterflies fluttering in her stomach and then risked looking up through the bars of the cage towards the ever-decreasing circle of light that signified how far she now was from the safety of Thomas's arms. This sense of isolation was not a feeling Rowan was relishing and yet she knew she would never forgive herself if she failed to see this task through.

Smells of old grease, discarded dust, untreated damp and sea salt assailed Rowan's nostrils, as her surroundings morphed into shapeless blobs too difficult to discern. She stepped to the edge of the cage and tried to see below but there was nothing except impenetrable inky blackness. Rowan took a deep breath to try and steady her nerves, her gaze latching onto the only thing that could give her some comfort in this menacing place, noticing to her annoyance, that the storm lantern she held in her fist appeared to be trembling.

Something skittered loudly away in the darkness, a long pale tail flicking once in the lamplight before plunging into the shadows. Rowan swung the lantern to investigate, only to gasp as she spotted four sets of red eyes balanced above each other, reflecting the light back towards her and creating the illusion the woman was staring into a bizarrely arranged set of vanity mirrors. A thick cobweb strummed like a guitar string as the cage bumped past and the four eyes turned away as one, eight hairy legs scuttling off, eager to investigate what succulent morsel fought to survive, trapped in its sticky web.

Rowan swallowed hard, choking back her feelings of unease. The rat's tail was easily five or six times her own current height. The vermin had to be some kind of monster! Rowan suddenly realised the danger she was in, shrunk to a perfect rat sized snack! She shuddered and then thought of what a spider bite could do to her in her current predicament. What would have been a simple irritant for a few days, easily treated with steroid cream or a course of antibiotics, would now be instantly fatal!

She stamped her foot angrily, gritting her teeth and making the cage tremble. Rowan did not want Thomas to feel less of her, to think her weak or not willing to help him and his ship. She was not prepared to disappoint him in any way and fought to keep her fears in check.

The cage continued to descend as Rowan's feelings of impotence continued to grow. This situation was getting worse and worse the more she thought about it. They were too far down! How much longer was this descent going to last? What if they ran out of chain, what if something happened to send her plummeting to her doom? What if...

The cage lightly landed, the chain quickly pooling up on the roof before sliding to the floor and causing clouds of dust to fly up into the air. Rowan pushed on the door glad to see that she was not trapped within the cage and stepped out onto the floor, only to find herself shuffling knee deep through the accumulated dust and debris.

"I suppose I should say something deep and meaningful?" Rowan muttered to herself. "Something like one small step for woman, a giant leap for womankind." She tried to focus her thoughts, securing the wrench at her belt as she tugged free the thin chain and safety pin but ironically all she could think of was the fact that the area needed a damn good clean! Anything could be under this dust, she could mis-step, put her foot between the planks of the ship and twist her ankle, or worse yet slip through a crack and plummet to her doom, landing somewhere in the bilges or breaking her body on the ballast stones of the hull.

Lifting the lantern high, she struggled to make out where the elusive chain and end goal of her unusual quest lay. It had to be lying in a discarded pile on the floor somewhere, yet as Rowan slowly extended her search area away from the cage, she could find no sign of it. This was ridiculous! The chain had to be here. It was not as if it had simply got up and walked away of its own volition!

Rowan continued cautiously navigating the floor, the thin chain snaking across the ground behind her as she slid first one foot, then the other, across the uneven surface. Dust piled up around her boots, soiling the leather. Well, one thing was for sure. When she got out of this Thomas was going to buy her some new boots and maybe even a nice feminine dress as well. Something slinky, that complemented her figure and felt exciting to wear, unlike the rough, coarse fabrics and hardwearing garb favoured by the fashion-retarded crew of the *El Defensor*! A smile crossed Rowan's face and a flush of colour sprang to her cheeks, temporarily lifting the gloom that had settled upon her in this dank place.

A huge cog wheel, at least from Rowan's tiny perspective, sat vertically in a hole in the floor. This was clearly where the loop of the chain ceased, where the action of turning the helm above converted the movement of the ancient rudder at the stern of the ship. Rowan lifted her lantern higher, letting the pale light illuminate the cold chain links descending to the floor and engaging with the teeth of the cog, interlocking before running down beneath the deck, passing around the cog and then rising up towards the helm.

Rowan cursed as her limited view followed the chain as it rose into the darkness; she realised that her goal was not lying loose in a discarded pile upon the floor, like she had been led to expect. Instead it appeared that the end of the chain was hung up somewhere in the darkness above. There was nothing for it, she would just have to climb.

Threading her left arm through the giant safety pin, Rowan approached the chain and shook her head. Just how far up was she going to have to climb? This thing looked as big as the beanstalk in the fairy tale stories she loved as a child. It looked to be a long way! She gripped the chain and felt the greasy surface sliding beneath her fingers.

Oh, Thomas was going to owe her far more than a pair of boots and a nice dress when she finished with this. He was going to have to buy her a completely new wardrobe! She jumped up, locking her hands around the link above, before pulling herself up, gripping the cold metal with her thighs as she started the long climb into the shadows. The thin silver chain snaked across the dusty floor behind her, unravelling from where it had landed near the cage and wriggling as if it were alive.

* * * * * *

"I just can't believe this has happened," wailed a dejected voice. "Of all the bad luck! How could we possibly have had two inns burn down around our ears?"

"It's like we rolled a 'critical miss 'whilst wielding an enchanted long sword!" came a mournful reply. "The outcome is always messy and you are left with a nagging doubt that something you have become attached to is missing from your life."

"The gods are against us," stated a third voice. "I guess it is our lot in life to suffer."

"I'm going to miss the bowls of chilli and the garlic sand prawns, they were to die for.," added a fourth.

"I think it's all relative to time and space," boomed a fifth. "And we are clearly not in the right time and are never in the right place. Would anyone care for a candied gelatine infant?"

"Please be quiet, I'm trying to write down the words of a song that just came to me!" said the sixth voice, before its owner reverted to humming a tune that only he could hear.

Scrave turned his attention from placing one weary foot in front of another and pulled his headscarf more tightly around his face as his ears isolated the discussion from amongst all of the grunts, curses, animal cries, cracking whips, wailing babies and creaking wagons from the caravan train in which he was now hiding. He knew those voices! The Elf carefully began to slow his pace, causing curses and less than flattering comments to rise from the mouths of the people in the caravan walking past him, as they had to change direction to avoid a collision. A scruffy camel plodded past on massive flat feet and deposited a pile of dung directly in Scrave's path, causing a few insolent laughs from other travellers who felt the offering would have been better if it had landed on the Elf's head.

It took several moments of skilful weaving throughout the confusion of the column, before the Elf managed to draw level with the group of despondent travellers and confirm his suspicions. He hunched his shoulders to reduce his height and leaned more heavily on the staff in his left hand, taking small ponderous steps as of a weary old man, whilst he let an unseen smile slide across his face. He was right. It was the young men from the inn, the gaming group.

One burly youth pushed hard at another, causing him to tumble into the path of a pair of oxen, only for the fallen youth to be snatched back with a handful of tunic by the aforementioned offender who then delighted in informing his shaken colleague that his life had just been saved. These young men seemed so innocent and carefree. Scrave shook his head. He had never been innocent and being carefree soon meant being dead where he came from.

A disturbance at the back of the caravan tore Scrave from his dark thoughts; voices raised in anger and alarm reached his ears. Moving silently away from the youths, Scrave made his way to the outer edge of the caravan and stared back across the desert sands, his eye tracing the snaking line of traders right back towards the city of Al Mashmaah, where slender minarets gleamed golden in the clear sunlight of the early dawn. One glance was all it took to confirm the Elf's fears.

Guards seated upon giant salamander were making their way up the line, their huge amphibian mounts hissing angrily at anyone who dared resist, large tails swishing in frustration or thumping down onto the sand, causing travellers to jump and start away. Irate guards pushed over boxes, emptying carts, causing a general disturbance as they made their way along the line searching for something, or more likely someone. It did not take much imagination to guess who that someone was!

Scrave cursed his own stupidity, having already debated at length with himself, that leaving in a trade caravan was the most obvious and therefore the least wise choice of actions opened to him. Yet here he was, despite his mental protests, feet pounding the sand along with all of these other travellers, destination unimportant as long as it was away from Al Mashmaah and its prying eyes.

These desperate actions made no sense! He knew that it was dangerous to leave, so why was he here now? The Elf reached up and subconsciously touched his eyepatch, then paused, hand raised, as his mind caught up with his actions and started filling in the blanks. A dawning realisation of horror swept over him, the thoughts sending shivers down his spine as the only possible cause squirmed within his right eye socket. It had all felt so natural at the time, as if Scrave were the one leading the way and making the decisions but now as he thought about it, there could be no other reason why he was in this ludicrous position. The Elf almost believed he could hear whatever it was chuckling at his horrific discovery.

Shouts and cries of protest became progressively louder as the guards continued to advance. A couple of excitable chickens ran out from the column straight into the path of one loping salamander that simply flicked out a long sticky tongue and drew the creatures, feathers and all back into its maw with a sickening crunch. The guards pulled traders aside, making them stand apart from their families and fellow travellers, whilst they ransacked their belongings, the contents scattered cruelly across the sand.

Scrave's initial instinct was to run away, find somewhere to hide but the desert was a barren and desolate place with nowhere for him to run without being exposed as the fugitive that he was. He considered pushing through the crowds, making his way towards the front of the column and then just as swiftly reconsidered, there was an established hierarchy to these trade caravans and if he were to try to push past, towards the more affluent travellers, looking as he did, his discovery would be certain. The thought of his current camouflage betrayed by the very people he was using to hide within gave the Elf an uncomfortable moment to pause and consider his options.

A bright flash of light cut the air over the tradesmen isolated to one side and a stench of strong ozone started to filter through the convoy. A slender figure stepped from the light, followed by a group of heavyset guards. Long silky robes flowed about her form, accentuating curves and offering a brief glimpse of tantalising flesh that would be the dream or death of any man whose gaze lingered too long.

The Elf took a deep breath in shock and tried to steady himself; how had the sorceress found him so fast? His sudden, unexpected inhalation coincided with a mischievous gust of wind and a handful of blown sand from the desert that lashed Scrave's face and entered his open mouth, resulting in a coughing spasm he was powerless to stop. Worried stares from the traders and wayfarers around him resulted in merchants starting to ease away from this unexpected risk of contagion.

Scrave tried to smile, tried to reassure everyone with a waving hand that he was fine but he just ended up coughing more, bringing tears to his eye. He tried to blink rapidly and cover his mouth in a futile attempt to quell the outburst even as he gained another glimpse of the beauty that pursued him at the corner of his eye. The Elf would have recognised those legs anywhere, even with an eye that streamed with tears!

Justina stepped away from her guards and slinked over to the first hapless trader, shouted something at him that Scrave could not hear, then cast a spell that made the unfortunate man's head explode in a blossom of gore. His smoking corpse dropped to the sand, the stump of his neck still smoking, as cries of anguish rose from his family back in the main convoy. Unperturbed by this reaction, Justina advanced towards the next in line and repeated her fearsome questioning.

Having seen enough, Scrave turned away to lose himself back into the crowd only to find to his surprise that during his coughing fit, he had been left standing well apart from the convoy. He looked around in shock, trying to gauge the best direction to head without drawing attention to himself and slowly started to move back, only to hear a loud voice demand that he stopped and identified himself.

The Elf bowed his head, cursing his poor luck, turning on the spot, as a mounted guard charged up to him on his salamander, the amphibian skidding to a halt in a blast of sand that threatened to set off Scrave's coughing all over again. He tried to hunch down lower, tried to make himself look pitiful and poor, only to feel his breath catch in his throat as the figure of Justina paused in her interrogation and stared directly at him.

"State your name and business." The guard demanded, pointing his lance directly at Scrave's chest. The Elf pantomimed another cough, theatrically clutching at his robes, before slowly slipping his hand inside to feel the cool metal of the enchanted serpent dagger wrap almost sensuously around his wrist. He checked the tip of the lance, noting the skill of the guard and the fact it barely wavered. The guard's reach with the weapon was a distinct disadvantage and moving in close would put the Elf dangerously near to the snapping salamander. Scrave licked his lips nervously, his voice still hoarse from the cough and prepared to act.

"Speak up man." The guard demanded, alighting from his mount as it pawed impatiently at the ground, its long tail flicking from side to side in excitement, possibly in the hope of having another Elf-sized chicken for lunch. Scrave risked a quick glimpse over the guard's shoulder and noticed that Justina was now taking slow measured steps towards him. He needed to act now!

"Oh father, what are you doing out here?" A voice rose from behind him, making the tense Elf jump, as an arm draped across his shoulder and tried to guide him away. "I have told you so many times not to wander off."

The surprise was total as Scrave took in the features of the dark-haired youth alongside him and instantly recognised him as the shy lad from the gaming group. In the sunlight, the young man's acne appeared truly brutal and his swept over hair gleamed with grease but at that precise moment, Scrave could have kissed him.

"Sorry son." He mumbled, instantly catching on and taking his role. "I get so confused sometimes. When are we going to reach your sister's home again? Is it this way?" He waved his staff and appeared unsteady, leaning his weight on the youth and almost making him fall over, before veering off towards the guard and making the man jump back or risk skewering the Elf by accident.

"Soon father, soon!" the youth stated aloud, snatching at Scrave's robe and almost jarring the Elf's hand, complete with dagger, from within its folds. The boy leaned in close and whispered into Scrave's ear. "You are so right about living in the real world. Just think of the stories I'm going to be able to tell now."

"They won't be much good to you if you are dead." Scrave shot back, before continuing to stagger dramatically towards the amused faces of the people in the trade caravan.

"Hang on." The guard interrupted. "Where are you headed?"

"He's with us!" shouted several other voices, diverting the guard's attention away and further down the column, to where an extremely tall man appeared to be pointing towards someone behind him and out of sight. The guard turned back in irritation only to realise that the addled old man and his carer had somehow moved much faster than expected and had made it back to the caravan and disappeared into the confusion. As they merged into the relative safety of the crowd, the young man breathed a huge sigh of relief.

"Thank you." Scrave whispered as they parted the people before them.

"I just hope my friends are okay." The young man replied, only to be jostled as the other gamers materialised around them from the crowd.

"By Solomon what did you think you were doing? You could have gotten yourself killed!"

"Are you insane? Who was that old codger anyway?"

The youth turned to speak to the Elf only to find that somehow in the excitement he had managed to slip away. He frowned at his friends' lack of empathy, then set off in pursuit, threading through the crowd, pushing a flea-bitten donkey out of the way and slipping underneath the neck of a large docile camel, leaving his friends yelling pointlessly after him. The edge of the caravan came into sight and the youth pushed through. All the people around him were staring in shock at an unfolding scene that stopped the young man in his tracks. A mounted salamander could be seen charging off across the dunes with the Elf bouncing upon its saddle and a guard was lying on the ground, his body warped, as if he had been sucked dry and left in the merciless desert heat.

"I have never seen the like." A trader uttered at his side. "It is the work of devils. Who was that man?" Guards further down the column started shouting alarms the mounted guards on the other side struggled to push their snapping salamanders through the caravan causing confusion and screams of terror from travellers and animals alike.

"To be honest I don't even know his name." came the youth's thoughtful reply.

* * * * * *

The two sword blades crashed together, first high, then low, not with the full strength of a life or death duel but still with enough weight to injure if the weapons struck home.

"Now faster," Colette demanded breathlessly, pushing back her hair and stepping back to bring Kerian's long sword back around to face her opponent. "You are holding back on me."

The two blades met again, striking dull tones that echoed across the deck. Colette meeting Aradol's tame ripostes with lunges, flicks and parries, knocking her opponent's blade from high to low, left to right, as the two stepped backwards and forwards in their dance.

Colette slid her sword edge down the length of Aradol's ancient blade and grinned, blowing air up across her face to make one of her blond curls bounce mischievously against her forehead before winking and blowing a kiss, then attacking again. She tried to get a reaction from Aradol's solemn face but the young man was clearly preoccupied and failed to respond to her light-hearted gestures. There was nothing for it, she needed to be more spontaneous and catch him out.

Aradol sighed deeply, his mind trying desperately to focus on the training session and the beautiful woman before him but he kept seeing the image of the grave of his friend on the quiet beach and the placement of the final stones of the cairn by his shipmates. It was so hard to concentrate at times like this. How could he continue as if nothing had happened, as if life was normal once more? It felt like a betrayal to Ives memory. Knowing he would never see his friend's happy smile, ever...

"Look out!"

Colette's attack came in high, Kerian's blade slicing through the air, its momentum accelerated by the weight of the weapon as it practically dragged the young mage's arms down with it.

Aradol observed the attack with disbelief, caught completely unaware, realising he was wide open and in no position to parry. He started to swing his weapon up to try and deflect some element of the blow, already knowing that he was going to be too late and realising that he should never have taken his eyes off his enthusiastic student. He stared into Colette's deep blue eyes noting her innocent smile and watched as her whole expression changed to one of horror in a heartbeat. Who would have thought it was going to end like this? The crewman closed his eyes and prepared for the worst.

The clash of steel on steel jarred Aradol's eyes open again and he looked up to see another blade had intercepted Colette's attack and held it bare inches from his skull.

"Can we please concentrate on keeping my remaining crew alive?" Thomas grunted, his cutlass squealing its protest as the long sword scored down its edge. He pushed up, shoving Kerian's magical blade aside, out of harm's way, allowing its tip to crash onto the open deck.

Colette shrieked, letting go of the hilt and dropping the whole sword to the floor, before she ran forward and grabbed Aradol by the face, twisting him around in her direction.

"Are you alright? I'm so sorry, I never realised how heavy the blade was. If anything had happened to you, I would never have been able to forgive myself."

"It is normally common courtesy to warn me when you are going to attack." Aradol stammered. "I can't teach you if I am dead!"

"Not unless you are one with the force." Thomas quipped. "Be wary young Padawan. If you strike him down, he shall return moodier than ever."

He smiled at his own witty attempt at humour, imagining Aradol glowing with a ghostly luminance not entirely dissimilar to Kerian's enchanted blade, coaching Colette in the art of swordplay, only to find that neither Aradol nor Colette were even listening, being absorbed with each other. He turned and walked away muttering to himself and considered finding a more responsive audience to perform to.

There had to be someone to speak to onboard, something to do, anything to take his mind off what was happening at the helm and the repairs going on below decks. Rowan was tough, she was going to be fine but there was a growing feeling of unease Thomas could not shake. Maybe he should go back and ask Commagin to pull Rowan up out of the steerage and back to safety.

The captain shook his head, no he could not do that to her. Rowan was trying to prove her worth to him and the crew; if he stepped in and took this opportunity from her then she would always resent him for it. He was damned whatever he did and he felt terrible leaving her in a situation he had no control over.

Taking the ladder down to the main deck, Thomas tried to whistle a tune to himself and appear casual as he quietly patrolled the ship. The *El Defensor* creaked and groaned gently beneath him, as if she were alive and breathing in and out softly in time with the gentle waves lapping at her hull. The rustle of canvas drew the captain's gaze upward, to note birds with crescent shaped wings of scarlet and green, darting and scything between the masts and swooping across the sky. Their colours so vibrant and alien against the cornflower blue backdrop that for a moment Thomas could almost believe he was looking at the paintbrush results of an eccentric expressionist painter rather than seeing these magnificent creatures in real life.

A school of flying fish leapt from the waters of the bay, arcing gracefully before falling back into the depths from which they came, drawing Thomas's thoughts back over to the looming pyramid set high up on the bluff and the green mantle of jungle it wore. He knew there was a maze beneath the massive monolith but from down here upon deck the details were lost to the eye. Even so, the captain could see the smoke of several fires and hear the sounds of construction originating from the base of the pyramid. Whatever was going on over there the pace had picked up dramatically since he had last considered it.

He reached the ladder to the forecastle and began to climb staring out towards the long bridge that connected the city of Taurean with the jungle and the pyramid beyond. People in brightly coloured garb ran along its slender length, stringing bunting and flags from the statues and hanging banners from the rail. There was almost a carnival air about the place.

His ears picked up the sound of quiet whispering as the captain neared the prow of the ship. Not sensing any threat in the sound upon his own ship, he rounded the corner and found Brother Richard sitting cross-legged on the floor, a large dusty book lying open in his lap. The priest appeared lost in thought, staring intently into the pages as if the very secrets of the universe where here for the taking, the man talked to the page before him, clearly mouthing the words aloud as he focused on crafting a small mannequin out of sticks.

"I used to do that when I was learning to read." Thomas asked, eager to engage in conversation, "especially with the hard words."

Brother Richard tore his gaze from the page as if slapped. His face flushed crimson, his eyes darting about as the actions of someone who clearly had something to hide. Richard gently closed the volume, his faded and stained blue robes covering the tome protectively, his accusatory gaze piercing and angry. He checked to see if the captain had anyone else alongside him, placing the hand with the stick figure out of sight within his robes as he did so.

"What are you reading?" Thomas continued, edging closer, only to note the frustration rising in the monk sitting before him.

"It's private." Richard replied. "Please would you leave me in peace to undertake my studies?" The captain paused, noting the hostility, not sure why it was being directed at him.

"That book has to be a best seller if your face is anything to go by." Thomas replied flashing a disarming smile. "Its fine, I'll just leave you to go on reading. I just thought you might like a little company, instead of talking to yourself." He shrugged his shoulders and walked on, noting that Richard was moving his upper body and robes to shield the book and prevent the captain from glimpsing what he was looking at.

"Maybe you can tear yourself away enough to stop and chat on my next lap." Thomas smiled. He turned back towards the main deck and started to navigate the harbour side of the ship where the view was no less majestic but now there was an uncomfortable chill to the air.

The city of Taurean loomed now above him, crowned by the palace containing the matriarch who had tried to have him poisoned. He itched to make Mora see the error of her ways but with the guards and populace so suspicious of him and his crew, the chances of getting anywhere near her with a weapon was as likely as the captain ever seeing the Manhattan skyline again.

The gangway shook ahead, as someone started to board the ship. Thomas took the opportunity of the distraction to push Brother Richard from his mind and slid down the ladder to meet the person coming up.

Weyn, looking more battered and bruised than ever was in the lead, his arm bandaged and held in a sling. Mathius came up behind him holding a curled document in his hand.

"Any luck finding Ashe or Rauph?" Thomas opened.

"Well we found one of them alright!" Mathius replied in a tone that left Thomas honestly wondering why he had even asked. "Just wait until you see this."

Thomas allowed Weyn to squeeze by then watched Mathius unroll the paper and display the illustration upon its surface. The dark font proclaimed a great event but the writing blurred into insignificance to the illustration set below it.

"I don't believe it." Thomas muttered, as he took in the likeness on the bill. "How in the world did he get himself into that mess?"

* * * * * *

"I know him!" Ashe squealed through a mouth of half-chewed cinnamon swirl pastry that he had found just lying around abandoned on a bakery stall. He pointed excitedly at the poster plastered on the wall before him and turned his head to where Sinders sat perched on his left shoulder, looking into the scruffy bird's deep black beady eye. "And you know him too, that's Rauph. I wonder what naughty thing he has done to be put up on a poster?"

The Halfling, covered in grime from head to foot, looked a sorry state for having slept in the gutter beneath a pile of refuse the night before. His four-foot high frame had attempted to return to the *El Defensor* back in the harbour but every time he did, he had found the way blocked by rather stern looking Minotaur guards who by the sound of their gruff discussions appeared to be searching high and low for a diminutive escaped convict.

Looking more like a walking vagrant than his usual happy go lucky self, Ashe had tried to push the misery he felt at not being able to return to his friends into something more positive and had took up the chore of finding this terrible prisoner by himself. Although the Halfling had to admit that finding the elusive felon had been more of a challenge than he had expected, especially with all the distractions Taurean had to offer.

Ashe tapped his foot and scrunched his little face up thinking carefully. He had been on a poster once and it had not been a very nice experience. For one thing, everyone knew what you looked like and in another because of the unkind words scrawled beneath his face everyone had placed their hands in their pockets or over their valuables when he had wandered near. Did this mean Rauph was being kicked out of Taurean? The Halfling moved closer, wrinkling his little nose and mouthing the words of the poster.

"Welcome to the grand event. By the decree of the Matriarch, it begins at dusk tomorrow. Come see your heroes, including the Prince Regents, Drummon and Kristoph, battle deadly monsters, navigate lethal traps and fight each other to the death for your entertainment and the greatest of all prizes. The Labyris Axe.

"Gosh! That sounds exciting." Ashe stated to Sinders, "Maybe Rauph is not being thrown out after all. Doesn't he look all ferocious and brave, snarling at that ugly Minotaur Drummon. I'm not so sure about how Drummon is holding that huge mace, if he is not careful, he might hit Rauph with it!" The Halfling continued to scan the poster stopping with the small writing at the bottom.

"Don't forget to queue early to get your seats."

Ashe turned around and reached for a passing cloak trying to snag the man's hand and ask the most important question regarding exactly where these seats might be found, only to discover his hand filled with the man's coin pouch. These people were so careless with their belongings!

He turned to another passer-by and came up short, noting the scruffy youth that had been talking to him by the fountain when he had been collecting all the thrown away coins.

"I know him." He pointed at the poster. "He's my best friend."

"That's nothing. I'm sleeping with the matriarch." The urchin replied, scratching his spiky hair.

"Really?" Ashe replied wide eyed. "Then I suggest you get a new girlfriend because believe me she is a very nasty person with a very bad temper." Ashe turned to point out Sinders on his shoulder.

"This is my bird. The one I was looking for before I got into that misunderstanding with the guards. Sinders meet... Umm. Meet..."

"Porthon."

"Porthon... of course!" Ashe turned back to the poster. "Where exactly do we go to get the best seats?"

"You are in luck." Porthon replied. "I happen to be going there myself. The earlier we get there the better view we can secure." He gestured over towards the mainland and the huge pyramid. "It all happens over there and from the gossip I have heard, I would not miss this event for the world!"

"Then Sinders and I shall tag along." Ashe replied enthusiastically. "Maybe if we are lucky, we will also spot the villain everyone is looking for on the way. Whoever it is, they must have done something really bad. Maybe we can claim a reward!"

* * * * * *

Rowan leapt up for the next link in the chain, feeling her arms starting to tire from the long climb. The more she ascended the more she felt she should have spent time climbing the rigging of the *El Defensor* to stay trim. A smile crossed her face. What a great idea... and Thomas would have had kittens if she had done so.

She grabbed the link firmly and tried to pull her knees up, gripping the cold metal between her thighs. The long thin chain dragged relentlessly at her shoulder where it remained fastened to the safety pin, every link advanced resulting in a heavier and more cumbersome burden to manage.

It was no good, she had to rest, had to stop and catch her breath. The chain tugged gently at her shoulder as if it had snagged on something and then became free again. Rowan shrugged her shoulder and yanked the chain back again, sending a silvery wriggle back down through the slender links.

The snagging at her shoulder came again, a sharp tug down followed by no resistance at all. It was as if the chain were caught up on something. She needed to move on, needed to keep climbing the chain and find the end. Taking a deep breath Rowan jumped up for her next handhold, only to find her shoulder wrenched painfully and her hand slip from its grip. She scrabbled at the huge links, her breath held in horror, trying to find a way to stop her fall, shoving an arm out instinctively into the hole in the metal only to have her full weight yank on it as she arrested her descent.

Rowan hung there, eyes closed, trying to fight through the pain, momentarily breathless and confused as to what had just happened. The pain in her arm started to ebb and she sucked in a breath and looked up the chain, willing that the last link be hung up just above the one she was on, even though she knew it was wishful thinking on her part.

The safety pin at her shoulder tugged again. What was wrong with this stupid chain? Rowan frowned and tugged back, determined to free it from whatever it was stuck on, only to find the safety pin snatched back hard against her shoulder, pulling her out and away from the chain into open air.

She screamed as she fell into darkness, watching as the chain she had so laboriously climbed slipped away from her as she plummeted. Rowan had no thoughts as to looking towards what had pulled her from her lofty perch, no courageous need to turn about and stare down towards her ultimate demise. Instead, she closed her eyes and screamed.

* * * * * *

"What do you mean he has escaped into the desert." Justina hissed angrily, like the snake she so vehemently desired. "Kaplain. I swear to you if you have let him slip through our clutches." The *Bearer* looked down at his sandals and shuffled his feet. Looking like a schoolchild caught doing something he knew was wrong.

"Well we had no supplies to give chase. He is bound to be running out of water. The salamanders were not equipped for a long expedition."

"If the Elf and my dagger are crossing the desert, then we are going to go after them. Do I make myself clear?" Kaplain looked up towards his mistress, his eyes lingering on the horrific demon sitting upon her lap, currently occupied with chewing on a shrivelled child-sized hand. Hamnet paused in its meal and stared back, eyes gleaming coldly from the bony sockets of its skull.

"Completely clear mistress." The *Bearer* replied. "Your will shall be done."

"It had better be." Justina replied, stroking the skull of her demonic pet.

"Or I shall know the reason why."

Chapter Thirty-Six

The look on Octavian's face told Kerian all he needed to know.

"We split three water skins." The gypsy confirmed, holding up the deflated bladders and letting them flap in the wind to reinforce their predicament. "There is no way we are going to get to Al Mashmaah with the water we have left and these are beyond repair."

"We have a perfectly good oasis behind us." Kerian gestured. "The horses have already had their fill and I can see there is plenty left for the likes of you."

"But I have nothing to carry it in." Octavian replied. "I'm not sure about you but I think my pockets might leak!"

"What about if just one of us goes?" Kerian snapped, raising an eyebrow and staring at Octavian with barely contained ire.

"Really?" Octavian shot back. "After us spending the night together? Shame on you Mr Denaris. I say shame!" Kerian tried to remain mad, tried to avoid catching the contagious smirk showing on the gypsy's exhausted face and found he could do nothing but crack a smile.

"Damn you." He whispered to himself, turning to gather his scattered belongings and pack them onto Toledo's already overloaded back.

"We need to reduce our baggage. Throw away everything we don't need." Kerian stepped off the blanket and started to pull other items from Dorian's corpse, waving his hand rapidly to dispel the flies that had already descended on the donkey's decomposing carcass. A roll of faded material came away from the sand and Kerian noted the faded insignia on the pennant that had fascinated Octavian so much.

"Well we don't need this anymore." He grunted, pouring sand from the flag.

"Give me that." Octavian yelled, running across the sand and yelping as his bare feet touched the burning surface. "You are not getting rid of my keepsake."

"Then carry it yourself." Kerian replied, throwing the flag in Octavian's direction.

"Have you come across any of my clothes." The gypsy asked, scrabbling through the sand and struggling to pull more items from the deceased donkey as Kerian rolled up the first blanket, tugging it away from beneath Octavian's feet exposing him to the hot sand again.

"I'm not worried about your clothes," Kerian replied, struggling not to laugh as Octavian pulled a battered boot from the sand only to yelp and drop it as a silvered serpent slithered from its neck. "I am more concerned about finding us a safe haven on the supplies we have left. I had one destination in mind and had not considered any others."

Octavian hopped about the remaining blanket, pulling on the solitary boot before standing up and turning about, shading his forehead from the rising sun and the prevailing wind with a raised hand.

"I am going to need to get up onto one of the taller dunes to be sure." Octavian commented, as Kerian pushed him aside and rolled up the second blanket. "But I think we are closer to one edge of the desert than the other. If we take it steady and conserve our supplies, we should make it out of here but it won't be easy."

"Here's your other boot." Kerian threw the sand filled boot over to his companion then continued to tug at the debris littering Dorian's corpse but the donkey seemed almost sucked down into the sand and a faint vibration near Kerian's hand made him draw back warily. "I don't think we are going to get much more out from under him." He sighed. "We will have to make do with what we have got. Are you ready?" Kerian drew himself up into the saddle, tugging Toledo's reins and easing the horse up towards the crest of the nearest dune.

"Wait for me." Octavian yelled, stuffing the last few objects he could salvage into his stallion's saddlebags, whilst lamenting the supplies he had to leave behind. "I don't think my horse is going to be able to take my weight with this wound to its back leg. Is there any chance I can hop up with you?" Kerian scowled down at the gypsy, his features clearly showing what he thought of that idea.

"You were the one that attacked the horse. You deal with the consequences!" Kerian pulled up at the top of the cream and crimson striped dune and looked about. There seemed to be a storm on the horizon back over towards Tahl Avan but otherwise the open desert appeared to stretch for miles. Octavian slogged up beside him, struggling to pull his ragged shirt about his shoulders, before giving up with a curse and casting the whole lot aside.

"Are you sure you never found my spare clothes?" he whined.

"For the last time, I have not got your clothes." Kerian shouted. "They must have been under Dorian. If you want them, go back and dig them out by yourself. It is too hot to dally and I want to be well on our way before the sun gets too high in the sky. Now, which way do we go?"

Octavian looked down at his ragged clothes in resignation then sighed deeply before turning about to check his bearings. He tutted and scowled, looking up at the sun, taking in the distant smudge of a mountain range on the horizon and the endless expanse of desert before he turned back towards the fiery orb hanging in the sky and pointed to the horizon below it.

"We have to go that way." He muttered, clearly not happy with his choice of destination.

"What's over there?" Kerian asked, noting, that Octavian's skin was already turning a reddish hue from the kiss of the sun. The man really did need some clothes to shelter him from the elements or he would be too ill to travel by nightfall.

"Blackthorn." The gypsy muttered. Kerian shook his head, remembering full well the path the ghostly woman had warned him he would take, it appeared he had no control over his own fate. Everywhere he went problems beset him, leading him on to dangers anew. He dismounted, deciding for now to keep the information of his clandestine meeting close to his chest and moved to one of the saddlebags, tugging it open and pulling out a roll of clothing he knew lay there.

"Here, you can borrow this." He remarked, throwing the clothes over to his companion who caught them in mid-air and started to unroll them to reveal a familiar moth-eaten set of armour that appeared to be a mish-mash of multiple suits roughly stitched together.

"I know this suit of armour." Octavian remarked. "This is the set I got from the crypt back in Tahl Avan."

"I know." Kerian replied, remounting the saddle, before lifting his hood up to protect himself from the wind and pulling his cloak tighter about him. The knight turned Toledo in the direction Octavian had indicated and then started to ease the stallion down the far side of the dune before shouting back over his shoulder.

"I don't seem to need it anymore."

Octavian struggled to pull the musty clothes over his head and cinched the belt at the tunic's waist before wrinkling his nose in disgust. The armour smelt foul; the thought of sand fleas and lice sprang vividly to his mind. He was sure he would end up itching by the end of the day!

The gypsy tugged at the reins of his stallion and led the horse as he started to follow his companion then he paused as something made him halt. A growing sense of dread swept over him, as if someone had walked over his grave. The feeling was unexplainable and something told him it was not just down to the troublesome thought of their ultimate destination. He twisted about and stared over at the storm on the horizon, furrowing his brow.

It made no sense, the clouds seemed wrong, misplaced somehow. He licked a finger and held it up. The wind was definitely blowing in the other direction, towards the cloud, yet it still appeared that the cloud was heading relentlessly towards them.

Octavian shrugged his shoulders before tugging hard on the reins and started coaxing his horse down the rise, its forelegs sinking into the soft shifting sands, right up to its fetlocks.

The mysteries of the Vaarseeti desert were many and no matter how often Octavian travelled here, there was always something new to alarm him.

* * * * * *

Rowan hit the spider's web with such force that her spine felt as if it had snapped, her head jerking back so hard that she saw stars. There was a sensation of dropping into a sticky trampoline before she found herself flung back up in the air again as if on a wild carnival ride.

The swift rise ended just as roughly, the sticky filaments at her back clutching so tightly that when she reached the apex of her ascent, she felt the exposed areas of her skin rip as the adhesive prevented her from leaving its clinging embrace. Rowan cried out as her body snapped back, her wounds adhering to the sticky web and coating the grey like strands crimson.

Rowan found she had no choice but to close her eyes in an attempt to prevent herself from being violently sick and waited for the up and down movement of the web to cease its vibration. Her ears felt like they were humming, her breath came in shuddering gasps but she could not move to assess her wounds due to the unbreakable grip of the resilient weave she was mired in.

"Damn it!" she cursed, trying to lift her head and examine her situation, only to feel the sharp pull of the web from behind her. This was ridiculous! How had she managed to get herself in this mess? It was like something out of one of those Mrs Pepperpot books by Alf Proysen her father used to read to her when she was a child. The main heroine used to shrink to miniature size at the least expected moments and have all kinds of adventures. Rowan started to chuckle, imagining meeting her childhood hero, walking up, curtseying and offering her hand in welcome. The chuckle became a full-fledged laugh.

Somewhere in the back of her mind, Rowan knew the hilarity was wrong. She was stuck to a giant spider's web, had not achieved her goal at all and was in danger of reverting to her normal size at any time. This was if she did not end up being eaten by whatever had crafted this sticky death trap in the first place! I must be in shock, she realised, the laughter dying on her suddenly dry lips. Rowan took a few deep breaths, then angled her head to take in her surroundings. The wrench lay off to her right side, stuck fast to the web. A glow behind her head explained where the lantern had landed, shadows cast from its stuttering flame indicating the light was off balance and the fuel tilted away from the wick.

Well, she could lie around here all day and wait to see what happened, or she could pull herself together and try to get out of here. Rowan tried to move her hands, and started patting down her pockets, first one side then the other, feeling the skin on her exposed arms pulling taut and threatening to tear. She had a penknife somewhere in her overalls; she just had to find it.

A faint vibration ran across the web towards her, causing Rowan to lift her head and strain against the webbing pulling at her hair, trying to discover where the disturbance was coming from. There was nothing but shadows over there, nothing but... A large hairy leg reached out from the shadows, causing Rowan to catch her breath.

This could not be happening! This had to be a nightmare that she was going to wake up from. Rowan struggled to tear herself free, sending vibrations through the web and causing the huge leg to lift from the web surface before another and then another hairy limb eased out from the shadows. Eight beady eyes glowed in the darkness as the spider's body moved out into the illumination cast by the flickering lantern.

Rowan stopped her struggling instantly, remembering that spiders homed in on the vibrations of distressed prey trapped in their webs. She renewed the search for her pocketknife, trying to remain as still as possible as she tried to find the lump that meant her goal was nearby but these damned overalls had more pockets in them than she realised and the search was taking too long! The spider was going to be upon her before she...

The safety pin still strung over her shoulder snapped down, drawing Rowan deeper into the web and snapping her head painfully backwards. Two further tugs followed, yanking her arm so hard she feared her shoulder would dislocate, as whatever was pulling on the thin chain yanked down hard. The web thrummed beneath her and the arachnid rushed over to investigate the movement, mistaking the pull as that of its prey, its thick bristling legs scuttled across the web, advancing in rapid jerky movements.

Rowan barely had time to scream, as the web stretched downwards again, bowing beneath her, the excruciating tension from below increasing the pressure on her shoulder. Whatever held the end of the chain it was worrying it backwards and forwards, pulling first one way then the other as the sticky strands of web cut deeper into her arm, releasing a fresh trickle of blood. Rowan tried to move, tried to angle her body to release the safety pin and free the chain but the adhesive in the web had her so firmly secured that she could not even scratch her nose, even if she had wanted to!

She finally located the pocket containing her knife, slipping her right hand inside, closing it around the tool, only to find that it was then incredibly difficult to remove it from her overalls with her hand formed as a fist. She flattened her hand and tried to encourage the pocketknife towards her with her finger, only to have her whole body jolted as the web yanked down again.

The spider suddenly loomed over her, fangs bared, legs twitching as it prepared to bite its prey and paralyse it before cocooning Rowan as a tasty morsel for its larder. Rowan looked up at the eight black eyes staring down at her, taking in her own bloodied reflection and stark look of terror, just as something flared to life behind her. Heat blossomed above Rowan's head as the lantern, now tipped completely on its side finally ignited the spilled fuel from its reservoir and sent it racing along the web.

Reacting to the unexpected flare, the arachnid reared up, its front legs waving aggressively towards the unexpected threat that dared to get between it and its meal. The web yanked down once more drawing another scream from Rowan and dropping the arachnid right down on top of her. Thick bristling hairs scratched at Rowan's face as she tried to turn her head to the side to breathe, the terror of her situation now as paralysing as the web strands holding her. She was going to die in a dirty ship hold as a spider's snack!

The web snapped without warning. One second Rowan was snuggling up close to a ravenous hairy spider, the next her heart was in her throat and she was tumbling down into the darkness, falling end over end, web, spider and all.

Rowan hit something soft that broke her fall, heard a disgruntled meow, then found herself landing hard and generating a large cloud of dust. She rolled as she hit the floor, gathering more debris and wrapping herself about with the long chain, before her motion was arrested with a sudden violent stop that left her shoulder feeling as if it were on fire.

The dust settled gently around her, alighting on the errant strands of web still wrapped about Rowan's form and coating her in a fuzzy layer of grey. She staggered unsteadily to her feet, shaking her head before looking around, trying to grasp her bearings, only to realise that the only light source now available came from the opening in the deck far above. The lantern and its earlier conflagration now a distant memory, in a world where everything lay cloaked in darkness, shadows and unseen menace.

Shrugging the loops of thin chain free from her body, Rowan ran a hand up her arm, wincing at the dampness she felt there, before she reached the safety pin and went to remove it from around her shoulder. One exploratory feel confirmed her worst fears. Her shoulder was swollen and hot to touch from the abuse it had taken. The safety pin ran across the joint like a hot poker, digging into her flesh and resisting opening due to the fact it required squeezing to do so. She tugged at it gasping in shock and found herself light headed as fresh agony lanced through her body.

Rowan took a deep breath and tried to push the pin free again but the renewed agony that assailed her almost dropped her to her knees. It was better to leave the pin in situ and worry about it later. She gathered up a loop of the chain and wrapped it about her waist before tugging the rest towards her. Something rattled across the deck, behind her and not in the direction of the loops of chain, freezing her in mid-action. She reached her right hand into her pocket and pulled out the errant pocketknife, clicking the small tool open and feeling merciful that in the darkness she was unable to see just how puny and pitiful a weapon it really was.

A soft padding sound moved around her as if something were purposefully circling her. Was it the spider? Was the creature that large and heavy that to her smaller ears it could make such a noise? She stepped away, angling towards where the tiny circle of light from above kissed the deck, pulling the chain after her and wincing at the rattling hubbub it caused.

The padding stopped.

Rowan stopped too, her ears listening for a clue to her stalker whilst her eyes strained in the darkness, seeing nothing. An aroma of fish wafted across her nostrils, causing Rowan to wrinkle her nose in disgust. She turned her head aside and choked back a scream as the darkness beside her appeared to move like a wall of liquid. She stepped away in horror, only to trip over the trailing thin chain, her hand reaching out for balance, her fingertips brushing across a soft pelt. Rowan spun about, her eyes trying to lock onto the circle of light as if that one slim beacon could save her from whatever demon now stalked her. A giant furry head suddenly materialised out of the darkness, glassy feline eyes gleaming despite the subdued lighting.

Socks! The damned priest's cat was down here! In a flash Rowan realised who had been pulling on the chain. Hell, she had seen cats play with balls of string before and now she found herself the perfect bite sized treat!

She slowly started to back away, as the cat's head came down to her level, its nose twitching inquisitively as it sniffed her small form. Its tail flicked in the shadows, an excited movement matching the actions of the cat as it sank lower and stretched out its claws, wriggling its bottom as it prepared to pounce.

Rowan spun about, dug in her heels and ran, knowing her very life depended on it, blindly rushing out into the darkness, the thin chain rattling behind her as she sprinted. She tried to put out of her mind the possibility of running into something hard and hurting herself, of tripping over a crack and breaking her ankle or worse her leg. Terror gave her strength she never knew she had, as she simply ran as fast as she could, hoping against hope she would find cover. She did not get very far!

Socks watched the chain whizzing across the floor before him as if vaguely disinterested, before lifting up a paw to stomp down on the links to prevent them from moving any further. Rowan felt the chain about her waist pull tight, then her feet snapped out from beneath her and she fell down onto her back, sending fresh agony lancing through her arm. The breath crashed out of her body but Rowan still had the sense to roll away, just as a huge paw swiped the area where she had lain, long claws scoring the wood and setting Rowan's heart beating faster.

Fleeing to the right, feeling her foot slip on the edge of a plank as she threw her body across the gap, landing hard and breathless, only to have her back pushed by another paw swipe that sent her tumbling again. Rowan crashed down, screaming at the frustration and injustice of it all. The cat was playing with her. It was only a matter of time before its claws would sink into her flesh.

She lashed out with the penknife just as Socks lunged forward, striking a blow on the cat's nose that made it sneeze sharply in shock. Socks rubbed its face with a paw then stared around, initially unable to locate its prey in the darkened hold space, its ears twitching to locate the sound of the chain slithering across the deck. Then the feline hunter was off, padding after its prey with uncanny accuracy. The cat was not in a rush, the outcome of the encounter already assured.

Socks would feed tonight.

* * * * * *

Commagin scratched his nose with a jagged fingernail and glanced at the sand timer beside the hole in the deck. His low grumble into his beard said what words could not. He was concerned; Rowan should have been on her way up by now, yet the chain remained lax and the signal had not come. The grains of sand were now well past the half way point and Commagin knew that once all had slipped through the bottle neck of the timer Rowan would swiftly revert to full size again.

He leaned over the hole and tried to gaze down into the darkness but could see nothing of the drama unfolding below. Another grumble followed the first. If he did not hear from her soon, he was going to have to pull up the chain and just hope for the best. Hope that she was in the cage, the job completed, not left down below in a claustrophobic small space that would crush her body like an egg if the magic spell failed.

Commagin did know that Thomas was not going to be happy if anything became of Rowan and that he would never forgive the engineer if this occurred. He grumbled into his beard for a third time then reached into his stained apron and pulled out a dented flask.

With a deft twist of the wrist, the Dwarf had the flask open and to his lips, swallowing the fiery liquor and letting its caress slip down his throat, coating it in velvety warmth. He lowered the flask from his lips and stared at the warped reflection on its side and considered what life would have been like if he had simply stayed at his forge in the mines instead of following the *El Defensor* on her adventures.

He lifted the flask to his lips again, then paused. He did not think it would do to face Thomas's wrath intoxicated. He owed the man that much at least! Grumbling much louder now, the Dwarf screwed the top of his flask firmly closed then stared back down into the hole, the sand particles trickling by at the corner of his eye.

"Come on Rowan." He muttered. "What's taking you so long?"

* * * * * *

Rowan's shoulder hit the huge chain and cogwheel with such force that she spun out to the side and ended up sitting on her rear holding her hand up to her face to feel the egg already forming on her forehead. For a moment, she had no idea what she had crashed into, until she heard the unmistakable chink of the chain as the vibration from the collision transferred along its length.

She picked herself up; feeling shaky from the impact; her hands outstretched, blindly feeling for the cold hard surface in the darkness, before she began a slow walk around the cog, feeling for the side where the huge links were not as taut. This was definitely the loose side of chain; yet the all-important link she needed to thread her own slender chain through may as well have been miles above for all the good it did.

"So we meet again." She muttered angrily to herself, slapping the chain in frustration and sending rattles up its length. How was she ever going to reach the top? She was exhausted; the very weight of her own head seemed too great for her shoulders. Rowan rolled her neck, hearing the click in her spine as she tried to ease some of the stiffness she felt there, before running her left hand up under her hair to angrily rub at her knotted muscles. Her eyes strained to pierce the darkness and identify the whereabouts of the damned cat she knew was out there somewhere, waiting, watching for that moment when her guard was down to pounce and eat her alive.

The cat materialised from out of the shadows, its hunter's body sleek, feline eyes luminous, claws razor sharp. Rowan stepped behind the cog, daring to peek through the holes in the great wheel, sensing the deadly predator turning this way then that, slinking ever closer as she crouched down in fear.

Socks pawed at the thin chain lying on the floor, toying with the silver line as if it were twine from a ball, instead of attached to the safety pin stuck at Rowan's shoulder. She rubbed her left hand in response, worried that the pins and needles she was feeling in her arm were signs the swelling in her shoulder had worsened to the degree that it was starting to cut off the circulation in her arm. Her fingers on her left hand felt like sausages they were swelling up so fast...

Richard's cat rolled across the floor dragging the thin chain along with him, which whipped across the deck then snagged on the safety pin around Rowan's shoulder, yanking the hidden woman out into the open. She shrieked with pain as she found herself pulled into the cat's view. Socks paused in his play, his head slowly turning from its current upside-down position, to almost the right way up, its body appearing to unwind, until the predator was now the right way up and preparing to attack again.

Rowan tried to hold her breath and ease back into the shadows of the cogwheel, just as Socks pounced, claws scratching and scrabbling at the wooden floor in its haste to catch the little engineer. Rowan grabbed up all the loose chain she could manage and ran back behind the cog, dragging the spare links with her as one of Sock's huge claws slashed through the air, missing her by inches.

She dodged to the left, only to find a claw slicing in from that side of the cog, then darted back to the right, only to find herself face to face with the huge snout of the massive cat. Another lunge, another slash, the cat started to come around the cog, forcing Rowan to break from cover or risk being eaten, its tail flicking backwards and forwards in clear excitement.

This was insane! The coils of the chain gathered at her feet threatening to trip her at any moment and added yet another hazard to Rowan's worsening plight. Socks whipped around and jumped, quick as lightning, as Rowan instinctively dropped to the deck, the cat crashing head first into the vertical chain and setting it clanging loudly from side to side. The cat's reaction was to lash out at the inanimate object that had caused it such pain, swiping with its paw and setting the whole chain swaying from side to side.

Rowan turned to run, daring to risk the open deck in the confusion but Socks was faster, claws slamming down onto her back, knocking the breath from her body and drawing another scream of agony. The cat bent its head to sniff, sent forth a rough barbed tongue from its mouth and licked Rowan's head before opening its mouth wide and lunging forward to bite.

Something unseen finally worked loose high above, sounding a loud 'ping' that cut through the shadows, an ominous portent for the tumult about to begin. Socks froze, his mouth wide open about Rowan's head, before it sensed something was wrong and turned its attention from its meal.

A cascade of chain fell from the heavens, a thunderous waterfall of cold metal links piling up in a roar that was deafening. Huge lengths of chain fell down upon the cat, causing it to meow in protest and try to leap away, but other links continued to pile up faster than the agile cat could manoeuvre, knocking it down to the deck.

Rowan slipped and skidded about on all fours, trying to gain her feet and dodge the rain of greased links as they crashed down about her. The descending chain whipped about, delivering a glancing blow across Rowan's temple, dropping her back to her knees stunned, the downpour of chain continuing to crash and tumble about. It seemed endless, link after link freefalling through the darkness, a relentless torrent offering no salvation from its cacophony of noise.

Her left hand hit the floor first, the sensation both numb and alien to her. It was like pushing her hand down into a vat of warm dough that encompassed her fingers and wrist. Her right hand landed on top of it, feeling the same strange puffy sensation of a swollen inflamed limb. Her hand was grossly misshapen, it was the most bizarre thing, even with all of the chaos unfolding around her. Rowan's mind laughed at the absurdity of the sensation, it was almost as if her hand belonged to someone bigger, as if she were...

As if she were starting to grow again! The realisation hit like a sledgehammer, causing her heartbeat to rise and the breath to catch in her throat. She was growing again!

The spell was starting to fail!

Chapter Thirty-Seven

Rauph sat as if in a daze as the palace attendants fussed about him. They polished his horns, washed him, clipped him and groomed him until his chestnut coat gleamed in the evening light. Others buffed his armour and oiled his weapons as if their very lives depended on it.

Greaves were strapped to his muscular forearms, shin guards placed over fine leather boots, double laced to ensure nothing came free during combat. A black and gold breastplate, with a matching rear, a thick leather skirt secured over a chain waist coat that dropped to the Minotaur's thighs. They placed an ornate helmet upon the prince's brow, with slots allowing his majestic horns to be slid through, before a black silken cloak with embroidered gold filigree was laid around his shoulders and clipped into place on the breast plate, capturing the hero that everyone within the room believed they were serving.

"It is done." Whispered the head valet, stepping back with the other servants to run his eyes over Rauph's form and nod in satisfaction. Here indeed, stood the regal prince, Mora wanted them to portray. "Can you turn for me, Kristoph. I need to check the cloak is lying just right?" Rauph looked up, registering the man was talking to him but not really comprehending the simple instructions given.

"I want you to turn." The valet repeated. "Come on stand up." He gestured wildly with his hands, then upon noting that his charge was not responding, moved forward, forgetting his station to grip Rauph firmly by the shoulder.

If looks could have killed, the servant would have instantly become a pile of ash.

"I do not wish to stand." Rauph growled in warning. "In fact, all I want is to be left alone."

"Come now Prince." The valet continued to encourage him. "We need you looking at your best for the tournament tomorrow. I need to see how your cloak hangs to arrange for any last-minute adjustments."

"I don't care!" Rauph roared, grabbing his helmet and throwing it across the room, narrowly missing an antique vase filled with flowers as it clanged into the darkness. "Just leave me alone!"

The servants rushed away, scattering into the shadows and taking the shortest route to avoid Rauph's wrath, before closing the door swiftly behind them. Silence settled over the room like a shroud, leaving Rauph angry at himself for displaying such an outburst, even as his mind replayed his mother's words.

She had killed Ashe. The little Halfling who had done nothing to warrant such deadly action. Condemned all because he was Rauph's friend. The Minotaur wanted to sob, feeling the responsibility as heavy as any chains, sapping the resistance from his massive form. Ives had died because he was Rauph's friend too. How many more would he lose because of the cruel machinations of his mother?

The faces of his fellow crewmates flickered through his brain, Thomas, Colette, Marcus, Mathius, Commagin. How many more would be murdered just because of his birthright, his bloodline? The thought of his friends in pain crushed his spirit even further, eroding the navigator's resilience, leaving him open to the tendrils of despair and depression lurking at the edges of his mind.

A throat cleared in the shadows, drawing Rauph from his indulgent self-pity, making him turn to see the captain of the guard step towards him, the discarded and now dented helmet held in his hands.

"I see the burden of being a prince rests heavily upon your shoulders young Kristoph." Aelius commented. "But be wary of your temper. Your servants are under Mora's instruction, your rage is misplaced and wasted if you take it out on them. Never lose sight of who your true enemies are, nurture your rage, don't squander it. Use it to strike when the time is right. When your aim is true and your blow most effective."

"This is easy for you to say." Rauph replied sadly. "I am like a predator that has had its spirit broken, its venom sacs emptied, its claws and fangs pulled. Any actions I take will have severe repercussions for my friends. They will suffer for any resistance shown and I have already lost Ives and Ashe."

"Ashe Wolfsdale the Halfling?" Aelius asked, tilting his head to one side and thinking about the last time he had seen a little pair of legs scrabbling over the keep walls. "How did he supposedly die."

"Mora had him hung." Rauph replied, bowing his head as the sadness surged back in like the incoming tide. Aelius moved closer, placing a hand on Rauph's shoulder and passing the dented helmet back into the Minotaur's hands.

"If I have taught you anything." Aelius advised. "It was that you should never believe what anyone tells you, unless you see absolute proof. Wars have started this way, misunderstandings that spiral out of control, a misjudged word, an act of bravado that has led to thousands being slaughtered for nothing." The captain shook his head sadly.

"Do you not recognise the potential that you have?" Aelius asked. "Tell me, can you not see that you have the opportunity to strike for change within the monarchy?"

"But how am I to take a stand against them?" Rauph replied looking up into his concerned tutor's face and seeing the sorrow reflected in his aged eyes before staring down at the hazy reflected image presented in his helmet. "I am but a humble navigator. I have no power, no means to stop the injustice I see everywhere I walk about Taurean."

"If that is what you see in the reflection of your helmet then you have already lost." Aelius replied. "I on the other hand see someone who's heart is pure, whose friends are loyal and strong and whose people stand behind him with a zeal I have seldom witnessed in my lifetime. Mark my words. Mora's time on the throne is limited and I know just the Minotaur who will replace her, he just hasn't had the right motivation to do so."

"Who is that then?" Rauph asked, tracing the image on his helm with one huge finger.

"Oh Kristoph, if only I were as naive as yourself. If only I could see the world in your shades of black and white. Life would be much less complicated." He leaned in closer, whispering into Rauph's twitching ear, as if afraid someone would overhear his treasonous words.

"You are the Prince Regent. Your family may try to cheat you, may try to kill you but somehow you will prevail. I have a feeling in my gut that this is so. Remember my words. Control your temper, use your strengths when you can and rely on the guidance of others when you cannot. I know you can win this competition despite the odds placed against you. Strike for justice, for truth and for the right to rule Taurean the way it was meant to be. I want you to make Taurean great again."

"At the cost of my friends?"

"If that is the sacrifice required to allow you to fulfil your destiny, then yes. Especially if they believe in what you stand for and if this is the case, what right have you to take their choices away from them?" Rauph looked back up at his mentor, insecurity still visible within the depths of his eyes.

"But Drummon is so strong. How can I beat him?"

"By using this." Aelius tapped Rauph on the forehead, then sighed. "Or if this fails, rely on this." He lowered his hand and placed it over Rauph's heart. "They say love and compassion for others can move mountains. In your case it only needs to move a stupid thug of a Minotaur and his manipulative mother."

"I need to leave you now; you will need your rest for the morning when the competition starts." Aelius moved to exit the room, then stopped when he saw that Rauph still appeared downcast.

"By the way." He smiled. "That Halfling friend of yours. The last time I saw him he was climbing over the palace walls and escaping from our dungeon with his scruffy black and white bird. If he has been hung, he is definitely a very lively corpse!"

"A lively corpse?" Rauph muttered, frowning. "How is that better than being hung?" Aelius smiled and knelt down, bringing his head level with his young charge, before staring into Rauph's deep brown eyes.

"Your little friend is on the run somewhere in the city." Aelius grinned. "And he's stolen the royal seal. Just make sure tomorrow that you kick Drummon's arse for me."

Rauph sat open mouthed as Aelius left the room. Ashe was a lively corpse? How could this be so. His mother had told him Ashe was dead. Did this mean he had become undead? He stood unsteadily, his mind going over the words delivered by the captain of the guard, trying to make sense of them. Even if he ignored the thought of Ashe staggering around the city searching for fresh brains and warm flesh to eat, how could he, Rauph defeat Drummon and subsequently overthrow the Matriarch? He walked over to a mirror and gazed carefully into its depths at a much clearer image of himself than the helmet had presented.

The Minotaur staring back was nothing like the navigator Rauph knew. For one thing he appeared proud, charismatic and not the least bit shaggy. He moved his arm to check the creature in the mirror was indeed himself and nodded when he saw the Minotaur within mirroring his move. It was like the real Rauph was wearing a mask in there and if he could reach into the mirror and peel back the covering the navigator knew he would find the terrified Minotaur he was, cowering beneath. Rauph was hardly hero material. He suddenly felt the room was too warm and that his breathing was becoming a struggle. He needed some fresh air.

He moved in the direction of the balcony and stepped out to fill his lungs with the sultry evening air. Somehow being outside away from the confines of the room made him feel a little brighter. Taurean stretched out below him, hundreds of citizens running this way and that as they scurried to do their overseers wishes, fearful of violence if they failed in their duties.

The navigator looked down at the ship he had called home for all these years and thought fondly of his crewmates. The noise and bustle of the city acted like a soothing balm to the Minotaur's mind and he was grateful for the distraction. Rauph took it all in, the birds wheeling through the sky, the sun starting its slow descent towards the horizon and the ominous pyramid squatting on the mainland over the twisting labyrinth beneath. What horrors would be lurking in the darkened corridors of that maze? What challenges other than Drummon, was the navigator expected to face?

Rauph tried to make out the layout of the labyrinth from his elevated spot but the pyramid obscured more than half of its elaborate twists and turns. He could see the walls in some areas were heavily covered in vegetation, other areas where torches seemed to have been assembled to provide illumination to those navigating the twisted passageways below. People appeared to be milling about on the top of the maze, flickering camp fires showing where eager spectators were already taking their places to ensure they missed none of the grand spectacle due on the morning. Rauph suddenly realised just how massive the maze had to be for so many spectators to gather upon the top of its walls.

Maybe he should have been training for the competition? It instantly occurred to him that he had no idea of what was expected of him as a contestant. Where was he supposed to go? Was he supposed to pass under the pyramid, or scale its outer walls to get to the top? The magnitude of the situation was not lost on the Minotaur. He briefly wondered what they contestants were given as a packed lunch when they competed. Violetta normally made his expedition sandwiches. He suddenly missed her cooking, especially her gumbo.

A scrabbling in the ivy climbing the wall, drew the Minotaur's attention away from his thoughts of food and his suddenly rumbling stomach. He stared over the edge and took in the ragged figure of Mathius scaling the wall towards him, the man's breath coming in short gasps, his hands and face criss-crossed from the scratches of wicked thorns.

"Hullo Mathius." Rauph waved down, almost causing the assassin to miss his hand hold and plummet to the courtyard below. "What are you doing down there?"

"Shush!" Mathius gestured, plunging his hand into the ivy to try and get a secure handhold only to scare two roosting birds that took to flight in an explosion of feathers and frustrated squawks.

"Are you coming up?" Rauph asked leaning over and sending some loose mortar crumbling down upon his friend's head.

"Stop it. Just stop it!" Mathius spat, glancing about nervously and checking that his noisy crewmate had not roused the attentions of the guards manning the walls. Satisfied that there was nothing barbed or pointed heading in his direction the assassin looked up again, only to find another crumbling piece of pottery bouncing off his head.

"Listen," he snapped. "Thomas has sent me to tell you that we know what is going to happen tomorrow and we will be there in the crowd to help you. Do not fear, we shall be there when you need us to be."

"Where will you be?" Rauph asked, his brow creasing in worry. "I would not like to miss you, there seems to be a lot of people over at the labyrinth already and it will be easy to get lost." Mathius waved his arm trying to quieten the Minotaur down.

"Don't you worry about that. Just know that you are not alone."

"That's probably a good thing." Rauph replied. "Aelius tells me I'm going to be the new king and all I have to do is win the competition and beat Drummon and Mora to do it. The trouble is, the way he says it, he seems to think this is going to be easy and I know for a fact Drummon is very strong."

"Well don't worry. All you need to know is we will help you in any way we can." Mathius looked down searching for a foothold to help make his way back down the wall. "We shall look forward to seeing you tomorrow."

"Oh by the way." Rauph shouted down excitedly. "Ashe is a zombie now."

* * * * * *

Panic blinded Rowan for a second, adding to her sense of disorientation caused by the darkness and the blow to her head. She needed to get back to the cage, needed to be lifted up and out of the hold before the spell failed completely. How was she going to find the cage in the darkness? How was she going to find her way back? She took a few faltering steps one way and then the other. Which way should she go? She was going to die here trapped below decks, her body crushed, her bones snapped. She turned, stumbling over the thin silver chain, her mind was in such a turmoil it initially failed to recognise the lifeline the chain represented.

Of course, she could follow the chain!

Rowan dropped to her knees gathering up the silvery links of metal into long loops as fast as she could, then began to follow the lifeline out into the darkness away from the larger piles of huge chain still clattering and settling on the deck. The silvery links passed under a length of the larger chain, temporarily stopping her in her tracks. She pushed the larger chain aside with a grunt, sliding it across the deck, pulling the smaller silver chain out from underneath the last solitary link there.

The last link! She had found the final link but there was no time left to secure it properly and anyway, she could not pull her swollen arm free from the safety pin! She looked down at the centre of the link and frowned. To find it now, of all times, when she had so much else to worry about. The tingling creeping up from her hand to her wrist reminded her all too well of the urgency of her need to depart swiftly and return to the cage, yet she still found her steps faltering as she turned away.

Rowan took several more tentative steps then shook her head, bringing her hands down to her sides, clenching her fists angrily as her onward passage came to a grinding halt. She thought of Thomas and the others relying on her and cursed under her breath, her anger directed as much at herself and her need to escape, as it was to the impossible situation that she now found herself in. She shook her head, then turned back to the final part of the chain and gazed down at it, her mind tumbling over and over.

The solution to her problem was not an easy one. There was no way she could drag this huge chain and the rest of its length over to the cage. One link she could perhaps slide along the floor but never several massive links all interlocked! How was she going to do this? How was she going to show Thomas his faith and love of her was deserved? Her mind scrutinised the link carefully, all the time trying to ignore the swelling spreading up her arm.

There was more space through the centre of this link than a chain with links at both top and bottom. Could she possibly squeeze through it? A crash of cascading links sounded behind her as Socks angrily extricated himself from beneath the heavier piles of chain, spitting and snarling in anger. Rowan pushed at the link, trying to lift it up and tilt it on one edge so she could slide through then took a deep breath.

"Why do I think I'm going to regret that extra cookie at lunch time." She muttered, as she started to wriggle and squeeze her body through the opening, twisting to allow her shoulder and then her arm to slide through the link, before lifting one knee, bending, breathing out, attempting to squeeze her slim body through the grease stained hole. The patter of approaching paws fed the anxiety rising in Rowan as she struggled to get through. Socks, damn that stupid cat! Why did he have to be down here? The cat was rapidly heading in her direction. She tried to speed up, only to find that her hips would not pass through the gap.

"Oh come on!" she snapped angrily. "My hips aren't that big!" She wriggled impatiently, trying to bend her neck to identify why she could not pass through, cursing every stolen pastry that ever passed her lips and promising if she could survive this she would diet until she was looking like a twig! She tugged again, still feeling the stubborn resistance, an increased pressure on her right hip, then realised with some embarrassment that her tool belt was the reason she was unable to squeeze through.

The padding of paws came closer, causing Rowan to fumble with her belt buckle as she tried to squeeze through the small gap and open her belt at the same time.

"It would be easier if my fingers were not like a pound of sausages!" she screamed, tugging violently until the belt suddenly came free and slid down to her ankles, allowing her to pass through the hole and tumble out the other side.

Socks jumped over the piles of chain and slid to a stop to sniff at the link now sitting empty apart from the tool belt lying beside it. The cat turned its head to the left, then the right, then noticed the thin sliver of chain scooting off across the deck at its feet. It licked its lips hungrily then set off in determined pursuit.

* * * * * *

"That's long enough." Commagin snorted, watching as the final grains slid through the sand timer and dropped onto the gravitational dune below. He flexed his shoulders gripped the rope in his hand and started to haul up the line, hurriedly taking in the slack. "You better have done the job." he muttered through gritted teeth.

"Just don't let me down girl. Be safe and don't let me down."

* * * * * *

Rowan slid to a stop before the cage, trailing the thin length of chain behind her and stared at the battered container as if it were a palace. She had never wanted to see something so much, instantly feeling safer at the prospect of stepping inside.

Something huge jumped over her head. Rowan had a glimpse of black and white fur then her feline nemesis smashed into the cage, sending it toppling onto its side and rattling across the floor. The cat twisted its body in the air, extended its claws and dropped in a spitting snarl blocking Rowan's route of escape.

"Oh you absolute bastard!" Rowan cursed as her sanctuary clattered off into the darkness. She sized up the cat as it moved a few steps to one side before retracing the route, getting closer to her with every step along its arcing path. Sock's tail flicked from side to side, the cat's slitted eyes not daring to shift from its prey.

Rowan ran to the left, then cut to the right hoping that her change in direction would confuse Socks but the hunter's instincts allowed it to pounce with unerring accuracy, its claws outstretched. She found herself smashed to the floor, lines of fire slicing through her lower leg as the cat struck. Rowan screamed her frustration to the world; trying to tuck and roll like she had been taught when learning parachute landings in another world far removed from this one.

Adrenaline took over, squashing the fear back down as she lowered her head and tried to escape into the darkness, her left leg threatening to buckle beneath her at any time. Somehow, she reached the cage, grimacing at each agonising step, only to have her hopes crushed, finding the cage toppled on its side, all dented, with the entrance blocked, now impossible to gain access.

Rowan stole a quick glance behind her, horrified to see the cat slinking deliberately towards her, showing no hurry in its deadly advance, clearly understanding that its prey was tiring and the game was nearly up.

"Oh please give me a break!" Rowan cried her frustration aloud. Was she ever going to have something go her way? The rope lying alongside the cage suddenly shifted, shooting upwards, the slack whipping across the floor, making Socks jump back, suddenly skittish of the unexpected movement.

Rowan's eyes followed the rope then realised what was going on. The cage was being lifted up, she needed to get on and fast! She ran for the prone pen, arms outstretched, desperate to grab the cage and hope she could hang on for long enough, only to watch in horror as her makeshift elevator scooted up into the darkness, inches from her fingertips.

"No!" Rowan screamed "Commagin! Please send the cage back down!"

Her cries fell on ears too far away to hear her pitiful calls and the cage continued to rise. Rowan realised she was stuck in the darkness and stared around her with panicked eyes, pleading to find a way out, knowing there was no way she would find an escape from the confined area in time to avoid her fate. Her left hand was now twice the size it should have been and her wrist and forearm were catching up fast. Fresh tingling was racing up and down her legs, indicating these limbs were about to grow as well. She was going to die and all she could think about was the warm touch of Thomas and the time they had spent earlier that afternoon in his cabin.

"Oh Thomas. I really loved you." She confessed, turning around, tears in her eyes, watching Socks padding towards her, death reflected in his eyes, wishing she could just click her heels together and magically transport home. She looked down at her dust coated boots and tried to smile. Unfortunately, they were not ruby red slippers. She realised she had never felt as alone as she now did.

The cat batted Rowan with an outstretched paw, knocking her to the deck and blasting the air from her lungs before she could sob. She fell heavily, her resistance all but gone, the silver chain she had been following lying beneath her.

Socks opened his mouth, baring his fangs, before meowing his triumph to the world.

"Please make this be quick" Rowan prayed, clenching her fists and closing her eyes tightly. She drew in a deep breath, feeling the cat's claws pushing against her chest. All Socks had to do was extend those claws fully and her heart would be ripped from her chest.

The silver chain snaked away across the deck alongside her but Rowan was too terrified to care. She just kept promising to herself that if she kept her eyes closed it would all be over soon.

"I hope I make you really sick!" she cursed aloud at the cat, as it drew it's head up and licked its lips in preparation for the feast to come. Pain speared through Rowan's left shoulder, making her scream anew. She felt herself roughly dragged along the floor, cat claws scraping down the front of her overalls as she was hoisted up into the air.

The pain was excruciating, almost beyond bearing. Rowan tried not to cry out but the pain, oh the pain, it was simply too much to bear. She felt she was going to pass out as she hung all of her body weight from her injured shoulder. She just needed to keep her eyes closed and it would all be over soon. Please let it be over soon.

* * * * * *

Commagin pulled the rope up as fast as he could, all the time aware that the sand timer now showed the safety margin of time was also up to get Rowan out. Feelings of dread enclosed him as he pulled faster and faster, hand over hand. Why had Rowan not signalled to be pulled up? What if something had happened to her, what if his premonitions of doom came true? If Rowan was not in the cage when he pulled it up, his time aboard the *El Defensor* would be over. Thomas would never forgive him and for that matter, the Engineer knew he would never be able to forgive himself!

Somehow the perilous scenario with Rowan made the concerns Commagin had for his Gnome apprentice even worse. They should never have left Barney behind in the ship's graveyard, never abandoned him in his hour of need. Commagin knew that if they returned through the magical portal and found no sign of his little friend, he was going to have to take his leave of the ship and spend whatever time was necessary searching that terrifying place, ship by ship until he found his little apprentice again.

His arms ached and his lungs burnt, as he heaved on the rope, hand over hand, drawing the cage ever closer. He needed to be faster, needed to keep pulling, needed to rescue that cage from the depths of the ship he called home. The Dwarf gritted his teeth and kept on pulling determined he would not lose another member of the crew.

The dull clang shocked him when it came, pulling the engineer from his focus. Commagin gave the rope another firm tug, wrapping it tightly around his waist to stop it from sliding back down into the hold, the force of his pull dragging the cage clear across the deck, then he turned to regard the dented and squashed container and found his worst fears realised.

He ran to it, dropping to his knees, his stubby hands wrenching open the door and staring inside through his thick glasses, pleading, praying that his young charge was inside. However, one look was all it took to confirm she was not there. How was he going to tell Thomas? How was he going to explain that this terrible accident had happened? What was he going to do? His mind conjured up the horrific scenario of Rowan screaming as she grew, her limbs filling the small space and then the intense pain as she realised there was no space left to grow in. His eyes filled with tears, the image overwhelming.

Commagin sucked in a deep breath, not realising that he was actually holding onto it so tightly. Well, he would make sure he was near her when it happened. He would not desert her, he owed Rowan that much. He crawled over to the hole in the deck and stared down into the darkness, knowing that the chance of seeing anything or even of hearing Rowan's final screams would be slim to none, whilst also realising that if he did hear them, they would haunt him for the rest of his life.

He stared down into the hole and blinked once, then twice, then instantly brushed the tears from his eyes and quickly grabbed onto the thin silver chain that lay over the edge of the hole and disappeared down into the darkness, its other end still firmly attached to the base of the beaten cage.

Commagin pulled as fast as he could, his cataract misted eyes determined to confirm the miracle he saw attached to the end of his line. He pulled faster and faster, confirming the lumpy knot of silver links and the small figure dangling motionless from it. He reached out grabbing the miniature form of Rowan and took in her shredded clothes, the bloodied and dust streaked face, her shoulder swollen purple from the safety pin and chain snagged there.

The engineer plunged his hand into his apron pocket and pulled free some battered wire cutters he had there, using the tool with a skill and dexterity that confirmed a lifetime of using such items. The safety pin snapped clear and Commagin drew Rowan's arm gently from the ruins of the spring-loaded vice. She moaned in his hand, her chest rising and falling, her eyes squeezed tightly shut. The Dwarf leaned in closer, Rowan's lips seemed to be saying something.

"It will be over soon. It will be over soon." She stated repeating her mantra over and over.

"Hello beautiful." Commagin whispered, a smile spreading across his face as he realised that the end of the silver chain was looped through the helm chain he required. "You are right; it is all over now."

Chapter Thirty-Eight

The dawn sun rose gently over the city of Taurean, its warm yellow glow bathing the thick emerald carpet of overgrown jungle, waking the indigenous creatures within, raising them from their slumber to crawl, fly, run, maim and rip each other to shreds. The same light kissed the capstone of the ancient pyramid, sending golden rays of illumination shooting out across the bay towards the sprawling city and bathed the labyrinth below in a beautiful glow, unaware that its warming actions would soon have the same effect as it had on the creatures of the jungle. Creatures would run, fight, scream and bleed beneath its radiance before the close of the day.

Mora stood on her veranda taking in the sights and the smells, barely containing the tremors of excitement running through her form. She had barely slept the night, tossing and turning, unable to get the inner peace she desperately sought, until she had thrown the covers aside and came out to meet the dawn head on. Today was the day, the coming together of years of planning and subterfuge. Tonight, when the celebrations finally finished, the Labyris axe would have a new easily manipulated owner and her position as Matriarch upon the throne of Taurean would be assured until the day that she died.

She breathed in the air, believing that it somehow tasted sweeter for what the day was yet to bring. Every conceivable problem had been resolved. Drummon had spent the night revising the plans of the maze, identifying the best route to take and how to disarm the traps under the games master's expert tutelage. Kristoph was safely secured and ready for the one-sided combat that would result in his untimely and tragic death and his enslaved shipmates and craft would be shared out amongst the richer families of Taurean, securing political favours for her years of governing to come.

Nothing could spoil this day.

Mora breathed deeply again, relishing the taste like a fine wine, then turned from the balcony to meet her serving staff who stood patiently by, ready to bathe and dress her. This went without a single snag of a comb, without a cross word or punishment administered to the serving girls. Mora felt more relaxed than she had in months and attacked her breakfast with relish, before her final chiffon gowns of blue and gold were wrapped about her form and a golden tiara bedecked with sapphires rested regally upon her head.

The Matriarch glanced at the mirror, taking in the female Minotaur within. She looked perfect, powerful enough to rule Taurean with an iron fist, yet demure enough to still entice a suitor for the entertainments after the celebrations of the evening. Maybe one of the newer more eager and athletic bulls from the elite guards would serve. Mora closed her eyes relishing the thought.

"Summon my transport." She ordered, clicking her fingers to send two servants off with her command. To think that this evening Taurean would finally be hers to rule as she saw fit. The Matriarch gazed out towards the pyramid and imagined the pomp and circumstance that would occur in the throne room set just beneath the golden capstone. There she would be crowned the undisputed leader; no Empress... yes, she liked the sound of that! Her clinging lecherous clique of pampered replacements would soon be smiling from the other sides of their faces when they realised that their chance to rise and occupy Mora's place in the hierarchy would never come to pass. It was almost too great a feeling, knowing that on the morrow she could sign their death warrants and have them all executed, leaving her with a lasting peace to her inner sanctum that she would relish.

Mora took a slow walk through the receiving room, allowing time for her guards and servants to gather about her before she progressed from the entrance, quite elegantly she felt and descended down the marble staircase. Her palanquin awaited, ready to carry her over the bridge to the viewing platform reserved for the favoured families of Taurean elite. Her eyes glanced over the servants who all paused in their tasks to stand with heads bowed as she passed.

Everything was as it should be, all was as planned. Mora slowed as she approached the vestibule leading down to her transport. A line of palace servants stood awaiting her pleasure but there was no sign of the games master and she had expressed her desire that he meet her here so she could discuss the finer points of the games. The servants shook their heads at her query as to his location. No one knew where the Minotaur had gone, his whereabouts a mystery.

The Matriarch tried to brush the annoyance away. It was a minor irritation to concern herself about, nothing of real importance. Every detail had been examined time and again. Perhaps he was already at the games, rushing to ensure all was prepared for the visiting dignitaries.

Speaking of the dignitaries, where were the others? Where were Karlar, Ammet, Chane, Shuesan, Pascol and Wanessa? Did they not realise that today was the last day of freedom they would have? Mora chuckled to herself, causing a couple of servants to edge away nervously. It was strange though. Mora could not believe that Wanessa would be early to anything given her immense size.

The servants plumped her pillows and offered delicacies on golden platters before Mora was hoisted up onto the litter and her procession began. The Matriarch tried to contain her excitement as every step taken brought her closer to her goal. Normally she never bothered looking through the velour drapes but today she did not want to miss a moment.

Guards snapped to attention as she passed. Citizens and servants waved and cheered as her carriage moved past, some people held flags and wore ribbons on their arms in gay colours that did not match the colours of their tunics. Hues of silver, purple, orange, gold, blue, red and green flowed through the crowds of cheering people. The excitement was palpable; Mora felt her heart beat just a little faster. Huge banners showed her two sons in mock combat, Drummon all in black and intimidating, a silver ribbon tied on his arm, Kristoph all chestnut and proudly wearing a golden ribbon on his arm...

Mora blinked twice at the poster as she remembered the colours of the ribbons worn in the crowd, only a handful of people wore silver ribbons! Surely, these ribbons did not indicate allegiance to a contestant. She looked again at the ribbons upon ribbons of gold as the palanquin moved serenely past and grimaced. Kristoph wore a golden ribbon on his arm!

An uncomfortable twitch suddenly developed in her left ear. She raised a hand pressing her ear back into place until the involuntary movement subsided.

Her transport crossed the Plaza of the Fallen, weaving its way past the statues of heroes long passed into legend. Crowds of citizens cheered and threw rice and paper streamers into the air as the litter passed by, the masses crowding the route to catch a glimpse of the dignitaries and contestants as they paraded across the plaza. Flags waved enthusiastically as the procession passed, cheers rose to the heavens, spooking the green parrots to fly about the sky, high above the chorus of upraised voices.

Despite the adoration, Mora suddenly found a rising sense of disquiet within her. She tried to smile as the palanquin moved to exit the plaza only to have her smile slide from her face when they moved past the statue raised to Kristoph. The magnificent sculpture of the heroic Minotaur now proudly displayed a golden ribbon about his arm!

Mora lent back in her seat fuming! How could this have been allowed to happen? She tried to understand where the swelling of support for Kristoph had come from, her mind racing over the events of the last few days. None of her spies had informed her of a growing disquiet. She tried to calm her heart, take deep breaths and relax. It did not really matter whom the support was for when the outcome was already decided. Let the populace wave their little flags and live their moment of fantasy. Reality would swiftly follow, sweeping all this ridiculous behaviour before it.

The Matriarch tried to smile but even she knew it was strained. She gazed out through the velour drape, hoping the passing scenery would take her mind off her troubled thoughts as the procession commenced crossing the bridge, the vista changing from city streets to the cool blue of the Taurean waters and the vibrant lush green of the jungle beyond. The crowds lined the bridge several deep, Mora watched other members of the crowd run by with green, blue and red coloured ribbons on their arms and smiled to herself; clearly some of the populace had misjudged the coloured ribbons they needed to buy.

The breeze from the waters was cool and refreshing after the heat of the city and Mora finally began to put her thoughts aside as she looked ahead and noted the ancient labyrinth approaching and the open plaza before the huge ancient archway leading into the twisting and turning passages beyond. Mora could not wait to take her seat at the royal enclosure ensuring she had the best views of the contestants and to smile sweetly at her female courtiers for one last time.

The Palanquin lowered gently to the sand alongside several others and Mora stepped from the sheltering transport out under the cornflower blue sky. Attendants rushed about adjusting the Matriarch's blue dress, remarking how beautiful she looked, before Mora finally lost her patience and pushed them all away, ascending the tall wooden staircase leading up to the seating area with the roar of the crowd ringing in her ears. She offered a demure wave, rewarded by more enthusiastic cheers, turned the final landing to walk out into the viewing box, and paused for effect as those influential members of the Taurean nobility turned towards her and started clapping loudly and enthusiastically.

Mora progressed slowly past them all, shaking hands, kissing those deemed fortunate enough to be in a position of power and finally made her way to the front of the viewing area to where the seats for the privileged few were located. The Matriarch frowned in confusion when she noted that only one seat was occupied. She was sure she noted the travelling conveyances of her colleagues down below, yet the only Minotaur sitting, no, make that lounging before her was Wanessa.

"Good morning Wanessa." Mora opened, her face still wearing a look of confusion. "Where are all the others?" The obese Minotaur, wearing a ludicrously sheer yellow dress that hid nothing from the imagination and made her look like a giant over ripe lumpy plantain, turned from the silver platter alongside her and pointed to her mouth as she chewed furiously. Crumbs of cake and crushed delicacies fell from her chops to the deck below.

Mora scowled as she waited for the, well there was no other words for it, fat cow, to stop chewing and barely contained her rage, as Wanessa seemed to draw out the masticating action, bobbing her head from side to side and holding up a finger repeatedly to indicate she was almost finished.

"Oh, hello Mora." Wanessa finally replied, spitting some food from her lips as she did so. "The others are here; they are just getting ready."

"Ready for what exactly?" The Matriarch replied, moving forward to take her seat, checking before she sat that no morsels of food had landed in her chair.

"It's a surprise." Wanessa giggled, reaching for another succulent treat.

"Have you not had breakfast this morning?" Mora enquired.

"Oh yes. Of course. It's the most important meal of the day." Wanessa replied plopping a sweetmeat between her lips and chewing on it noisily.

"So what is this one then?" The Matriarch asked, trying to keep up the pretence of friendship whilst secretly imagining roasting the lumpy banana over an open fire pit.

"Lunch appetisers." Wanessa mumbled between mouths of food. Mora turned away, fighting the urge to vomit. The obese Minotaur was such a slob, a complete simpleton, like all of the others, occupying a position bestowed by birthright and not ability, the sooner she was free of them the better!

The Matriarch stared over the handrail, her mind searching for a distraction, gazing across the sand coated arena that lay before the platform, scanning the musicians all bedecked in violet sashes, the bugles and trumpets gleaming in the sun, polished so heavily it was as if the celestial orb had seen fit to drop from the sky to rest upon the sun-baked sand. Her gaze wandered from the band to the gates of the huge archway, locked gates barring access to the labyrinth beyond. A large golden gong hung suspended beneath the arch and sentries stationed on the stonework above appeared to be struggling with something that Mora could not make out.

Movement from the right caught her eye, a line of pavilion tents each with resplendent coloured ribbons flying from the top stood in silent formation. A young servant was running from tent to tent putting his head between the flaps to announce that the tournament was about to begin, warning the contestants that their time to shine was nearly here. Mora had to admit the games master was making good on his promise that everything would look amazing and run as clockwork. Where was he anyway?

An explosion over at the maze wall made the Matriarch jump, an errant firework spiralled off into the sky, fizzing and banging to the roars of laughter from the people standing below. The crowds were getting excited; Mora allowed herself a smile, this was going to be the spectacle to end all spectacles. She took a moment to look at the packed terraces set along the top of the very walls making up the maze; it was standing room only up there. The crowds of people kept jostling each other, trying to stare down into the sand paved trenches, within which the contestants would soon be running, fighting and dying.

Mora found her thoughts returning to the line of tents. Where had the games master found additional competitors at this late hour? She found the thought quite exhilarating, a mystery to solve. She reached out for a sweet cake only to find Wanessa guarding them fiercely, hugging the platter and gazing at the Matriarch with a furious scowl.

"I'm sure there is enough for all of us. Mora exclaimed, snatching a delicacy from the tray and lifting it to her mouth despite the venomous stare directed at her. "The others better hurry or they will miss the opening ceremony. Oh too late…"

The sound of bugles cut the air, a fanfare to draw the attention of the crowds and to signal that the tournament was about to begin. Mora swiftly brushed the front of her dress down acting as if the populace could see the offending crumbs on her dress from so far away, then moved to the front of the platform and waved to the crowds drawing rapturous applause from those around her as the seething masses looked on expectantly.

The bugles sounded again, the roars of the crowd quieting down as Mora turned to a serving page who rushed forwards with a small scroll and held it out for her to read the opening speech from. Mora glanced quickly around the box again, searching for the games master and realising with a sinking heart that he was not going to appear. This was very peculiar. The Matriarch cleared her throat, tapped twice on a golden brooch at her breast depicting two horns set side by side, wrapping around each other into a point, then she began to speak, knowing each word would now be magically transmitted across the crowds.

"My lords, ladies and peoples of Taurean," she began, the crowds noise dropping so that every word the Matriarch offered sounded clear to everyone attending. "Welcome to the 23rd Labyris Tournament…"

The crowd erupted into cheers and yells, causing Mora's eyebrow to rise in annoyance. She was not used to being interrupted, however from the chorus of cries and clapping going on in the box behind her as well as from the crowd she wisely knew when to bite her lip and let the crowd's enthusiasm ebb of its own accord.

"This tournament is by Taureans, for Taureans and is an opportunity to showcase the mightiest and strongest our society has to offer," she continued. "When Autio, the first Labyris Knight, rose up and shook off the yoke of our overseers, taking on the cruel slave masters by facing down the gods and stealing away the mighty Labyris axe, he ensured that Taurean became a prosperous nation that was both feared and respected. Today in honour of that feat, the greatest warriors Taurean has to offer will have the honour of fighting for you. Many will die for your entertainment but only one will win through to raise the Labyris axe." Mora paused, as two guards came in and moved to stand alongside her and at a nod from them, she continued with her oration.

"Behold, Autio's mighty Labyris: Weapon of the Gods."

The crowd roared their approval as the two guards dropped the covering draped across the object they carried, revealing the heralded ancient weapon to the spectators. They hoisted the huge axe up high above them, grunting at the effort, allowing the sunlight to reflect off the mighty double-headed blade, its bronze edge gleaming sharply in contrast to the satin black finish of the rest of the blade. Mora had seen the weapon many times before but today the eerie weapon appeared to emit a luminous halo of light.

From sharpened edge to edge, the span of the weapon was nearly three feet, with the top half of the axe head sheared across its centre and the bottom half of the weapon twisted into two wickedly sharp spikes that pointed down towards the ground. The shaft of the axe, constructed as legend told from an ancient Harkiss wood, had a deep reddish umber to its grain, with two grips made of wrapped leather strips set further down its length for a wielder to hold to prevent the weapon slipping.

The roar of the crowd seemed to go on forever and this time Mora let them have their moment, allowing the guards to continue turning and hoisting the magical blade, lifting it high for as many spectators to see as possible. Mora let the adoration sweep over her, imagining the same delight when she took the position of Matriarch forever and her son Drummon finally lifted the magical blade. Let them all cheer, her time was nigh.

Mora turned towards Wanessa only to find the idle courtier smiling at her in a way that the Matriarch found uncomfortable. It was as if she knew something that Mora did not and this was unsettling. She wracked her brain trying to figure out what it could be as the guards finally lowered the axe and covered it again, ready for transportation back to its resting place at the tip of the pyramidal tomb looming over everything. No, Wanessa probably had indigestion and her face looked that way due to accumulated gas.

The Matriarch stole another glance and noted the smug grin that remained on her face. This was not a trick of the light, nor was it gas. Something was going on that Mora was not privy to and that little worm of doubt continued to twist within Mora's brain.

The page cleared his throat, and Mora realised that she was staring like an idiot and that she had forgotten she was in the middle of her proclamation. She looked down at the scroll in her hand and rolled her eyes. It was the most boring part of the announcement; explaining to everyone what was about to happen, despite the fact that every spectator knew exactly what to expect.

"At the sound of the archway gong, the gates will open and the competitors will enter the labyrinth, one at a time, one combatant every ten minutes, until all contestants have passed through. Once they had entered the maze, some of the deadliest trackers and most cunning predators from the jungles of Taurean will be released into the labyrinth to pursue them." Mora smiled as she said this, knowing that Drummon already knew the weakness of the creatures assembled and how best to throw them from his scent. She took a deep breath and continued her announcement.

"Other beasts have already been set within the labyrinth, lying in wait for the unwary." She announced, hearing the roars of approval from the people around her. "Fiendish traps have been designed by our games master, set to snare those competitors who are not worthy to progress from the maze, weeding out the weak, highlighting the strong and the cunning. All competitors have until the sun sets this evening to make their way through the passageways and negotiate the exit."

"The twisting *Stairway of the Triumphant* leads out of the maze up into Autio's mighty pyramid. If any contestant fails to ascend the staircase, before the last ray of the setting sun touches the capstone on the pyramid, the exits to the maze will be sealed and the monsters remaining permitted to consume those who are still wandering its passageways."

Wanessa yawned loudly, snatching Mora's attention away from the scroll. She scowled before allowing her eye to roam down to the small writing once again. The Matriarch noted what came next and smiled. This part of the rules was written in stone, yet none ever considered the implications, although they would after today!

"At this point any lucky contestant who remains alive will face a choice; they can stop at the base of Autio's pyramid and collect their reward or consider scaling the rest of the stairway to reach the summit and gain even greater rewards." Mora paused letting the words sink in, knowing that she was now about to reveal her plan before all of these witnesses. "Few have undertaken this perilous act in years past but a true hero, mighty of heart, with the will of the people can consider this option. I am facing retirement and am proud to announce that the winner of this year's competition will become our new leader, if they successfully wrestle the Labyris axe from its resting place." An excited roar resonated from the crowd as they suddenly realised this competition had the potential to be really special. A new ruler to be decided that day! The excitement rose to fever pitch.

"Who knows, maybe this year, one of our lucky competitors will be courageous enough to take the challenge. Maybe, if we give our competitor's a sign of encouragement, they may consider it!" Mora looked down at Wanessa and then at the empty seats alongside her as the crowd roared enthusiastically, despite most onlookers knowing that by the end of the maze, any competitor left alive was normally happy just to limp home with their winnings collected at the base of the pyramid, rather than risk it all on the almost certain death that came with ascending the stair and taking the axe from the orb at its summit.

"So without further delay, let us introduce you to the contestants..." Mora opened her mouth to announce the two contestants listed on the scroll when the page hurriedly placed another piece of parchment in her hand.

"What is this?" Mora whispered, looking down at the list in her hand, her eyes widening as she saw what was written there.

"Last minute changes." The page replied. "We did not have the time to change the main scroll; the games master sends his sincere apologies."

Mora felt a lump forming in her throat and her voice suddenly went dry as Wanessa turned fully towards her, clearly wanting to witness Mora's expression as she read what was written before her.

"I give you the green contestant, Karlar!" Mora choked, looking down to the pavilions and watching as the blond Minotaur threw open her tent flap and stepped out onto the sands waving to the crowd, her armour golden and green, a gleaming trident held high in her hand. The Minotaur turned and raised her weapon firstly towards the crowd, gaining a roar of delight, before turning towards Mora and pointing the blade directly towards the Matriarch, the intention of the gesture anything but one of respect.

Mora swallowed hard then looked down at the next name.

"For your entertainment, the red contestant, Ammet!" The next tent flap flung back and the almost skeletal black Minotaur stepped out onto the sands, red ribbons curled within the braid of black hair that hung down her back, a long crimson cloak, embroidered with strange symbols flapping about her. She waved to the crowd, getting cries of appreciation before also turning to the viewing box and offering a low bow.

"Did you think we were stupid?" Wanessa whispered, just loud enough for Mora to hear as she began to voice the next name.

"The indomitable blue contestant, Chane!"

Chestnut hair, moulded into pointed spikes, adorned the top and back of Chane's head, making her countenance quite fierce to behold. She held aloft a blue and silver weapon that looked like an elaborate cross, the edges gleaming in the sunlight. As the Minotaur turned, she threw the cross out before her, watching as the weapon spun out in a slow arc. Impossibly the device picked up speed, spinning rapidly out over the heads of several ceremonial guards before turning back towards the umber coloured Minotaur, completing its arc and flying safely back to her hand.

One guard shouted out in surprise as the tip of his ceremonial flag suddenly toppled from its haft, the flag sheared clean through, much to the delight of the cheering crowd. Chane smiled and gestured to her servant who ran forward and offered a lit cigarette for the Minotaur to inhale, before blowing the smoke out in rings as she turned for the spectators to see her ornate gleaming silver armour.

"Your games master was most forthcoming given the right incentive." Wanessa continued. "He wanted to keep his other eye after we forcibly removed one from him. Who would have believed the ancient clause about the Labyris axe and getting to rule Taurean if you capture it and have it in your hand at the end of the day?"

Mora tried to maintain her smile but Wanessa's comments were like wicked barbs in her skin and she felt her carefully manufactured demeanour slipping from her as she struggled to maintain her composure.

"Your Purple contestant, Pascol" Mora croaked finding each word harder to speak than the last and gesturing for a drink to wet her dry palate.

Out walked Pascol onto the golden sands, her leather armour patched and threadbare even from this distance, a solitary purple ribbon marking her contestant status wrapped around her left arm. The thin Brown Minotaur flicked her mane back and spun a long slender spear about her body, whipping the weapon about her body before planting it at her side and lowering her head to smile up at Mora and the viewing platform.

"Everyone wants to have a go for the throne." Wanessa continued to goad. "Let's be honest the competition is not stiff. Drummon may be strong but he is several eggs short of an omelette."

"Shuesan wears the orange ribbon!" Mora squeaked as the dark-haired Minotaur stepped from her tent and lifted her mace high for the crowd's approval; her armour tinted a rusty red, the ribbon wrapped about her forehead like a bandana.

"To be honest they are more concerned about Kristoph." Wanessa announced. "It appears he has the support of the crowd behind him."

"Your silver champion, Prince Regent Drummon!" Mora stated; her voice now husky. The crowd did not applaud at this announcement as Mora's son emerged from his tent, his body encased in matt black armour rimmed with silver. He held up his long sword and turned to the crowd, expecting the adoration shown to the other contestants, only to find boos, hisses and laughter coming from the spectators at his appearance. Mora watched as her son's brow furrowed and he roared his anger at the crowd who continued to goad him, feeding off his frustration.

"Why are you not competing?" Mora whispered, directing her question at Wanessa before completing her announcements.

"Your final contestant. Wearing the golden ribbon. Kristoph!"

The crowd erupted in a deafening round of applause and stamping of feet. The floor of the viewing platform vibrating through its timbers causing Mora to gasp aloud at the support shown for her recently returned child. Golden ribbons flickered through the crowd like ripples across a pond, as people enthusiastically waved their banners and showed their support but the tent flap to the final contestant did not open. Guards moved forward flanking the opening and still no contestant came forth. Mora leaned forward craning her neck to catch a glimpse of the Minotaur she so desperately needed to give credibility to Drummon's challenge.

"So why are you not competing?" Mora asked, as the guards finally ran into the tent and forcibly pulled Kristoph into the open. The Minotaur stood proud, his head free of a helmet, his body encased in worn salt lined leathers and not the ceremonial armour painstakingly designed for him. Mora realised with shock that the chestnut coloured Minotaur was wearing the garb that she had first seen him in on the floor of the restaurant in the harbour, all those days before. His tattered brown cloak scuffed black leather boots and the twin worn scabbards strapped to his back holding his scarred and battered long swords.

The crowd screamed their appreciation as the Minotaur looked towards Mora, his eyes burning with hatred. The spectators did not seem to care that the Minotaur was not playing to the crowd. His brooding looks as he stood encircled by the guards, their spears all pointed at him, only fuelled his image as one rebelling against the Matriarchal society, and the crowd loved it.

"Let them kill each other." Wanessa replied, as Mora tore her gaze from Kristoph and looked up towards the archway where the bundle struggling between the guards stationed there was revealed to be the missing games master. They pushed him towards the edge of the platform as Wanessa's comments rang in Mora's ears. "There is no point in competing myself, I am not fit enough. However, I am not stupid. If they all die, I am the only one left in line to replace you when your term as Matriarch expires. In addition, if anyone by chance does survive, well... I never raised a finger against them. As long as I have food and access to Minotaur of my choosing, I am no threat to anyone..." Mora tried to focus on the last words written on the scroll, the words that signalled the celebration should begin.

"The god's willing, as the sun sets on the eve of this day, whichever Minotaur holds the Labyris axe will be our new ruler! On behalf of the people of Taurean..." the Matriarch held her arms wide before the crowd, barely containing the tremor in her voice. "Avete Fos... fare you well and may you all die with honour!" Wanessa turned towards Mora fully as, at the signal, the games master was dislodged from his perch and swung down onto the gong, the rope around his waist snapping tight, practically cutting the Minotaur's body in two as he hit the large metal disc and set it ringing with a wet thud.

"Apart from you." Wanessa continued to threaten her voice turning icy cold. "Apart from you." The gong sounded ominously as Karlar ran for the gates to the maze as they slowly creaked open. The first contestant turned and waved towards the spectators, before she slipped through the opening. The crowd roared its appreciation as she ran under the cascade of crimson drops from the gong and she disappeared into the darkness.

The Labyris tournament had begun as it would end... in blood.

Chapter Thirty-Nine

Kerian looked out across the cooling desert sands and sighed deeply to himself, letting his dry tongue run around his cracked lips in a forlorn attempt to leave some moisture on them. He was so tired he just wanted to lie down on the hard stone beneath him, close his eyes and sleep forever but Octavian was still out there somewhere hunting for food. In a curious way, Kerian doubted he would ever be able to sleep properly again, knowing that his companion was scouring the dunes hunting for prey.

The horses stood asleep behind him, shoulders touching, skin sagging, their coats dull, the odd nicker of discontent signalling that the scrub grass and sparse vegetation foraged from along their journey had barely kept the horses fed. Octavian's mount was suffering the most, the wound on its flank so slow to heal, despite the fact that the gypsy was walking alongside it.

Their water supplies were another problem all together. The horses had to come first if they were to make it across the barren sands and Kerian was stunned at just how much water a thirsty stallion could consume. He licked his lips again, feeling the crusty skin rasping across his tongue as he considered what he would give to magically fall back into the cool depths of the Mereya River.

Thirst was a torture Kerian had never really experienced before. His tongue felt swollen and kept sticking to the roof of his mouth and he had small painful ulcers developing. Cracks had formed at the edge of his mouth making talking uncomfortable and eating an agony, that was, if any food actually ended up on his lips!

On the third day of their trek, Octavian had recommended sucking on a small pebble to make saliva in Kerian's mouth but after a while the knight had forgotten what he was doing and had tried to bite down on the stone, stopping with a nasty jolt back to reality. How many days ago was that? Kerian tried to focus on the landscape about him as he struggled to think the simple question through, his burning red-rimmed eyes straining, looking for a sign of a charging wolf like beast, an approaching caravan or possibly armed raiders. He felt his eyes growing incredibly heavy.

How far had they travelled today? Kerian had no idea, some distance he hoped, following Octavian's nose in the direction of Blackthorn and the doubtless terrifying horrors that awaited them there. Octavian's spectral wife had told of petrified forests and monsters that ran in the night, of a castle in the woods where she was captive. It made Kerian shudder just thinking about it. After all, if she was trapped and could still wound Kerian with her magic, from this considerable distance, just imagine what she could do if she was liberated?

He shivered and pulled his cloak further around his shoulders. If he could just get some sleep, rest his eyes for just a moment. No! He had to wake up, keep alert and protect the horses so that tomorrow they could travel further over this accursed dustbowl! The thought of another desert trek sapped what little strength and resilience Kerian had. Why was he doing this? Did it really matter? The *El Defensor* was worlds away; he needed to face the fact that he would never see Colette again. A smile played across his cracked lips as he thought of golden tumbling curls and cornflower blue eyes. It had been so long since he had held her in his arms. He wondered if she ached for him as much as he longed for her. He just needed to rest his eyes for a small moment. Just...

Kerian awoke with a start, sitting up in fear, knowing that in his exhausted state he had let his guard down. His cloak had stuck to the side of his head and reluctantly peeled away as he moved, tearing small flakes of dried skin from his cheek. A windrow of the shifting sands had accumulated at his back, making an uneven pillow that he needed to remove if he were to get comfortable again. He tried to rub the sleep from his eyes and instantly regretted the gritty feeling, as if someone was scouring his eyeballs with sand. Well, in a strange way this was exactly what he had done. He blinked, praying for tears and felt the blessed coolness of them as they slowly slid across his blurred vision.

He swivelled to check the horses and then took a slow look around from his vantage point on the rocky outcrop, his tired eyes struggling to confirm if a flickering shadow was a threat or simply a result of an over active imagination. Satisfied no danger was near, he slowly got to his feet and arched his back, feeling his joints cracking in protest as he took a few steps across the stone outcrop to gaze out over the valley where Octavian's direction had taken them.

This was a desolate place, made worse by the overcast sky which had leached the lunar brightness from his surrounds as he had slept. Stumps of trees littered the ground, their life bleached from them, their boughs now skeletal bones. Even the serpents, present every night with a tenacity that would have put a well-paid mercenary to shame, found the terrain tough going, tending to slither rapidly across the rocks in ribbons of gleaming quicksilver rather than burrow beneath its rocky surface.

What had he been thinking about when he had drifted asleep? Kerian knew it had meant something important to him but for the life of him, he could not remember what it was and the effects of the heat had made it so hard to concentrate of late. There was much to consider, Octavian had not explained how much further it was to their destination and had scolded him like a child for repeatedly asking the question, yet it was a valid one with their provisions nearly gone. He did not wish to die out here, a victim of exposure, scoured by the relentless sand and baked by the oppressive heat.

He realised they could not allow their mounts to perish if they wished to cross the desert and make good distance each day but the creatures needed more rations than Kerian had believed possible. He was starting to begrudge every morsel Toledo devoured! He had no control over the current situation, no means of improving his lot and that of his fellow traveller. Kerian hated feeling so impotent, having to rely on another to survive. He felt like a man adrift, powerless to swim against the currents of a turbulent river that he knew he was floundering in, largely due to his own mistakes.

Kerian let his hand slip around the hilt of the sword now hanging at his belt and gently slid the blade free, marvelling at the balance of the weapon, the keenness of its bevelled edge and the way its flawless length shone despite the darkness. Somehow, just holding this blade gave him a feeling of calm, a semblance of normality in his currently chaotic world.

Shimmering lines of reflected light moved across Kerian's worn features in time with the dark clouds scudding across the heavens. Dimmed slivers of lunar illumination painting his thoughtful face with silvers and shadows, mirroring the turmoil of feelings with which the knight wrestled. He hefted the sword's weight in his hand, taking it carefully by the blade to examine the hilt and the golden circle set at its base. Engraved flickering tongues of flame etched across the grip and the cross-guard represented the celestial orb of light today's dawn would bring.

Kerian took up the weapon by its hilt again and looked down the blade, noting the symmetry of the fuller, the sharpness of the edge and the way it tapered into a deadly gleaming point. The blade had been so bright when he had first used it against Octavian, yet now, under this increasingly overcast desert night sky, it stubbornly failed to flare with its earlier brilliance. He moved to sheathe the sword then paused.

A smile slid across his lips. In the romantic tales of the old knights that Kerian had read as a boy, the heroes always named their swords. The thought appealed to Kerian's poetic and chivalrous image of what it was to be a true paladin, fighting the evil monsters and foul creatures that infested the darker corners of the world. He chuckled to himself, realising that with his own chequered past and the rather dubious life choices he had made, he could hardly be considered a paragon of virtue or stalwart foe of darkness in all its forms. Indeed, in times he had been the very darkness people had feared but the thought of naming the blade seemed right somehow. He sat and pondered. Now what should it be called?

He thought back to the way the blade had lit up in the darkness, how its radiance had turned the desert night to brightest day. It had to be something connected with that light, something about the clean brilliance of the blade and the way it had shone as a beacon in the darkness.

Aurora. Somehow, *Aurora* sounded the right thing to name this strange weapon. He slid it home in the scabbard hearing the cross hilt click softly against its mouth as the weapon rested firmly in place. This scabbard had to have been made for the weapon; there was no other way it could have sat so well. Indeed, the whole outfit he wore appeared connected, both in construction and colour. For a second Kerian's mind wandered, considering what the previous owner of the outfit must have looked like and how he had met his end and then he shrugged turning his attention back to the dark horizon and the other problem he had yet to address.

The storm that had been pursuing Kerian and Octavian relentlessly since they departed the oasis remained hanging ominously low in the sky behind them. Each day it inched ever closer and each time Octavian promised that the prevailing winds would sweep the clouds past, yet somehow, they never overtook them. Hypnotic patterns of dust and sand writhed through the air in a banking wall of debris that howled as it stalked them, displaying a shrewd cunning and intelligence as if alive, rather than the mindless atmospheric feature it was supposed to be.

Kerian's eyes scanned the line where the wall of dust kissed the dunes but with the low level of moonlight filtering through the overcast night sky, it was difficult to identify if anything actually lay hidden within the mysterious wall of billowing sand. One thing was for sure, it made Kerian uncomfortable and he always trusted his instincts when the little voice in his mind warned him something was wrong. That little voice was practically screaming at him now, warning him to mount his horse and flee but where would he go, especially with the inherent dangers involved when travelling the desert at night? The way he felt right now, dehydrated and sapped of strength, meant that anything more than a short jog would soon find him on his back, begging whatever irrational fears he believed were after him to quickly end his misery.

"Come on Octavian. Its time you were back!" he whispered to himself, subconsciously gripping the hilt of his magical weapon tighter as he continued to scan the monotonous landscape. The damned gypsy had to be out there somewhere! He said he was going to try and find some food for them and Kerian was starving!

A shadow wriggled across the distant dunes, angling its path of travel so that it would cut past the very front of the cloud. Kerian squinted hard, crunching up his eyes, trying to get a clearer glimpse. It looked like a giant lizard... with a rider upon its back! The creature ran lightning fast, flicking its tail rapidly from side to side in an effort to maintain its balance, its hind legs scooting across the sand, propelling the beast in a wiggling line that was closing rapidly on Kerian's position.

Something suddenly detached itself from the cloud mass, falling forward and splitting apart, crashing down upon the sprinting lizard as it charged past, pinning the lizard's limbs, dragging it squealing in protest to the desert floor. The rider became unseated, falling from his thrashing mount and hitting the desert sands, rolling over and over as the huge dust cloud surged forward and swallowed both rider and lizard from view.

Kerian's blood turned to ice in his veins. What had just happened? The reaction of the cloud was so fast! Were they human figures that spilled from the cloud and attacked the lizard? He continued staring at the swirling mass of dust, his eyes straining, searching for some sign of the rider and mount, some clue as to the person's fate. Somewhere in the base of the cloud brief, bright, flashes of coloured light flared, illuminating a mass of silhouetted creatures hidden within the swirling mass of dust before the wall of sand ominously darkened again and continued its slow advance towards where Kerian stood.

That was the final straw! The dangers of travelling the desert at night be damned! Kerian would rather take his chance with the silvery serpents and crimson scorpions than face whatever it was he now knew was definitely pursuing them. He rushed to his bedroll, lifting the blankets and supplies from the floor and packing them upon the horses as swiftly as he could, his eyes noting the shifting walls advance towards him, close enough now that he could hear the roar that accompanied the moving sand. The horses reacted instantly, stamping hooves and pulling at their reins as they sensed Kerian's agitation to the approaching menace.

"Come on, come on." Kerian snarled to himself, struggling to strike the campsite as quickly as possible, his fingers frozen almost numb with fear, as he wrestled with the obstinate buckles and straps. Stuffing blankets into holdalls, bundling dirty pots, pans and utensils into a sack and swiftly fastening them to Toledo's saddle. Piling supplies haphazardly onto each other, quickly tied with belts, only to bounce up and down precariously on the rumps of the overburdened horse that shied and rolled its eyes with fear.

Kerian paused to check that nothing important had been left behind, before he took up the reins of the horses and started to lead them from the campsite and down into the stony valley, trying to keep to the larger exposed slabs of stone jutting from the ground as much as possible and making wider paths around areas where treacherous pockets of sand had collected. All thoughts for Octavian fled his mind, the gypsy was just going to have to track him down and catch up later. There was no way he was going to wait for the roaring wall of dust to envelope him with the inherent consequences such an encounter would bring. He needed to move faster, needed to get up onto his horse.

Toledo snorted in protest as Kerian moved to mount the stallion, stepping sharply away to the side and aiming a well-earned nip towards Kerian's hand. There was no way the horse was going to let him climb aboard in its overburdened state and despite the weakness the horse was experiencing it refused to yield, crab walking away every time Kerian moved to place his foot in the stirrup.

"Oh to hell with you!" Kerian cursed, snatching up the slack of the reins, having no choice but to resort to leading the two mounts across the rock-strewn ground as the cloud continued to creep ever closer. Where was he going to go? He noted the winding path of the valley floor, the way it meandered and twisted, realising that he was inadvertently following an ancient dried up riverbed offering very little in the way of options for a choice of direction. A well-placed kick sent an over inquisitive hissing serpent slinking off into the scrub as he pressed on, the knight now noting the roaring sound of the storm as it moved closer, a constant reminder of the horror that now harried his every move.

The banks of the dry river started to rise on either side as Kerian struggled on with the horses. Dust began vibrating on the desert floor, small grains of crimson and beige shimmering and dancing across the rocky surface, whipping about around the legs of the mounts and their determined guide, errant gusts funnelling dust plumes along the riverbed and blasting past him as the oppressive clouds advanced. The route became steadily darker, more cloaked in shadow, certainly more difficult to follow and before long, Kerian found his footsteps faltering and unsteady as the walls of the river course rose up about him, curtailing what little light remained.

Toledo suddenly stopped in his tracks, wrenching Kerian's arm and pulling him around. The knight turned, determined to give the horse a piece of his mind but the stallion pulled sharply away, heading towards the bank and practically dragging Kerian along with him. Sharp branches clawed at Kerian's face and his boots slipped on the rocky scree, his vision practically useless in the darkness of the ravine. Off balance, he had no option but to rely solely on the stallion's instincts in finding a way forwards, so he let his resistance towards Toledo's actions ebb and tried to protect his face with his spare hand as much as he could.

The roaring of the cloud started to lessen as Kerian felt, rather than saw, the surprising presence of a roof over his head. Toledo continued to drag Kerian along with him, pulling him through a rickety doorway and further into the darkness, until, apparently satisfied with his destination, the horse stopped and let the reins finally go limp. Octavian's horse snorted and stamped his hooves as Kerian quickly struck up a flame and gazed out at his unlikely sanctuary.

They seemed to be inside a small abandoned dwelling that had been fashioned from an old cave; at least it may have been habitable as a home a long time ago. Faded pictographs and hand drawings covered the walls, there were dried palm leaves scattered across the stone floor and a small fireplace, still marked with soot, stood cold and stark in one corner. Broken and discarded ancient furniture lay in pieces about the hovel, with piles of drifting sand settled in the furthest nooks and crannies, no doubt blown in by the breath of the desert winds. Withered shrubs and desiccated vegetables lay forgotten within raised flowerpots, something the horses soon set to work on, chewing frantically on the rubbery carrots and wrinkled apples foraged from a stunted fruit tree and a cracked terracotta trough. A sunken well lay in the far corner and a small alcove set off the main room appeared to be the main sleeping quarters.

Kerian found a dusty lamp, the glass cracked, fuel minimal upon shaking and swiftly lit it before he set about building a fire in the derelict grate out of the crumbling pieces of wood lying about the room. A warm glow soon issued from the fireplace, sending a thin tendril of smoke spiralling up into the darkness. Confident that he could extinguish the lamp and conserve the fuel, Kerian blew it out, then reached over for the last remaining apple on the stunted tree and bit down on the heavily dimpled surface, chewing slowly, relishing the saliva squirting into his mouth with each heavenly bite. It may have been the rubberiest most pathetic apple Kerian had ever had, but it tasted simply divine.

The horses shuffled about within the cramped quarters, jostling for position and nudging each other away from the remaining rubbery vegetables, chewing nosily and seemingly agreeing with Kerian's verdict of their meagre faire. The knight tried not to laugh aloud in his relief at finding shelter and brushed himself down before moving to the entrance of the home to wrestle with the warped and sagging door. He struggled to push the door to but the wood was badly warped from its exposure to the elements and failed to hang true, allowing the swirling clouds of dust to still seek ingress about its poorly fitting frame.

Kerian reached out and grabbed an old table leg, wedging it beneath the door handle, before digging the bottom edge into the floor. He quickly checked through the gap in the door as to the progress of the storm. The sand whipped along the dry riverbed, borne by a wind that heralded its passage with a piercing whistle. A tremor vibrated through the wooden door, a repetitive booming, once, twice, a third and fourth time, before the pattern repeated again, growing in intensity and volume.

The knight frowned at the sound; boom, boom, boom, boom, it was like a marching beat, the tremors causing dust to spiral down from the ceiling in a slow spasmodic trickle. Clumps of soot crumbled away and dropped into the open fire with a clatter, causing the flames to spit and spark. The knight blinked his eyes and then returned his attention to the doorway and the raging storm without. The sight he saw made him freeze in place. Sinister figures were moving along the riverbed, mere feet from his place of concealment; dark shapes, marching onwards, ancient spears held high, faded pennants cracking in the wind, footsteps in time and synchronised. It was an army on the move, intent on traversing the desert to a destination unknown. But what was an army doing here?

Toledo nudged Kerian hard in the small of his back as he continued to shuffle about the cramped living space looking for more food, causing the knight's head to bang loudly against the doorjamb. Kerian bit back a curse, rubbed his forehead in a bid to try to relieve the discomfort and then noted with concern that his mild concussion had caused more than just a throbbing pain. It had also grabbed some unwanted attention.

A foot soldier within the passing shadowy ranks had paused in his march, turning his head towards the hidden doorway and Kerian's current hiding place. Kerian pulled himself back from the door, gasping at his discovery, whilst hoping that the darkness within the small ravine would be enough to hide the entrance to the soldier in much the same way it had been masked from Kerian. However, the knight's wishes were not to be. The soldier took one faltering step, then another, causing others within the ranks to file past him as he walked unerringly towards the cliff face hovel and the knight hiding within.

Kerian slowly drew his sword, his eye still pressed against the gap in the door, studying the figure advancing but not yet sure if this was a friend or foe. Two other soldiers shuffled to a stop, pausing in their march to turn and follow their curious brother in arms into the shadows, their hands reaching for their weapons.

Toledo snorted in delight at discovering another withered carrot and nudged Kerian again, reinforcing the fact that there was very little space to manoeuvre in here should a melee develop. Kerian shoved back hard with his bottom and stared back through the gap, vainly attempting to identify some sign or insignia, some idea of what army these troops belonged to. The first soldier moved closer, his actions stiff and unnatural, perhaps even stilted, now that Kerian could observe the figure up close. Something about the way the soldier moved caused the hairs to rise on Kerian's forearms.

The foot soldier stumbled in the darkness, falling hard against the door, making the table leg creak ominously and Kerian step instinctively backwards, before the unidentified figure regained his unsteady footing and stood up tall. The sparse light from the fireplace passed over Kerian's shoulder, beaming through the gap in the doorway to capture the soldier's state of decay in vivid detail.

Kerian took in the sight of the withered flesh, the bleached pieces of skull showing through the flaking face, the yawning hole where a nose would normally be, and the stained teeth that grinned due to a lack of lips with which to do otherwise. He stepped back in shock, pushing against Toledo as the shambling undead creature brought its face up to the opening through which Kerian had been spying. It stared through the opening with its one remaining shrivelled eye, acting as if it could see clearly. Half a ragged eyelid blinked closed, the other half missing, probably food for desert scavengers' years ago.

Aurora slammed between the boards of the door, the flawless blade taking the creature through the neck, severing its spine and dropping its head to the floor. There was no shriek of alarm, no opportunity to call for help. Kerian's strike was clean and almost surgical in its precision. The skeletal soldier dropped to its knees, hitting the door hard and causing the table leg wedged beneath the handle to finally snap in two. Kerian did not hesitate, tearing open the door, allowing the dust from the storm to swirl into the room and causing the horses to snort in alarm. He charged out, leaping over the monster at his feet as it collapsed in upon itself, swinging his blade in low, hacking the legs out from underneath the second skeletal warrior before bringing his blade up, then back down hard upon the skull of the third, cleaving it in two.

The second soldier tried to get to its feet but a swift backhanded chop with *Aurora* stopped that idea before it could reach fruition. Kerian brought his weapon around before him, clutching the hilt in both hands, feet slightly apart, eyes squinting out into the clouds of dust, watching for the next wave of monsters he knew would come towards him, even as he realised that he had attacked the three undead foes with a fluidity he had not experienced in years!

Kicking at the tabard of the nearest corpse, Kerian tried to make out the faded insignia inscribed upon its tunic but the light from the doorway only reached so far and it was so dark out here in the ravine that he could not see sufficiently to throw much needed illumination onto his predicament. Why did *Aurora* not shine brightly, why did the weapon not light up the night sky as it had before? He shook the blade as if by somehow agitating the weapon it would flare into searing light but the blade remained stubbornly dull.

Another large shadowy figure stomped over in Kerian's direction, causing the knight's questions about his mysterious blade to be set aside. A tattered cloak whipped about the tall figure, its ragged length snapping in the wind, the hood shading a grinning skeletal face that stared at Kerian with such intensity that the knight could have almost believed the creature still had its eyes instead of dark sockets.

Several other indistinct shapes marched past behind it, oblivious to their fellow soldier's change of direction, intent on heading further down the ravine, the rank and file of hundreds of warriors marching in step to a destination known only to them. The sound of their passing creating a level of noise that almost matched the intensity of the storm whistling about them and set the sides of the ravine trembling.

Kerian moved forward to intercept the charging creature, figuring it was better that he took the initiative, swinging his blade in at waist level, only for the huge undead soldier to lift up his arm and deflect the attack on an ancient shield carried within the cloak. The skeletal warrior tilted its head, first one way, then the other, then dropped the shield and drew out a huge spiked mace from within its cloak before leaping forward in a rush.

Aurora parried the first and second crushing blows, sending a ringing out into the darkness as the weapons collided. Kerian noted an opening, leaping forwards, lunging at the skeleton, beating the mace out to the side as he swung his blade in with deadly accuracy, piercing the monster's cloak, once, twice, only for his weapon to pass out the back of the material having managed to damage nothing. The mace swung back, barely giving Kerian time to withdraw his longsword and make a quarter turn to the inside, concealing his vulnerable front but exposing his back as the mace whipped by overhead.

Kerian struggled to recover, finding himself up close to the monster, enveloped in the decayed smells that lingered about its person. He took a deep breath and almost gagged before attempting to turn around, beating his blade against the haft of the mace, desperately trying to hit the monster's hand, to dislodge or remove a few fingers and send the weapon spinning away into the sand.

The grinning skull seemed to mock his attempts, ignoring the flicks of the blade that Kerian offered in its direction. It parried his next lunge, bashing his blade down with a *bind knock* that slammed the blade from high to low, dragging Kerian along with it. The knight overbalanced, stepping past the huge undead soldier, more fully out into the dry riverbed and the roaring tempest.

The sandstorm slammed into Kerian, stabbing at his eyes, ripping at his skin, making him lose his focus on the foe before him and instead start panicking about the hundreds still left unseen, marching ever onward through the debris and dust. However, Kerian need not have worried about this, as the skeletal soldier apparently held a grudge and charged right after him, straight back into the vortex of grit and sand.

Kerian just managed a *Sixte* parry, bringing his longsword up in a deadly arc to knock the mace out to the side, before he reversed the swing in a two-handed chopping action. *Aurora*'s keen edge skidded across the monster's armour, striking sparks off some rusted chain mail to catch the creature right beneath the chin, knocking it back several steps. It crashed into another marching infantryman, sending the skeletal creature spinning out of step, to collide with a rank of spearmen who spilled about like children's dominos, one losing its head, another an arm as they fell to the rocky ground.

The huge skeletal warrior lashed out angrily with its mace, striking left and right as the next two skeletal infantrymen marched up, inadvertently pulverising a bony chest and permanently realigning a lumbar spine before the weapon located its enemy within the dust storm and clanged heavily into the mirrored shield hung at Kerian's back. Kerian found himself lifted up and thrown forwards several feet, before he managed to stagger about to regard the monster bearing down upon him. He needed to figure out the best attack to slow the creature and leave it vulnerable. Go for the leg, the neck, its weapon arm? He needed to decide and swiftly, before the creature was upon him.

Kerian smiled as an opening made itself clear, bringing his sword up above his head as he timed the precise moment to strike. The skeletal warrior strode closer, swinging its mace from side to side, its boots striking the stony floor in measured strides that brought it within striking range. The knight watched the steps, measured the rhythm to the swing of the mace, waited until the creature was almost upon him, then as the mace moved to the left, he spun to the right, bringing the gleaming sword about in a glittering arc, to strike not at the front of the monster but to its rear.

Aurora slammed into the back of the soldier's left knee, shearing fibrous tendons and ligaments, splintering the monster's tibia and cracking its femur, sending a gristly kneecap spinning out across the sand. The skeletal warrior spun with its mace, not realising that this very movement only served to snap the knee further apart, sending the skeleton crashing to the floor, its cloak billowing out around it. Kerian continued his turn, arcing the longsword up and then down, shearing the monsters now exposed neck, snapping the vertebrae and finally laying the unholy creature to rest.

Kerian turned, sword outstretched daring any further warriors to attack only to realise that an eerie silence had now descended on the riverbed. The wind inexplicably died down, the marching boots and clattering bones all stopped. Kerian blinked his eyes in disbelief, not sure what was happening but preparing for the worst.

The marching soldiers all stood at silent attention, not moving, as still as in death, except they were vertical instead of horizontal and lying in their graves. A faint bugle call sounded from beyond the ravine wall where other warriors had apparently halted their march as well. It hung in the air, a call to assemble the ranks, to inform the troops that their march, for this day at least, was over.

The silence was almost deafening. Not an animal stirred, nor snake hissed, even the nocturnal desert owls dared not break the sanctity of the moment. It was as if the whole world had decided to take one large breath and everyone but Kerian had been included in the message. The knight looked at the skeletal statues all so still about him, rows upon rows, rank upon rank of undead soldiers stretching away as far as he could see; wondering if they were all looking at him, watching him to see if he would turn his back and let down his guard. He half expected them to suddenly charge and bury him alive with their incredible numbers alone!

What army was this? Why was it following him? Kerian wanted answers, he looked down at the ruined skeletal warrior at his feet and the long flowing cloak the monster still wore. It was a senior figure, judging by the faded braid upon its uniform, yet Kerian recognised enough that it was not the commander of the unit. That warrior was still out there somewhere, possibly moving among the ranks of soldiers now standing motionless about him.

He knelt down to examine the faded uniform more closely, realising he was the only person moving within sight. The unsettling sensation of being watched sent tingles up the back of Kerian's neck, he kept imagining the soldiers turning and springing upon him at any moment, filling the air with gleeful shrieks as they chopped him to a thousand pieces but despite his jittery feelings nothing happened.

Keeping a tight grip around the hilt of his sword, Kerian moved his free hand down to lift up the edge of the cloak and examine it more closely. The blade in his hand suddenly flickered, as if a tongue of flame had just raced along its glittering length, before it instantly extinguished, returning the blade back to its normal appearance. Kerian froze, caught between looking at the longsword, the cloak of the skeleton at his side and keeping a watchful gaze out of the corner of his eye at the troops standing to attention.

Aurora stayed dull, just a steel blade reflecting back the clouds scudding overhead. Kerian counted to three inside his head, then shook the sword again just in case he had inadvertently activated its magical illumination then cancelled it again. The sword remained stubbornly dark. The damned weapon made no sense...

Aurora flared back to life, the blade shining as bright as the sun, just as something large hairy and wolf like leapt through the silent ranks of sentinels, only to find itself yelping and squealing in horror as it moved into the magical sphere of radiance, crashing to the ground in a writhing heap.

Kerian looked up with a start, shocked that anything could close in on him so quickly without him noticing, only to recognise the humanoid figure transforming on the ground beside him and shrug his shoulders at the gypsy's obvious discomfort. It served Octavian right, trying to sneak up on him and scare him in this way. He looked back down at the cloak, now brilliantly lit, noticing the spider insignia and confirming his thoughts on who this mysterious legion was.

"Provan" Octavian growled mid-transformation. "Kerian we have to run. The Provan legion are after us." Kerian ripped the cloak from the dead skeleton at his feet and threw it over to Octavian's naked form before grimly getting to his feet.

"I already know." He replied firmly, gesturing at the eerie soldiers standing motionless around them. "They are already here. The question is, why?" Octavian got to his feet shivering, pulling the cloak about his frame to protect his modesty.

"Seriously Kerian, there was no need for the sword. I can change back myself now it is no longer a full moon. You pulling that blade makes me feel like I've run into a barn door." Octavian looked about, sniffing the air, hoping about on his bare feet trying to avoid the worst of the sharp gravel covered ground. "Where have you hidden the horses? I need my clothes and boots back."

"Over here." Kerian replied thoughtfully, leading the gypsy back to the cave and the rickety doorway through which the two horses stared out at them wide-eyed. "Did you see any sign of a giant lizard in your travels?"

"No not a single giant lizard, which is a shame because I hear they taste like chicken." Octavian paused when he saw the errant apple core Kerian had dropped on the floor of the cave. "Did you keep me an apple?" he enquired with a raised eyebrow.

"Apparently the apples were off." Kerian replied, looking back out over the ranks of silent troops. "Why do you think they all stopped like that?" He turned back to Octavian only for the gypsy to stare at him with a frown.

"Excuse me." The gypsy remarked. "Please can you turn your back? I need to get dressed." Kerian moved to comply, still struggling to understand what was really going on. If the Provan legion were really after them the question remained why? If there was a need to capture or even kill them then surely the troops would have kept attacking? It simply made no sense.

"Come on, let's go." Octavian urged, pulling at the reins of his mount and turning to exit the cave. "We need to get out of here. All these piles of bones standing here are giving me the creeps!"

"And a guy who changes into a wolf and eats people doesn't?" Kerian shot back, leading his horse after the departing gypsy and staring longingly at the small shelter they were now abandoning.

"Sounds just like my kind of guy." Octavian joked before looking at his horse and frowning. "Who the hell packed my saddlebags? I'll never get the creases out of my tunic!" The two adventurers moved cautiously out across the riverbed, weaving their way through the skeletal troops as quietly as they could, waiting for the inevitable scream of a battle cry or the creak and clatter of old bones moving together as the soldiers prepared to attack.

"Hang on a moment." Kerian whispered. "Where's my food."

"In the same place as my apple." Octavian shot back.

* * * * * *

The fire in the little fisherman's cave had slowly burnt itself out, the fuel for the fire so rotten that the flames had consumed it incredibly fast. Clumps of soot continued to tumble free into the fireplace, causing hissing and spitting from the few hot coals that remained alive. The wind began to pick up again, gusting into the cave, lifting the disturbed sand upon the ground and blowing it back into the furthest reaches of the room. The discarded lantern toppled onto its side, the little lantern fuel remaining, glugging mournfully from its reservoir. The tracks of the previous visitors began to smooth out, forming gentle waves upon the surface of the floor.

A loud horn sounded outside, the echo of the call ghostly and haunting as it resonated down the chimney, then the relentless stomping of hundreds of feet vibrated throughout the cave. The Provan legion were on the move again. A larger clump of soot dropped from the chimney, rolling over and over, bouncing down into the fire pit and incredibly as it landed, the debris muttered a loud curse. There was a flash of light and suddenly a man appeared, stepping out of the fireplace and brushing his soot covered robes down whilst further oaths fell from his mouth indicating his surprise on how he had ever avoided being burned alive.

He turned, taking in the small room, his hands pushing back his lank hair, only pausing to adjust the eye patch covering one eye. His boot came down heavily on a chewed apple core, almost causing the figure to stumble and further curses come from his mouth.

Scrave reached down and picked up the mushed apple core before throwing it away. He stopped and sniffed the air. Something flared brightly from behind his eyepatch, illuminating the Elf's face in a cool green glow. Scrave's lip curled up, his face becoming more bestial in an instant as the twisted creature coiled within his right eye socket sought control.

"Dennarrrisssss!"

Chapter Forty

The immense doors to the labyrinth boomed shut behind Rauph, sealing him inside a dimly lit world where the sky above was a thin strip of cobalt blue, hemmed in on all sides by dark granite walls twenty-five feet high and fifteen feet thick. The surfaces of the walls were festooned by colourful jungle plants, moss and creepers, some dark and slimy and adorned with thorns, whilst others displayed gloriously vibrant flowers and variegated leaves. The floor of finely raked sand indicated the tracks of the other contestants who had entered the maze before the navigator, starkly marking the trail Rauph needed to follow.

Pausing for a moment, the navigator suddenly found himself showered with brightly coloured ribbons and streamers, thrown down onto him by the spectators crowded around the top of the massive walls. They fell about his feet like confetti, serving to impair the Minotaur's keen vision as effectively as the roaring appreciation of the crowd deafened his chestnut ears. He had memories of this place, vague shadowy ones of wandering the maze with governors and later with friends but the actual route into the heart of the labyrinth remained a mystery lost in a history that his fractured recall was at present not party to.

Burning brands, set at regular intervals along the walls, served to light the solitary path ahead, leaving Rauph with nothing to consider apart from his bearings, which was no easy feat, considering all of the Minotaur's surrounding landmarks were obscured by the towering walls and the bobbing heads of the braying crowd. The only obvious structure of note was the imposing pyramid, stretching up to the sky. The navigator scrunched up his face and tried to ignore the roar of appreciation. This situation needed to be carefully considered; he could not simply charge headlong into it like a Minotaur in a porcelain shop, as that quite often resulted in a severe scolding, losing your allowance and a lot of broken crockery!

Rauph realised his situation was serious and that the decisions he took next could have fatal consequences. He knew he was often seen as stupid or slow; however, neither of these descriptions accurately portrayed the complex inner workings of the navigator's mind. The navigator was aware how he became confused when people talked to him, sometimes misunderstanding sarcasm and humour. This innocence often left Rauph responding to situations by saying things that others would never consider, leading to the Minotaur stumbling through uncomfortable social situations and making his ability to balance the fine art of politics a suspect one. It was always so easy to upset people's feelings, even when Rauph meant nothing untoward at the time.

He recalled that as a youth, his first encounter with politics and social niceties had been an unmitigated disaster when he had attended the funeral of a local noble woman. Her husband, a keen hunter, had shared his grief widely, exclaiming he would have an empty house and could not imagine life without her. Rauph had tried to offer comfort, suggesting that maybe he should have her stuffed and mounted like his other hunting conquests, because his grace always remembered those adventures so well. That way she would never be far from his thoughts. Surprisingly, to Rauph, these comments caused sheer outrage and bluster from the grieving widower, demanding instant redress, threatening duels and demanding compensation.

They also caused amused titters from the assembled courtiers, who instantly imagined the departed lady's head mounted on a wooden plaque and stuck on the wall between a stuffed Penades tiger and Berelian antelope. The cheeks of female serving staff also coloured, knowing that there was more than one way of interpreting the young Minotaur's naive comments and that mounting and stuffing had been going on under their mistress's nose for years!

Displaying such poor tact, Rauph often found himself with a lot of time alone. He would spend it in quiet contemplation, carefully replaying scenarios and mulling over problems or situations that were confusing to him, sometimes these revelations occurred in the middle of conversations with others, leading to people finding his behaviour and unexpected outbursts strange. The Minotaur laughed aloud for no apparent reason, sometimes several days after hearing a joke or experiencing something that had confused him. More often than not, these chuckles occurred in lessons of mathematics or Taurean language, resulting in stern punishment for causing a disturbance in class from the tutors who mentored him.

Despite these setbacks, Rauph remained genuine, fair and kind, his quiet behaviour gaining him more friends and supporters than he realised, as he quietly sat and pondered his day-to-day problems within the security of his own imagination, allowing the politics of Taurean to continue on without him.

Those very same thought processes were happening in Rauph at this moment. He knew the object of this competition was to get under the pyramid and to climb up the stairway to the ancient halls above. The Minotaur also realised he could not get to his goal by simply scaling every wall that he came upon, travelling in a direct line until he reached the centre of the labyrinth. After all, he knew the pyramid actually rested upon the maze, meaning at some point the sky would disappear from above and his passage would be to all intent and purpose, subterranean, making climbing over the walls an impossible act. He also had no rope or climbing tools. Tunnelling through the walls was equally problematic. He would need supporting struts, digging tools and... well it was simply too much work.

Leaving a trail of breadcrumbs or unravelling a ball of string were two other options quickly rejected. Rauph had eaten all of his bread at breakfast time and had not considered that he would have needed more loaves for this endeavour, otherwise he would have asked for a very large packed lunch! He also knew of no one in Taurean with a ball of twine as large as the one he would need to trace a way through a labyrinth of this size. The resulting sphere would have been as wide as the very passageway he was travelling, making such an idea totally impractical, let alone impossible to hide beneath his tunic.

The Navigator considered tracing his hand along one wall and letting the maze take him wherever it would, before he factored in the other contestants and the rules to this contest. The competition was time restricted, so tracing up, down, in and out of every blind alleyway and twisting pathway would be yet another time-consuming way to end up finishing last and it was strongly suggested that finishing last was not conducive to good health and longevity.

Rauph scowled, deciding to apply his thoughts as if this were a navigational problem. The Minotaur prided himself in his sense of direction and his ability to find any course on any map. If he followed the logical thought that ahead was towards the centre of the maze, or for today's purposes North, he might just have a chance. A smile crossed his features, as he finalised his plan, then he frowned again. Unfortunately, he had no labyrinth map currently in his possession.

Well, in that case, he would just have to make one!

The navigator scrunched up his eyes and tried to imagine what such a map would look like. First, he needed to imagine a blank sheet of paper. That was not too hard; most people thought his mind was a blank anyway! He then decided what colour pencil to mentally draw his image with and let his imagination sketch the purple passageway along which he travelled.

A rough picture of the maze started to appear in Rauph's mind. He mentally enhanced the image with every forward footstep taken, adding little notes to his mental picture of wobbly pencil lines, recording a scraggly bird's nest up on the right complete with chirping young, and a large gouge taken from the stone on the left. He took another step and felt the floor sag slightly beneath him. That was strange; floors seldom sagged in Rauph's limited experience. He paused in his mental cartography, filing the information away before considering the mystery before him.

The navigator noted the tracks in the sand, noticing that every set moved to either the left or the right, before tracing along the stone walls, rather that striding straight across the sagging floor. Was this some kind of trap that would be triggered if Rauph walked across it? The Minotaur considered this option carefully, weighing the idea as he gently bounced one foot up and down on the edge of the sagging area, sending sand slipping down through a crack that ran directly across his path and making the floor squeak loudly. A loud growl came from beneath the ground and the sand visibly flew upwards as something huge slammed into the underside of the passageway.

Rauph quickly ignored the growl, after all floors rarely snarled, although the squeak could mean he had inadvertently disturbed a large mouse. Rauph knew he could not allow himself to be distracted by a cuddly mouse with big floppy ears and a button nose no matter how big it would have to be to make all of these sounds. He briefly wondered if he could find some cheese then shook his head as he realised that he was losing focus. He had to concentrate on the clues before him. If the other competitors had considered this area a threat, then maybe there was something in their beliefs, because as of yet Rauph had not heard any announcements informing him of a departure of one of his rivals, either out of the maze exit or via a gory death and there were no sticky dead bodies lying about the sand either.

The crowd roared loudly somewhere over to the right, suggesting something exciting was happening in that direction, distracting Rauph yet again. He decided to act, tiptoeing carefully along the left edge of the pit, despite the fact that whatever was below him was now clearly agitated at his passing, before finding himself back on firm ground.

The navigator scowled as he recalled his scratchy purple picture in his mind and added an important squeaky mouse note to his diagram, then he placed a huge imaginary gold star on his sketched route to remind him to return and find said mouse, before he continued along the passageway, only to find it terminate at a 'T' junction with two possible choices now offered. Rauph suddenly wished he had something to chew on whilst contemplating this unexpected situation. Indeed, a piece of crumbly cheddar seemed a great idea at this time! He looked left, then right, noting that both appeared to run straight as far as he could see. So would it be port or starboard?

The Minotaur turned to port remembering that his starboard side now faced towards the centre of the maze and jogged a few confident strides, hearing the screaming from the crowd lessen as he ran along the passageway, away from the uproar. Rauph noted the moisture slick walls here, vivid deep purple blooms, a hint of honeysuckle in the air and a dark blue-black squirrel foraging for food before he realised that the sandy floor before him was smooth, showing no sign that any competitor had selected this new route. His footing became less confident, his pace dropped and doubts crept in. What if he had gone the wrong way?

If everyone else had chosen to turn to starboard, then maybe he needed to go that way too. He swivelled on the spot and slowly started to backtrack, confirming as he jogged along that his footprints were the only ones marring the sandy surface. Rauph started to pick up pace as his confidence returned and his imaginary purple pencil scribbled out the wrong passage from his map. He knew he was the last contestant to enter the labyrinth, so by definition he was therefore the last contestant in the race and he intended to rectify that unfortunate situation as swiftly as possible.

The Minotaur reached the same 'T' junction he had recently departed and stole a quick glance down it to try and spot the giant mouse, only to notice that the floor of the passageway, right about where it had appeared to sag, seemed to be rising up from the ground. There appeared to be a cage of some sort, rising from the floor, with something large pacing angrily around inside its confines and it was definitely not a mouse.

Rauph shook his head, chastising himself at his lack of concentration and focused on charging ahead down the other branch of the junction in pursuit of his rival contestants, the purple illustration in his mind growing more complex with each measured pace. He did not have time for trivialities now, he had to follow the others, then overtake them and he also wanted to find out what had had the crowd in such an uproar. What was behind him did not matter at this time, even if it did have a cute button nose.

The cage clanged loudly as the door at its front dropped away, raising a ripple of excited shouts from the crowd, answered by the monstrous creature that charged out with a primeval roar. The menacing challenge echoed around the walls of the labyrinth and the crowd roared their appreciation in return, struggling to see the spectacle of the exotic creature crawling below them.

Rauph heard the loud noises from behind him, his brow creasing with confusion. Had he somehow been turned around in his travels? Rauph double checked his imaginary purple drawing and shook his head. No, the crowd had definitely been cheering more loudly up ahead, not behind him and the direction to the centre of the maze was definitely on his left side. Had someone doubled back? He considered this for a moment as his feet pounded along the passageway. That was ridiculous! Any contestant would have had to get past him first and he knew he had not bumped into anyone on his travels, so why the excitement of the crowd?

This whole scenario made no sense.

Another wave of sound echoed hauntingly behind Rauph, growing nearer and louder as the creature from the cage swiftly closed the gap towards its prey. The navigator turned about, stealing a quick glance behind but upon seeing nothing but shadows, returned his attention to his chosen direction of travel, only to slide to a stop at a second intersection. This time a choice of three passageways led him forward: Port, starboard or dead ahead. Dead ahead... somehow Rauph did not like the sound of that! The centre of the maze was to port, so the navigator turned left, continuing to extend the purple map in his mind's eye.

Something huge extracted itself from the darkness and swiftly skittered up the wall of the labyrinth behind him, eight blade-like legs stabbing through the vegetation, gouging the stonework beneath. A razor-edged tail whipped about in excited agitation, as its yellow eyes narrowed and zoomed in on its fleeing meal.

The crowd screamed their delight at seeing the exotic beast closing in on the first victim of the competition, delighted that they knew something the clueless competitor below did not. Spectators leaned over so close to the edge of the wall and so dangerously near to the stalking beast that they ran the risk of also becoming its prey but this was apparently lost on the crowd in the anticipation of seeing first blood spilt.

Rauph continued his charge along the corridor, hearing the baying of the crowd but simply deciding it was better if he ignored them. He noted the passageway turned to port a short way ahead but there was also a narrower overgrown side passage to starboard heading the way he wanted to go. The navigator pushed his way into the side corridor just as the screams of the crowd reached a crescendo and the monster launched itself from the wall above.

The beast hit the edge of the passageway in an explosion of foliage and frantic scrabbling, just ahead of where Rauph had turned off the main walkway. It snarled its anger and frustration at miss-timing its leap, clawing at the vegetation and ripping apart everything it could get its teeth and claws into. A spiked hood of loose skin flared up around its neck, adding to the creature's fierce look as it skittered and slid down to the floor before shaking its head and wheeling about, charging off after the Minotaur prey that had not even bothered to look in its direction.

Rauph, oblivious to the frenzied pursuit, continued running along the new passageway, noting the way the ancient gallery twisted first to the left, then to the right but always orientating himself in the direction which the pyramid lay, whilst hoping that a new corridor would soon present itself, allowing him to move closer to his goal. The navigator tried to blot out the eager screams of the crowd of heads peering down at him from the walls and focused on the details of the labyrinth as he ran.

Filtered sunlight had permitted vegetation to thrive here in vivid greens and vibrant flowers, whilst other walls, where predominant shadows and darkness remained, led to the growth of tightly spiralled ferns, waving fronds and lush clumps of green and brown mosses that clustered tightly around pools of rainwater collected in the cracked and tired masonry.

"Behind you!" a voice screamed in warning from above, clearly very excited at watching the action unfolding beneath, drawing disgruntled looks from fellow spectators who did not want the surprise of the pursuing beast spoilt for the fighter apparently fleeing below. Rauph shook his head, determined to keep his gaze focused firmly ahead. He did not intend to turn about, besides, the purple map in his mind's eye told him he was currently moving in the right direction! Sometimes people just went out of their way to cause trouble and make you doubt yourself, which was too much of a distraction whilst he was trying to make up time.

The Minotaur turned another starboard corner, disturbing several birds scratching at something brown and leathery lying on the sand, their explosive flight upwards causing him to shy and throw his right arm up in reflex, as the corridor about him ended in an area approximately thirty feet square. An unexpected mace blow crashed down upon Rauph's right arm, yanking it down, pulling him off balance and making him bellow in pain as he tumbled out into the daylight.

Rauph fell to his knees, swiftly putting out his left hand to stop himself falling on his face, only to find the mace catching the front of his chin, clicking his teeth painfully together then striking his nose as the rust coloured cudgel rose up for yet another strike. The navigator reached for his snout, checking it was still attached and noting it felt wet to touch, his hand coming away to reveal a bloody streak across his chestnut pelt.

"You and your bastard brother!" snarled his attacker. "You have no right to try and usurp us from our birthright. We have waited on Mora, supported her government dictates and legislation, even put up with her idiotic prince, only for her to backstab us in this way. How dare she…"

Rauph tried to dodge away, knowing from the emphasis of the voice that another blow was coming, only to feel the mace crash into his right side, thudding into his leathers, lifting him clear from the sandy floor and bowling him out across the sand. He staggered up onto his knees, coughing out a wad of bloody phlegm and wheezing heavily as he struggled to inhale enough air to stop his head spinning. After agonising moments, he finally managed to gather enough breath to stare up into the face of his attacker.

Shuesan stood before him in her rust tinted armour, her orange headband at an angle, her hair dishevelled and matted in blood that Rauph was positive was not his own. The female Minotaur appeared strangely lopsided, her face off kilter and no longer symmetrical, her armour dented and crushed. The navigator shook his head, trying to quell the ringing in his ears, his every breath painful, his right arm still numb and tingly as if a thousand fire ants had set up a colony beneath the Minotaur's skin.

Rauph tried to suppress the pain from his injuries, tried to take in the image of the foe before him and comprehend why he had been attacked in this way. He blinked again, allowing his eyes to focus through the pain and realised that something was clearly wrong with Shuesan's head, she was all bruised, her face battered and swollen, the armour dents also appeared fresh, silver metal glinted from within the virgin creases and deep scoring across the breastplate. He considered all of the visual clues then stated the obvious.

"Where has your ear gone?"

"Your evil twisted sibling did this!" Shuesan screamed. "He caught up with me, maimed me and left me for dead but if he thinks I will die in this godforsaken labyrinth, he is mistaken. I'm going to make sure that at least one of Mora's brood perishes here first."

The mace swung in again but the small reprieve had given Rauph time to catch his breath and balance on the balls of his feet, allowing him to spring away just as the weapon whipped past him. He reached up reluctantly unsheathing his swords in a move practiced time and again, only for hot searing agony to flare through his side, eliciting a loud grunt of pain as the muscles across his ribs rebelled against the unexpected movement.

Shuesan's wicked mace angled in again, forcing Rauph to bring up his right sword arm in an attempt to parry, only for him to watch in shocked betrayal as his blade flew out of his numbed hand and thudded onto the sand. He reacted swiftly, snapping up his left longsword barely in time to parry the heavy mace before staggering backwards.

The crowd roared their approval at the contest of strength unfolding right below them, throwing their coloured streamers into the air to show their gratitude and support for the two gladiators battling upon the sand.

Rauph ducked his head as the mace whistled by, then swung his sword up in retaliation, scoring a fresh silver wound across his adversary's auburn plate armour, sparks jumping from the weapon as it caught on each seam. Shuesan's mace whooshed back in with a lightning fast backhand that almost caught Rauph unawares. He had no choice but to give valuable ground, the sand beneath his feet kicking up as he retreated from the advances of her brutal weapon.

"I have no quarrel with you." Rauph stated, circling warily just beyond Shuesan's reach. "If my brother has grieved you, then surely he is the one you should direct your anger towards?"

"You are all from the same bloodline." Shuesan spat, jabbing her mace forward, then darting back beyond the reach of Rauph's blade. "By killing you, I hurt your brother and mother, spoiling their plans and diminishing their legitimacy."

"I'm not sure how." Rauph replied, dodging to the left, sidestepping a wild swing from his opponent before circling warily again. "They both seem equally keen to kill me by themselves, without any help from others. You would just be doing them a favour." Shuesan mirrored the navigator's moves, ending up with her back towards the passageway from which Rauph had first entered the small arena. A bird hopped across the sand with something furry in its beak and Rauph noted with some surprise that it was the ear missing from his attacker.

"Oh look, your ear!" he remarked. Shuesan smiled and shook her head.

"Do you think I would be that naive to fall for that one?" she smirked. "Really I would have expected better from you Kristoph." Rauph tried to explain, tried to point out he was telling the truth but then he noticed something else moving stealthily through the shadows behind Shuesan preparing to pounce.

"Look there really is something behind you!" he gestured, pointing with his right hand only to have to snatch it back again as the mace whipped across the space his hand had occupied.

"Seriously." Shuesan smirked. "That's almost as bad as there's your ear..." The beast leapt from the shadowy passageway, eight razor sharp legs raised like shining daggers, punching straight through the plate mail of the female Minotaur. Metal parted as if made of paper, as the steely limbs pierced her right arm, left leg and several places on her torso, showering the sand with crimson blood.

Shuesan crashed to the ground amid a chorus of enthusiastic chants and cheers from the spectators above, all appreciative of the fact that they were lucky enough to be seated in such an excellent position to witness such fantastic gore and relish the violent spectacle.

Rauph wanted to move and assist, wanted to charge forwards and help but something about the frenzy of the attack had him pause in his tracks. The beast opened its angled jaw and clamped down hard on Shuesan's exposed neck causing her to scream in terror and the crowd to roar even louder, their applause rewarding the horror as it unfolded before them.

The creature shook the female Minotaur hard, making Shuesan drop her mace as she valiantly tried to keep her face from rubbing across the sand floor. She hurled vitriol and verbal defiance at the monster despite her pain, struggling to get up onto all fours, even under the sheer weight of the monster on her back and the grievous wounds it had inflicted.

There was a sickening crunch as the beast bit down hard, severing Shuesan's spine. Her head instantly sagged, her limbs losing the ability to fight and dropping her back to the floor in a heap. The monster's long tongue darted out, licking the fresh blood and gore from her armour and fatal wound, savouring the taste of its fresh kill, before burrowing its head into her ravaged neck. Flesh parted in ragged chunks as the creature feasted in earnest, its neck fan vibrating with each large gulp as it relished the luxury of the warm meal.

Rauph edged towards his dropped blade, carefully inching across the sand to the weapon, not daring to take his eyes from the monster as it gorged itself. He carefully retrieved the long sword then considered running for the nearest passageway and exiting the area as quickly as possible. He paused at the opening, stopping to take one last look at the woman who had tried to kill him.

The beast continued to feast, aware of the navigator's presence but not concerned that the Minotaur offered any threat. It pulled away a fleshy mouthful of shoulder, stretching the muscle from the bone and ripping the bloody meat away, swallowing it in a great gulp, pausing only as a tall shadow fell across its form.

Rauph's longsword speared down, slamming into the base of the creature's neck before it could even issue a warning growl. It squealed loudly, its tail lashing around from the side, only to be parried by the Minotaur's second blade. Claws scrabbled and gouged at the floor, causing further trauma to Shuesan's corpse as the monster struggled with the intense pain. Rauph pushed down hard and twisted the blade violently to one side, hearing a snap and feeling the death spasm of the creature writhing beneath him, before it finally lay still, pieces of Shuesan still dripping from its open maw.

The longsword dripped gore as it slid from the creature. Rauph moved to wipe it on the carcass as best as he could, then turned to examine Shuesan to see if there was anything that he could do to save her. He looked down, taking in her ravaged body and then the limbs of the monster he had just dispatched, before freezing in place as he counted the eight razor sharp limbs, his eyes going wide in horror.

The crowd above looked down on the scene not understanding what they were seeing. Their champion initially ran from the slain monster, backing up swiftly to the wall, before hiding himself in the vegetation. Several long moments passed before the Minotaur extracted himself from the plant life, shredded vines hanging from his horns like a deep green curtain. He slowly returned to the corpses, his movement skittish as if expecting the dead to rise and leap at him once again. Then he stood over the bodies, his head bowed as if in discussion.

Was he thanking the gods for his victory? Saying a prayer for his fallen competitor or simply catching his breath? No one knew for sure. The cheers lessened as spectators leaned forward, desperate to hear the words of their hero, golden ribbons spiralling down to the arena floor to mark his victory and show support for the showmanship the Minotaur had displayed. Cries rose once again as the Minotaur finally sheathed his blades, then the champion looked up at the crowd, checked his bearings and choose from one of four possible exits to pursue his journey into the deadly labyrinth. A resonating horn blast echoed from the labyrinth walls confirming Shuesan's grisly demise and the spectators roared.

The crowd grew sombre as the champion departed, knowing that they would be unlikely to see more excitement without moving seats and advancing along the crowded maze walls. Everyone wondered what the champion had said, the mystery discussed in whispers. Only Rauph knew what he had uttered and it was not directed at the fallen female Minotaur. Instead it was aimed at the creature he had slain and was an admission of guilt at having attacked it and stopped it from finishing its meal. Instead, if the crowd had fallen dead silent and listened carefully to the haunting echoes of the battle still reverberating from the canyon like twisting passageways of the labyrinth, they would have heard nine confusing words.

"I'm sorry but for a moment there, I thought you were a spider!"

Chapter Forty-One

"Steady Cornelius, steady!" Miguel whispered, daring to take one hand away from the rusty rung before him and swat at the lizard's massive tail as it swung from side to side, close to the buccaneer's head. "You are going to knock me off the ladder if you aren't careful!"

The giant lizard uttered a guttural murmur, mocking like a chuckle and then lightly tapped Miguel on the head with the tip of its tail before leaping further up the ladder and disappearing into the darkness of the listing elevator shaft. The buccaneer bowed his head to protect his eyes from the shower of rust slivers dislodged by the lizard's rapid climb and soon found himself alone in the shadows with only the constant drip of water and the ominous creaking from the huge cruise liner "*The Neptune*" for company.

Miguel nervously wiped his hands one at a time on his trousers and then confident no more rust would fall, looked up after his companion wondering for what felt like the hundredth time why he was doing this.

The plan seemed fine to begin with, salvage Pheris the cyborg and then access his memory banks to reactive a portal. Then use his parts to re-float and energise the barge and high tail it out of this hellhole but now he was deep in the lair of the beast that held his mercenary crew in thrall, he was starting to have second thoughts about its success.

Those damned spooky hounds patrolled the graveyard of wrecks and derelicts with a tenacity that Miguel had to admire. His three-man expedition, well two lizards and a man, had to halt several times whilst the Scintarns had stalked nearby, collectively holding their breath as the hounds slunk by searching for food and unfortunate shipwreck survivors.

At least when they were outside, clambering over the slippery creaking wrecks they had a slim chance of spotting the beasts but now deep inside the listing cruise liner the shadows held an ominous quality that placed the privateer on constant edge and made him feel as if a heart attack was imminent.

He took in a deep breath and continued to climb hand over hand, cursing the pains in his legs, arms and lower back as he tackled the ascent. Clearly, he was weaker than he had realised. Living on a diet of raw fish and rotted scraps was taking its toll, sapping more of his strength by the day. Where was the top of this damn access ladder? In this darkness, it seemed to stretch for miles.

Something metallic dropped down from above, ricocheting off the sides of the elevator shaft, setting Miguel's teeth on edge and his heart pounding to the point he felt it would pop out of his chest. It passed by him unseen, clattering and clanging away into the darkness, only to crash loudly into a pile of debris at the base of the shaft, setting the ladder vibrating beneath his hands.

The buccaneer swallowed hard. He tried to put the fall to the back of his mind and tried to ignore the fact that a similar end would befall him if he lost his grip and plummeted to the bottom.

Echoes of movement sounded all around him. Creatures stirring within the structure, the padding of paws and scratching at the elevator doors informing him that they would not avoid detection for long. So much for the stealth part of this mission. The Scintarns knew they were here now and the job of salvaging the cyborg had suddenly become that more difficult.

Miguel swallowed hard and continued to place one foot above another, pulling himself up shakily rung-by-rung. After what seemed an eternity, he finally arrived at an elevator doorway that had been violently wrenched apart. Miguel struggled to pull himself through the opening, before getting to his feet and turning, to come face to snout with Horatio's grinning maw and forked tongue flicking inches from his face.

He staggered back in shock, almost falling back through the ruined doors and down the very shaft that he had worked so hard to ascend. Cornelius shot out a claw and caught him around the arm, pulling him back to safety then the two lizards stood side-by-side and chuckled wetly again.

"Ha, ha! Very funny." Miguel whispered. "Stop fooling around so we can just get on with the mission okay and for heaven's sake Horatio take that stupid racoon skin cap off your head." The lizards turned as one, tails swishing across the stained marble floor as they headed off into the shadows, their chuckles still hanging mockingly in the air.

* * * * * *

Kerian risked a glance behind him and confirmed his worst fears. The Provan legion was closing in again, the cloud of dust roaring towards them with a speed the strung-out adventurer would be unable to match. Toledo gasped and shivered with every step, clearly close to exhaustion, despite Kerian's urgent coaxing. The knight realised he might have to consider the unthinkable, of leaving his stallion behind to die.

In desperation, he turned towards Octavian, staring through the sandstorm blowing about him intent on asking the gypsy if there was any end to this nightmarish landscape and the relentless pursuit that followed them. His companion was off to the side, slogging through the drifting sands, his head down low, his steps measured, leading his emaciated mount onwards, the animal clearly in the same dire state as Toledo. Why was this happening to them? Why was the legion so determined to hound them in this way?

The dunes still stretched ahead as far as Kerian's limited vision could make out, miles upon miles of peaks and troughs, a punishing enough trek for a healthy man in his prime but a certain death sentence for two men who were dehydrated and had not eaten properly in a week! The same horrific vista stretched away to the left, whilst on the right, a rock-strewn dune stretched too high to even contemplate climbing.

Kerian stumbled, his weary foot catching the top of the dune, pitching him forward, to yank hard on Toledo's reins and wrenching his shoulder as he nearly fell on his face. He staggered back to his feet, spitting grit from between his parched lips, beyond caring at the line of drool left dangling from his chin. He was exhausted, tired beyond all measure of the word.

They needed to stop, needed to conserve energy, to stand and take on the hordes of undead relentlessly pursuing them. Kerian knew with a sinking heart that he would be too exhausted to even lift his blade, let alone mount a sustained defence against the creatures in his present state. He noticed froth was forming on Toledo's nostrils and the stallion had developed a stumbling gait. The situation was bad, possibly the worst Kerian had ever endured. Was he going to die here in this accursed place? His shoulders sagged with the realisation that he could be trudging across his own grave.

"Come on Toledo." Kerian willed, "Please just hang in there a little longer. For the both of us." The stallion rolled his eyes, his breath coming in louder snorts. They needed to get Octavian to stop, needed to find a way out of here or a place of shelter so they could mount a defence. He turned to signal the gypsy but Octavian was already cutting across his path and heading towards the huge mountain of rock and sand on their right.

"Are you insane?" Kerian tried to scream, only for a hoarse whisper to escape his cracked lips with no hope of reaching his companion's ears. Kerian tried to surge forwards, tried to force his way through the wind-blown sand, only to stumble once again. He felt the strength ebb from his legs, found himself dropping to the ground again, his knees sinking into the soft sand, his arms and legs as heavy as lead.

"I just can't do it." he whispered to himself. "I don't think I can go on. Not anymore." Kerian stared around as if in slow motion, trying to spot Octavian through the storm with eyes that were so caked in sand that pulling them apart required a herculean effort. He tried to cry out with a throat that betrayed the urgency of the situation and refused to issue anything but a muted croak. Kerian groaned inwardly, despair crashing over him in an invisible crushing wave, before he pitched forwards onto his face and was finally still.

* * * * * *

"We must have taken a wrong turn." Miguel commented, scratching his head as he tried to interpret the warped deck plan displayed across the wall before him and decode what all the faded colours upon it might signify. He wiped his hand across the sign, hoping that by cleaning the map he would somehow translate its secrets, only to leave smudged fingerprints. "Now what floor was the cafeteria on again?"

Cornelius licked his lips nervously and moved to the side, his interest suddenly peaked by the scent of a trail of blooms, sprouting several feet away from a creeper that had tumbled down an open stairwell and through a broken skylight. Horatio had also suspiciously moved far enough away that Miguel could not touch him and was examining a statuette of a semi-naked man, holding aloft a trident, with particular fascination. Miguel knew that secretly the two giant lizards were laughing at him and this infuriated the buccaneer even further.

He squinted at the sign, hoping for a revelation, looking at the oval set to the side of the deck plan that the buccaneer was sure should have the deck number printed upon it but the disc was coloured too and Miguel could never see colours well if they were laid one upon the other like this. It was as if some colours were simply invisible to him. There had to be a clue here somewhere, it had to be easier than this! If they were here at the *Porpoise Reception*, then the cafeteria should be to the left.

His gaze traced along the length of the curved reception desk and the grand sweep of the crafted surface, noting the access point where reception staff could lift the desk and step through to the work area. The doorway past this had a tarnished plaque on it saying the *Coral Lounge* but from the look of the wrecked furniture, water damage and ominous shadows no one had been lounging in there for quite some time! He looked to starboard and noticed signs for the *Guppy Crèche* adorning two doors hanging open due to the list of the deck. He turned back to the plan even more confused than before. Where on here did it mention a stupid crèche?

This ship was a maze, why were the directions so damned confusing? An angry flutter of wings drew his attention to the sight of two birds fighting over scraps perched high on a chandelier that swung backwards and forwards as they fought, the green creepers and curtains of algae wafting about like drapes caught in a pleasant breeze. Miguel wrinkled his nose. This place really needed much more than a pleasant breeze! The place reeked of death, rot and mildew!

He turned back to the sign only to find that in his distraction he had unwittingly dragged his finger across more of the display, creating a clean furrow through the sludge and revealing another smeared image besides the one he had been looking at. Miguel stared at the blurred cross section of the cruise liner, then wiped his hand further along the sign revealing several more decks and gaining a black stinking hand for the privilege. There was a restaurant on the deck on the left, also one on the deck to the right, one up above and another... damn it there seemed to be a bloody restaurant on every damn deck! Why did people need so many places to eat on a ship? And for that matter how many decks were on this ship anyway?

Miguel went to wipe his hand on his breeches, then paused, deciding that even he would not sink so low as to coat his already soiled clothing with yet another foul-smelling blemish. He flicked his hand, trying to dislodge the sludge from his palm, then when that did not help, he smeared it all over the reception desk. Damn! Why had he not paid more attention to what deck they were on when they were led from the ship to take part in Malum's trap building exercise?

He shook his head in frustration, knowing that it had been pretty hard to focus on anything, especially when the psychotic monster in question had been munching on his first officer at the time! He bit his lip and returned to the dilemma of the decks. Somewhere here there had to be a clue. Was that smudge there something he remembered? He really could not be sure.

A low growl issued from behind him, causing Miguel to whip about and reach for his newly acquired duelling pistols. The padding of heavy paws and clicking talons on marble drew his eyes to the ebony figure of a large Scintarn hound that stepped out from the shadows of the crèche, licking its lips at the possibility of a feast, its dark eyes blazing with intensity.

The buccaneer twisted back towards the sign, torn between the unwanted new arrival and the fact he was sure he had just seen something he remembered on the map. The heavy panting of the hound seemed really loud as it moved closer but Miguel needed to focus on finding Pheris. He was the brains of the operation; the lizards were the hired muscle. They could deal with the oversized dog.

Another growl joined the first as a second Scintarn entered the reception area, slinking past the statue of the man with the trident, hackles raised, lips curled back and teeth bared, its black crystalline spinal ridge catching the light and glinting in the corner of Miguel's eye.

A bark from behind him and to the left, forced Miguel to turn from the deck plan for a second time, only for the buccaneer's annoyance to turn into a gasp of shock. There were now five Scintarns advancing towards him all growling menacingly, apart from one that appeared to be munching something within its jaws. Yet, even this action stopped when it saw the fresh food standing before it and the hound dropped down, ears back, legs spread, ready to pounce along with its brethren. Miguel frowned, looking about the room, noting his avenues for escape were being swiftly narrowed down and then he realised that Horatio and Cornelius had disappeared.

"I'm definitely making them into handbags!" Miguel cursed, as he reconsidered the merits of employing two giant lizard cowards as henchmen and slid along the wall, the eyes of the Scintarns watching his every move, saliva dripping from their jaws as if he were a moist chicken slowly turning on a rotisserie.

"How do I keep getting myself in these situations." Miguel muttered, angry at the interruption to his quest and a little concerned about the number of hounds now squeezing through the doors and heading in his direction. He took another step, only for one Scintarn to lunge forward nipping with its jaws, forcing the buccaneer to step back or risk losing part of a limb.

Miguel fixed the monster with a stern gaze, raising an eyebrow in mild annoyance, before he calmly levelled one of his duelling pistols and pulled the trigger. The gun roared, bucking in his hand, its stock belching egg scented smoke as the lead ball ammunition shot from the muzzle and smashed through the Scintarn's skull. The hound dropped instantly to the floor and was still.

Another Scintarn slammed through the double doors to the reception lobby, clearly drawn by the sound of the discharging firearm. Miguel turned smoothly, his coat flaring out behind him, arm outstretched. He sighted along the barrel, squeezing the trigger, the gun recoiling in his grasp, its lead projectile leaping from the barrel with a flash of fire and accompanying egg scented smoke. The bullet smashed into the doorway, cracking the wood, leaving the hound ducking down but otherwise unhurt.

The buccaneer did not hesitate, raising the first pistol and moving to pull the trigger. This was how the privateers of old must have been in combat, unstoppable a force to be reckoned with, terror of the high seas... The pistol refused to fire.

"What?" Miguel looked down at the gun in shock, incensed by the weapon's betrayal after such a spectacular opening act. He swung the second pistol around and tried to fire this one with the same dry click as a result. Surely these weapons fired more than one damn shot! Miguel cursed as he remembered these were duelling pistols! One shot was normally all anyone needed to achieve satisfaction. A second shot was simply overkill and was not expected unless both parties missed on their opening salvos!

One quick look at the drooling maws moving cautiously towards him confirmed that he did not have the time required to reload now! Miguel slammed the pistols back into their holsters as the Scintarns advanced, clearly picking up on the change of their prey's demeanour from calm and in control to becoming on the edge of panic. The buccaneer reached out behind him, not daring to take his eyes from the sleek monsters advancing his way. He felt along the reception desk, searching for anything he could use for a weapon, something to mount a defence against the creatures advancing determinedly towards him.

His hand slid through something wet and slimy and the thought of the two birds sprung to mind, making him shudder just before his hands closed on something hard. He grabbed it and swung it about just as the next Scintarn leapt. Teeth flashed inches from Miguel's face as the ship's directory slammed into the side of its head, making the beast drop to one side and the air fill with loose leaves of paper as the binder sprang open.

Two other hounds leapt into the opening, getting a swift boot to the jaw and a punch on the nose. Miguel was not going to go down without a fight! The other hounds were more cautious, snapping from both sides, forcing him further back against the reception desk and making the buccaneer cry out in fear. The other Scintarns were already getting to their feet and then four attacked at once. Miguel jumped backwards, bringing his legs up and sliding his bottom across the work surface, nearly losing his left foot in the process as two sets of jaws snapped inches from each other along the path that he took. Miguel smiled as he realised that he had avoided the attack, only to cry out again as he overbalanced and crashed off the reception and down into the space behind.

One Scintarn leapt up onto the desk, eager to close on its food, only for Miguel to leap up with a letter opener in his hand and plunge the weapon deep into its eye. The hound fell back on the far side of the desk scrabbling and yelping in pain, only for its fellow hounds to jump on the wounded animal and tear it to pieces.

Miguel dropped back down behind the shelter of the reception, briefly considering if it was safe to reload but the rapid skittering of claws on the floor soon put pay to those thoughts. He shuffled along on his knees heading for the opening in the desk and the only possible exit past these creatures. Pieces of water stained paper, office litter and accumulated muck covered the ground, cluttering up his escape route and making his attempt at a stealthy departure anything but. He shuffled around the corner just as another hound leapt up onto the reception and started to pursue him along the top of the desk, the remains of its fellow Scintarn dripping from its jaws.

The buccaneer risked a quick glance up at his ebony pursuer then crawled rapidly towards the exit, heart beating in his throat, his nose wrinkling at the stench through which he crawled. Oh what he would give for a good, long sonic shower when, if ever, he got home! He moved to pass under the desk, only to come nose to snout with another growling Scintarn.

Miguel shrieked in surprise, pushing up with his hands to get out of reach of the hound before him, slamming his own head on the underside of the desk, which lifted up and clouted the Scintarn padding along the top of the reception, catching it under the jaw and dropping it back out into the main lobby. The other Scintarn leapt up just as Miguel staggered backwards, his actions dropping the desk surface straight back down onto the leaping creature and making it yelp and stagger about stunned.

The buccaneer saw his chance and took it, sprinting for the doorway into the *Coral Lounge,* several sets of sharp teeth snapping shut inches from his fleeing hind quarters. He ran into the darkness, not sure which way to turn, only knowing that if he stayed where he was, he would soon be dog food and that option had little appeal to him. He ran across the spongy carpet, noticed an opening in the wall and ran for it, hearing the hounds frantically scrabbling after him in pursuit.

He charged through the opening, finding himself in a stairwell that spiralled downwards and stank like a charnel house. There was little choice but to take the route offered and the pirate ran down the steps, noting the blood spatter arced across the walls of the stairwell but having no alternative but to follow the carpet treads and see where he ended up.

Miguel leapt from the stairs and fled into the shadows, the hounds tumbling down the stairwell behind him in a rush. The buccaneer came up short with a groan when he realised that he was running through a large area filled with what looked like piles of rubbish, battered packing cases, bundles of clothes and discarded keepsakes. Where had he got to now?

The stark image of a tall metal cage standing in the middle of the room barely entered Miguel's thoughts as he ran around yet another pile of clothes and jumped over a battered red suitcase that appeared to have tumbled from its pile. The huffing breaths and thumping of paws from behind indicated that the hounds were closing in. Miguel headed for the far wall of the room, throughout the refuse, changing direction, body swerving randomly, cutting left and right, as fast as his footing on the wet carpet allowed him, his eyes frantically searching for a way out, his ears hearing the collisions and scrabbling of the hounds as they struggled to keep up. There had to be a way out of here. There just had to be!

He saw a doorway in the bulkhead and ran towards it, noting the viewing port set in the door. Miguel slammed into the entrance and grabbed the handle, pulling as hard as he could but it refused to budge. Miguel's breath fogged up the glass as he grunted and pulled with all his might, trying to open the portal but it would not yield. He tried to readjust his footing and slipped on something in the darkness, smacking his head against the glass, seeing stars before finding himself looking into what appeared to be a swimming pool, although the water was missing and instead it was filled with...

The Scintarn crashed into him, dropping Miguel to the floor as it snapped repeatedly. The buccaneer tried to push the creature away, its huge teeth catching the tips of his hand and painfully drawing blood. He kicked out, feeling satisfied with the connecting crunch before back pedalling away, his hand coming down on the item he had slipped on and instinctively closing about it as he crabbed away backwards. Miguel collided with a pile of suitcases, sending them tumbling down about him, filling the terrified man's vision with glimpses of flashing teeth, faded luggage tags and *Samsonite* labels.

He rolled to his feet and fled, noting other Scintarns angling in to cut off his route and prayed for some way out of his predicament. There was an opening ahead and he took it at a run, only to slide to a halt in absolute horror as he realised that he had arrived in what could only be described as a slaughter house. Blood streaked bones and offal lay everywhere! Flies buzzed about the room and masses of maggots oozed and wriggled in the corners.

It was like seeing one of those medieval churches with the bones stacked in the catacombs, only there was no reverence shown to these remains. They lay where they had been dropped, snapped ends clearly displaying where marrow pulp had been sucked from the bone, gnaw marks indicating that the end of these people's lives had been nothing but horrific. Miguel looked over and noted the throne assembled in the centre of the room and the mass of bloody skulls discarded about it, puncture holes in the top of the cranium clearly identifying who had feasted on these particular delicacies.

Miguel's heart ran cold. Dear god! He had stumbled into Malum's lair! His eyes darted about frantically, taking in the horror and praying that the master of these dark demon hounds was out at the archways at the edge of the graveyard rather than sitting here waiting like a spider in the centre of a web that the buccaneer had accidentally blundered into.

A mildew coated doorway in the far wall drew his attention and he fled past the throne just as the hounds sped into the room and bounded after him. Miguel ran for his life, knowing he could not hope to save himself in a fight with so many demon dogs. He found another stairwell, leading upwards and leapt the stairs two at a time, his fear filling him with adrenaline and making his body tremble as he ascended. He threw himself from the stairwell and burst out into a room filled with corridors branching off in all directions. Cabins numbered in their hundreds spreading fore and aft.

Miguel chose a direction and ran, not pausing to check for landmarks, just determined to get as far away from the creatures that pursued him. He tore around corners at random, ran through shadowy rooms and slammed door after door to foil his pursuers, his heart hammering in his chest, his journey an experience of sheer terror. He slid across a marble floor, skidded past another deck plan, before sliding down a curved bannister and jumping off straight into the back of Cornelius, who turned and growled menacingly his tail whipping about in anger.

"What are you doing here?" Miguel snapped breathlessly. "Where were you when I needed you, you oversized newt?" Miguel tried to push by, knowing the hounds would not be far behind but Cornelius stubbornly refused to move and instead continued shuffling backwards towards him.

"Why won't you let me by?" the buccaneer snapped irritably, checking back over his shoulder for the shadowy dogs he expected to be closing in. "I need to get by." Cornelius turned again and Miguel managed to wriggle past on the left, only to find the lizard was accompanied by his brother Horatio and that they were carrying the mangled form of Pheris between them.

"Where did you find him?" Miguel stood open mouthed. The lizards shared a look between them and a hissing as if to say it was obvious where the mangled cyborg had been. They kept edging backwards to an opening that led onto the listing deck of the liner and out into the eerie mustard light.

Miguel tried to usher the lizards on, terrified his pursuers would arrive at any minute but the lizards seemed unconcerned and relaxed as they shuffled over to a lifeboat that hung lopsided from its davits.

"What are you doing?" Miguel asked. "We need to get off this stupid ship and get out of here. We are not sinking!" Horatio lowered Pheris to the deck and worked the mechanism to free the lifeboat, struggling at first with the corroded mechanism before it freed with a sharp crack and a mighty thump from the lizard's claw.

Pheris was hoisted into the craft and the lizards clambered up beside him before turning and offering a scaled claw for Miguel to come aboard as well. The buccaneer stared at the lizards as if they were mad, then reluctantly accepted the offer and clambered aboard, closing his eyes as the lifeboat swung out over the edge of the listing cruise liner and swung gently from side to side.

Cornelius hissed a signal to Horatio and the two lizards started to lower the boat over the side and down to the mangled wrecks below. The descent was slow and noisy, drawing the attention of several hounds that whined in exasperation when they reached the railing of the cruise liner and found that their prey was frustratingly out of reach. Howls filled the air, requesting reinforcements but the haunted echoing replies came from beyond the twisted hulks and derelict vessels and sounded far away, signalling that any support would be a good while coming.

Miguel sat quietly, watching the two lizards complementing each other for their actions and realised he was totally reliant on the monstrous reptiles. The life boat continued to creak slowly downward before the mechanism finally came to a juddering halt. Miguel looked up at his bodyguards and opened his mouth to voice a sarcastic comment about how great their situation had improved by leaving them hanging defenceless, suspended in the air but his words died in his throat as the two lizards drew out rusty knives they must have salvaged from somewhere upon the Neptune and slashed the ropes.

The scream that uttered from the buccaneer's lips, died almost before it began as the lifeboat dropped barely ten feet, then splashed down into a small canal of murky water that snaked its way between the rusting wrecks lying alongside the Neptune. Miguel's hand shot open and something golden flew from his fist, bouncing along the bottom of the boat, to end up wedged beneath one of the seats.

Miguel stared after the object in shock, not realising that he had held the metal disc in his hand for so long. He stood up, setting the boat rocking and the lizards hissing in anger but ignored them as much as they ignored him, dropping to his knees and sliding his hand under the seat to recover the golden prize before holding it up to the sickly light.

The coin was the size of an 'o' formed by a thumb and index finger and it glinted, despite the mustard tinged light. On one side was a cross with the legend *Hispanirum Et India Rex* engraved around the circumference.

Miguel's heart quickened and he swiftly ignored the grunts and curses from his lizard companions, his eyes widening with delight. He turned the golden coin over and noted a regal figurehead of a man who was obviously of some importance. The writing beneath proclaimed him to be *Philipus*.

Miguel looked back up at the listing liner and this time he no longer had a look of fear in his eyes. He may not have recognised the writing or the meaning behind the Mexican royal escudo he held in his hand but he recognised pirate treasure and he now knew where a whole room of it lay for the taking.

* * * * * *

"It has to be around here somewhere." Octavian thought, lifting his head and shielding his eyes against the persistent biting sand. The entrance to the Alicieus Span had to be here. This had to be right, the landmarks were right, it even smelt right! He pushed on, dragging his feet through the drifting dunes as he ascended the rocky slope, his stallion snorting in distress at the punishing gradient.

Damn this storm! It made everything so difficult to see. Octavian tugged on the stallion's reins coaxing the beast up the incline, doubts rushing in at every step. Should he have turned sooner? Where were the Givrea sentinels. Did they slumber under the sands here, or further back in the desert? Had he somehow missed them in the storm?

An odd shaped wedge of pale stone jutted from the side of the dune ahead, its outline becoming clearer with every step as Octavian advanced. He felt an odd glimmer of hope rise in the pit of his stomach. Could it be? The gypsy redoubled his efforts, churning through the sand despite the weariness assailing him. Yes! This was it! He was sure!

Octavian led his stallion around the marker and dropped to his knees, frantically scooping away the red and white sands with his hands to uncover another stone and then another all of them linked together, each one slightly larger than the one before. The gypsy looked up the dune and smiled, his eyes tracing the line of where the rest of the sleeping sentinel lay. Yes, this was definitely the place. He glanced to the left, recognising a similar submerged line in the sand that led to another buried shape further along the dune face. Where one Givrea sentinel lay, its twin was never far away.

"Kerian, look we have found the way out." Octavian shouted over the storm, turning his head to share his delight with his travelling companion, only to find himself alone on the exposed sand dune. "Kerian...?" Where the hell was he? The gypsy regained his feet and staggered a few steps, shielding his eyes and squinting into the gale to try and spot just how far behind Kerian had fallen but his companion was not to be found. A sense of dread rose up to smother the hope that had briefly bloomed within him.

"Kerian, where are you?" Octavian started to slip and slide down the sand, small avalanches spilling down the dune in pursuit of him. "Kerian!" He called out again turning his head from side to side and seeing nothing that would help him in his search. Oh where had the idiot got to? If he had known how much trouble meeting Kerian would cause him. Octavian would have run screaming as fast as he could in the other direction.

The gypsy slid a few more feet before he finally reached the base of the dune and set to trudging along its base, following his own already blurring tracks. The swirling sand slammed into his face, scouring his hands and stinging every piece of exposed flesh as he advanced deeper into the swirling cloud bank. Visibility rapidly decreased, there was every chance Octavian would blunder past his companion and never be the wiser.

He risked raising his head, hoping to scent the man but the overpowering stench of death that accompanied the advancing legion permeated everything. He could not believe it. To have come so near and fall at the last fence. No this was not to be. Kerian was going to help him rescue his wife and child and nothing was going to stop that from happening. He turned, stealing a glance back at his tracks, determined not to get lost in this confusing world of spiralling columns of red sand, swirling white grit and choking brown clouds.

A terrified neigh carried on the wind reached the gypsy's ears, drawing Octavian's attention off to the left, deeper into the whirling clouds. He staggered in that direction, noting dark shadowy figures shambling in rank towards him and he veered away, determined to give the troops of the Provan legion as much space as possible. A foot soldier jumped out from the cloud cover, moving to slash the air with his sword but then it paused, inexplicably, letting the gypsy slip past and angle to the left; the skeletal warrior staggering and almost losing its balance as it turned to keep up with him.

The silhouette of Toledo loomed from the darkness and Octavian slogged his way over to the terrified steed, where it stood trembling and stamping its feet, determined, despite its exhaustion, to defend the warrior it had come to respect and rely upon during this hostile trek. Octavian's reassuring pat on Toledo's nose did little to calm the beast and it snorted in distress, pawing at the ground inches from Kerian's half buried form. The gypsy looked down at the unconscious traveller then considered the dune he had to climb. He almost gave up at the very thought, then remembered his family and bent down to pull Kerian from the sand.

"No, just leave me!" Kerian moaned, spittle running down his chin, his face caked in sand.

"The hell I will." Octavian shouted. "Now get on your feet soldier!" Kerian sagged back down to the floor, almost dragging the weakened gypsy down with him but somehow, through sheer determination and a plethora of curses, Octavian started to lead his colleague back along the tracks that he knew led towards the sentinels.

"Come on, not much further!" Octavian coaxed, noting to his relief that Toledo staggered along after them, clearly worse for wear but apparently as determined to see Kerian to safety as Octavian now was.

Step by weary step, the two men struggled against the elements, pitting their wills against the storm as it cruelly buffeted them. Octavian had one moment of indecision where the tracks of the undead troops had crossed his own but by looking at the darkness of the storm clouds he was able to identify an area that seemed lighter than the rest and he pushed on, determined to breach the wall of sand, then drag his partner up the dune to the span he knew would lead them to Blackthorn.

Octavian allowed himself the barest of smiles as the clouds parted, grunting against the ever-increasing weight of the man leaning on his side whilst congratulating himself at his ability to lead them out of the cloud. The side of the dune loomed before him; its incline transformed in his absence into a precipice that seemed impossible to conquer.

The gypsy shook his head. No it was not impossible. He had already managed it on his own. Now all he had to do was manage it with a dead weight on his arm and a lame horse dragging behind. No problem at all! He gritted his teeth and started taking the first few steps feeling the crushing weight of his charge pushing him deeper into the sand, making each heavy footstep more treacherous and difficult to extricate from the enveloping sand.

Kerian slipped several times, leaving Octavian struggling to hold the man upright. The gypsy attempted to reposition him but Kerian was simply too heavy and awkward. He kept slipping to the ground, groaning with distress as if in some delirium, only for Octavian to have to hoist him up again and struggle on a few more steps, ever aware of the closing ranks of the Provan legion behind him.

Time crawled, mere moments seemed eons of agony as the two men battled with their exhaustion, yet Octavian refused to give in, drawing on a reservoir of energy he never knew he had.

The scent gave the stranger away, seconds before Octavian noticed his shadowy figure striding out from the clouds, he was swaddled head to foot in rags taken from the Provan legion which may have accounted for the smell of death about him but there was something else here, as if the man carried another with him. The long grey cloak emblazoned with the Provan legion spider could have been the man's shroud, he appeared so thin and emaciated, his face, where Octavian could make it out, a mass of healed scars as if the man had been trapped in an inferno at some point in the past and narrowly escaped with his life.

However, it was the intensity of the man's gaze that really snapped the gypsy out of his agony. It was the look of a man who wanted something badly, a look that was driven and all consuming. Octavian tried to reach for a weapon of sorts but Kerian hung on him wrongly and it was impossible to get a grip on anything as the strange figure advanced.

Kerian slid from the gypsy's arm and slumped to the floor, just as the stranger leapt forward. Octavian prepared to morph into his animal form, despite his weakened state and the dangers such a metamorphosis could do to both himself and his companion, especially as he had not fed for several days but the actions of the stranger made him pause.

Instead of attacking them both, the emaciated figure took Kerian in his arms and lifted him up from the ground before turning towards the gypsy and indicating everything was under control. The stranger looked Kerian up and down, a confused frown on his face, as if he expected to see someone else. Then he shrugged and looked over towards the massing legion, then up towards the summit of the dune, where Octavian knew the sentinels awaited.

"I believe you are travellers in need of assistance," the thin man smiled. "The law of the sea dictates that one must always render aid when it is requested and from the look of our surroundings, your choices for onward travel appear somewhat limited." Octavian instantly found himself relaxing at the unexpectedly jovial response and nodded his head, thinking that if the man had two eyes, he would probably have been winking at him right now. The eye patched man tilted his head, his face still displaying some confusion.

"I must ask, why in the world would two people such as yourselves be wandering around in the middle of this god forsaken desert?" Octavian tried to voice a suitable reply but the shock of finding someone willing to aid him, just when he was in such dire straits had left him gasping like a fish abandoned on dry land.

"Then after that amusing tale, I would like you to confirm the name of the gentleman I hold in my arms."

"Who are you?" Octavian asked, finally managing to form the words and discovering to his surprise that the stranger's smile was contagious.

"My name is Scrave," the one-eyed Elf replied, "and it's a pleasure to finally meet you."

Chapter Forty-Two

"Can you see him?" Thomas shouted, squeezing himself through the tightly packed screaming crowd to where his shipmates had secured seating on the labyrinth walls. "He has to be down there somewhere." The captain leaned forward, regarding the arena below with a troubled frown, the hood of his cloak firmly in place to hide his face from the Minotaur guards stationed along the walls scanning the crowd for potential troublemakers.

"Well he doesn't appear to have reached this part of the maze yet." Mathius confirmed, his eyes scanning a large open area below, in which ravenous monsters swam slow circles in pools of dark water and ancient stone columns of varying heights formed supports for rope bridges that hung above pits containing spikes, snakes and snarling beasts. He looked on fascinated as a large armoured creature suddenly charged from an overgrown section of the arena, intent on crushing a female Minotaur trying to cross before it. Although the contestant dodged the initial charge, the creature's flailing tail caught her a glancing blow to the temple, sending the contestant stumbling away, her golden trident dropping from her grasp, much to the delight of the baying crowd.

"Didn't we see some of those creatures in the jungle?" Weyn asked, rolling his shoulder and trying not to wince at the tightness of the knots he felt within. It appeared that the rushed magical healing Violetta had performed was only able to do so much with his injuries. "I don't understand this part of the maze. There only seems to be one entrance and as yet I can't see any exits. It's like this is just one massive cul-de-sac."

"Well if it is," Thomas replied, "I doubt Moira's darling boy Drummon would still be waiting here." He raised his spyglass to his eye confirming his findings, then lowered it again, a scowl playing across his features. "And it is no surprise that he's not playing fair."

"Where is he?" Mathius took the glass from Thomas's hand and stared through it, the lens bringing the sight of the combatants much closer and clearer to the eye.

"Over by the entrance, left side, hiding behind those bushes, far back in the shadows." Weyn replied, pointing to where the Prince Regent had secreted himself, whilst the other Minotaur fought for their very lives against the voracious beasts the hunting parties had captured and released into this arena. Mathius locked onto the image of the black-haired Minotaur and noticed how he was almost perfectly camouflaged within the shadows cast by the gently swaying foliage.

Is he reading a map?" the assassin hissed. "Damn… wouldn't it be great if we could get that for Rauph? He would clear this maze in no time then." A roar raced through the spectators as one monster let loose a torrent of spikes from its arched tail, peppering the wall behind another contestant and spearing her leg before she threw a cross bladed weapon in retaliation, clipping the monster's tail and slicing it clean off, leaving the beast writhing in agony. The gleaming weapon twisted out in a lazy circle, then came back to the Minotaur's outstretched hand before she painfully limped off in one direction and the wounded creature slunk off in the other, back towards a patch of dark shadows beneath a stand of huge palms.

"But why is he just standing there waiting?" Thomas muttered. "It doesn't make any sense."

"Maybe the exit doesn't reveal itself until something specific happens." Weyn commented. "I guess that may explain why he hasn't even attempted to leave the bushes and expose himself to any unnecessary danger."

Thomas cast his eyes across the arena, taking in the varying heights of the stone pillars and the bridges swung between them. His eyes roamed the far side taking in the solid stone wall that appeared to show no indication of any possible doors. Exotic plants curled and twisted across the stonework, bright cornflower blue trumpet flowers, large enough to make hats from, nodding gently up and down in the breeze as if they were enjoying the spectacle of gore unfolding beneath them.

"Well if there is an exit, I can't see it." he confessed. Another roar went up from the crowd as a spindly insect like creature charged towards a female Minotaur wearing a red cloak. The contestant pulled the crimson cloak about her, then simply disappeared, leaving the insect clicking its mandibles in frustration and Thomas thinking his ears had just popped. "Now that's clever!" he remarked, as the air shimmered just behind and to the left of the insect and the female Minotaur rematerialized. She moved swiftly over to the monster's hind leg and draped her strange red cloak across it. The air popped, the insect screamed in pain and then it collapsed backwards, its hind leg now lost, green sticky ichor jetting from the stump. The Minotaur cloaked herself again, quickly disappearing before the wounded creature could retaliate.

"Very clever!" Mathius stated quietly. "I know someone who would give their back teeth for an item of clothing as useful as that."

Screams from another creature thrashing about at the side of one of the flooded pools snatched the assassin's attention towards a large crab-like creature being shocked with lightning blasts from a Minotaur wielding a strange spear. Every time she shocked the creature, forcing it back towards the water, she would flip the weapon about, as if by doing so it somehow recharged the device. The crab monster dropped one foot into the pool as it retreated, just as the next blast hit; the resulting shock blowing the creature apart, sending fleshy lumps of meat and hard shell spinning about the arena and dropping the spear wielder down onto her backside.

"There he is!" The spectator standing alongside Thomas shouted out his appreciation, standing up and slopping wine from his goblet down the front of the captain's clothes and almost knocking the hood from his head. Thomas bit back his annoyance and followed the enthusiastic spectators' gestures, staring over towards the arena entrance and noting Rauph just stepping down onto the sun-kissed sands. The air exploded with golden ribbons as the audience screamed and threw their favours of support into the arena. Rauph just stood there, his face bemused, apparently studying the scene unfolding before him. The Navigator stepped further out into the arena and the passageway rumbled closed behind him, sealing all of the remaining contestants into the arena.

A clarion call of trumpets sounded and high up on the far wall a section of the labyrinth slid to one side with a loud rumble, making Thomas appreciate how the clever use of the foliage within the maze served to camouflage things. The captain automatically traced backwards across the arena, taking in the varying heights of the columns of stone and the precarious pathways the contestants would need to traverse to enable them to reach up the wall to the height of the exit. This would be quite a challenge for even the fittest of decathlon athletes at home!

Rauph appeared to have also analysed the puzzle, apparently deciding that the lowest stone pillar was the place to start. He jogged across the arena floor and moved to ascend the crumbling pillar, much to the delight of the crowd. The thin, red headed female Minotaur carrying the lightning spear and sporting a purple ribbon came up behind Rauph and shouted up to him, asking if he would help lift her onto the pillar. Rauph had paused in mid-climb, staring down at her, seeming to consider her request for aid, after all, Thomas had always told him to be kind to the ladies on the *El Defensor* and help them if he could.

"Don't do it." Mathius hissed. "She's suckering you."

"I don't think I can watch." Weyn confessed, lifting his hand to his face and staring through his fingers.

Rauph dropped down to the arena floor from his lofty position and cupped his two hands together, urging Pascol to place her foot in them so he could boost her up the column. It seemed the gentlemanly thing for a

Minotaur to do and Rauph immediately felt good about himself for doing so. She placed her boot in his hand and Rauph could not help but notice the frayed threads holding the leather together and the fact that the heel of her boot shifted slightly as she put her weight upon it.

He hoisted Pascol up onto the pillar with a mighty shove, allowing her to scrabble amongst the ancient masonry and secure a hand hold so she could clamber up to the top of the column. Rauph held his head down until the worst of the debris had stopped falling on his head from her boots and then proceeded to clamber up after her, his huge hands easily finding purchase on the eroded stonework.

"Hey Kristoph." Pascol shouted over the roar of the crowd, just as Rauph's head came level with the top of the pillar. "I think you only helped me because you wanted to look at my rump in my tight leather armour."

"What?" Rauph replied, pausing in his climb, bemused by the comment, then mortified at what the female Minotaur was suggesting.

"Just avert your gaze for a moment." Pascol teased, fluttering her eyelashes provocatively at him. Rauph, still eager to please lowered his head and stared back down the column, noting out of the corner of his eye that other contestants were making their way towards him from across the sands.

"Here it comes." Mathius groaned. "What a glutton for punishment our navigator is."

"Tell me when it's over." Weyn sighed, now covering his eyes with both hands. Pascol leaned down and callously jabbed her spear into the side of Rauph's head; A blast of lightning lifting the hapless navigator clear from the column and dropping him back down onto the sand of the arena where he lay jerking as sparks danced along his horns.

"Ouch!" Thomas winced. "That was a dirty trick."

Weyn lifted his face from his hands only to cover them again as another competitor charged across the sands, her spiky hair flattening as she ran, blue ribbons dancing at her shoulder and blood streaming from a wound in her leg. The Minotaur screamed as she hit Rauph square in the back, just as he got to his knees, using the poor navigator as a spring board to launch herself up the granite column and gain purchase on the crumbling stonework. Rauph crashed back down, face first, the air rushing out of him, only for the air to shimmer and pop as another contestant materialised out of thin air in a swirl of cloak and delivered a skilfully placed boot into Rauph's side, just where he had already been injured by the mace attack.

The navigator groaned, guarding his side and rolling away as the female Minotaur's red cloak billowed out above him, the material threatening to settle upon his body, the insides of the material revealing row upon row of black barbed teeth. Rauph rolled again, desperate to avoid being enveloped in the tooth-lined interior of the cloak, only to feel the ground disappear from beneath him as the Minotaur dropped into one of the deep pools with a mighty splash.

Ammet pulled the hood of her magical cloak from her head, allowing her curly black hair to bounce free as she stared down at the dark waters below, her eyes as dark as the serrated teeth lining the inside of her deadly cloak. Her gaunt face shivered as the teeth of the cloak lying across her back dug into her flesh, sucking a little more of her life force away and explaining why she always appeared so gaunt.

Ripples arrowed through the water towards her, signifying the path of deadly predators arrowing through the depths towards where a fountain of bubbles marked the descent of Kristoph's sinking body through the murk. It was a shame; her cloak had hungered for the chestnut prince and the sentient clothing had missed this opportunity to feed. Another shudder ran through her body as the cloak extracted its price for her failure.

She stared up at her colleagues, who were already making their way across the first rickety bridge that swung above the dark pool and frowned in frustration. Maybe she would have better luck feeding her cloak with another one of her competitors. The problem was that she knew there was no way she would be able to climb up the granite column like her rivals, as she lacked the height required. Pascol, already making her way across the first rickety bridge seemed to realise this, looking back and laughing before goading her challenger by throwing a playful wave in her direction; an action which she instantly regretted as the bridge wobbled dangerously beneath her. Ammet gritted her teeth, staring at the back of the Minotaur with eyes like daggers, wishing with all of her might that the waving bitch would just miss her step and fall.

A gleaming black arrow shot through the air, turning Pascol's smug look into one of surprise as the razor-sharp hunting head of the projectile sliced straight through one of the bridges supports ahead of her. The guide rope she was holding suddenly snapped, leaving the female Minotaur windmilling her arms, trying desperately to stay upright before she lost her balance and tumbled from the bridge with a scream, dragging the rope with her.

"What a terrible spot of bad luck. Who would have suspected such a structural failure?" Mathius grinned, standing beside Thomas, the both of them using their bodies to obscure the fact that Weyn was swiftly unstringing his bow before anyone in the crowd glanced behind to see where the arrow had come from. "had to be an 'Act of the Gods'."

"I call it Karma." Thomas grinned, patting Weyn on the shoulder. "Damn fine shot by the way!"

Pascol hit the water and carved a huge wake through the surface as the rope swung to a stop, spluttering and crying out in shock as the cold water washed over her. Despite this, she stubbornly held onto the line, struggling to pull herself out of the water with every intention of ascending the rope to make her way back up to the ruined bridge. The structure rocked and swayed from side to side at her struggles, much to the annoyance of Chane who still clung onto the remaining hand support as she attempted to make her own way past where her fellow opponent had fallen.

"Keep still you fool!" Chane yelled down. "I have no intention of joining you and the more you thrash about the more the predators will be attracted to you."

"Like you care." Pascol spluttered, pulling herself arm over arm, inch by inch from the water. "You just want to win. You have never cared about anyone but yourself." She pulled herself higher, managing to lift her top half clear from the water and bit back more curses as she watched Chane finally limp across the gap and make it onto the next pillar. She was such a bitch. Watching that Minotaur overtake her ignited a hatred and energy Pascol never knew she had.

Pascol lifted herself further, using her upper arm strength to lift her bottom from the water, just as something hit her legs hard, pushing the Minotaur physically across the surface of the water and almost tearing the rope from her hands. The competitor froze in terror as whatever it was that had hit her swam past, leaving the Minotaur to arc back through the water to her original starting place just below the bridge. She shivered, not knowing whether to start climbing or simply stay still, her nerves alert for a sign of whatever it was that had attacked her in the water.

Ever so carefully, she wrapped the rope back around her leg and started to inch up the line, her eyes flitting left and right for signs of the creature returning. Another inch, another chance of life. The rope slowly turned Pascol around, allowing her to see the bubbles from where Kristoph had fallen into the water. The surface appeared to explode in a frothy maelstrom, clearly whatever was in the water was now attacking the prince. Taking this as a sign the creature was occupied, Pascol renewed her efforts, straining to pull herself from the water, lifting herself arm over arm, as first her body and then her legs lifted free.

Pascol hugged the line tight, letting the fluid drip from her body and finally allowed herself a moment to catch her breath. Something appeared to ripple through the water beneath her, something that caught the sun and reflected it back from several mirror-like scales that moved just below the surface, their edges defined by a golden glow.

The Minotaur could not help but be mesmerised as the tip of a dark green snout slowly rose from the water. Golden crest spines arched along its neck, a thick grey webbing stretching between them. Orange eyes stared up at her as two widely spread webbed claws swept through the water with incredible power.

"Is that a turtle?" Thomas asked, rubbing his eyes in disbelief as he took in the sight of the monster's neck stretching further and further from the surface as if it was made of elastic. The dark snout opened wide, then lunged, snapping the air just inches below Pascol's feet. The Minotaur struggled to grip the rope securely before pulling her spear free, lifting it high to clumsily jab down at the monster as it lunged again. Lightning flickered down the spear, jumping from Pascol across the gap into the turtle's open maw. The monster instantly withdrew its head, re-submerging in a gush of steam.

"Looks like it was nearly a bowl of soup for a second." Weyn remarked. "Oh there he goes. Drummon is moving now."

"Why hasn't Rauph come up yet?" Mathius asked, leaning further forward in his seat, trying to catch a glimpse of the churning waters. "He should have come up by now." As if in answer, the water marking Rauph's descent into the depths suddenly turned still and its colour darkened.

"That doesn't look good." Thomas stated getting to his feet. "I think Rauph's in trouble. We need to get down there and help." Weyn turned towards his captain open mouthed, as if to ask exactly how Thomas expected them to do this with all the Minotaur guards present, just as Mathius laid a hand on Thomas's arm and calmly gestured to the form of a soggy chestnut Minotaur pulling himself from the water, sword in hand, the end of the blade dripping with a viscous slime.

"I think our navigator has it all in hand." The assassin replied calmly, despite the fact that even he was feeling the racing of his heart. The emotions of the crowd reflected by the deafening roar that rippled around the arena as Rauph finally pulled himself to his feet and turned his attention back towards the smallest pillar.

The water exploded behind him, the giant turtle in the centre of the pool hurtling up from the depths, its neck stretching from the water, sharp jaws snapping together to bite deeply into Pascol's midsection where she swung helpless on the rope. The Minotaur managed one wailing scream, flailing ineffectively with her spear, her lungs crushed by the force of the bite. Pascol's body came apart like the ragged seams of her armour, the lower half dropping with the giant turtle, leaving her top half hanging suspended from the rope, her entrails slopping wetly into the water. The crowd roared their appreciation at the gore but Rauph was oblivious to his fellow contestant's demise and was already clambering up the pillar, preparing to cross the rickety bridge.

"What is Drummon doing?" Mathius murmured, pointing as the black Minotaur angled away from the pillars and ran along the far side of the arena, only stopping to hack away a questing pincer from an over eager crab-like creature.

"More importantly where is he going?" Thomas asked, following the path of the Minotaur as he ran to the base of the wall below where the new opening loomed high above. "He's never going to attempt to scale the wall, is he?" Thomas frowned, thinking the action would be highly unlikely, before he observed the prince regent scrabbling through the undergrowth as if he were looking for something.

"Go for it Rauph!" Weyn cheered, gaining several confused looks from the nearby spectators who had no idea who Rauph was. Weyn pointed back to where their navigator was wobbling his way across the bridge with a grim determination and surefootedness that could only come from spending time in the rigging aboard the *El Defensor*. He reached the other side and another roar of appreciation came from the crowd, just as the giant turtle breached the water below and snapped its jaws together on the gory remains of Pascol, ripping the corpse and the remains of the bridge down with it. Another sombre horn blow heralded her demise.

"That's an interesting development." Mathius commented. With the bridge out of action we have two female Minotaur that are going to be hard pressed to make it up to the height required to gain footing, especially the one with the trident. She looks a little dazed from the injury she sustained earlier. Look she isn't even walking in a straight line.

"Maybe they will just use the ladder Drummon has magically found." Thomas snarled. "Of all the cheating...." He shook his head in dismay as the black minotaur continued to pull a ladder from the undergrowth he had been so enthusiastically searching and positioned it against the wall just beneath the exit. The crowd seemed to notice at the same time, loud boos and catcalls coming from the spectators who quickly quietened down when the Minotaur guards along the walls looked in their direction.

Rauph paused in his journey, staring out across the network of rickety bridges he needed to traverse and coming to the same conclusion that his spectators had; that somehow, he had let himself be suckered into taking the long way around.

A trumpet blast echoed through the arena, causing Drummon to start climbing up the ladder as fast as he could. Rauph had no idea what the trumpet call meant but if the urgency of his brother's ascent was anything to go by, he needed to move fast!

The first granite pillar exploded, dropping down to the ground with a crash. Rauph reached the third pillar in a rush just as the second pillar also toppled with a groan. A flash of crimson near the base of the ladder tore Thomas's attention from his shipmate back to Drummon and the fact that the female Minotaur in the strange red cloak was racing up after her Prince.

Drummon noticed the vibration through the ladder and started tearing vegetation from the wall, hurling debris and leaves down on his pursuer who simply disappeared as the branches and foliage fell only to rematerialize after they had passed by. Karlar, sporting her green ribbon staggered to the base of the ladder and after staring at her trident in a confused manner started to climb unsteadily after her two adversaries, setting the ladder wobbling ominously under their combined weight.

Rauph raced across the bridges, setting them swaying dramatically as he charged. He almost got half way across the next bridge, that swung precariously over a large pit lined with spikes, when a blur of silver and blue whistled out from the pillar ahead of him and arched back in towards his head making him duck in surprise.

The strange object whirled back to the pillar ahead, only to be thrown out again, offering Rauph a quick glimpse of its owner, a flash of spiky hair and a blue fluttering ribbon. The weapon arced out with deadly accuracy, whistling past the navigator to slice through the handrail behind him instantly dropping the bridge to one side.

Rauph threw himself forward towards the far side of the bridge, his huge hands scrabbling for something to secure himself to, just as the bladed weapon sheared through the second rail as it continued its lazy curve back towards its wielder. The granite pillar behind him suddenly exploded, sending jagged shrapnel flying out across the sands. The bridge trembled and then snapped, leaving Rauph with a split-second feeling of weightlessness before he plummeted towards the spike laden pit below.

Chane could not hide her superior smirk as she observed the Prince dropping away. She held out her hand and caught her weapon almost by reflex, securing it at her belt before limping off across the next bridge, intent on getting through the exit as soon as possible. This was almost too easy.

Rauph slammed into the granite pillar with a grunt that blasted the air from his lungs and almost made him release his grip on the shattered remains of the bridge. He scrambled to find purchase on the granite pillar, glancing over his shoulder at the gleaming tips of the spikes that had so nearly claimed his life, knowing that if the timings were right, he had but seconds to ascend the pillar and make it across to the safety of the next one.

"Come on Rauph!" a piercing voice screamed. "Get a move on, she's getting away." The Minotaur shook his head. Obviously, he was suffering from some kind of concussion. He could have sworn he heard Ashe but he knew Ashe was a zombie now, stalking the darkened alleyways of the town searching for fresh brains to consume. He shook his head and continued to climb, straining to ascend hand over hand.

Rauph finally pulled himself onto the top of the granite column, noting a tell-tale vibration within the stone signalling it was about to follow the fate of the previous columns. He ran for the next bridge, head down, arms pumping, his breath coming in snorts as he charged across the swaying obstacle, barely noting that the pit below was filled with wriggling giant poisonous centipedes. The navigator lunged for the next column, just as the one behind him exploded, dropping the bridge just as he reached the granite sanctuary.

"Go Rauph!"

There was that voice again. The navigator shook his head from side to side. He had to have hit his head harder than he thought! He looked up, noting that only two bridges remained and spotted Chane already dropping down from the final pillar and disappearing through the entrance into the next part of the labyrinth. He set off in pursuit, spotting that the other contestants were nearing the top of the ladder.

Drummon reached the top first and pulled himself over the lip of the exit, then he got to his feet and tried to shove the ladder aside but the weight of the other two contestants climbing rapidly after him made it hard to dislodge it from its position. He placed a boot against the rung and pushed as hard as he could, lifting the ladder away from the edge by about a foot before it bounced back down again, the vibration of the drop almost causing the two female Minotaur to lose their grip.

He grunted his disapproval and tried again, pushing the ladder away, noting that the hostility of the crowd was rising. Movement out of the corner of his eye showed Kristoph was making up swift ground and the initial thought of slicing through the bridge supports and dropping his brother to his doom briefly played through his mind. Then the image of Mora berating him also appeared, scolding him and reminding him that he needed Kristoph alive to add credibility to the competition.

A grasping hand reached out and grabbed his boot, making the black Minotaur reconsider his actions. He kicked out at Ammet, and then pulled his boot swiftly back as she tried to drape the edge of her cloak across his foot. The top rung of the ladder disappeared with a 'pop' and its instability increased further. Drummon checked where Kristoph was and to his chagrin discovered that his brother was already running across the final bridge towards him. He growled to himself, angry that he had no time to get rid of his troublesome pursuit, then the Prince regent turned and ran through the exit, deeper into the labyrinth, leaving the three competitors to fight it out amongst themselves.

Ammet pulled herself over the lip of the sill and rolled through the exit, disappearing into the maze in a swirl of red cloak, just as Rauph jumped from the final granite pillar and landed in the exit way. He took a split second to take in the passageway beyond; noting the smooth walls that seemed coated in a shiny slime like a slug would leave behind. The vegetation appeared strange too, as if nothing would grow in the area where the slimy residue remained.

He stepped forward intent on following the other competitors and heard another ominous trumpet blast as his foot touched the sloping floor. The stone doorway immediately began to grind its way slowly across the sill.

"Please don't leave me!" screamed a voice behind him. Rauph spun about, trying to locate where the voice was coming from and noticed the ladder rattling below his feet. He stepped back through the opening, brushing against the rumbling block of stone slowly moving out to seal the portal and stole a glance down the ladder where Karlar was struggling to ascend. The blonde Minotaur painfully drew herself up, one rung at a time, a huge swelling blossoming above her left eye.

"Hurry up!" Rauph tried to encourage her. The exit is sealing itself, we don't have much time." Karlar ascended another step then slipped and fell back two rungs. She stared at Rauph with pleading eyes and looked far from the pampered, blond haired Minotaur that he knew. Now her hair lay matted to her brow, the strands grimy and damp with sweat, her left eye was swelling shut, her makeup smeared and the nails of her right hand chipped and splintered. There was even a dribble of spittle running across her chin. Karlar had never looked so pitiful.

"Pass me your trident. Maybe I can wedge the door somehow." Rauph suggested, swinging his head to check that the door was grinding ever closer.

"Never!" Karlar shouted her defiance. "I will never give up my..." The explosion from the pillar directly behind the female Minotaur made her shriek and nearly drop from the ladder. The column splintered into large jagged fragments, the top half dropping towards her. Karlar looked up in horror as the granite tilted over then fell directly towards her. She struggled to rise up, get out from beneath the shadow looming over her, her actions now as rapid as the dazed Minotaur could make them. The tumbling stone smashed into the ladder just beneath her feet, missing her by inches and pulverising the rickety construction, dropping the Minotaur as the remains of the ladder and the destroyed pillar fell from beneath her. Karlar screamed, just as Rauph's hand reached out and caught her wrist, leaving her swinging over the rubble.

"Drop the trident." Rauph grunted, "I need your other hand."

"I will not give up my trident!" Karlar reiterated shaking her head and causing more spittle to run down her chin. Rauph grunted with the weight of the Minotaur, gritting his teeth and snorting his pain as he struggled to heave her up the side of the wall. The grating of the stone slab sliding shut behind him mimicked the grinding pain he felt coming from his ribs as he struggled to lift her inch by inch up and over the ledge.

"Come on!" he snarled, lifting Karlar high enough that she could finally get her boot on the sill. Their muzzles kissed, causing Rauph to start and throw himself backwards, taking Karlar and her trident with him as he tumbled through the exit. They landed with a crash, Karlar on top and Rauph underneath, just as the doorway closed shut, sealing the arena behind them.

The crowd laughed aloud at the compromising position their prince now found himself in, lying flat on his back with a female Minotaur straddling his stomach. They started shouting down rude comments and making obscene gestures. Rauph looked up past Karlar's ruffled blonde locks, realised what everyone was staring at and blushed.

"Did the earth move for you?" someone shouted, laughing raucously. Rauph's gaze moved from one laughing face to another and spotted a small child like face staring down at him, his face as flushed as Rauph felt his own should be.

"Ashe?" Rauph was totally embarrassed as their eyes met. The Halfling surprisingly looked quite pink for someone supposed to be a zombie, he thought. Maybe he had just eaten someone? Karlar moved sluggishly on top of him, weakly pushing herself up from his chest with her right hand and staring about dazed. She looked to the left then the right, then looked down at the navigator with bleary eyes that suddenly sharpened into deadly focus. A dull sound to the left of the two figures signalled that another piece of labyrinth was slowly moving away but neither Rauph nor Karlar dared to take their eyes off each other.

"Trident!" Ashe screamed, jumping up and down and waving dramatically. "Look out Rauph she has a trident!" Karlar swung her left arm up, bringing to bear the gleaming golden weapon which she then moved to plunge deeply into Rauph's chest. Rauph had already spotted the cruel betrayal in Karlar's eyes the second that she moved and he acted on reflex turning towards her left arm, knowing she was not balanced on that side, before hurling her from him with a roar. There was a wet splodge like sound and Karlar stared to scream.

Rauph staggered to his feet, turning towards where he had thrown the female Minotaur and froze at the sight that beheld him. The section of wall that had slid aside contained a huge blob of gelatinous material that stood as tall as the slime marks on the passageway walls. Marks below which no vegetation dared to grow. Inside this massive jelly hung the remains of rodents, birds and small mammals, all in various states of translucency, their bodies appearing to look like they were trapped in amber; only if you looked closer you could see they were slowly dissolving as they were absorbed into the gelatinous whole of the creature they were trapped inside.

Karlar hung on her side, one arm and half of her face embedded in the gel. Each time she screamed the blob seemed to pulsate and then suck her body further into its mass. Rauph froze, not sure what to do. He grabbed her free arm but could not find a way to gain leverage on the smooth scoured floor. Karlar screamed again as he pulled at her arm and then the gel oozed over her lips and raced inside her mouth filling every part of her lungs and slowly suffocating her before Rauph's horrified eyes.

The blob of gel started to wobble then it slopped forwards, oozing and squeezing through the gap that had opened out into the corridor, causing Rauph to step back onto the sloping floor or risk suffering the same fate as the now slowly dissolving Karlar. Another horn blast echoed from the walls and the crowd roared again.

The navigator looked down at the slope beneath his feet and suddenly realised why the walls of the maze were so clean, why they had that tinge of slime about them and also why the floor beneath him had a slight downhill gradient that led off into the twisting turns of the labyrinth. The gelatinous blob slid forward again, confirming his fears, its mass conforming to the walls and leaving no space for the Minotaur to escape on either side. He had no option but to turn and head down the slope in the hope he would find a way of avoiding the jelly as it slowly began to pick up speed.

Ashe peered at the scene unfolding below him through his little fingers, trying to decide if he was about to be violently sick as the twisted lifeless body of Karlar slowly rolled within the gelatinous blob and stared up at the crowd, her mouth forever frozen in a silent agonising scream. The Halfling closed his eyes, grimaced and said the first thing that came into his little mind.

"Oh, but that was just so gross!"

Chapter Forty-Three

So this was what it was like to be dead.

Everything felt cool and dark after the intolerable heat of the desert; the ever-present wind that had not only scoured his exposed flesh but also the edges of his sanity, was now an echo, still present but subdued in the background and more like a whisper. Vague demonic shadows flitted about around him and somewhere in the distance, the clarion calls of horns sounded over the tumbling roar of an avalanche.

Yet despite this, Kerian felt at peace. Given, his arms felt like they had suits of armour tied to them, his head felt the size of an enormous watermelon and his body felt it was sinking deeper and deeper into the soft bedding on which he lay but it felt so good to just let go and rest. No more fighting undead monsters in dusty tombs, no more dealing with that rogue Octavian, just simple peace and quiet.

The voices rising and falling about him tried to drag his attention from these pleasant thoughts of tranquillity. He recognised them but it was such an effort to remember, such a struggle to identify them from a memory that was as fogged and incoherent as his own. Something wet touched his lips and splashed across his face. For a second, he could not breathe, stunned by the alien sensation, as the cool water trickled into his mouth and ran across his swollen tongue. He arched his back, reaching for more like an infant stretching towards the sustenance of a mother's teat.

"Not too much Kerian, you will only make yourself sick. Only little amounts first." Another tantalising trickle of fluid passed Kerian's lips as he suddenly recalled who the voice belonged to. Octavian. That's who it was! Still bossing him around, still dictating terms! Well that confirmed it, he was clearly destined for one of the hells and part of his eternal torment would be a pale shade of that damn gypsy guide haunting his every tortured moment.

"Are you sure that is Kerian Denaris?" Another voice, this one from further back in his memory. He knew that voice but from where. It was infuriating, as if the answer was right on the tip of his tongue.

"Why do you ask?" Octavian enquired. Would this man ever stop with the incessant questions?

"Kerian Denaris is an old man of at least sixty summers. This man has lived maybe forty, if that. This man must be an imposter."

"How do you know of Kerian Denaris?" Octavian's voice more cautious this time. "Why were you out in the desert all alone. Were you following us?" A loud crash resonated through the area causing Kerian to startle and move to sit up, only to smack his head on the underside of a drinking bowl that Octavian was using to deliver the water.

"Kerian stay still. You need to gather your strength. We cannot cross the Alicieus span without you being well. The Givrea guardians have permitted our passage but they will not save us from the perils of the crossing."

"Where are we?" Kerian muttered, rubbing his head and taking in the sight of the cool cavern in which they dwelt. Reflected golden ripples off a welcoming pool flowed across the red and white striped ceiling, their motion created by the horses drinking deeply at the edge. He opened his mouth to ask another question, only for Octavian to pour more heavenly water into his parched mouth.

"I already told you. We are about to cross the Alicieus span into Blackthorn but the winds across the span make the storms in the Vaarseeti seem like gentle zephyrs. When you are ready, we really need to depart. The Provan legion are still trying to follow us but the guardians will never permit such an army to cross." Octavian paused and turned to a shadowy figure standing over by the horses. "We shall need to rope ourselves together. Scrave throw the rope please."

The soothing water in Kerian's mouth turned to vinegar. He turned his aching head, his eyes widening as he took in an improbable sight. An emaciated vagabond stalked across the floor of the cave towards him, cloaked in torn rags and coated by the dust of the desert. The figure threw back his hood, exposing scraggy shoulder length Elven hair bleached from exposure to the sun and a face impossible to forget: the diamond tattoo on his right cheek and the wicked scar running from his left eye socket and down along his jawbone. This could be but one person, despite the fact that the last time Kerian had seen him he was stabbing the cold-hearted bastard through the heart with his own sword before leaving him to bleed out on a bed of gold coins and exotic gems.

But why the eyepatch?

Scrave continued moving closer, his sharp Elven features becoming clearer as he moved from the darkness of the cave and into the flickering torchlight, his dark eye scrutinising Kerian intently as if searching for a clue to an enigma that only the Elf was party to. The killer tilted his head to one side, as if taking in the view from another perspective, the light accenting the sharp bone structure of his face and highlighting a pointed ear poking out from his headscarf. He nervously licked his lips, his hand dropping to pat the side of his robes, as if checking that something valuable remained secreted there.

Kerian met Scraves's cold gaze head on, not wishing to show any sign of weakness, despite how wretched he felt. Indeed, if Scrave was thinking of taking revenge he had chosen the ideal moment to exact it and the knight realised he would be powerless to stop him. Kerian had witnessed the incredible speed and skill of this callous fighter, the deadliness of his cold-hearted attacks and yet he remained lying on the floor allowing the killer to move closer! He needed to do something, needed to prepare for the inevitable one-sided battle that was about to shatter the sanctity of their refuge. He inched his hand towards the hilt of his sword, trying not to break his gaze from this impromptu contest of wills and inadvertently telegraph his intentions.

The Elf allowed a cold smile to slide across his face, stealing a glance at the unguarded movement of Kerian's hand, before returning to scrutinise Kerian's face with even greater intent.

"Who are you?" he asked, his suspicion emphasised by the dry husky tone of his voice.

"Excuse me?" Octavian butted in, causing Scrave and Kerian to break away their gazes and stare at the gypsy in clear annoyance. "What? I need the rope, okay?"

Scrave's hand moved from behind his back, drawing Kerian's gaze towards his adversary again. This was it; this was where the Elf would use his sword and the cave would become the scene of a blood bath. The movement was lightning fast, making Kerian draw his breath in a gasp, even as he commenced drawing his blade. The coil of rope Scrave had been holding behind his back sailed across the room and slapped Octavian firmly across the face, even as the Elf's boot moved forward and incredibly hooked Kerian's blade from his hand and flipped it up into the air, where the Elf then caught it and weighed the weapon in his hand, turning it over and admiring the workmanship.

Kerian tried to rise from his prone position, tried to get his hands beneath him and prepare to move away but Scrave's dusty boot planted squarely on his chest and the Elf leaned closer, causing the front of his robe to part slightly. Kerian's eyes widened in recognition at what he saw, as Scrave leaned further towards him to increase the pressure on the knight's chest.

"If you wish to impersonate someone you really need to do more research." Scrave hissed. "For one, Kerian Denaris is an old man. You might fulfil the part in another twenty years or so."

Kerian tried to remain calm, tried to keep his emotions from betraying him. How had Scrave managed to get his hands on it? He tried to focus on anything but the object swaying before him and locked onto Scrave's eyepatch and the untold mystery surrounding this, only to find himself suddenly feeling afraid that what lay behind the eyepatch was a greater danger to him. Scrave took in the frightened look and failed to understand its relevance, believing that the look was in response to this impostor being caught out.

"You also need to know that Kerian's sword is not silver and the hilt is two roaring dragons, not a crude rendition of the sun." He flipped the sword about, presenting it hilt first to Kerian so he could recover it, much to the knight's open-mouthed astonishment.

Octavian approached, unaware of what had just transpired, too occupied with securing the length of rope about his waist before offering his hand to Kerian and hoisting him to his feet. The gypsy set about securing Kerian to the line, wrapping the rope about the knight's waist in a figure eight after leaving roughly thirty foot of rope between Kerian and his own body. Kerian noted that several knots had been tied along the length of the rope at regular intervals but he did not understand the rationale behind this, his brain was simply too busy trying to comprehend what had just transpired.

Scrave somehow did not recognise him.

"So come now." Scrave continued. "What is your real name?"

"Kerian. My name really is Kerian."

"Of course it is." Scrave grinned, as if sharing a private joke, leaning forwards to brush some errant sand from Kerian's tunic, only to transfer more from his own desert scoured clothing in its place. Octavian bustled in beside the Elf and moved to loop the rope around him as well.

"What are you doing?" Scrave snapped, slapping Octavian's hand down and pushing the rope away. Octavian stepped back in shock, a snarl escaping his curled lip as Scrave's hand dropped back to the place on his tunic that he had patted earlier. Just what was the Elf hiding there?

"I'm sorry." Octavian held his hands up in a display of apology. "I never meant to offend you, I just wanted to secure you to the line."

"I have no desire to be tied to another." Scrave replied, his tone now civil and smooth once he realised no threat was intended. "Relying on others has never worked out well for me in the past. I prefer to be independent."

"Suit yourself," Octavian replied, "but I have travelled across the Alicieus span before and I must warn you, the trip may be a little disorientating for the uninitiated."

"Story of my life." Scrave replied coolly, moving away from the two men to collect supplies from the floor and pack them on the mounts. "The horses are watered, so when do we leave?"

"Once Kerian feels strong enough to do so." Octavian gestured. "Are you?" he turned to note Kerian's thoughtful expression, just as another loud roar echoed through the cave.

"I think we had better hurry or our departure may be forced upon us." Scrave gestured towards the cave entrance where the sunlight continued to beat upon the sand and project a blinding glare.

"Are you ready to go?" Octavian asked again.

"...am I what?" Kerian turned to the gypsy, his mind torn by the enigma that Scrave represented and the unanswered conundrums that seemed to be weaved about his emaciated person.

"Ready to go?" Octavian prompted.

"Sure, lead on." Kerian replied, purposefully hanging back and gesturing that Scrave should also move ahead of him. He had no intention of having the Elf at his back where he could not see him. "You first."

"No, after you." Scrave replied, acting the gracious host and stepping back as Octavian moved past him and gathered the reins of his horse.

"But I insist." Kerian pushed.

"Oh for Adden's sake." Octavian butted in, "I'll go first." He walked by, leading his horse between the two men, making Kerian break eye contact with his acquaintance as he passed, his rope sliding forlornly along the floor in his wake. Kerian used the opportunity to walk over to Toledo and gather up the stallion's reins, hoping that as he did so Scrave would take the opportunity to trail after Octavian but as he turned to follow the Elf still stood alongside him, obstinate as a shadow and as impossible to shake. Toledo pawed at the ground, eager to set off but both Kerian and Scrave stood in the stallion's way. It snorted loudly as if ordering the men to make way.

"You know, the name Kerian suits you." The Elf offered, looking intently at Kerian again, his head tilted to one side. "I knew a Kerian once and he was a suspicious bastard too!"

Kerian tried to disarm the tension with an exhausted smile, only to be yanked forward, colliding with Scrave as the rope pulled taut. The two men jumped apart, Scrave angrily brushing himself down as if contaminated, even as Kerian was tugged out of the door.

"What's at Blackthorn anyway?" Scrave asked, trying to avoid the embarrassment of the collision.

"A haunted castle and a petrified forest." Kerian shouted back, trying to put out of his mind that when he had touched Scrave's side something at the Elf's waist had moved under his hand. Was it his imagination, or had he heard an unmistakeable warning hiss? "Apparently it's the region where Octavian comes from." There was another yank on the rope and Kerian slipped out through the cave entrance back under the brutal glare of the sun.

"Sounds like the ideal vacation." Scrave mumbled to himself, checking his dagger was still comfortably beside him before he turned and followed.

* * * * * *

Kerian left the cave and entered a world of noise and heat that initially left him stunned. The sun's heat instantly hammered down upon his shoulders, offering no mercy, delivering what felt like a sustained hammer blow to his head after the relative cool of the sanctuary in which they had rested. His head pounded repeatedly, threatening to make him sick and lose what little moisture he had taken into his stomach. The glare subsided as his eyes adjusted to the brightness of his surroundings. He realised that the pounding was not just regulated to his head. It was happening around him as well.

They stood in a courtyard of sorts, the floor of marbled stone, created with the same coloured reds and creams of the sands that rose on all sides about him. Behind them a pathway led out back into the sandstorm that had been shadowing their every move. As he watched huge creatures moved in and out of view, roaring their defiance to the creatures marching within.

Huge claws, easily eight feet long, swept through the cloud, sending tens of little figures tumbling away, only for them to get back up on their feet and charge back towards the huge creatures again, weapons waving, advancing once more into the fight. A tail, easily thirty feet long swept up into the air, its surface covered in little fighters hacking and slashing at the sand coloured stone that made up its bones. The tail crashed down onto the ground making the dunes tremble so violently that other little fighters simply fell to the ground, their legs unable to hold them up.

Kerian blinked his eyes trying to understand the scale of the scene before him, but with the swirling cloud and the fact he was only getting glimpses of the creature and not its whole body it was hard to make out particulars. Then he realised with amazement that the little stick figures attacking in droves were indeed the Provan legion, fighting this gargantuan creature, trying to overwhelm and smother it with their apparently limitless numbers.

A loud trumpet call signalled another attack, only for the ground to tremble behind Kerian, causing him to turn only to witness a monster bearing down towards him. The beast was gigantic, a huge triangular sand stone coloured head, twin horns spiralling up from above armoured brows that shadowed deep set eyes the colour of nightmares. The beast moved towards the party like a land lizard, its huge pointed snout swinging from side to side, teeth clicking as it hissed warning to those who dared oppose it and its brethren. Massive claws slammed into the ground as the creature pulled its immense bulk over them, ignoring the party as if the travellers were totally inconsequential.

Kerian watched in part amazement, part fear, as the beast rumbled past him, each section of the creature the same sand coloured stone, each segment moving and creaking as the dragon slithered past. In his mind he found it impossible to fathom the spectacle of the beast, his eyes drawn from each gleaming armoured plate to each cruel wicked claw. He marvelled at the way the dragon breathed so deeply, its sides moving in and out with a crackling sound as each stone scale coating its torso clinked against its counterpart as it moved. Yards upon yards of the monster swept past and still it had not stopped blotting the sun from the sky. Kerian eased over to Octavian his mouth opened wide as the creature moved by.

"I know." Octavian shouted. "I felt the same way when I first saw the guardians! Come on we need to move fast if we are going to get to where we need to be." The gypsy gestured that the others follow him and led them to where the dragon had come from, its massive stone segmented tail rippling past them, swaying backwards and forwards as the monster finally moved by. The three men and two horses moved to the opening and paused there, their eyes beholding yet another wonder that struggled to be defined by words alone.

"May I present..." Octavian gestured. "The Alicieus span."

The span was an ancient stone bridge, its colours a continuation of the patterned stone floor of the courtyard. It stretched out into nothing, its length becoming slimmer and slimmer until you had to blink to check you were still looking at it. The width of its path was barely enough for a single caravan to pass, with small bricks set proud of the brickwork on either side of the path to help guide cart wheels along its length. The sight was dizzying to behold, the colours running into each other making it seem even longer than it already was. A pillar set about waist height, stood to the right of the span, a softly glowing orb set upon its top emitting a pale rose coloured light.

Scrave moved forwards to the edge, feeling his robes start to whip about him as he advanced to take in the view. The world dropped away at his feet, the landmarks he would have expected to see mere dots, impossibly far, far below. Despite having climbed the rigging of the *El Defensor* many times, he found himself suddenly experiencing a nauseating sense of vertigo. The Elf could not help but step away from the edge to prevent himself from vomiting. How could they be so high? It made no sense. He took a deep breath, trying to stop the world from spinning, trying to blot out the angry roars of the dragons attacking the legion and concentrated on focusing with his one good eye along the edge of the span.

He noted the first impossibility within seconds. The span was incredibly thin from the side view, like a sword blade presented with the flat of the blade upwards and its keen edge set towards and away from him. It looked so fragile, so delicate. There was no way such a structure could sustain any substantial weight upon its surface. It looked as if it would snap and crack apart like thin ice on a barely frozen pond.

Then he realised the second thing that was wrong with the span. Despite the bridge stretching out over nothing, there appeared to be no way the bridge could support itself. There were no struts, arches or cables, no signs of suspension, support columns, trusses or cantilevers. The whole structure was clearly magical in nature but who would have the power to create such a feat of sorcery?

"My kin have used these magical bridges to travel for centuries." Octavian shouted across to Kerian. "They are a way of crossing the world faster than conventional means but the journey is not without its dangers. Over years the traffic has reduced as the travelling community has dwindled but the guardians remain ever vigilant and protect those with the right blood line, offering access to those that require it."

"And this span takes you to Blackthorn?" Kerian asked, observing Scrave out of the corner of his eye as the Elf walked towards the edge of the bridge and carefully placed his boot upon its smooth surface as if expecting the whole structure to disintegrate and drop into the abyss below.

"It will take you wherever you wish to go." Octavian replied. "As long as civilization has not encroached too heavily in the area and disrupted the natural flow of magic. Come on we must make haste. I am only granted passage for so long."

Octavian moved forward and gently ushered Scrave to one side. He approached the pillar and held out his hand, laying it gently upon the orb. The gypsy started to speak in a strange language not known by either the

Knight or the Elf. It sounded like Octavian was asking for permission to cross and the name of Blackthorn was mentioned several times.

The span began to shimmer, its surface colours appearing to run over the edge as if the entire surface had become liquid. The reds and creams of the desert started to change to deeper more sinister blues and greys that appeared to well up from the centre of the stone. Octavian bowed his head and lowered his hand from the orb, his face drawn as if requesting the use of the span had taken something from him that he would never recover.

"Let us hurry." He gasped. "We must leave now." Octavian stepped forward, leading his horse out onto the bridge, their footsteps echoing loudly on the stone pathway. Kerian watched the lifeline between the two of them snake after the gypsy, the knots bouncing and tumbling along the floor making the rope dance and jiggle with every step. For a second, he had the most terrifying thought that when the rope pulled taut, he would be dragged over the edge and fall to his doom.

He turned around, taking one last look at the waystation where they had found refuge, soaking up its beautiful, yet ancient appearance, then beyond to the opening where the two monstrous dragons held the Provan Legion at bay, their gigantic forms thrashing about within the sandstorm swirling angrily around them.

Scrave moved past him, reaching down to grab the rope as it bounced along and swiftly winding it about his left wrist before he took a deep breath and stepped out after the gypsy. Kerian watched him take the first few tentative steps, which soon became faster as the Elf realised the span would not fail beneath his feet.

Kerian took a last look at the glowing orb on the pillar, noticing a flickering image within the rose colour. It offered a glimpse of forests of skeletal trees blanketing a bleak landscape in which a foreboding castle sat perched upon a rocky outcrop. He moved closer to get a better look just as the rope snapped taut and tugged him away. Scrave was clearly as impatient as ever!

Toledo snorted nervously as the knight took his first step out onto the cool smooth surface of the span. The floor felt slick, as if it were coated by a thin layer of frost. Kerian took his next step, feeling his boots give just a fraction as he set his weight upon them. He was going to have to be careful walking here! The rope snapped taut, tugging him onwards out onto the main body of the bridge and making him slip further. A cold wind suddenly swirled around the span, making his cloak snap and billow at his shoulders, threatening to steal the breath from his lips. He found himself shivering as the warmth from the desert sun was inexplicably blasted away the further he stepped out into the haze.

He watched the back of Scrave slowly becoming indistinct, despite the fact the Elf was barely fifteen feet away from him, it was as if Scrave were stepping into a light morning mist that had no place on a bridge with a gale blowing about it. This was insane. What was he doing out here?

Kerian had no choice but to follow, feeling drops of strange moisture start to collect on his clothes and face, the liquid shimmered eerily in the hazy light. He rubbed one bead between his finger and thumb and noted the oily residue it contained spreading out under pressure only to reform once his thumb had passed over it. A tug at his waist set him forward again, the haze moving to envelope him completely.

The knight felt a sense of anxiety building. This was all so very strange and alien to him, so far removed from anything he could have possibly believed. He needed to focus on his footsteps, watch carefully where every step landed but his mind kept racing. There were so many questions he needed answered. So many things he needed to understand but it was so hard to concentrate when his spirit felt depleted and his reserves of strength were so low. How long had it been since he had eaten anything substantial?

His initial quest to find Colette was slipping further and further from him. She could be anywhere, she could be hurt, she could even be searching for him. He had no way of checking. If only he could find the damned pendant and gaze into its depths to have one more glimpse of her. What he would give to hold her in his arms, to tell her that he loved her and that he would never leave her side again if she would have him. It was impossible, a pipe dream. He suddenly believed they were destined never see each other again, despite what Octavian's wife had foretold. The thought came as a crushing blow. His right hand dropped to the bag at his side and fumbled with the flap as he continued to take each precarious step. He knew the damned pendant was in there somewhere, he had watched it fall inside, so why could he not now find it?

Speaking of pendants, what about the one he had spotted dangling around Scrave's neck? He had noticed it immediately, recognised it in seconds. It had to be his. The glimpse of the emerald light and the casing that contained it was too much of a coincidence. There were no others that he knew of. It had to be his. He had stolen that gem to keep the effects of aging from crippling his body as he had searched for a cure to his curse. The very same necklace that had saved him from the effects of the heat in the subterranean temple back on Stratholme when the magical bracelet Colette had enchanted had expired. He had thought it lost along with Colette's pendant in Wellruff and that the market traders had taken it. So how had Scrave come to find it?

Kerian's hand continued to fiddle with the flap of the bag, his thumb and finger rubbing the smooth material as he tried to gather his turbulent thoughts. Then there was the whole unanswered conundrum of the Elf himself to consider. Kerian had slammed three feet of forged steel through Scrave's heart! He had to be dead! There was no getting up from such a mortal wound. He had left him bleeding out on the floor of the temple, his life blood seeping into the golden coins scattered beneath him. So how could he be here, walking as plain as day in front of him with no obvious disabilities other than the strange eye patch? Was the pendant to blame? Was it healing the Elf as it had Kerian?

Then he had to understand how Scrave had escaped the temple. How could he be here right now? Wherever here actually was. Stratholme was many leagues away. Was he somehow tracking him?

The odds of finding Kerian in the inhospitable terrain of the Vaarseeti desert were incalculable; the desert simply too vast. Octavian and Kerian had managed to become lost simply following the trail markers. The Provan legion had remained lost in the desert for generations until Kerian had blundered into them. Even the city of Tahl Avan had been scoured from its ever-shifting surface. If a desert could wipe a civilization from the map and swallow an entire elite legion of soldiers, the passage of two men and their horses would be simple to erase. There was no way he could have been followed. No one knew where he was heading. Indeed, up until a few days ago Kerian had been heading for Al Mashmaah, his course not set. They had only just changed direction in their quest for Blackthorn and he still thought this was a hair brained idea. How had the Elf managed to find him?

It was one hell of a coincidence and Kerian had lived too long and seen too much to believe in coincidences. He rubbed the flap of the bag faster, finding the action soothing in his current state of mind as he struggled to make sense of the mystery the Elf represented. Then there was Scrave's eyepatch. There was something about the sight of it that made Kerian's skin crawl. He took a deep breath and shuddered as his footsteps continued to pace through the haze. It seemed such a little thing but there was something very wrong about that unseen eye, something more dangerous than even the Elf.

His nose twitched; he could smell something strange. It was a scent of mulled spices and warm bread. He sniffed again, clearly in his weakened state with lack of nourishment he was starting to hallucinate! He sniffed deeper, there was definitely a spicy smell coming from somewhere. He looked down at his side and noticed that in his deliberations he had inadvertently opened the pouch and a tantalising aroma was now wafting from the opening. He slid his hand into it and felt something warm beneath his hand.

No, it could not possibly be. His mouth started salivating as he lifted out the warm spiced roll its surface pitted with olives and rouged with the orange of baked tomatoes. He held it up to his nose, breathing in the scents, not believing his eyes. It had been so long since he had taken any food! He ripped a chunk from the loaf, noting the steam rising from the bread as if it had just come from a hot oven and placed the morsel in his mouth.

He stopped walking, the sensation of the food passing his lips making his stomach roll in anticipation, his eyes flood with tears of pleasure. The rope snapped taut at his waist tugging him forward, almost making him drop his new-found bounty as his feet skidded across the surface of the span but he was determined not to relinquish his grip on his prize.

Kerian shot a scowl towards the front of the group, even though he could barely make out the shadowy shape of Scrave and nothing of Octavian at all, before he turned his attention back to the treasure in his hands. The bread was simply divine, he ripped off another mouthful. Feeling the crust crack as he bit into the surface and the warmth of the springy interior inside his mouth as he chewed ravenously. Tomato juice dribbled from his chin as he bit into a hot chunk of the fruit, nearly scalding himself in the process but he was beyond caring.

Then it hit him. He had smelled these scents before. Where was it? In the market place at Wellruff? No that wasn't it. The vendor stalls at Lichfield? No that wasn't right either. It was more recent than that. Then it hit him; an image of himself and Octavian hanging upside down over a boiling pot of molten gold. He had smelt it then, the time... oh gosh, the time when Colette's pendant had fallen into the bag!

He plunged his hand inside the pouch, feeling several more loaves, small urns and amphorae pass beneath his questing fingertips. It had to be here. It just had to be! He did not want to raise his hopes up higher, dared not wish that his thoughts could be true. Then his fingers fell upon the unmistakeable shape of the one thing he had thought lost forever...

And Kerian's heart soared.

Chapter Forty-Four

"Rauph! The trident; don't forget the… oh excuse me, mind yourself, watch your hand. What was I saying? Oh yes …the trident!" Ashe yelled down into the labyrinth, struggling to make his way along the edge of the spectator packed wall, pushing and shoving, ducking and diving and somehow managing to find himself with two purses sticking from his pockets, holding a small roll of hot chicken in one hand and a fistful of assorted coloured ribbons in the other. "Yum… ou ave to take the… oh too late." Ashe swallowed a mouthful of the food as he watched the acidic jelly surging forwards, rolling over the discarded weapon and collecting it up along with the other detritus from the arena floor.

So much for that idea! Ashe thought as he took another bite, before lifting the skirt of a plump observer blocking his path and slipping between her legs, shielding his eyes with the fist of ribbons, just in case he saw something he would wish to forget.

"Sorry, nice bloomers by the way!" He darted between two stern Minotaur guards and risked another quick glance down into the labyrinth at the rapidly departing figure of the navigator as the stubborn Minotaur continued to head away from him down the slope. "You need to wait for… watch it, I nearly dropped my chicken roll, excuse me, please breathe in, sorry was that your foot? …wait for me." It was so strange. Ashe had never known Rauph to be so deaf before. What was the Minotaur playing at? Why was he ignoring him? Was the noise of the crowd so loud he could not hear his voice? Come to think of it there was an awful lot of noise from the crowd behind him as if they were somehow agitated.

The Halfling risked a quick glance, noting to his surprise that there was an angry surging mob heading in his direction. He faced front, anxious to see who had upset them, only to collide with the posterior of a Minotaur guard who was bent over looking down into the maze and observing the action. The guard snorted in surprise, clearly not expecting to be run into and then spun around angrily, causing Ashe to throw his hands up in the air in surprise and send brightly coloured ribbons and chunks of steaming chicken onto the guard's uniform.

"Oops, I'm terribly sorry. I never saw you there." Ashe confessed, trying to squeeze by on the left where the crowd was tightly packed. The Minotaur snorted again, his anger clear for everyone to hear. Sinders swooped down, precariously scrabbling for a perch on the Halfling's shoulder, only to see the hulking Minotaur bearing down. The bird swiftly buried its head under its wing, hoping that if it could not see the angry Minotaur then the angry Minotaur could not see it.

The guard stomped down a huge boot, blocking Ashe's way, forcing the Halfling to dodge to the right and dart along the very edge of the maze wall. A burst of speed, then he was through, feeling the air part inches above his head as a huge hand reached out to snare him. Ashe held his breath, head down, he had to catch up with Rauph, had to... The spear haft caught his back foot as he ran, snagging the Halfling and spinning him off balance.

"Cracking conkers!" The Halfling cursed, stumbling on the crumbling edge, sending fragments of mortar and dust tumbling down into the passageway from beneath his scrabbling feet and accidentally dropping one of the pilfered purses to the ground, where it split open, spilling coins indiscriminately and causing yet more chaos as the crowd surged in to pocket the windfall.

Ashe's little hand reached out, grabbing a scarf, yanking the poor unfortunate spectator forward, whilst somehow correcting Ashe's own pendulum line of trajectory, allowing the diminutive thief to regain his balance and sprint off through the milling crowd, leaving the Minotaur guard to thrash his way through the people clawing at the coins on the floor and smash aside the choking man still struggling to release his scarf.

The Halfling pushed past a young couple more intent on each other than the spectacle below, before suddenly finding himself out of wall space, with another cross passage lying below him, that traversed left to right with several side branches clearly visible. Ashe looked down into the maze, noted the scoured stone floor, far below and watched as a female contestant charged by, her crimson cloak spread out behind her like a flying carpet.

Oh this was a right bowl of hazelnuts! Where was Rauph? Somehow, he had lost sight of his friend. This part of the maze had to be further along the route as he had seen the Minotaur in the red cloak pass his earlier position minutes before Rauph had even entered this section of the labyrinth. Ashe's eyes scanned the crowds lining the walls, trying to figure out what way the passage went. Clearly the route must have twisted away somewhere back along his path and was ultimately going to come back in this direction. That would mean that if he waited long enough Rauph would be along.

The female Minotaur suddenly reappeared, from the direction she had taken, backtracking before taking another side passage that ran almost straight ahead. Spectators roared their excitement as she returned again in mere moments, her agitated actions showing how the ways she had chosen were clearly not the path to take. Ashe studied the crowd before him, noting how they stood across the Minotaur's proposed path, therefore making that passageway another dead end and confirming that her latest choice had indeed been fruitless. She ran along the path, her actions frantic now, her hands pushing and shoving against the stone walls, looking for some means to escape.

"Gotcha!" snarled a voice from behind, causing Ashe to turn around and come face to face with the Minotaur guard who still pursued him, lumps of cooked chicken still sliding down his smart tunic, leaving unsightly greasy marks.

"You really ought to get that seen to or you will never get the stains out." Ashe pointed out helpfully, feinted a charge to the left, before running right, wriggling his way between the tightly packed spectators gathered about him. A groan of disappointment issued from the mouths of the people behind him but Ashe could not stop to see what they all were looking at, his attention focused on escaping the clutches of the huge creature lunging madly after him, bowling spectators over like nine pins.

Ashe slipped past a man with a thick bushy beard playing drums and a young woman with short spiky hair that played a tune on a flute mimicking the excitement of the chase they were witnessing, before he dived between a fat man eating a large pastry and a parent balancing an infant on their shoulders, the child waving a blue stuffed toy monkey with pure enthusiasm. The guard roared his disapproval but was unable to squeeze between the spectators easily and started grabbing people and yanking them back past him causing the flute to toot loudly in protest before it was snatched and smashed to kindling under his boot.

The Halfling shoved and pushed his way along the wall, making his way around to the end of the first dead end, dancing beneath the outstretched arms of a drunken sot who wanted to kiss him and leaping over the scuffling bodies of two men who were clearly not seeing eye to eye. He raced through a column of smoke ascending from a brazier hung below, little orange flecks of cinder and curling spirals of smoke sent spinning in his wake.

He slipped beneath a silver lanyard hanging from a bugle held by a Minotaur who was waiting to announce another death to the crowds and stole a quick glance down into the labyrinth. The crimson cloaked Minotaur was now nowhere to be seen. Where had she gone? He looked over the side checking to see if she was against the wall but she was not there either. How could she have simply vanished? Rauph arrived, huffing around the corner and came to a stop, just as Ashe paused above him to draw breath.

"Hi Rauph." Ashe waved down eager to see his friend again. Rauph glanced up, his eyes growing wide, then he scowled and shook his head before setting off down the first passageway the cloaked Minotaur had explored.

"It's a dead end!" The Halfling shouted down helpfully but his calls fell on deaf ears. Soon enough Rauph retraced his steps and took the only remaining passage available.

"That's a dead end too!" Ashe screamed, only to watch Rauph disregard him with a flick of his wrist and shake of his head before he charged down the pathway anyway.

"Told you so." Ashe remarked, as Rauph came back to the main passage, this time with his enthusiasm clearly waning, a look of total confusion on his face.

Someone barged into Ashe from behind, causing the Halfling to stumble forwards, his little hands scrabbling for a hold on the ledge to prevent him from tumbling over. Sinders exploded into flight from the thief's shoulder, flapping its wings before turning about in a tight circle and dropping like a stone to the floor of the maze, where it pulled up at the last moment, before crashing comically and rolling over on itself.

"Now there is no need to push!" Ashe snapped angrily, trying to resist the mass behind him, only to hear the screams from several upset and shocked spectators as they surged forwards to crash against him again, harder this time. "What are you doing?" The Halfling turned about and found several people squashed up against him and shoving through them, the towering Minotaur guard. The creature lashed out catching one complaining spectator on the nose, crushing it like a ripe tomato. A mist of crimson puffed in the air as the man stepped back, then stumbled and fell over the side.

Rauph had noticed the scrum of people crushed to the edge and struggling not to fall. He had also noticed zombie Ashe clawing at these figures as they screamed. The first spectator fell to the floor beside him, his short dark hair soaked with blood from his broken nose, his leg cracking as he landed, the sound echoing down the passage like a dry twig snapping.

"Stop you'll tip us all over!" Ashe yelled, struggling to move away but the pressure of the crowd was too much and he could not find grip on the crumbling edge to push back. His heels slid over, leaving the Halfling balancing on his toes and still the force increased. A huge hand burst through the spectators grabbing Ashe by the hair and lifting him squirming from the ground.

"Aww let go you are hurting me!" Ashe squealed, struggling to hold on as the Minotaur guard swung Ashe clean over the edge, sending another two spectators screaming into the pit as the brute laughed aloud. Rauph dodged as a large woman fell, landing awkwardly, dazed, her head striking the stonework with a sickening thud. More spectators screamed, whilst others cheered, as the second man fell, a scholar by his robes, his hair thinning atop his head. He landed better than the other spectators had, rolling with the fall only to find himself further down the passageway, flat on his back, further along the passage Rauph had come from.

This was horrific, these poor people had thrown themselves down into the labyrinth rather than be eaten by a zombie Halfling! Crowd members panicked trying to rush away as the angry Minotaur guard continued shoving people aside with little concern for where they may end up.

Zombie Ashe, now clearly frustrated by his fleeing meals, had apparently turned his attention to larger prey and seemed to be clawing at a Minotaur guard's huge hand, clearly trying to sink his little incisors deep into the creature's flesh. Those poor people, Rauph wanted to help but they were all on top of the wall, there was nothing he could do.

"I will teach you to abuse me you little bug!" the guard snorted. Ashe's hands fumbled at the Minotaur's hands, trying to lever up a finger, grip onto the wrist of his uniform, anything to stop the pain from his hair but he could not find any way to gain purchase. He looked into the guard's eyes and suddenly realised what the creature was going to do to him.

"Rauph help me!" He pleaded. "I'm going to fall."

A wet, squelching noise sounded behind the navigator, as the gelatinous mass that had been sliding down the passage slowly oozed around the corner behind him, blocking any chance of escape. Rauph looked back at the two exits remaining, knowing each ran to a dead end, then up at the dangling flesh-eating Halfling zombie then back again at the jellied mass slowly sliding towards him down the ramp.

A quick mental note of his purple maze diagram confirmed to Rauph that he was boxed in, there was nowhere to go. He tried to quell the panic rising within him but he knew what the corrosive touch of this jelly creature could do having seen it first-hand. He checked the distance thirty feet, twenty-five feet. It was surprising how fast this wobbly lump of gel could slither!

Ashe screamed as the guard let go, dropping him into the maze. Sinders squawked too, loudly warning Rauph that something was up and the Minotaur stepped back just as a certain small Halfling landed atop of him with a grunt before tumbling to the floor. Ashe bounced up only to come level with the pointed edge of Rauph's twin swords. He looked down at the blades in disbelief, bewilderment on his face at being welcomed with such aggression. He wasn't sure if he should check his hair to make sure it was still there or ask the dumb Navigator just what the hell he was thinking!

The scholar further down the passageway screamed as the acid jelly oozed across his wrist and moved to suck him inside. Snatching the man from his dazed state and forcing him into agonising reality.

"You will not bite me undead fiend!" Rauph snarled, to cheers from the crowd above.

"Rauph what are you talking about?" Ashe remarked, putting his finger on the tip of one sword and pushing it to the left so he could step away to retrieve Sinders and place the bird back on his shoulder.

"I will not let you eat my brains." Rauph stated.

"Why would I want to eat your brains." Ashe asked bemused. "I don't like brains. They are all rubbery and slimy. Yeuk!"

"Oh yeah! So what's that on your tunic Zombie Ashe?"

The decidedly not a zombie Ashe, looked down and discovered an errant chunk of chicken from his earlier lost roll, tucked in amongst the folds of his clothing.

"Oh that's just chicken." He confessed with a smile, picking it from the front of his clothes and popping it in his mouth with a grin. "See, lovely."

Rauph backed up a step and almost threw up.

"But Thomas tells me everything horrible tastes like chicken." The navigator stated in horror, the tips of his swords trembling.

Ashe, uncharacteristically lost for words, took a moment to check his situation and noted the quivering jelly mass sliding steadily towards them, its gloopy interior having sucked the unfortunate squealing man deeper inside, right up to his chest, despite his desperate struggle to pull free.

"Come on we have to get out of here." Ashe started, taking control and walking towards the jelly his keen eyes checking the floor and the walls. There had to be something here, the crimson cloaked Minotaur had only been out of his sight for a few moments. There had to be a doorway they could not see or a secret passageway that led deeper into the maze and if there was one thing Ashe was good at, it was spotting secret doors and corridors, because that's where people hid their valuables.

* * * * * *

"So where do you think they are going?" Rowan asked, looking up at the covered seating area where Mora and Wanessa were being ushered from their seats towards the exit.

"I'm more interested in seeing where the prize goes." Colette replied, pushing back against several spectators who were jostling for space on the cramped labyrinth wall where they stood. She turned to the man behind her, her eyes blazing. "If you do not remove your hand from my arse, I'll shove it so far up yours, you will have to open your mouth to pick your nose!"

Rowan jumped at the outburst, accidentally elbowing a shawl covered spectator alongside her, causing the woman to grunt and turn her wrinkled face up towards her.

"What is it lovey?" the crone asked, her smile revealing a mouth with more gaps than teeth and a tongue that was coated in thick white fungus.

"My friend wondered where they are taking the axe?" She replied, trying to smile back and be apologetic whilst trying not to breathe in the stench of the crone's halitosis wafting towards her, nor stare at the enormous hairy wart squatting on the end of the hag's nose.

"Up to the pyramid." She replied, licking her lips with her pale slug of a tongue, before issuing a wet cough that made Rowan think of people who had been smoking several years and made her want to step away, despite the fact that the pressing crowd made it impossible to do so. "See the opening far up there, inside is the burial chamber where past rulers sit in state and it is where the Labyris Axe will be handed to the winner, isn't this exciting?"

"What? Up there?" Rowan allowed her gaze to wander up the side of the massive pyramid, shading her eyes with a hand in an effort to make out a thin black line cut into the side of the ancient monument right beneath the capstone. "How do they get right up there?"

"My sister's niece's cousin says she has seen inside the pyramid and that it has several levels and stairs with interconnecting passages that lead up to the burial chamber but she is a terrible gossip and I would not believe half of it." She smiled, then descended into another hacking cough before spitting a gob of sickly lime green phlegm off the wall to the sand below. "Oh but you can't go up there dear, despite how pretty you are. Only royalty, select Minotaur and their servants are permitted and that balcony far up there, where the winner steps out, is the only part we common people are permitted to view."

"So that's a balcony?" Colette frowned, leaning closer before suddenly turning towards the leering spectator behind her and landing a punch that lifted him off his feet causing the crowd to roar in laughter.

"I warned him," she muttered, blowing a stray blonde curl from her forehead before grabbing hold of Rowan's hand. "Don't' let go, no matter what happens."

"Why where are we..." Rowan turned towards her friend and listened as arcane words flowed from Colette's lips. Her arms suddenly felt cold, goose bumps rising up beneath her clothes as if insects had just crawled across her skin. She felt herself stretching out, the feeling increasing in intensity. Then with a clap that set her ears popping, she found herself stepping forwards but instead of falling from the labyrinth wall and down onto the sands, she staggered out onto a cool stone veranda.

Rowan's head spun and she flushed, a light feeling in her stomach reminding her of sending her little yellow Cessna into a dive. She tottered forwards a few more steps before ending up against a balustrade only to stare down the side of the pyramid onto the intricate maze and throngs of the packed crowds far, far below.

"Steady!" Colette's hand landed on her shoulder pulling her back from the edge and into safety. "Teleporting can cause you to feel a little queasy."

"H...h...how?"

"It's a kind of magic." Colette winked, before lifting her finger up to her mouth. "Come on let's look around quickly before anyone sees us up here."

Rowan blinked twice, taking deep breaths as she stared down at the pattern of the stone labyrinth, noting how the passageways and open areas formed an intricate geometric pattern that no one at ground level would ever behold. "Oh my! It's so beautiful from up here." She reluctantly turned from the wide balcony and followed Colette as they cautiously stepped into the shadow and out into the large chamber within.

"Oh wow!" Colette whispered. "Just look at this place." Her eyes roamed around the cavernous area, approximately one hundred feet across, soaking in every detail of the circular room, noting the flickering torches evenly set around the walls illuminating hieroglyphs of Minotaur and humans building Taurean in harmony. Spiced incense teased her senses, the pungent odour mixed with a hint of dust and the promise of secrets from ages past. Three exits led off into the darkness, probably to the passageways and stairwells rumoured to lie below. Thirteen huge thrones all sat facing inwards in a circle, with smaller chairs set between them. A soft yellow glow rose up from a pit that lay at the centre point of the room.

Rowan moved slowly forward, slipping between the chairs, awed by the size of the thrones, set high above her, only to hesitate when she noted that the thrones across from her were occupied by huge shadowy figures, their armour glinting in the torchlight.

"Colette. I don't think we are alone here." She whispered, her finger lightly tracing along the side of throne nearest to her. She paused when she was able to see into the huge seat and stifled a shriek at the huge Minotaur sitting there looking directly at her. His horns were dipped in gold and silver, his armour painted an ornate black and scarlet. One gauntleted hand rested on the hilt of the biggest broadsword Rowan had ever seen and a dark red cloak swept from one shoulder and cascaded down the pedestal of the throne to the floor.

Her first instinct was to run, then something made her pause, her eye caught by the furious activity of a small spider weaving an intricate web between the sword and the arm of the throne. Then she noticed other signs; thick dust in the folds of the cloak, the way the Minotaur's head lolled to one side and then she realised that the dark openings in the creature's helmet held a secret she was beginning to comprehend.

This Minotaur had not moved for some time.

Rowan paced over to the next throne and studied the occupant sitting there with the same keen eye. This creature had an open-faced helm making it plain to see why it no longer wielded the huge crystal Warhammer laid across its lap. An ivory skull regarded her from beneath the ragged remains of its desiccated hide.

This creature had also been dead for a long time!

She stepped away from the threatening throne, only to feel a hand come down upon her shoulder. Rowan moved to scream, only for another hand to come down across her mouth, stifling her shout as Colette moved around to her side her fingers at her lips.

"Be careful," she whispered, pointing towards the centre of the room. "It's a very long way down." Rowan turned and realised she had been backing towards the centre of the room and into the pit that lay there. The area was a large sunken bowl about thirty feet across with most of the floor removed. The peril was only really apparent when this close to the edge or seated raised upon one of the thrones. Stone walkways barely as wide as a decent sized boot spiralled in from the edge towards a round dais at the centre of the pit, the paths sometimes rose, sometimes dropped, interweaving and crossing until they all ended up at the centre of the bowl. Here stood a statue of two kneeling Minotaur gazing up to an empty pedestal. The dust lay disturbed here as if something had recently been removed.

"No guesses to what normally sits there." Colette murmured as she took in the sights through the openings in the floor, then took a deep breath to steady the sudden vertigo that assailed her at the immense drop down into the workings of the ancient monument. "You can see everything from up here. Look..." She gestured for Rowan to follow her example and gaze down at the inner levels of the pyramid.

The view reminded Rowan of the inner workings of a chronograph watch, the type with the open face revealing the working clockwork parts within. The mesmerising assembly of moving parts formed a mechanical golden staircase, where individual stairs solidified then folded, spun out, then retracted. Outside the vertiginous spectacle, tier upon tier of seating ran around the inside of the pyramid, offering spectators an unobstructed view. As she watched, several Minotaur entered the auditorium and took their seats.

"It's just like the maze outside." Rowan gasped, suddenly realising how beautiful the interwoven pathways of the bowl were and what they actually represented. "This whole thing is like a giant rose."

Colette stepped away, her attention captured by several thrones that still were empty, still awaiting their eternal occupants. A table sat to the side of one of these, its surface draped in an ornate cloth that dropped to the floor. Two of the smaller chairs sat vacant upon either side.

"What do you think this is all for?" she asked, indicating to a jewelled goblet upon the table, a piece of fine white linen draped over its top. She touched a parchment scroll, quill inkpot and candle adjacent to the goblet then moved to pick it up, only to freeze as she heard something in one of the stairwells. The noise grew louder, causing the two women to find a hiding place as a slender figure came from the left and walked carefully across the floor.

Only as the girl approached did Rowan recognise this was one of Mora's personal servants, her head bowed, an amphora clasped in her trembling arms. The girl approached the table with unsteady steps, clearly exhausted from the strenuous climb and no doubt relieved to have managed to carry the jar all the way up to the burial chamber without dropping any of the precious liquid within. The servant girl placed the jar carefully on the floor, stood up, sighed, then turned to leave, only for a fearful clatter to stop her in her tracks as an ancient shield slid from one shadowy throne and crashed onto the floor. Rowan cursed loudly, realising any attempt at stealth was now pointless and stood up, her arms open wide to show no threat as she stepped from the gloom.

"Look I'm really sorry. I did not mean to scare you." She opened.

"You should not be here. It is forbidden" the servant shouted. "I must summon the guards. I must..." she yawned, shook her head as if confused, rubbed her eyes and then crumpled to the floor as if felled by an invisible blow. Rowan rushed over fearing something had happened to the girl only to note Colette brushing her hands together as she stepped from her place of concealment, the remnants of a destroyed gemstone crunching beneath her boots.

"Don't worry, she is going to be sleeping for hours!" she winked mischievously. "Now pick up that shield and then we can hide this girl and decide what we are going to do next..."

Heavy footsteps sounded from the entrance to the right. A steady march of feet in step.

"Hell, now what?" Colette cursed. "Help me quickly!" She gestured to the unconscious serving girl, lifting her by the arms and with Rowan's help dragged her behind the table before rolling her under the tablecloth.

The footsteps came closer accompanied by raised gruff voices cursing the stairs they had needed to climb. Colette grabbed Rowan by the arm and shoved her under the table on top of the gently snoring girl before joining them and wriggling to the edge so she could see out from underneath the heavy cloth.

From her sheltered vantage point Colette noticed eight ceremonial guards entering the hall carrying the axe upon a bier between them, the gold of its blade resplendent upon the bed of royal blue velvet on which it lay. The Minotaur moved to the edge of the recessed pit and a faint rumbling sound arose, the tremors of which vibrated through the stone floor and up through Colette's delicate fingers. She craned her neck to see better, wishing the guards would move aside, instead they seemed to be all gathered around the axe and were passing it amongst them.

"That's it done!" One guard announced, finally stepping back for Colette to finally see the axe was now carefully positioned between the two minotaur statues, their outstretched hands cleverly sculpted to hold the axe and its velvet backdrop without the items tumbling through the gaps in the floor and down into the pyramid below.

"Can I just request something." One guard asked, still gasping and out of breath from his earlier climb. "Please don't let me have to carry lady Wanessa up here. She's been gorging herself all morning. The last time she did that she threw up all over the place."

"You will carry who you are instructed to." Came a stern response, as a grey-haired Minotaur stepped from the shadows. The guards snapped to attention as Aelius approached them, pulling themselves up onto the ledge of the pit and forming a line as the last guard pressed something that caused a ramp Colette had previously not noticed to slowly retract back into the lip of the pit, leaving any move to the pedestal where the Labyris now lay, one of great risk.

Aelius paused and looked around the room, sniffing the air. There was a scent of something here that was not normal. Was it lavender?

"Gentlemen I think we need to make this entertaining." He stated, his eyes still searching the room for signs of something not right. "The last four of you down the stairs will be given the honour of transporting the titanic lady Wanessa. I suggest if you do not wish to be in this unfortunate group you will make haste to ensure you get down the stairs first." He clicked his fingers indicating they were to set off and all eight guards charged for the exit, like a bunch of rowdy school boys being summoned by the home bell, any semblance of ceremony now sacrificed in the race to avoid lifting the obese Minotaur.

"Are they gone yet?" Rowan whispered. Aelius turned in the direction, where Colette was hiding, his eyes appearing to penetrate the thick cloth and locate the young women hidden beneath, before he smiled and stepped off into the darkness to follow his troops loudly clattering down the stairs.

"Why?" Colette replied, deep in thought at the actions of the captain of the guard and not really paying attention to the shuffling and wriggling going on behind her as Rowan tried to find a comfortable way to lie. If he had seen them and Colette really believed he had, why had he not come over and dragged them out into the light?

"Because I would really like to move this serving girl's toe from my nose." Rowan replied, breaking into Colette's thoughts and leaving her questions unanswered.

Colette slipped out from beneath the table, ignoring the comments from her companion as she walked back over to the pit and gazed across at the ceremonial weapon, a thought forming in her mind. If Mora did not have the Labyris axe at the end of the tournament they would be unable to confirm a successor, the mantle of power could not be handed down causing unrest within the population because by its very nature a vacuum needed to be filled. If the crew of the *El Defensor* had the axe they would be in an excellent position to negotiate if things became tricky, maybe even be able to discuss the release of Rauph.

Rowan walked up alongside Colette, still moaning about the indignities of hiding under the table and voicing her concerns that they would be caught if they remained here much longer. Colette ignored her, instead, dropping to her knees and moving her hand along the lip of the pit. There had to be something here, there just had to be.

"Ah, ha!" she smiled, feeling the carefully hidden button beneath her finger and pressing it to make the walkway rumble out across the pit and click into place at the base of the isolated pedestal.

"Well what are you waiting for?" Colette asked, turning to Rowan.

"What are you doing?" Rowan replied in confusion. "We need to get out of here. Please don't tell me we are not leaving."

"We are not leaving." Colette replied calmly, causing Rowan to bite her lip in frustration and mutter under her breath. "Because you are going to steal that axe."

"I am going to do what? Are you mad! We shall get caught for sure." Rowan stared across at the pedestal and the treasure lying there glinting softly, her eyes wide as if expecting a troop of burly Minotaur to charge back into the room at any moment.

"Of course we won't." the mage replied. "After all I shall be right here standing guard whilst you go and get it."

"No! I'm not going to do it." Rowan replied shaking her head. "Let's go back to the ship we can grab more crewmen to come and get it now we know where it is."

"The axe is unguarded at the moment." Colette replied. "It's now or never." Rowan shook her head, feeling hot, flustered but having to and agree with her stubborn friend's assessment.

"I'm going to get you for this." she promised, before stepping out onto the ramp and walking as quickly as she could through the spiralling and intertwining pathways, over the dizzying drops and certain death that waited below. She arrived at the pillar, her legs shaking like jelly, gasping with relief, her hands skeletal white due to the grip she had on the Minotaur statues.

Up close the Labyris axe looked very heavy. What if she dropped it? She slid her hand beneath the haft of the ceremonial weapon and moved to lift it down from the stand, grunting at the weight. Carefully, ever so carefully, she eased the weapon free and started to slide it from its resting place, trying to put her worries out of her mind. Positive thinking was the key. She wasn't going to drop this, accidentally cut her foot off or do anything silly. This weapon would be theirs in mere moments. No one would even know... Oh yes, they would.

With this weapon so prominently displayed it stood to reason the Minotaur were bound to notice if the damn thing went missing and it wasn't the easiest thing to smuggle away. She could hardly hide it down her trouser leg!

"Hang on a minute!" Rowan paused halfway. "What if they notice it has gone?"

"That's the idea." Colette smiled. "Come on. Hurry up!" Noises rose from the stairwell adding credence to Colette's sense of urgency. The guards were coming back. Rowan froze, the axe half in and half out of its resting grooves.

"Damn!" the mage cursed under her breath. She had not expected them to be coming back so soon. She stared urgently about the area, her eye noting the serving girl's foot now sticking out from underneath the draped tablecloth, the shield still lying on the floor out of place the Warhammer alongside it teetering dangerously. Then she looked back at Rowan trying desperately to shove the axe back into its resting place so she could turn and run back across the ramp.

"Stay right there!" Colette hissed.

"No way." Rowan shook her head. "I'll be seen!" She took a step onto the ramp and let go of the Labyris, only for the weapon to start slowly sliding down towards the end of the pedestal. Colette took one look then dropped to her knees sliding forwards and pushing the button that retracted the ramp, forcing Rowan to remain behind clutching the statues and hanging on for all she was worth.

"What are you doing?" Rowan hissed. The pain of betrayal etched into her face.

"I'm sorry," Colette replied, meeting Rowan's furious gaze and not backing down. "You have to trust me. I have a plan."

Chapter Forty-Five

Kerian swallowed his last bite of the bread and picked up his pace, eager to share this divine bounty and sudden change of fortune with Octavian who was leading somewhere ahead of him in the mist. His boots slipped on the slick surface as if he were on ice, making the going more comic than actually productive, with every determined quick step swiftly deteriorating into a slither by its end.

The length of knotted rope attached to his waist lay on the floor before him, an umbilical cord fastening him first to Scrave and then to the gypsy Octavian, the only person in this strange place who he hoped could lead him to safety. How he yearned to see a sunrise again, to lift the pendant and start searching for Colette. Out here on the span, the thickness of the mist was such that he could barely see fifteen feet ahead of him, let alone spot the sun. A supernatural wind shrieked and pulled at his clothes threatening to shut the flap of his pouch and risk him losing access to the sustenance within. Kerian had a feeling that If the pouch were to close, the chances of locating the food again were slim, as he had no way of understanding the workings of the enchanted bag.

The knight refused to acknowledge the strange phenomena of the bag, or his travel on this magical bridge. It was an impossible scenario his mind could never understand. By rights the wind should have blasted this magical mist to shreds leaving him a clear view of the span and his fellow travellers. The bridge had no means of support, it defied logic and gravity. The magical pouch was a law unto itself. So much of his life was fantastic now that trying to comprehend the situation and unravel the enigmas that he faced would probably unravel his own mind as well. He shook his head. It was better just to take the situation at face value and just keep on walking, hoping that everything would work out alright in the end.

A blast of wind gusted, shoving Kerian from behind and causing him to slither and wobble closer to the edge of the path. Scrave's faint silhouette came into focus for the first time, just a few metres ahead of him, the guide rope rising up from the span where it wrapped around Scrave's left arm. For a second Kerian debated if he should share his magical fare with the dark brooding Elf considering their turbulent history. His new-found elation at finding Colette's pendant, now safely inside his tunic next to his heart, pushed such petty differences aside. Life was looking up! Kerian was going to start looking for Colette again. If he closed his eyes, he could almost feel her back in his arms. Little else mattered... As he moved to offer Scrave some food Toledo snorted loudly and stopped Kerian in his tracks, snatching his arm back and spinning him around like a clumsy ice skater.

"Oh come on stupid! We need to keep going." Kerian scolded, Toledo's ears flattened and his eyes rolled nervously. "Don't be silly, the rope will pull taut in a moment and I have no intentions of leaving you behind." He checked over his shoulder noting that Scrave had once again disappeared into the mists and that the slack in the rope was being taken up.

"Come on Toledo! Whatever this foolishness is I want no part of it." The spare slack at Kerian's feet started to snake away leaving him with a stark choice. "Okay, if you want to be stubborn, I can fix that." He grabbed at the spare length of rope hanging from the end of the guideline at his waist and unwound it, before tying the loose end around the pommel of the saddle and tugging hard to ensure the knot was secure. Then he set off with Toledo now firmly tethered behind him. The stallion snorted in protest, shaking his head before reluctantly taking one step, then another, his ears down and his head held low.

"Come on Kerian!" came a ghostly voice through the mist. "You are slowing us down, get a move on."

"I'm trying," Kerian shouted back, looking over his shoulder at the stallion and its reluctant walk. "It's Toledo he's dragging his feet. I think something has got him spooked."

An ear-piercing shriek cut the air as a dark shape sliced through the mist between Kerian and his companions. Toledo instantly reared up, hooves flashing, only for its back legs to scrabble on the slippery surface and cause the horse to crash back down onto the span. Kerian lost his balance, as the stallion yanked him, his legs sliding out from under him, dropping him heavily to the ground. There was a crack, like thunder, a heavy beating of wings, then another dark form swooped through the mist. Kerian had the impression of massive claws outstretched and snatching at the air right where he would have been standing, had he not fallen.

Cries of alarm rose from the mists ahead, indicating that those in front were experiencing similar troubles but Kerian was too busy trying to get back to his feet, his boots scrabbling on the slick marbled surface. He crashed down again, his open palm slapping the multi-coloured surface of the span with such force that his hand went numb. He snatched it up, shaking it, trying to coax back some feeling, then realised that the whole bridge was shuddering beneath him as if something huge moved along it.

A haunting clarion call echoed along the length of the bridge, sending shivers down Kerian's spine. He knew that call, it signalled the

Provan legion were coming. Somehow, they must have broken past the dragon guardians. An image of hordes of undead swarming the span and charging in their direction filled his mind and he reached for his sword as the bridge trembled beneath him.

He moved to shout a warning, only to feel the rope about his waist suddenly snap tight, crushing the breath from him. Kerian found himself spun around and dragged physically along the span, violent tremors vibrating along the rope's length as he was pulled. Toledo snorted as the rope then snatched at his saddle, hauling him along after his master.

Disembodied cries of pain filled the mist as Kerian slithered to a stop. His mind instantly sensing that something had to be wrong. The cries sounded as if they were coming from above. He got unsteadily to his knees then quickly pulled on the rope attached to Toledo's saddle in order to pull himself fully to his feet.

"Octavian? Scrave?" Kerian hissed, stepping carefully forwards and following the rope further into the mist, his hand finally freeing his sword from its scabbard. "Where are you for Adden's sake?" He moved further along the span, his breathing ragged, his footing unsteady, Toledo's hooves clopping along the bridge behind him. Where had they gone? This damned mist made everything so hard to see.

Toledo let out a scream and side stepped as a huge claw came up over the edge of the path, sinking its talons onto the patterned surface of the bridge and shattering the pattern into a spider web of fractures. A dark, sharply angled triangular head, haloed with long black feathers reared up from underneath the span, screeching in the stallion's direction. Kerian's blade lunged out instantly, his military training leaping to the fore, the gleaming steel incredibly batted aside as a huge wing arched over him, placing Kerian under its shadow. Huge wing hooks latched onto the far edge of the span, anchoring the monster and stopping it from falling.

Kerian screamed as the creature's head came towards him. It was an old woman, her eyes cold and dark, set beneath brows of thick feathers. Her nose swept down from her high forehead terminating in a sharp angular point. The mouth was an impossibly wide 'V' shape that even as he watched, yawned open to reveal rows of wicked yellow teeth. The thick muscular neck swept down to a rounded breast covered in dark feathers and the shoulders became mighty wings slapping in the air, stabilising the horror's balance, battering the knight and his stallion and forcing them down.

Toledo kicked out hard, his back hooves stamping into the wing hooked on the span, the attack cracking several thin bones in its delicate structure, making the beast release its grip. The monster shrieked in anger, not sure now if it should attack the horse or turn its attention to the knight trying to slash at its claw. Its wings flapped furiously, struggling to maintain its position as its head darted forwards, determined to scoop Kerian up and crush him in its maw.

Kerian dropped back, missing the snapping attack by inches, then retaliated, darting swiftly forwards and skewering the monster's left eye, making it shriek in pain and drop off the edge with another ear-splitting crack of its wings. He slithered to the edge, staring into the murk, desperately trying to locate where the creature had gone, only for Toledo to neigh in alarm as the horror pulled itself up from the other side of the span and lunged for the undefended stallion.

Toledo reared up instinctively, yanking Kerian back towards him as he lashed out with a hoof and brought it crashing down on the monster's claw, just as Kerian stabbed upwards with his sword, striking the underside of the monster's jaw and forcing the creature to painfully shut its mouth. Kerian swung his blade around, looking to score a hit on the creature's breast, hoping its heart would be similar to a human one and lunged, only to find himself wrenched away as the guide rope snapped tight again. He was wrenched forwards into the mist away from Toledo and then to his horror felt the guide rope dragging him upwards, pulling him away from the surface.

Kerian struggled on tip-toe, still trying to remain upright as the rope brutally tightened about his waist and hoisted him up, only to drop him down again as if finding the additional weight too much. The knight was powerless to act. He debated cutting the rope as he was hoisted into the air again but had no idea what would happen if he did. Chances were that he would slide right off the span or miss it all together. At least whilst they were tethered, he still had a chance of survival, however slim it might be.

Several bright flashes of light lit up the sky, darting purple orbs streaking around in circles as if homing in on target, their paths winding closer and closer to slam into something above and explode. Kerian looked on as dark objects started to rain down about him, slack lengths of rope dropped past, pieces of quivering charred flesh, blackened feathers, a piece of claw. Kerian hit the bridge hard, dropping to one knee and crying out in pain. The scent of burnt flesh reached his nostrils, the harrowing sounds of his stallion in distress coming from behind him. Octavian appeared, dripping blood from several gashes across his ragged armour, his body limp, suspended at the end of the rope, his descent not quite the free fall, its progress slowed by the tautness of the rope stretching up into the mist above.

Kerian struggled to reach out and clutch the rope as Octavian's body fell past but the stretch was too dangerous to make without risking falling over the side. He watched, agonised by his impotence as the rope continued to snake past. Scrave descended through the haze, surrounded by a cloud of blackened and singed feathers swirling about him, his vertical speed keeping pace with Octavian's, his Elven face a mask of concentration, his left arm tightly constricted by the length of rope attached to the falling gypsy.

"I can't slow us." Scrave cried in dismay as he fell. "My spell cannot arrest our fall." He dropped past, following Octavian to be swallowed up by the mist. Kerian felt the coil of rope slide at his feet as it started to whip off after the two men. No! He could not be pulled over after them. He set off back towards Toledo, knowing that each staggered step was only a momentary respite from the yank that would send him tumbling after his companions.

Toledo neighed loudly, as he suddenly charged out of the mist, eyes rolling in fear, causing Kerian to dodge to the side or risk being trampled as his mount came through, its flank awash with blood from talon marks scoring its side. He snatched at the stallion's reins holding on for all he was worth as the rope at his waist finally snapped tight, yanking him off his feet and dragging him to the edge of the bridge.

The rope slowed as he dropped down, the reason for the knots along its length now clearly understood. As each knot hit the lip of the bridge, they slowed the rate of descent of the rope, juddering and shuddering as each knot caught in turn before jumping over the edge. Toledo dropped low, his hooves clattering, struggling to find purchase.

Kerian's legs scrabbled on the slick surface, his boots slipping and sliding as the rope continued to yank one knot at a time over into the abyss. He looked up at Toledo, noting the terrified look in the stallion's eyes as it took the strain of the two men and the weight of Kerian hanging from its saddle. It was an impossible task, something Toledo could never hope to manage but Kerian refused to give up without a fight. One of his boots slipped off the bridge, kicking out at thin air with nothing to prevent a fall. His other boot lashed out in panic pleading for grip and miraculously caught a foothold.

The weight snapped across Kerian's waist, making him scream. It felt like he was being cut in half! He struggled to hold firm, tried to bring his other boot around and gain purchase. His armour creaked and groaned, incredibly taking the brunt of the force and preventing his fears of being ripped apart from becoming reality. He spat his anger between clenched teeth and sucked in a breath, fearing he would soon pass out.

"Back up Toledo, please back up." He begged, knowing that if he let go of the reins then he, Octavian and Scrave were all finished. The stallion struggled to place itself, shaking its head, its body trembling as it strained against the incredible weight it was holding. Kerian held his breath as the titanic tug of war initially remained a tenuous stalemate.

"Come on boy." He willed. "I know you can do it." Toledo shuddered, his breath snorting from flared nostrils, blood dripping from his many wounds. Kerian dared not look behind him, knowing that if he stared into the mists, he would probably give up the fight and admit defeat. His boot scrabbled again then caught on something, finally giving him two legs with which to hold ground. Toledo wheezed loudly, then pulled with renewed vigour as Kerian strained to straighten his own beaten frame, his spine creaking and crackling in tune with the armour he was wearing. The rope shuddered as one knot popped back onto the span, making Kerian think it was his spine breaking and not the rope actually moving.

"One thing is for sure." Kerian grunted as he locked his legs. "I'm going to be a lot shorter when this over." He strained at the rope, trying to help Toledo pull back and was rewarded by first one, then another knot popping free over the edge and back onto the bridge. Toledo continued to retreat, his breathing laboured, the strain visibly telling on the stallion as it struggled inch by inch to pull back. They were doing it. They were actually doing it!

Something large and black swept across the bridge, wings cracking as they beat at the air.

"Come on!" Kerian screamed. "Pull damn you!"

The return of the winged monsters galvanised Toledo into action making the horse pull harder than ever, drawing on every reserve it had as it struggled to pull the rope back onto the bridge. A claw landed on the span beside them, crushing the rope beneath it and giving Toledo and Kerian an unexpected reprieve as the weight they were holding suddenly ceased.

The knight recognised the chance for what it was, rolling backwards as another claw came down before darting between the creature's legs, pushing his way through the monster's tail feathers and back towards the edge of the span. The massive bird hopped as it felt the spare rope coil about its legs. Jumping up only for the rope to snap tight again, pulling its legs out from under it and smacking its face onto the bridge.

Toledo judged the moment to perfection, kicking out in a last-ditch effort that caught the creature in the face making its neck snap back and it suddenly went still. Kerian dropped to his knees and stared down off the edge of the bridge, following the rope down and was surprised to see the struggling figure of Scrave just below him. The rope was still constricted around Scrave's left arm, the limb now at an unnatural angle, the hand swollen and black as the weight of Octavian kept the rope tighter than a vice.

Kerian watched the Elf twist one way then the other, his right arm flailing at the left, beating the useless appendage in frustration at his failure to free himself from the ropes so cruelly binding him. Scrave reached into his robes with his free hand, struggling for a moment then let out a cry of triumph as he drew out a weapon, confirming Kerian's suspicions.

He stared down upon the malevolent dagger, not daring to believe his eyes that the cursed blade had managed to find itself near to him again. Ruby eyes sparkled, gilded scales gleamed and a cold chill seemed to penetrate Kerian's bones causing him to shiver. The dagger writhed about Scrave's wrist settling itself easily within the Elf's grasp displaying a familiarity that could only have come with experience. Scrave grunted as he tried to stop himself swinging about, then moved the blade to beneath his arm and began sawing at the rope.

"Put your blade away!" Kerian shouted down. His eyes still mesmerized by the gleaming snake. "If you cut the rope Octavian will fall to his death."

"He's dead anyway." Scrave snapped back. "Let the Harpies have him."

"He's not dead until I say he is." Kerian retorted angrily, alarmed at the callous reply. "Now put away your blade and let me haul you up."

The serpent hissed angrily in Scrave's hand, as if urging the Elf to continue hacking at the rope. Scrave moved to do so, determined that the young knight above him was nothing he could not handle.

"Maybe I'm not making myself clear." Kerian replied, an icy tone to his voice, causing Scrave to look up mid-saw and see that the knight had placed his own blade against the rope just above the Elf's reach. "If you cut my friend free. I shall have no hesitation to do the same to you."

"Do you honestly feel you can take me?" Scrave threatened. "I was killing people before your father was a gleam in your grandfather's eye. I can get up this rope in seconds. I doubt you can cut through the rope in that time." Kerian looked down at Scrave and muttered under his breath. It was possible the Elf could make good on his promise. It was time to up the ante.

"Maybe you are right." He replied drawing his blade across the rope, allowing several strands to part with ominous twangs.

"What are you doing?" Scrave cried out in disbelief. "Are you mad? What about your friend?"

"What about him. You have already told me he is dead. Now put the weapon away or I drop you both." Something moved behind Kerian, a rustle of feathers moving across stone, a snort of alarm from Toledo. "Now! Before I make good on my threat."

Scrave scowled angrily then, recognising he could not win, slipped his hand back into his tunic and let the dagger slide reluctantly back into its sheath.

Kerian staggered to his feet and grabbed the rope with both hands, trying not to think about the weight hanging on the other end and pulled for all he was worth. The Harpy lying behind him on the span jerked its leg, inadvertently aiding him and yanking the Elf up higher as its claws became more entangled in the rope.

Inch by inch, grunt by grunt, Kerian pulled the Elf higher, until Scrave was suddenly hanging onto the lip of the span with his good hand and then was rolling onto the bridge and gasping in pain, as he finally managed to free his arm from the rope's tenacious grip. Kerian grunted as Scrave rolled free, realising that the Elf weighed almost nothing. The burden on Kerian's back remained as crushing as ever but he dared not give up, pulling hand over hand gritting his teeth and cursing aloud as he pulled. Slowly but surely, the limp figure of Octavian rose from the mist's embrace.

"Never, ever, threaten me boy." Scrave whispered in Kerian's ear, poked his dagger hard into the small of Kerian's back, causing the knight to falter in his rescue attempt and curse at his own stupidity. "With one thrust I can send the two of you to your graves. So tell me, no plead with me, as to why I should not finish you both now."

"Well I for one have no idea what to do at the end of this span." Kerian replied, trying to keep the anger from his voice, not daring to move. "We could travel all this way and find the gateway onwards locked, our way forward barred. Is that a risk you are willing to take?" Toledo whinnied anxiously as the Harpy struggled to move again, kicking out with its legs and uttering a keen shrilling sound of distress as it gently fluttered its wings.

"You have a choice to make Scrave but hurry, I cannot hold Octavian all day." Kerian warned. A shriek of alarm cut the air, the Harpy finally regaining consciousness, one wing thrashing towards the two men, causing Scrave to spin around and duck as the black feathers passed inches above his head. The Elf ran over to the struggling beast, reaching into his robes and pulling free the serpent dagger, to strike repeatedly at the creature's neck, causing it to thrash and moan in pain as its ichor stained the bridge beneath it.

Kerian refused to look, shuddering as he heard the monster's inhuman shrieks at each plunge of the cursed weapon. He pulled hard at the ropes before him, desperate for his body's punishment to be over with, pleading with himself that he had the strength to achieve the impossible, until with a monumental effort, he finally pulled the gypsy to safety and collapsed beside him shaking with exhaustion.

Octavian looked a mess. His clothes had been ragged to start with and where his body was exposed it had been lacerated by the wicked claws of the creatures Scrave called Harpies, yet despite the gory mess, the wounds were not as grievous as Kerian had initially feared and more superficial in nature. A ragged breath passed the gypsy's lips causing Kerian to finally release the breath he never realised he was holding. Octavian's eyes flickered open and he looked about confused, unsure where he was.

"Nice to see you are joining us in the land of living once again." Kerian joked, the relief palpable in his tone. He staggered to his feet, his joints on fire and walked back past the still twitching Harpy towards Toledo and rubbed the exhausted animal behind the ears.

"Oh Toledo. If only you understood what I feel for you right now." He ran his hand along the stallion's flank, noting the ragged wounds, the shaking of the stallion's frame and its loud snorts. He reached out to untie the guide rope, realising with surprise that his own hands were shaking with the shock of the moment. He clenched his fist tightly, trying to calm himself, before reaching up and finally freeing the rope.

"I guarantee you when we have finished this journey you shall have a thorough rubdown, rolled oats and as many mares as you can sire." He smiled reaching out to stroke Toledo's neck.

The blast of wind hit Kerian like a wall, making his ears ring, knocking him to the floor and hitting his head. He heard Toledo scream, felt warm blood splashing across his face and when his vision finally cleared Toledo, his stallion, the loyal mount that had carried him across the desert, faced down ghouls and terrors that would have sent normal men screaming for their beds, was gone, several solitary black feathers spinning on the bridges surface the only explanation to his fate.

* * * * * *

"Now that is ridiculous! I mean how is a Halfling supposed to reach that?" Ashe gestured, pointing up to a brick in the labyrinth wall several feet higher than he could reach. "Come on Rauph, I'm telling you that is the way out. Push the button quickly."

Rauph struggled to tear his attention from the sight of the scholar being sucked into the jelly. He winced as the man screamed and turned his face towards the Minotaur, allowing Rauph to witness the horrors of seeing the skin of the man's face sucked hungrily from his skull, starbursts of crimson erupting inside the gelatinous mass and colouring its yellowed surface in a scarlet mist.

"What did you say?" the navigator mumbled turning back to his diminutive ally.

"The button Rauph, the button on the wall!" Rauph followed Ashe's gaze and noticed the worn brick set at his eye height, a small mark carved upon its surface setting it apart from the rest of the wall.

"What do you want me to do with the brick?" Rauph asked, his gaze being dragged back to the figure of the scholar, still struggling despite his horrific injuries, as he was finally consumed by the jelly.

"Push it!" Ashe screamed. "Pull it! Move it! I don't care just do something! Before that jelly gets to us. The way out has to be here. It just has to be." Rauph pushed at the brick and felt it click beneath his stubby fingers.

"Now what?" He asked, warily eyeing the jelly sliding towards them. Barely ten feet separated them from the creature now and Ashe was showing no signs of avoiding the danger. "Do you think you should be moving away from that thing now?"

"I don't understand it." Ashe shook his head, as the roar of the crowd rose above them and the jelly bore down on them. "That should have worked. It makes no sense. Hit it again." Rauph reached forwards and pushed the button again, feeling the same click as he let go. He turned to Ashe and shrugged his shoulders.

"I think it's broken. We need to go now." The jelly was now only six feet away and Rauph was considering grabbing Ashe and running with him.

"Where to?" Ashe screamed. "Push the damn button again."

"I told you it doesn't work." Rauph replied leaning over and pushing the brick once again. "See?"

"I don't understand. You must be doing it wrong. Lift me up so I can have a go."

"We really need to run now." Rauph replied.

"Pick me up!" Ashe screamed waving his arms about and causing Sinders wings to flap in agitation. "I'm telling you that's the way." Rauph leaned down, swung Ashe up onto his shoulders and moved over to the wall to let Ashe examine the brick.

"Well it doesn't come out of the wall; it doesn't move up or down. It has to be a push." The brick clicked into place once more and then popped out again. "Damn it! What are we doing wrong?" Rauph moved a nervous step away from the jelly nearly upsetting Ashe and accidentally dropping the Halfling into it.

"Where do you think you are going?" Ashe snapped angrily. "I'm telling you that's the way out of here." He stretched his arm out, pulling at Rauph's hair as he tried to shift position, obscuring the Navigator's vision and causing the Minotaur to put out an arm to steady himself. His hand swept bare inches above the surface of the gelatinous blob causing Ashe to shriek out a warning, just as the Halfling's hand hit the brick again.

Rauph continued to struggle, reaching out his other hand to touch the far side of the passageway. His hand brushed the masonry and touched another brick set at exactly the same height, in exactly the same place. Both bricks pushed in, both bricks clicked and the floor of the passageway suddenly opened up and dropped Ashe and Rauph into the darkness before rising back up and closing with a boom.

"Well that was unexpected!" Ashe coughed, struggling in the pitch darkness. "A trapdoor in the floor. Who would have seen that? Are you okay Rauph? I can't see you as there are no lights on down here. If only they had served me carrots in prison."

"I am now you are off my head." Rauph replied, his voice booming in the darkness. "Why is it so quiet down here?" Ashe stopped scrabbling about in the darkness, trying to ignore the gooey strands of something that kept coating his hands wherever he put them down.

"It does seem odd that there are no spectators down here." Ashe replied. "Maybe we pressed the wrong button? Can you find a way to make a light please because there is something on the floor and it's all gooey and not in a nice way?"

"Well it's obvious why there are no spectators," Rauph replied helpfully. "I mean how would they see what was going on? Hang on." There was a scraping in the darkness. Flint sparking and suddenly a small flame flickered into being, cupped inside the Minotaur's massive hands. Ashe looked down at his feet and took in his surroundings with his usual tact.

"We definitely pushed the wrong button."

The flame went out plunging them both into darkness again. Sinders shuffled nervously on Ashe's shoulder causing the Halfling to 'coo' gently to reassure the bird.

"We need something to feed the flame." Rauph mumbled.

"Hold on." There was some scrambling in the dark then Ashe said "I have some things you can set fire to. Damn now my fingers are all sticking together."

"Ashe are you ready?" Rauph enquired. "I'm going to strike the flint now." An explosive flare lit the darkness as Rauph turned towards the sound of the scuttling. Ashe looked up at his hairy friend as the light flared and noticed the Minotaur had stupidly turned his back to him. He stepped lightly around the sticky corpses lying at his feet, kicked aside a dusty skull and ran around in front of the Minotaur, holding a bundle of rags in his hands.

"Okay Rauph use this stuff." Ashe held up the rags trying to catch the flame but the Navigator's hands were too high above him. "Down here stupid!" Ashe laughed, jumping up and down trying to reach the tinder box in the Minotaur's grasp. He knocked Rauph's hand plunging the room into darkness again.

"Oh come on Rauph. Let's be serious." More scrabbling sounded in the darkness as Ashe felt about on the floor, finally finding the box so he could strike the tinder and make a fire. The sparks caught on the dusty rags and Ashe had a fire going in moments "There you go, no problem at all…" Ashe looked up and noticed that Rauph was still staring past him up at the ceiling. He turned around anxious to see what the navigator was staring at.

"Oh!" Ashe exclaimed. "Wow… That's got to be one of the biggest spiders I have ever seen."

Chapter Forty-Six

When the wounded Octavian finally led the group of weary travellers off the span and through the gateway at the end, there was no feeling of elation, no sense of relief at having completed the dangerous trek. Not one voice was raised in triumph, instead the three sombre men stepped off the span's streaked colours, out onto a loamy forest floor and shivered at the cold weather swirling around them.

"What is this place?" Scrave whispered, turning about, his worn leather boots scuffing up the heavy carpet of grey green pine needles at his feet, releasing an acrid odour of decaying fungus spores into the air. He stared up at the towering heights of the silvered coloured trees standing silently around him, almost to where they kissed an anaemic sky, noting the skeletal, naked limbs upon which nothing appeared to grow.

The gateway swirled itself closed, leaving a huge tree trunk exactly where the path terminated. Kerian noted this with a grateful nod and relaxed his grip on his sword. There would be no going back that way. The nightmare of the span was now behind them. He just wondered what terrors they had replaced it with.

"Welcome to Blackthorn" Octavian sighed, sinking down to the floor and dropping the bloodied remains of his saddlebags beside a large clump of yellow and white spotted toadstools. He rested his back against the bark of the tree trunk and dropped his chin to his chest. "Now If you don't mind, I would like to catch my breath."

Kerian stepped away from the group, his mind thinking back over their ill-fated trip, still stunned that Toledo was gone, brutally snatched from him by one of the Harpies that hunted in the mists. Octavian's mount had fared little better, its remains discovered further along the bridge. The poor animal torn to pieces, leaving just the saddlebag that Octavian had managed to salvage.

At least the gypsy had saddlebags! All of Kerian's belongings were gone, snatched away in a second. His mother's mirror, his diary, even his old black outfit, stolen by the accursed birds.

He hoped they choked on them.

Kerian let his eyes scan their surroundings. Row upon row of trees stretching away, branches devoid of any vegetation, dark blues, slate greys as far as the eye could see. The ground was not much better, dips and hollows choked with rotten vegetation and windfall strangled by wiry brambles and briars adorned with wicked thorns. Occasional clumps of bright fungus added much needed colour to this painter's palette of gloom.

A pathway snaked away through the trees, drawing Kerian's eye to follow, only for the sinister figure of Scrave to step into view. Damn that Elf. He looked the healthiest amongst them and that was saying something. Even his arm where the rope had crushed it on the span appeared to have miraculously improved in colour and plumped out again, the skin smooth, the limb no longer bent at a strange angle. Dark magic to be sure.

Kerian refused to meet the Elf's eye and continued his survey of the landscape, completing his sweep, noting where the path climbed via slow switchbacks to the left, surmounting an imposing granite cliff, its ominous grey dotted in orange mosses and clumps of red grasses, making it seem like the rock face was haemorrhaging blood.

"Where have you brought us this time, Octavian?" Kerian whispered to himself, exhaling deeply, his breath fogging the cold damp air.

The trio settled into an uncomfortable silence. Octavian winced at every intake of breath; his wounds clearly troublesome. Scrave leaned against a tree, his right hand inside his tunic, probably gaining comfort from his cursed blade and shaking his left arm as if the Elf was trying to regain circulation to the crushed limb. Kerian rubbed absentmindedly at his clothing, hoping the blood stains from Toledo's violent departure would come out of the desert fabric. After all, this was the only outfit he had left to his name! He wrinkled his nose feeling an itch on his face and lifted his blood-stained hand to his forehead, feeling the scab-like texture of congealed blood spattered there.

"So where does the road lead?" Scrave opened, breaking the silence. "Which way do we go now?" Octavian looked up at the Elf, his face a picture of weariness.

"The road leads two ways: Glowme Castle lies in that direction," he pointed towards where the path climbed up the cliff face. "Or you can go the other way to the hamlet of Thernout."

"What's at the castle?" the Elf asked, his eyes tracing the route and clearly not happy at what he saw.

"My wife and daughter." Octavian replied as if the weight of the world were upon his shoulders. "They are ransomed there and I have no treasure with which to free them."

"I'm sure we can come to some arrangement." Kerian stated confidently, despite the fact his face clearly betrayed the fact, that he was not exactly sure how this miracle would be achieved.

"Well I never signed up for anything like that." Scrave replied. "Thernout you say! I shall look forward to good food and warm company. Join me once you have finished having fun storming the castle." He waved in Octavian's direction then paused in front of Kerian.

"Damn if there isn't something about you that reminds me of my Kerian." Scrave offered. "It's like you are his younger brother. Be careful you don't live long enough to turn into him. He was also a suspicious bastard. It might just get you killed."

"Many have tried." Kerian replied arching his eyebrow, his hand inching towards the hilt of his blade.

"Until we meet again." Scrave responded, his gaze looking down to Kerian's moving hand and then back up to meet Kerian's gaze, before tutting, shrugging his shoulders and turning to throw a wave over his shoulder as he walked away.

"I'll look forward to that." Kerian replied, walking over to where Octavian still sat against the tree and offered his hand. "Are you ready to rescue your wife and child?" Octavian looked up at Kerian's hand then reluctantly took it and let the knight pull him to his feet.

"Kerian you look a state!" he remarked, taking in that his friend was covered in dried blood from head to toe.

"You don't look much better." Kerian replied pointing out the hodgepodge armour the gypsy wore and the lacerations covering his body where his skin dared show itself. "We are hardly dressed for the occasion."

Octavian winced as he threw his saddlebag over his shoulder, then gazed wistfully after the departing Elf.

"You know for all his sombreness and unpredictability I was rather hoping that Elf would help us rescue my wife and child. He was quite good in a fight. What's the story between you two?"

"He's not that good a fighter." Kerian replied with a smile. "I killed him once."

Octavian looked after the Elf, watching him make his way determinedly through the trees towards the road.

"Well take it from me. You didn't do a very good job!"

* * * * * *

The two companions found the trail tough going, the persistent inclines and switchbacks sapping the little strength they had remaining. Their boots frequently slipped in the slurry at the edge of the road where carriage wheels and animal tracks had rutted the trail before them. Frequent pauses for breath and the repositioning of Octavian's saddlebag made the thought of restarting the climb a distinctly unpalatable one.

Every muscle of Kerian's back ached, his calves felt like they were on fire but every time he looked over towards Octavian and caught an unguarded look, he saw a man with defeat clearly etched across his face. A failure who knew with certainty that he was walking towards his doom. Kerian had to admire Octavian's spirit, for the gypsy never faltered in his steps, his lip never trembled. Instead he stared resolutely ahead and prepared to meet his fate head on.

There was no way Kerian was going to let him face that fate alone.

The track ahead of them curled gently to the left and slowly started levelling out, giving the companions much needed respite from their arduous climb. As the trees thinned, a breath-taking panoramic view of the grey spindle covered valleys presented itself. Slate grey lakes dotted the landscape, nestled in the cupped valleys between mountainous peaks frosted delicately with snow. As the track wound perilously along the edge of the cliff, it revealed a dizzying drop and finally allowed Kerian his first glimpse of castle Glowme.

It was perched on a column of stone, set apart from the surrounding mountain. The sides of the peak on which it rested dotted with yet more grey spindle-like trees. Access to the castle was via a misshapen stone arch that reminded Kerian of a withered arm and spindly hand that reached out from the ground they were traversing and appeared to grip the base of the castle in its withered grasp as if it were trying to throttle the keep.

Four square towers set the corners of the castle, with a stark portcullis marking the entrance between two huge stone gargoyles armed with spears. The main keep grew from within the towers like a child's sandcastle, the walls not quite true, several areas of the keep crumbling where ivy and briars had consumed them. Tall windows lit from within by sickly yellow light dotted walls of cold slate grey that looked stark and unwelcoming despite the orange glow of the setting sun. Smaller towers sprouted from within the walls, guard posts set behind crenellations, their sharp roofs looking like arrows pointing to the cloudy sky. Behind these, set to the back of the castle, there rose a larger more robust tower, a huge stained-glass window set within its curved walls.

Kerian took a long look, judging the defences of the place, how difficult it would be to scale the walls and the long drop that any invaders would face if they were to fail. It was quite a fortress; all be it one falling into ruin. Something about it made the knight shiver, he felt ill at ease and turned to voice his concerns to Octavian but the look on the gypsy's face stopped him from speaking. It was a look of reminiscence but no good memories were being recalled here. Octavian looked like he was reliving a nightmare.

"His laboratory is in the taller tower." The gypsy whispered aloud, nervously licking his lips. "That's where he does all of his experiments." Kerian took a deep breath, feeling the chill in his companion's words but determined to put on a brave face for his friend. He needed to act on this whilst he could still feel the courage to do so because just standing here staring at this gothic citadel was making him feel more and more like running for the hills.

"Then I guess we had better let him know he is having guests for dinner." Kerian replied, nonchalantly, patting Octavian on the shoulder before setting off down the path

"That's what I'm hoping to avoid." Octavian replied ominously.

They walked side by side following the track until they reached the bridge that led to the castle. Two gargoyles stood sentry on this end of the bridge barring entrance with their spears. Kerian stared up at the towering stone carvings, easily twenty feet tall. Admiring the artistry in the creature's tails, spiralled horns, curved talons, pointed teeth, stubby wings and protruding tongues.

"They are quite intimidating." He confessed, moving to step onto the bridge.

"Halt!" boomed a voice. Kerian looked about for the source but could only see the gargoyles so he took another step, then jumped back as the two spears slammed down onto the bridge in front of him.

Octavian pushed Kerian aside and stepped forward as the two gargoyles creaked and grated, their tails dropping across the pathway to prevent anyone passing below their spears, whilst their lips pulled back in a fearsome snarl.

"Tell our master that I have returned." Octavian replied, staring up at the nearest gargoyle, his arms crossed as if he were ordering about something that was half his size instead of the other way around. Kerian flinched as the other gargoyle leant down, its stone skin rasping as it moved, nostrils flaring to sniff at Octavian, before turning to sniff at Kerian.

"We know you." It confirmed turning to Octavian, "but we don't know who this is." The stone monster drew itself up and raised its spear, its threatening stance unmistakable. "What is his business here?"

"He is with me and is helping bring tribute to pay ransom for my wife and daughter." Octavian growled, his voice taking on a noticeable animal snarl. The gargoyle stood up and stared into space for a moment as if communicating with someone unseen, then leant back down again.

"Our master bids you welcome and enter." He replied his voice all gravely and rough. The gargoyle's tails rolled aside; their spears parted, revealing the entrance to Glowme castle. Kerian stepped through the animated statues and pretended to act confident, striding purposefully across the bridge with Octavian at his side.

"Can I let you into a little secret?" Kerian whispered, his face set in a stern look as he took in the portcullis slowly cranking up before them revealing the dark sinister throat of the keep.

"What's that?" Octavian replied, struggling to keep his own stern countenance, despite the fact his saddlebags were slapping against his legs and ruining a lot of the effect.

"I'm really not that confident going in here." Kerian confessed. Octavian's footsteps staggered and he choked loudly.

"What?"

"I mean now we are getting closer the castle does look rather foreboding. I mean just look at this place. It's like a bad horror story. I expect to see bats flying around! I've an image of a cloaked maniac sitting at an organ playing depressing music, suffering from a serious dental problem and a bad case of photophobia."

"Well you've got the psychosis and the rotting teeth right." Octavian replied solemnly but he doesn't need an organ, the spirits haunting the halls make enough noise for that. And instead of bats, he has hounds like me."

* * * * * *

Scrave's eyes followed the meandering track ahead and wondered for what seemed like the hundredth time how far it was to this damned hamlet. He felt like he had walked for hours, surrounded by nothing but spindly trees and prickly briars. Nothing seemed to live here. Not a hopping rabbit, a bouncing squirrel, a foraging boar. No birds sang, hooted or squawked. Indeed, the only sound he heard was his own footsteps, a wet squelching soundtrack to a boring monotonous journey.

The scenery never appeared to change. He was sure he had seen the clump of fungus on the ground, sitting over by the large dead tree on the left several hours ago. Even the tree over to the right with the twisted branch and the lopsided slant looked suspiciously familiar.

He looked down at the tracks on the road and noted the fact that someone had been walking the path before him, quite recently too from the look of the fresh boot prints. Well if someone else had walked along here then it stood to reason the path went somewhere.

Scrave looked around again and noticed that the sun had appeared to jump across the sky. He had no recollection of the time passing but now there were more tracks on the road ahead of him and they seemed to be wearing the same sized boots. He slowed to a stop, a strange suspicion rising in his mind.

His boot squelched into the mud alongside the nearest footprint, then he carefully withdrew his muddy footwear and stepped back feeling his heart sink as his eyes confirmed the nagging feeling he was dreading. The tracks were his. He had walked this length of the road several times already. The Elf swallowed the curse rising to his lips and stepped over to the other side of the track, sure enough his boot marks were there too.

How could this be. It made no sense. Something slithered behind his eyepatch causing him to start.

"What is going on?" he muttered.

"Denarisssss." A voice whispered in his ear.

"No!" he screamed aloud. "You're messing with my head again! You've been turning me about!" He thumped his forehead with the heel of his hand, striking himself just above the eyepatch, venting his fury and frustration, before calming himself to lower his hand and realise what a ridiculous situation he found himself in.

He needed to think, needed to figure out what was going on but with that infernal worm squirming at the back of his eye, controlling his actions, he was powerless. He felt like ripping the eyepatch off and sticking his finger into his eye socket and rummaging around in the gore, not quitting until he had pulled the parasite free, consequences be damned! Then he stopped himself.

"What do you mean Denaris!" Scrave snapped, shouting the question out and making himself jump at the loudness of the sound as his breath rasped in his ears. "Denaris isn't here!"

"Yes he is..." the little voice in his mind whispered. "You had him and you let him get away."

"That wasn't our Denaris!" Scrave shouted again. "He's too young! He's..."

Someone was standing in the road ahead of him. Scrave uttered a cry of shock, his hand reaching for the dagger inside his tunic and getting caught in the folds, he looked down then up again and the figure was gone. He could have sworn he'd seen someone. A knight, ancient clothes armour, the works, looking directly at him.

"Hello? Is anyone there?"

He spun, feeling as if someone were standing at his shoulder, his feeling of unease growing. Was that a tree or another knight? A rock or a man observing his every move? He needed to flee but what way, the damned thing inside his head had got him so confused he did not know which way was to the hamlet and which way was to the castle.

Someone was behind him; this was not his imagination. He could hear breathing and caught a scent of perfume.

Scrave spun round, coming up short, his face inches from the tantalisingly beautiful sorceress who had been such a part of his dreams these weeks past. Her beautiful long hair, the tight bodice of her outfit drawing his gaze down from her piercing eyes and sultry smile for just a split second to admire her smooth cleavage.

"Oh hi gorgeous, fancy seeing both of you here…" The sword hilt struck him right above the eye dropping the Elf to the floor and leaving him senseless, his skin swelling almost instantly.

Justina looked about her, taking in their bleak surroundings and shivered as the magic portal spiralled shut behind her. She pulled her cloak tighter around her shoulders then clicked her fingers, feeling the material turn from silk to a thick fur coat.

The bearer stepped up alongside her, his book in his arms, beckoning for his knights to step away from the trees they were hiding behind and drag the groaning Scrave up from the ground. Justina walked over to where they supported the Elf and traced one beautifully painted nail down the Elf's face to his chest before she slid her hand inside his tunic and finally grasped her prize.

"You see Kaplain," she purred. "That is how you get your man."

* * * * * *

The courtyard of Glowme castle revealed itself in all its glory as Kerian and Octavian stepped out from under the creaking portcullis and passed through the outer wall of the castle. The floor beneath their boots was uneven, making walking unsteady and the flags were slippery with algae in areas where the light of the sun rarely shone. On the mud splattered flagstones remaining, some lifting at the edges, others cracked and broken, the companions could identify where nature was attempting to re-establish a foothold, with spindly blood red grass stalks and ferrous coloured clumps of moss occupying areas not often traversed.

A stained fountain gurgled as if being strangled, yet failed to produce a stream of water, its bowl half-filled with foul smelling dark sludge upon which clumps of buoyant moss from the gables and eaves of the keep, bobbed gently. An obligatory gibbet cage, complete with skeletal occupant, swung from a large hook in the castle wall, alongside limply hanging rotting flags coated in fungus, their designs too faded to discern. Two spluttering braziers set either side of the main doors raised cloying smoke into the air.

"What a dump!" Kerian remarked. "You say someone actually lives here?" He glanced towards Octavian expecting to see the gypsy's usual cocky smile and instead faced an expression full of concern. They advanced towards the oak doors and Kerian raised his fist to knock then paused, remembering the face of the man alongside him and that Octavian's wife and child lay within. Instead of knocking he pushed the heel of his hand against the door, his other hand dropping to the hilt of his sword.

The door creaked open as if on arthritic hinges, popping, crunching and shuddering, somehow managing to catch on a stone under the bottom edge of the door and scraping along the dusty stone flooring beyond, with Kerian wincing at every agonising inch. The corridor beyond lay in shadow, stone pillars stretching ahead into the unknown, a wide sweeping staircase lazily gyrating up to a level above them. Ivy grew over the walls, poking through holes in the doorframe, winding its way up and under the tapestries hanging forlornly on the stonework. Rugs exhaled dust as the two men stepped across them, their footsteps clearly marked as they made progress.

Glass cases were set back into alcoves along the right wall, from which a soft illumination flickered, as if the source of the light were alive. Kerian cautiously advanced, his senses alert for sounds that the castle's occupants were aware of their presence. Glowme castle creaked and groaned about him as if breathing. It was like being back on the *El Defensor* when she gently rocked at berth but this sound was menacing. He reached his hand out to part the leaves of a plant positioned before the first alcove and found his gloves holding nothing but powder, that crumbled at his unwanted touch.

Now he was closer to the alcove Kerian was finally able to see into the glass cases and the grisly secret contained. He leaned closer, taking in the pile of rags and dried bones heaped haphazardly at the base of the cabinet, staring in fascination at the gently spiralling column of vapour that appeared to dance about them, pausing for a moment in an area before jumping across to another and examining the remains as if searching. He shook his head, was he imagining a sound coming from the glass, like a wailing, sobbing sound? Kerian moved closer, gently placing his hand against the glass.

The column of vapour turned instantly, rearing up and transforming into a ghostly figure that charged the glass surface, mouth wide, screaming its anger to the world, only to crash into the other side of the glass and explode like a ripe fruit, dripping ghostly residue down the inside of its prison, to pool on the floor beside the bones that had belonged to it in a past life. A keen wailing rose anew from the ghost as it sought to collect itself again.

Kerian jumped back, only to step directly into Octavian and jump again. Whipping round as he struggled to bring his sword to bear in the confines of the passageway and finding himself entangled with Octavian's saddlebags.

"By Adden!" he cursed, realising that the ghostly glow he had been witnessing was the spectral remains of the creature in the case. He looked at Octavian's face, made ghostly in the darkness and the reflection of the supernatural luminance; taking in the gypsy's wide eyes, before Kerian turned to stare off into the darkness where alcove upon alcove flickered and wailed. "How many of these cases does he have?"

"Hundreds" Octavian whispered solemnly. They moved on, carefully walking down the passageway, ghostly wails from apparitions trapped in their glass tombs heralding each step. Here a spectral woman sobbed and wrung her hands in shimmering ectoplasm, there a ghostly knight, pushing against each corner of the glass, struggling to find a means of escape from his entombment.

"Is your wife and child in one of these?" Kerian whispered, horrified by the suffering and torment he was witnessing. He glanced back over his shoulder and realised that Octavian was struggling to contain his emotions, his eyes swollen with tears. The gypsy bit his lip and simply nodded. Kerian turned, his features grim. This could not be allowed to continue. These spectral phantoms needed to be laid to rest, given proper funerals and allowed to pass over rather than serve as ghostly lanterns for a ruined castle.

"He keeps them here to remind others what will happen if they fail to pay ransom." Octavian offered.

"But they are all dead." Kerian replied. "Do these people not know this?"

"They still pay to release the bodies, even if their loved ones have passed." Octavian replied grimly. "And there is always the slim hope that the ransom will be gathered and paid in time for their family to be released alive." Kerian noted the timbre of his friend's voice and shuddered, realising this was Octavian's forlorn hope that the gypsy was describing. The two men slipped into an uneasy silence, heading towards a door at the end of the passageway, Octavian paused to actually sniff the air.

"What is it?" Kerian hissed. "What do you smell?" Octavian shook his head as if something were buzzing about his ears, then gripped it in both hands, his face contorting in pain.

"He's in there waiting." Octavian grunted, dropping to his knees, his hands still gripping his skull. "Kerian you have to get away from here. He is too strong he is too..." the words were lost as Octavian fell to the floor, his skin warping, his body making sickening snapping and crunching noises as his limbs started to re-shape and metamorphose into the creature Kerian had fought in the desert.

Kerian felt torn between staying and helping with his friend's agony or trying to find a reason for it. Even as he edged away from Octavian's snarling form, the door ahead of him creaked slowly open revealing a room with bookcases on the walls and a roaring fire in the hearth. Kerian stepped forward, relieved to leave his friend in the passage, whilst taking in the sight of tables and chairs covered in large dusty volumes, stacked on every available space apart from a high-backed chair around which lay several dark and snarling figures.

A slender, blonde haired man sat in the chair, his hair wild and wispy, his thin slitted eyes scrutinizing the knight from behind a pair of wire framed spectacles of smeared glass. He wore a dirty, stained apron over patched trousers and a linen shirt streaked with grime. In his lap was an open ledger showing pages of tight dark script and drawings of what looked like coloured prisms. The man leant forward, his hand dropping to stroke the hair of a warped creature laying at his side, his pale fingers pulling tightly at a luminous stripe of white fur running down the creature's back. Her lip curled back and her hackles rose as Kerian stepped further into the room but her dark eyes showed nothing but pain as her master pulled at her hide.

"Steady. Agnezkia. Steady. Is that any way to greet our guests? Please, do come in." The man gestured towards a small stool that sat in front of him, a tray of something red, moist and shiny perched upon it. "Just move the tray, place it carefully on the ground." Kerian stepped closer and identified the morsels as pieces of dark flesh sitting in a pool of congealing blood. He had no intentions of moving the tray and made no move to do so. If this upset his strange host then so be it. Kerian swallowed hard and tried to ignore the tightness he suddenly felt in his throat.

"I have come to pay the ransom on Octavian's wife and child and wish them and Octavian released into my custody," he stated, with more confidence than he actually felt. The door crashed open   behind him and Octavian, now fully transformed into his animal form, prowled into the room and stalked over to the tray, his long pink tongue lapping the congealed blood before hooking a succulent piece of meat into his jaws and swallowing it with relish.

"I don't think my hound wishes to go anywhere." The man stated calmly. "And I for one have no intentions of giving him up." He clicked his fingers and Octavian immediately stopped eating, blood dripping from his jaws. He padded over to the strange host and bowed his head before him in subservience, before turning and fixing Kerian with a dark emotionless stare.

"Welcome home my hound." The mysterious host began. "You are a little late but your arrival is not unexpected. Now, why don't you introduce me to your new plaything."

The Labyris Knight

-: Part Four :-

The Descent of Darkness

"You must experience the depth of terror in darkness,
before you can truly appreciate the wonder of light."

Ana Silvestri Gypsy Fortune Teller

Chapter Forty-Seven

"I think Captain Aelius that your men need to improve on their fitness." Wanessa snapped, swinging her stubby legs from the litter that had carried her substantial bulk up the stairs. "I was going to invite one or two of your men back to my bedchamber after the tournament to celebrate in style but they don't look able to draw breath let alone satisfy my needs."

"Guards fall in!" Aelius roared, making his wheezing troop stagger back to their feet and form the semblance of a line. "The Lady Wanessa says you are all a disgrace. I tend to agree with her." He moved closer to his troops, approaching one who was really struggling with his wheezing. He leaned in close as if to examine the Minotaur's uniform then whispered in his ear.

"Looks like you dodged a crossbow bolt eh? I know she likes you!" He moved away winking. "Now I am so disappointed I want you all down those stairs patrolling the lower levels no one is allowed up here but me! Do you understand? And when I summon you to carry these fair ladies down again, you all better be fit and ready. Now jump to it!"

The Minotaur ran for the stairs, eager to get away, leaving Aelius alone to guard the two most powerful members of the Matriarchy. He moved over into the shadows by the archway and took up his post, his grey eyes observed Mora and Wanessa walking towards the table upon which the ceremonial goblet and wine awaited.

Aelius knew the procedure. The goblet was filled once the Labyris was gained, then the departing Matriarch would pass the goblet to the winner as a mark of allegiance and fellowship. The victor toasted from the goblet first, signifying to all that the departing monarch was willing to serve her replacement, that she held the Labyris knight in higher esteem than herself. A drink to herald an arrival, a drink to seal a departure.

He watched as the serving girl moved to offer wine to the two female Minotaur, then offered a tray of finger food that Wanessa snatched from her hand, before pushing her away. It showed the arrogance of the two women that they failed to acknowledge those who worked for them and whom they deemed lower than their own exalted station.

Aelius took a deep calming breath and moved back into the alcove his mouth suddenly dry. What he was doing was incredibly risky, it was treason, punishable by death but he knew he had to make a stand for what was right, needed to give Kristoph every advantage he could. His eyes may have started to fail him but he knew for a fact that the serving girl who came up the stairs had black hair. The one serving them now was distinctly blonde.

* * * * * *

The crowd were clearly upset, loudly voicing their disapproval, pushing and shoving, trying to stare down into the maze to see with their own eyes the thing that others had only dared to whisper. In some places scuffles had broken out, people crying, tempers fraying, whilst others sat in their seats not daring to believe the impossible.

Thomas pushed his way through the agitated crowd and stared down into the labyrinth alongside several angry spectators who were shaking their fists at the Minotaur standing about them. He observed a bewildering scene of several guards poking at the floor of the maze with their spears and scratching their heads, whilst others held back a large jelly like mass with flaming torches, causing it to shy away from the naked flame any time one was waved too close to its viscous surface.

"So what's going on?" Mathius asked squeezing through the crowd and coming up alongside the captain. "I don't like the mood of this crowd. It looks like there is about to be a riot at any moment."

"I have absolutely no idea." Thomas confessed, risking a quick glance back down into the labyrinth, as if by taking a second glance something new and useful would be seen. As he watched, a section of the maze wall swung open to reveal a dark passage. A guard exited shaking his head, confirming that their quarry had not passed that way. The door slid closed with a soft rumble, its carefully shaped stonework appearing to merge with the rest of the wall, making it nearly impossible to spot if you were not aware it was there. "They seem to have lost something."

The guards held an agitated conversation. The guard who had previously left the passage stabbed at a stone situated at the bottom of the secret doorway revealing the opening once again.

"That's actually quite clever positioning the button on the floor." Mathius commented. "These Minotaur with their self-indulgent thoughts of grandeur would not consider looking down to where their servant race resides, never stoop that low. Hey... stoop that low. That's quite funny." Mathius turned towards Thomas smiling, then stopped when he saw the captain's face.

"This isn't helping us." Thomas murmured, staring about the terraces for an explanation of what was going on. People were throwing their ribbons down onto the floor and starting to walk away towards the entrance of the labyrinth, the looks of disgust and disappointment not dissimilar to baseball fans leaving Yankee stadium in the Bronx, if a game had not gone their way.

"Kristoph has gone," one spectator sobbed as she walked past, clutching a corn doll of a Minotaur that was decked out in black armour and wearing a golden ribbon tied about his left arm. "He's gone, leaving us in our hour of need." The words made Thomas stop and focus more intently on the young woman, noting her red puffy eyes from crying, the golden ribbons that she had tied in her long ponytail and her worn green dress, patched in a couple of places.

"Excuse me? What happened to Kristoph?" The spectator stopped her sad slow walk and wiped her eyes, staring up at Thomas in disbelief. How could this man not know the horrors she had just witnessed? She gasped in some air, as if by simply mentioning the words she would cause herself yet more distress, then began theatrically relaying the terrible news.

"The labyrinth opened up and swallowed him." She wailed. "There was a disturbance, a small child was fighting with a guard, he was probably a pick pocket or something. Then the child and several crowd members fell into the maze, it was horrific. People were terribly hurt." She paused taking in another shuddering breath.

"I don't suppose this child had a black and white bird by any chance?" Mathius asked, a suspicion rising in his mind.

"What? I... there might have been." She looked flustered, annoyed that her story had been interrupted. "Look... do you want to hear my story or not?"

"And...And?" Thomas beckoned with his hands, trying to coax more out of the young girl and giving Mathius a warning look, causing the assassin to cross his arms and scowl.

"Then someone shouted something about a zombie. Everything got confused. The child climbed up onto Kristoph and it looked like it was trying to eat Kristoph's brain, he was flailing about in the maze, clearly in pain. Oh... do you think maybe the child was the zombie?" Her eyes widened, suddenly excited at this revelation. "Where was I? Oh yes... Then the floor of the labyrinth swallowed up the zombie and Kristoph and several spectators got eaten by the jelly."

"Can you show me where?" Mathius asked, indicating towards the edge of the seating area.

"Right there." The girl wailed, pointing down at the gelatinous mass. "You can still see parts of them floating inside it." Mathius opened his mouth to reply, then shut it again, rolling his eyes to the heavens as the girl started crying again.

"I know this is really upsetting." Thomas said quietly, stepping forwards and shoving Mathius to one side, "but it is really important that we know where the maze swallowed Kristoph."

"Right under the jelly." The spectator replied, her face flushed with anger now. "Right where I told you. If neither of you are going to listen to me then I shall take my leave." She spun in a huff, hugging her miniature Kristoph to her breast and stormed off through the crowd.

"Well... I think she likes you." Mathius stated sarcastically. Thomas followed the girl's path through the crowd, suddenly lost for words, then turned back towards the maze. The gelatinous flood reached out and snatched an inattentive Minotaur guard by the leg, dragging the shrieking creature into its body with a wet sounding splotch. All the other guards instantly retreated in shock, then started beating at the jelly with their torches in a vain attempt, to rescue their kinsman. The surface rucked up, leaving painful black marks on the creature's skin.

"There is no way we are going to get down there to help him." The captain muttered. "We don't have a hope of coaxing that creature away and there are way too many guards. Whatever mess Rauph is in, I'm afraid that for now he's on his own."

"At least Ashe is with him." Mathius replied. Thomas turned towards his companion and fixed him with an incredulous stare.

"That's what scares me." He murmured.

* * * * * *

The huge spider stared hungrily towards Ashe, its intense black beady eyes surveying the succulent morsel that had magically fallen into its lair. If it had had lips and a tongue it would have been running one over the other in an enthusiastic display of anticipation for the meal it was about to receive. Instead, the massive silvery blue headed arachnid quivered it's black and white striped hairy legs in excitement, lifting its two front pedi-palp to paw gently at the musty air.

Ashe stood open-mouthed, awed that something he normally found about the *El Defensor* no bigger than a silver bit and which normally met a grisly end crushed beneath the sole of the Halfling's boot, or dropped in Marcus's socks could be found on such a massive scale!

"Look Rauph! Look…" he whispered breathlessly. "Isn't it beautiful? I think it's waving to us."

A huge crash sounded behind the Halfling, as something equally hairy and large, eight-foot-tall in actuality, thudded to the floor in a dead faint. Clouds of dust billowed up into the air, dried bones from long dead spider meals snapped and crunched, a dented helmet went spinning off across the floor sliding to a stop near Ashe's feet and tendrils of dusty web danced excitedly within the unexpected currents of air.

"I'm really sorry about my friend." Ashe apologised, turning back towards the spider and noting that it had inched ever so slightly closer than when he had last been looking. "He's not normally this shy. I don't know what has come over him. Clearly running about in the maze upstairs has taken it out of him." He bent to retrieve the helmet from the floor and lifted it up only to discover, much to his distaste, that it still had its previous owner's shrunken head inside.

"Oh dear. Whatever has happened here?" he asked himself, looking up to see if the spider could help illuminate the situation, only to find that it had moved closer still. Eight images of Ashe's questioning face reflected back from the surface of the spider's onyx eyes and a little voice suddenly recommended caution in the back of an inquisitive Halfling's mind.

"Have you not heard of respecting someone's personal space?" Ashe remarked, taking a cautious step backwards, only for the spider to match him and shuffle forwards the same distance. "I mean we hardly know each other. That's how accidents happen."

Ashe looked about the rectangular chamber, taking in the thickly cobwebbed corners of the room where vague human-shaped forms hung cocooned in sticky webs, then over to a grate set low in the far-left wall where a shrivelled-up torso of a Minotaur lay on its side, a hole in its chest exposing dusty desiccated innards. He then looked back at the helmet and head he still held in his hands and suddenly realised that there had been a fair share of accidents in this room.

The Halfling turned the helmet over slowly, then jumped as he caught a reflection of the spider advancing closer within its tarnished surface. The helmet slipped from his hands in shock, the desiccated head rolling out from inside it as it bounced. Ashe bent to pick it up, just as the arachnid pounced.

Ashe shrieked as the spider jumped, its hairy legs instantly forming a tight trap about him and knocking him to the floor. Sinders squawked loudly and flew away in an explosion of feathers, swooping about the subterranean chamber and crying out a cacophonous alarm. The arachnid gazed down at the squirming Halfling and slowly, almost lovingly extended its sickle shaped fangs, already beading with clear drops of deadly venom.

"Oh mouldy acorns!" Ashe screamed, his little hands struggling furiously.

The arachnid lunged and bit down hard on Ashe's head, its fangs striking hard into each side then recoiling with a dull clang, before it pinned the Halfling securely in place with its abdomen and struck again, its fangs spearing down once more in an attempt to crush the little thief's skull.

Ashe grunted as the blue spider bit him, its bulk crushing him to the floor, forcing a submission where all the Halfling could do was lie there and let the creature feast. Venom oozed from its fangs, running down the outside of the dented helmet that Ashe had miraculously managed to clamp onto his own head seconds before the deadly fangs had struck. He stared past the fangs into the spider's maw and could not help himself screaming at a view he, unlike scholarly arachnologists, would never truly appreciate.

He kicked out with his feet, sending the crispy skull that had once occupied where his own now resided, out across the floor, bouncing and spinning in a lopsided lazy curve. The spider heard the sound and paused, still frustrated at its lack of success in stopping its prey from wriggling around. It looked up, dropping Ashe from its fangs and stared about the room, looking for the source of the disturbance and wondering if further food had arrived, whilst still bouncing hard up and down on the Halfling.

"I...could...really...use...a...hand...here!"   Ashe   squeaked. "Stop...or...I'm...going to...throw...up!"

Sinders swooped down in a blur of black and white feathers, claws extended, beak pecking aiming right for the arachnid's black eyes. The spider backed up, raising its long front legs aggressively, giving the Halfling just what he needed, room to slip free.

Ashe slithered out from between the spider's legs and crawled rapidly towards Rauph, grabbing him by the breastplate and banging on it as hard as he could.

"Wake up you idiot. We are in trouble!"

Rauph opened a bleary eye and struggled to focus, hearing an annoying little voice and not understanding why he could not just sleep until it was his turn on watch back on the *El Defensor*. He shook his head, moving to sit up, noting that Ashe was wearing a lopsided antique helmet that looked battered and dented to hell. Then he looked past the Halfling to where Ashe's stupid bird kept darting and diving about making such a din that it was giving him a headache. His blurred vision finally focused on a huge spider jumping and sidestepping at the end of the chamber, its blue fuzzy head bobbing and weaving, hairy black and white legs waving about angrily. A spider... oh yes, he had forgotten about the spider.

The navigator crashed back onto the ground, dragging Ashe with him and causing the Halfling to verbally deluge the comatose Minotaur with every variety of nut curse he could imagine. The thief got to his feet and as soon as he did, he heard the scuttle of hairy feet heading in his direction. His eyes dropped to Rauph's battered swords sheathed on the Minotaur's back. At last a weapon! He gripped the blade and was amazed how easily the weapon slid free from its scabbard and kept sliding and sliding! Gosh this was a big sword!

The point finally slid free scoring the stone floor as Ashe moved to lift the five-foot long blade from the dust. It required a herculean effort on the four-foot Halfling's part, his little face flushed red with bulging veins standing proud on his forehead. The spider charged towards him, hairs bristling, eyes gleaming.

"Take this you hairy fiend!" Ashe announced, lifting the sword back over his head as in the pose of heroes from tales of old, before finding the weight of the blade dragging him backwards and nearly pulling his arms from their sockets. He skidded, trying to balance himself and spread his legs wide, then with a Halfling battle cry, he swung the blade mightily... and missed.

"Oh pickled pistachios," he cursed as the blade crashed down and hit the dusty flagstones sending vibrations up its length and along the Halfling's arms. The spider jumped backwards from the blade, then charged back in, intent on biting its elusive prey once and for all, only for Sinders to swoop in, slashing with its claw and cutting a groove in the creature's blue head which knocked its trajectory off track, hitting Ashe a glancing blow, to send him sprawling one way and Rauph's sword in the other.

The thief ended up squashed against the half-consumed Minotaur over by the grate and found himself desperately rolling over its grisly corpse, his hand coming down on something long forgotten in the dust. The spider darted in swiftly, its beady eyes narrowed in hatred for the tender morsel that just would not lie down and accept its fate.

Ashe got to his knees, frantically brushing strands of web from his face so that he could observe the arachnid scuttling furiously towards him. It's black and white striped legs moved so fast it was like following a blur. He watched as it darted to the left, then to the right, always advancing in rapid bursts of speed. The Halfling swallowed hard. It looked so big, so hairy and so blue!

The Halfling firmly gripped the weapon he had discovered buried in the dust and tried to lift up the ancient spear but it was still held tightly by the hand of the Minotaur guard. The Halfling yanked the spear up, then found himself pulled down again as it snagged on the corpse.

"Oh come on!" Ashe screamed his frustration, wrenching the spear this way and that, desperate to free the weapon, just as the spider finally charged towards him. The arachnid leapt up into the air, legs outstretched, fangs bared as Ashe gave the spear one last almighty tug.

There was a dry crack, a sickening squelch, a sense of frantic wriggling and then Ashe found himself covered in hot, wet liquid that absolutely reeked! The spear snapped, the bottom of the shaft still retained by its deceased owner, giving the Halfling an entirely new perspective into the term 'death grip'. Ashe went down and the wriggling spider came down on top of him, squashing him to the flagstones for one final time, its legs feebly twitching as it curled in tightly upon itself and suddenly appeared very small.

Ashe pulled himself free, coughing and spluttering, spitting pieces of furry spider from his mouth as he staggered back to his feet. Sinders swooped in towards Ashe's shoulder, then squawked in horror and aborted its landing, veering off at the last moment with a staccato chatter of angry birdsong.

"Oh come on!" Ashe yelled defiantly, flinging his arms wide and splattering spider guts everywhere. "It doesn't really smell that bad!"

* * * * * *

"Now heave!" Commagin yelled, his eyes bright at the prospect of finally completing the repairs to the *El Defensor's* helm. "That's it, watch your fingers Marcus, watch your fingers!

The Dwarven engineer inserted his crowbar and pushed down with all his might, trying to slip the newly repaired chain links over the cog so they would mesh with the teeth that controlled the rudder movement.

"Harder!" he grunted, gesturing that Marcus needed to pull the chain more towards the cog so that it would help with his own efforts. One link clunked into place, then another. "Come on, nearly done!" There was a mighty bang as the final link slammed into place, Marcus snatching his fingers away with inches to spare.

"Man the helm." Commagin ordered, his breath coming in gasps. "Turn the wheel a quarter to Starboard, then do the same to Port but do it slowly, understand?"

"Don't worry, I've got it." Marcus smiled smacking the dwarf on his back. "Give me just a second." Commagin wiped his brow with his handkerchief and held his breath as the cog took up the tension then began to slowly creak, then turn, one chain link at a time clicking into place and meshing with the cog. His eyes stared intently through the thick glass lenses of his spectacles, watching as the newly forged link he had used to repair the chain rose into view and clicked smoothly into place riding over the cog inches beneath the engineer's nose.

The link fitted perfectly into the teeth of the mechanism and showed no signs of rough edges or hairline cracks indicating his metalwork was sound. The chain stopped turning then reversed motion the new chain link rolling back over the cog as smoothly as it had traversed in the other direction. Commagin exhaled with relief, confident now that the rudder would hold. He reached into a bucket at his feet and smeared grease over the links with a brush to protect the chain from rust and wear, then pushed the bucket and crowbar out onto the deck and climbed out of the hole. Marcus was already there waiting, his face beaming as they both slid the hatch back into place.

"A job well done." Commagin sighed, content that this engineering challenge was now resolved and allowing himself the first smile he had taken in a long time.

"The rudder responded to the helm." Austen confirmed walking over from the stern where he had been positioned to check its movement, Thomas will be pleased, well done Commagin."

"Not a moment too soon." Marcus pointed towards the jetty where a Minotaur troop were marching down towards them.

"Free the lines! Unfurl the sails!" Commagin snapped, "Take us out Austen."

"Where to?" the helmsman replied. Commagin looked across the strait to where the huge maze rose from the jungle, the roar of the crowds reaching them despite the distance. "Let's go where all the excitement is."

"Are you sure?"

"Positive." Commagin replied, as the sails above him unfurled with a snap and instantly filled with the breeze. He stared up through his glasses at the blurry shapes of the two brothers Plano and Abilene moving about the rigging and realised he could never wish for a better crew. The stomp of marching feet turned into a run as the Minotaur troops now charged down the quayside but it was too late, the *El Defensor* had been held in port too long and was already easing away.

Marcus suddenly staggered, as if struck and sank down onto the deck beside the dwarf, his face suddenly pale, his skin clammy.

"Are you alright son?" Commagin asked, concern etched across his aged features. "You don't look very well."

"I'm not sure." The monk replied, "Maybe I have overdone it. I feel empty as if all of my energy has just been drained from me."

"Just sit there and rest a moment." Commagin replied. "You city folk just haven't got the stamina of us seafaring lot. You sail with me for a few more years and I'll make a man of you. Mark my words you will be fine in a moment." The Dwarf got to his feet and walked across the deck to the nearest crewman and whispered into his ear.

"Fetch Violetta quickly. Something is wrong with Marcus." Commagin ushered the crewman away, then walked slowly back towards the monk, not liking the sudden change that had come over the youth. One minute he had been vibrant and full of strength, now he looked a shadow of himself, aged and in such a short passage of time. That meant only one thing. Sorcery was at work.

* * * * * *

Rauph wrinkled his nose in disgust. There was a terrible odour wafting up his nostrils! It made him want to gag. It was the smell of snails caught out in the noon sun, when they all bubble up and froth inside their shells. It was like… oh words were just beginning to fail him and whatever it was, it was just inches from the end of his nose! He dared to crack open an eye and groaned.

"Hiya Rauph!" Ashe beamed, waving a slime covered hand and looking as if something massive had just blown its nose on him. "Here, have your sword back."

The navigator sat up sharply, instantly alert, not sure if it was down to the brown slime dripping from the Halfling all over his armour or the thought that Ashe had been playing with his sword. To Rauph each scenario was by itself horrifying! He got to his feet, trying to brush off the sticky residue from his armour, snorting and wrinkling his nose at the foul odour, before reaching out and taking the offered blade.

As soon as his hand closed around the grip, he knew he had made a mistake. The hilt was wet and sticky and as he moved the sword to sheathe it, he realised that long slimy strands were still firmly attaching the Halfling to the hilt. Rauph's eyes narrowed as he took in the goo oozing down the fuller of his weapon, then stared around anxiously looking for something to wipe the longsword clean. Ashe stood as patiently as he could, hands on hips, helmet askew, slime dripping from his nose.

"You know this place is very interesting." Ashe commented as Rauph darted from one pile of rags to another, trying to find something to clean his weapon on. "We seem to be beneath the maze. There are passageways everywhere going off into the darkness and I wanted to go off exploring but with you sleeping I knew I had to…" Rauph stifled a squeal as he turned around and noticed the corpse of the giant spider all curled up upon itself.

"Oh don't worry about him." Ashe shrugged. "He's dead. No one messes with me and Sinders." Rauph looked towards the Halfling in disbelief, his face set in a look of doubt.

"As I was saying, there are long straight passages everywhere with torches on the walls. I've brought some in here for us to use but come on its exciting, there are loads of places for us to explore."

"You tell me the passageways run directly beneath the maze." Rauph stated slowly. "And that they go everywhere."

"Yes, yes!" Ashe gestured impatiently. "Everywhere. Where would you like to go?" Rauph stopped moving for a second and closed his eyes as if gathering his thoughts or seeing something only he was privy to.

"I want to go that way." the navigator pointed, indicating with his huge hand over towards the right, a grin crossing his bovine features. "And I want you to stay several steps behind me."

* * * * * *

Miguel Garcia looked down at the open console with disbelief. Someone had come here whilst he was on the *Neptune* and had stolen all of the tools he had kept here! He stared around the barge, taking in the panorama of the crushed and decaying ships listing and groaning under the mustard sky and cursed whatever bastard had done this. Whoever it was had even eaten his favourite candy bar, one he stored here just in case of low blood sugar emergencies. He was not diabetic but you could never be too careful!

The waters swirled and gurgled, lapping over the far edge of the barge and slopping up the deck every time Horatio or Cornelius stalked towards that end. Sleek grey shapes knifed through the depths, circling in anticipation at the vibrations made by the huge lizards, hoping that a missed step would deliver food. Beyond the open stretch of treacherous water, a line of archways marched one after the other into the distance.

The buccaneer shivered, risking another look over at the cluttered skyline, his eyes searching for the hounds or any signs of their terrifying master and his strange glowing lights that heralded his arrival. The slow grinding turn of the shipwrecks meant that the construction site around the arch Malum expected the *El Defensor* to sail through, had slipped past an hour ago. Miguel estimated it would be several more before his barge completed the circuit and returned to the point where the danger lay.

Miguel dropped to his knees and started inspecting the assembly of broken remains that made up Pheris. How was he going to pull lose a wire and jump start the barge if he had no tools? He turned the cyborg's torso over, checking for an access port, a power outlet, something he could jury rig. His mind turned to the wires in the console. If he could strip a lead of its insulation and plug it directly into Pheris, then maybe he could get enough energy to fire it up.

He bent to the task, peeling the insulation free with his teeth and twisting the leads together before sticking the makeshift flex directly into Pheris's discovered power output. The barge shuddered, its lights flickering on and off.

"Come on! Come on!" Miguel willed the machine to catch, willed the turbines to kick in, only to watch everything splutter and stop again. He looked up from his project, searching for someone to blame and noticed Cornelius and Horatio sniffing the air and moving towards a pile of rubbish dumped at the corner of the barge. Horatio still had that stupid racoon hat on him and appeared to have adopted it as a fashion trend all mercenary lizards should follow.

That was funny he never noticed the pile of refuse there a minute ago. Miguel considered investigating himself, then felt the hairs on his arms rise as if there was a massive build-up of static electricity.

"What in the worl…" the sky split apart just above the water, revealing a rapidly flickering scene, fading in and out of focus. The energy pouring from the rift made Miguel's teeth chatter and his hair stand on end. There was an annoying buzz in his ear like tinnitus but in the next second it sounded like a musical instrument playing beautiful tortured music.

There was a bright flash, forked lightning shot across the sky, an explosion of parchment papers, glass vials, even a suit of armour fell from the fissure, then three people appeared, falling from the sky to splash into the murky water. The rift spluttered then disappeared with a bang, knocking Miguel off his feet. Electricity crackled and surged over the barge, arcing through Pheris body and down into the console making its engines ignite and roar, lifting the stricken vessel free from the water's grip for the first time since Miguel's ill-fated mission had brought him here.

Miguel looked down at the console and all the green lights as the power banks filled to capacity, a smile spreading across his face at his good fortune, just as the sea bubbled furiously in front of his vessel and a large sphere, or some kind of opaque bubble rose from beneath the surface with the three people inside.

The sphere crackled and then collapsed in on itself with a thud, dumping seawater and the cargo of three people down onto the deck. Miguel quickly ran his eye over them as they groaned and coughed up water, his hand reaching for one of his reloaded pistols. A scholar of some kind clutching a large book like a lover, a thin man with pointed ears who had his hands tied together and reminded Miguel of someone he had known in the past, all be it this man was much thinner and... his heart beat faster.

A woman of impeccable beauty, porcelain skin, long black ebony hair and wearing a sodden fur coat over skin-tight robes that revealed more of her body than they covered. Never one to pass up on an opportunity to help a pretty lady, especially one clearly in distress, Miguel shrugged his shoulders tried to straighten his hair, then stepped forward to offer his assistance.

"It is not often that an angel falls from the sky and lands on my ship." He began, offering his free hand. "My name is Miguel and by the look of you, I am sure you have a fascinating story to tell me."

Chapter Forty-Eight

Kerian scrutinized his strange host from across the room, careful not to react as the man stood up and casually walked towards him. Now he was closer, Kerian could see that his long blonde hair was unkempt, his skin sallow as if he rarely saw or ventured out into the sunshine. His clothes were grubby, as if they had not been washed for some time and his leather boots were stained with black marks.

The knight tensed as his host approached, detecting a scent of musk from the man that made him feel decidedly uneasy. His instincts told him to strike this person down despite the fact that no hostility had yet been shown towards him. Warning growls from Octavian and Agnezkia stopped Kerian from reaching for his sword. Two other snarling creatures emerged from behind a large table and padded across the room, dropping down to the ground against Kerian's boots, their teeth bared.

His host reached out a pale hand, the nails ragged, the skin bitten and rough. Kerian thought he was offering his hand in greeting, only to realise that the man was reaching past him for the tray still perched upon the stool. Facial nerves twitched in irritation, as his host removed the tray, clearly unhappy that Kerian had disobeyed his order to put the tray on the floor. His smile was forced as he turned back towards his chair, his pale, blue-tinged lips parting to reveal brown decayed stubs of teeth set into anaemic gums.

Kerian suddenly had the strangest sensation he had seen this man before but before he could ask, his host dipped a slender finger into the plate of meat, the slimy viscosity of the blood staining his pale fingers as he traced patterns through its contents. He selected several choice pieces of flesh, then threw them towards his thralls, the meat thudding to the floor, just in front of the creatures and splashing up the side of Kerian's boot. Eyes filled with longing stared down at the offerings, two beasts whined softly, one shifting itself as if uncomfortable, tilting its snout and staring up towards its master. Not one creature moved to eat, instead they trembled with anticipation, their ears cocked, saliva dripping from their jaws.

"So, you have ransom for Octavian's wife and child." The man began, settling back into his chair before picking up a crystal glass half full with a heavy amber liquid. He took a slow sip, then closed his eyes to savour the experience before gazing intently in Kerian's direction.

"Yes." Kerian replied coolly, not failing to notice the crystal glass was now smeared with the dark crimson residue of his host's soiled hand. The man stared long and hard through his spectacles, the tension growing between them across the warm room. The empty silence made Kerian want to talk or move but the warped creatures lying at his feet were stopping him from moving anywhere and he knew that talking during a silence was a sign of weakness that he did not want to show at this crucial juncture. Kerian knew he was in trouble, that he did not have the means to pay this ransom but he was not giving up his necklace. He would die rather than lose her again. He watched as his host continued looking Kerian up and down before shaking his head solemnly.

"Well, I have to confess that a man who doesn't even have his own means of transport and arrives dressed in such attire, hardly raises my hopes for a suitable payment. You do understand that the fee for the two is quite..." He paused taking another slow sip from his glass before licking his lips. "...substantial."

"I can assure you, that you will be satisfactorily rewarded." Kerian replied, his mind racing for a means to turn this situation to his advantage. Maybe he could bluff the ransom, delay the inevitable conflict until he had a clear plan of escape? Now where did he know this man from? He had never travelled to Glowme castle or even near this region, so how come he had this continuing feeling that their paths had crossed before? What was more, he had a growing belief that they had not parted on amicable terms. The only positive thing positive about this encounter was that the man clearly had no apparent idea who he was. "Anyone who has had dealings with me knows my reputation is sound and my credentials impeccable."

"That is reassuring to know." His host replied, his pale face still portraying his scepticism. "Are you going to sit, or are you expecting to simply stand here all day long? I have to warn you that hounds will be hounds and if you remain standing for too long, they may mistake you for a fence post. It would be a real shame to stain your attire further."

Kerian looked at the four twisted monsters drooling and whining about him and realised his host was playing with him. These were not hounds, far from it. They were warped beings, constructed from several creatures. Here was the pelt of a bear, the spots of a snow leopard, the horns of a goat, all of these creatures were chimera's, experiments that his unsettling host seemed to have been party to. Octavian had warned him of the danger of being bitten by these creatures and how their taint had warped him into what he was today.

He knew was never going to be allowed to sit down and if he did, it would be a tactical mistake that would lose him his means of movement. There was no mistaking the fact these beasts could rip him apart in moments if they managed to pin him down! He needed a distraction and quickly!

Kerian stared about the room, taking in the white mould blooming from the shadowy corners, the faded portraits in chipped gilt frames that hung on the walls and stared at him with solemn, dour expressions. There were no clues here, no answers to the enigma of this man's identity.

The cupboards and bookcases were filled with documents and ledgers but the spines were so dusty he was unable to make out any of the titles. He knew from Octavian's descriptions that the man was a scientist, yet Kerian never knew any scientists! He could not keep the man waiting, he had to introduce himself and try to present at least some semblance of control.

"My name is Styx." Kerian replied, watching his host for any tell-tale signs that he recognised him but the response was just an acknowledgement of the fact supplied, followed up with another sip from the crystal glass. It was time to use flattery. "Octavian told me you were a generous host and that you were a renowned scientist." His host's eyebrows rose in surprise.

"Quite a prestigious one in fact." Kerian continued. "I would love to see around your home and see where you make these scientific advancements. Maybe spend some time in discussion and understand your motivations." He smiled, waiting to see if his prose would have the desired effect. The scientist placed his glass down and licked his lips, a delighted grin lighting his face and giving Kerian another unwanted glimpse of his atrocious dental state. He turned towards a water clock set upon the dresser beside him and adjusted his glasses.

"Well, as luck would have it, I do need to go down to my laboratory before I arrange for dinner. One of my experiments is nearing fruition and I feel I am very close to achieving my goal. In some respects, Mr Styx, you are quite honoured to be here on the eve of such a momentous occasion."

"Why, what are you attempting to achieve?" Kerian asked, playing along with the ruse.

"Why, what everyone wants of course." His host replied, getting to his feet and walking towards the door they had entered through. He clicked his fingers and his creations lunged for the food lying before them, wolfing it down.

"Control. Absolute control."

* * * * * *

"Glowme castle was originally constructed in 221 and has remained guardian of these mountains for over seven hundred years. Our family have resided within its halls for nine generations. Here within the great hall there are portraits of the founding family members. Lord Thadeus, Lady Elzbeth, even Sir Oliver, quite a tyrant in his time. It was said he once chopped three men in half with one mighty swing of his broad sword. Personally, I have my doubts."

"It's a shame it is so dark in here." Kerian replied drily, his eyes taking in the faded canvas displaying a rotund man, decked out in heavy plate, his gaze staring down at Kerian with a look that made the knight feel like an intruder. A huge dragon's head lay at the man's feet and he was posed with one boot resting upon the gory trophy. He held a massive broadsword in one hand, holding the heavy weapon aloft as if he were about to be blessed by a divine presence for his successful kill.

Kerian tried to hide his smile. Such a pose was not only ridiculous but with a blade that heavy it was likely impossible to maintain without both hands on the weapon and then only for the shortest of times. His smile died as he turned back towards the enigmatic man who was making his way over to the far side of the hall, a lit candelabra held high, his footsteps echoing loudly across the cavernous space. The twisted results of his experiments escorted him, padding almost silently across the floor in a diamond formation, one in front, one behind, the others side to side.

Pale ghostly forms of an elderly couple gave off a luminance that barely pushed the shadows away. They writhed in torment, repeatedly trying to touch each other and offer love and support, only to be frustrated by the cruel glass layers of the case between them. The knight swallowed hard, imagining if he and Colette could ever be in such a position; unable to share the love and compassion they held for each other. Kerian licked his lips and tried to push the haunting image from his mind. He needed to focus, needed to gain the advantage they sorely needed if they were to complete this rescue attempt.

"The daylight fades the paint, so we rarely open the drapes." His mysterious host replied from across the hall, unaware of Kerian's dark brooding thoughts. The scientist placed his candelabra down upon a dark low desk and reached up to grab hold of a set of heavy drapes and drag them apart, allowing pale beams of anaemic afternoon sunlight to stream into the chamber through clouds of dust disturbed by his actions.

Kerian blinked as the light flooded in, his eyes taking in the hall clearly for the first time. This castle was in worse condition than he had thought. Everywhere he looked there were signs of neglect; cobwebs hung densely in the upper corners of the room, furniture riddled with woodworm, gilt peeling from frames, black mould creeping along the walls where damp had seeped into the stonework, displays of halberds and swords arranged upon the walls, were pitted with rust and in much need of oiling. He took in the vaulted ceiling, the faded tapestries, his nose tickled by the disturbed dust and the scent of the mustiness. There was a stench of decay hanging over everything, leaving a sour lingering taste in the back of the knight's throat. Kerian looked back at the painting, now clearly seeing the cracks in the oils and the grime that had built up overtime.

"If you don't mind me saying, everything here appears a little tired." Kerian commented, trying to keep up his confident act as he reluctantly walked over to the window to stand beside the scientist and stare out into the cheerless light. "The upkeep for such a place must be enormous. I presume keeping such a magnificent stronghold in this condition is quite demanding for someone residing here all by themselves?"

"Oh, I am not by myself." His host replied ominously. "I have my hounds and a few select staff that have been kept on after others were unfortunately let go." He stared out the window through a jagged hole where a piece of glass had fallen away. Kerian followed his gaze, taking in the jumbled rooftops, the crumbling gargoyles and the secret courtyards, where any trace of ornamental gardens had been strangled by voracious weeds. Forlorn statues cried petrified tears of injustice as they silently drowned in seas of brambles, carved limbs raised pleading to an owner that no longer cared.

"So can you tell me more about your experiments?" Kerian turned back towards the man, only to find to his surprise that his host had already walked away, his candelabra held aloft. "Are you trying to improve the life of those around you, change this world for the better?"

"What I do, I do for myself." His host laughed coldly. "What is the point of doing work for the betterment of man, when the only man I want to enrich is myself? Imagine if you were to work on making someone stronger, faster, more intelligent than yourself and you succeed. What happens if they want to keep those advances you have discovered. How can you stop someone who has such a physical advantage over you? Why would I put myself in such a ridiculous predicament? My working practice ensures I have no such worries."

Kerian moved to catch up, walking past some large porcelain vases decorated with sinuous mythical creatures. One vase had a large crack running up the side and as Kerian passed he was sure something looked out at him from the darkness. They stopped before two huge doors, whereupon his host extracted a heavy bunch of keys from his pocket and unlocked one door with a heavy clank. He winked at Kerian as he dropped the keys back into his trousers.

"You can never be too careful." He whispered. "We would not want just anyone walking in here by mistake. Too many accidents happen that way. Now if you will allow me." He gestured with his arm, bowing low. "Welcome to my laboratory."

The doors swung wide and Kerian found himself instantly wrinkling his nose from the stench that emanated from within. His eyes watered at the chemical irritation, the smell of unwashed flesh, the scent of old blood and the unmistakable tang of salt water. His ears rebelled at the assault of sounds; bubbling, hissing, bells ringing, steam escaping, creatures whimpering and suffering extreme pain. He looked over towards his host and noticed the man seemed to be relishing the knight's discomfort. Kerian gritted his teeth, forced a smile in response and stepped through the doorway.

They stood on a balcony overlooking a large split-level cluttered room with a large floor to ceiling window running the entire length of one wall. The view of the snow-covered mountains, kissed cotton pink and auburn by the setting sun had the look of a lost masterpiece that artists would have given their life to paint. Here, in this macabre setting the backdrop was jarringly and glaringly out of place. Nothing artistic would ever be created in this room!

The walls behind Kerian were lined with shelves that groaned under the weight of archaic books and scrolls. Suits of ancient armour stood solemnly at regular intervals along the wall as the balcony continued around the room's perimeter with identical staircases on the left and right walls spiralling down to the main laboratory floor.

Kerian cast his eyes over the handrail, noting the work benches set about the room, their surfaces littered with glass bottles bubbling and steaming, cages of creatures running about and throwing themselves against the bars in what appeared to be signs of madness. One bench had a dissected animal upon it, the assorted implements that had been used to explore the innards of the unfortunate subject scattered haphazardly about the work surface.

In the centre of the room was another table, this one set with places for dinner. Kerian counted the spaces. There were five in all, silver cutlery framing gold edged plates. Napkins folded into elegant swans that nestled alongside crystal cut glasses. It was beautiful and yet, just like the scenery so alien when considering the overlying ambience of menace about the room. Several pedestals stood before the huge window, glass cloches covering items of apparent value, keeping them free from dust and contaminants. The one to the left appeared to hold an ancient violin that slept upon a bed of crushed velvet.

Kerian's host was already descending the left staircase, moving across the room with clear purpose, his passage leading him to a basket on the floor where several mewling sounds arose. Kerian noted that all of the larger beasts had followed their master down to the ground floor, so he placed his hand on his sword hilt and gently freed the blade from the scabbard, exposing a sliver of *Aurora's* metal that gleamed brightly, before he clicked the weapon back in place again. He considered drawing *Aurora* now, knowing that it would change Octavian and these other creatures back into their proper forms. He considered that their combined numbers would easily overpower the man, yet somehow, something held him back. There was more going on here, too many questions and riddles and Kerian was determined to extricate the answers.

"You know the problem with scientific research is that it's so damned expensive." Kerian's pale host continued, as the knight descended the stairs towards him. "Funds only go so far, there are peer reviewers to bribe, critics to be silenced, laboratory costs, subjects to be located and experimented on. I mean scientific papers don't write themselves you know. You have to raise funds any way you can..." He paused, checking his lab notes before tutting loudly and reaching down into the basket to lift out a small puppy covered in dark fur, ridges along its spine and above its eyes reflecting back the light as if they were made of flint.

"That's better! See Agnezkia, gaze upon your offspring. Together we have created the future. Undying loyalty, obedience, strength and aggression in a form that is as beautiful as it is deadly." He gripped the puppy hard by the scruff of its neck and drew out a large syringe, plunging the needle into the wriggling creature, making it yelp loudly, before injecting the red liquid within into the squealing animal. Kerian moved up alongside him and stared down at the basket as his host grabbed the pups one by one and repeated the action. Six puppies. Six unmistakable creatures from nightmare.

"You see here we have a classic example of my work. I have been trying to combine animals and humans together for years, with limited success. They are always so unstable, the human part always rebels, always tries to fight back until I have no choice but to put them down. If only they were as predictable as the animal side. I expect Octavian will meet the same fate eventually." He shook his head, then smiled at the wriggling puppy in his hand. "Now look at this, I have finally managed to breed my own hounds. I no longer need human subjects to experiment upon. I can have litter after litter of totally loyal creatures."

The hound in his fist turned and sank its teeth into his hand with a growl, shaking its head violently from side to side. Kerian looked on as his host smiled sadistically, then flicked his wrist sending the pup skidding across the workbench and off the far end, back to the basket with its siblings.

"So much for loyal." Kerian replied, noting that the puppy that had fallen from the bench had managed to land outside of the basket and was now wriggling about trying to get back onto its front and clamber back in with the litter, mewling in distress. Another pup moved across the basket and Kerian noticed its back leg was all bent and twisted.

"Not quite as perfect as you are leading me to believe." He stated, pointing out the disability.

The scowl across the scientist's face bore witness to points scored in Kerian's favour. However, the smile on Kerian's lips failed when his host grabbed the puppy and lifted it high poking and prodding at the deformed limb as if horrified such a thing could exist.

He turned away from the desk, holding the squealing puppy in his hands and marched towards the underside of the balcony, his purpose not apparent but he was definitely under a thunderous cloud. Kerian bent down to retrieve the dropped pup and stroked its head, just as a glass vial of bubbling blue liquid overbalanced as the scientist charged past, knocking it with his arm and sending the glass spinning off the work bench to smash into pieces on the ground.

Kerian started at the sound, his gaze following his host as he moved under the balcony. Two corridors led off, to the left and to the right, each one lined with yet more glass containers. A huge aquarium stood centrally between them, its walls coated in dark green algae, obscuring whatever horror lurked inside. There was a sense of something large and ghostly pulsating through the water, its physical features difficult for Kerian to make out from this distance.

"I don't have many visitors coming here, out in the middle of nowhere, from whom I can seek sponsorship or who care enough to drop by to see how I am." His host shouted as he headed towards the large glass tank, "Equally, it's not as if I can go door to door to beg for scientific funding. 'He has such a big castle; why should we lend him money?'" Kerian noted the distain and emphasis the man placed on the latter sentence as if this were a scenario he was replaying in his mind.

"Instead, I have to rely on the bounty from tempests, lost travellers and carriages mired in the mud. So when strangers seek shelter, ask directions, or request help to mend their carriage wheel, I am always happy to play the good host and help out. It isn't my fault when they can't pay the price for the service I provide?"

He banged angrily on the glass of the aquarium, making whatever was inside flash brightly. Orbs of light appeared to dart and swirl around inside the murk, clearly agitated at the sound.

"If you can't pay for my aid, then I either hold your family to ransom until you can, or experiment on you... Or both in Octavian's case. Oh would you like a biscuit?" He turned offering a plate of stale oatmeal cookies as if this conversation were completely rational and sane. Kerian noted that several of the offered biscuits had bites already taken out of them.

"I would not like to spoil my dinner." Kerian apologised, moving to follow and remembering the place settings at the long table as he passed. "Are you expecting more guests?"

A pale hand reached out, adjusting the flame below a bubbling beaker, turning the heat to a low simmer before the scientist's piercing eyes turned their attention back towards Kerian.

"My hounds are already bringing our latest visitors towards the keep. I expect them shortly, despite their reluctance to accept my invitation. I get very angry when people don't accept my charity." He looked back towards the discarded cookies as if making a valid point. "I'm starting not to like you Mr Styx. I think we should talk business. Where is the bounty that you have promised me?"

Kerian met his host's gaze and frowned, causing the man's facial expression to darken and match his own. The pup squirmed desperately in the scientist's grasp but he showed no signs of noticing, his focus now entirely on Kerian.

"We shall discuss payment of ransom when I have seen Octavian's wife and child. Not a moment before." Kerian replied coldly. "I feel there is no need to pay you if the goods have been damaged."

"Damaged." The laugh was humourless and dry. "The welfare of the goods depends on how quickly Octavian returned with payment. How long ago was it my hound? How long since I sent you out into the big wide world to gather ransom for sheltering your wife and daughter from those hill bandits?" His gaze looked over to where Octavian was sniffing at one of the glass cases in the left corridor and whining softly.

Kerian started to edge towards the cases, his passage taking him close to the glass aquarium. Orbs of flickering light raced towards him.

"What's in here?" Kerian asked, trying to change to subject and calm the scientist down. "Is it some kind of aquatic will-o-wisp?" One of the creatures slammed against the inside of the algae coated glass, red and white pulsating colours flared in the water and where the colours faded at the tips of the creature's limbs. Kerian noted the image and frowned. His suspicions were coming together now, the mental jigsaw puzzle pieces slotting into place but he did not like the picture he was beginning to perceive.

"Is something the matter?" His host asked. "You look as if you have seen a ghost Mr Styx. I can assure you they are perfectly harmless as long as you don't fall in the water. These creatures use colours in the most unusual ways. The way they communicate forms a large part of my experiments." He tapped on the glass again, watching with glee as the lights within flared red and white.

"I often find if I leave them long enough, they can become extremely aggressive, especially when they are hungry." A smile filled with rotted teeth flashed towards Kerian, before the scientist turned and started to climb a metal staircase set at the side of the tank.

"Do you know a Lampren can also live for hundreds of years without any signs of aging?" The scientist climbed a few steps, wrestling with the pup that was clearly very aware of where it was heading. "They like their food to be particularly energetic. It's something to do with how they process the chemicals found in their prey's brain at the time of the kill. I hope to unlock that secret and figure out how they do it. I also want to figure out how they mesmerise their prey."

The scientist opened the lid of the aquarium and without a sign of remorse threw the puppy inside the tank where it immediately started splashing about in the water, desperate to escape, its claws frantically paddling at the surface. The lid slammed back down, sealing the creature inside its watery tomb and the lights in the tank started flashing wildly.

"Mankind has always wanted to outlive the years they are given," the scientist continued with his lecture as he descended the staircase. "They pluck at straws to extend life beyond its natural limits. I know of two such pitiful attempts, there is a cursed knight that has managed to live for hundreds of years on an island to the north of here, his keep filled with the wailing spirits of his doomed family who do nothing but torment him every night, leaving him in abject misery." He brushed his hands together, then wiped them on his trousers before continuing his tale.

"Then there are rumours of a lich wizard who has managed to use his obsession with magic to keep his body functioning, despite the fact that pieces of him keep rotting away over time. I understand he has to mask his body in enchantments of illusion just so he can sit with people and not cause them to vomit." His host grinned again before turning to a workstation and flicking a beaker filled with a viscous purple fluid. Kerian tried to focus on his host but felt his gaze drawn towards the aquarium and the pitiful sounds coming from within.

"Then there are the vampires and the were-creatures. I've tried that. The failed experiments are here for you to see. Only existing during the twilight hours, responding to the cycles of the moon or having an unquenchable thirst for blood. No...none of these ideas appeal to me. If I can harness the Lampren's power, I will not simply extend how long I live, I shall remain fit and well enough to enjoy those years and will have the power to make anyone obey my commands."

"Rattling around, all alone inside your ruined keep. How is that any better than a cursed knight or an undead wizard?" Kerian spat, his horror tainting each word as the water inside the aquarium frothed and churned as the Lampren circled the struggling puppy. Colours flashed inside the tank, then suddenly the puppy stopped struggling, its movements weaker, before it slipped beneath the surface and slid down the glass. The creatures inside the tank attacked as one, ripping the pup apart in a frenzy.

Tiny barbs on the end of their feelers shredded the drowning creature into small parts, lumps of flesh swiftly swallowed by the monsters, presenting Kerian with a sickening view as larger barbs lanced out and sought ingress to the puppy's skull and the moist brain inside.

"Oh I don't intend to stay here. I intend to travel, see the world, feast on the sights, the sounds, the smells. If you can live forever you can amass wealth and live in style as long as you don't spend too long in one place. The world is my mistress and I am keen to indulge in everything she can give me."

Kerian swallowed hard, suddenly feeling a little light headed. He walked unsteadily over to the glass case where Octavian continued to scratch and whine. He gazed past his friend's shaggy form and noted the beautiful woman that appeared to be sleeping at the base of the cabinet, her body curled tightly in the small space, her legs drawn up, her hair a cushion against the glass. Ana had never looked so radiant in all the times she had visited him. A luminous ghost stood over her body crying softly, her phantom hand tenderly touching the glass above her transformed husband's head where he continued scratching at the glass coffin that held her corpse, his claws working frantically around a small crack at the base.

The knight tried to clear his throat but suddenly found it raw with emotion as his host laughed coldly behind him. Ana looked as though she had been dead for a long time.

"Oh my dear Octavian," the scientist stated sarcastically. "You always were too slow. I bet you regret knocking on my door now don't you."

"Where's the child?" Kerian asked his voice barely a whisper, his eyes not moving from the crack in the case. "Where is Iolander?"

"Why Mr Styx. Where else did you think I got the fresh food for my hounds?" He laughed, slowly licking the blood-stained fingers of his hand.

Kerian felt the gorge rising in his throat. The room suddenly felt too hot. He needed to sit down. The knight turned and headed over to the dinner table, sinking down onto one of the chairs his body shaking as he realised the horror that he faced.

"Now, now Mr Styx. Don't look so pale." He slid a crystal glass in Kerian's direction and poured a clear liquid into it. "Have a drink, relax. Then we can get down to business. You still have my ransom to discuss."

The scientist smiled, then slapped his pale forehead with his open palm.

"Oh where are my manners?" he chastised himself, tutting loudly. "I realise I never introduced myself. How extremely rude of me. I hope you can forgive me."

Kerian looked up at his host and fought the urge to be sick. He knew what the man was going to say. Had known it long before this moment yet hoped against hope it could not be true.

"Welcome to Castle Glowme Mr Styx. My name is Lord Okubi" He held out his hand in greeting, his fingers still streaked with blood.

"...But you can call me Malum."

Chapter Forty-Nine

The stone block grated as it slowly raised up from the floor of the maze, allowing two deep brown Minotaur eyes to stare out across the darkened arena towards the *Stairway of the Triumphant* where it rotated at the very centre of the labyrinth. Nostrils flared as the creature sniffed, trying to see if he could detect any other contestant's scent but there was an amount of pungent smoke slowly sliding across the ceiling in dark black clouds and all that his nostrils detected was something that smelt like roasted pig that contrasted sharply with the scent of dead snail currently at his feet.

"What can you see? Come on Rauph boost me up so I can take a look. I want to see where we are." Ashe complained.

"We are at the centre of the labyrinth." Rauph replied. "I can see the staircase but I can't see anything else."

"Then what are we waiting for?" Ashe pushed from below. "Come on let's win this stupid competition and then we can finally leave Taurean." Rauph frowned, the Halfling's words weighing as heavily upon his mind as the stone slab currently balanced upon his head. To be honest, despite everything that had happened he was not sure if he really wanted to leave Taurean.

The stone slab slid fully over to one side and Rauph climbed out, his chestnut hair covered in white dust and grime from navigating the underground passage. He turned and offered his hand, pulling Ashe up through the hatch as if he were catching a fish off the stern of the *El Defensor*, yanking the Halfling clear out of the hole as if he weighed little or nothing at all.

Ashe stared around as soon as his feet touched the ground, his eyes wide with excitement, taking in the tall spiralling staircase that remained in constant motion, the bladed steps folding away, whilst others opened up like petals from a flower kissed by the rays of the morning sun. The staircase wound its way up through the ceiling and into what had to be the innards of the great pyramid but from where they stood, Rauph and Ashe were too distant to see into the centre of the ancient monument. Beams of fractured light shone down through the opening at the top of the stairwell, bathing the shifting steps beneath in a golden glow that winked on and off as the steps subsided and then reformed.

The arena floor also glowed with a shimmering light, highlighting a grid pattern of perfect squares each ten foot by ten foot with a gleaming silver edge. It reminded Ashe of a massive board of *Knights and Castles*.

Rauph and he were on the edge of it, with the shifting stairway standing at the middle of the far side. The Halfling's eyes scanned the floor, realising that the square pattern was repeated both to the left and the right and probably on the far side of the staircase as well. Four boards overlapping, so that whatever way a contestant approached the stairs, they would have to cross the patterned floor. Ashe found the floor a delight to behold, the squares shimmering about the base of the stunning, golden stairs as if they were ripples rolling out across a bejewelled pond.

"It's beautiful!" Ashe whispered in awe. He took another long look around the large area, frustrated that he could only make out the vague edges of the massive arena from where they stood due to the thick smoke in the air. There were no clear signs of the entrances into this space, so he had no idea from where the other contestants were expected to appear. Ashe shrugged and stepped away from Rauph, eager to gain a better look at the spinning stairway.

The square beneath his little boot clicked as he stepped on it, freezing the Halfling in place.

"Oops!" he winced, rocking backwards and forwards on the stone and feeling it move beneath him.

"Oops?" Rauph turned from sliding the slab back into place. "What do you mean 'Oops?'"

A razor thin sheet of metal shot up vertically from the floor, separating the two companions placing a gleaming wall directly between them. Ashe uttered a nervous laugh, then stepped to the left to try and walk around the barrier, feeling the stone shift again as his weight was positioned. Another sheet of metal flew into the air, preventing him from stepping from the stone, its passing edge catching Ashe's left shoulder and spinning him about.

"Oww! Mouldy acorns!" Ashe steadied himself and rubbed his shoulder only to find his hand came away wet with blood. He stepped to the right, moving reflexively away from the new wall and the stone moved beneath him again. "Umm Rauph, these walls are really sharp. Don't get too..."

Another barrier rocketed towards the ceiling, this time on the right, boxing Ashe in on three sides and forcing the Halfling to either stay where he was and risk getting trapped if the final side rose, or to step out further into the large open arena and risk further dangers. Ashe knew he had to think fast but there was really no safe option to consider. He could not risk getting trapped, yet neither did he fancy stepping across the gleaming silver line on the floor that now had much more sinister connotations than a simple artistic pattern.

He felt the floor rocking gently beneath his feet and had a thought. If he could just jump all the way out to the centre of the adjacent square, without touching the edge, then he would probably not trigger further reactions. Ten foot of stone lay before him, who was he kidding, there was no way he was going to jump ten feet! He took a deep breath, then leapt out onto the only available space left and felt a rumbling beneath his feet confirming his fears. He had jumped too short!

The fourth side of the square shot up behind him with a bang, completely surrounding the area he had just left. The sound ominously echoing around the arena. There was a loud clanking, then all four metal sides slowly started retracting down into the floor, revealing a yawning black pit where the floor space had once been. Loud grating sounds descended from the ceiling as long openings started to part, revealing the faces of the spectators eagerly craning their necks to stare down into the killing ground whilst other holes opened up in the floor to raise smoking torches that spat and popped upon tall tripods.

Rauph looked across the pit at Ashe and held up his hands, indicating to the Halfling that he needed to stay still. The Minotaur's face was stern in his concern for his little friend but then turned to confusion as a faint clattering sound arose far behind the little thief. Ashe spun, watching with interest as a row of metal sheets shot towards the ceiling in a vibrating wave, marking the determined passage of someone charging across the floor towards the staircase.

"Run for the stairs, Ashe." Rauph ordered. "Don't you stop for anything, you hear me. Don't look behind you, just make for those stairs and whatever you do... Don't fall over." Ashe looked down at his feet, then the squares ahead of him and tried to figure it out. Running was all well and good but if he was running and missed a step by even the slightest margin, he could end up half a Halfling, or even less and he was not very keen on that image. He was already small enough!

Ashe shook his head and edged his foot carefully towards the left side of the square he was standing on, all he needed to do was make sure he did not trigger the slab. There was a click, barely felt through his boots and the metal sheet slammed up, blocking his escape to the left. Ashe looked at the distance remaining between his foot and that gleaming metal edge and frowned. It was nearly three feet, meaning that he would need to jump well before the edge if he was to avoid triggering the trap. He did not have the stride that Rauph had. He was never going to be able to do this!

If he could not leap across the yawning pit behind him, then he had no choice but to move forwards. He swallowed hard, it was too much, he'd be sliced and diced before he had even crossed two squares!

"What are you standing there for?" Rauph bellowed. "Can't you see what is happening?" The navigator gestured urgently towards the clattering sheets of metal and Ashe looked that way, initially not knowing what he was looking at. He did not have the advantage of Rauph's height and could not see the jagged line of open pits yawning across the playing board.

"Go!" Rauph roared, before he started to sprint across the squares, metal sheets rising towards the heavens as each mighty stride hit the floor, the razor edges missing the Minotaur by seconds as he charged determinedly towards the advancing wall of metal angling towards them. Rauph instinctively knew that if he waited too long and allowed that jagged pathway to cut across his path it would leave the two companions isolated and unable to reach their goal. Ashe inhaled deeply and balanced on his toes, as if he were about to run a race, then sprung lightly on his feet, only to hear yet another ominous click.

"That's not fair." The Halfling screamed. "I never moved!" The right side of the square blocked as another razor-edged sheet shot for the sky, leaving Ashe with only one exit and it was not in the direction he wanted to run. The staircase was over to the right meaning he now had to go forwards and then leap sideways to regain his path.

"Oh amorous almonds!" He screamed, charging forward and out onto the next square realising that if he put just one step wrong, he was going to be literally kissing his nuts goodbye. He landed on the next slab, feeling it click but kept running, the air behind him rushing past as the metal barrier launched up from beneath. Sinders squawked loudly in protest from its perch next to Ashe's ear, flapping its wings and obscuring the Halfling's vision.

"I know, I am rushing, I really am." The Halfling responded to his feathered friend, spitting feathers from his mouth as he leapt to another stone, missing amputation by the barest of inches. "Just hold on tightly and close your eyes, like me." Sinders stared at his master, in shock, then ducked his head down into his black and white plumage with a further terrified squawk.

Ashe hurled himself to the next slab, his lungs burning, the metal barrier physically pushing him forward this time with the shockwave of air, causing the Halfling to windmill with his arms to prevent falling. The little thief was not stupid, he realised he was not getting the distance he needed with each step, he was going to end up missing his footing and the result was too gruesome to contemplate. He looked over towards one of the torches set about the arena floor and noted that the slab upon which the nearest smoking flame stood appeared different from the others. He needed to change direction anyway, so he leapt to the side, his chest heaving as he ran across and dived for the sanctuary of the spitting brand, just as something whistled past his head and scythed through the air in a slow crescent, right where he would have been, had he not changed direction.

The line of metal barriers standing up behind him, blocked Ashe's sight from identifying who had just thrown the strange missile towards him but his eyes had recognised the strange silvery weapon arcing back around. It had to be the blue competitor. He got to his feet, realising his hands were greasy from the surface of the slab but all too pleased that where he stood was solid and not threatening to slice him to ribbons at any time. His eyes started to smart almost instantly from being close to the spitting torch suspended above him.

He looked up, then realised his mistake and quickly stared back at the ground again, hoping vainly that his mind would erase the terrible image he had just beheld. The thief finally understood the real concerns of the street urchin Porthon, regarding the strange disappearances of his street friends. Ashe swallowed hard and tried to concentrate, despite the wobble in his throat and the tears in his eyes. How could these people be so cruel to those less fortunate than themselves?

The Halfling gritted his teeth and waited for the barrier to rumble back down again so that he could see the blue and silver armoured Minotaur that was limping determinedly towards him, her orange hair all spiked and hard, her arm already back, ready to throw her deadly weapon.

Ashe swiftly took in the scene, looking around for Rauph and spotting the Minotaur far across the arena floor, charging alongside whoever was trying to cut them off. There would be no rescue from his friend. The gleaming staircase was directly ahead of him and the blue champion was rapidly closing from behind with a stride the Halfling could never hope to match. Rauph had told him to run for the stairs and by every nut analogy in the book, that was what Ashe was going to do!

* * * * * *

Rauph surged ahead, angling towards the advancing line of barriers with a dogged determination, his own pounding movements initiating a matching boundary of cold metal. His eyes judged the passage of whoever was moving to cut them off, the competitor shrewdly triggering both of the sides of each slab as she ran and allowing her own forward momentum to trigger the metal sheet behind, completing each square and dropping the whole into the chasm below.

It was a clever play but it did not allow for what Rauph had in mind. At the last moment he leapt diagonally across onto the slab directly in his opponent's path, slamming his right heel down hard on the rear edge just before his rival could reach it. His actions activated the metal barrier just as the competitor moved to jump across after triggering the left side of the square. There was a loud thud and a curse as they rebounded back off the barrier. Rauph did not hesitate and leapt to the other side, ready to activate the wall on the right, there was another frustrated cry and Ammet appeared in a swirl of red cloak, materialising out of thin air before the navigator's eyes.

"I've got you." Rauph roared menacingly, knowing he had his victim boxed in, due to the fact that Ammet's own path had resulted in the metal wall triggering between this slab and the one she had just leapt from, leaving her with nowhere left to run apart from through himself.

"I don't think so." Ammet replied, glaring venomously at Rauph from where she stood, her curly black hair soaked in sweat and plastered to her brow. Her gold earring glinted in the torchlight and there was a desperation and hunger in her dark eyes that made Rauph realise she was not going to back down without a fight. "You don't even belong here. Why didn't you stay dead? I mean what do you care about winning? You gave up your right to the throne when you abandoned us."

"I care for the Taurean people." Rauph confessed. "...And I care for my friends. That's all the reasons I need." He watched intently for a reaction from the female contestant and watched as she bowed her head and stared up at him through her long eyelashes coltishly.

"Can't we work together, beat Mora and then figure out what to do next?" She asked slyly, a treacherous smile spreading slowly across her features.

"I don't think there is much to figure out." Rauph confessed. "I have to beat Drummon to save my friends. If this means accepting the mantle of king, then so be it. I do not want the position but I shall not shirk from my duty if called."

"And I can be your bride?" Ammet smiled moving sensuously towards him. "We can rule Taurean side by side." A clattering sounded behind Rauph making him check over his shoulder to see Ashe was now cut off from crossing the slabs. The ominous figure of Chane walked towards the Halfling. She was repeatedly throwing her deadly weapon out towards him, forcing Ashe to cower at the base of one of the flaming torches, instead of allowing him to head across the slabs towards the rotating stair. Rauph immediately felt uncomfortable with the growing conflict within him, he needed to act and save his friend but Ammet was the more immediate danger here.

"Come on, don't say you haven't thought about us being together?" Ammet continued, gathering her long cloak in her hands and pulling it tight across her body to accentuate her Minotaur curves. "Once you have lain with me you will never want anyone else." Rauph licked his lips nervously, not sure what to do as she swayed towards him, swinging her hips and confusing his emotions. She was quite exotic for a Minotaur despite her obviously psychotic personality flaws. Ammet winked, offering a gleam in her eye that offered nights of long hot smouldering passion, then her arm snapped forward sending her evil cloak fanning out towards him.

"You are so stupid..." She laughed, knowing that Kristoph would never have the time to get out of the way before her ravenous cloak engulfed him and teleported a large part of his torso away, leaving him bleeding out on the floor. Her eyes gleamed with excitement, the surprise was complete.

"...So I'm told." Rauph replied, stomping his foot down and triggering the final metal barrier. The sheet sliced up through the leading hem of the cloak, cutting free a scarlet ribbon that fluttered harmlessly to the floor at Rauph's feet. There was a loud bang as the wall surrounded the slab then a muffled thump as the stone dropped away inside. Rauph had no time to congratulate himself over his ingenuity. He instantly turned about and started to retreat across the slabs eager to assist his little friend.

* * * * * *

Ashe shrieked as the deadly silvery blue blade arced in on yet another glittering orbit, just managing to duck before the swirling blade took his head off. This was ridiculous! He was literally a sitting duck standing under this torch which meant he had to risk it, make a break for it and run for the stairs like Rauph had told him to do, despite the inherent risk it involved.

The weapon scythed back and was deftly caught by Chane who sent it whirling out almost instantly, this time swooping it in low, causing Ashe to jump or risk losing a limb. He jumped, stepped back a few unsteady spaces and caught himself just inches from the gleaming edge of the nearest slab. Sparks flew as the weapon skimmed the stone surface, before it looped up again and arced back around to its mistresses' outstretched hand.

"Hold on Sinders." Ashe yelled running for the next slab and throwing himself through the air. He landed with a thump, feeling the slab click and hearing the metal sheet launching from the ground behind him, only for it to clang noisily as Chane's deadly toy collided with it. He did not want to know how close the weapon had come to hitting him and swallowed hard before jumping to the next slab causing the same automated reaction from the trapped arena floor. His eyes darted from side to side, noting the walls of metal slowly retracting around the floor about him, some near, others far, opening up different views and opportunities of pathways to take.

One wall squealed loudly in protest, shuddering to a stop in mid descent, a jagged hole cut through the metal appeared to be preventing its smooth surface from sliding back into place. Ashe had no idea what had caused the damage but as Rauph was not focusing on it and was instead staring intently in his direction, he figured it wasn't that important. He gazed back over towards the golden staircase and took a deep breath before throwing himself towards the next slab, his arms and legs flapping, as if he were some kind of gangly frog.

The navigator angled towards his little friend, noting Chane stopping to collect her weapon from the floor and eyeing up her target as he hopped ridiculously from one slab to another. It would have been quite amusing if it had not been for the terrible danger the Halfling was in. She drew back her arm waiting and watching for each wobbling jump the thief made, then threw her weapon.

Rauph bellowed in horror as he watched the deadly throw, already knowing in his heart that this time her aim would be true. Ashe landed awkwardly, pulled himself up to jump again, then bent his legs and bounced high, twisting in the air just as the blade whirled in and pierced his right side. The thief dropped to the floor like a puppet with its strings cut. A wall of metal shot up as he fell, activated by the Halfling's landing, blocking Rauph's view. He charged for all he was worth, noting the vindictive smile upon Chane's face as she watched him coming, aware that he would never be able to reach his fallen friend in time as she moved behind the barrier chuckling.

Chane strode purposefully over towards the downed Halfling, intent on causing the pitiful creature pain and suffering, knowing it would further enrage Kristoph, to put him off balance and therefore easier to defeat. She knew it took a cool head to beat her in unarmed combat and by goading the prince in this way, she knew he would be blinded with rage by the time he arrived. Kristoph's pet lay on the floor groaning, his hand clutching where her weapon had penetrated his tunic, its blade wedged in his bulging side.

She moved closer, stepping carefully over onto the slab and leant down to retrieve her blade, tugging hard at the weapon, only to find it was caught up inside the little man's tunic. Chane tugged again and something bright blue started to emerge from his clothing. Was this the colour of a Halfling's blood? She pulled harder at the tangled mess bulging out through the rent sliced in Ashe's tunic, its edges stained dark with blood. What was this? Some kind of inner organ? Chane braced herself and pulled harder, drawing another groan of pain from the thief as the object finally popped out, making the Minotaur stagger back towards the edge of the slab, her boot stopping just short of triggering the mechanism.

The female Minotaur gazed down in disgust at the wet blooded thing she held in her hands, initially unsure as to what it could be. Then she turned it over in her hands and started to laugh. A bright stuffed toy, fashioned in a shape of a monkey, stared back at her, its eyes wide, its nose formed from a button, the right ear shredded and hanging limp at the side of its head. She struggled to free her weapon from the tangled material but the threads were all wrapped around the blade and it was knotted tight from her pulling.

Why on earth had this pitiful creature been carrying a stuffed toy inside his tunic? She looked down at the little man still lying on the floor and allowed herself a moment of rare maternal emotion. He looked so defenceless lying there, so sad, so pathetic.

"I think I know why Kristoph liked you." Chane whispered, still working at the toy as she attempted to free her weapon. "You are quite cute for a pet. I bet you were constantly keeping him on his toes." She turned away, confident the Halfling was no threat to her plans and prepared to face the angry chestnut Minotaur charging across the board towards her. One final traumatic wrench and the weapon ripped free from the toy monkey, allowing Chane to drop the ruined toy to the floor where she stepped on it and ground it under her left boot.

It was time for Kristoph to meet his doom.

"Surprise!" A small voice groaned from behind her, causing Chane to start, just as a small hand shoved her hard in the small of her back making her stagger off balance, her left boot lifting from the crushed blood-soaked monkey and scuffing forwards, leaving a smear of scarlet in its wake. She reacted quicker than Ashe gave her credit for, her left hand sweeping behind her to grab a handful of the Halfling's hair, just as he bent down to retrieve his toy.

Ashe shrieked in pain and reacted the only way he could, pushing towards the Minotaur to relieve the pain, just as Chane's slick boot came down on the edge of the slab and skidded forwards.

"Look out!" Ashe cried. "Don't pull me anymore. You'll drag us both over..." He struggled with the Minotaur but she was simply too strong for him.

"You stupid creature. You dared to lay hands on me? Me! Do you think you of all creatures have the right to tell me what to do?" There was a click, a responding metallic swoosh and a sickening thud as the metal sheet shot upwards. Sinders took to the air in an explosion of feathers. The crowd roared in delight, causing Rauph to scream out his fear, the view to whatever grisly spectacle they beheld still blocked by the row of triggered metal barriers, letting the Minotaur's imagination run wild. Ashe was dead, Chane had killed him, he had not been fast enough, it was all his fault! He charged around the end of the barrier and stopped breathless, his eyes horrified at what he beheld.

Ashe lay slumped against the metal barrier, his little body covered in gore, his eyes closed as if he were sleeping, the lower half of Chane's body still spasmodically twitching on top of him. His little hand clutched a blue furry toy that was turning black as it soaked up the crimson pool around him. Rauph jumped over onto the slab, ignoring the click and swoosh of the metal barrier behind him as he dropped to his knees, snatching the Halfling out from beneath the Minotaur's corpse. The navigator's chestnut eyes filled with tears that he desperately tried to blink away as he scrutinized Ashe's body for some clue to the fate that had befallen his friend.

Rauph scrabbled at the Halfling's side, pulling Ashe's tunic away from the worst of the gore, finding himself retrieving pieces of adhered blue fur away from a shallow wound in the thief's side. This made no sense, Ashe had to be hurt somewhere else? Rauph turned the little thief over, noting a large egg had formed on Ashe's left temple, as the Halfling's head lolled to one side. The navigator's huge hands continuing to frantically search for a more serious wound but found his friend was covered in so much gore that his task was simply an impossible one. Everything was covered in so much blood!

The crowd screamed for more blood, making Rauph wish he could climb up through the observation ports and lay waste with his swords. Maybe if it was their own blood being spilled, they would not be as vocal in demanding more tribute from the contestants they clamoured over.

"Ashe! Wake up." Rauph yelled. "Come on you stupid Halfling, open your eyes!" The body in his arms remained unresponsive. A low groan sounded from the Minotaur's lips as he gathered up his little friend and bundled him in his arms, collecting the ruined toy and Chane's discarded throwing blade as he did so. He was not going to leave Ashe alone out here, under the eyes of these disgusting vultures!

For a moment, Rauph considered walking back to the tunnel entrance where he and Ashe had first come from but a quick glance at the cavernous floor where the stone blocks had dropped away made it clear there was no way back. He had only one choice, to ascend the rotating staircase. The navigator started walking solemnly across the arena floor, beyond caring as rows of metal barriers lanced into the sky behind him, the deadly blades missing him by the narrowest of margins. His attention was totally focused on his fallen companion. This was his only friend and he had failed him. No one had been as good to Rauph since Scrave had left. How could he be expected to focus on the challenge now? How could he continue up the staircase of the triumphant when the only thing that truly mattered to him lay lifeless in his arms? There was nothing triumphant about this.

Rauph paused in his passage and looked up to realise with some surprise that he had arrived at the base of the spiralling stairs. He stared up at the dizzying array of collapsing and extending steps, the whirling and spiralling cog work mechanism and the way some steps rolled into each other or peeled away out over nothing. The climb was undeniably daunting, the steps folding and opening at set times, the very design of the intricate structure meant to confuse and befuddle anyone challenging it.

The mechanical movement had been constructed to make people falter in their steps, made them question the route, look down at their feet or up above them at the intermeshing cogs, the movement drawing the eye, distracting the unfocused, making them plummet to their doom or risk being crushed in the machinery of the stair.

However, Rauph did not think about looking ahead, planting his feet or picking a route. He just wanted to get his little friend to safety. The navigator placed his boot down on the first step just as it opened, then continued to place his feet one after the other, his mind focused entirely on Ashe and therefore he was not distracted or fooled by the optical illusions created by the movement of the deadly monument.

Each step took him further up into the spinning structure, each descending boot landing just as a stair extended and each step lifted just as the support beneath it collapsed. Rauph remained totally focused on the still Halfling and did not flinch as a stair above him extended right where his own would have been if he had not stepped forward at just the right moment. He did not balk as the step beneath him swung out and then drew him back into the staircase at a higher level, just in time for him to step off and continue his treacherous climb.

Within moments he was passing through the ceiling and out amongst the seated crowds within the pyramid. They roared their appreciation, pointing and cheering the champion as he continued to ascend without pause, then one by one they started to notice the bloodied figure the Minotaur supported in his arms and their cheers died away. This champion who could literally be their king, refused to wave or acknowledge his supporters, his forlorn face indicating something terrible had happened here.

It was a display of compassion that left some murmuring and others speechless. Where had this small child come from? How had it ended up in the deadly maze? Why had Kristoph taken this loss so personally? His actions were so uncharacteristic. Here was a Minotaur that truly cared for his people no matter what race they were.

A complete unnatural hush descended inside the pyramid as more and more spectators noted the humbling and moving sight, the smooth click and whir of the oscillating and rotating stair suddenly loud to everyone gathered. Rauph remained focused on his friend, still placing one foot after the other and trusting that he would keep Ashe safe until they reached the very top. He refused to look away from his charge, refused to be distracted, even when the throwing blade, still slick from blood, slipped from his arms and clattered down the stairway. He did not care, all he wanted was for Ashe to be alive and well.

"Kristoph." Initially, the call was from just a few lowly spectators, a low murmur of appreciation shown the only way they knew how, by calling out their champion's name. It remained low but slowly gained momentum. "Kristoph, Kristoph!" The people were showing support for the Minotaur they believed would be their king. Some started to cry, others to simply hug those standing beside them. In their appreciation no one noticed how the forgotten throwing blade suddenly disappeared from the stair upon which it had landed.

Shadows started to lengthen around the inside of the pyramid, the torchlight becoming a deeper hue of orange and yellow as the natural light from the opening in the capstone high above started to leech from the sky and the sun began to set behind the Taurean mountains.

"Rauph I think they are getting your name wrong again." A little voice murmured, causing the Navigator to stumble. "Did you see what the blue contestant did to my toy monkey? I was saving this for Katarina. Someone in the labyrinth crowd must have dropped it so I picked it up to keep it safe for her."

Rauph stopped completely, the rhythm of his steps rushing completely from his mind as he stared down at Ashe in disbelief.

"Ashe, you're alive." Rauph gushed. "You're really alive. I thought I had lost you."

"Oh you will never lose me Rauph. I mean you are so tall that you stick out easily in a crowd. I could see you from a mile off." Ashe smiled as the Minotaur threw back his head and laughed, only for Rauph's laugh to change into a bellow of pain.

Ashe tumbled from Rauph's arms as the navigator dropped to the metal floor, colliding with the next step ahead, before sliding across its rotating metal surface and over to the one beyond that. His fingers scrabbled for a hold as his little legs slid away from beneath him, his body sliding rapidly across its golden surface as the whole length of the step started to fold away.

Rauph looked down at his leg in horror, noting the blue and white throwing blade jutting from his calf. His mind could not fathom how this had happened. He had been holding it in his arms, or had he dropped it? He could not be sure but the pain was so intense. He moved to grip the weapon and draw it from his flesh when the air shimmered before him and he found himself staring into Ammet's piercing black eyes, her scarlet cloak swirling about her.

"I will teach you to turn your back on me!" she spat venomously. "I will make sure you regret that choice until your dying breath."

"How?" was all Rauph could stutter through gritted teeth as he felt the step beneath him starting to slowly slide inwards, towards the hub of the stairway.

"My cloak saved me." Ammet snapped. "It removes anything it touches apart from its wearer. I just laid it on the barrier and stepped through. I intend to reward it with a feast of royal blood. I'm going to let it take you a piece at a time." She snapped the cloak down and Rauph snatched his hand back, the fibres of the cloak brushing his fingers and making them feel numb.

Rauph felt the step suddenly lurch beneath him and he was swung backwards, away from Ammet and over towards Ashe, who was himself barely hanging on to the step he had skidded across. His little legs kicked at the air, desperate for a foothold, as the bladed step he was upon, started to slowly rotate towards him, risking dropping him further down and off the edge. Rauph knew that despite it appearing as if Ashe had several lives, there would be no way his friend would survive such a plummet.

The crowd held their breath, watching this spectacle unfold. Sinders continued to swoop about the stairway, darting in towards Ashe then swooping away again, unable to land. The step continued to turn, Ashe slipped further down the surface. He could not hold on; his fingers were still slick with blood. His eyes widened as he watched first one finger, then another, drop from the thin edge he clung to.

His hand slipped one last time and he fell out into nothing...

...just as Rauph's huge hand snatched him by the back of his tunic and threw him bodily upwards into the air, where he crashed down onto another step, only a short distance below the strange ball-like structure situated at the very pinnacle of the staircase. The navigator slid along, propelled by the motion of his upward swing and nearly dropped himself off the ledge, much to the gasps of the crowd. He struggled to swing his leg up only to scream again as Ammet materialised behind him and tugged the weapon violently.

"Rauph look out." Ashe screamed, as he scrambled across the steps, finally managing to pull himself up inside the ball to relative safety. "She's still below you." Rauph swung his legs clear, just as the crimson cloak fell across the tread he had vacated, tearing it away and leaving a gaping hole and a piece of golden metal spinning away towards the floor far, far below.

"Come on Rauph, come on!" Ashe urged, shuffling along the walkway to try and get a better view of his friend struggling to vault another step and clamber up a clanking gear towards his little friend's outstretched hand. Their fingers brushed just as the gear beneath Rauph dissolved under the voracious attention of the scarlet cloak. He dropped down, crashing through two steps and slid to a stop on a stair that was folding back towards the central column.

"Shame you didn't fall the whole way." Ammet appeared above him laughing at Rauph's fall just as another stair telescoped out above her and smacked her on the back of the head. She turned to react, snarling, then realising she faced a solid object turned back towards where Kristoph had landed, only to find the chestnut Minotaur was gone, leaving a blood trail dripping around the corner.

The light flickered and a shudder ran through the stair. Rauph took in a deep breath, gritting his teeth from the pain in his leg, feeling the warmth of his blood dripping down his leg. The stairway trembled again and Rauph suddenly realised why. He thought back to the rules of the game.

"If any contestant fails to ascend the staircase, before the last ray of the setting sun touches the capstone on the pyramid, the exits to the maze will be sealed and the monsters remaining permitted to consume those who are still wandering its passageways."

The sun was setting! The stairway was about to fold closed like a flower tightening its petals to protect the insides from the coldness of night. He leapt up to the stair above him and pulled himself up in agonising grunts. Scuffling sounded from below but Rauph leapt just before the cloak swirled about him leaving Ammet cursing in his wake.

"She's still behind you Rauph!" Ashe screamed.

Rauph dodged a scything stair, slid down another, then threw himself through the air, his arms wrapping tightly around the curved walkway, his legs swinging below him. Ashe leapt forwards trying to help pull him up but Rauph was way too heavy.

There was a snarl from below and Rauph screamed again as Ammet leapt for his leg, wrapping her arms around his wounded limb and bringing her whole weight down on him. She tugged and pulled but her thin frame was not enough to make Rauph lose his grip. She started to pull herself up his leg, her hands like claws reaching for the weapon embedded in the Minotaur's limb.

"I'm going to enjoy killing you." Ammet growled. The whole staircase suddenly stopped spinning and folding. The golden light flickered through the entire stairway then every step started to fold in upon itself. Ammet screamed as the steps below her disappeared, leaving her hanging out over a long drop. Her struggles grew more intense as she tried to claw her way up Rauph's body.

He yelled and bellowed, trying to shake the determined competitor from his leg but she clung on like a predator, intent on finishing off her victim. She lifted a hand free to lunge for the blade in Rauph's leg when a wet sodden blue mass smacked her in the face. She sputtered and raged, pushing the toy to one side, just as Rauph's boot kicked her, knocking her free.

Ammet screamed as she fell, the crowd roaring their approval as she dropped like a stone, her arms windmilling as if she were trying to fly, her crimson cloak billowing out behind her but doing nothing to slow her fall. She crashed into the floor, smacking down hard against the stone, bones cracking as her crimson cloak fanned out and landed on top of her. She groaned impossibly still alive, then the cloak dissolved the floor and she fell again down into the darkness below.

Rauph pulled himself up onto the walkway and lay there panting, his leg shaking from the pain of the weapon still punched through him. Ashe walked over arms outstretched on either side to keep his balance and winked.

"See I told you I would never lose you." He smiled, staring down to the ground far below. "I don't suppose anyone will give me my monkey back." Ashe jumped across his friend and ran to the edge of the walkway, just as Sinders swooped in then pulled up sharply with a shriek and darted away again. Burly hands reached down and yanked the Halfling up into the throne room above. Rauph pulled himself to his feet and somehow managed to stagger after his friend, totally exhausted but determined to keep Ashe safe. He reached the edge of the walkway and found the same massive hands pulling him from the gap and dropping him to the floor of the throne room.

Rauph lifted himself from his knees and froze as he beheld the torch-lit scene before him. Several Minotaur guards stood before him, one with a sword at Ashe's throat. Mora sat to the left with Wanessa beside her. A serving girl stood back in the shadows, her features indistinct but her scent somehow familiar and sitting on a throne to the right sat Drummon, his pelt gleaming, his eyes shining, whilst in his hands, he held the Labyris axe.

"You finally got here brother." Drummon smiled. "But I'm afraid you have arrived too late. The Labyris axe is mine and Taurean has a new king."

Chapter Fifty

"Now the introductions are over, why don't we get down to business." Malum hissed, leaning forwards and resting his chin on one pale slender hand. "I understand you promised a ransom. So... why don't you hand it over?"

Kerian swallowed hard, determined not to look towards the monster before him, his heart thumping in his chest. Malum... How could this be Malum? That was the name of the monster in the ship's graveyard, not a mad scientist that lived in a ruined castle, miles from anyone. His mind raced, looking around the room for some inspiration as to how he could bluff his way out of this, finding nothing within the myriad of bubbling bottles and creepy science experiments to explain his lack of funds.

"I feel that there has been a misunderstanding." Kerian replied, swallowing hard and trying to put on a face "I expected to pay for live hostages I could use as house slaves, not corpses. They are no good to me!"

"That's Octavian's fault not mine." Malum replied, spreading his free hand as if this was a moot point. "He knew it was a time limited offer and he simply ran out of time. Enough of the stalling, the ransom... now!"

Kerian's hand felt for his sword but it never got there. Two huge monsters came from nowhere and their hot jaws closed around his wrists before he could even lift them from the arms of his chair. Their teeth formed restraints more efficient than any manufactured manacles. Kerian struggled but this only made the creatures snarl and tighten their painful grip so he could feel the fangs pressing into his skin. The pressure made him instantly freeze; Octavian's warning of the consequence of a bite of these creatures replaying in his mind.

Malum clicked his fingers and Agnezkia padded over to Kerian, placing her huge paws onto his shoulders and pushing him further back in the chair with her immense weight, her jaws dripping saliva as she moved close to his face and gently licked his chin with a low warning rumble deep down in her throat. Her uncomfortable administrations continued to make Kerian squirm, her hot fetid breath against his skin, a long pink tongue licking down the side of Kerian's neck, lingering over the beating pulse of his carotid artery, before slipping down to his shoulder where she suddenly lunged and bit through the shoulder strap of his magical satchel.

Kerian's heart beat faster as he felt the hound tugging at the strap, knowing there was nothing inside the bag with which to pay Octavian's ransom. Even the exotic bread he had been eating on the span had disappeared. He knew this because he had checked when they walked through the forest. The bag had remained frustratingly empty. Powerless to do anything, he watched as Agnezkia pulled the bag free, retrieving it for her master. Kerian knew if he did not get his hands free in the next few valuable seconds and stopped Malum from opening the satchel, then the masquerade would be over and both he and Octavian were as good as dead. He watched as Agnezkia returned to her master's side and placed the bag obediently in his lap before she tilted her head so that Malum could rub behind her ears to show his appreciation.

"I must say this bag feels a little light to be carrying the amount you will need." Malum stated, lifting the bag up and jiggling it to see if he could feel anything moving inside before reaching for the flap. "Are you paying in gemstones? I'm not so keen on those, it is always so tricky to judge the value of them and I will need to get them converted into cold currency which is always a bother."

"I think you will find my form of tribute quite unique." Kerian replied, knowing full well that his 'currency' would definitely not be viewed favourably. He tested his living bonds once again and felt his skin pinch as the teeth clenching him gripped tighter. The hounds responded by salivating long stringy threads of drool that dribbled from his fingertips to the floor. Malum grabbed the flap of the bag and started to lift it.

"What guarantee will you give me that you will cure Octavian and let the two of us go?" Kerian blurted out, making Malum pause with the flap half lifted.

"Oh I never gave any guarantees." Malum smiled, his two fingers still holding the flap. "Octavian can never be cured of his condition but I would not let that worry you. You just need to make sure you take him for long walks, feed him regularly and lock him up every lunar cycle." The scientist looked up and grinned as if pleased at his pitiful attempt at humour.

"Look... just wait a moment. I would not want you to be disappointed in what I have brought." Kerian remarked. "If I can just... well... you know, if what you have there does not meet your needs, maybe as time is no longer an issue you can let me find something more suitable for Octavian's life. I am sure I can find you an alternative that is more appropriate to your needs." Malum scowled as Kerian continued talking, making the knight realise that maybe he had said too much, then, with one eye on Kerian, he lifted the flap and stared down inside the satchel.

Kerian held his breath as the deranged scientist's eyes narrowed, then strangely widened in surprise. This was it, any second now Malum was going to click his fingers and the hounds would tear out Kerian's throat! Malum cleared his own throat loudly, then sat back and re-examined the bag, slowly turning it around on the table, then he patted the outside of the bag with both hands before pushing the sides in towards each, practically making the satchel go flat. He sat there, for what felt like an eternity and then he looked up at Kerian and shook his head making the knight's heart sink.

"Well, well Mr Styx. I have to say when you first came here, I doubted your credentials. Now I am faced with this surprising development." Malum indicated the satchel, causing Kerian to swallow nervously again, his throat suddenly, painfully, dry. The knight's eyes darted nervously about the room, searching for anything that he could use to get himself out of this situation. He needed something to go his way for once.

Octavian was sadly oblivious to his predicament and was instead intently scraping at the bottom of his wife's casket. There was no knife near to hand, even if he could lift his arm to wield one. No way of distracting the creatures on either side of him without losing several fingers. He had run out of reasons and his time for stalling was over. Kerian slowly drew back a boot, intent on at least kicking out at something when the time came, whilst wondering why there was never a stray cat around when you needed one.

"I have to say this is not what I expected at all." Malum said slowly, emphasising every word as he shook his head from side to side. "How do you manage to do this? It is really quite incredible. Although I must confess this is not a currency that I am used to dealing with."

Kerian went to open his mouth, to joke one last time that the exchange rate for a bag of nothing was probably more valuable in Wellruff right now, or that maybe the bag was a high fashion item in Catterick and was therefore worth more money than it looked like, then resigned himself to the fact that his charade was over.

Malum slowly lifted his hand and inserted it carefully into the open satchel, before starting to rummage around inside. He pulled out a golden circular brooch with tiny rows of sapphires and diamonds rising up like a fountain of water on the front.

Kerian's mouth dropped open in surprise, just as Malum returned to the magical bag and extracted a small golden statue, a short dagger and a bronze goblet, placing them reverently on the table, his eyes gleaming with avarice, as a low gleeful chuckle issued from his pale lips.

"Where did you get all of these treasures from?" Malum gushed. "And this bag, wherever did you get such a wonderful satchel?" Kerian suddenly remembered where the unexpected treasures had come from. An image sprang to mind of Octavian scrabbling amongst broken crates that had fallen from the burial ship in the lost city of Tahl Avan. Oh Octavian, if he were not a dog right now, Kerian could have hugged him but time was short and Kerian recognised a slim advantage when he saw one. A plan of sorts started to form in his mind and he smiled.

"They are just a small sample from my own collection." Kerian replied, deciding to take the chance whilst it was offered. "You can keep everything from the bag if you wish but Octavian goes free, his wife and daughter get a proper burial and I'm afraid I keep the satchel." It was time to see how far he could push the scientist.

Malum looked down at the treasures on the table, his face clearly displaying the turmoil about responding to such demands, then weighed it all against the value of the items laid before him and the glittering jewels still waiting to be removed from the bag. He reached his hand over to the satchel and started to push it about the table, clearly conflicted.

"But I want the satchel." Malum finally responded getting to his feet and stamping the floor, much like a spoilt child. "Somehow it was not heavy, despite all of these wonders, yet when I squash it, it doesn't feel as if there is anything inside, despite the fact there are still so many treasures within. I want to know how it works. I need to know how it works."

"It is quite unique." Kerian admitted, nodding his head. "That is why I find it so useful to transport my wares. However, this bag has sentimental value and I could never part with it." The knight looked up at Malum and stared intently, knowing he had baited the hook but was yet to reel the scientist in. It was time to apply the pressure. After all, he had nothing to lose. The scientist's look of longing turned instantly into a thunderous frown. He lifted the flap on the satchel, toying with it, then moved to close the bag.

"I would not do that, if I were you." Kerian warned, mentally twitching his fishing line and teasing his opponent to bite. "I think it is time you released Octavian and myself and let us go on our way."

"You are not in a position to make demands." Malum screamed. "This is my home, this is my laboratory and as this satchel is in my home it becomes mine by right." Kerian continued to meet the scientist's fearsome gaze, not daring to flinch. This was going to be the gamble of his life.

"I warn you. If you close that bag our negotiation is over. I will not permit you any more treasure." Kerian stated, his tone adding a threat to his words. "My reputation is not only based on how reliable I am. I have powers the like of which you could never imagine and that satchel only answers to me."

"Powers... Oh of course you have." The scientist laughed, theatrically flicking one long finger and allowing the flap to flop shut. "You can make this bag do whatever you want, even though you are sitting over there. I think not. However, you are right about one thing. Our negotiation is indeed over. Agnezkia, please silence our impertinent guest."

"By the dark shades of *El Defensor* and the evil spirits of Commagin," Kerian shouted dramatically. "I command you demons… transport my treasures away." He nodded his head for dramatic effect, mainly because his hands were currently occupied doing chimera dental examinations and stamped his boot to give emphasis to his words, all the time thinking Colette would be splitting her sides laughing if she could see him right now.

Agnezkia growled, licking her lips expectantly as she stalked slowly across the floor towards him, her rear legs tensing ready to pounce. Malum looked down at his pet, then about the room with his mouth open and his eyes wide as if expecting something magical to occur then when nothing happened, he turned back to Kerian with a superior smirk and a cold look in his eye.

"Your treasures are still on the table." He stated coldly. "You never had any magical powers. If you had, you would never have let my hounds hold you so easily. I'm going to let Agnezkia take her time with you."

"Are you so sure?" Kerian replied mysteriously, trying not to react to the sleek death advancing towards him. "I don't remember saying anything about the items on the table." He stared at Malum, not daring to break his intense gaze and hoping that something in his stare would give the scientist food for thought, whilst inside he was mentally crossing his toes and fingers and praying the satchel would remain true to its stubborn nature.

"You bore me." Malum dismissed him with an outstretched hand, then turned and opened the satchel to gloat over his new treasures once more.

"No!" He muttered, his hand delving into the bag and coming up empty. "No, no, no!"

Kerian smiled darkly. No more would he simply react to things happening about him. It was time to take charge. The mysterious Styx was back! It was like an old battle cloak that always kept the wind and rain away; slightly musty in nature but comforting and warm in all the right places. His fish was now wriggling furiously on the line.

Malum's eyes narrowed, his face flushed and he stormed over towards Kerian, bag in hand, angrily pushing Agnezkia aside, just as she rushed to take a bite from Kerian's leg.

"Make them come back!" Malum demanded. "Bring back my treasures or I shall have my hounds rip out your throat right now."

"Go ahead." Kerian replied calmly. "But if you do, the bag will never reveal its secrets to you. It answers only to me and I no longer wish to give you any of my wealth unless you release me." The knight tried not to smile as his host struggled with this unexpected reversal. He clearly wanted to kill Kerian, it was written all over his twisted face but he wanted what was in the satchel more. If he ordered his hounds to kill and then found out that what Kerian said was true, he would never gain another treasure from the bag. Kerian was confident that if the state of the castle matched the state of the scientist's funds then this scenario would not be an option Malum would pursue.

"Aargh!" Malum screamed, dropping the satchel to the floor and kicking it under the table in frustration. "Can we re-negotiate? Maybe start over. Clearly, we have both got off on the wrong foot. Perhaps we can address this matter further over dinner."

Kerian allowed himself a smug grin then gestured to his hands.

"Oh, of course, please forgive me." Malum smiled, his awful dental problems appearing through his tight-lipped attempt of a smile. "I'm so sorry." He clicked his fingers and the two hounds released Kerian's arms causing pins and needles to rush painfully into the knight's fingers.

"That's much better." Kerian replied, getting carefully to his feet, trying to hide the tremble running through his limbs. He moved away from the chair, purposefully walking around the table, taking the time to dry his hands on one of the napkins and carefully examine his wrists and hands. Relief flooded through him when he noticed his skin had not been broken. He picked a set place where he could have the large window at his back and the rest of the room open and visible before him, then lowered himself into the chair. Kerian hooked the satchel with his boot, drawing it across the floor and near to his side before he looked up at Malum and rested his chin on his bridged hands.

"So, what's on the menu?" Styx asked.

* * * * * *

"You cannot come in without a ticket." The hulking Minotaur remarked, snorting his disgust that the ragtag group of humans before him would even consider trying to gain access to the great pyramid. "Seating is for those of a higher standing in Taurean society and by the look of the three of you, I believe you all fall considerably beneath that mark. Now be gone before I forget I'm in a good mood." He snorted again for emphasis, his black and white fur bristling and his golden nose ring swinging as he moved his enormous head.

Thomas looked down at his travel stained clothing, taking in his attire and nodding his agreement, before turning to Weyn and Mathius and beholding similar dishevelled individuals. All three resembled having been pulled through a hedge backwards whilst traversing the angry crowds situated around the labyrinth. It was times like this he wished he had the same 'access to all areas' given by his police badge back in his previous existence.

"He appears to have taken offence at our appearance." The captain confirmed. "Apparently if he lets us in, he is concerned we will lower the tone of the establishment and upset its ambience. I have asked him politely several times and he is not for changing his mind."

The Minotaur guard frowned, struggling to overhear from the noise and not sure if he had just been insulted or not.

"Maybe we should just stop being polite?" Mathius replied, clearly frustrated. "I mean, what right does he have in saying we don't belong inside where all the fun is?"

"I hardly think it's fair, judging us on our attire. I'll have you know I have dined with royalty." Weyn replied, his face pouting from the insult before he looked down at the guard's feet. "At least we aren't wearing sandals!"

"Sandals!" The Minotaur growled. "I'll have you know these are grade A military issue boots."

"Of course they are." Thomas replied, holding his hands up as the guard reached for the sword at his side. He rolled his eyes and nodded his head towards the two men behind him suggesting they did not mean what they said, then looked down. "...Although I can see their point."

"What do you mean." The guard snapped his hand releasing the hilt of his sword as he bent over to take a look and found to no surprise that his feet were within highly polished, military issue footwear. He looked up again snorting his hostility at their childish remarks, only to find a bright shiny dagger tip pointed right between his eyes. Before the guard could back away, Thomas snatched one arm, Weyn snatched the other and Mathius, still holding his dagger steady, yanked down on the nose ring bringing tears to the guard's eyes. The guard looked at the hovering blade cross eyed and froze.

"I think you need to reconsider our entrance request." Mathius stated coldly. "I think you need to reconsider it most carefully. Do you agree?" The Minotaur bobbed his head as Mathius pulled on the ring causing further tears to run down the guard's face.

"You see, I told you he would understand." Weyn remarked smiling. "What an excellent guard this Minotaur is. I knew it all had to be some terrible mistake."

"I'm terribly sorry." Thomas shook his head. "I tried to be nice. I really did."

"Stay there and be quiet." Mathius hissed into the guard's ear. "In a few minutes stand up and forget we were ever here. Just remember we will be watching you and my friend Weyn here can hit a bull's eye at 100 yards with his bow. I don't suppose you have preference which one he should take out first?" The assassin tapped the Minotaur lightly on the nose, then waved his dagger once more in a threatening manner before easing backwards through the doorway and into the pyramid proper.

"It's called a gold." Weyn whispered in the assassin's ear. "Not a bull's eye."

"Does it matter." Mathius shouted, craning his neck up to take in the throng of cheering spectators crammed into the seating inside the huge torch lit arena. "Dear lord how are we going to find anyone in here?"

"Kristoph, Kristoph!" the crowd chanted, people screaming and pointing at several small figures struggling right at the very top of the golden staircase.

"I'll give you one guess." Thomas replied, noting the darting figure of a little black and white bird as it swooped up into the ornate lattice of an orb situated in the roof high above.

"The stairs are over there." Mathius pointed to a series of steps hewn into the walls that went up and up into the heavens.

Thomas found his own gaze rising with the steps, his head moving backwards and forwards as if he were watching a tennis match, his mind counting the switchbacks and balking at the thought of what he would need to do.

"There's never an elevator around when you need one." He muttered threading his way through the cheering crowd.

Someone screamed from high above and a body wrapped in a crimson cloak crashed to the floor.

"It's okay." Weyn shouted back to his companions. "Don't panic. It wasn't Rauph."

"You know who that guard reminded me of?" Mathius shouted over the din. "The landlord of the *Bloated Badger*. He never wanted to let us in either."

"With good reason!" Thomas replied. "We burnt his inn down."

"I've noticed that happens a lot with your crew." Weyn replied, squeezing between several unruly spectators. "I remember it was a bit of a dump. Back in *Dodderington* if I remember. You know, I still don't recall why it was the *Bloated Badger*."

"Oh that one's easy." Thomas shouted back. "He said he wanted to name the place after something you always find at the side of the road."

* * * * * *

Commagin brought the eyeglass up and scanned the coastline ahead, looking for a suitable place to drop anchor and await the return of Thomas and the remainder of the crew. The sails of the *El Defensor* snapped in the evening wind rising from the bay, the galleon surging through the water, her passage as smooth as her decks.

The Dwarven engineer allowed himself a brief moment of a smile, feeling the vibration of the ship thrumming through the helm beneath his fingers and the breeze whipping at his beard. He realised that he never felt more alive or proud than he did right now. Sure, this ship needed a crew to man her but she ran this smoothly because of her engineer.

He watched the sun slowly sinking behind the mountains, turning the cobalt waters into a darker velvet as they sailed into the shadows and noted the torches flickering into light, one after another along the cliff face ahead. The pyramid already glowed with all of the torches set about it and the roar of the crowd reached his ears even over the creaking sounds of the ship.

"Kristoph, Kristoph!"

Commagin grinned. He recognised that the spectators were calling Rauph's name as known on Taurean. He also knew that it was a bad idea to think that Rauph was as stupid as he acted. Rauph had proved repeatedly that you underestimated him at your peril. Someone, somewhere was no doubt finding that out, to their cost.

"Where are we going?" A voice enquired at his shoulder.

The engineer started, not realising someone was standing so close. He turned to find a hooded figure beside him and it took him a moment to realise that the black coloured robes the man wore were actually blue and that he also held a large book clasped tightly under his arm.

"Oh Brother Richard. What brings you up on deck at this hour. Are you tired of all your studying?"

"I shall never tire from learning the mystical arts." Richard replied mysteriously, staring off into space. "I just needed some air."

"Well it is fortunate I found you." The engineer continued. "Marcus is unwell and Violetta is trying to help with what ails him. Do you think you could offer your expertise and opinion? He is a delightful young man and I would hate for something serious to be happening to him."

Richard looked over at the Dwarf and for a second Commagin thought he could have sworn he saw the priest smile. The engineer suddenly felt cold and took a small step instinctively backwards.

"Well that is terrible news." Richard replied after a long moment of silence. "I shall indeed look in on him when I have finished my walk about the deck."

"Can't you look at him now?" Commagin asked raising one hairy eyebrow as he asked. "I understand he is really unwell."

"I shall see what I can do." Richard stated. "Good evening to you." The priest set off across the deck and descended the ladder to the lower deck, not looking back once but not hurrying either.

"There is something very wrong about that man." Commagin muttered under his breath. He shivered again and suddenly wished they were back out under the warmth of the sun's rays. The engineer made a mental note to discuss this concern with Thomas when the captain returned. He looked up at the pyramid and wished he could somehow hurry them up and hand over the helm. The sooner the better.

* * * * * *

Richard carefully cracked open the cover of the large blue ledger and looked inside at the beautiful illustration of the prison cell. This he had sat and stared at every night, since he had first laid eyes on the plate after dismantling the magic book and springing open the clasps.

As the lantern light swinging gently from the bulkhead fell across the open page, it started to transform from its intricate painting into an image that was as vibrant as it was real. A knight within the picture slid a lizard playing piece across an ancient chequered board sitting upon one bunk and was immediately taken by his opponent's sorceress game piece.

"Cranfelt, Providance." Richard whispered, his summons making the two knights look up from their game. "Cranfelt, watch your tower, Providance is drawing your pieces out so he can take it with his warhorse. Oh and please tell Tobias that it is nearly time for us to be moving."

"There is no need to tell me." The knight in question replied, stepping out from the shadows, his body now transformed from the thin and emaciated figure he once was into a formidable warrior all bulked out and strong once again. "Your magic seems to have worked, my strength is returned."

"Did you have any doubts?" Richard replied smiling. "I told you I would look after you. You have to have a little faith sometimes Tobias. After all that is the currency I deal with."

"No doubts, Bearer." Tobias responded. "We know you are always looking out for us." He pulled his sword from his sheath and dropped to one knee. The other knights in the shadows copied their leader.

"When you call we shall be ready."

* * * * * *

"How are you feeling Marcus?" Violetta enquired as the monk finally cracked his eyes open at her tender administrations. "For a second there you had me worried. It was like all of the life was draining out of you."

"I don't understand what happened." Marcus groaned. "One moment I was fine the next I was falling to the deck and could not catch myself." He closed his eyes and groaned anew.

"Just lie there and take it easy." Violetta replied. "Luckily for you I can fight magic with some of my own."

"My head is killing me." The monk confessed, dropping his head back down onto the pillow. "Maybe something bit me in the jungle, or I am dehydrated but I'm always so careful so I don't understand... magic did you say?" Violetta nodded.

"I would stake my 'top secret' gumbo recipe on it." she smiled.

"But why would Colette do anything to me?" he spluttered. "I haven't hurt her."

"I don't think it was Colette, Marcus. She has her hands full enough with her own problems if I know her. It's something on this ship. Luckily it stopped what it was doing before it killed you. Have you any idea what it could be?"

"No idea." Marcus confessed, his mind racing as he tried to sort out his thoughts through the mental fog.

"It was draining your very vitality." Violetta mumbled. "Absorbing your life. I hope you figure out what it could be before it chooses to attack you again."

Marcus closed his eyes to stop the room from spinning and offered a tired smile.

"I hope so too." He confessed.

Chapter Fifty-One

Kerian watched Malum noisily devouring his meal and tried to assemble his chaotic thoughts by gently pushing a root vegetable around his plate with a fork and crashing it into a roast potato. He was not that hungry and the blue steak oozing blood on his plate was hardly appetising after watching the man before him eat.

Surely, this scientist could not be the same Malum as that in the ship's graveyard, because, by Thomas Adam's own admission, that Malum had been there for a very long time and he had no bright flashing lights bobbing about him. He clearly did not recognise Kerian despite the fact Kerian had previously faced the monster down with Thomas. The quandary in question, Malum, suddenly regarded Kerian with an inquisitive look. He clearly wanted to know if there was something wrong but he could not ask, as he was too busy chewing on an oversized chunk of meat he had torn from the steak. Kerian smiled politely and feigned eating a sliver of carrot, gently shaking his head to reassure his host the food was fine. Fine if you wanted food poisoning that is.

Something pawed at Kerian's leg and he shot a quick glance under the table; his mind wondering what other laboratory experiment had slithered there, only to note that it was the little puppy that had earlier escaped its bed and it was now happily chewing on the leather tie that dangled from the back of the knight's travel stained boots. Kerian nudged the jet black creature away but the puppy simply growled, then leapt back onto his boot and started chewing at the leather all over again. Kerian looked down into the Scintarn's jet black eyes, noticing the little nubs jutting through its fur showing where the flint like armour would eventually form along its spine and across its forehead. To think this creature would grow into a monster? A loud banging from Malum, as he hacked at his steak, drew Kerian's attention back to his own meal and he suddenly thought of a way of hiding his lack of interest in his food.

Two hulking automatons constructed of sewn together body parts, lumbered into the room and placed extra tureens of vegetables and rare steaks down in front of the empty place settings. Then they produced covered desert plates they positioned alongside Malum and Kerian's positions. Kerian risked a quick glance under the cloches and was amazed to see how delicate the desserts appeared to be, lines of gleaming sauce decorating folded pastry lattice, with fruits carved into small exotic blooms. There was no way such cumbersome flesh golems could have made them.

Clearly, there was a chef somewhere in the castle depths, probably locked away and serving his own ransom enforced stay by preparing such delicacies.

He quickly dropped a piece of steak on the floor and chuckled as the puppy ran after it, its front half stopping to pick up the morsel before the rear half of its body was aware its head had stalled, causing a floppy forward roll and a quick scamper to turn about and seize the prize. Malum looked up from his meal, juices running down his face and frowned.

"You don't seem to be eating much." He remarked. "Is everything not to your liking."

"Everything is fine." Kerian replied feeling the tell-tale tug at his boot once again. "I thought we were expecting another three guests? It would be a shame for all of this food to go to waste."

"We are. I'm not sure what is keeping them." Malum paused and gestured to Agnezkia, whispering in her ear before the hound bounded away up the stairs and out the doors. "I am sure they will be along shortly."

Kerian followed the path of the hound, then found his eyes drawn back through the workings of the laboratory to where Octavian still lay at the base of his wife's casket. He had apparently exhausted himself scratching and was now guarding the remains of his wife and child. Kerian noted the luminous ghost standing above Octavian and would have choked if he had been eating, she was glaring at him with a venomous stare and gesturing with her arms and then staring back at him again. What on earth was she doing? He knocked another piece of meat on the floor, using his napkin to mask the action and smiled at the skittering of claws on the stone surface.

"Have you always wanted to be a scientist?" Kerian asked, trying to bring his attention back to his dangerous host and masking the sound of the claws below his feet.

"I seem to have a certain aptitude for it." Malum replied coldly.

"Well your results do seem to speak for themselves." Kerian remarked, watching one of the behemoths struggling to fill a crystal goblet with wine and slopping half of it on the table. He reached across for his dessert spoon, judging this course at least, should be safe to eat only to find the implement violently jump across the table and smack him on the knuckles.

"What?" Kerian looked up towards Malum thinking this was some kind of trick, but Malum was too busy sucking the marrow from the ring of bone lying at the side of his plate to notice anything. That was strange! He tried again and this time the spoon smacked him hard on the wrist, causing him to swear and drop the hidden contents of his napkin onto the floor. He lifted his feet and tried to spot the meat, only to find it had dropped onto his satchel. Kerian quickly tried to flick it off before the juices stained the bag but the puppy pounced on the treat and shook it from side to side growling, before diving under the satchel to eat its meal, its bottom up in the air and its tail wagging furiously.

"Do you suffer from nervous tics?" Malum enquired. "You keep dropping your food and now you can't seem to hold your spoon. I can cut a hole in the top of your skull and stop that from happening if it bothers you."

"No seriously, I'm fine." Kerian replied glancing over at one of the serving golems and looking at the bolt protruding from its left temple. "I am absolutely fine." Malum shrugged and resumed eating, leaving Kerian to look around the room again, his gaze finally returning to the casket where the spirit within continued to glare daggers at him. As soon as his eyes registered her ire, she flicked a finger towards him and the spoon jumped off the table, flipped and smacked him on the temple before dropping to the floor with a clang.

"I'm really sorry." Kerian apologised, bending to the floor to retrieve his spoon and cursing under his breath.

"I can get my trepan set any time you want." Malum suggested helpfully from the other side of the table, offering a smile that would leave Kerian with nightmares for weeks.

"It must be the altitude." Kerian joked, before turning back towards Octavian's wife and doing his best to scowl back. The tragic ghost shrugged her shoulders and pointed again but this time Kerian finally realised she was pointing beyond him and not at him, instead directing his attention to something over by the window, then mimed something with her hands which again made no sense. He turned towards the window taking in the glorious sunset then remembered the cases standing there. In particular, the one holding the violin. She was mimicking playing the instrument! That was it! Although, surely, she could not expect him to play? All he could do was beat a drum and that was often at the wrong time! Give him a weapon and he was a master, give him an instrument and people often begged to be killed rather than listen.

"You have a beautiful violin in that case over there. Do you ever play it?" Kerian asked, causing Malum to snort loudly into his wine goblet and splutter its contents across the table.

"Play it dear lord no!" he laughed. "It was part of Octavian's agreement. Along with his wife and child."

"Can I have a look?" Kerian asked. Malum's eyes narrowed, then his face turned into a forced smile as Kerian lifted the satchel from the floor and folded it tightly in his lap, the implied threat instantly changing the scientist's demeanour."

"Of course, of course." Malum gushed. "Help yourself." A huge golem clomped down the stairs and stomped into the room, thankfully diffusing the tense moment. It walked over to Kerian's chair, dropping Octavian's saddlebags and Kerian's shield down at his side with a clatter.

"Thank you for being such a graceful host." Kerian smiled, getting to his feet and straightening his gathered possessions, checking everything was there before the golem stomped off again. He walked over to the glass case and stared down upon the violin that Octavian had told him about all those weeks previously. Looking at it up close made Kerian's skin crawl.

There was something foreboding about this instrument, something tortured in its shape and design that he could not immediately decipher. The main body was like a traditional violin, a squat figure of eight design shaped from an unusual grey hued timber. There was a rare sheen to the wood, enhancing the depth of the grain and the whirls within its surface, making the pattern appear to swirl as his eyes beheld it, almost as if it were liquid rather than wood. The neck and fingerboard appeared normal, four golden strings stretched taut across its length, until Kerian walked around the violin and noted the instrument from the other side. Then he realised it was carved in the shape of a woman in torment, her arms stretched out above her head, the peg box a cruel form of torture device crushing her hands together and forming them into the scroll situated at the tip. Her mouth screamed silently and anguish lines marked her face. The detail was disturbing but also exquisite, a long braid of hair coming down from the violins head curling over her left shoulder and snaking down between her breasts to where it was looped and knotted at her waist.

Kerian walked slowly back around the case, placing the disturbing carving away from him and examined the front of the violin again, noting the piece of bone that had been utilised as the bridge, adding tension to the strings and the bright silver metal tailpiece that glinted rose pink in the sunset. The chin rest was worn smooth by many hours of playing and the bow lay lightly across the strings waiting for a maestro to wield it. He glanced back over towards the casket, noting Octavian's wife nodding and gesturing that he picked it up. Kerian's eyes roamed back over towards Malum, only to find the scientist watching him intently, suspicion in his malicious eyes.

"Can I hear it play?" Kerian enquired.

"Be my guest." Malum stated. "Then afterwards I think we should look at my treasure once more."

"Oh not me." The knight confessed. "I could never hope to do such an instrument justice. What about Octavian? I hear he can play incredibly."

"Really?" Malum's eyebrow shot up in surprise. "He never told me." He snapped his fingers and Octavian lifted his shaggy head from the floor and growled angrily in the scientist's direction.

"Now!" Malum screamed, stamping his foot. Octavian rose onto his paws and slunk over, voicing his disquiet with every step, his whole body quivering. He arrived at Malum's feet, ears and head down. "Kerian wants you to play the violin. You will do as our guest asks or I will punish you." Octavian yelped loudly, dropping to the floor, writhing in pain as Malum used his unearthly power to morph the gypsy back into the body of a shivering young man once more.

"You bastard!" Octavian gasped, his body wracked with pain at the transformation. "I promised you I would be back. I did everything you asked but you still let my family die."

"The violin." Malum ordered. "Now!"

"Come on now." Kerian snapped, throwing Octavian's clothing towards him. "You heard the man, play me some music whilst I eat." The gypsy stared at Kerian with his eyes blazing in hatred, his fists down at his sides.

"How could you even dine with this monster? I knew you were a bastard but this is a new low even for you. After all the time we travelled together and the many times I saved your life. I should have left you to die." He spat out a globule of spittle, hitting Kerian in the face and shocking the knight. Kerian stepped back, slowly wiped the spit from his cheek, then slapped Octavian hard across the face dropping the gypsy to the floor much to Malum's delight.

"Just get dressed and play as if your life depends on it." Kerian warned before turning to Malum. "You will need to teach me how to house train him."

"I'll be delighted." Malum replied; a flush rising to his pale cheeks. "Please don't let this impertinence worry you. I shall have him suitably whipped later. Return to your dinner. Eat your fill." Kerian walked back to the table and carefully angled his chair so he could still see the ghostly presence in the casket and also Octavian backlit against the sunset, his head bowed, shoulders slumped, violin in one hand, bow in the other.

As he sat, Kerian trod on something on the floor under the table, his boot skidding out from beneath him, making him drop heavily back into the chair. He lifted his boot and noticed a smeared piece of moist steak on the tread. Of the baby Scintarn there was no sign. It appeared that even the puppy knew when it had enough of Malum's cuisine! He placed the satchel on his lap and pulled the frayed ends of the strap together tying them tightly before lifting the crystal goblet from his place setting to take a mouthful of wine.

Octavian drew the bow across the violin's strings, causing the instrument to squeal in protest and Kerian to almost drop his glass. Malum looked up from his dessert and laughed.

"I think someone has clearly been exaggerating their skills," he stated drily.

"Sorry," Octavian coughed, drawing himself up and placing the bow upon the strings again. A bitter sweet melody echoed across the laboratory. The effect was hypnotic, as if every bubbling potion, dripping pipette, whistling pipe and gushing hiss of steam froze and held its breath to listen to the tune that flowed from the magical instrument. The hounds turned in fascination, cocking their heads to one side and even Malum looked distant as if remembering something from long ago.

Kerian suddenly found himself thinking of Colette, of how the sun would shine on her long blonde hair, how her eyes would sparkle with warmth when she entered the room. He reminisced the tender moments they had shared in their too short time together causing a deep ache to grow in his breast and his hand to reach up to the amulet hanging about his neck. He held it as if he were holding Colette's very hand, feeling a tear forming in the corner of his eye as the music rolled over him and he acutely felt his loss.

The images of the subterranean temple sprang to his mind; golden coins spilling around his ankles, jewels and priceless artefacts sliding down mounds of treasure, the wealth of which could never be spent in a hundred lifetimes. The sword fight with Scrave, the heat from the lava and that final ill-timed throw of the serpent dagger.

The images ran so fast, so fluid, he knew they were just memories but they felt so real as if his life were being replayed and was rushing before his eyes. The swell of the music lifted him onwards, the painful memories filling his mind and stripping him bare, leaving him vulnerable and helpless.

Colette's look of surprise as the dagger struck home. Her shock and hurt as she crumpled to the floor. Cradling her in his arms as she slipped away and knowing that this was something he could never allow. Using the wish to save her life and teleport her safely away to the *El Defensor* knowing it would ultimately spell his doom but knowing he would have it no other way. Kerian was weeping openly now, unaware of the table in front of him, the laboratory around him, the monster sitting opposite. Instead he remembered Colette magically teleporting away, crying that she loved him, yet leaving him alone.

A low growl stopped the flow of poignant memories, snapping Kerian back to the present with a start. He opened his eyes, blinking rapidly, immediately noting that the room had darkened whilst he had been reminiscing. Just how long had he been sitting here? Malum still sat entranced across the table, the music swirling about him and showing the scientist images that clearly had him terrified. The hounds had deserted his side and were over by the huge windows, growling at the glass as if they knew something lurked just beyond.

Octavian continued to play, his own face now streaming with tears, his gaze locked with the spectral eyes of his wife, his playing becoming more frantic, more powerful, angry and emotional, the gypsy now a slave to the musical enchantment, gripped by the melody and playing because the music willed itself to be so, his body now an extension of the violin, swept along with everyone else in the room.

Kerian forced himself to concentrate, his gaze reluctantly turning towards the ghost in the casket, despite the music beseeching him to do otherwise. He gritted his teeth, fighting the magic of the eerie serenade, forcing his head around, watching as she moved her lips, speaking arcane words and clearly using her limited powers to make Octavian play; her fearsome gaze locked firmly on the evil scientist. He squinted his eyes noting a pale ribbon of sparkling motes snaking from the crack in the base of the casket and wrapping around Octavian's leg.

His friend was drawing the bow across the strings of the violin without pause, his fingers moving as fast as the bow, violently drawing sounds from the instrument that a virtuoso would struggle to create. Sweat was dripping from his forehead, his hair was slick to his skull and his clothing hung on him damply as he continued to play as his wife demanded.

The scrabbling grew louder at the window. What was it, a pigeon? Kerian could not make it out from the corner of his eye. Whatever it was scampered along the outer sill making the hounds rush along the window after it, backwards and forwards like some mad game. He glimpsed a skeletal tail, a small squat body. Was that a large skull with glowing green eyes? Then it was gone, leaving the hounds pacing, clearly agitated as the music played on, more intense, angry and vengeful. Kerian started as Malum slowly lifted a knife from the table, a trickle of blood oozing from his left nostril.

Octavian continued to play, his eyes closed, his body swaying, the backdrop through the huge windows no longer a rose-coloured sunset, instead dark clouds rumbled across the vista, thunderheads clashing as they collided above the rocky peaks on the far side of the valley, monstrous titans battling in tune to the magic that the gypsy created through his use of the bow. The strings hummed, the sounds shriller, louder more urgent, causing Kerian to want to cover his ears and the hounds to whimper in distress on the floor.

Malum seemed more intent on the knife slowly inching its way towards his neck. The veins in his forehead pulsed, his nostrils snorted and his face flushed as if he were desperately trying to push the weapon away. Instead, the blade drew closer, the tip of the weapon pricking his neck. Kerian suddenly realised that the enchantment within the music was forcing Malum to kill himself.

Octavian staggered, drawing the bow across the violin and making the instrument shudder then shriek before stopping abruptly. He fell to his knees gasping, clearly exhausted from playing, his energy spent.

"I'm sorry." He wailed looking towards his wife's remains. "I can't Ana, I simply can't."

The sudden break in the music seemed to shatter the spell, the apparatus on the laboratory desks beginning to bubble, hiss and pop again. Malum screamed, suddenly resuming control of his hands and hurling the blade aside from his neck as if it were a diseased thing, with no thought as to its trajectory. The blade glinted in the candlelight as it spun across the room, then the casket shattered and the world turned insane...

The very air appeared to fill with static, hairs lifted along Kerian's arms and he felt as if all the oxygen was being sucked from the room. The phantasm of Ana Silvestri stepped free of her prison, threw her arms wide and every glass vial, bottle, vase and tube on the work benches exploded sending gleaming splinters of glass rocketing out across the room. The huge glass windows running the length of the wall shattered, raining jagged shards down onto the floor and across the table. Sparks arced about the room and Kerian ducked instinctively as one large piece of glass smashed down and speared the chair alongside him.

"You did this!" Malum screamed, pointing at Kerian with one blood streaked finger. "You and that damn gypsy bitch!" He clicked his fingers and two hounds leapt up onto the table snarling, whilst one of the golems lurched forward from where it had stood against the wall.

"That bitch is Octavian's wife!" Kerian shot back, drawing his sword in one smooth motion and letting the light of Aurora bathe the two creatures, making them whine and writhe in pain upon the table top.

"My hounds." Malum shrieked, throwing up his arm to shield himself from the light as he staggered forwards to grab them. Kerian moved to tackle him, only to be forced back by the lumbering golem that swung a fist in his direction making him duck and step away.

He swung his blade in, piercing the creature's side, only to watch it grunt, then reach for the gleaming steel as if it had not been hurt at all. He retreated just in time, the monster's stubby fingers closing on thin air. Kerian stepped back, stamping down onto the edge of his shield and flipping it up to catch it with his free hand, just as the golden statue he had given Malum for ransom flew across the room and clanged loudly upon the shield's polished surface. Kerian looked up over its rim and noticed Malum reaching for his serving plate and throwing that in his direction too. Porcelain cracked as he deflected the throw, only for Kerian to then jump aside as the golem lumbered past swinging its arms wildly, trying to connect a punch from which there would be no coming back.

He ran towards his chair, then used it to leap onto the table, kicking aside the transforming chimera and turning to find the golem now at head height and lumbering towards him. He lunged with his blade, the steel glancing off the creature's forehead and snapping the bolt from its skull. Foul smelling ichor started to bubble from the automaton's head, thick viscous fluid that dribbled down into its eyes blinding the creature and enraging it further. It crashed against the table, its arms swinging wild then lumbered off across the room to crash into a suit of armour which it pounded intensely thinking it had finally found its target.

Kerian turned back towards Malum, only to find the scientist lunging at his back, his hands open, going for Kerian's neck. The knight only had time to swing his shield around and smash the scientist in his face, making his nose explode and knocking him away. Malum screamed in pain, dropping off the table.

He spun around, noting more snarling creatures advancing from every entrance, all of them reluctant to move into the light, as if, by instinct, they knew this would cause them pain. Just how many of these failed science experiments did Malum have? The spectre of Ana materialised alongside Kerian and threw him a smile.

"I'm glad Octavian and I never had you around for dinner at our place." She remarked, taking in the chaos about them. "Thank you for bringing him back to me. I knew you would not let me down." She smiled tragically, turning firstly to see her exhausted husband weeping by the window, then back down towards the focus of her hatred crawling away across the floor.

"You are going nowhere!" she snarled, flicking out a hand and dragging the scientist squealing back across the floor towards her. She lifted him up, turning him about to face her, then snarled, allowing her spectral face to transform into something horrific and skeletal causing Malum to scream anew.

"Malum, if you truly care so much for your experiments, I suggest you become one." Ana stated coldly, raising Malum from his feet and hurling him across the room, smashing him through the test tubes, swiping clean table tops and crashing straight into and through the wall of the glass aquarium.

Water thundered across the room. Kerian saw it coming and swiftly grabbed his equipment, lifting it above the torrent just before the water surged past, washing over Octavian and pushing him under, as the wave cascaded out through the destroyed window. The gypsy surfaced gasping, still on his knees, his head bowed, the violin and bow still firmly grasped in his hands.

Malum screamed from the back of the room, the creatures inside the tank, flopping and thrashing on the floor suddenly latching onto his body and starting to attack him, their barbs arcing in and ripping chunks of flesh from his torso, despite knowing that their removal from their natural habitat would eventually lead to their demise.

Ana continued to throw her powers towards the thrashing scientist, piling on her magic, venting her anger, melting his features, transforming his body and melding the monsters from the tank with the very creature they were trying to consume. Kerian held up his hand to shield his eyes as the intensity of the attack continued to course into Malum, with Ana pouring all of her anger, pain and venom into her assault.

"Consider yourself cursed!" Ana spat, lowering her arms and sighing, her ghostly image fading from alongside Kerian, leaving the knight looking across at the scientist's warped body with a shudder. Barbs and limbs twitched like fish left on a riverbank, whilst steam curled up from Malum's mangled remains as he breathed raggedly.

Octavian suddenly felt a warmth wash over his body and he looked up to find the phantom of his wife kneeling before him, her glow brighter than ever, her smile as radiant as he remembered, in all the nights they had been forced apart.

"Oh my love, Ana, how can you forgive me?" he wept openly.

"There is nothing to forgive." She smiled sadly. "You kept your word to me darling. You came back, despite suffering so much for your family. You never forgot us. How can I hold anger in my heart towards you?"

"But I failed you." He sobbed. "Our child is dead, you are dead. We have lost everything."

"Iolander is beyond suffering now. She is free from pain. You were never going to return in time. Malum would have seen to that." Ana replied gently shaking her head. "But you have not lost everything, for you have gained a friend, one that is more loyal than you realise and you have become a better man because of your trials." She reached forward to tenderly slide a wet lock of hair from her husband's forehead.

"Kerian Denaris will lead you to greater things. You will see worlds much better than this one. You just have to remain true to your heart and ultimately you will be rewarded." Her ghostly image flickered and waned before she became clear again, her magic clearly weakened with the powers she had used.

"I love you so much." Octavian confessed, his body shaking with grief.

"I know my love." Ana smiled. "And I love you too. Don't worry, when the time comes, we shall both be waiting for you in the afterlife." She stared off as if hearing something Octavian could not, then looked back at him again, her face suddenly urgent once more.

"The danger is not yet over. You must still experience the depth of terror in darkness before you can truly appreciate the wonder of light." She announced cryptically. "More people are coming, evil people that aim to do you harm. You need to play the violin again, call down a storm. Just like your grandfather. Kerian will know what to do."

"I cannot play without your guidance." Octavian confessed. "The violin is not my instrument."

"It is now." Ana smiled knowingly, leaning forward to kiss him lightly on the forehead. Octavian closed his eyes feeling her lips in his imagination, then when he opened them Ana was gone. He looked about dazed, noting Kerian still standing on the table, sword held high, the light from his blade flickering and flaring every time one of the hounds dared draw near. The golem continued pounding the suit of ancient armour, its fists now taking chunks out of the staircase and the mangled remains of Malum groaned on the far side of the room. People, what did she mean by people? Everyone was here.

The doors at the top of the balcony exploded inwards, splinters of wood flying out in all directions, one chunk lodging into the golem's skull with a 'splat', which it totally ignored, being intent on killing the stair rail in its confused state. The hounds turned snarling towards the new threat and charged for the stairs, leaving their master groaning on the floor.

Kerian jumped down from the table and quickly walked over to Octavian pulling him to his feet, his face turned towards the new threat, not knowing what to expect. A knight smashed his way through the ragged remains of the door, his sword swinging as he cleared the opening and then stepped aside, making way for an exotic dark-haired woman bedecked in a long fur coat that flipped open as she walked revealing tantalising glimpses of skin-tight robes and long tanned legs.

"Well this is not what I expected at all." Justina confessed, walking up to the rail and placing her hands upon it to stare down into the wrecked laboratory. More knights filed into the room behind her and took up position along the balcony as her eyes took in the ruins of the room, the snarling hounds, the mindless golem and then the two men standing by the ruined window, one of which was armed with a sword and a shield, the other soaked to the skin and holding a violin.

"My, my, it looks like I have missed one hell of a party!"

"I have to play the violin now." Octavian whispered.

"Play the violin?" Kerian shook his head, his eyes wide. "What the hell were you just doing if not playing the violin?"

"Ana told me to do it. She has told me to call down a storm. She said you would know what to do when the time was right." Octavian stared up at the knights as another two figures walked through the ruined door. One of them he recognised instantly, whilst the other held a dagger to that person's throat.

"It appears Scrave never got very far." Kerian commented, noting the Elf and the fact that his hands were tied. He did a quick headcount and noted fifteen people above him. Something told him Malum had miscounted the invitations he had sent for dinner.

"Just hold them off for me will you." Octavian stated, walking back to the window and putting his bow to the violin once more.

"Hold them off!" Kerian remarked, muttering to himself, hesitantly walking towards the staircase, noting the first few knights already starting to step down the stairs purposefully towards him. "Oh sure. No problem. Fifteen to one. Piece of cake really. So any great ideas on how I'm supposed to do that exactly?"

The golem reacted to the advancing knights first, just as the lilting sounds of Octavian's violin started to fill the room. It rounded on the vibrations from the stairs and grabbed the nearest knight pounding the man into the wall so hard Kerian expected to see an explosion of blood, instead he was stunned to see the knight step away and swing his sword, hacking through the monster's left arm, making it moan. However, if the knight had expected this to be a blow that would put the golem out of action, he was sorely mistaken, because it reached around with its other arm and grabbed him by the head before crushing his helmet flat.

Kerian winced only to look on amazed as the knight disintegrated, not into crushed blood and bone but magically into pages and pages of loose manuscript. The golem thrashed about for a moment, then snarled and advanced up the stairs towards its next victim.

The remaining door at the top of the stairs flew off its hinges and another golem lumbered in snatching knights left and right, throwing them over the banister and down into the lab. Kerian watched the first one fall, hearing the man's neck snap as he landed, then his eyes moved to trace the second knight who had grabbed the rail to stop his fall and was now dropping down to the floor. The first knight started impossibly getting up, moving his head straight, then drawing his sword and advancing back towards the stairs where Kerian stood.

"Uh oh!" Kerian uttered, as the second knight regained his feet and then determinedly started in his direction. "This is not good. Is there any chance you can play a little faster?" Octavian appeared to be ignoring his request, slowly building the tempo on the violin, tapping his foot and letting the music swell about him as the clouds outside continued to crash and flicker threateningly. Movement out of the corner of Kerian's eye made him snatch a quick glance in Malum's direction, only to see the horrific blooded figure of the scientist impossibly struggling to draw himself up from the floor.

"My eyes!" The scientist screamed. "What has happened to my eyes? I can't see!" He staggered to his feet, the barbed tendrils of the Lampren swaying like a nest of vipers and glowing eerily as if they were tasting the air for prey. Malum threw his arms out to the side, feeling for something to touch and steady his balance, his eyes permanently scarred by the magical powers of Ana's spells.

"Where are you Styx? I am going to make you pay for this." The tendrils stopped and slowly turned in Kerian's direction. Kerian looked at the knights picking their way through the destruction, then at the nightmare creature that Malum had now become.

The gypsy really needed to pick up the pace with that violin!

"Styx." Scrave muttered, his Elven ears picking up a name he thought he had left in the past. It could not be! The golem landed a lucky strike, knocking Kaplain a glancing blow and jolting the Bearer's grip on his magical book. The knights froze momentarily before the man could focus his thoughts and order them back into action. It was the shortest of moments but Scrave read it well, ducking the next blow from the monster and taking the opportunity to step away from the chaos, just as four warriors charged in and started hacking and slashing at the huge behemoth. Scrave got to the bannister and stared down at the young man he had been travelling with.

Styx, there was no way that the Kerian below could be Styx. Could he? He watched as the younger Kerian stepped back to engage the first knight and whipped his sword through a salute that was identical to the one Styx had displayed in a darkened alleyway in Catterick all those months before. No it could not be! Yet, in his heart he knew it was. This Kerian Denaris was his Styx. Scrave's eyes narrowed as his anger rose to the surface. How could he have been so stupid? A little voice in the back of his mind chuckled and the worm in his eye socket shivered. He needed a sword. Right now!

A cold wind rattled the empty window frames, gusting into the room as a staccato rush of raindrops hammered over the sill. Lightning flickered outside and a loud rumble of thunder added percussion to the violin's musical enchantment.

Kerian parried the first strike from the nearest knight, their blades meeting high, then stepped back and 'beat' parried the knight's low lunge, slamming his blade down hard and knocking the thrust away. A flick of the tip of his sword nicked the knight's elbow but nothing came out of the wound except a scrap of aged parchment. A swift riposte followed by a lunge, a counter parry, then a 'bind knock' intercepting the knight's attack from the left and knocking it out to the right, before Kerian lunged and plunged Aurora deep inside the man's chest. Kerian's grin of triumph ended prematurely as his foe head butted him, striking his nose with the iron rim of his helmet, making Kerian see stars.

He staggered back, just as Justina sent several balls of fire flashing from her fingers to detonate against the golem's hide at the top of the stairs. The creature finally showed signs of pain, stepping away from the flames and beating at its chest as they licked hungrily at its clothes. The knights also stepped away, their faces reflecting the respect they had for such a hungry blaze.

Click Clack, click clack. Malum's tendrils snapped out, stabbing the second knight at the neck, the face, the axilla and the groin tearing free tissue that turned into manuscript pages. His attack spun the magical fighter, then the tendrils realised that the creature could not sate Malum's appetite and turned towards the only sources of flesh and blood available to them.

Octavian played faster, the storm outside the window matching the ferocity of his playing. Lightning arced across the sky, this time striking the castle and causing the foundations to shake. Scrave staggered on the balcony, still trying to snatch a weapon from one of the knights hacking and slashing before him but with his hands tied, it seemed every time he grabbed a hilt of a weapon he felt it slip from his grip and his fingers ended up grasping air! He needed to get down into the laboratory, he needed to kill Kerian. No he did not! He needed to do something else but he could not remember what it was. Kill Denaris! No everything was becoming muddled again. He staggered as a knight suddenly whipped his sword around catching the Elf across the temple, drawing blood.

Kerian pushed against the knight facing him, then felt his ears pop. The air at the centre of the laboratory shimmered and twisted, swirled and crackled and the loose items on the floor started to dance about the room, filling the air with loose sheets of manuscript, ruined bottles and pieces of armour that bounced about as if caught in a tornado. Quickly stepping back, Kerian fooled the knight into lunging forwards and over extending, leaving the enchanted warrior off balance. Kerian pushed as hard as he could and smiled as the man fell, then dodged back as another sword slashed the air before him. A stray candelabra flew through the air, smacking this second knight on the head, knocking him down on top of his comrade as a strong smell of ozone filled the room.

Kerian turned, searching for Octavian through the swirling debris, then struggled towards him, the twisting wind at his back clutching hungrily, making him feel as if he were slogging through a morass. He held his shield up to guard his face, deflecting errant objects and scientific paraphernalia that flew madly about the room. The deflected items tumbled and bounced towards the maelstrom forming at the centre of the laboratory. A ball of blue lightning flashed into being, hovering above the debris, then it snapped wide open, revealing the haunting image of a familiar mustard coloured sky above a landscape of skeletal masts.

The suction from the open portal increased tenfold, everything not bolted to the floor now started slipping and sliding towards the flickering maw. Kerian felt his eyes hypnotically drawn to the scene within the crackling gateway. Could it possibly be? Were his eyes playing tricks on him? The ships all forged together; shifting, spinning, grinding their rusting and rotting hulks in a torturous dance that would ultimately lead to their destruction.

He finally reached Octavian but did not dare tear his gaze from the one thing he had spent all of these months chasing; the ship's graveyard. Kerian placed his arm carefully around the gypsy, using his shield to guard his friend from the worst of the debris whipping through the air, whilst leaving Octavian free to continue playing as the tempest screamed. It was almost impossible to hear the music now, as the storm produced by Octavian's playing roared so loudly.

The images in the portal suddenly shuddered, the number of ships in the graveyard rapidly diminishing, then inexplicably multiplying again, as if the portal was opening at different periods, showing snapshots in the life of the decaying wrecks. There seemed no pattern to it, sometimes lots of ships filled the scene, other times practically none, calling into doubt the stability of Octavian's magical gateway. The bannister suddenly tore from the wall and was sucked through the opening and whisked away, instantly disappearing as the scene through the portal flickered and changed. Knights tumbled to the floor and slammed against the walls as the storm took them and threw them about like rag dolls.

Kaplain, clearly worried for the welfare of his magical fighters, shouted words instantly torn away by the storm but the enchanted knights responded instinctively and started crawling, staggering and walking back towards him, some suffering grievous wounds from the flailing arms of the flaming golem as the bearer held out his magical ledger and ordered his charges to sanctuary within the book. One by one they disappeared, as the bearer struggled to hold his ground against the shrieking winds threatening to tear the precious volume from his hands.

The golem at the bottom of the stairs tumbled backwards and disappeared through the portal, then the one at the top of the stairs found itself dragged from its feet and sucked through, its mouth open in clear surprise. Justina cast a spell, hoping to shield herself and her troop from the relentless howling draw of the magical portal, encapsulating herself, Scrave and Kaplain in a sphere of energy which immediately set off bright sparks as debris pounded its magical surface. Her superior look of satisfaction instantly turned to horror as the larger surface area she had created made it easier for the vortex to gain a hold and wrench them from their position at the top of the stairs. Kerian caught a quick glimpse of the sphere being sucked through the opening in a flash of electrical blue sparks, along with a battered suit of ancient armour and assorted debris from the imploding laboratory.

Kerian could barely stand, let alone see; the storm continuing to snatch at his clothes, stealing his breath, making him duck and use his shield to deflect the dangerous items flying about him. Malum suddenly lunged through the wall of flying debris, his pincers snapping, hands clutching, mouth open in a vengeful scream, just as a massive bolt of lightning crashed through the open window, lifting several work benches with the force of the explosion, striking Malum and knocking him flying through the portal. His hounds skidded and clawed at the floor trying desperately to avoid the fate of their master but one by one they were swallowed by the yawning opening.

The knight` caught a rare glimpse of the graveyard in its infancy, then this too was snatched away, more shipwrecks falling into the necropolis even as he watched. He squinted against the dirt and grit flying about him, desperately trying to shield his face and eyes still not believing what he was witnessing. The ship's graveyard was right before his eyes, all he had to do was pick the right moment and he could be back with Colette again. It was a dream located within a nightmare, if he chose wrong they could be lost in time. If he chose right, there was still the possibility that the *El Defensor* would be months returning through a portal, if ever. He gritted his teeth, cursing his indecision. He was too close. This was the chance he had been waiting for.

The view changed, showing several cargo vessels crashed together, their containers scattered like fallen building blocks. He knew those ships. It was time. He tightened his grip on Octavian's waist then leapt, throwing away caution for the hope of finding Colette, dragging his friend with him into damnation.

The storm stopped almost as swiftly as it was created. The rain easing as the clouds rolled away, revealing the darkness of the night. Stars blinked across the velvet sky and a gibbous moon appeared as the last ominous clouds magically melted away. Castle Glowme settled and creaked into an uncomfortable silence, then from out of the shadows a new sound arose. A steady marching of skeletal feet, the relentless beating of a rotting drum. Those in the know would have trembled in their beds and held their loved ones tightly. However, the creatures that lived in the petrified forests of Blackthorn knew only pain and terror as this army swept across the land killing everything in its path.

The Provan legion were on the march and they would stop at nothing until they reclaimed what was rightfully theirs.

Chapter Fifty-Two

Rauph hung his head in defeat, waves of nausea rolling over him as he replayed his brother's words and tried to pull free the throwing blade in his calf.

"The Labyris axe is mine and Taurean has a new king."

After all that work, all the trials he had faced, his brother Drummon had beaten him to the prize. Drummon would be king, the crew of the *El Defensor* would be sold as slaves or sent to the mines and his friends likely slain; all because Rauph had not been fast enough. He tugged at the blade once again, gritting his teeth as he heard it slide wetly from the muscle. Blood welled up from the wound and started to trickle down his leg as Rauph carefully folded the weapon closed and placed it on the stone floor beside him.

"Let me help you." The serving girl offered, moving forwards.

"After I have had my fill of the sandwiches and not before." Wanessa ordered, yanking the slave back towards her, demanding that she be fed.

The navigator barely noticed, absorbed in a sense of despair that crashed down upon his shoulders with a weight the Minotaur could never hope to resist. Rauph pulled his competition ribbon from his arm and tied his leg as tightly as he dared, before slowly moving to stand. It was all over now. He just had to accept his fate. He knew Drummon would not let him live, not with the cries of the crowd calling out the name Kristoph in ever louder voices.

Rauph looked over to where Ashe struggled, his shoulder squeezed tightly by one of the guards, a sharp blade resting against his throat, then over towards the serving girl who was being berated by Wanessa for not putting her mistress's needs before a male Minotaur. He knew who the serving girl was, recognised Colette from her scent, she could not hide it from him but the others here seemed to be none the wiser to her identity and thought she was simply hired help and therefore eligible to be abused.

Sinders swooped across the room, irritating some of the guards by dive bombing them whilst being careful to stay out of sword range. The bird dipped one wing and gracefully pivoted around before flying to the centre of the orb, where it landed on the shoulder of a statue of a young woman holding an axe.

"Come on brother. It is time to see me crowned King." Drummon taunted. "I would hate for you to miss such a prestigious occasion." He hefted the axe in his hands and walked out onto the balcony, determined to show the Taurean people that Mora's successor had been chosen and that a new ruler now held dominion over their lives.

Rauph watched him go, his shoulder's slumped, his breath coming in ragged gasps, too tired to fight the inevitable; only to watch Drummon pause just before the balcony and motion to the guards. They leapt forward at his command, clearly anticipating this prearranged signal and grabbed Rauph roughly by the arms, dragging him after his brother and out under the twilight sky.

"What are you doing?" Rauph demanded, as the coolness of the air wrapped around his body, the breeze from the water making his hair ruffle and a clarity return to his thoughts.

"Why brother. It suddenly occurred to me that this is such a spectacular weapon and surely I as the new king should have the benefit of christening it." Drummon stated, a wicked gleam in his eye. "I need a chair please!"

"I simply cannot miss this." Wanessa got to her feet and wobbled unsteadily, before regaining her balance, then she waddled over to the balcony, leaving her chair for one of the guards to retrieve and take over to their new king.

Rauph suddenly realised what his brother was suggesting and tensed, trying to pull himself away. He freed one shoulder, threw a wild punch that set one guard's helmet rattling and pushed another away, only for three more to grab him and restrain his arms making further struggle futile.

"About there will be fine." Drummon motioned, indicating that the chair should be placed right before Rauph. "Now kneel Kristoph and this time I shall finish the job properly. I understand a true headsman can take one with a single swing. I'm a little rusty myself so I may have to settle for two or three."

The pressure on Rauph's arms intensified and two well placed kicks to his wounded leg had him dropped to his knees. Within seconds, his hands were tied around the back legs of the chair making it almost impossible for the Minotaur to pull free.

"No!" Ashe screamed, struggling to pull away from the guard who held him, before finally slipping from his jacket and leaving the Minotaur holding nothing but the Halflings clothes. He dropped to the floor, rolled, then crawled away only to come up short against a long blue dress.

"Ashe Wolfsdale. It appears we meet again!" Mora hissed, reaching forwards to grab him firmly by the ear and the scruff of his neck.

"Ow! No, let me go! I have to save my friend." Ashe yelled, wriggling furiously, his hands reaching out and grabbing at the Matriarch's robes. She shook him hard, rattling Ashe's teeth in his skull and lifted him free of the ground before walking out onto the balcony to join all of the others.

"It is time for you to see what is about to befall you." Mora stated coldly. "Kristoph is to die and then you are to follow."

"Look I'm sorry about the ring. I'll give it back, just let my friend and I go." Ashe sobbed, tears running down his face.

"That time has long passed." Mora replied. "Now be quiet, I do not want my son to hear the shrieks of a child as he dies. He fought hard for his prize and even though he failed, I wish for him to die with honour."

Rauph found his head roughly pushed down upon the chair seat and ended up facing the crowd of witnesses. Mora looked on, as cold and frigid a mother as ever was known, having got what she desired out of him, he was now to be disposed of. Wanessa was jiggling on her feet, excitedly clapping her hands and tittering. Drummon was smiling so broadly he was in danger of getting lockjaw. Aelius stood away from everyone, half hidden in the shadows, his face grim. Yet the face that broke Rauph's heart, was the little Halfling's. Ashe looked so tired, so bloodied, battered and bruised; covered head to foot in dust, spider guts and blood, his hair matted and sticking up in all directions and tears streaming down his face.

"I'm so sorry I let you down." The navigator whispered. His heart knowing that Ashe would soon be joining him.

"Where are my delicacies?" Wanessa suddenly snapped. "I can't watch an execution without nibbles!"

The serving girl rushed over with a plate of food, her face a picture of concentration. Drummon swung the axe about, gauging the weight, his face frowning, as if he discovered that upon wielding the weapon it was off balance and not behaving as it should. He moved up close to Rauph, swung the axe and laughed as it swished through the air close to his brother's skull, then leaned down and whispered into Rauph's ear.

"Don't go anywhere. I'll be right back." He winked, before walking to the edge of the balcony and holding the enchanted weapon up high for all of the Taurean populace to behold. The crowd roared their approval at seeing the royal party, high up on the balcony, many in the crowd using specially purchased eyeglasses to stare up and witness the spectacle of a new ruler for Taurean being crowned.

"See, I am your king!" Drummon roared, holding the enchanted axe up high for everyone to see. "Behold your ruler." A loud clatter sounded behind him and he turned to see Wanessa slapping the serving girl about the face and knocking her to her knees.

"Next time bring the grass balls and cheese! I don't know how many times I have had to tell you girl!" Rauph tried to see what was going on unaware that the serving girl was staring up at Wanessa with hate filled eyes, her look of concentration now lost. The floor about her scattered with small sandwiches and finger food that had been swept aside by the arrogant Minotaur.

Drummon frowned and turned back towards the crowd, moving to hold the Labyris axe up for the crowd to see one final time before he turned and took up his position to take his brother's head and cement his coronation. He lifted the weapon high, only to hear a gasp from Mora and some mutterings from the guards. Rauph felt the pressure release at his head just as Ashe opened his mouth and announced to the kneeling navigator what was happening.

"Where has the axe gone?"

* * * * * *

Another black arrow streaked through the air, slamming through sinew and bone and knocking a Minotaur guard off the steps with the force of the blow.

"To the left." Mathius pointed calmly and Weyn fired another deadly shaft, piercing the unfortunate target's eye and dropping him to the floor, his bow hand instinctively reaching for another arrow even as the latter left the string of the taut bow. The third arrow ricocheted off a minotaur helmet and twisted away off into the crowds.

"Oops!" The archer winced as it slammed into a spectator's seat pinning a high up member of the Taurean society to their seat whilst others screamed and ran for the exits.

"Careless." Mathius remarked, tutting loudly. "You pulled your shot."

"No I didn't." Weyn retorted. "I'm still having issues with my arm." Mathius grinned then looked over his shoulder at Thomas still climbing the stairs, then down towards the floor where a stream of guards clambered up the stairway towards them. "How long did he say we had to hold them back?"

"Until he gets to the top." Weyn replied loosing an arrow that took one Minotaur in the knee and felled him. "Uh oh."

"Don't you 'uh oh' me!" Mathius snapped. "What is the problem? Oh, on the left" Weyn fired his bow to where Mathius had indicated, his arrow slamming through plate and stabbing cleanly into a Minotaur chest, before he indicated the far wall, away over the sea of spectator heads, where another staircase rose from the floor. Guards were swiftly charging up the stairs, hoping to cut the three men off.

"Uh, oh!"

* * * * * *

Colette fell to the floor, her face stinging from the slap administered by Wanessa, her concentration holding her magical illusions in place broken. The spell shattered just as Drummon swung the axe up high and with the illusion removed the weapon reverted back to its true form in the black Minotaur's hands growing heavier and throwing off his downward swing.

The Warhammer Drummon was now holding smashed into the back of the chair, missing Rauph's head by inches, driving the back legs down into the floor and causing them to shatter. The chair disintegrated under the force of the blow, dropping Rauph down and freeing him from the hands of the guards who had been holding him.

The navigator did not need to be told twice. This was the only opportunity he was going to get to escape. He lashed out with his hands, the remains of the chair legs still tied to his wrists now impromptu weapons that he flailed left and right with, feeling satisfying 'thwacks' and 'thunks' as he took out the legs of those nearest him.

Drummon roared his frustration, finding himself over balancing as the Warhammer dragged him off to the side, the head of the immense weapon chipping the stone floor and leaving the Prince Regent with no opportunity to reverse the swing and kill his brother. He spread his stance, gripped the haft of the weapon and finally wrenched it from the floor, spinning it around, just as one unfortunate guard received a blow to the back of his knees from Rauph and dropped his face directly into the hammer's path. The Minotaur's skull cracked like an egg, blood flowed and the hammer dropped to the stone floor again, dragging Drummon down and invoking another roar of frustration from him, as his brother finally regained his feet.

As soon as Rauph stood up, the pain in his calf exploded making the navigator stagger backwards, directly towards Wanessa, who drew a dagger from the folds of her robes and raised it to strike. Ashe tried to cry a warning but Mora yanked on his hair, making his cry a sob of anguish, drawing her son's attention towards concerns for the Halfling thief rather than the Minotaur about to plunge her dirk between his shoulder blades.

Colette grabbed the sandwich platter and swung it with all her might, smashing it into Wanessa's head and leaving her staggering before she reversed the swing and slammed it in behind the Minotaur's legs, dropping her to the floor, her face now a mess of blood, bruises and egg and cress sandwiches.

"The statue." Colette gasped. "It's over at the statue."

"What is?" Rauph stood there perplexed, looking this way and that but not any clearer as to what he was supposed to be looking at.

"The Labyris axe!" Colette pointed, banging the tray down onto Wanessa's head once more for good luck. "The axe is where it has always been, over on the central pedestal. Rowan has got it."

Drummon roared again, pushing the guards aside. His gaze meeting Rauph's as Colette inadvertently revealed where the prize lay. Both Minotaur turned towards the lattice orb noting the petite figure of Rowan still struggling to keep the axe from sliding from its station, then their eyes turned to each other, they snorted a challenge, then the chase was on.

Rauph was further into the room and had a clear head start but Drummon was still fresh having clearly faced very little of the trials and tribulations met by the other contestants. He leapt forward with a battle cry, swinging the Warhammer to the left and the right, sweeping the scrabbling guards from his path without any concern for their wellbeing. They were between him and his birthright and as such their lives were expendable.

The navigator turned and ran for the orb, feeling fresh pain lancing through his leg each time he placed his weight upon it. He could almost feel the floor shaking as his brother charged relentlessly towards him, could see the fear etched on Rowan's face as she struggled to support the Labyris axe and stop it slipping from her grasp. She was so far away, the distance between them closing in agonising slow motion.

Drummon swung the war hammer in a clumsy arc, meaning to knock his injured brother from his feet, maybe break a few ribs or crack his skull but Kristoph's unsteady gait from his injury threw off the Prince's aim and the hammer merely smashed into the navigators left shoulder.

The blow threw Rauph forward as if he had been hit by a tree. He stumbled out of control, falling flat on his face and sliding over to the edge of the twisting walkways, just short of where he had originally climbed up into the room. He slid across his own bloody boot prints, his chin hitting the ground, painfully snapping his teeth; his shoulder screaming in agony as his arm bent back against the joint, his chest landing on something that had been left discarded on the floor, the collision pressing the wind from his lungs.

Drummon laughed as the blow landed, then struggled to control his own momentum as the swing of the hammer made his own feet skip. He allowed the massive weapon to follow through on its momentum slamming the head of the hammer down hard onto the very edge of the opening in the floor, cracking the stone and sending tremors through the delicate structure of the orb.

Rowan squealed in alarm as the vibrations ran through her body and the axe tilted further towards the edge. The damned thing was too top heavy, too difficult for her to hold onto. She tried to pull it back, standing on tiptoe, her arms outstretched. How had she let Colette talk her into this?

"Hello puny human." Drummon shouted. "Why don't you give the axe to me?"

"That is going to be easier said than done." Rowan replied, her outstretched fingers barely touching the huge axe.

"Now!" Drummon roared, swinging the war hammer down and smashing it onto one of the delicate walkways leading out to the pedestal. Rowan screamed as the pathway cracked and the axe shuddered beneath her fingertips. Drummon laughed at her distress and casually walked around to the next pathway.

"Do I need to ask you again?" he warned.

"You will have to come and get it yourself." Rowan shouted back. "I'm barely managing to hold onto it."

"Wrong answer." Drummon replied swinging the hammer, sweeping it up then letting it crash down onto the second slender walkway, demolishing the path and causing the whole pedestal to groan at the weakness of having two supports removed.

"What are you doing?" Rowan screamed, her eyes glancing down through the gaps in the stonework, seeing all the little people running around down there like ants from a disturbed nest. A wave of vertigo passed over her and for a second, she felt she would lose her balance and fall. "You will make me drop the axe."

"I can always retrieve the axe." Drummon grinned swinging the huge hammer around in a circle as he walked calmly towards the next support. "Only three left now."

"Please don't." Rowan cried out. "I can't pass you the axe, it's too heavy and I am afraid I will fall."

"Too bad." Drummon replied swinging the hammer again with equally devastating results. The pedestal tilted, sliding the axe back into Rowan's outstretched hands just as further structural cracks raced along the remaining struts. One Minotaur statue slowly leaned out then tumbled away into the pyramid base, causing Rowan to scrabble to regain her footing. The whole orb was unstable now. Rowan knew she had to get off before the whole thing dropped sending her to her death and the idiot Minotaur was continuing his walk around the perimeter of the hole swinging his hammer and actually whistling to himself.

She looked over at Rauph, still prostate on the floor, struggling to rise, noted the others advancing between the thrones, silent witnesses to an execution of someone who was not guilty of any crime towards the Taurean people. She saw Mora screaming at Drummon to stop, Ashe thrown from her grasp, landing hard, rolling away across the floor. Then she saw Colette who was clearly trying to gather enough magical power to cast a spell in Rowan's direction but by the look on the young mage's face, it was clear she recognised the futility of trying to do so. There simply was not enough time.

Then the orb dropped.

* * * * * *

There are 1860 steps from the main foyer of the Empire State building up to the 102nd floor, taking an average person approximately forty minutes to complete the strenuous climb. Thomas knew some keen athletes who ran as far as the 86th floor, managing 1576 steps in a little over ten minutes. However, in comparison to his current ascent, he knew deep in his heart that such an undertaking would have been a walk in the park.

His knees ached, his lower legs screamed at each step, his clothes were stuck to his body with perspiration and his lungs were sounding like old bellows wheezing. If he had been an old jalopy, he would have been condemned to the junk pile! Just how had he managed to get in such a poor shape?

The scream from above diverted his attention from his own woes and he looked up, initially bemused, as the orb in the ceiling appeared to snap on one side and drop downwards, swinging over to the side, where it was still attached to the stonework. A pale Minotaur sculpture dropped away, falling end over end, only to smash into pieces on the ground far below. He shrugged, not concerned with the fate of a statue, only to realise that the screaming continued.

He looked back up to the orb and felt his heart skip a beat. A small, petite shape was hanging from it, her hands grasped around a staff of some kind that was wedged into the intricately carved design that made up the ball. Vague shapes were moving towards the edge where the structure had come away from the ceiling but Thomas was unable to see exactly what was going on, his eyes repeatedly being drawn towards the slim figure swinging in the air. He knew that body, he knew that scream... Rowan. Dear lord it was Rowan!

Thomas felt a sudden rush of energy as the terrible desperation of the situation sunk in. He had to get up there, had to strive to save Rowan, although in his mind a little voice was already warning him it was pointless to attempt. He could only save her if he got down onto the slowly spiralling staircase but it was all folded up, its point bent over under the weight of the stone orb sitting on top of it. Thomas gritted his teeth, clutching his cutlass firmly in his hand and started to take the steps faster, knowing he had to try, no matter what the cost.

He turned the last corner at a sprint, charging up the steps, only for a huge Minotaur to drop down onto the step above him and bring to bear a halberd it held, the huge blade gleaming brightly in the torchlight. The captain did not miss a step, leaping aside as the guard lunged, before swinging his cutlass down hard across the shaft of the huge weapon. The halberd staff snapped, the blade ringing loudly on the stair, the guard staring at his weapon in disbelief as Thomas charged towards him. Then the cutlass swung again and the guard's left horn was sheared cleanly off.

"Move!" Thomas yelled. The guard felt for his horn then staggered to one side leaving the stairway clear for Thomas to ascend to the final landing. He only hoped it would not be too late.

* * * * * *

"Drummon stop what you are doing!" Mora roared. "You need the axe."

"I know and when it falls, I'll send one of the guards to fetch it." The huge Minotaur shrugged, moving over towards one of the last two remaining supports. "This won't take long."

"And then that Minotaur will become king." Mora replied quietly, her nose and nostrils flared. "For whoever holds the axe this eve becomes the new ruler of Taurean. Drummon, you did not think this through, did you?"

Drummon's confident smile dissolved as he regarded the young woman swinging under him, her hands tightly clutching to the shaft of the axe, her face a mask of terror, her legs swinging out over nothing but a terrifyingly long drop.

"Oh." The Prince looked about confused. Just in time to see a human erupt from the nearest stairwell, a cutlass held in his hand, his face set like thunder.

"Humans are not permitted up here." Mora shouted. Then her eyebrows rose as she realised who she was addressing. "Thomas Adams? But that's impossible. You're dead."

"I'll take that as a confession and will deal with you later." The captain replied coldly. "Don't just stand there! Somebody save her!" He turned in desperation to Colette, saw the resignation in her eyes, then to

Rauph who was crawling over to the opening and peering down inside it, his arms reaching for the woman Thomas loved. The captain dropped to his knees and stared down towards where Rowan swung, her face red, her fingers white from holding on. Rauph's arms were painfully short of his target. It did not take a genius to realise he would never reach.

"Don't worry Rowan, I'm right here!" Thomas called down to her, feigning a smile to try and put her at ease. "Don't look down, just keep looking at me. We are going to have you out of this mess before you know it." He glanced about, desperate for more help, noting the hulking shape of Drummon hovering on the other side of the orb. The Minotaur appeared to be in some kind of conflict, smacking his head in agitation as he watched the unfolding spectacle, as if unsure of what to do.

"Please hurry," Rowan tried to force a smile in response but the strain was telling on her arms. "I don't think I can hold on much longer."

"Let me assist." Aelius replied stepping forwards and dropping to his knees alongside Rauph. "Hold me, I can reach out further than you and I am not injured." Rauph looked at his mentor's eyes, read the sincerity in them and reluctantly nodded his head, gesturing that his help was needed.

"Guards, arrest these people!" Mora shouted, indicating that Aelius and Rauph be taken away. Thomas regained his feet and viciously whipped his cutlass around, making the guards swiftly step back.

"The first one that tries is dead." The captain's face was set like granite, his eyes blazing with emotion. More Minotaur came out of the stairwell the other side of the room and started to charge towards them. Thomas took one look, swiftly counting the odds but refusing to back down. He would die before he gave up on Rowan. He turned and offered the approaching troop a salute with his cutlass and turned side on ready to meet them.

"Just get my girl up fast." He spat, fighting back his panic and preparing for what he thought would be the inevitable. "Or I will personally ensure you all face the consequences."

"Hold!" Aelius shouted making every guard stop at their commander's stern tone. "That human can wait. I need help here now!" The guards looked at each other and then leapt to assist, grabbing Rauph around the waist and sliding him forwards, so that he in turn could lower Aelius into the opening.

"Just a little further." Aelius ordered, his fingers outstretched for the young woman swinging desperately beneath him. "I can almost reach her." Rauph suddenly slid forwards off the edge, almost dropping the commander along with himself, the guards holding him grabbed for his legs and piled onto his lower body causing the Minotaur to roar in pain as they landed on his wounded leg.

"Steady Kristoph." Aelius warned, aware that his life and the young woman entirely depended on the strength of his young charge. "Don't you dare drop me or I shall be very disappointed in you." The orb groaned and creaked alarmingly.

Rauph gritted his teeth, tears running down his face, his breath coming in short spasms, the agony in his lower limbs almost more than the Minotaur could stand, yet he remained focused, refusing to let his mentor fall. Something snapped loudly in the masonry as the tension on the structure increased.

"Human, look at me!" Aelius stated calmly, trying to ignore the troubling sounds around him. "I'm going to grab your wrist, then I want you to let go of the axe. Do you understand me?" Rowan stared up at the old Minotaur and saw the concern in his eyes. The inner belief in the majestic animal that it would not, could not fail. She nodded her head and stilled her kicking.

"I don't know if I can let go." She confessed, a tremor to her voice. "I'll fall."

"If you don't, you will fall anyway." Aelius replied, reaching out, his fingers inching down across her tightly clenched fist. "And I for one would not like to face your man and admit I had failed to save you. He looks very intense."

The Minotaur grunted above him, voicing their concern over the weight they were supporting. Rauph had a glazed look in his eyes as he pushed down the pain in his legs and focused on a purple line drawing in his mind that was turning into the largest scribble he had ever seen. His hide was slick with foaming bubbles of sweat but he refused to give in, refused to pass out. There was too much at stake.

"On three." Aelius stated, inching his hand further down to her wrist. "One... Two..."

The crack was explosive; the orb's remaining supports finally giving up with the tension placed upon them. There was an explosion of stone dust, Rowan screamed and the orb crashed down into the arena below.

"Pull me up." Aelius cried, from somewhere within the dust cloud. "Quickly, pull me up." The guards grunted and groaned, working as a team, gripping clothing, arms slick with sweat, hands covered in blood from Rauph's injury and slowly they began to pull the two Minotaur away from the dizzying drop.

"Rowan?" Thomas asked, stepping into the masonry dust cloud. "Where's Rowan?" He looked numbly down at Rauph groaning on the floor, blood pooling around his leg, then to the hole, now slowly clearing of dust, revealing a yawning gap where the lattice orb once rested. Guards sat on the floor coated in dust, patting each other on the back and coughing. Thomas started to panic, where was Rowan? She had to be here. She just had to be!

He stepped over towards Aelius who had just pulled himself to his feet and had his back turned from the captain of the *El Defensor*, his cloak and clothes torn and covered in bloody hand prints, visible proof to the struggle that had just taken place.

"Rowan? Do you have Rowan?" he pleaded, placing his hand on the Minotaur's shoulder just as the captain of the guard turned around. For a split second, Thomas's eyes failed to register what he was seeing. The huge minotaur turned, his cloak swirling; In his right hand he held the Labyris Axe and tightly held against his left breast was a pale, shivering figure.

Rowan.

Thomas stepped forwards and held her tightly, weeping with relief. Rowan sagged in his arms, her head against his. No words needed to show what they felt for each other. Just an overwhelming feeling of relief and the security of having each other in their arms. As they held each other tightly the sun finally set behind the distant mountains, casting the pyramid into shadow.

A loud clattering rose from behind them, guards dropping to bended knee, swords and weapons lowered in a sign of respect. Thomas turned from his embrace, unsure why everyone was kneeling before him and Rowan, then he stared up at Aelius who was looking equally confused. Even Rauph was on his knees, bleeding battered and close to collapse but still offering his penitent pose to match all of the others.

"What is the meaning of this?" Aelius remarked, frowning. "Get up all of you."

"No!" Mora screamed, taking in the scene. "No, this cannot be!"

"What is it mother?" Drummon asked, suddenly emerging from the shadows, dragging the war hammer along the floor behind him. "Why is everyone kneeling?"

"Aelius has the axe!" Mora spat. "If you do not have the axe, you cannot be king."

"I thought you said that whoever holds the axe when the sun sets is the King?" Colette stated loudly. "Aelius holds the axe. Therefore, by your own reckoning, he is your new ruler."

"Never!" Mora screamed.

"The axe was supposed to be mine!" Drummon bellowed, exploding into action, charging madly across the room, the war hammer discarded in his fury, his head lowered, horns glinting, determined to gore anyone who got in his way.

Thomas reached for his sword but he was still embracing Rowan and was in no position to defend her. Rowan was still dazed and Aelius was still stunned to find out the revelation that he had just received a promotion he could never have expected. There was no way they were going to get out of this rampaging animal's path!

Rauph's hand shot out as Drummon charged past, purposefully catching Drummon's right leg as he ran and pulling as hard as he could. Drummon's forward momentum meant he overbalanced almost straight away, his head lifting up as he fell. A dark arrow streaked up through the hole in the floor, piercing the Prince Regent's throat and punching into his brain. Before the Minotaur could even register, he was dead, a second shaft slammed in beside it, dropping him to the floor with a terminal sigh.

* * * * * *

"I bet he never saw that coming!" Weyn winked, turning towards Mathius and holding out his hand, beckoning with his fingers. The assassin stared at the archer in awe, his mouth ajar, not believing the archery shot his friend had just pulled off from here, kneeling on the staircase that Thomas had just scaled. He reached into his pouch and flipped a silver bit towards Weyn who grinned and snatched it from the air.

"Remind me never to get on your bad side." Mathius replied.

"I told you I would get him back for striking me in the jungle." The archer replied; his face suddenly grim. "We better get up there and check if everyone is okay."

"After you." The assassin replied, bowing his head theatrically and sweeping his arm in the direction of the stairs. "Never let it be said that Mathius Blackraven gets between an archer and his arrows."

"Oh, I could so get used to this." Weyn replied, walking past and stepping over the bodies of several Minotaur guards. "I shall have to let Thomas know that from now on I will no longer be at his beck and call and if he wishes someone to 'go high', then he will just have to find someone else to go."

"In your dreams…" Mathius smiled, taking up pursuit. "In your dreams!"

* * * * * *

"Seize them." Aelius commanded, pointing his finger at Mora's stony figure and then at the unconscious figure of Wanessa lying on the floor. "I want them removed from my sight. I know of a nice comfy jail cell that has recently become vacant that they can sit in whilst we consider their fate." Thomas looked up at the elderly Minotaur and noticed a twinkle in the commander's eye that the captain had never seen before.

"I can tell you enjoyed saying that." He whispered. Aelius tilted his head to one side and leant in close.

"You have no idea." He smiled. "Now if you can excuse me for a moment." He stepped away, leaving Thomas to comfort Rowan, hold her close, stroke her hair and breathe in her scent. The captain leant in close to kiss her and felt the kiss returned hungrily. He looked down into Rowan's smoky eyes and tried to clear his throat from the emotions he felt welling up inside him.

"Rowan, I want to ask you something right now, before my courage fails me." He stated. Rowan gazed up into his eyes and smiled.

"Yes." She muttered huskily. "Yes, of course I will."

"Thank goodness." Thomas smiled. "I never thought you would agree to giving me a foot massage so easily." Rowan swung her punch hard into Thomas's left arm causing him to rub his bicep and wince.

"Look I was willing to face an entire troop of Minotaur to save you." He moaned. "That's true love that is."

"Now ask me properly." She teased. "And if you don't hurry, I may just change my mind on the answer." Thomas dropped to one knee, cradling Rowan's hand in his and looked up into her eyes.

"I never want to be with another woman as long as I live." He whispered. "You are my life. Please do me the honour of being my wife?" Rowan looked down at Thomas, then brought her right hand up to her face placing a finger thoughtfully on her chin.

"I thought it was traditional to have some sort of ring?" she smiled. Thomas looked at her hand and frowned, his face wrinkling in frustration. Damn. This was the perfect moment but how could she expect him to produce a ring in the middle of all this chaos? A little hand tapped on his shoulder, causing the captain to turn and see a messy dishevelled and bloody Ashe standing beside him.

"What... Ashe can't you see I'm busy. I mean, really? Do you have to interrupt? Now of all times?" Ashe continued grinning and started fishing in his pockets.

"Hang on, just wait a minute. I know I have it in here somewhere." He muttered, pulling funny faces and patting numerous pockets before he finally beamed and put his hand into his sock to pull out something he then offered to Thomas. The captain took the item from the Halfling's hand and stared down at it in surprise.

"Where on earth did you get a ring from?" he asked, his eyes filling with emotion. He looked up but Ashe was already gone, flitting across the room to examine the jewel bedecked thrones with his unique professional eye. The captain shook his head in amazement only to hear a throat clearing alongside him. He turned back to see Rowan staring impatiently towards him.

"I think you find it fits on this finger." She smiled.

* * * * * *

"Kristoph how are you feeling?" Aelius asked dropping down on one knee alongside the battered and bloodied Minotaur navigator. "I hope you do not feel bad of me. I never intended for this to happen. I wanted you to have the axe and lead the people of Taurean."

"That's okay." Rauph stated, staring up into the eyes of his mentor and offering a kind smile. "I was only competing because you told me I had to. I never wanted the axe, your majesty."

"I will always be Aelius to you my friend." Aelius looked across at the wounded Minotaur who had risked so much to save the people from their tyrannical rulers. "I promise you I will work with both humans and Minotaur to ensure there is no longer such a divide between us."

"I know you will." Rauph replied, looking down at his bloodied hands and fiddling with a broken and bloodied nail. "I guess it is time for us to be leaving then."

"Only if you want to." Aelius replied. "I could do with your judgement in the times ahead."

"I don't think so." Rauph responded. "If I don't leave with the *El Defensor* they will more than likely get lost. After all, I am their navigator."

"But you have done so much. Surely you want a reward of some kind. Name it and it shall be yours."

"I don't want anything." Rauph replied. "Maybe some jewels for the captain and supplies for the ship but that is all."

"Consider it done." Aelius replied, staring long and hard at the humble creature before him. "Never change, Kristoph. You are such a fountain of virtue and honesty." Aelius paused, looking about him and then gestured to one of the guards.

"Here, give me your sword." The guard walked over and offered the blade automatically, bowing his head and backing away. Aelius got to his feet, then lifted the blade up before his face.

"I must confess I am not adept at this but I shall do my best." he began clearing his throat. "Kristoph…"

"Umm," Rauph held up his hand. "Please, don't call me that. My name is Rauph, it is the only name I really remember and from what I have seen I do not wish to be called Kristoph anymore."

"Okay. Kris… Rauph, for gallantry and courage, for piety and honesty. For basically being the best student and friend I could ever hope for." He dropped the blade down and lightly touched first one of Rauph's shoulders and then the other.

"I dub you and bid you rise… my Labyris knight."

Chapter Fifty-Three

Sometimes life surprises when we least expect it; treasures are discovered in jumble sales, small fortunes are squandered on the roll of a dice, Minotaur navigators can be regal Princes and true love can be waiting in the most undesirable of places.

I still cannot believe that she said 'Yes!' I keep expecting to wake up and find this is all just some feverish dream caused by the Nirschl poisoning, yet people are telling me I have a ridiculous grin upon my face and a lightness in my step which truthfully, I cannot deny. Aelius has kindly allowed us to keep Mora's ceremonial seal, which Rowan is delighted about. He wants nothing to do with the old regime and is making good with his promise to sweep clean the remnants of the old order.

The days have definitely become a blur since Aelius was proclaimed the Sovereign of Taurean and already there are improvements visible everywhere. There are designated stewards ensuring the poor are adequately fed and clothed, the homeless housed and the unemployed who are able given work. Promoting self-worth has been key and it shows in the populace and how they eagerly go about their ways, whilst the money thrown into the fountains has been used to pay for the greater portion of these initiatives.

Mora and Wanessa have been exiled to a far-off island where they can retire in peace. Personally I feel this is too good for them and they should have incurred greater punishment. However, Aelius seems to be a compassionate ruler and tells me they will never be permitted to meddle again. I also understand that supplies are delivered on a weekly basis and that strict amounts will be issued. Wanessa's days of gluttony will soon be gone.

On board the El Defensor, life continues apace. Repairs to the ship have been given priority. Minotaur workers, seconded by Aelius, are stronger than anyone else on board and at the pace they are working, we should be shipshape within the week. That is, as long as Commagin is satisfied with the results. He has planned some sea trials over the next few days to iron out any snags but I think ultimately, he will never be happy unless he is the one carrying out the work. The El Defensor is his responsibility after all.

Supplies are plentiful in the hold; fresh water, fruit, cured meats and dried pulses mean Violetta will be busy for weeks cooking new exotic recipes. Rauph now walks the decks in his splendid black and gold armour. He wears a small badge on his breast in the shape of the Labyris and reminds everyone that he is a knight now. I do not believe we will ever hear the end of it. Secretly I think he seems quite relieved that the competition is over.

Marcus has been confined to Violetta's care following a health scare but he appears to be improving and I think he will be up and part of the crew again before he misses us too much. Colette has a full casket of cut jewels that she knows will be strong enough to power open the gateway and keep us searching for home. It is such a great feeling knowing that we can travel again... that is, once we pass through the gateway and deal with whatever awaits us in the ship's graveyard.

Truth be told, this is my biggest concern. For this time, Malum knows where we are. He knows what gateway we passed through. I must confess, I find my thoughts on this matter troubling. I can only hope my crew will be strong enough to face the dangers, whatever they may be, in whichever shape they come.

I must put these dark thoughts behind me and not wallow in them, for I have much to celebrate. Last night we had a sending off party at the fully refurbished 'Fickle Fish'. The owner was delighted at having royalty attend his opening night and the crew enjoyed the sumptuous food and company to their usual excess. I feel I have made good on at least one promise; leaving this man and his family with a legacy at our passing. Having Aelius the Emperor and Kristoph the Labyris knight as guests has set his restaurant's reputation for life.

And at the end of the evening, for the first time in our crew's history...

No inn burnt down.

* * * * * *

"Are you sure that you want to stay with us Rauph?" Thomas asked, standing alongside his huge chestnut navigator as the city of Taurean slowly eased away from their stern. "I mean you are giving up so much. You have a life of luxury back there. A people that support and respect you?" Rauph adjusted the helm slightly, letting the ship roll gently across the swells as the sails snapped taut above them, then he looked at the captain with his deep brown eyes.

"I'm not cut out to be a king. I'm a navigator. It's in my blood. Anyway your sense of direction is terrible. Think how long you have been looking to find your way home." He tapped his head, just beneath his right horn with a giant finger. "I always know where my home is, right here. That's why I never get lost or feel lonely."

"I can respect that," Thomas replied patting his friend reassuringly on the arm. "I'm hoping for similar with Rowan." He could not help himself, just saying her name made him smile.

"My home is on board the *El Defensor* and my friends are all the family I need." Rauph commented. "That is more important than wealth."

"Not to me." Mathius remarked as he walked past, spinning a dagger through his fingers.

"Then I am honoured to be counted as one of your friends." The captain replied, ignoring the mercenary comments of the assassin. "I mean not everyone can say they have a genuine Labyris Knight as their friend."

"I have a badge." Rauph beamed, pushing out his chest. "See?" Thomas looked up at the golden medal and smiled again, before turning away and heading across the deck.

"I feel safer already. Just keep her steady. I'll let you know when Colette is ready to open a gateway."

Thomas climbed down the ladder to the main deck and noted Commagin stomping towards him.

"I'm not happy about this at all." The engineer confessed. "Not at all. I've armed every able-bodied seaman but we have no idea what Malum has in store for us. We have lost Ives; Marcus is as weak as a kitten." He shook his head, a worried look across his face. "We simply need more men."

"Well in that case you will have to settle for more women instead." Violetta stated kicking open the door to the main cabin and marching out on the deck with a huge cast iron skillet in her hand. Rowan marched out behind her armed with a large wrench and Colette brought up the rear with Kerian's sword resting upon her shoulder. "Where do you want us?" Thomas looked at the unlikely troop and smiled in an attempt to hide the sudden feeling of dread he faced at seeing Rowan standing proudly amongst them.

"Anywhere you feel best suited." He replied, swallowing hard, staring quickly around the deck, knowing that if he said something to Rowan, she would never forgive him. Aradol stood to starboard, ancient armour on, sword in hand leading some crewmen to set up position along the rail whilst Mathius did the same to port. Weyn was already climbing the rigging heading for the crow's nest, his bow slung across his back.

Commagin was right, there wasn't enough men. He turned to the Dwarven engineer and winked, trying to avoid letting his gaze follow Rowan. This was ridiculous, he could not remain like this, every time they went into danger! He would end up a neurotic mess! The engineer looked at him with a knowing eye and slapped the side of his ornate crossbow.

"They will have to get through us first laddie." He grinned. "Don't you forget that."

"I wish Kerian were here as well." Thomas confessed.

"He could definitely handle himself in a fight." Commagin agreed. "But whatever we have, will have to be enough. We have to return regardless. My lad's there and I'm for rescuing him no matter what." The dwarf looked up at Thomas's face, only to find the captain's face flushed, his mouth opened in surprise. The Engineer's expression turned hard and he shot Thomas a withering look.

"Of course." Thomas spluttered, kicking himself for forgetting the little Gnome Barney. "Of course!" He turned away, embarrassed, his gaze catching Colette's attention.

"When you are ready." He barked, his throat suddenly dry and scratchy. "Take us through."

* * * * * *

The *Forget-Me-Knot* lay on her side terminally wounded, her hull ruptured, a wicked gash on her starboard side exposing her *Ashok Leyland* engine to the corrosive elements of the ship's graveyard; her life as a trawler now nothing but a distant memory.

With an overall length of 12.8 meters and a beam of 4.28 meters she had been designed and built by the Central Institute of Fisheries in 1985 to fish the seas off Gujarat with a crew of six. However, cruel fate had decided that her fishing career end here, lying on her port side, wedged alongside a wrecked three-masted 1861 Barquentine christened *Amazon* and crushing the prow of a thirteenth century Carrack whose name was obscured somewhere beneath her damaged port side.

An inky shadow dropped down from the *Amazon's* deck and paced across the starboard side of the marooned fishing vessel, its huge Scintarn claws finding secure hold on the rusting metal carcass of the wreck's hull, before it leapt lightly down onto the smeared glass windows along the side of the wheelhouse, its huge paws padding across the surface with an agility that seemed impossible for a monster the size of a full grown panther.

The hound paused at the last window, considering its path carefully, its dark nose sniffing the air about the chimney jutting from the roof of the listing vessel, as if it could smell the scent of cooking from the hob inside the wheelhouse. Then it turned, its dark eyes narrowing at the scent of something else, something faint but exciting.

Prey had been here recently.

The Scintarn licked its lips and drooled hungrily, its long tail curling around as it continued its agitated pacing about the ship. The flint-like markings tracing along its back glinted wetly, despite the fact they were actually dry and as cold and hard as the creature they sprouted from. It checked the access hatches, nosing them to see if they would swing open at its touch, then pawed at the windows, razor sharp claws scratching at the glass. The hound whined at its lack of success, then dropped down off the fishing vessel and carefully checked if it could gain access by slithering under the wheelhouse to reach it from the underside. The Scintarn noted the thick slime and coarse corrosion that it would have to rub its gleaming coat across to get in there and then reconsidered its actions.

A large crab, suddenly disturbed, scuttled across the deck, eager to escape the Scintarn's search and bury itself in a dark shadowy pool of water and hide from the voracious predator. However, it was not fast enough, its ill-fated charge ending by being flipped up into the air and having its shell crushed between the hound's huge jaws as it fell.

Another scent, fainter that the other overlying smells. The hound paused in its feasting, realising with disappointment that this discovery signified the ship had already been searched. Its brethren had been here recently. It turned and sniffed the air, huffing at its own disappointment before confirming its findings and padded away, slinking off across the twisted hulls and disappearing between the buckled gantries, broken masts and sagging sails with a flick of its dark tail.

Something squeaked from inside the wheelhouse and two little circles appeared in the condensation on one of the windows. Two dark eyes stared out through the holes before pulling away and turning to regard the other occupant of the stranded vessel.

"That was close." Octavian announced. "I think it has gone now." He wiped a grimy hand across his face and blew out a relieved sigh.

"How much longer do we have to stay here? Can't we go now. I'm cold and I'm hungry and I never want to eat Spam ever again." Kerian looked up from the ledger he held in his hands and rolled his eyes. It was impossible to concentrate on reading when his travelling companion was in such an aggravating mood. He closed the water-stained log book and slid it into his satchel for safe keeping, dropping the flap closed before realising with intense irritation what he had done. Now he could never find the damn thing!

"I have no idea what animal a 'Spam' is." Kerian confessed, clearly exasperated. "Look we have food in the pantry, we have the means to cook it and at the moment we are relatively safe. Whilst the doors and windows on this ship remain secure, we are sheltered from the elements and we can't be eaten by any hounds. Just sit down and relax. I'm trying to formulate a plan and I can't do it with you making all this noise."

"Well the bad news is that we appear to have eaten everything in the pantry that looks substantial." Octavian confessed, digging into the lop-sided cupboard and dragging out two sorry looking bent and mangled cans. "This is all that remains of our extensive supplies. All we have left is these two sorry specimens. Baked beans. Well I don't know about you but to me that sounds disgusting?"

"Look, we need to keep quiet and we need to keep a low profile. Malum is out there somewhere and he will be searching for us."

"I don't even think he knows that we are here!" Octavian snapped. "Come on Kerian. We can't keep hiding here on this ship. We need to get out, we need to explore. Maybe we can use the life raft from this ship and we can survey the surrounding waters. Then we can come up with a plan once we get the lay of the land as it were. After all, if we stay here, we could miss this *El Defensor* you keep talking about?"

"And if we go out, we could be eaten for dinner by a big black hound that appears to be one of your distant relations." Kerian retaliated.

"They look nothing like me!" Octavian shot back. "I mean, just look at the size of those things! Nothing Malum ever created was that big?"

"Nothing looks like you." Kerian smiled, taking in the crest fallen gypsy and his travelled stained clothing. "Indeed, nothing looks like either of us at the moment." He shook his head despondently, not sure what else to do, allowing an uncomfortable silence to descend on them, punctuated by the ominous creak and groan of the stricken vessels constantly shifting.

It had all seemed so simple at the start. Jump through the portal, await rescue by the Spanish Galleon *El Defensor,* meet up with Colette and then sail into the sunset. Things were never that easy. He thought back over the last few weeks, the two of them scrabbling like rats across the skeletal remains of the wrecks, hiding from the Scintarns and trying to salvage food to survive. Looking for places to sleep that would keep them safe and warm, when everything about them felt so damned cold and dank. They had both become weak from lack of food, making agonising progress across the morass of splintered boats and shattered ships, slipping and sliding down listing decks and climbing slime covered rigging until they had stumbled upon these magical metal containers.

Somehow, Octavian had been able to identify the fact that these hand-sized rusty containers held food stuff. Kerian would have cast such objects aside without thinking but the gypsy's keen nose had sniffed out these magical supplies with a skill that had stunned the knight. By keeping their searches restricted to the more intact vessels, they had discovered more of these strange containers, however, opening the damned things was another matter entirely. He rubbed his finger, remembering the painful cuts he had gained trying to open one that contained some congealed white sludge with grey and pink lumps floating in it. The gypsy had tentatively identified chicken, the label proclaimed soup but it had been absolutely foul, until they had realised that they needed to heat the contents before consuming it.

"Your bag is moving." Octavian stated, breaking Kerian's thoughts.

"What?" the knight replied, lifting one eyebrow in irritation. "Don't be stupid. My bag is not moving."

"I'm telling you that damn satchel just moved!" Octavian scrabbled away from his seat and backed away as far as the confines of the wheelhouse allowed. Kerian lifted his satchel up and stared at it, not noting any suspicious bulges or any signs of the flap moving.

"Very funny." He snapped. "Why don't you spend some time getting acquainted with your baked beans and leave me alo…" The flap lifted a few centimetres and a strange noise issued from the darkness within. Kerian nearly dropped the magical bag in shock. Octavian moved closer, his hand rummaging through a half open drawer of battered kitchen utensils, before grabbing a wooden stave and holding it menacingly above the satchel.

"Maybe it's a rat! We have seen enough of them around here." The gypsy announced. "When I say, open it and I'll brain it with this thing." Kerian looked at his companion and nodded in agreement.

"Okay." He licked his lips nervously. "Now!" Kerian threw back the flap and a moist little black nose poked out of the bag sniffing warily at the air. The knight instantly recognised it for what it was. His hand shot out, even as he warned Octavian not to make good on his threat. The rolling pin slammed onto Kerian's hand making him yelp in alarm and the sniffing little black nose disappear back into the shadows of the magical bag. The two men moved in closer and opened the bag fully, exposing the little wriggling creature inside.

"Oh my!" Kerian remarked. "How on earth did you get here?" Octavian placed his hand on Kerian's shoulder and grinned.

"Oh, please say we can keep him?"

* * * * * *

Marcus awoke to noises above deck and the unmistakable movement beneath him as the *El Defensor* raced across the waters. The ship was moving! He groaned at his own weakness. He needed to be up on deck, part of the crew, not down here being nursed by Violetta and her daughter.

He called out to Violetta, hungry for information, only to find there was no reply when he called. Little footsteps sounded and Katarina poked her head from around the corner. The young girl tilted her head to one side, swiftly taking in the signs her mother had told her to look out for and figured that the patient was not in imminent life-threatening danger.

"What's the problem Marcus?" she asked, her little smile beaming and radiant.

"I just wondered what was going on?" he replied. "It sounds like we are on the move again." Katarina stared up at the ceiling as if her eyes could see through the decking, up to where her mother stood with the crew.

"They are preparing to open a gateway and go back to the ship's graveyard." She confirmed. "Mum has told me to stay down here and keep an eye on you." Marcus face paled.

"They are going to go back through. I need to be up there with them." He moved to stand then realised that he had nothing on but his underclothes. "Um, excuse me please."

"Oh Marcus I have seen much worse than you know." Katarina tittered, before turning around to leave her back towards him. Marcus reached out, his fingers stretching for his blue robes folded on the chair by his bedside, determined to get dressed but not believing that Katarina would not turn around again just to see him blush. His finger caught the edge of the robe and he yanked it towards him, only for something to fall out from the deep folds of his hood.

The monk swiftly dressed then reached down to collect the object which had fallen, only for his hand to stop short as he recognised what lay there. It was a little stick man fashioned from thin dark twigs of a hawthorn tree, a sliver of hair was intertwined around its head, a small strip of blue robe fastened around its neck and there was some dark residue within the trunk of the figurine that looked wet and shiny. Marcus swallowed hard, noting how the figure was crunched over, its head buried in its hands whilst it knelt.

He picked the creation up with shaking hands, spreading out the blue piece of robe and noting the sign of the *Bearer* crudely etched upon the cloth. His fingertips tingled as he touched the crafted item confirming the monk's fears.

"Did you make this?" he asked, slowly turning around towards Katarina.

"No." the girl's reply was too definite for this to be a lie.

"Your mother?" A shake of the head. "Do you know what this is?" Katarina nodded, stepping warily away.

"Black magic." She replied ominously, marking the air with a sign, as if she could ward the evil from the figurine away. Marcus stood there for a moment undecided, then grabbed his boots and tried to pull them on, feeling a wave of nausea wash over him as he bent down. Someone was trying to curse him! He needed to do something, needed to tell someone. Richard. Brother Richard would know what to do.

"Wait here and don't touch that thing. It's dangerous." He warned, staggering out into the main passageway, his legs feeling like jelly as he tried to spread his stance and prevent himself from falling over with the movements of the ship. Why had he let this happen? He should have been more aware, of what was going on; should have been paying more attention.

He collided with the bulkhead then staggered around the corner. Where could Richard be? His addled mind refused to work, still struggling with the after effects of the debilitating spell. Marcus's first thought was that the priest was above deck with everyone else but Richard was never one to put himself in the path of danger, he was not that kind of man. Danger! They were in danger. He needed to get the book. Maybe he could summon the knights to help them?

Marcus slithered down the ladder to the berths, barely controlling his descent and headed unsteadily towards his own sparse cabin, pushing his doubts about controlling the book from his mind. He was the *Bearer*; he had the bestowed right to order the book and the knights within to carry out his wishes. His friends could be in danger, whoever had cursed him could also be cursing other members of the crew. They needed his help, no matter what the risks.

He reached the door of his cabin and pulled it open, staggering forwards as the ship rolled into the trough of a deep swell. The monk fell unsteadily to his knees as the galleon rose again, his legs like jelly. He cursed, placing his hand on the floor to steady himself and shake his head clear, then lifted his head to find that the room was full of shadowy figures. Marcus blinked twice trying to understand what his confused mind was screaming at him, his eyes darting instantly towards where the ledger lay.

The hiding place where he had secreted the book lay wide open, the dark hole beyond appearing to mock the monk for his naivety at leaving such a dangerous ledger unguarded. The shadows stepped forwards as one, armour rattling, boots stamping on the wooden floor responding to a call to arms. His shaken mind realised that they were the knights from his book, summoned forth, called to action by forces unknown but there was no way that the warriors could be outside of the tome without Marcus calling them. It was impossible! The magic could not work that way! It had never worked that way! Hands grabbed roughly at his robes, heaving him up from the floor, pulling Marcus further into the cabin. The monk was too shocked to respond, his eyes straining in the darkness, struggling to make out who his assailant was. Clarity slowly registered with the troubled monk as his surroundings were revealed. Was that the silhouette of Tobias?

"Tobias. Why are you out of the book? I never gave you permission. I never summoned you. Return now from where you came." The magical knight sneered, then incredibly bounced Marcus's head maliciously off the ceiling, making the monk see stars.

"You have no hold over me." Tobias spat. Marcus tried to push down the rising panic he felt within himself, tried to squash any self-doubt that remained. He needed to focus, needed to channel his command with authority.

"Return to the book." He ordered.

"I don't think so." Tobias threw Marcus back through the cabin door, smashing him into the wall on the other side of the passageway. The monk groaned, slumping down to the ground as Tobias strode purposefully from the cabin to deliver further punishment. One gauntleted hand reached forward to grab him at the throat as the other pulled back to throw a fearsome punch.

Marcus instinctively shoved down with his left hand, pulling his right hand up between them and sweeping it to the side, deflecting the punch, letting it crash harmlessly into the wall behind him, even as his right hand swept back and slapped Tobias hard on the side of his helmet. The knight loosened his grip at the monk's throat in shock, staggering backwards, shaking his head, only for Marcus to lift up one leg and propel himself from the wall, using his momentum to crash into Tobias, causing the warrior to stagger backwards into Marcus's cabin.

The novice landed lightly on the floor, his splayed hands catching his fall and allowing him to place his feet and flip back into a combat stance. Tobias quickly regained his own balance and charged back in, his fists lashing out first left, then right, each attack parried by the exhausted monk who repelled them, or dodged the blows, so that Tobias became increasingly frustrated and even angrier. Marcus feinted right then, slipped left, determined to find more room to counter the unprovoked attack.

Other fighters started to march from the monk's cabin, following the furious melee as it backed into a larger open area of crew sleeping quarters; where crude sheet partitions gave the junior crew an illusion of privacy, enclosing hammocks swung between wooden posts in the middle of the deck and the small cupboards or sea chests bolted to the floor in which they stored their personal belongings. Cannon had once occupied this space and their runners still crossed the floor making the area a trip hazard for the unwary, whilst several shuttered lanterns cast meagre illumination doing little to relieve the gloom.

Tobias lunged forwards, just as Marcus snapped out a kick, launching a small footstool in his direction, that knocked the knight's feet out from under him and sent him crashing to the floor. Marcus dropped through one partition, rolled across a sea chest and off the other side, determined to give himself some space, only to find his pathway being rapidly blocked by several knights advancing towards him.

Cold steel glinted as the knights drew their blades and charged. Marcus acted on impulse, his training coming to the fore. He stepped in towards the nearest knight, his hand catching the tip of the sword, pushing it out to the side, just as another assailant lunged from the left, attempting to skewer Marcus's foot to the floor. The monk lifted his boot seconds before the tip dug into the deck, then used the blade as a spring when his foot came back down, launching his body up high, letting him lash out with a kick as he turned.

His boot connected with the first warrior's head, smashing him to the side and sending him crashing over a wooden sea chest. Marcus reached out as he fell, snatching a partition sheet from its line and snapping it out to whip it painfully across the nose of the fighter who had tried to skewer his boot, making the man stagger backwards howling.

"Stay still damn you." Tobias cursed, lashing out, his arm sweeping high. Marcus ducked back under the sheets, jumping over the knight who had tumbled over the chest and scooping up the fallen warrior's blade. The monk knew that his ability to use this magical weapon would be limited, indeed his competence with a blade was mediocre at best but in the close confines of the deck he felt the odds would be roughly even. He turned sharply, swirling the loose sheet about his left hand whilst lunging with the sword, catching another magical knight beneath his helmet, flipping it up into the air. The warrior automatically clutched for his headpiece, lifting his arm up, allowing Marcus to plunge the blade he held all the way to the hilt, burying it in the man's chest amid a bloom of manuscript pages.

He spun about, leaving the weapon in his foe, using his protected left arm to deflect another blade, before he struck a further knight in the chin with the flat of his right palm and rolled under another flimsy partition that was immediately shredded by scything blades. Marcus was determined to cross from one side of the deck to the other and staggered his path to throw off his persistent enemies.

He dodged left, emerging near an alcove set in the hull of the ship, barely registering the faded posters plastered across the walls proclaiming the acrobatic prowess of the 'Rinaldo Brothers', Abeline, Plano, and their departed brother Lubok, from their days back in the Parisian circus. Marcus charged for the passageway, hoping to slip past his cabin and get help, just as another figure walked out into the shuttered lantern light.

"Brother Richard!" Marcus yelled, sliding to a stop, then ducking as a knight's arm swept over his head. He turned, delivering two rapid blows to the magical warrior's kidneys which sent the knight staggering backwards, only to trip over one of the runners on the floor and crash down onto the deck.

"Brother Richard, I am cursed. The ship is in danger. We must flee, gather the others. Someone is controlling the knights. I swear I did not summon them." Marcus tried to explain as best he could, yet his mentor remained strangely calm, despite the urgency of his warning and the chaos of the knights crashing around them. It did not make sense.

Tobias charged from the shadows, catching Marcus in the side and dropping him to the deck. He followed up with a gauntleted punch that rocked the monk's head back with the force of the blow. Marcus rolled to the side, scrabbling to regain his footing, trying to get into space, rapidly fending off the blows, as he struggled to find a way to get Richard away from the danger rapidly closing in from all sides.

"Fight them Richard. We need to get away." Another vicious blow landed, snatching the air from Marcus's lungs. He crashed back to the floor gasping, just as Richard stepped out from the shadows fully, revealing his betrayal by exposing the large blue book he held openly in his hands. Brother Richard looked down at Marcus disdainfully, his face turning into a wicked sneer. His expression clearly displaying the disgust he felt for the weak monk now being overpowered at his feet.

"You poor deluded fool." He stated disdainfully. "I am their master now."

Chapter Fifty-Four

The Taurean sky split apart with an angry crackle, yawning open several feet ahead of the prow of the *El Defensor* and belching forth a foul smell that instantly raised anxiety amongst the crew. The waters surged beneath the galleon's hull, sucking hungrily at the ancient ship and drawing it relentlessly towards the magical portal that had claimed so many vessels in times past.

Colette sat on the deck of the aft-castle, her eyes closed in concentration, her slim legs crossed. Kerian's dulled sword lay across her lap, the steel naked and ready to hand, whilst a large sapphire, probably worth a small fortune, slowly crumbled in her left hand as it sent forth the magical tendrils of power contained within its heart.

Rauph manned the helm, the Minotaur navigator carefully adjusting the heading of the aged galleon, so that she entered the gateway cleanly, ensuring the pitted stonework of the massive archway had clearance to both sides. Thomas stood alongside him, fighting hard to keep his emotions in check, straining his eyes towards the portal, scanning the mustard coloured sky beyond for any clues as to what terrors lay waiting within the graveyard. His nerves were on edge, his hand hovering near the hilt of his cutlass. This was it, there would be no turning back now.

Almost instantly cries of alarm and distress started to ripple towards the captain from the prow of the ship. Nervous voices rose above the sound of the churning waters. The crewmen snatching up weapons as they noticed ominous dark lines criss-crossing the way ahead like some grotesque fishing net.

"Turn around, turn about!" crewmen screamed but Thomas already knew with a sinking heart that their heading was set and they could never hope to manoeuvre the galleon when the current from the ship's graveyard had already taken hold.

"Brace! Brace! Brace!" Commagin screamed, reaching out and wrapping his arm about one of the lines, the crew around him scrambling to do the same. Thomas could only watch in horror as the crew he relied upon milled about in panic. Then the ship hit the net and the panic turned to terror.

A gut-wrenching, splintering sound reverberated through the *El Defensor*, as first the figurehead, then the spars from the foremast became tangled in the lengths of chain strung across their way. Yards splintered and folded, canvas sails crumpled, whilst others teared as the galleon struggled to make headway.

Smaller lengths of chain within the net first strained, then parted with sounds like gunshots, the separated links shredding sail and tangling with the rigging. Others held firm, snapping the smaller spars of the ship. The bowsprit bent ominously as it felt the strain, creaking loudly in protest before exploding, the forestay-sails dropping to the deck in an avalanche of cream canvas, the lines threatening to tear other rigging down alongside.

Thomas started shouting orders to his crew, his eyes tracing the construction of the metal cage they were sailing into, noting the points where the chains had been secured to the ancient stone archway on either side.

"Abeline, Plano, take the port side. Mathius and Austen take the starboard, we need to free those chains, do everything you can to give us some room. Weyn…" Where the hell was Weyn? Thomas looked up towards the crow's nest and instinctively winced as the main mast became entangled with the rusty trap, stretching it taut and revealing that the net was secured to the top of the archway as well. The archer was still up there, valiantly struggling to free himself from his lofty perch before it also snapped like kindling. Weyn dropped down towards the next stay and hugged the mast, bowing his head to try and protect it as the mast above him was torn away.

"We have a problem." Rauph stated, causing Thomas to turn towards his colleague and shoot the Minotaur a withering look for stating the obvious. "The ship is too long to pass through the gateway with the net across it."

"The what…?" The blood in the captain's veins turned to ice as he noticed the navigator spoke true. The *El Defensor* had not yet cleared the ancient stonework pillars of the archway, she still jutted several feet back into the world of Taurean. If Colette's portal magic now failed, if the ship was caught between the two worlds, the gateway could slam closed, shearing off the stern.

"Damn!" Thomas cursed. They needed to get the ship through the arch. They needed more slack in the net. He looked up at the stonework of the port side pillar, noting the tricky footholds and the rough scaffolding assembled alongside it. The pillar was close enough to jump to from the rigging. If he could climb up to the top of the archway and sever the anchor points the net should fall away giving them the space to move safely through the gate. The captain knew his cutlass could cut through almost anything. He suddenly realised what he had to do. He turned to his hairy companion and stared up into his eyes.

"Hold the fort. Don't leave the helm, keep Colette safe."

"Hold the what?" Rauph asked looking confused but Thomas was already gone running for the rigging and starting his ascent. "Keep who's safe?"

Loud screams arose amidships as ragged figures suddenly swung from the port scaffolding and dropped onto the deck, rusty weapons swinging wildly, eyes glazed with madness, actions of half-starved animals rather than the sane crewmen that had once accompanied Miguel Garcia on his ill-fated barge.

Some of the crew moved to meet the onslaught with what they had, whilst others tried to free the wounded galleon from her shackles. They met the new threats with a clash of swords and the clang of a heavy skillet but even as the crew moved to engage, eerie howls sounded from starboard and Scintarn hounds started to leap down upon the deck.

Thomas tried to ignore the screams of the crew as the hounds jumped aboard below him. He tried to ignore the howls and the wails of those meeting their grisly ends. He had to focus, he needed to save his ship first and just pick up the pieces later. The captain gritted his teeth as he climbed, not wanting to admit to himself just how many pieces that may actually be.

* * * * * *

"Seriously Octavian. Did you have to?" Kerian wrinkled his nose in disgust as he lent forward to pull the oars, therefore putting himself closer to his travelling companion and the noxious stench he had just created.

"I told you those beans were dodgy." The gypsy replied sheepishly, shrugging his shoulders in apology. Octavian pulled back on the second set of oars, helping the lifeboat skip across the deep waters as they rowed their way down a treacherous channel between a ruined steamship named *Pioneer* and a schooner whose faded name appeared to be *The Turner*.

"How many ships are wrecked here? This place seems to stretch for miles." Octavian asked. Kerian stopped rowing in mid-action and used his hand to push up a streamer of green slime that stretched across their way, before leaning back on his seat and staring about him as the small rowboat exited the tight constricting channel and finally moved out into a small lagoon.

He noted the decaying hulks piled high around them, the sad state of the warped decks, the gaping holes in the hulls allowing dank water to lap loudly inside the dark cavernous interiors and the broken windows that whistled when the wind passed through them. Everything here felt so sad, so pointless; much like his fleeting fantasy of finding Colette again.

"All of these ships had to have been filled with people." Octavian continued. "So where did they all go?"

"I can only assume Malum tortured and ate them." Kerian replied. "You know his hounds are trained to track survivors down and deliver them to him. Thomas and I rescued some crewmen from him in the past and I have seen the room where he feasts. It is not for the faint hearted." He shuddered, remembering the grisly scenes deep inside the cruise liner Neptune. Octavian lifted his oars, letting the water drip from the blades and make ripples across the surface of the sea as he considered the gory revelations Kerian relayed.

"But all of these people. Just think of the size of this place. That's going to take some commitment. It must have taken a lifetime, no several lifetimes for him to manage this." The gypsy paused, before a sudden thought occurred to him as he realised the enormity of the casualties involved. "Where are their belongings, their jewellery, their treasures? We searched many vessels for food and yet I never found a single travel bag or chest. Not a single personal item... Oh watch out!"

Kerian ceased rowing and glanced over his shoulder just in time to spot a jagged mast jutting high from the water. He adjusted their course, dipping one oar into the water to help swing the boat around and avoid the obstructing mast. The fighter gazed down through the opaque surface at the spectral shape of a main deck submerged below them, its surface draped with green curtains of weed that waved and swirled in the current. The little boat cast a shadow on the wreckage like a dark ink blot that slowly drifted across the sunken emerald backdrop.

"It just doesn't make any sense." Octavian confessed, dropping his oars back into the water and pulling again. "Their belongings have to be somewhere." He paused, leaving Kerian struggling to understand if a question had been asked or if he was supposed to respond in some way. Octavian tilted his head as if hearing something that the knight was unaware of, then gestured with his hand.

"Something is going on over there." He pointed. "I think we should investigate." He pulled at the oars again, shooting the lifeboat along and gestured for Kerian to do the same. Kerian observed his companion row then timed his own strokes to match, pulling hard and easing the boat around the hull of a listing freighter called the *Suduffco*, its wreckage creaking ominously as they neared.

As soon as they cleared the bow and passed beneath the rusty anchor, the sounds of a distant conflict reached Kerian's ears. He turned in his seat, his eyes widening in shock as he drank in the sight of the square masted vessel he had been questing for all of this time; the waters foamed angrily about her hull, the rigging damaged and misshapen, the galleon appearing to be stuck like a fly in a huge web. People milled about the galleon's decks, darting one way then the other, pursued by dark shapes and sword wielding foes. A chilling howl cut the air. There was no mistaking that sound. Scintarns.

Kerian swallowed hard, trying to steady his rapidly beating heart. Despite the *El Defensor's* injuries, she remained a regal looking classical vessel and he knew in his heart that Colette was upon those decks possibly fighting for her life right now. He needed to get over there as quickly as possible.

The huge freighter groaned in protest alongside them, its stern lifting as the rush of water from the open gate flooded towards them. Indeed, the force of the water was setting the whole morass of ruined ships nearest the gateway creaking and grinding in response as they jostled with the force of the current jetting into the graveyard. Kerian tugged furiously at his oars, feeling the little boat struggling to make way as it too became swept up in the force of the water rushing beneath her hull.

"Come on damn you!" Kerian cursed, pulling for all he was worth. "I can't let her go again. I need to get on that ship!" Octavian threw himself into the task, pulling on the oars as hard as he could but for every foot that they gained, they were swept several more away. Kerian's mind fought back the panic threatening him. To come so far and be so close.

The *Suduffco* loomed closer as the rowing boat inched towards the battered hull; a chill falling upon the two rowers as they were swept into her shadow. Several loud snaps echoed through the substructure of the wreck and the vessel began to turn, her prow inching out into the force of the flood, her stern crushing several ships lying beside her to kindling. The prow loomed over them, sweeping everything before it in a surge of water and accumulated debris.

"Pull damn you!" Kerian screamed as the huge structure creaked and cracked its way towards them, jetsam from the deserted decks tumbled down her rust eaten sides and sank into the depths as she swung her tortuous turn. In that exact moment, as the freighter's slow arc brought it between them and the *El Defensor*, the current pounding the little row boat was cut off by the ships heavy bulk.

"Row now!" Kerian roared, pulling at the oars until his muscles ached and his body felt coated in sweat. They both bent to the task, refusing to look up at the huge wall of rusted steel, flaking paint and weeping rivets that rolled relentlessly towards them. The little boat surged forwards as the ship edged closer, then with a huge groan the *Suduffco* slipped past them, pushing the boat away with its wake and sending it bobbing over towards the line of archways surrounding the graveyard.

Kerian looked along their unexpected direction of travel and regarded the line of silent gateways, his gaze tracing along the top of the archways and back over towards the trapped Spanish galleon. There were hand holds available to him, evidence of the erosion these huge stone pillars had experienced over the millennia they had stood here. It would not be easy but it was worth a try. He pulled sharply on the starboard oar, easing the small boat towards the nearest darkened archway, then pulled on the oars allowing the small vessel to cut diagonally across the current rather than row against it, determined to bring the pillar closer.

The current continued to roll around them, making the relatively short distance to travel an agonisingly slow one, especially with the sounds of the skirmish from the *El Defensor* ringing in his ears. Kerian bent his back to the task and rowed using reserves he never knew he had before the boat finally crunched up against the stonework. He dropped his oars, stood up and turned towards the monument, noting the holes in the stonework as the boat rocked up and down.

"Hold her steady." He requested, reaching out and then suddenly jumping across the water to the crumbling edifice, leaving Octavian staring at him with a look of sheer surprise.

"What exactly do you think you are doing?" The gypsy yelled, fumbling with the oars. "Get back into the damned boat Kerian. We can find another way around."

"There is no time!" Kerian snapped back. "I'm not letting that ship out of my sight ever again!" He turned and started to scale the stonework, scrabbling for holds and kicking free loose pieces of masonry, his scabbard dangling at his legs, his satchel bouncing from his right hip and his shield dulled a mustard yellow by the threatening bleak sky.

"Are you just going to leave me here?" Octavian enquired as the boat continued to slowly drift away from the pillar, now that only one set of oars was powering it. "You can't do that to me Kerian. I don't know where to go!"

"Don't worry." The knight replied. "I'm not going to be long. It's a quick race across the top of the arches, then I can get on board the ship and I can introduce you to Colette." Octavian looked back across the churning water at the chaos and screams ensuing aboard the *El Defensor* then shook his head in concern. Listening to the noise the strange galleon was the last place they needed to go. It seemed no matter where Kerian went trouble was never far away.

"Just row between the archways and I'll meet you there soon." Kerian shouted, leaping up to a hand hold and sending grit cascading down. "It will be fun!"

"By the sounds of it, it's probably a private party and we should really wait until we are invited." Octavian replied, really not sure what the best course of action should be.

"And miss all the excitement?" Kerian grunted, swinging his right boot up and levering himself further up the pillar, his fatigue all but forgotten, his spirits boosted by the thought that the woman he loved was only a few arches away.

"Can I at least keep the pet with me." Octavian ask, pulling valiantly at the oars and only finding himself spinning in a small circle as he tried to stop the lifeboat drifting completely away.

"Octavian you should know better." Kerian replied. "You know dogs can't row!" He turned back to his climb and inched up another few feet, continued his ascent with focused determination.

"You know dogs can't row." Octavian mimicked, putting on a squeaky voice in parody of Kerian's own as he watched his colleague incredulously leaving him behind. He cursed under his breath then turned away, pulling on the oars. Maybe, Kerian was right, if he angled the boat correctly, he could eventually work his way along the gateways and get closer to the galleon but he wasn't sure he wanted to.

"At least I'm loyal and don't leave my colleagues in the lurch." Octavian muttered to himself, struggling to adjust the direction of the boat as he reluctantly inched the small vessel towards the sounds of the battle. The gypsy watched Kerian climbing up the column until a sudden cold shiver ran up his spine. He shook himself, trying to banish the overwhelming sensation that he was seeing his companion for the last time.

"More loyal than you deserve, you clod. Just be careful..." He muttered, fighting back his emotions and bending to the oars before whispering one last adieu after the distant figure.

"And watch your back."

* * * * * *

"It's not breaking!" Abeline cursed, hanging from the rigging high above the deck and pulling furiously at where two lengths of chain joined together. "I need something to lever it apart."

A crazed figure jumped down onto the deck and charged screaming towards Plano, swinging a rusty sword that had clearly seen better days. The acrobat frowned at the interruption and turned from watching his brother struggle above him to address this new problem.

"Excuse me for just one moment." he grinned, before swinging himself up by the ropes and bringing his legs around in a beautiful arc that collided right under the charging thug's throat, momentarily lifting the man from the deck. He dropped to the ground holding his neck and gasping, whilst his sword flipped up into the air. Plano swung out again, caught the blade as it started to tumble and threw it up to his sibling.

"Thank you!" Abeline replied deftly catching it, inserting the blade into the link and levering with all of his might. The chain parted with a snap but unfortunately, so did the end of the blade the acrobat held. The weapon jumped in his hand and he instinctively dropped it, only to observe the sword bounce from the rail and sink into the frothing waters.

"We need another sword." He cried down to his brother.

"Another one!" Plano replied. "What happened to the last one?"

"I guess they don't make pirate swords like they used to!" Abeline exclaimed, inching his way along the spar to untangle another length of chain. Plano looked across the deck where a crazed fighter was chasing Violetta sword held high and grabbed hold of a rope secured to the mast beside him.

"I'll see what I can do." The acrobat muttered, wrapping his leg around the rope before he dropped down and swung out across the deck, in a move reminiscent to which he used to perform in the circus. His body swooped through the air, his legs scissoring forward as he reached the bottom of the arc, propelling him up and alongside the screaming fighter. Plano reached out and snatched the marauder's sword from his hand as he passed, leaving the attacker running towards the skillet wielding cook with nothing to fight with.

Violetta instantly stepped forward, swinging her cast iron pan with a skill learnt from years of use within the ship's galley, smashing her assailant in the stomach and then smacking him over the head when he doubled over. Plano continued his swing, leaving the formidable cook in his wake and mentally noting never to criticise her cooking again. His path of travel took him out over the skirmishing crew, towards the starboard side of the ship. He reached the apex of his swing just as a huge Scintarn hound leapt for him, its jaws wide open.

"Sacre Bleu!" the acrobat yelled, pulling back against his rope in shock. The hound's teeth snapped together inches from his heel as Plano started to wobble back across the deck, straight towards the raging melee he had passed. The acrobat realised he was never going to make it back to where he started, so he let go of the rope, dropping to the deck and rolling, just as Commagin let loose with his silver crossbow.

The air above the tumbling acrobat filled with bolts that peppered attacker, hound and ship alike as the weapon that was the Dwarven engineer's mightiest achievement roared. Plano scrambled across the deck on all fours, passing beneath the Dwarf, only to find his back suddenly used as a make-shift bench when Commagin placed the *Lady Janet* down upon him to reload.

"Thank you." Commagin grinned, swinging his crossbow up again and squeezing the trigger to produce another flurry of deadly shafts. Plano shook his head and continued to crawl off across the ship, the cutlass clunking off the deck each time he placed his hand down. Rowan suddenly screamed at the acrobat to duck, charging at him and swinging her wrench. The acrobat threw his head down, almost kissing the deck, his hair parting as she swung the tool missing his head by inches.

A loud yelp sounded as the wrench smacked across the nose of a Scintarn hound that was about to bite Plano's neck and it shied away, nursing its snout, its pride hurt more than the wound it had received. Plano looked up into Rowan's sparkling eyes and threw a clumsy salute.

"Mademoiselle, I am forever in your debt." He laughed, getting back to his feet, before swiftly parrying a portly attacker charging in from the side, slashing the blade across his sternum and letting the body drop to the deck.

"I am sure you will return the favour." Rowan replied, nodding her head in acknowledgement before stepping away to tackle another foe. Plano noticed a gap between the fighting figures and set off at a run, dodging a wild swing from a vacant-eyed assailant, then dropping to slide beneath the clashing blades of Mathius as he took on two fighters single-handedly.

The assassin thrust one of his daggers directly into the ear of his nearest opponent, then snatched the sword from Plano's grasp as the acrobat slid beneath him, using it to keep his second aggressor at bay whilst throwing his remaining dagger straight into the throat of yet another foe closing in. He launched into a dizzying counter, before flicking out with the tip of the sword and slashing it across the man's abdomen dropping him to the deck.

Mathius spun around and threw the sword back into Plano's hands. The acrobat deftly caught the weapon before continuing his charge towards the port side rigging. He slid to a stop beneath his brother and swiftly scrambled up alongside him before breathlessly offering the blade.

"What took you so long?" his brother enquired, before wrinkling his nose in distaste at the state of the weapon and the gore now running across his hands.

"What's wrong with you Plano?" He remarked, shaking his head in disappointment. "You could have brought me a clean one."

* * * * * *

Thomas swung himself inside the scaffolding, only to come face to face with an enraged man who immediately charged towards him and tried to hit him with a large metal pole. He parried the first blow, knocked the bar out wide and hoped that this would be enough to cool the assailant's rage towards him, only to hear the fighter angrily roar and then attack again.

The captain stepped back, shocked by the ferocity of the man's actions, especially as he held the superior weapon and was likely better trained. Yet the crazed man before him continued to charge, his eyes glazed, not focusing on Thomas at all. It was as if the man had been programmed just to batter anything he encountered. The fact that the man's eyes gave no clue of what he was about to do was truly unsettling. This was Malum's work, of this Thomas had no doubt.

Thomas stepped to one side, allowing his attacker to swing his pole at thin air, then shoved him hard, watching with pity as the dazed man simply stepped off into space, still swinging his pole as he fell down towards the *El Defensor*, smacking his head on the side of the ship before crashing into the waters below. Thomas had no time to watch the fall and continued his anxious climb up the wobbling structure, trying to put out of his mind that the whole scaffolding could fall apart and crash into the waters at any moment, taking him with it!

His ship was in danger this was all that mattered.

He finally reached the top of the pillar and pulled himself up onto the stone of the archway, noting the six huge chains secured across the opening that were holding his ship and crew captive. He swung his cutlass as hard as he could, watching the magical blade cleave through the rusty metal with a spark and chip into the archway. The portside edge restraint shot off the wide bridge of stone with a loud rattle and disappeared into the void as Thomas wrenched his blade free and charged towards the next anchor point. He chopped his cutlass down onto the next chain, hearing it snap cleanly and bounce off the edge of the arch.

That was two. Four to go.

He looked towards the next chain and noticed some movement at the far end of the arch, something was clambering rapidly up through the scaffolding, something moving fast with a spider-like motion that was unmistakable, using many more hands that a normal human would have at their disposal.

Thomas froze. He knew who this was, knew that this encounter was inevitable. The very thought of getting close enough for Malum to dazzle him with his coloured barbs and rend him limb from limb made the captain doubt every skill he ever had. His confidence started to diminish like a sand castle washed by the tide.

Malum pulled himself upright and rolled back his shoulders, his pale face turning this way and that sniffing the air, seeking the man he had waited so long to punish. He turned to the left, then to the right, his barbs extending like the tendrils of a dangerous man-o-war, their colours pulsing black and red, the endings opening and closing.

Click clack, click clack.

Malum turned slowly towards the sounds of running feet heading in his direction and smiled, his translucent skin threatening to tear as his lips rubbed over the ragged stubs of his ancient yellow brown teeth. His nostrils flared, confirming the smell of the man his sightless eyes could never see.

"Ah, Thomas. It appears you have finally been let out to play."

* * * * * *

Commagin held his crossbow up to his shoulder and swung it about the deck looking for another target. Several of the *El Defensor* crew dived to the deck as his sights passed over them, dreading the aged Dwarf might accidentally wound them with his wayward aim.

A huge hound pulled itself over the rail of the ship and dropped down upon the deck, its paws as large as dinner plates, its armour plating flashing as bright as any polished gemstone. Commagin swung the *Lady Janet* in its direction and drew a bead just below its heavy brow and directly between its pitch-black eyes.

"Just a little closer." The Dwarf whispered. "Just one more step."

Something slammed into the starboard side of the *El Defensor* setting the whole ship juddering. Commagin's quarrel shot from his crossbow, ricocheted off the Scintarn's shoulder and shot over the ships rail.

"Damn! Now what?" The dwarf shouted, only to find himself staring open-mouthed as the monster Scintarn charged towards him. He pulled his crossbow up, determined to stop the beast in its tracks, only for the quarrel to snap as the string missed the nock, jamming the beautiful weapon.

"Oh hell." Commagin mouthed as the hound pounced.

Several black arrows streaked down from above, punching the creature in its shoulders, neck and head, just as it jumped. The Scintarn piled into Commagin, its momentum too fast to be simply stopped by a volley of

Weyn's arrows, burying the Dwarf under its huge mass, its body limp and lifeless, squashing the engineer as its life blood dripped out across the open deck.

Weyn looked down at his latest victim from his viewpoint high on the mast and grinned, noting the tell-tale sign of Commagin's wriggling boot sticking out from under the massive black pile of fur which confirmed his shipmate was still alive and 'sort of' kicking.

He drew another arrow from his quiver and turned towards the collision that had just happened on the starboard side and watched in amazement as two giant lizards started scrambling over the side of the ship from a sleek slate-grey ship that appeared to be floating in the air! The lizards hit the deck running, charging from one person to the next, attacking crew and attackers with equal enthusiasm. One of them appeared to have a dead cat perched on its head, whilst the other pounced on to a growling Scintarn and wrapped its muscular tail around the unfortunate hound's neck, crushing the creature to the deck, even as the lizard's claws tore into another attacker's chest.

Weyn narrowed his eyes when he noticed that the lizard with the bizarre headpiece had chosen to run towards Rowan and Austen but both of them were occupied struggling to lever a length of chain free from the starboard rail. They would never see the attack coming. His hand quickly reached for an arrow and he pulled his bow back to full draw, fixing a bead on the reptile and judging its path of travel before letting the shaft fly.

The enchanted arrow hit Horatio's armoured snout and physically snapped in two, making Weyn blink in astonishment and the lizard spin around angrily, his tail flicking with agitation, his nose sniffing for his attacker.

"I don't believe it." The archer gasped, feeling for the return of his magical arrow and finding nothing but an empty hole where it should have been. "I just don't believe..." The lizard suddenly looked up, its reptilian eyes blazing with fury, its ire clearly directed in Weyn's direction to where he balanced on the spar.

"That's not good." Weyn muttered, reaching for another arrow as the lizard zig zagged across the deck towards the rigging and then started purposefully climbing up the ropes towards him. The archer fired another arrow, begging and pleading for it to be effective, only for the reptile to dodge to one side sending the arrow shooting over the side. Another followed, equally avoided by the sinuous creature as it scrambled up the lines towards him.

"Definitely no good!" Weyn started edging back along the spar, moving away from the main mast, wishing he had a sword, anything to protect himself from the armoured monster, other than the totally inadequate dagger he had sheathed at his side. Horatio pulled his huge body up onto the far end of the spar, his tail wrapping around the wood to aid stability, then hissed angrily in Weyn's direction before charging across the narrow beam towards him.

Another arrow bounced off its belly, a further ricocheted off the lizard's armoured brow and still it relentlessly advanced as the archer backed further away. Weyn's boot wobbled as he placed it and he looked down to realise that he had run out of places to run.

No, this was definitely not good at all!

Chapter Fifty-Five

"So this is the ship that is going to take me home?" Justina enquired, stepping down onto the *El Defensor's* deck, her fur coat from Blackthorn now replaced by glowing magical armour that appeared barely practical for the amount of flesh that was shown and equally distracting to Scrave as he stepped down alongside her.

"I must confess I find it a little rustic for my taste." The sorceress commented, "but I do like the rug." She kicked at the corpse of the huge Scintarn hound that had flattened Commagin, before walking purposefully out onto the deck, pausing only to lift her hand and lazily flick an explosive magical dart at one boarder who made the mistake of charging towards her with a weapon in hand. He fell to the deck seconds later, his boots smoking, missing a large portion of his skull.

"Yes. This ship can take you back to Catterick." Scrave replied, suddenly distracted by the twitching boot he noted sticking out from under the 'rug'. Justina turned revelling in the chaos unfolding around her, listening to the wails and the screams, soaking it all in and relishing the excitement after spending several weeks afloat on the barge with two large lizards, a boring and overly clingy buccaneer, a neurotic priest worried about his damned book getting wet and an elf that had become somewhat more useful than she had initially anticipated.

"Why do you covet this ship so?" the sorceress asked, her gaze catching sight of one of the lizards, what was his name, 'Horror show' or something, clambering up into the rigging after a man armed with a bow.

"This is Thomas Adam's ship." Miguel replied, climbing over the rail after them and leaving Kaplain struggling to follow him and not drop his ledger in the process. "He won't let you take control of his ship lightly."

"He has no choice." Scrave replied icily. "He marooned me and left me for dead. He owes me now."

"Now, now boys!" Justina replied sarcastically. "Let's play nicely. Now what did you say this captain looked like." Scrave started to recall his memories of Thomas, only for the ship to suddenly lurch beneath them, her deck timbers creaking in protest as the net holding the ship suddenly came free along one side. The galleon surged to its starboard side, the stone pillar looming closer until the *El Defensor's* hull collided roughly with the ancient stone, sending tremors vibrating through the ship and making a cloud of stone dust fall from the archway.

Scrave reached out reflexively to steady Justina, gripping her slender waist as she staggered, only for the sorceress to push him roughly away and turn with a twirl of her cape that almost took his last remaining eye.

"There's your captain!" she remarked, pointing high up, past the crumpled sails to the top of the archway where a pyrotechnic display of flashing lights appeared to in progress. Justina paced swiftly across the deck towards the aft-castle access ladder, leaving Scrave struggling to keep up as he angrily rubbed his forehead where her swirling cape had struck him.

So much for being the chivalrous type, the Elf thought. He admired her sensuous figure as she moved calmly across the deck, blasting anyone who got in her way with a mere flick of her wrist. She had such a mastery of the art. Oh the things they could do together. This woman was either going to show him the time of his life or end it! He climbed the ladder after her, only to find that Justina had come to a stop, staring out across the deck at the helm where Rauph stood.

Rauph...? Scrave swallowed hard. How could he have forgotten Rauph? All eight-foot tall, chestnut coloured hair, thick as two short planks, longsword wielding... The Elf paused, taking in the scene again. This was not the Rauph he once knew. This one had short hair, gleaming armour and a scowl that spoke volumes.

Justina continued across the deck, causing Rauph to become agitated. He did not know what to do. Thomas had instructed him to stay at the helm but how could he when enemies were running rampant about the lower decks and now this strange woman was walking towards him? He tried to take his hands from the wheel but as soon as he did it started to turn, pushing the ship further against the stone pillar of the archway. He turned the king spoke straight up, signalling dead ahead then moved to draw his swords. The wheel spun as soon as he let go, leaving him with one sword in his hand and the other still sheathed at his back.

"Oh my, aren't you simply magnificent." Justina stated, recognising the fact that the Minotaur was unable to move.

"I am a Labyris knight." Rauph replied. "I must ask you to surrender or leave this ship." The navigator's eyes glanced past the strange woman and took in the eye-patched person standing behind her. He sniffed barely believing what his eyes told him. Was that...?

"Scrave?" Rauph asked. "Is that you?"

"So quaint." Justina moved closer, making Rauph release the wheel and reach for his other sword, only to find the wheel turning beneath his hands as soon as he let go. He fumbled with the weapon, dropping it onto the deck so that he could wrest the helm back to midships, whilst struggling to pick his blade from the floor.

"It's so difficult to choose in situations like this." Justina mocked stepping nearer. "Let go of the wheel to attack me and you crash the ship, stay still and I will get close enough to..." She reached into her robe drawing forth the golden snake dagger letting it writhe around her wrist, the snake's head on the hilt hissing enthusiastically at the prospect of the sacrifice about to be offered.

Justina shivered inside knowing how Pelune, the head of the serpent order would relish a killing of something so strong. How the power of their life force would surge through the blade into the wielder, making them more powerful and with so much energy in this creature, the rush would simply be delicious. She eased closer, taking the darting eyes of the Minotaur to be those of someone afraid and relishing the power she held over such a magnificent creature.

"I told you to leave the ship." Rauph stated calmly, causing Justina to raise her eyebrow in surprise as he continued to fumble with his blades and also attend the helm.

"I know you asked nicely." Justina smiled, "but I simply don't want to." She lunged forward with the dagger; her eyes bright at the excitement of the strike. The Minotaur met her blade with his own, causing sparks to jump from the ceremonial weapon and causing the dagger to hiss angrily in frustration, the snake's head striking out repeatedly but unable to reach its prey.

Justina looked down at her weapon in shock, stunned as to how the Minotaur had managed to parry her, when just seconds before he had both hands full. Rauph flipped the dagger out of her hand, easily disarming her and sending it flying back over her head. Then he stepped away from the helm and Justina realised what the clever Minotaur had done. The helm tried to turn of its own volition, then became caught on the dropped long sword, now firmly wedged between its spokes.

"I asked you to leave!" Rauph growled, his brows creasing as he let his ire be known. "You will do as I ask or face the consequences. I am a Labyris knight and I have a badge to prove it."

"I'm sure you do dear." Justina shrugged, then fired off a magical spell in his direction, sending two energy bolts streaking out from her wand to hit the Minotaur at close range. The magic hit Rauph's breast plate then fizzled and died.

"Was that magic?" Rauph growled, as the sizzle of the magical residue died on his breast plate leaving a small spiral of smoke. "I don't like magic." He stamped forward towards the sorceress and raised his sword to strike her, just as a huge shadow fell over the navigator's shoulder.

"Rauph, look out!" Scrave warned as the second lizard, Cornelius pounced, his tail whipping up around the Minotaur's neck as it tried to yank his body backwards. Rauph snatched the tail as it coiled over his left shoulder and pulled hard, in a move the giant lizard simply did not expect. The monster squealed as the tail pulled tightly, its claws striking the back of Rauph's armour as it was dragged over his shoulder and slammed onto the deck.

Cornelius was up in a moment, wriggling around with an agility that even caught Rauph by surprise. The lizard jumped back onto Rauph, the two huge creatures now grappling with each other upon the deck, two titans wrestling desperate to find and exploit any weakness. Rauph tried to push the lizard's head up and avoid its snapping jaws but its tail kept whipping in and slapping at the side of his face, knocking his sword from his hand.

Justina stood back, letting the two monsters fight it out, recognising the second lizard, the one called 'Cornbread', as her ally. She suddenly remembered that Rauph had disarmed her and spun around, her eyes darting about the ship, desperately seeking the weapon. Justina's gaze fell upon another woman slowly getting up from the deck, her long blonde hair spilling across her slender shoulders, her face a mask of complete concentration. One hand raised behind her using magic to keep a crackling magical gateway open, the other struggling to hold a dull rune-etched sword.

"Interesting." Justina muttered to herself. Scrave had not told her there was another mage to contend with. Her skeletal familiar rushed across the deck and clambered up her cloak chattering loudly in her ear. "Don't' worry Hamnet, I have this in hand." The creature continued to chatter loudly but Justina was not concerned where her golden dagger was, not at this time, not when faced with such a potential threat. It was time to find out just how big a threat she was.

Justina summoned magic from her wand, building a small charged sphere of crackling energy to life at its tip, then sent it streaking across the deck towards where Colette stood. The spell dissipated as it struck an energy barrier shielding the young mage. Justina frowned, annoyed that her spell had been countered so easily and released a larger globe of energy that howled as it shot across the space between them.

Colette winced as the magical energy cascaded around her shield, licking at the edges seeking entry but dying out before it could do so. Her head was pounding! She risked a quick glance back at the archway and noted that although the port side edge of the galleon was almost through, the skewed course of the ship's travel meant the starboard side was even further back through the gateway than before. If she dropped her spell now the *El Defensor* would be crushed to kindling! She could not lose her concentration, she had to maintain it no matter what the cost!

Another magical detonation raked across her shield. The dark witch seemed very confident in her manner, not appearing to be in a rush, clearly taking her time testing Colette's magical defences. The mage swallowed hard, knowing all too well, that whilst she was struggling to hold open the gateway, she had no means to retaliate to the spells being hurled towards her, she was simply not powerful enough.

A streak of lightning jumped from the sorceress's wand, scrabbling across Colette's shield and making Colette close her eyes against the glare. As the spell sputtered out, the air around the mage shimmered brightly then cracked apart. Colette's heart sank. Her magical shield had failed.

She quickly scanned the deck, noting the strange figure in the distance dressed as if he had just stepped from somewhere dusty and desolate, discarding him as a potential ally, as he had accompanied the long-haired sorceress and her disgusting skeletal pet gargoyle.

Rauph was still wrestling with the huge lizard, rolling about the deck throwing punches and struggling to reach his sword but being constantly outmatched by the lizard's muscular tail which tangled with any limb he had free, pulling him back, dropping him to the floor, snatching his hand away from the sword and slapping him about the head each time he tried to gain an advantage.

Weyn was up in the rigging dealing with the twin of the monster struggling with Rauph and everyone else was down on the main deck facing the boarders. There was no one else left on the aft-castle to turn to. Colette was all alone. One lone mage with the long sword of a man she loved, pitted against a sorceress armed with a powerful magical arsenal and a condescending smirk plastered all over her face.

Colette extended her lower lip and puffed upwards, blowing a stray golden ringlet of hair from her face, her normally warm gaze from her cornflower blue eyes now chilling to tundra ice. The mage turned side on as Aradol had taught her and pointed with the blade.

It was time to show this bitch how a real mage fought.

* * * * * *

Aradol plunged his father's sword into the breast of a charging hound, then slashed with the blade to take the claw from another, catching a third across the snout with his backswing before disengaging. Yet for every creature he wounded, three more seemed to take their place. It was like facing a never-ending flood, despite the determination he showed, no matter how many corpses fell to the deck about him and no matter how much blood was spilt across the decks of the ship, the remorseless tide of slashing claw and snapping fang would ultimately overwhelm him.

He caught another Scintarn in the throat, leaving his left side exposed and the hound to that side of him immediately closed its jaws about his arm and tried to drag him down with its weight. Aradol smashed at the creature's skull with the hilt of his sword, thumping the monster several times before it dropped him and spun away, turning almost instantly and curling its lips back to expose its blood-stained fangs. The young warrior launched a kick in the Scintarn's direction only for two more hounds to barrel in from his blind side, teeth snapping and paws raking across his armour.

There was no way he could keep this up! His breath was becoming laboured, the dogs were yanking at his limbs, trying to drag him down to the deck. An armoured tail whipped around, the flint-like ridge slashing across Aradol's forehead, causing blood to drip down his face and further excite the hounds as the copper scent reached their sensitive nostrils. He staggered back across the deck, blinking rapidly, trying to clear his blurred vision, Scintarns bowling over each other in their stampede to claim this wounded prey as their own.

Someone came up alongside him, swinging a blade, cleaving a hound from throat to abdomen, beheading another on the backswing. Armour glinted in the corner of the warrior's eye as a fighter approached from the other side, slapping one creature down to the deck, dazing another, then plunging a blade deeply into the side of one more Scintarn making it howl in its death throes.

Aradol watched the two knights walk past him then realised he had no idea who they actually were. He risked the opportunity to turn around and noted several other knights climbing out of a book laid out on the deck. They turned to a man who knelt beside the book, a man wearing robes similar to those of Marcus. Aradol frowned. He did not recognise this person either. The fighters nodded as if receiving orders then drew their swords and advanced purposefully towards Aradol, two peeling away to either side to engage the Scintarns and push them back whilst the last one continued towards him. Aradol stepped forward relieved only for the mysterious knight to lunge at him with his sword.

The young knight barely dodged the weapon, swinging his blade to parry the attack with just enough contact to alter the path of the knight's thrust, it still struck his shoulder, scoring across the metal of his armour and leaving his left arm feeling numb. The warrior spun around, bringing his sword back down low, trying to sweep Aradol's legs but the young fighter recognised the move and dropped his own sword, intercepting the swing and moving inside of the knight's reach, bringing his own weapon up and slamming the hilt hard under the warrior's chin. Aradol did not hesitate, bringing his weapon across between them and swinging it down across the knight's outstretched arm, cleaving it away at the wrist, only for the sword and hand to magically transform into loose pages of manuscript that tumbled about the deck.

Paper! What manner of creatures were these? Aradol stepped back, disengaging from the fight, leaving the wounded warrior to scramble about, trying to gather up the paper sheets that had once been his limb and weapon. This made absolutely no sense. The young fighter risked a quick glance over towards the blue robed priest still kneeling upon the deck and then realised with some concern that even more warriors were climbing out of the book, apparently at the behest of the acolyte.

He moved to engage with them, realising this man added another threat to the dangers the crew were facing. A bright flash caught his eye from up on the aft deck, followed by another and another in sharp succession, bringing the young man to a stop. That was magic being cast up on the deck where... Colette was up there!

Aradol hesitated, torn between trying to stop this mysterious priest from calling more supernatural fighters from his book and wanting to assist the young woman he had spent so many training sessions with. His logical mind told him to attack the priest but a feeling deep inside his chest told him he needed to protect Colette.

"Damn!" Aradol cursed, then turned and ran towards the ladder. Colette needed him and his sense of chivalry, nay his honour, demanded that she was the priority.

* * * * * *

"Get off me you damn dog!" Commagin cursed, shoving with all of his might, pushing the huge Scintarn from his body. He struggled to extract himself, finally getting to his feet with every intention to leap to the aid of anyone who needed his help, only to realise that the ship's deck was now a scene of total chaos and that the choices of target were simply too many to prioritise. There were ragged fighters charging towards the crew with mad glazed eyes, Scintarns piling onto the deck from the prow, ripping apart any crewman unlucky enough to find himself near their jaws, knights hacking at the hounds the crazed fighters and the *El Defensor* crew. Knights! Where in the seven hells did the knights come from?

He snatched his crossbow from the deck and wound back the mechanism, his fingers numb, his mind racing. His tired eyes trying to make sense out of the bedlam within which he stood. There was a priest wearing blue robes out on the deck apparently summoning the knights but he did not look like Brother Richard or Marcus. The crew were falling back under the relentless onslaught, being pushed away from the sides of the galleon towards the centre of the deck.

A piece of shredded sail rippled down from above, dragging the Dwarf's gaze back along its path up towards the rigging where two people appeared to be fighting on the top mainsail yard. He blinked and rubbed his eyes, one of them appeared to have a tail!

Another piece of sail crumpled onto the deck causing the crew beneath it to split in different directions. There was no discipline here. It was everyone for themselves. The galleon slammed into the gateway pillar sending groans and shrieks of torment through the hull of the ship. Commagin turned his gaze towards the stern, instantly realising that there was no one manning the helm and that the ship had not yet cleared the portal. Where was Rauph?

A loud clang sounded amidships as Violetta used her skillet with devastating effect. Rowan was there too swinging her wrench and connecting more often than not, breaking jaws, sending teeth spinning across the deck and making any hounds near enough shy away from her deadly swings, their tails flicking angrily back and forth.

The ship shuddered again as a loud rattle sounded and a length of chain crashed to the deck. The *El Defensor* surged valiantly forward again, only to be snatched back as the net tightened its grip about her once more. Commagin looked at his friends then back towards the helm. He needed to be there, needed to keep the ship safe. The engineer pushed his glasses back up onto the bridge of his nose and marched off, firing his trusty crossbow at anyone that dared get too close.

One quarrel took a hound in the shoulder, another lifted a fighter from the deck punching into his chest just as he was about to swing his weapon at Austen. Everywhere the Dwarf looked someone needed his help. He just hoped that the choice he was making was the right one.

* * * * * *

"I'm telling you Sinders. There is no trust in the world anymore." Ashe muttered, trying yet another cabin door and finding it locked. "I mean how can I check everything is securely put away if everyone keeps locking their doors?" He continued along the corridor rattling and jiggling door latches, lantern held high, trying to justify the fact that Thomas had told him to remain below decks whilst the *El Defensor* passed through the gateway.

"I personally blame you for why we are down here." He remarked to the pet perched quietly on his shoulder. "If you had not made all that noise the last time we went through the gateway, we could have been up on deck right now looking at all the spooky scenery but no you had to open your big mouth and make a nuisance of yourself."

Sinders shot Ashe a bemused look, tilting its black and white head to one side, listening intently to its master despite having no idea what he was talking about and just hoping it would lead to Ashe offering another seedcake.

"A-ha!" The Halfling grinned, lifting the latch on the next door and pushing it open, before realising that it was Rauph's cabin door. He moved inside, holding his lantern up high, pausing to let the supernatural chill of the room sweep over him and make him feel all tingly inside.

"Now we have to be careful in here." Ashe warned his pet, moving over towards the chart table and standing up on tip toe to see if there was anything interesting left out on the table he could play with. "Don't worry about the dead body sitting in the corner. I've noticed if I don't go near him, he doesn't go near me." A loud bang sounded up above and the ship groaned alarmingly, sending a chart sliding from the end of the table to bounce across the deck and fall down near Rauph's huge bed.

"Sounds like something is going on upstairs." Ashe remarked, staring at the ceiling as several muffled bangs resonated through the planks towards him. A loud roar seemed to be growing under his feet and the deck started to vibrate. Was that water sounding against the hull?

"It's not fair. I always miss out on all the fun." He scooped to collect the chart from the floor, then turned about to place the map back on the chart table, just so that Rauph had no idea he had been here, because Minotaur could be quite tetchy sometimes, despite the fact Rauph was clearly Ashe's best friend. His eyes swept over the bed and then froze as he noticed the shape of the blue and silver throwing weapon used by the lady Minotaur in the labyrinth.

"It's as if..." What was that doing here? He moved over, forgetting the door swinging open behind him and looked down at the beautiful cross-shaped design. There was a small button at the centre of the cruciform and Ashe just had to find out what it did. He leant forward and pressed the button, then jumped back as the blades within the ends of the arms sprang out, one of them slicing through the top of Rauph's blanket.

"Oops." Ashe muttered, lifting the weapon from the bed and leaning forward to examine the damage. The blades had to be really sharp to do that! He put his lantern onto the bed and tried to push the pieces of the blanket together. No, that was not going to work. Ashe frowned and pushed up his *bycocket* hat scratching his forehead. He was not really that good at sewing and something told him that if he tried Rauph would notice. He looked at Sinders and shook his head. This was going to need some serious thought.

Voices and footsteps sounded in the corridor, heading towards him. Ashe snatched at the blanket in an attempt to pull it away and hide it, forgetting for a split second that the lantern was perched on top of it. Everything seemed to move in slow motion. He had no hands free to catch the lantern as it tipped. One was holding the boomerang blade, the other had a fist full of blanket. The lantern tipped, fuel flowed out of the reservoir and soaked into the bedding and the blanket caught fire.

"Oh mouldy acorns!" Ashe wailed, staring at the flickering flames and realising he was now in deep trouble. He tried to pat the flame to extinguish it, using the piece of the blanket he held in his hands but this just spread the flames further. What was he going to do? That had to be Rauph coming down the corridor. The Minotaur was going to be really mad. He dare not think how Thomas was going to take it.

He went to run away and hide somewhere, preferably several worlds away, then realised he could not leave the fire unattended. He scooped up the flaming blanket and ran for the door screaming an alarm as he ran, charging through the doorway, only to slam right into Brother Richard who was walking towards him holding Marcus's large blue book.

The flames caught Richard's robes instantly and licked hungrily across the surface of the blue book, causing the priest to shout in surprise, then alarm as the surface of the book blackened and bubbled. Several people behind the priest started to scream and dropped to the deck thrashing about as if in serious pain.

"I'm sorry. I'm sorry!" Ashe screamed, dropping the blanket and fleeing through them all, jumping over some flailing people and dodging the terrified bodies of others, his eyes tearing up as he ran, his anxiety not allowing him to recognise that he had jumped over several knights he had never seen before.

Marcus reacted instantly, head-butting the knight behind him and snap-kicking another, struggling to free himself from the magical fighters that had him hemmed in on all sides. Ashe dodged through their legs, too scared to stop, too embarrassed to confess to the damage he had just caused, just desperate to get as far away from the scene of the fire as possible.

Richard dropped to the floor, using his bare hands to beat at the flames trying to consume his magical ledger. His skin blackened and blistered as he beat at the blaze but he would not relent, would not allow this magical book to be taken from him, not now, not after coming so far. He snatched at the blanket and threw it aside, not realising where he had inadvertently thrown it.

Tobias screamed in terror as the burning blanket landed upon his leg. He tried to kill the flames, tried to stamp them from him but his magical construct was based on paper and this was fuel for the inferno. Marcus barrelled past him, smashing the knight in the face, dropping Tobias to the floor, only for the ship to slew violently to one side, making the monk lose his balance and stagger, then trip on something left on the floor of the corridor. Whatever it was shrieked loudly in the darkness, then tumbled back inside Rauph's cabin.

Richard hugged the ledger to his chest determined to extinguish the last of the flames, gritting his teeth as his flesh seared, then he turned to see Tobias being consumed by the fire and screamed. The knight wailed his own funeral dirge, his body crumbling away to glowing ash.

"Hold him!" Richard screamed, as Marcus tried to regain his feet to escape. The other knights sprang back into action as the flames extinguished and the threat to their form was removed. Marcus tried to fight them off but there were too many of them within the close confines of the restrictive corridor for him to do anything but fend off the worst of the blows. He moaned in pain as he was crushed back to the deck and Richard suddenly appeared above him. Marcus took in the fresh burns across his mentor's chin, the blackened and split fingers that desperately clutched the precious ledger, leaving bloody prints across the blackened and blistered blue leather of the cover.

"Oh Richard please stop this." Marcus begged breathlessly. "Nothing is worth this, nothing." Brother Richard regarded his fallen student and fixed him with a look of pure hatred. He flexed his fingers, feeling the skin upon them start to tighten and split, the tissue still hot from the kiss of the flames. He knew the pain would soon be unbearable. This was all Marcus's fault. He turned to the other knights, his face suddenly cold and lacking emotion.

"Shut him up and make him pay." He snapped. The knights nodded their understanding then carried out their orders. Marcus tried to dodge the blows as they landed but there was no room left to manoeuvre. He felt a tooth crack, another loosen; he felt his eye swell, his lip split and then a terrific blow to the temple. He tried to tell the knights to stop, tried to beg that they leave him alone, screaming as someone stamped on his hand and the bones shattered but the knights were carrying out their orders and they simply would not listen to reason.

* * * * * *

Kerian jogged along the top of the archway, watching the scene unfolding below him in disbelief as the crew of the *El Defensor* fought for their very lives. He could not believe the crippling damage being inflicted upon the vessel. Even as he watched, the foresail and topsail crashed down upon her damaged decks, scattering crew and foes alike as the ship tried to push against what appeared to be a massive net entrapping her.

He tore his gaze from the decks, giving up on the faint hope he would be able to identify Colette from this far distance and instead traced the lines of the net back to the top and sides of the gateway the ship was trying to negotiate. He noticed several figures ahead of him; one clearly swinging a sword, the other a mass of swirling colours and snapping tendrils, then felt his stomach go suddenly cold.

Malum. He did not need to see much clearer to recognise the horror that awaited him. He swallowed hard and pushed down the worries and fears running rampant within him. That monster was between him and Colette. He had faced him on the *Neptune* and in Glowme castle, so he could face him here now!

His footsteps slowed despite his resolve and he took the opportunity to pull the mirrored shield from his back, slipping it over his left arm. Kerian drew *Aurora* and let the sword's light illuminate the stone pathway beneath him, noting with some surprise how the lights from Malum's tendrils became muted when regarded from *Aurora's* own luminance. He took a deep breath, tried to steady his racing heart, closed his eyes and then slowly reopened them. He could do this. He had to do this. He took a step towards the monster, rolled his shoulders and then took another, this one more confident than the last.

Then he charged.

Chapter Fifty-Six

Another energy sphere crackled towards Colette. She reacted on instinct, dodging to the right, dragging the spectral thread of energy behind her that tethered her conjuring to the magical gateway. She recalled Aradol's lessons, raising Kerian's sword in preparation to parry the attack, knowing that this was pure folly on her part. Her skill with a blade only went so far and the power of the magic rushing towards her was such that it would probably incinerate her as soon as she swung at it. She needed to get closer to the sorceress attacking her if she were ever going to be able to fight back as Kerian's blade was so heavy. The thought of the confrontation scared her but she had no choice, she could not give up when the crew and ship were at stake.

Colette swung the dulled blade wildly, the sword colliding with the magical spell just before it hit her. She screamed as she attempted to deflect it away and felt something race up her arm, setting all of the hairs on her body standing as if she had received a large static charge. Her teeth snapped together, nearly removing the tip of her tongue as the runes on Kerian's sword lit up and then dulled as the magical attack was impossibly absorbed by the metal.

Justina frowned, her superior smile fading. Her spell should have turned the young mage into a dirty red smear and scattered parts of her across the deck. How could she still be standing? She pointed with her wand again, letting forth a blistering ball of fire that roared across the deck, narrowly missing the head of Cornbread who was astride Rauph and smashing him repeatedly on the nose. The lizard saw the flame approaching and ducked only for one of Rauph's horns to score him viciously across the jaw.

Colette noticed the fireball advance, watched it grow in size as it closed on her and knew she would never avoid the magical spell. She closed her eyes tightly and swung up the long sword, not even having the time to step aside. A wave of heat washed over her; the sword in her hand growing uncomfortably warm. She staggered, dropping to one knee, then carefully got back to her feet, checking her concentration remained focused on the conjured gateway before opening her eyes.

"Impossible!" Justina uttered, pushing up her sleeves. Her fireball had failed to detonate, its arcane power also absorbed by the smoking blade in the young woman's hands. The runes flickered along the sword's length, then went dark again. Colette stifled her feelings of surprise as she felt the sword become lighter in her grasp, the metal cooling as it rushed through the air. Something strange was happening here but Colette was not exactly sure what it was. Her fingers snagged a ribbon from her hair as she moved; it was a simple spell she was considering but if it gave her just a second of advantage then that would be enough. She just needed to close the distance of deck remaining between them.

Rauph landed several heavy blows to Cornelius's skull, rattling the lizard so he had to shake his head to refocus, his tail twitched angrily, slamming on the deck. Colette darted past them, heading towards Justina as fast as she could, hoping the shock of seeing her spells fail would rattle the sorceress just long enough for the mage to carry out her plan. She dodged and weaved, trying to make herself a harder target to hit, the tendril of her magic writhing over the deck behind her. If she could just land one blow with Kerian's sword and get close enough to throw her ribbon before the sorceress gathered her wits.

The navigator managed to get his foot under Cornelius and kicked him off, sending the lizard towards Colette. The reptile bounced off the deck, tail flicking out to give balance, only for it to crack across the mage's hand, forcing her to drop Kerian's sword and jolting the ribbon up into the air.

Her heart sank as she watched the violet ribbon complete its upward path then arc back to the deck, only to land on the snout of the surprised lizard. The ribbon instantly lengthened before it tightly wrapped around Cornelius, binding him tightly, strapping the creature's limbs to its sides and leaving him struggling helplessly on the deck.

Justina flicked her wrist, sending a barrage of magical darts out across the deck as Colette dived for the floor in an effort to recover Kerian's blade. The darts split apart and wheeled away, one right, one left, the other straight ahead and coming in fast. Colette looked on in despair, completely helpless, her hand still reaching for the dropped blade. She realised she would never be able to intercept this attack whilst still on her knees.

Rauph dived between the two women, turning his back to shield Colette just as the third magical dart hit him, staggering the huge Minotaur and making him roar with pain. He snatched at Colette's robes, physically lifting her from the deck, just as her hand closed upon the hilt of the sword. She felt herself snatched bodily from harm's way as the navigator's free hand reached out and caught the second dart, batting it down to the deck. Colette closed her eyes as Rauph tried to turn again, this time spinning her about as if they were dancing, so that the final dart impacted on the Minotaur's right flank. He roared again, bloodied and battered by Cornelius, burnt and wincing from the explosive darts and the after effects of the powerful dark sorcery still smoking where his hide was singed. The navigator sank to the deck with an agonised gasp; despite being resistant to most magic, it was clear this sustained attack had nearly overwhelmed him.

Colette rushed out from behind Rauph, Kerian's sword in hand, determined to drop the dark witch down. She swung the weapon as hard as she could, aiming for the sorceress's neck but Justina ducked as the blade sailed past. The sword clipped a trailing lock of hair and struck Justina's precious wand, shattering it into a thousand pieces.

The detonation threw Colette and Justina from their feet, dropping them to the deck and blasting Kerian's sword from the young mage's hand. Power surged through the weapon, causing the runes to glow and the blade to vibrate. It bounced once, then appeared to halt in mid-fall, hanging perpendicular, the eyes of the roaring dragons on its hilt now ablaze as the weapon hovered menacingly several inches off the deck.

Commagin felt the explosion rush over him as he charged up the port side ladder, his crossbow levelled out before him. A man knelt in his way, scooping something up from the deck, his clothing marking him as a stranger on the ship and therefore a potential threat who was annoyingly obscuring the Dwarf's view.

"Get out of my way you fool!" the engineer snapped, shoving the man to one side so he could scan the scene for other dangers; Colette lay there as if dead, another woman lay prone opposite her, Rauph groaned loudly sitting up holding his head, his pelt marred with scorch marks and a giant lizard lay close by, wrapped up in a huge purple ribbon.

Commagin shook his head worrying if he had taken too much spirits the night before, then blinked several times to confirm the lizard still lay there. He lowered his crossbow, Initially thinking there was nothing here to shoot at; then quickly reconsidered as the strange female started to stir. The Dwarf swung the *Lady Janet* across and sighted down the quarrel, only for the *El Defensor* to slam into the pillar of the archway again, the collision making the engineer stagger back into the man he had pushed aside and finally allowing him to meet his gaze.

"Scrave?" Commagin gasped, recognising the Elf even as he felt a sudden pressure on his sternum.

"Her life is not yours to take." Scrave stared coldly into Commagin's eyes, watching the horror suddenly dawn on the engineer that something was terribly wrong. The Dwarf looked down at his chest and noticed the golden serpent dagger writhing there, the hilt still held firmly in Scrave's clenched hand. The *Lady Janet* tumbled to the deck, Commagin's fingers now too numb to hold onto his beautiful crossbow.

"S... Scrave?" Commagin clutched at the Elf's clothes, his hands twitching as he struggled to hold on, fighting to keep upright. His legs felt numb, there was a coldness seeping through his body as if someone was literally draining the strength from him.

"You bastard!" The engineer spat through gritted teeth, his face a mask of pain. "I hope you rot...in...Hell." He tried to push Scrave away, tried to pull the dagger free but these actions required strength that the Dwarf suddenly found he no longer had.

"I was born in Arnreith." Scrave whispered, trying to prize the Dwarfs bloody fingers from his clothes. "So Hell does not scare me." Commagin's eyes blazed with fury at this betrayal but his strength of will could not stop the evil magic of the dagger from doing its insidious work. The Dwarf tried to suck in another breath, tried to gather the strength to throw a meaningful curse, fighting the serpent for every second of life that it drained from his body.

And then he could fight it no more.

* * * * * *

Weyn nervously licked his lips as the giant lizard continued to advance along the beam towards him. Despite the perilous situation the archer now found himself in, his mind was thinking the strangest things. He slung his bow over his shoulder and snatched a quick look down at the deck far below. It was a long way to fall! He considered using his dagger as a defence against the monster but if his magical arrows could not harm the beast the chance of his secondary weapon even scratching its hide was at best debateable.

He considered diving from the mast, the absolute image of a swashbuckling hero, knife firmly clasped between his teeth, then realised that he would need to miss the remaining sails still snapping angrily around him and avoid hitting the strange skiff that had collided with the *El Defensor* and had of all places decided to hover right where he needed to jump!

He also wondered if it was a dead squirrel on top of the lizard's head.

The reptile hissed again, its long, forked tongue tasting the air. Its approach no longer rushed as it now toyed with its prey. After all, Weyn had literally nowhere left to run. The archer swore under his breath. If he ever got out of this, he was never 'going high' again!

"Jump!" a voice shouted from the left.

"W...What?" Weyn turned towards the sound and noticed Plano waving urgently at him from the wreckage of the fore topsail, a rope in his hand.

"Jump!" the acrobat gestured again waving his hand anxiously. "Hurry there is no time to wait. Don't worry I will catch you!"

"Now?" Weyn's voice wobbled as he looked down at the deck. "Are you sure?"

Horatio growled at the unexpected development, recognizing he could lose his meal and immediately tensed up his legs. His tail twitched, before he lunged forward, jaws snapping, claws outstretched. Weyn threw himself from the stay, his hands frantically snatching the air as he jumped towards Plano. The lizard's claws missed his boots by inches. Horatio clutched at thin air, then overbalanced dropping from the end of the mast, his massive limbs windmilling as he fell, his racoon skin hat plummeting after him.

Weyn screamed as he fell through the air, he could not help it, he was absolutely terrified but as he dropped Plano swung smoothly from the mast, a rope wrapped around his legs and swooped in to snatch the archer as he tumbled past. Weyn grabbed urgently at the acrobat, inadvertently pulling him off balance and making him fumble the simple catch. Plano's hand slipped on the rope and the two of them crashed backwards into a canvas sail that immediately folded. They slid down the canvas, desperately trying to slow their fall.

Plano remained calm, reaching out to snag the rigging as he passed, whilst Weyn stabbed into the canvas sail with his dagger, tearing a huge rent in the fabric in an effort to slow his own rapid descent. The two men collided with each other and hung there gasping.

"See I told you it would be alright and I would catch you." Plano smiled, just as the sail collapsed in on itself, dropping the two men down onto the tight curve of another sail beneath. They slid down the impromptu chute before emerging right over the chaos of the main deck, where they dropped and rolled over groaning, only to be buried by the ruins of the canvas sail that followed them down. Weyn cursed and kicked, burrowing his way through the billowing heavy material, until he was finally able to free his head. He came up facing a ring of swords held by grim faced knights and paused his struggles only for Plano to pop up beside him.

"Yeah everything is going to be fine." Weyn stated sarcastically, placing his hands behind his head in surrender. "Just fine."

* * * * * *

Thomas swung his cutlass with all his might, bringing it down on the third anchor point, shearing the chain in a rain of sparks. It whipped off over the stone edge, generating further slack in the net, permitting the *El Defensor* valuable space to inch forwards through the magical gateway. The captain risked a quick glance over the precipice, confirming his valiant efforts were not yet enough, noting his ship was still dangerously stuck between worlds. Magical spells crackled across the aft deck and then an explosion knocked Colette and her female adversary off their feet.

The energy trail snaking across the deck that linked Colette to the gateway stuttered, then flickered out as her head hit the floor and Thomas cursed as he recognised the consequences. With mystical energy no longer forcing the gate open, it would start to close. His head pounded at the implications. The galleon was not yet through; the *El Defensor* would be crushed!

Malum's taunting laugh echoed above the sounds of the ongoing battle. Thomas looked over and noticed that his nemesis seemed well aware of the events unfolding below and was relishing them.

"If you want to free your ship, you have to come to me." He hissed, one fine tendril dropping to the stone archway, the barbed fan at its end opening up and tapping the chain secured at his feet for emphasis. "You should never have run away. This punishment has been long overdue."

"As is your painful demise." The captain snarled, taking a deep breath to try and steady his nerves and lighten the heavy sense of responsibility he now felt pressing down upon his shoulders. He gripped his cutlass tightly, facing the horror that haunted his dreams and charged forward. There was no luxury of time, his hourglass was empty. Everyone's fate depended on him now!

Malum's tendrils flared wide like a peacock in a mating display, the fans at the end flickering vivid colours of greens and purples. Then each one collapsed, the barbs forming into angular darts all primed, ready to strike, swaying like agitated cobras and equally as dangerous. Thomas lunged once, twice, three times, trying to force Malum back and away from the anchor chain. The monster sensed Thomas's desire and calmly dodged each thrust, ensuring every attack was wide of its mark, before setting his feet and sending his barbed tendrils spinning angrily in from the left flank.

Thomas turned to face the onslaught, swinging his cutlass in a glittering arc, causing the fans to retreat, only for others to arrow in from behind, tearing flesh from his shoulder and a laceration to his right leg, causing the captain to gasp in pain as he tried to escape.

"Oh Thomas, you are really out of practice." Malum taunted, his attacks streaking in from high and low, forcing Thomas to hobble back into the clear or risk further injury. The arch started to tremble beneath his feet, vibrations racing up through the stone. The gateway was closing! He had to act now! Thomas feinted left, dodged right, swinging his cutlass towards

Malum's translucent midriff, batting the tendrils swarming towards him, turning himself in behind his swing and stepping closer, dropping his head to avoid a barbed fan, angling his attack so he could get inside the radius of the monster's deadly reach.

Malum sensed him coming and smiled, allowing Thomas to believe he was beating his attacks on purpose, before he lashed out with his withered hands, his thick yellow nails gouging skin from Thomas's cheek before an overhead fist slammed down into the captain's skull.

"You are so predictable." Malum hissed as Thomas dropped onto the stone of the archway.

"I think you will find that is mutual." The captain grunted, swinging his cutlass towards Malum's feet. The monster hissed in alarm, stepping back from the sword's deadly path, then uttered a malicious laugh as the cutlass missed him. He turned his head, sniffing the air, trying to ascertain what action Thomas would attempt next, only to realise, with some surprise that Thomas was returning the laugh, his blade's glittering path slicing through the real target and severing the anchor chain.

It rattled off across the stone, the end whipping around like a live serpent instead of an inanimate object, the links pulling tight and catching Malum's emaciated foot as the chain shot past. Malum shrieked as it dragged him over the edge of the archway, his body all folding in on itself as he was pulled over the stone lip, the colours of his fans flaring black and yellow in distress. Tendrils whipped out defensively, fans slamming into the stone, the barbed teeth gripping the lichen coated surface, scrabbling for holds, missing the prone captain's body by inches.

Thomas pulled himself to his feet, not believing his luck and turned his attention towards the next chain. A loud crack sounded behind him as the chain finally fell free but the captain was not willing to spare himself the time to see if Malum had fallen with it. Instead, he prayed that his actions would give his ship the valuable inches she needed to save her stern. There were still three more to go, three more chains to sever if he wanted to grant the *El Defensor* her freedom. He dropped and slid like a New York Yankee stealing home base, swinging his cutlass and smashing the fourth chain, before he was up and running again, determined to give the crew every fighting chance. If he could just sever the last two...

Something scrambled rapidly along the edge of the archway to his right, causing his heart to pound in his chest. No not now. Not when he was so close! Angry red and black coloured fans whirred and buzzed like agitated hornets, flaring brightly, moving faster than Thomas could possibly run. The captain threw everything he had into his charge, his eyes tearing in frustration as Malum overtook him, before scrambling up onto the path ahead, his translucent body blocking Thomas's passage like some huge billowing Portuguese Man O War waiting for its prey to swim right into its venomous tentacles.

Thomas screamed his frustration aloud, charging in with abandon, cutlass swinging, only for the fans to flicker brightly, faster and faster, the beautiful colours calming him, making him want to stop, reconsider his actions. Everything was going to be all right, all he had to do was surrender himself to the will of the monster who had held him captive and whose evil presence had lingered in his nightmares ever since.

His mind warned him what was happening, screamed at him to close his eyes, fight off the temptations emanating from the creature that could control his mind but as much as he was horrified, he was also transfixed. The captain felt his resistance crumbling, his free will betraying him. His mind slipped into a pleasant fog where he felt liberated and free of the cruel burdens that life had laid upon him and despite his concerns he started to smile. The voices in his head were telling him to let go of his cutlass, to surrender to the inevitable.

Footsteps echoed on stone, rapid closing fast but Thomas did not care. He just needed to open his hand and throw his sword away.

"Styx!" Malum hissed, his voice fading as if he were turning away and addressing someone. "...but that's impossible."

What was impossible? What did that have to do with him dropping his sword? Thomas felt the fog starting to clear the suggestive hypnosis evaporating from his mind. He opened his eyes, immediately noting that Malum had turned his back to him, his focus now on something that had engaged with the monster. He looked down at his hand noticing that the hilt of his cutlass still remained tightly clenched in his fist, then realised he was on his knees. When had he dropped to the stone? He had no recollection of it.

Thomas looked up at Malum, noting the whirling and buzzing fans slicing through the air, darting around trying to score a hit on the unknown saviour that had come to the captain's aid. He tried to see past the tendrils whipping around Malum's body but could only make out lightning fast fragments of image, intersected by a sword that glowed so brightly it made Thomas squint.

Travel stained brown boots, dusty cream trousers, golden links of chainmail poking out beneath a leather tunic, a beige travel cloak that hung down over the fighter's face. This was no one the captain recognised. The dazzling sword swept up banishing some of the shadows from inside the cloak's hood revealing a split-second glimpse of a debonair smile that appeared so out of place that it seemed surreal.

A loud crash sounded from below, killing Thomas's curiosity. His ship! The *El Defensor*! How could he have forgotten? He looked around the stone, quickly orientating himself to the anchor currently set between Malum and the man who fought him. He needed to get to the chain!

Thomas stood up and snarled, stabbing his sword towards Malum's exposed back. The cutlass lunged towards the monster's pulsating skin but some sixth sense must have alerted Malum and several barbs shot towards Thomas intercepting his sword and causing the captain to roll his shoulder and dip his head, as one fan ripped across his bicep, drawing a line of scarlet that quickly soaked through his torn shirt. His cutlass chopped through one tendril, sending gouts of sticky liquid into the air and drawing a shriek from Malum as the monster reacted fully, spinning around, determined to face the captain and deal with him once and for all.

As Malum turned, Thomas kept close with his back, running along the very edge of the stone archway, his boots scuffing loose lichen as his cutlass parried and blocked the angry barbs sent his way. He spun out into the open running for the fifth anchor point, only to have his leg snatched out from under him by a seeking fan that dropped him to the stone.

The captain kicked out, frantically trying to free his boot, the chain he wanted to sever painfully close but not close enough.

Malum roared as his mystery assailant scored a telling strike and the fan recoiled, withdrawing into a mass of tendrils that writhed in pain. Thomas rolled and swung his cutlass, watching with relief as the chain snapped and disappeared over the edge. Five had been destroyed. It had to be enough. He willed it to be enough, because somewhere in his mind, he knew the archway below had already closed.

* * * * * *

Ashe burst out onto the deck, his eyes filled with tears, his actions not those of someone with clarity of thought. He just wanted to run away and find somewhere to hide. He knew that the one inviolable rule of sailing on a ship was never to start a fire and he had broken that rule, putting the lives of all of the crew at risk by his actions.

He was so upset he never even saw the Scintarn hound that turned towards him and charged, thinking a Halfling mouthful was just what it needed. Never noticed the sword thrust from the magical knight who put it down, or the crazed privateer who then smashed that knight to the ground using a cudgel, creating a flurry of loose manuscript pages before he too was dispatched by a thrust from Austen as the crewman moved to protect Rowan and Violetta.

Ashe pushed through a group of people and someone kneeling, before tripping over something, sending both the Halfling and the object spilling across the deck.

Kaplain threw his arms up in horror as what appeared to be a small child ran over his precious tome before falling flat on their face, sending the magical book skidding over towards a group of three individuals the child had appeared to be running from. He stood up enraged, already ignoring the cries of apology as the child scrabbled to his feet and kept running towards the ship's rail.

Rowan moved to retrieve the book but was caught short by the magical electrical charge meant to dissuade people from picking it up. She licked her finger looking up to see the priest angling towards her, his face a mask of fury.

"Violetta, 2 o'clock!" she warned, bringing her wrench around as Violetta moved up beside her.

"Give me my book." Kaplain demanded, not slowing as he approached, clearly expecting the two women to cow to his demands.

"I don't think so." Rowan muttered, purposefully lifting her boot and placing it upon the book's surface.

"How dare you!" Kaplain screamed, throwing a wild punch. Rowan instantly had a flash back to her older brothers fighting her; how they used to tease and how she had learned to defend herself from a young age to become the toughest brawler of them all. She ducked, allowing the punch to sail over her head, before she retaliated by slamming the wrench into the priest's midriff. He doubled over, allowing Violetta to step in and slam her skillet across his head with a backhand that would have put most tennis players to shame. Kaplain staggered, dropped to his knee and then fell to the deck senseless.

"That's what you get when you don't say please!" Violetta scolded.

His knights turned as one towards the disturbance, several pausing in mid-fight, allowing their opponents a free shot that served to simply showcase how outmatched they were. Several Scintarn ran away with maws stuffed full of yellowed pages of manuscript, whilst crewmen lost their weapons, still plunged deep within the knights' sturdy bodies.

The warriors turned towards the book, marching across the ship determined to protect their magical resting place, two of them physically dragging the protesting forms of Weyn and Plano along the deck after them.

Violetta and Rowan backed away, pushing Austen with them, there was no way they could tackle twelve magical knights by themselves.

"I'll take that." Mathius stated, scooping the book up from the deck using the edge of his cloak and running with it towards the prow, only to find a warrior step purposefully across his way, sword swinging. The assassin dodged to one side, changing direction, angling back across the deck, drawing more of the knights after him, knowing from previous experience that getting close to these creatures was not a prospect he wished to experience again.

He moved towards several Scintarn that had cornered some of the *El Defensor's* crew, leaping up onto a crate and herding the knights after him, much to the horror of the sleek ebony hounds who immediately felt the bite of their enchanted steel swords. Mathius grinned at his own ingenuity. If he could keep this up, he could clear the deck of the opposing forces all by himself! He stole a quick glance over his shoulder, only to trip over the corpse of a Scintarn hound, sending the ledger flying from his grasp, right into the back of Ashe's head.

The Halfling did not see the book coming towards him and had no idea he was about to be closely acquainted with such heavy literature. He was peering over the side of the ship at the skiff that was still hovering there, wondering if this could be his way off the galleon and a good place to hide until the aftermath of the fire had died down, when he was literally pushed onto it. He fell down onto the steel deck, the magical ledger thumping down alongside him. Almost as soon as he landed, he felt the vibrations in the strange craft increase as it moved away from the galleon.

Ashe got to his knees, shaking his head, watching in shock as the skiff eased away, leaving a row of angry looking warriors lining the rail of the *El Defensor*, all powerless to follow unless they wished to be eaten by the gigantic eels now swarming hungrily around the galleon's hull.

What had he done now? He swore he had not touched anything! The skiff wobbled out into the channel then laboriously swung itself around the prow of the *El Defensor* giving Ashe a first-hand view of the damage that had been sustained to the majestic vessel. It certainly did not look so good from out here when you had moved back in this way.

A huge net appeared to have been strung across the structure of the ship. It was still firmly in place on the starboard side but the rest of it now hung loose, draped over the splintered masts and crushing the sails. The whole ship was turned at an angle, appearing to be almost wedged inside the archway, straining against the net. It reminded Ashe of a majestic bird with its wings broken in a trap and he suddenly thought of Sinders. Where had that stupid bird gone?

The skiff wobbled to a halt, then suddenly accelerated at full speed towards the starboard side of the *El Defensor*. His heart leapt into his throat.

"What...? No don't hit the ship, don't!" He closed his eyes tightly and braced as the skiff scraped along the side of the galleon and slammed into the stone pillar of the archway, sending Ashe tumbling across the deck. Scaffolding groaned, wobbled, then plummeted into the water, dropping hypnotised crewmen and Scintarns into the churning current only for them to be dragged to the depths by the sleek predators circling the ship.

The Halfling was up on his feet in a moment, terrified he would be blamed for this further catastrophe, before he noticed what appeared to be a small pile of refuse hunched over the helm with two scuffed boots sticking out of the bottom.

"What are you doing?" he screamed, as the craft vibrated again before shuddering backwards, pulling away from the pillar, only to line itself up for another charge. Ashe staggered across the deck, determined to snatch the wheel away from this walking garbage pile, only to find himself staring into two eyes and a grubby face hidden deep within the mobile trash heap.

"Barney is that you?" Ashe asked, just before the Gnome slammed the throttle forwards and rammed the gateway again, sending cracks shooting up the ancient stone structure as the vessel rose from the water and snapped the lowest chain attached there. "Do you think this is a good idea?"

The rubbish nodded its head in confirmation, then tried to put the skiff in reverse again but it seemed to be suddenly struggling as if it were losing power. Barney struggled with the mechanism as Ashe wiped his nose and his tear streaked cheeks on his sleeve, suddenly caught up in the excitement of the moment and forgetting his earlier distress. He had no idea what the Gnome was trying to achieve but there was no denying it was fun!

* * * * * *

Mathius parried a sword thrust, rolled to the side to get clearance, then retaliated with three quick slashes across the magical warrior's face, parting his skin to reveal the tightly packed pages beneath. The knight shrugged and lunged again forcing the assassin back away from the rail over towards the cabin entrance Ashe had recently ran from. Mathius tried to goad the fighter into over extending, to leave himself vulnerable but the knight was too sure and much too confident to fall for such a simple approach.

The assassin's left dagger parried an overhead chop and he tried to twist the hilt and catch the blade either to force it from the warriors hand or at least make him drop the enchanted weapon but instead he found the brute's strength such that he started to twist back forcing the strain into Mathius wrist leaving him the choice of disengaging or dropping his own weapon.

Mathius stepped backwards instinctively and walked into another person emerging from the cabins. There was an unmistakable sound of chainmail moving and the assassin risked a quick turn only to note, too late, the downward swing of a sword hilt that struck him on the temple, dropping him to the deck.

More knights spilled out onto the main deck, causing Rowan, Violetta and Austen to pause as they noticed there were now duplicate fighters, mirror images of each other, stepping forwards and wielding their swords, the only difference being the colouring of their cloth. One set had blues as their predominant colour whilst the others had highlights of green.

"I think we need to stop fighting now." Austen remarked, lowering his sword, fully aware the battle was over when faced with such overwhelming odds. Abeline dropped to the deck from the rigging, eager to engage with the enemy, only for his face to drop when he noticed the sheer volume of foes approaching them.

"I tend to agree." Rowan replied, trying to keep the tremor out of her voice as the warriors advanced menacingly and Abeline's weapon clattered loudly to the deck behind her.

"Bring them on I say!" Violetta snarled, bringing her frying pan up before her. "No man is ever putting me back in chains again." Rowan laid a soothing hand upon her arm.

"I hear you." She whispered, dropping her wrench. "but now is not the time for heroics." Violetta shook her head and dropped her shoulders in defeat, gently placing her skillet to the deck as if it were a priceless treasure and not something that she had been bashing the opposition with but moments before.

"What?" she remarked, raising an eyebrow in annoyance. "Do you know how hard it is to get a good frying pan!"

* * * * * *

Aradol charged out onto the aft-castle, aware something was happening to his right but unable to take his eyes from the woman crumpled on the deck. He charged across the space and dropped to her side, taking in her beauty with a heart that ached. If anything had happened to her he could never forgive himself.

Rauph staggered to his feet and moved past the kneeling knight, his attention focused on something to the stern of the ship but Aradol's intent was to the woman at his side and refused to be distracted. He lifted her head tenderly from the deck and gently stroked her brow.

"Colette, can you hear me?" He asked, breathless with fear that she could not. He gasped aloud, praising the gods as her eyelids fluttered open and her beautiful cornflower blue eyes focused on him.

"I thought I had lost you." He sighed, scooping her up into his arms and cradling her softly against his chest. Colette looked confused, her mind clearly racing to catch up with the events that had been developing before she had blacked out but Aradol was caught up in the moment.

"Everything is going to be okay." He smiled warmly. "Don't worry I shall protect you with my life."

"No you don't understand." Colette replied, her memory suddenly becoming very clear. The sorceress, the gateway, the spell. Oh no! The spell. She looked down at her hand in shock, realising the magical power holding the passage open from Taurean had now been dispelled by her lack of consciousness.

The ship would be crushed! She turned her head towards the stern, noting Rauph leaning over the rail, pushing against the stone pillar of the gateway for all he was worth, trying to hold the ship from the closing aperture with a feat of strength that she would have thought impossible.

She turned back to look at Aradol in disbelief. Did he not realise the danger they were in? Aradol looked at her wide-open eyes and leant in even closer.

Then he kissed her passionately on the lips.

* * * * * *

Kerian thrust with *Aurora*, trying to strike a telling blow to the monster, only to find he had to step back as more tendrils darted in towards his arm, forcing him to swing up his shield and deflect the barbed fans away. One fan hit the top edge of the shield, razor sharp little teeth scratching the highly polished surface as it struggled to gain purchase and rip his protection away.

"That's it! Just keep him busy." Thomas shouted from the other side of Malum. Kerian tried to see what it was the captain was doing and even take the time to say hello, re-introduce himself but instead the man suddenly ran away along the top of the archway, leaving Kerian to fight the tendrilled menace all by himself.

"What...?" he could not believe it! Thomas had run away and left him! He could not believe the captain had done such an improbable deed!

However, before he had time to think about it, Thomas was gone and Malum turned all of his attention towards Kerian. Barbed tendrils whirled in from all sides, brightly coloured lights flashing pre-programmed messages to suggest Kerian drop his weapons, let down his guard so that Malum could feast on his brains but with the light from *Aurora* as dazzling to Kerian as it must have been to his foe, the coloured lights from Malum's display were muted and thankfully ineffective.

Kerian struggled to pull his shield free, then decided to do the opposite and shield charged the monster, pushing back hard in a move Malum clearly had not expected. Malum's feet slid across the surface of the stone, his barbed fans initially frozen by the actions of Styx, the man who had forced him to this desolate place and conspired with others to curse him with his current form.

With this unexpected success, Kerian shoved all the harder, until he physically pushed Malum over the edge. The monster dropped from sight with a scream and Kerian immediately turned towards Thomas, eager to have words with the man.

Thomas had other ideas and was intently focused on hacking away at a chain attached to the top of the archway. Kerian initially had thoughts that this was a fine way to break your blade but the captain seemed quite determined and who was he to warn him that he would need to see a good blacksmith to get the kinks worked out of the metal afterwards. Thomas's triumph as the chain fell free, instantly turned to concern as the entire archway shook and cracks coursed through the structure.

Kerian nearly overbalanced as the tremors shook the stonework. He staggered near to the edge where Malum had fallen over and risked a glance down onto the deck of the Spanish Galleon to which he had been so desperate to return. His eyes roved over the deck in that split second, noticing crew gathered midships, some in the clothes of knights, others in more common seafaring garb. Octavian's rowing boat was not far away on the port side of the ship, the gypsy's rowing clearly not his strong point but at least he was safe.

Not so the numerous corpses lying scattered about the ship, mainly hounds but also people who Kerian silently prayed were not crewmen that he knew. His gaze moved to the aft-castle, this would be where Colette would be because she needed to open the gateway. He just wanted one glimpse of her, one quick look to sate his need for her, to see that she was safe.

Thomas started shouting something but Kerian was not bothered about the man right now. He needed to see Colette. His eyes fell upon her and he blinked several times, clearly confused with what he was seeing.

She was in Aradol's arms and they were kissing!

Thomas continued his screaming but it fell on deaf ears. The captain started charging back towards Kerian, sword in hand. Let him come, Kerian did not care. He felt a pain in his heart, as real as if someone had stabbed him there and was now maliciously twisting the blade. After all this time! All the days, weeks and months of pain and suffering he had endured to get back to her and she was kissing someone else!

He blinked back the tears, not daring to believe what he was seeing, only for a movement to his left to drag his attention towards a strange vessel that skipped over the water and slammed violently into the stone arch in an explosion of sparks.

The whole structure swayed alarmingly beneath Kerian's feet making him stagger to the side, giant cracks appearing between the blocks of stone that created the monstrous arch. He fell to one side, putting his hand out to catch himself, in an act that probably saved his life.

Several of Malum's barbs shot forwards, the fans opening out, buzzing over Kerian's head as he dropped, opening when they expected to hit, the trailing edges scoring the flesh across the top of his scalp. Kerian spun on one knee, horrified to see that the creature was looming high above him, other barbs swaying and ready to strike. He had no time to swing his sword, no time to go on the offensive. He swung up his shield and winced as several barbs struck the surface, hitting with such force that his shield slammed down hard onto Kerian's chest blasting the air from his lungs.

Thomas rushed in, cutlass swinging, hacking and slashing for all he was worth, catching a couple of barbs and sending them flying away trailing ichor. Malum roared in fury, torn between the two men, not knowing which one he hated the most. Kerian rolled to one side, coming up right on the edge of the archway and only just stopping himself from overbalancing and falling onto the ships far below.

Colette and Aradol! The thought galvanised his emotions, pouring out a hatred and bile that had *Aurora* lunging, striking, stabbing at Malum as if by these actions Kerian could purge his mind of the distress he held deep inside. Malum shrunk down onto the stone then leapt just as a huge tremor ran through the arch, sending a buckling force rippling through the stonework.

Malum landed past them both, tendrils waving anxiously as he charged towards the next arch along, determined to place as much space between himself and the damaged column as possible. Thomas gritted his teeth and turned to follow, determined to finish this battle once and for all. Kerian fell into step alongside him and noticed the strange looks the captain was throwing his way as he ran. He appeared confused, as if he knew Kerian but could not place from where.

The keystone at the centre of the Taurean arch dropped away, setting off a chain reaction that dislodged the blocks either side and raced through the stone the two men were running upon. The stonework trembled beneath their feet, huge slabs of masonry tumbling down just as they leapt from one stone to another. The column behind them wobbled then stabilised but the tremors beneath them raced past and to the next archway which started to vibrate as the magic sustaining it threatened to disappear.

Kerian threw himself over to the next slab, Thomas landing beside him, Malum just ahead. They could feel the stonework buckling beneath them as they ran out onto the next gateway. There was an almighty groan, then the slabs ahead of them physically jumped before the whole arch cracked and gave way beneath them. This new gateway flashed, its arcane magical energies crackling as if knowing it was working for the very last time. The portal roared open, revealing a fleeting glimpse of a storm swept night and a skyline of tall structures illuminated with lights, then it surged closed, before the whole arch collapsed in on itself sending chunks of masonry crashing into the murky waters below.

Chapter Fifty-Seven

Colette felt a tingling rush as Aradol kissed her. A cascade of emotions, feelings of security, the excitement of knowing someone truly cared for her. She wanted to enjoy it, bask in it, surrender to the warmth of his muscular arms but the timing of this passionate embrace was so wrong. She broke the kiss, looking up into his brown eyes, noting the total devotion and love reflected back at her from this charismatic man who had spent all of that time training her to use Kerian's sword.

Kerian's sword! She pushed Aradol away, suddenly horrified by her own behaviour, angry at letting herself be this vulnerable, her mind battling with the feelings of guilt and insecurity whilst deep inside secretly wishing she could enjoy the feelings more. Her gaze stared over his shoulder and lingered on the erect blade that vibrated at the centre of the deck.

The ship! Damn, how could she have been so stupid?

Colette turned around, disorientated, the whole scenario playing out before her surreal and as if in slow motion. She noted the bow of the ship, the gateway slamming closed, huge splinters of wood shearing off and tossed up into the air, Rauph collapsing on the deck his body shaking in sheer exhaustion. She spotted the dark witch being helped to her feet by the strangely garbed man and then she noticed Commagin lying still, his hand outstretched, fingers curled, the *Lady Janet* abandoned at his side.

Aradol placed his hand on Colette's shoulder, unaware of the drama unfolding behind him, his emotions completely focused upon the beautiful mage. The ship rocked violently beneath their feet as something crashed against the side of the galleon, before it slammed into the stone pillar. A mighty crack sounded as the net restraining the ship finally gave, allowing the wounded vessel to surge forward into the clear, huge masonry blocks crashing down into the waters of her wake.

Magical knights stormed up onto the deck from both ladders, swords gleaming. Another crash, another crackle of static, the hairs on her arms rising as the adjacent gateway roared into life, revealing an alien landscape, a stormy night and tall closely packed buildings, before this too disappeared in a cascade of falling masonry and stone.

"Drop your weapons!" the knights roared. Aradol turned towards the sound, bringing his sword to bear, his mind not thinking clearly, prepared to take on an entire battalion.

Colette glanced over to Commagin's still form, tears welling in her eyes and everything rushed back into perspective. She placed a hand on Aradol's shoulder and leant forward to whisper into his ear.

"Stop. Just stop!" Aradol turned back to her, confusion written clearly across his face, his emotions running high. "We can't win this one Aradol. We simply can't." She lowered her head and Aradol's shoulders slumped, his sword reluctantly dropping to the floor as the warriors moved in.

* * * * * *

Colette looked around in a daze as she was pushed roughly to her knees, noting the remaining crew all gathered there, hands upon their heads, shoulders slumped in defeat. Nineteen fearsome knights surrounded them, swords drawn, their faces devoid of any emotion. She tried to count heads, tried to note which of the crew had survived. Commagin's body was dropped roughly on the deck in front of her making her gasp at the insensitivity shown to her friend, whilst vividly asking the question of what had happened to those who were still missing.

Another crash snatched her attention to a metallic creature being hauled over the side of the ship's rail, then Ashe and finally... was that Barney? All of them herded into the remainder of crew gathered upon the deck. Rauph was hobbled, his head pulled over to one side his horn tied to his back leg, his arms trussed to the same line. He looked so sad and dejected a far cry from the happy Labyris knight he had been mere hours before.

Weapons clattered onto a pile, Rauph's swords, Commagin's crossbow, Mathius's daggers all discarded, together with other weapons assembled following the aftermath of the skirmish. A monk dressed in the same robes as Marcus scrambled back onto the deck, clutching a huge blue ledger in his hands as if he were worried it would be snatched away from him.

Marcus thudded onto the deck, senseless, his face a mass of bruises, blood dripping from his lips. Richard remained, standing outside of the circle, his face red and blistered his hands clearly burnt. He also held a blue ledger, this one damaged by the same conflagration that had seared his face and hands. Marcus's book, Colette surmised. She looked back at the crushed monk taking a moment to notice his breathing, spiking fears he had also fallen in battle but Marcus appeared to be made of sterner stuff and a laboured wheeze issued from his lips. It was a minor gain, for everywhere she looked the crew showed the signs of crushing defeat and it was breaking her heart.

"My skiff is dead in the water." A figure stated climbing over the rail after the monk. "Whatever power it once had has gone." He threw a dirty rag down onto the deck in disgust, then walked over to his two lizards, one nursing its head, the other angrily hissing at anyone that came near, clearly unhappy and apparently missing it's hat from all of the angry gesturing.

Miguel Garcia. Colette recognised him and shook her head in disgust. What was that pirate doing here? Miguel paced up and down impatiently before he stopped in front of them and addressed the remains of the crew.

"Where's Thomas?" he demanded. Colette gasped, turning around rechecking the crew, scanning the faces, realising that the captain was not among those collected here.

"He was up on the arch the last time I saw him." A voice sounded across the deck. Colette looked up and noticed the sorceress walking towards them, her robes swishing around her. "Maybe he fell."

"If he did, then he is dead." Came a dry voice, as another figure walked up alongside Justina to stand at her side.

Colette's eyes widened when she recognised the golden dagger openly displayed at the man's waist, her eyes moving up to take in an Elven face, all be it one drawn and aged since she had last seen it. Her blood turned to ice in her veins. Scrave.

A voice hailed from the side of the ship calling up to those on board. Knights moved to the rail and helped haul the stranger up. Colette glimpsed a mass of wild black curls, olive skin and a dazzling smile that fell the second he turned around and took in the crew kneeling on the deck.

"Oh." Was all he had time to utter, before he was ushered in amongst the group and forced to his knees, his saddlebags dropping to the deck beside him. "I'm not one of the crew honest." He muttered but no one seemed to care. He turned to Colette and flashed her a nervous grin.

"You must be Colette." He whispered. "Gods, you are as beautiful as Kerian said you were. The stars must have shone brighter on the night you were born."

"K...Kerian?" Colette whispered; her throat suddenly dry, her face flushing as guilty images of her kiss with Aradol flashed through her mind. "How do you know Kerian?"

"We have been travelling together for months. He was determined to get back to you. He said he would never give up hope and now that I have seen you with my own eyes. I can understand why." He flashed her another smile then looked around the deck. "Where is he anyway?"

"What do you mean?" Colette frowned. "Is Kerian here?"

"Well he was in the boat with me and then he said he had to come to you so he climbed up the archway and..." Octavian looked up at the sky and the gaping hole in the arches that was all that remained of the gateway the *El Defensor* had sailed through. "You don't think he was up there when that all fell do you?"

* * * * * *

"I cannot keep my knights out of the book indefinitely." Al Mashmaah's bearer paced the captain's cabin, his blue ledger under his arm. Scrave looked up at Kaplain from the captain's chair, his boots crossed and resting on Thomas's desk, a cut crystal glass with a snifter of orange liqueur in his hand.

"Neither can I," Richard replied, whilst tightly bandaging his burnt hand. "They are magical beings for holy crusades, not simple prison guards."

"What about the black hounds?" Justina dipped her finger in Scrave's glass and licked the tip of her finger provocatively. "They are still stalking us, taking those crew of Garcia's who are no longer under the thrall of that glowing creature with the tentacles."

"They appear to have become confused since the arch fell. Most of them ran off and are hiding in the wrecks. We cannot send the knights into that unstable area in the hope we flush them out. They are too busy guarding the *El Defensor's* crew." Miguel replied, clearly not impressed with the direction of the talks, his eyes constantly glancing down at where Scrave sat.

"Which brings me back to my first point." Kaplain interjected. "The knights cannot remain outside of the book indefinitely. What are you going to do with the crew?"

"Let's just kill them all." Justina suggested, leaning forwards across Scrave to reach for the bottle.

"We can't." Miguel replied. "We need them to get us out of here. My cyborg Pheris is broken and the only way we can open a gate is by using Colette's magical powers and sailing the *El Defensor* out of here and that is a problem in several ways. Firstly, I have no idea where the archway is to take me back to Maraket, nor do I have any idea how to identify it and secondly she refuses to work her magic for us."

"Maraket... I want to go back to Catterick not experience more trouble. I am sure that given enough time I can figure out how to open the gate." Justina purred. "But you are also forgetting the gypsy. He can open gates by playing his violin. We have witnessed this first hand." She nodded towards Kaplain and traced a finger across the back of Scrave's neck making him bunch his shoulders.

"What about the knights?" Kaplain stated again, his temper rising. "We need to do something with the knights."

"Why don't we maroon the crew of the El Defensor in the graveyard and just take the gypsy or Colette with us. Let the hounds have them. That way at least the poor creatures won't starve." Justina suggested.

"Leave an enemy alive in your wake." Scrave muttered. "That is not my way."

"Lock them in the brig then." Miguel stated, clearly growing frustrated and wanting to raise his own topic for discussion.

"Not with that Halfling." Scrave replied. "We tried that in the past and he escaped. I have yet to find a cell that can hold the irrepressible Ashe Wolfsdale."

"So we can't lock them in the brig, we can't maroon them and we can't kill them." Richard stated exasperated, his hands tapping impatiently on his book. "What is more, I'm not even sure my knights will return to my ledger." He ran his bandaged fingers over the damaged surface of the book. "I don't even know if it is safe for them to go back inside."

"Well that's easily remedied then." Scrave added, shaking his head. "Has anyone got something they wish to say that will not add to the list of our problems."

"I was wondering when you would get out of my seat." Miguel suddenly snapped. "You promised me that I would be allowed this ship if I got you on board. I have kept my end of the bargain. Now do me the service of keeping yours."

"You should know better than to trust an Arnreithian Elf." Scrave stated coldly. "If you want this chair why don't you come and take it." Garcia paled as the golden serpent in Scrave's lap hissed its enthusiastic opinion on the matter.

"You gave your word." Miguel muttered, clearly wounded by the betrayal. "You are using my crewmen to patch up the ship. All I need to do is say one word and they will down tools."

"And if they do, I shall take pleasure in killing them all." Justina snapped. "So I lied! Get over it." Miguel looked across at the dark witch and then at the confident smile plastered on Scrave's face and backed away. He knew a bad hand when he saw one and at the moment, he had nothing he could even bluff with, despite the fact his fingers itched to pull out his duelling pistols and shoot both of these traitors in the head at point blank range.

"I will get you all home." Scrave stated calmly, settling back in the chair and kissing Justina's hand. "Colette will help us or the gypsy will, it matters little to me. It is only the *El Defensor* I am concerned with. This ship has always been my destiny and she will sail where I tell her. After all, I am her captain now. This is where I was born to be."

"So what about the knights?" Kaplain sighed.

* * * * * *

"How long do you think they are going to keep us here?" Octavian muttered. "I for one think the on-deck gymnastics thing is going a bit far. If I ever bring my hands down from my head, I think my shoulders may snap in protest."

"Were you like this every day when you were with Kerian?" Colette enquired. Octavian nodded his head. "Then it's a wonder he didn't kill you."

A ripple of silence crossed the deck as the doorway to the upper cabins opened and the five ringleaders stepped out onto the deck. Colette let her gaze run over them, noting the scowls on Garcia's face, the sly smile on the witch and the indifference shown by the others.

Scrave walked forward and addressed the group.

"There is a problem that affects us all." He opened. "The *El Defensor* is stranded in this inhospitable place unless we can find a safe port to affect repairs. Miguel's crew are doing the best they can but we can only go so far with the manpower we have. I need volunteers to help repair the ship." Not a single member of the cowed crew moved to assist and Colette smiled despite herself.

"How about you Colette. We need you to power the archways. Will you join me." He held out his hand. The mage looked up into his one eye and shook her head.

"I will never aid you Scrave. You were a snake when you were a crewman on this ship and you remain a snake now. Thomas Adams is my captain, it is his orders only that I obey."

"That's an unfortunate and rather narrow viewpoint." Scrave commented. "You see we really don't need you anymore. We have someone else that can open the gates."

"I'd like to see you try." Colette spat her defiance. Scrave motioned with his hand, ignoring her bluster and indignation.

"Grab that one." he motioned, "and bring his saddlebags." Octavian looked up as the two surly giant lizards stomped across the deck towards him.

"You want me?" He asked pointing to his chest. "I knew this all had to be some huge mistake."

"You can open the gateways?" Colette stared crestfallen at her gambling chip being so easily pulled from her. "Why didn't you tell me?"

"Well we haven't really got acquainted yet." Octavian replied before he was jerked to his feet.

"Is the violin still in your bags?" Scrave enquired. Octavian nodded, only for his bag to be pulled apart and his belongings dumped upon the deck.

A shriek and a scuffle sounded as a knight climbed up from below decks, moving into view holding Katarina by the scruff of the neck. He roughly threw her down at her mother's feet and she hugged her fiercely.

"Oh Kat, why did you not stay hidden." Violetta whispered, holding her tightly clearly fearing for her daughter's life.

"I had to be with you." Katarina whispered back. "I did all that I could to help Marcus." She pushed the small magical saint into Violetta's hand, then sat down alongside her, her little face pale and frightened.

"What are they going to do to us?"

"I' don't know dear." Violetta squeezed her daughter's arm tightly. "Just remember I am never going to leave you. No matter what happens."

Scrave paced about the deck clearly unhappy with the lack of support shown to his request.

"I want you to know that I commend your loyalty to your old captain." He shouted. "Just remember, whatever happens next, you brought this on yourselves. Brother Richard, if you don't mind."

Richard knelt down on the deck and squared the book before him, sitting back on his heels, closing his eyes and chanting as he opened the burnt ledger. The page yawned wide exposing the heavily detailed illustration of the cell within, the edges of the page blackened and warped by the fire. He waved his hand across the page, invoking a mystical phrase unknown to anyone but Marcus who groaned as he heard the ill-fated words.

"This is going to be interesting." Justina smiled, cosying up to Scrave, her hand hovering near his waist, only for the Elf to bring his own down to guard his golden dagger and push hers away.

"Let Colette be the first." Scrave ordered, angry at her rebuttal. Two knights stepped forward, forcibly pulling her from the crowd and herding her towards the open book. Colette was unclear what was about to happen. She could not understand what they intended to do. If she was being led to her death then she was determined to go with her head held high. She put up a token resistance as she was marched towards the ledger.

"Put her in." Justina screamed. Put her in? What in the ledger? Colette's knees nearly buckled as the terror of the suggestion ran through her mind.

"Richard you bastard!" She spat. "We took you in, gave you a home and you repay us with this. I swear you will regret this for as long as you shall live." Her boots skidded across the deck as she was dragged towards the magical tome.

"Spare me the hysterics." Richard stated coldly. "If this goes wrong you will be dead in the next few moments. I will definitely live longer than that."

"Richard please reconsider what you are doing." She screamed. "You had a family here, people that loved you."

"People that held me back you mean." The priest replied coldly. The knights threw Colette forwards, she held out her hands trying to stop her fall only for her to find there was nothing to stop her tumble. She screamed as she fell, the magical forces shrinking her down, compacting her size to that of the scale of the cell and suddenly she found herself hitting a cold stone floor. The air blasted out of her as she hit, her head ringing as it took a glancing blow from the leg of an old bunk, a discarded game piece rolled across the stone near to her hand.

The mage turned about, looking up from where she knelt, taking in the oblong shape above her that was filled with the colour of a dull mustard sky. There appeared to be no way to climb back up to the light, no footholds or ladder to escape with. Richard's head filled the opening, his eyes staring down into the illustration, straining to see if she had survived the magical transformation. He nodded apparently pleased with the result as further screams of pain and terror echoed down into the book from beatings handled to the *El Defensor's* crew.

Plano dropped down into the cell, his face pale, his eyes wide with shock, his tumble turning into a roll, much more successful and dignified that Colette's own sprawl. Then Abeline, Austen, Mathius, Rauph, Aradol, the crew kept dropping into the book, filling up the area between the bunks and as each one fell into the room, the magical cell appeared to stretch and grow into the distance to accommodate them.

Violetta, Katarina, Rowan, then Barney fell in. Ashe, who made sure he bit the hand of the guard that dropped him. The metallic creature Colette had seen being retrieved from the skiff also clattered into the book, wires and cogs spilling from its insides and bouncing across the floor. Finally Marcus was dropped down into the darkness, his fall broken by members of the crew, who gently laid him down on the nearest bunk, trying to support his head and limbs as they did so, only to pull their hands away in surprise at how unnaturally cold the Monk's body felt. Colette tried to remain stoic, remain strong for the crew, even as the gravity of this horrifying situation hit her. She stared up at the opening of the book, shading her eyes as Richard's face moved back into view.

"I swear I'm going to get you for this." She screamed. "If it's the last thing I do."

Richard turned to the people she could not see and she watched as they took it in turns to stare down into the page. She focused on each face, memorising the details, determined to never forget the people that had done this to her and her shipmates. The traitor Scrave with his ominous eyepatch. The dark witch with the malicious smile on her face, Garcia who just wanted to look away and the other priest who appeared to be viewing this as some huge science experiment. Then Richard's face came back into view and his hand reached up to close the book.

"Please Richard. Don't do this." Colette pleaded as the room around her started to get darker and the opening above her slowly started to narrow. "We cared for you. We loved you." The fear from the crew became tangible within the close confines of the cell. Voices started to raise in protest, some whimpered, others shouted their outrage putting voice to their distress as the darkness closed in.

The yellow mustard skyline shrank even further, turning to a thin slit, the crew's pleas becoming screams of terror as the darkness descended upon them.

Then Richard closed the book.

Epilogue

Kerian fell towards the water, the remnants of the archway tumbling and spinning around him, his body giving the illusion that he was somehow weightless. The air rushed past his ears, teared his eyes and it was all the fighter could do not to struggle. Images flashed through his mind of his youth when he had jumped from the cliffs at his family estate, plummeting down into the crystal blue waters of the bay and hitting the sea, feeling the crushing blow of the water and the air pushed from his body before he shot up towards the sparkling surface much to the amusement of his step-brothers.

He opened his eyes, returning to reality with a start, noting the churning brown water below, the waves breaking as the stonework from the archway crashed into the depths. This was no sparkling bay! The air alongside him crackled, pulling at his skin, the vortex pulling him into a dark void where the wind howled and the waters ran dark and choppy. He had to control his dive, had to take steps to keep his sword out of the way or risk seriously injury when the blade hit the water.

The surface was rushing up towards him now, the wind biting in its chill. Kerian knew he had seconds to act, he swung *Aurora* up above his head and drew in the deepest breath that he could, just as he hit the sea with a force that felt like it had sent his knees up into his stomach. His mouth opened at the shock as the icy water closed over him, the brackish liquid forcing into his mouth making him choke and splutter. *Aurora's* light extinguished, leaving him with a vivid after glow pulsing red across the underside of his eyelids.

He tried to orientate himself, but everywhere was darkness, he had no idea what was up, what was down, only that he needed to breathe and soon, or risk drowning. He fought back the panic, waiting for his body's natural buoyancy to send him the right way then kicked in that direction, praying he had chosen correctly.

Kerian surfaced into the storm, his mouth gasping for air, his arms leaden, clothing and armour pulling at his limbs, threatening to drag him under the water again but he noticed something in the darkness and swam towards it, gasping with relief when his fingers grabbed the stonework of a huge pillar that rose above the water. It had to be one of the archways, somehow, he still in the ship's graveyard but why had it become so dark?

He tried to make out where the shipwrecks lay, then swam towards a likely area that was darker than his immediate surroundings, struggling to pull himself from water that not only tasted strange but was slick and had debris floating in it that both threatened to entangle his clothing and make his progress painfully slow. Kerian floundered in the shallows, struggling to pull his battered body from the icy clutches of the waves and slipping on the slick rocks that butted up to a grassy clearing. Grass… the graveyard did not have grass. His heart sank. Something was very wrong here.

A hand reached out from the darkness, catching him by the wrist, helping him clamber from the water to collapse on the ground shaking with the cold. He turned over, blinking his eyes clear from the relentless rain to make out who his unlikely saviour was and noticed the exhausted features of Thomas staring back down at him as lightning flickered across the sky.

"Is that you Thomas?" Kerian laughed through chattering teeth, struggling to sit up, his cloak tangled around his legs.

"Kerian?" Thomas stared down at the man he had rescued from the waters, the man who had battled alongside him against Malum. He could not believe his eyes. If this was Kerian then he was easily twenty years younger than the old man he had once known.

"I thought it was you." Kerian smiled, moving to stand then stopping as the satchel at his waist started to bulge out. He struggled to free the flap, then reached into the bag to retrieve the cause, pulling free the small black Scintarn puppy that had crawled in there under the dining table at Castle Glowme. The puppy coughed and spat water then looked up at Kerian with its wrinkled face and whined, clearly not happy with being in the cold.

"You know for a minute there, I thought we were in trouble." Kerian continued, looking up at the captain, only to pause in his conversation as Thomas's attention appeared to be drawn to the tempest and the darkened landscape around him.

Thomas looked over to the nearby bridge that Kerian had clung to and followed its span as it reached out across the water. He knew that bridge. He looked up at the sky, noting the flashing lights indicating aircraft flying miles above the storm, then let his eyes fall to the wet railings beside him and the sign erected there. He knew what the inscription on the sign would say even before he read it. It would describe the battle of Brooklyn and the evacuation of Fulton Landing. He turned, looking back across the grass towards the squat building in the distance, the one he knew held a carousel inside. Pebble beach was over in that direction. He was standing in the Empire Fulton Ferry Park! The lightning strobed across the bruised sky, turning everything monochrome like an old photograph.

The captain looked back towards the bridge, searching the night for some sign of the *El Defensor*, some glimpse of the ship's graveyard and realised there was nothing but the wind, the storm and over it all the tantalising smell of hotdogs.

"Oh, we are in trouble all right!"

-: The End :-

The Crew of the *El Defensor* Will Return

Acknowledgements

Okay, first off, I need to apologise for leaving the second part of this first trilogy on such a cliff hanger. The problem is that I have discovered writing is addictive and as I have been hitting the keys for the last three years, sharing my adventures of the *El Defensor* crew, I suddenly realised that this second novel was going to be a lot larger than its predecessor. Readers had already emailed me about the inherent risk of carpal tunnel, back strain and the hernias they had endured in reading *Styx & Stones*. Amazon's publishing platform equally did not permit novels with bigger page ranges than my first novel, so there was nothing for it. I needed to decide to cut the story, to end *The Labyris Knight* and start part 3, *Sinders & Ashe*. I hope you can all forgive me for where the editing axe fell!

Speaking of editing... Finishing a novel is not quite as solitary a process as the romanticists would have you believe, sure there are long times spent alone typing into the early hours but that is only the tip of the iceberg as regards the people who went into finishing this massive book. I need to thank Hampton Ewart my editor in chief, who has often regarded me from over the top of his glasses with a stony frown, an exasperated headshake and an authoritarian 'No!' I wish to thank him for his incredible patience with my 'tale of high adventure' over the last three years, for all of those Friday night sessions of tea and biscuits where we hammered out as many grammatical errors within the sprawling text of this mighty tale as we could find. Any errors that remain within the text are now solely this authors responsibility.

I also wish to thank Alex McCowan, a keen proof reader who sent complex emails on the structure of armour and the nutritional nature of hay for horses. Thanks also go out to Richard Wilson for late-night messages of support, even when struck down with the bubonic plague of Bristol and his insistence that someone, somewhere, ought to make a movie out of this. Dave Pannell also needs mention for corrupting my youth by introducing me to fantasy novels; tales about white gold wielders, swords of truth hidden in piles of junk and teaching me that putting a car in reverse actually involves depressing the clutch first! These novels are fired by your infectious enthusiasm!

Jay Eales of *Factor Fiction Press* came up trumps again with the title for this novel. That's two I owe you now. The Monday Night Lads need a quick nostalgic mention. May your dice never stop rolling. You all know who you are, despite the fact that over the years we have drifted continents apart. Thanks also to Dr Warwick Coulson for the dubious honour of crafting the *'Tale of the Bloated Badger'*.

Finally, I need to thank the three people that remain my inspiration. Ryan and Owain, two young men I remain extremely proud of, currently facing their university courses with typical Derbyshire aplomb and of course my wife Nicola, who ensured this book cover is as stunning as the last.

Now if you will all forgive me. I need to write a modern-day thriller, craft a world with citadels of ice containing exotic masked villains and spin tales of warships that scream. The *El Defensor* has a new captain and he is as cold and as ruthless as the place that birthed him.

Adam Derbyshire. April 2019

Author Notes

Adam Derbyshire has always wanted to write stories...
But real life and utility bills kept getting in the way.

Swiftly approaching his mid-life crisis, he decided it was time to
either buy the luxury sports car, or tell the world about the
ghostly ship and crew that sail throughout his dreams.

He lives in Northamptonshire with his wife and children
and sadly, could not afford the Aston Martin.

The Labyris Knight is his second novel.

Printed in Poland
by Amazon Fulfillment
Poland Sp. z o.o., Wrocław